PRÆTORIAN

THOMAS GIFFORD

BANTAM BOOKS
NEW YORK · TORONTO · LONDON · SYDNEY · AUCKLAND

PRAETORIAN
A Bantam Book / April 1993

BOOK DESIGN BY GRETCHEN ACHILLES

Library of Congress Cataloging-in-Publication Data

Gifford, Thomas.
    Praetorian / Thomas Gifford.
        p.   cm.
    ISBN 0-553-09371-1
    1. World War, 1939–1945—Campaigns—Africa,   North—Fiction.
I. Title.
PS3557.I284P7   1993
813'.54—dc20   92-39568
                                                         CIP

Published simultaneously in the United States and Canada

PRINTED IN THE UNITED STATES OF AMERICA
BVG   0 9 8 7 6 5 4 3 2 1

FOR PATRICIA

AUTHOR'S NOTE

I come by my affection for Great Britain and things British quite honestly. It's in my blood. My forebears—the Giffords, the Maxwells, and the Eatons—have done their bit for the old country in one way and another. They have shed their blood and in several cases laid down their lives from Murmansk to El Alamein. While it is not my intention to glorify war, I hold these Giffords, Maxwells, and Eatons who did their duties in high regard. And when in London on Remembrance Day, as I seem frequently to be, I have been stirred deeply when elderly men, some erect and jaunty, some with canes, some in wheelchairs, have passed in review and snapped the salute and I have known them as the Rats of Tobruk. They are the men who have endured and survived something I will never know. Thank God. But there is in me something that envies them.

Geoffrey Keyes, V.C., was a hero who did not survive, except in the hearts of his countrymen and in the respect of even his German enemies. Geoffrey Keyes led—and gave his life in the conduct of—the actual mission which served as my inspiration for the core event of this novel. The mission in my book, led by Max Hood, resembles Keyes's commando attack in many physical details and in its original purpose. None of my characters has any real-life counterpart; in particular, none in any way resembles the hero Geoffrey Keyes, nor any of the men who accompanied him. I am a writer of fiction; I deal in all the maybe's and what if's which make up the novelist's stock in trade. But if I were a biographer I would not turn to Geoffrey Keyes's life as a subject for the simple reason that his sister, Elizabeth Keyes, has brilliantly accomplished the job with GEOFFREY KEYES, published in England by George Newnes Limited, in 1956. It is a work which not only does honor to its subject but to its author, and to their father, Admiral of the Fleet Sir Roger Keyes. The Keyes family is typical, I suppose, of those families which punctuate the history of their island race with such reassuring regularity.

A little less than a year after young Keyes had been killed, Winston Churchill remarked to the Admiral that Geoffrey had been "a splendid son." The Admiral responded: "If Geoffrey had only succeeded, what a difference it would have made." Mr. Churchill said: "I would rather have Geoffrey alive than Rommel dead."

Rommel himself ordered the cross of young cypress cut for Geoffrey

Keyes's grave and it eventually was sent to the Keyes family in England, where it was placed in the chancel of their parish church. The old admiral died on Christmas night of 1945, having seen the war through to a successful conclusion. Upon learning of his death Sir Walter Cowan observed that surely "Geoffrey was there to take his hand."

I mention all this because it is—in a world of moral order—important that we remember such matters. It is a good thing to remember that once, a long time ago, there was a great moral conflict, a war not only worth fighting, but a war that had to be won. There was no margin for error, as has been the case ever since. To have been part of such an undertaking—when the world hung suspended between the light and the darkness, while men and women saw to the deciding of the issue—must have been a glorious thing, whether you knew it at the moment or not.

PRAETORIAN is my attempt to recapture lives lived at a moment in history when the stakes were altogether higher than they have been since. Yes, it was all a long time ago, but it was yesterday, too.

A year after the raid on Rommel in November of 1941, the great turning point of World War II had just ended. At El Alamein, out there in the Egyptian desert, General Bernard Montgomery—subsequently known to history as Montgomery of Alamein—drove Erwin Rommel, the Desert Fox, and his Afrika Korps back into Libya. Alexandria, Cairo, and the Suez Canal would never fall into German hands. Until El Alamein, Hitler's armies had never lost a major battle. After El Alamein, they would never win another.

Now, fifty years down the road, representatives and veterans of all the warring armies return to the desert to honor the fallen of that terrible battle. Roughly fourteen thousand Commonwealth soldiers, about sixty thousand Germans and Italians, were killed, wounded, or forever missing.

El Alamein is a remote and cruel spot, two hours on rough roads from Alexandria, six hours from Cairo if your car can take it. Yet those who remember make the journey each year to the three startling memorials rising at the site. The British cemetery most resembles a carefully tended country garden. The Italian memorial is a magnificent, soaring reminder of a cathedral of antiquity. The Germans have built a memorial described by a recent observer as "eloquently austere as a medieval fortress."

The desert, the war, the era writ in its largest sense provided a crucible for those who lived their stories in those long-ago days. I have tried to convey something of what it must have been like. But never have I forgotten that any creation of mine is only a moment, a ghost, and that behind the mist of fiction lies a reality which still informs the lives of those of us who make the effort to explore that faraway country, the past.

Thomas Gifford
New York City
1992

We do not know what is happening,
and that is what is happening.
—José Ortega y Gasset

If we fight to the end
it can only be glorious.
—Winston Churchill

PART ONE

LONDON
1940-1941

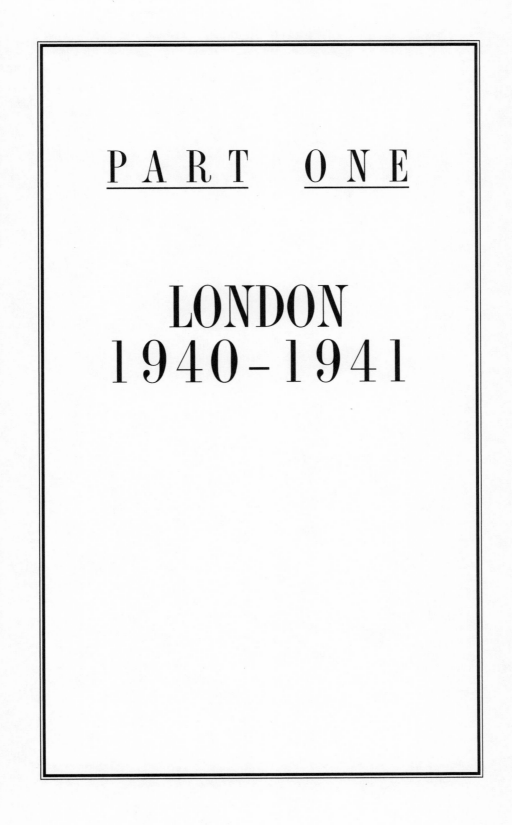

PART ONE

LONDON
1940-1941

CHAPTER 1

The Blitz was in full fury, but people in Rodger Godwin's circle ignored it as much as possible. To-hell-with-bloody-Hitler was the prevailing attitude. The restaurants and pubs and clubs were full in the evening, and people still gave cocktail parties. Godwin had just run into Monk Vardan at such a party, and they had decided to have dinner together. They were on their way to Dogsbody's.

The blackout was intense as always but the scene was given an eerie unreality by the bomber's moon, which made the stroll quite pleasant since the Luftwaffe had not yet arrived. The paving stones in Berkeley Square were slick with wet leaves. Great puffy barrage balloons floated high over the city, reflecting the silvery moonlight. They had a benevolent look, like a herd of sheep grazing against the moon. Sections of the streets were roped off where bombs had left craters, where skeletons of burned-out buildings might collapse without warning. Dogsbody's had survived unscathed, and behind the plain oak door with the brass knocker in the shape of a doleful hound's head it was dim, clublike, lots of shine on the leather and wood and silver. The blackout curtains looked heavy as chain mail. If you weren't an habitué of Dogsbody's you'd never have known the place was there.

Once they'd settled in at table, Monk Vardan wrapped himself into the heavy, carved armchair and quickly surveyed the evening crowd. No two chairs and no two tables were alike, part of owner Peter Cobra's plan. Nothing matched. Controlled chaos. Vardan waved a couple of fingertips, the gesture as subtle as a man bidding up the price at Sotheby's. He had removed a black slouch hat and wore a white silk scarf, a city suit quite out of date, a floppy red paisley silk square in his breast pocket, and a monocle clamped in his left eye; the candlelight was reflected in the glass disc. A black silk ribbon fluttered.

"Halloween, is it?" Godwin inquired patiently, even though he was developing the first rattles of a headache. "Let me guess. You're either Dracula or Bertie Wooster. I mislaid my costume." He pressed his temples. Vardan was ordering something obscure and expensive from the cellar. Cobra's *sommelier* hovered unctuously.

"Occasionally," Vardan said, "I affect a certain Puckish whimsicality. It is called style."

"Called pansy, if you ask me."

"Precisely why your opinion went unasked, old boy. You journalists are much too opinionated a lot."

Godwin looked away. Clyde Rasmussen was sitting near the fire, his face almost as rosy as his unmanageable shock of hair. In the years since they had met in Paris in 1927, everything about Rasmussen had thickened, changed, but the hair perhaps least. There were rumors that nowadays he hennaed the encroaching gray. The hayseed's face had grown puffy with sensuality and disappointment, yet there was no one in the room who could lay claim to greater celebrity. Clyde Rasmussen and His Society Boys Band were now and had been for years nothing less than the rage. The eagerness in his eyes showed you he was still in the hunt. He wore evening clothes. He was sitting with two girls who gave the impression of being out for an evening with a somewhat dangerous uncle.

Vardan laid his long forefinger aside his beaky nose, gimlet eye glinting behind the monocle. "Now let's get to the heart of things. You seem to have a secret sorrow. . . . Overwork? Despair? War getting you down?"

"You sound like a laxative advert."

"That's interesting. Leave it to you Yanks. So, if it's not constipation, it must be," Vardan clucked with quiet delight, peering the length of his nose, "a woman. Or perhaps women. The eternal variety? *Femme fatale?* A parlor maid? A new woman? An old love? Don't let me prattle on, my son, confess to the vicar."

Pâté arrived, a fairly fancy claret with lots of dust clinging like dandruff to the round shoulders of the bottle. Godwin begged Maurice, the unctuous hoverer, for something cold, something with ice, for God's sake. He had to get this said if only his head would remain attached to the rest of his body. "Monk," he began, remembering how Vardan had come to him with the tale of a pregnant girl years before, "I've worked myself into a tight corner . . ." He stopped. What the hell was that supposed to mean, anyway?

"Ahhh. Has a stagey sound to it, doesn't it? Shall we give conversational English a try?"

"There's this woman."

"And you need to confess. But the presence of a woman is normally cause for a peal of bells, rejoicing all round. Why the woeful countenance?" The restaurant was nearly full, a fire licking up the chimney, the bar in the other room producing a lot of noise, bits of song. Godwin saw three people sitting in the cozy booth in the corner and felt a frantic thumping in his chest at the sight of them. He turned away, clung for safety to the rubbish Vardan was talking: "Is this some toothsome new creature?"

"Not exactly. I've known her a long time. That is, I knew her a long time ago. Now I know her again." He sighed. "I'm putting this badly. It's a complicated story. Monk, you're the only person I could tell, I'm afraid."

"What about your old friend Rasmussen?" A sly smile.

"Well, you see, he's part of the story. . . . Believe me, there are very good reasons to leave Clyde out of this."

"Take it as read, old man. I don't suppose I know her . . ."

"No, you do know her. And her husband too."

"Ahhh. The picture, though still murky, grows ever clearer."

"She's in this room." Maurice arrived with a glass full to the top with ice, gin, and a hint of quinine water. Godwin could have sworn he felt blood vessels breaking in the whites of his eyes as he sipped the gin.

"In this room as we speak? With her husband?"

Godwin nodded. He dared look again, hoping she wouldn't catch his eye. Cilla and Max Hood were dining in a dim corner with the émigré playwright Stefan Lieberman, a German Jew. Or Austrian. Or possibly French. Godwin had met him casually at a party or two. Lieberman had, it seemed, taken the literary community by storm. He had lunched amid photographers at the Ritz with Noel Coward.

"Do you plan to reveal her identity? Or is it a game? I shan't play unless there's a prize."

"She's over there. In the corner."

Vardan peered across the crowd, past the shimmering shadows and firelight. Slowly his mouth dropped an inch, revealing his huge elongated horsey teeth. The monocle popped from his eye, swung at the end of the silk ribbon. "I *say*," he exclaimed softly. "You cannot possibly have reference to Cilla Hood. . . . Yes, yes, you can, can't you? You are a very sly old dog. Very sly. Among the slyest at the end of the day. Fancy that . . . Cilla Hood." His eyes moved from Godwin's face, then refocused on the corner. "You are a brave laddie, indeed. My respect for your courage grows apace. Foolhardy, however. Comes from being an American, I suppose."

"Brave? What the hell are you talking about?"

"What else would you call someone who cuckolds a Legend in Human Form? A Hero of the Great War? A man who rode the camel just to the left of Lawrence's? You must be insane or in love. Max Hood has made a specialty of killing coves with his trusty dirk."

"Bare hands, too," Godwin murmured.

"A quibble. Dying comes at the end. Which are you, mad or in love?"

"Obsessed. Dumb with passion. You know what I really am, Monk? I'm the man whose dreams came true . . ."

"You could do the wise thing in such cases—give her up and compose sonnets to love. Safest path."

"The hell with sonnets. I've as good as got her. It's a damn mess. So you do know her?"

"*En passant.* Max rather better. Winston dotes on him. 'We need more men like Max Hood!' That's the cry heard round number 10. I think he sees something of his own younger self in Hood."

Monk had made his mark early, in his twenties, as an historian, with several scholarly publications, but in recent years he'd gravitated toward the world of politics. With a certain prescience he'd hitched his wagon to Winston Churchill's star in the mid-Thirties, although at the time the great man's wattage had been desperately low, nearly extinguished, his future invisible to the naked eye. But Monk had fallen under the man's spell. Now he was seen to have played his hand brilliantly. He was close to the Prime Minister, though just how close was a matter of some dispute by the watchers of such rankings. He held no official post. Godwin had learned, however, that the relationship between the two men had a weight and density very few would have suspected.

Vardan laid aside fish knife and fork, dabbed his mouth with snowy linen, and sipped wine. "I've known Max Hood many years. Legend at Eton by the time I got there."

"Well, I'm in love with his wife."

"You say you've as good as got her. Customarily, one either has her or doesn't have her. Translation, please."

"We're in love. We're not adulterers. Not yet. . . . It's hard to explain. We have a history. I knew her years ago—"

"Surely she's very young now—"

"Younger then. Just a girl. There's more to this than sex, Monk. We're tearing our lives apart. . . . Sex is the least of it, in a way."

"That's odd. She's said to be an accomplished seductress."

"The thing is, I don't care. It's all irrelevant. There's never been anyone like her."

"You could be in the soup then, old man. Tell me what you will in the full knowledge that I remain as mute as the much discussed sphinx. The silent repository of scandal. It *is* a scandal, you *do* know that? You *are* Rodger Godwin. She *is* Cilla Hood. I expect Max would kill you."

"I've known him for dog's years. Since '27. He wouldn't *want* to kill me. He'd be sorry—"

"Ahhh. Well, cold comfort, that."

The air-raid sirens were going but it seemed to make no difference at Dogsbody's. Godwin paid no attention. The occasional *crrrummmmp* of the explosions outside was always somewhere else. Conversations tended to grow shrill during the raids, and when the building sometimes shifted on its foundation, grinding dust down from the ceilings as the detonations came closer, there were the odd, fleeting looks of alarm. But ignoring it was the done thing.

Vardan said, "Well, there is the view that God made husbands so we might have someone to cuckold. But I doubt if He was taking Max Hood into consideration."

"Max is more than that to me—I hate what I'm doing to Max. But Cilla . . . I've never felt anything like this. I feel as if I can't die, no bombs can kill me. Cilla can keep me alive, she has the power to make me feel so much. . . . But, Monk, I can't forget this sickness that's at the core of it. Max . . ."

"This is quite simple, as I see it," Vardan said. "It's the betrayal of Max Hood that's bothering you. Betrayal. One of the cornerstones of what we often think of as 'real life.' Well, I bring good tidings. Betrayal is the currency of our times. We may as well be in Byzantium or imperial Rome or knee-deep in the Renaissance. Betrayal is everywhere. We have all been betrayed, again and again. We were betrayed by the Great War which turned out to have been merely the first act of this one, and it certainly didn't make the world safe for democracy. Prosperity was dashed to bits in 1929. Our leaders have all betrayed us. History has betrayed us. Love has betrayed us. We constantly betray ourselves, and God has gone off and left no forwarding address. Europe is a charnel house . . . nothing but traitors, spies, brigands, blackguards, as far as the eye can see. Betrayal . . . well, your turn is coming. Plenty to go around. So get used to it, that's my advice . . ." Vardan raised his hand slowly, cocked his head. "I think they're coming closer. Listen." He smiled. "This could be the night, old chap. Listen to them coming . . ."

Peter Cobra was standing between the bar and the dining room, fitting a cigarette into his holder. His face suddenly lost all animation and he, too, cocked his head, putting a hand on the swinging door. It was a memory Godwin carried with him, the last thing he saw before the bomb hit.

The explosion was deafening, a terrible roar and slam and smash in a confined space. People were scrambling on the floor, glass was breaking and spraying like a blizzard of snow, tables were tipping over, the heavy blackout curtains were billowing and shredding. Godwin's chair fell over backward and the table landed on top of him and the air was full of choking-thick dust and he felt someone fall on his hand, grinding his palm into broken glass on the floor. He tried to pull his hand free, and the glass was ripping at the meat. A woman landed on his back and he saw her stockinged leg directly before his eyes, saw the strain running through her body, saw the stockings ladder as she struggled to right herself.

The noise which had been indescribably loud suddenly blew itself out and the scene turned into a kind of silent movie. Only later did he realize he'd been momentarily deafened by the insane decibel level of the blast. He peered up from between the woman's ankles, saw that she'd lost a shoe, and watched as one of the ceiling crossbeams came loose in a shower of plaster and swung down, striking Cobra's partner, Santo Colls, on the shoulder and knocking him down. The blackout curtain hung loose, and the windows were gone and there were fires burning in the street. Slowly he began to hear things again. People shouting, screaming in pain or terror. Cobra still stood in the doorway only now he held one of the swinging doors in his hand. It had been blown off its hinges.

Miraculously the lights hadn't gone. Some of them had been broken, some of the candles had been blown out as if a giant had had a go at his birthday cake, but there was enough to see dimly across the room. Colls had crawled across the debris and was pushing pieces of burning coal back into the fireplace. Sam Balderston of *The Times*, his fat face streaming with blood from a cut on his forehead, was stamping at the flames nibbling the edges of a woman's long gown. Godwin pushed himself free of the table and the woman who lay across his back; she had either fainted or been knocked unconscious or was dead. He struggled to his knees. Where was Cilla? He pushed his way through the chairs and tables and strewn wine bottles and the bodies all coughing and crawling and trying to stand up. A beautiful blonde was watching helplessly as the strand of pearls at her throat spilled, tiny white globules bouncing down the front of her black dress and into the wreckage on the floor. Cilla. . . . He might have called her name as he choked on the dust. Cilla . . .

There in the corner, Cilla sat braced against the sides of the booth, her face pale and framed by the Louise Brooks bob, not a hair out of place, looking into the eyes of her husband. Stefan Lieberman was sitting on the floor dusting himself off with great hairy-backed hands. Something had cut his head, and he was feeling gingerly for the sticky wound. Cilla slowly reached out and put her hand to her husband's cheek, reassuring him that she was all right, then let her gaze slide past and come to rest on Godwin.

Unexpectedly she began to laugh, tugging at Max Hood's sleeve, pointing at Godwin. It all seemed to be happening very slowly, as if they were all in shock. Hood turned, a quizzical expression on his face. There was a touch of gray at the coal-black temples. He began to grin when he recognized Godwin through the dust and smoke. He was relaxed, in command. Max Hood was where he was happiest. Under fire.

"Rodger," she said, leaning forward, color returning to her cheeks, "how very becoming!" She pointed at his head. Chaos was in full cry just a few feet away. Beams from electric torches were poking through the gloom from the street outside. There were only a few lights burning now in the restaurant. Godwin felt the top of his head, turned to a mirror mounted in the corner, now shattered but still in its frame. He glimpsed his fragmented image, looking like a figure dear to the heart of Mack Sennett. A napkin had landed on the top of his head. He seemed to be wearing a small tilted pagoda. He patted it. "It seemed," he said, as if they hadn't just been bombed, as if the street were not afire, "just the thing for a night out."

Hood slid out of the booth and slapped Godwin on the back, squeezed his arm affectionately. He was shorter than Godwin by half a foot, built like a middleweight contender, trained as always to fighting trim like Battling Terry Hardy.

Godwin said, "Max, how long have you been back?" Godwin heard his own voice. It sounded desperate and false and guilty.

"A month," Hood said. "Meant to ring you but you know how it is. Meant to ring you up—wanted to hear about your meeting with Rommel —go all right, did it?"

"I liked him—"

"Yes, yes, likable chap. Well, they've had me busy, you know. Trying to solve our problems in the desert. I got up to Stillgraves just once for a week. . . . You're looking fit for a sedentary scribbler." He looked up at Godwin, who stood well over six feet and felt, at 225 pounds, anything but fit. There was a small scar beneath Hood's left eye. Godwin had been with him long ago when he'd picked it up. A man had rammed a broken bottle at his eye. Paris again. A bloody night.

"Everybody all right over here?" Godwin looked from Lieberman on the floor to Cilla. He had to be careful. Like every guilty lover, consumed by his secret, he was sure he was giving himself away. "Cilla?" How could he keep from touching her? In the broken mirror he saw the reflection of a fire darting in the darkness in the street, the figures of the Auxiliary Fire Service struggling with hoses. Someone was tearing down the last of the blackout curtains, ripping it loudly.

"Rodger, darling," she said, standing up, swaying a bit unsteadily, "I'm perfectly fine. Max, take that silly thing off Rodger's head. He looks like Chips Gannon doing his imitation of Queen Victoria." As she came out from behind the table she reached up and did it herself, whisked the napkin from his head, then leaned down, knelt beside Lieberman, said something, dabbed at his head. Godwin could see her breasts floating as her neckline belled out. He saw her nipples and made himself look away. There was another explosion down the street and the mirror gave up, showered its countless bits across the table.

Hood had turned, as the smoke began to clear somewhat, and was helping a man to his feet. His wife was crying, trying not to show it. "I'm perfectly fine, Hubert," she said. The woman's teeth were chattering and she couldn't stop them. She'd just been bombed and lived through it. "Never better," she said, smiling at Hood, having no idea who he was. He was simply the man who helped her husband to his feet the night the bomb hit Dogsbody's.

Cilla was touching Godwin's sleeve. Lieberman had arisen and set off resolutely for the bar. Her eyes sparkled. She'd mastered the shock. Now she was enjoying herself. He felt her hand on his sleeve, looked into her eyes. She knew it was a wonderful scene to play. "Do you love me, Rodger?" Now that the worst danger had passed, the worst the Germans could manage for the moment, she was moving on. Was she raising the stakes? Well, it was her style, moving from the impersonal to the personal: Which was more terrifying? "Do you love me, darling?" She was speaking in a normal tone of voice. It was too loud. Hood's back was turned. She tugged at Godwin's sleeve again, a front tooth sinking into the outward jut of her lower lip. He hadn't seen her for five days. Now she was tempting fate: Max Hood might so easily have heard her.

"I love you," Godwin whispered. "Now for God's sake, shut up."

She gave her head a shake, brushed plaster dust from her hair. "I thought as much," she said. She produced her characteristic vixen's grin. "It's all over your face, you know. You can't help it."

Peter Cobra came to them, tall, almost supernaturally elegant. He was frosted with bits of plaster. He had rid himself of the door and was holding a bottle of wine and a corkscrew. He surveyed the wreckage of the establishment, nodding thankfully that the diners were all back on their feet. Where the bomb had actually landed was momentarily immaterial. The patrons of Dogsbody's had escaped.

"I've been waiting for this night. And all I have to say is this—" He swung his long arm out, taking in the entire shambles, ending with a wiggling of his fingers at the tall, stooped figure of Monk Vardan, who was leaning against a wall as if he just might be all that held it up. As Cobra spoke, the room went eerily silent so that only the sounds of the outside world drifted in. The street was lit by fires down the block. "This," he said, "calls for the Mouton Rothschild '18! Please, be my guests, ladies and gents—Santo, to the cellars! We'll drink our fill!"

The moment was recalled in later years by diarists who saw it as the symbol of something or other, the spirit of British insouciance while the bombs were falling. The remark made its way around London in a flash. By lunchtime the next day everybody knew what Peter Cobra had said. In America the next evening millions tuned in their radios in kitchens and parlors and heard about it from Rodger Godwin. It made one of his most memorable "War Is Heck" pieces. People in London and abroad took it up as a kind of rallying cry when the going in their streets got rough: *I say, Doris, this calls for the Mouton Rothschild.* And before you knew it Peter Cobra had become a legend. If he hadn't said it, he once observed, no one might ever have asked him to write his memoirs. The first volume of course had titled itself: *This Calls for the Mouton Rothschild.*

While the wine was being uncorked and poured, while the shaken crowd was dusting itself off and discovering it was alive, Max Hood beckoned to Godwin from the doorway where the heavy oak slab itself remained intact. It was like a scene from a battle, as if Hood were once again leading his men over the top and into the jaws of death. The street was glowing with hot spots, fires flaring up, bricks crashing from the darkness above, smacking into flames and showering sparks that caught on the wind like glow-worms. AFS workers were overwhelmed by the collapse of two buildings down the street and the road was cluttered with piles of bricks and up-rooted paving stones and wooden beams, mounds of broken furniture which minutes before had filled flats above the shops and pubs. A dining table was slanted on its two remaining legs in the middle of the street. A man sat on the curb, his shirt and trousers blown to tatters, otherwise only dazed. In the gutter a battery-operated radio lay on its back, dance music still playing loudly, Al Bowlly singing "Stardust." A building had collapsed inward on itself, had become a dark cave from some operatic underworld, lit by a few small flickering fires caused by the incendiaries.

Max Hood stood still, staring at the fires. "Listen," he said, "listen. . . ." The fires blinked at them from the darkness like the eyes of wild beasts, waiting in the wreckage to strike back. "There's someone crying . . ."

It was like Paris, the way it had been that August night back in '27. Godwin's mind flashed back to the night Sacco and Vanzetti had been executed in Massachusetts, and Paris had gone mad. *Listen, there's someone crying. . . .* Max Hood had said the same thing that night, and life had changed forever.

One of the AFS men, his face grim and sooty beneath a steel helmet, said, "Here, give us a hand with this fuckin' hose, mate. Make yourself useful." The leaks in the hose sprayed tiny delicate geysers of water, fountains of crystal in the firelight and in the play of electric torches and headlamps. The hoses curled like intertwined strands of spaghetti. Sheets of flame at the end of the street in Soho Square cast long shadows toward them. Someone grabbed the hose and set off behind the firemen.

Hood was right. Past the crackle of flame, the creak of buildings pulling apart, the dance music, the rumble and growl of a laboring ambulance engine . . . there came the thin sound of crying, muffled but insistent.

Hood led the way into the crumbling darkness, the smell of gas leaking somewhere like the hiss of a lethal snake. Godwin's stomach was turning at the smell. Odd, how a few steps into the dark, into the dripping water pipes and the brick dust and plaster dust and gas smell, and you'd left the real world behind. But this was the real world. You had to remember that. Hitler had made it real. Godwin tripped and scraped a knee on something broken and sharp. Hood was moving carefully, quickly aware of how everything becomes a booby trap in a bombed-out building. He knew a good deal more about bombed-out buildings than Godwin did. Fire bells kept ringing somewhere in case anyone hadn't noticed there'd been an air raid.

It didn't take long to find the woman in the wreckage.

Her blond hair was burnished by the light from a nearby trickle of fire, small, inconsequential, the smoldering contents of a wastebasket. There was a blue ribbon in her hair, beside her scraped face a pile of broken bricks. One arm was free but the rest of her had fallen through the floor. Only her head, her face, was visible, and though her lips moved she had difficulty making any sound other than a moan. Godwin dropped to his knees and began digging at the bricks. Hood braced a slab of wall, hoisting a heavy beam against it, then kicked a hole in the flooring big enough to squeeze through and drop into the basement. Godwin shifted the bricks, began talking softly to the blond head, saw her blink and nod, kept talking, heard the rotten flooring give way as Hood kicked through it, smelled the sickening gas stronger now from the cellar, realized a water pipe had ruptured above him and was sprinkling him with scalding water. He moved out of the way, kept pushing at the goddamned bricks. Scalding fucking water. Perfect. The woman blinked at him, terrified at the change in tone as he swore, and he cooed to her, and then he heard the high-pitched, thin wail again, realized it wasn't the woman, whose eyes seemed empty as her blinking slowed. It was a baby crying. When he had finally cleared the bricks away he gently shifted her head, tried to make her more comfortable, and felt his fingers sinking into the pulpy wetness where the other side of her head should have been. Something terrible had happened to her; her skull was crushed. She was trying to speak to him. She was going to die and she knew it and she had something she wanted to say. The baby was crying and he heard Max Hood coming back up through the floor like a messenger from Hades.

"The baby's weathered the storm," Hood called from below. He held the blanketed infant awkwardly, gingerly, shadows playing across his face as he handed the package up to Godwin.

Godwin leaned over the woman so she could see. "Your baby's all right." The blanket was pink and smeared with dirt and dust. "She's fine, just fine." The woman tried to lift her arm but the fingers barely moved. She gave up the effort. Something, life, flickered for an instant in her nearly blank eyes. She was trying to see her daughter through the gathering darkness. She knew she wouldn't be seeing her daughter grow up and live a life and find a husband and have kids; she knew she was going to miss all that, and still there was something she could give her before time ran out.

"Her name," the woman gasped softly, as if she were in the grip of a miracle, dipping into the well of strength that was all but empty, "is . . . Dilys . . . Allenby. Please . . . don't . . . forget . . . please . . . Dilys . . . Allenby . . ."

The baby must have been five or six months old. She was getting tired of the evening's entertainment. Her gown was smudged, her face was dirty and tear-streaked, and she was already half asleep.

"Give her to me." It was Cilla. She was standing behind them. "Give me the baby, Rodger." She was reaching out anxiously. "You're going to drop her."

He handed her the bundle. "Meet Dilys Allenby."

Cilla held the baby to her breast. The pale little face lay like a cameo on the black velvet.

Godwin looked at Max Hood. "We've got to get her mother out."

Hood shook his head imperceptibly. "Her legs are gone." He was whispering. "It's an abattoir down there." Godwin realized that Hood was soaked with blood.

Godwin knelt beside the woman again, put his face near hers. "Your daughter is just fine, Mrs. Allenby. Not a scratch. Can you hear me? She'll be . . . perfect."

"Her name is Dilys." The woman's eyes were nearly closed, as if she were falling asleep. "She's . . . a . . . dear . . . little . . . thing . . . No . . . trouble . . ." She managed to lift her hand a few inches. He took it, felt the slight pressure of her fingers, the end of her strength.

"Help's on the way," Godwin whispered into her ear. "You'll be okay. Just hold on a bit longer. Dilys is fine; she's waiting for you . . ." He kept whispering to her and finally her fingers were limp and he knew she was dead.

When he was leaving the building he saw an ambulance team with someone slung on a stretcher between them. "There's a dead woman back there," he said.

"She'll just have to join the queue, won't she? We're sorting through the live ones at the moment." They shuffled on like bit players in *Hamlet*.

Cilla and Max Hood were standing across the street where the buildings had escaped damage but for the blown windows. Cilla was cradling the infant, softly kissing the top of her head, the wispy blond hair. "Took your time, Rodger," Hood said, a kind of nonchalance bred on the battlefield. He nodded at the building where they'd just been. Godwin turned, saw the lonely brick wall collapse, burying Mrs. Allenby.

"Oh, for Christ's sweet sake."

Hood reached up, put his hand on Godwin's shoulder. "It happens, old man. Every damn night." He was holding an unlit cigar, rolling it between his fingertips.

"Come on, heroes. Peter may still have a bottle or two left." Cilla forced a smile. She held the baby carefully against her chest. They set off back up the road toward Dogsbody's, stepping over the tangle of hoses, trying to stay out of the way.

A photographer from one of the papers was standing in the street talking to Peter Cobra and saw them coming. He recognized Cilla and called to her. "Miss Hood, Miss Hood," ignoring the fact that it was Mrs. Hood. "Right here, Miss Hood."

Cilla looked up, clasping the baby to her, and the flashbulb popped.

"You only need the one," Cobra said easily to the photographer. "We've all had rather a frenzied evening. Actually, Norman, why don't you take some of me . . . 'Heroic man about town Peter Cobra insists it will take more than Hitler to close Dogsbody's.' We do like the sound of that, Norman." He struck a pose and Norman obediently snapped another picture.

A stretcher party was moving past them. A nurse stopped beside Cilla. They began to talk. Hood turned to Godwin. "The studio will love that shot, won't they? 'Cilla Hood rescues orphaned infant from bombed building.' If you've missed the lesson for tonight, old chap, it reads, 'It's a rum old world.' Let's have a drink." He turned to Peter Cobra. "And none of that filthy old claret you dragged up from the back of beyond. Gin's what's indicated."

"My goodness, Max," Cobra remarked with reserve, "a palate like a wagon tongue. And you, soon to be a field marshal."

"Your sources are hopelessly misinformed," Hood said. "What a joke. Field Marshal Hood."

"Field Marshal *Sir* Max Hood, I'm told."

"A simple gin will suffice, Peter," Hood said.

Cilla was handing the baby to the nurse. "Dilys Allenby. Is that clear? And what's your name?" She listened intently while the nurse spoke. "And how might I reach you?" The nurse said something else. Cilla said, "Then I'll call you at that number tomorrow. Mrs. Allenby was killed just now. I want to be quite sure all goes well for her daughter, you do understand."

"Of course, Miss Hood."

"And if I should miss you, this is my number at home. You may leave a message with my maid if I'm not there." She gave her the telephone number. "And thank you so much for being here. If Mrs. Allenby knew, I'm sure she'd be greatly relieved."

A cold mist was falling. A couple of blocks away the Ball and Hoop was burning. Santo Colls was inviting the victims of the raid to have coffee and sandwiches. His cooks were already carting platters and urns out to the sidewalk where they'd set up planks between chairs, a makeshift field kitchen. Cobra nodded approvingly, drinking from a wine bottle. Monk Vardan came out of the doorway, balancing a huge platter of sandwiches. "I've come to this," he said, "a waiter. My last ambition realized."

Cobra said, "Found your niche, have you?" and disappeared with Max Hood into the old establishment. Clyde Rasmussen, each arm around a girl, wandered off down the street, long muffler dangling from the belt of his polo coat and dragging in the rubble and water.

Vardan saw Cilla and Godwin, said, glancing at his tray, "For my many sins," and returned whence he came, Colls shouting instructions at his retreating back. The smell of coffee was drawing a considerable crowd. Cilla was standing in a doorway across the street, mist sparkling on her face. She touched Godwin's sleeve, drew him into the shadow. Her eyes followed Vardan until he was gone.

"Have you told Monk about us? I didn't know he was such a friend of yours—"

"No, of course not," Godwin lied.

"I'm glad," she said. "Monk is a gossip."

"Forget it," he said.

"Do you miss me, darling? Do you positively ache with longing for me?" She had worked her small hand into his, looked up, eyes glittering, reflecting firelight. "I ache for you, Rodger, I want you so . . . I go to sleep thinking of you and then I dream of you and wake up to the thought of you—oh, how has this happened to us?"

"You sound like a movie," he said. He touched the back of his hand to her cheek, the downy softness. "When can we meet? I want you in bed with me." Something exploded softly, somewhere else, blocks away.

"Oh, my love, my darling—"

"See? You sound like a movie. *My dahling.*"

"You call me darling, too."

"I know. You've got me sounding like a movie. The folks back in Iowa would throw up."

"Well, we're not back in Iowa, nor are we likely to be, so do stop fussing. Now, Rodger, about our meeting, that's what I have to tell you— I'm going to Stillgraves tomorrow."

"Rather sudden, isn't it?"

"Don't be angry, darling. I long for Chloe as well. She'll be three in a few days, I promised her that mummy would be there for her party. Stillgraves is a rather grim and bleak place for a child. You do understand, Rodger. Tell me that you do—"

"Of course."

"I'll be thinking of you . . ."

He sighed. "I'll miss you like hell."

"Will I finish by driving you into the bed of one of those BBC girls?"

"That's not a drive. More of a short putt."

"You *can* be so amusing. But I heard my father say that at the age of one year."

"Incredible. Most people can't talk at all at that age, let alone tell jokes."

"*I* was one, fool, not my father."

"Well, you have a helluva memory then," he murmured.

"I'll write to you. Now kiss me, darling."

"Max might see—"

"Kiss me, Rodger."

A week later he got the letter from Stillgraves.

It can't go on, can it, my darling? It's killing both of us. It always comes down to timing, doesn't it, my love? Perhaps we just weren't cut out for betrayal. Wouldn't that be funny—if we both turned out to be too good for this? Let's do try and be noble. I love you.

Cilla

After reading it he sat by the window of his flat and looked out at Berkeley Square, bleak and gloomy in the chill of a late afternoon. Ahead lay an evening promising bombs. He'd be broadcasting at midnight. He had to write the piece. But he felt empty and for a while inconsolable. He tried to find a name for what he was feeling and then he remembered the conversation with Monk Vardan the night Dogsbody's got bombed, and he knew what it was. Monk said there was plenty to go around for everyone and your turn would come. Well, it had. Rodger Godwin had been betrayed.

CHAPTER 2

ONE YEAR LATER

Godwin slammed down the telephone and said, "Shit!" He said it loudly, and the word bounced around the cramped quarters and finally rolled away, died. He wished he had a window so he could throw something through it. Where in the name of God could Cilla be?

He stood up and hurled a large dart at the Hitler dartboard someone from the Air Ministry had sent him a while back. The dart bounced off the Führer's preposterous mustache, shot back and struck Godwin's leg a glancing blow. Dear God, he thought, if You're listening, why not just kill me now? Get it over with. It's been a rotten day. Your humble servant is ready to go. . . . As usual, God wasn't listening, or had chosen to toy with him again. It was a cat-and-mouse game and Godwin knew who was the mouse. In any case, God was busy these days; maybe He was raising Cain on the eastern front. God was not consistent. He could not be trusted. He was not a pal.

Godwin's desk, deep in the steaming entrails of the BBC's Broadcasting House, was littered with scrappy bits of scripts he was writing for both evening broadcasts, the one for England, the other for America. He was, as well, trying to get some stuff ready to record for the stockpile. The office was stifling and he'd been there too long. The armpits of his shirt were soaked and clinging. His eyes burned and his throat was raw from breathing the hot air and smoking too many cigarettes. He leaned down, found the dart, and carefully—with a conscious effort at self-control—tossed it at Hitler once again. It managed to stick, barely, just below his left eye. It clung, drooping, like a sleeping bat surprised in the beam of an electric torch. Soon it would fall. That gravity business he'd heard so much about.

He wiped his moist and shining brow on the sleeve of his shirt. There was always something wrong with the heating deep down in the sub-subbasement. Too hot, too cold. He grabbed the telephone and once again placed the trunk call to the number in Cornwall. Waiting, he hummed "A Nightingale Sang in Berkeley Square," remembering the days when he'd thought it was pronounced *Berklee,* as it would have been back in Iowa, rather than *Bar-clay.* He smiled faintly at the memory. The telephone kept ringing at the other end. It was late afternoon. Where could they be? Finally he dropped the handpiece into the black cradle, stared unseeing at the various half-written scripts. His desk looked like the cat's box. He had to get things under control.

He knew Cilla had taken Chloe and driven to Cornwall, to Lady Pamela Legend's home, to celebrate—if that was the right word—her twenty-ninth birthday. He couldn't quite imagine the atmosphere between Cilla and her mother, but he assumed it was probably pretty poisonous. He wanted to speak with her, hear the sound of her voice which he never thought to describe but simply loved to hear. A low voice at times, throaty, but clear and precise at others. Maybe it was being an actress, maybe she'd worked on it. He wanted to tell her he was thinking about her and loved her and wished her a happy birthday. He wanted to do for her on her birthday what he wished she would do for him. She never would, of course, but that was life. In any case, how typical that she'd suddenly be unavailable. But where might she be? Lady Pamela was more or less housebound. There was Fenton, of course, thought by Cilla to be the oldest butler and majordomo in Christendom, and there was the nurse. . . . How could none of them be there? Could Max have shown up and whisked them away? No, that seemed a particularly farfetched idea. So what was going on?

During the year since the bombing of Dogsbody's, Godwin's relationship with Cilla had traveled a tortured, circuitous trail. They had become lovers, they had shared moments of emotional cataclysm—the fact was, it was pretty much her style—in places as unlikely as Cairo. They had betrayed the man who trusted them both. And, somehow, they had endured. Sometimes for better, sometimes for worse. The role of "the other man" weighed heavily on Godwin. The role of traitor to his friend Max Hood was a lot like an acid bath, searing away his conscience down to the bare, whitened bone. Still, he had to have her. They endured, though Godwin was often in the dark, waiting on things he couldn't control, wondering just what the hell was going on.

All that was the price of loving Cilla Hood.

•　　•　　•

When Godwin came out of the studio after completing the British broadcast, there was a five-hour wait until he went on live to America. He washed his face, changed his shirt and tie, and found Homer Teasdale sitting on the edge of his desk when he ducked back into the office. Homer was reading through all the letters and wires, notes, and miscellaneous private communications intended for Godwin. Homer Teasdale stood, kept on reading, and said: "Honest to God, Raj, I can't believe some of the secret reports you get hold of. I think maybe you could be looking at the Old Bailey here. Jail time. You wouldn't like it, Raj. Where do you get this stuff?"

Homer Teasdale looked at Godwin, pushed the hornrims up his nose. He was a bulky, well-upholstered man in his late thirties, tailored by Devlin and Musgrave of Oxford, shod by Bracewell and Jones of Edinburgh, shirted by Thomas Pink. His face was pure basset hound, his flat voice and open countenance pure evidence of his Indiana birthplace. His attitude and style produced instantaneous trust and liking in Englishmen as only a certain type of American abroad can. His mere presence seemed to proclaim that honesty was indeed the best policy. He gave the impression of being a very large dog in pants. He was a figure in London, not the least of reasons being his connection with Rodger Godwin. And Cilla Hood, for that matter. And Arch Petrie. And Clyde Rasmussen. And Reg Hasledon. His list was a long one, yet he was the kind of agent who always gave you the feeling that you were it, the only client in the world for him. It was a gift. He was a lawyer, a banker, a keeper, a representative of and agent for several people whose names were on everyone's lips. The attention he gave to his clients' affairs bespoke an ordered mind, a tenacity one discounted at one's peril, and a degree of loyalty that would have sent Damon and Pythias in search of their laurels.

Godwin put his hand on the huge shoulder. "I have my sources. Things arrive in my mail. Don't worry so much. Cheer up. Look at it this way: Hitler could be coming up Regent Street and dining at the Café Royal—but you may have noticed that he's not. Things, you see, could be worse."

"Worrying is my business, Raj. I'd be lost without it—and you pay me to worry for you. My God, it's hot as hell down here tonight. You notice the heat? Very nice broadcast by the way. Uplifting theme. Lots of bad news making the rounds." He spoke, nodding his head upward as if it were controlled by a kind of ratchet until he was bent slightly backward and was looking down his nose at you.

"Uplifting themes are my business. If it's the Germans who win in Russia, then it's *not* decisive in terms of the overall war. But if Ivan whips the Germans, then it *is* decisive—it'll be over." Godwin folded his trenchcoat over his arm, crooked the Brigg umbrella over his wrist. "It must be true. Cyril Falls of *The Times* told me so at lunch."

"Ah, yes, the Savoy. I saw you across the room. Did you try the jellied eel? Excellent. May I take that as a no? Well," he sighed heavily, "I expect it went down very well."

"I thought you had it for lunch—"

"No, no, the broadcast. Something hopeful for a change. Which reminds me, I have some good news for you." Homer was thrashing about, trying to get into his Aquascutum, in a room that was several sizes too small.

Godwin ducked a windmilling arm. "The network boys have okayed the bombing mission?"

"Look, let's go over it all point by point when we've had a drink. Dinner's on me."

"You always work it into my bill. Be honest."

"Raj, you are a cynical and suspicious man. I fear for your immortal soul at times. Dogsbody's?" They were winding their way up narrow staircases, toward fresh London air and the smell of the inevitable damp.

"Where else?"

The corner table was stuck off to the side of the fireplace, partially cut off from the rest of the room. It was frequently reserved for lovers but Peter Cobra had sized up the look on Godwin's face and given him an imperceptible nod, like a man buying a Renoir at Sotheby's. He knew when Godwin just might be in a mood to take a swing at someone. The comparative seclusion of the corner table seemed well advised. "Try to avoid disgracing ye olde establishment," he murmured.

"Beg pardon?" Homer was nearly stuck trying to squeeze into the booth. His tie was dangling within half an inch of the candle's flame.

Godwin plucked Homer's tie out of the fire. "He senses in me a certain disquiet this evening. Bring us strong drink, Peter. I may have to throw it in this man's face."

"Perhaps a pitcher, then," Cobra said, shimmering away.

"Now listen, Raj," Teasdale said, undertaking a flanking maneuver before things got away from him, "look at it from the network's point of view. You're a valuable commodity."

"Like a pork belly? Soy bean futures?"

"They don't want you to get killed."

"I'm supposed to be a war correspondent." If Clark Gable had been a war correspondent, would he be having days like this? Cilla had once told him he looked like a great big Clark Gable, minus the mustache, of course, and minus the big ears, and he'd said that she obviously meant he didn't look like Clark Gable at all. No mustache, no ears, what was left? Well, she mentioned something about the eyebrows going up toward the center sometimes and there was this dimple. What else? And she'd grinned the evil grin with her cat's mouth, the grin everybody knew, the grin that was usually twenty feet wide up on a screen in a darkened theater.

Homer was talking. "In their view, you're not a war correspondent. Foreign, yes. War, no. For one thing, the United States is not at *war*. That's a subtle distinction in your view, perhaps, but it makes a hell of a lot of sense to the network boys back on Madison Avenue. Look at those very large checks you get every two weeks. They sign those checks. There's a kind of geometric precision to it. There's you, there's the check, there are the network boys. Connect the dots."

In the ensuing silence Godwin realized he had to make Homer stop talking like a newsreel narrator. Otherwise he'd be forced to kill him with his bare hands. Cobra arrived with two very large martinis. "So far, so good," he murmured and was gone.

"Homer," Godwin said softly, "the network's concern is very touching. So is the concern of the American Newspaper Syndicate and, one assumes, of the *New York Journal Trib*. Really sweet guys, families and dogs and houses with lawns in Larchmont and Rye. But they don't quite seem to understand what we have going on over here. This is a war, you see. You've noticed it, I imagine."

Homer Teasdale grinned. "Look, I've noticed the war. I'm sure they have—"

"I'm supposed to be covering it. If I don't cover the war, people will begin to laugh— Has poor old Godwin lost it? Soon they'll be listening to Reynolds and Murrow instead. And finally my checks will stop. And I will have no need for your services except possibly to turn on the gas. Maybe the network boys don't actually listen to my broadcasts or read my column —would you say that's possible? What do you think?"

"Now, Raj, you know damn well they hang on your every word." He grinned halfheartedly, which was about the best a basset hound can do. "You have the biggest news-broadcast numbers of anyone, coast to coast, bigger than Gabe Heatter or Ray Swing or Hans Kaltenborn. . . . You are damn near as big as . . . Amos and Andy!" His voice had dropped to a whisper.

"Sodom and Gomorrah! Ham and eggs. You've got to relax, Homer.

Any day now you'll start taking little digestive pills, then liver nostrums—"

"Raj, we're being serious here."

"All right, Homer, let me put it this way. If—I say *if*—Amos and Andy wanted to make a bomber run over Berlin and then do a show about it, *then* I would say the network boys had a point. I'd be in their corner. But Amos and Andy don't want to fly over Berlin in a bomber—"

"And very wise they are too!"

"However, I do. Get it? Nobody gives a shit what Amos and Andy or Fibber McGee and Molly or Edgar Bergen and Charlie McCarthy have to say about the bombing of Berlin. But it is what I *do*. The Air Ministry has given me the go-ahead. Bomber Command says I'm just the guy they had in mind. I want to take that ride. I want to see Berlin burning. And then I want to tell the story. I want America to get excited, dammit—"

"What you want, my friend," Homer said in his flat, measured Indiana tones, "is to get America into this war. Am I right?"

"You're beginning to sound like an isolationist, Homer."

"I'm not an isolationist but a lot of people are. Some of the network boys may not share your desire to commit America to this war." He shrugged. "Maybe *the* network boy himself. Hector Crichton . . ."

"To hell with him. Getting America into this thing is the whole point of what I'm doing. It's how I'm fighting the goddamn war." Godwin took a prolonged drink, felt the Plymouth gin hit him almost immediately.

"Tell me something, Raj. Doesn't the thought of making a bombing run over Berlin—well, doesn't it just scare the dickens out of you?"

"Of course it scares me. It's supposed to scare you, if you're not nuts."

"Well, then . . . why press the point?"

"It's something the network boys wouldn't understand, Homer. It's called conscience. I'm making a hell of a living off this war. My name is a household word because of this war. Like Drano and Saniflush and Amos and Andy—"

"You were big before the war, Raj."

"Not like this. All I'm asking is one goddamn little bombing mission—"

"I'd be too scared. But I do see your point. You're an honorable man, Raj. I've always said that."

"You're a good chap yourself, Homer, old fellow. I don't care what anyone says."

"I am a good chap and sometimes I think you don't quite see it. Ah, waiter, another round here. Yes, a damn good chap. Loyal to a fault." He sighed, dewlaps flopping down over his collar. "But, Raj, getting America into the war is not your job. The network will stand for only so much—"

"Ah. You're not a good chap after all. I take it back."

"And you'd better get used to the idea that you're not going to be bombing Berlin. Should I keep saying this? Or is it getting through?"

"Quentin Reynolds, he gets to go." It occurred to Godwin that he was beginning to sound like a petulant child.

"Mr. Reynolds, regrettably, is not a client of mine and therefore not my concern."

Dinner had been served but Godwin couldn't remember actually eating any of it. He'd wind up with an ulcer if the goddamn network boys didn't ease up. He watched Homer dab at his mouth and rest both hands flat on the table. It was a way Homer had of organizing himself and his thoughts. It usually meant he was holding pretty good cards.

"Now listen to me, listen hard, because I'm telling you how it is, whether you like it or not. Before the war you were certainly widely known, but you were not as valuable to the network then. This war, the Battle of Britain, Raj, the Rommel interview, it put you on the map, broadcastwise. Before that it was your books people thought about. You had a kind of piecework contract with the network before the war began . . . but, by God, sitting down with Rommel, the Battle of Britain, broadcasting it like a football game, the fighter planes overhead, it made you a star! Now they *can't* let you get killed!"

Carried away by his emotions, Homer got a sip of his third martini before knocking it over. With a broadcast coming up at midnight, Godwin had limited himself to a pair. Homer's large and plaintive brown eyes sought Godwin's. "Do you mind if I finish your martini, Raj?" He took it and sipped again. "You are no longer 'our special correspondent'—you are a five-nights-a-week listening habit. You've swept the country like—like—"

"Influenza? The grippe?"

"Well, the principle is the same, yes. You're also a regular moderator of the Sunday night European round-up of correspondents. . . . Raj, they cannot and will not allow you capriciously to die on them and, somewhat more personally, you can't *afford* to die. You're on your way to being a rich man. And my second point is perhaps the only one that matters. The contract you signed contains an iron-clad clause the network insisted upon—the 'unnecessary risk clause'—which, simply put, means you can't take any. And the network gets to decide what constitutes necessary and unnecessary. My advice is simple. Don't tempt them, don't get under their skin, just let the ship sail on a bit." He sighed weightily. "Later on? We'll see. Maybe we can force them to let you call your own shots." He shrugged.

"You're telling me I'm a prisoner. Is that what you're saying?"

"A prisoner of your own success, your fame. Just enjoy it, for heaven's sake. Which reminds me, that good news I mentioned. It's about your BBC audience. Are you sitting down?"

"Homer . . ."

"The BBC says you're edging ahead of Reynolds! And you're closing in on Priestley and frankly that pleases them because they're getting pretty fed up with Priestley—"

"He's the most popular voice in the history of the BBC. Sure, no wonder they're fed up with him—"

"A lot of them say he's a Communist. Y'know, you listen to some of that stuff, when he gets to talking about what it's going to be like after the war, you kind of wonder—"

Godwin shook his head. "You know what I say, Homer. I say network boys are the same wherever you go. Godwin's Law."

"Well," Homer sighed, "you could have something there."

"But I know how to beat the bastards. I just figured it out. It's simple. All right, so they've got me on this bombing Berlin thing. The next chance that comes up . . . I'm just not going to tell the bastards. I'll tell them afterwards. They'll be so excited about the story, whatever it is, and my audience will be eating it up—and the network boys won't make trouble. *They* won't be able to afford it." Godwin smiled broadly.

"One thing I've learned, Raj. Never be too sure of what the network boys will do. Sometimes you get caught in their little games, stuff you never know about. Like this America First-er at the top, Hector Crichton, he's an honest-to-God isolationist, so, let's do it this way. I'm going to pretend you didn't tell me your little strategy. You never said it, I never heard it. But let me ask you one thing—don't go haywire on this thing about getting America into the war. It uses up your credit with Crichton. Do you hear what I'm saying?"

"How could I, Homer? We never had this conversation."

When he got back to his Berkeley Square flat, wearily picking his way through the blackout and the fog, he decided to give Cilla one last try. Her birthday had officially passed and he was angry that he'd failed to get through to her. Angry but also worried. He heard the call being placed, then the ringing. He was about to hang up yet again when he heard her voice. It didn't sound quite right. There was something wrong.

"Cilla! Where the hell have you been? Happy birthday, honey. I've been going nuts trying to get hold of you."

"Oh, Rodger! Darling! It's so awful!" She sounded as if she had a cold. Or had been crying.

"This is a lousy line. What's the matter?" The buzz and snap seemed to occupy the center of a gale force wind.

"My mother," Cilla said. "She's had another stroke. I got her to the hospital. She can't move, she's in a coma. I've wished her dead so many times and . . . oh, hell, Rodger!"

"Do you want me to come down there?"

"I'd give anything, darling. But you know it's impossible."

"Have you told Max?"

"In the morning I will. I just got here from the hospital. We've been gone for hours and hours."

"How's Chloe?"

"She knows her grandmother is sick. She was there when it happened. God, I don't know what I'd have done without her—she's my angel, Rodger. Listen, I've got to get some sleep. In another minute I won't be making any sense at all."

"My God, how I love you," Godwin said.

"I know, darling, I know." He heard her sending him a kiss. "I'll be in touch when I know more."

"I'm sorry as hell, Cilla."

"I know. 'Night, my love."

He sat in the darkened room looking out into Berkeley Square, two o'clock in the morning, and he knew men were dying in Russia and men were waiting to die in the desert and he was sick and tired of the network boys and he wished things were different with him and Max Hood and he missed Cilla . . . but what he was thinking about most was Cilla's mother, Lady Pamela Legend, and the first time he ever saw her—at the house on the Left Bank that summer in Paris.

It was a couple of days after the dinner with Homer Teasdale at Dogsbody's that Monk Vardan dropped by Godwin's office at the BBC. The chat with Monk turned out to change his life forever. It was the sort of moment that appealed to a professional journalist when he was summing up somebody else's life, but of course Godwin couldn't recognize it for what it was. He'd seen the gleam in Hitler's eyes one day in a hotel lobby, a chance meeting during the Munich crisis. He'd seen the moment engulf Churchill the day he was called upon to form a government, seen the flame leap up at a time when other men Churchill's age were packing it in. But when his own life was balanced on swordpoint he just didn't get it. It was simply Monk shooting the breeze.

The days were blurring together. Godwin had spent more hours than he could recount dashing about town, from briefing to lunch to interview to cocktails with a visiting American admiral and back to Broadcasting House to buckle down to business, then back out to dinner with a fellow from the food ministry who was trying to make sure that Great Britain didn't starve the way it looked like Leningrad was about to do. It was a typical day, no more nor less frantic than another. Just like all the others, that was the thing. In the normal course of things he'd have finally staggered on home but instead, weary and with a headache from the embassy champagne, he'd spent the night at Broadcasting House, the great bomb-damaged pile in Portland Place, the first night he'd not gone home since the previous autumn when Herr Hitler had unleashed his much discussed Blitz on London town. Back then Godwin had frequently found himself broadcasting to New York all through the burning and the screams and the explosions and the sirens in the firelit streets, all through the hours until dawn and the retreat of the scourge back across the Channel and the all-clear's sounding and the sun's rising.

Things were different now. The Hun weren't knocking at the door and the bombs were no longer blowing Londoners to bits. The big story was coming out of Russia, and as his old friend Gabriel Heatter was saying back in the States, *Ah, there's bad news tonight.* Old Gabe was saying it every night.

Godwin was planning to take the next day off, maybe two days, and get some work done on the galleys of his Blitz book and fiddle a bit with the final manuscript of the new one about how the English were reacting to the recurring spectre of the Hun, how they were pulling together—lots of personal anecdotes in the manner of another working stiff, Quent Reynolds. So, instead of going home he'd bunked in the third subbasement where they'd been broadcasting since fourteen months ago, back in August of 1940. He planned to grab a nap, write a couple more commentaries, and record them in the wee hours when he'd have the studio to himself, along with an underused night engineer. It was called Studio B-4. The studio was part of all the changes the war, the Blitz, had worked on what had once been the immutably upper-class ambience that had for so long been the trademark of the BBC.

The great bronze doors were the only reminders of the way the place had looked the morning he first arrived back in 1935. Now the Art Deco interiors had been chopped up, riddled with heavy steel partitions and gas-tight doors. Armed guards with live ammunition checked passes. The endless corridors were patrolled by volunteers with shotguns and the sandbags were still stacked outside. It was pointless to assume there'd be no invasion just because there hadn't been one yet. Ask the Russians. They'd even had the assurances of a nonaggression pact. Ask the good people of Leningrad.

The seats had been removed from the great underground concert hall, mattresses moved in to make it a dormitory for employees. Lower yet, at what someone pointed out was "the blue clay level" of ancient Roman London, a vaudeville studio had been obliterated by construction workers, replaced by desks, maps on walls, teletypes, typewriters, and a machine-gun nest in what had been the balcony. It never had occurred to anyone that the trouble would be pretty well out of hand if the Nazis had reached the third subbasement. The idea was to open fire from the balcony.

In this subterranean vault which could bring on a fit of claustrophobia in the bravest of men there had long been *trompe l'oeil* murals which created the feeling of open space. Now even they were gone, covered over by soundproofing for the sake of those using the small, newly constructed emergency studios, of which B-4 was one. It made for a troglodyte kind of existence at best, particularly when the bombs had been falling overhead, shaking the dust out of the spine of the building and rattling the pencils in the cup on your desk. The Luftwaffe of Herr Goering had targeted Broadcasting House as a prime military objective, the empire's communications center. They had set out to bomb it to rubble and while failing at that they'd certainly made their point.

As he lay on the iron-framed bunk bed he found sleep elusive. Memories of the Blitz kept taking shape in the darkness, prodding him with sharp sticks, not the memories of the camaraderie and the good times—yelling from the rooftops as the bastards bombed you—not memories of the rush to Savile Row in hopes that your tailor had survived another night, not the memories of the rakish days and nights, but the bad stuff. Memories of death and loss, memories of the night dear, loyal Beth Kilbane had been at her desk upstairs when the goddamn UXB came through the seventh-floor window and blew everything to hell. . . . A bad night, one of the worst. Beth, his secretary and producer—the dual roles a curious result of wartime staffing—had helped him in his skirmishes with the network executives safe in New York, an ocean away; it was Beth who had died at her desk in a hail of glass and shrapnel and flame. In the smoke and the dust he hadn't found her, he'd found her hand and half of her arm, identified by the charm bracelet wrapped around her thin wrist.

There was no point in trying to get back to sleep. Too many people were waiting for him there. Absent friends. He swung his legs over the edge of the narrow bed with its army issue blanket and ground his cigarette out in an ashtray from the Ritz. It was nearly five o'clock. There would be a touch of gray in the eastern sky. He thought about the Germans coming awake in the outskirts of Leningrad, deep in snow. He thought about Comrade Stalin, how short he was, how he stuffed his trousers down into the tops of his boots. He thought about morning dawning across the North African desert where Rommel seemed to hold *kismet* in the palm of his hand. He thought about how the first drinkers in the bar at Shepheard's Hotel in Cairo would be talking about the Desert Fox, enlarging on the legend. . . .

Godwin stood up and went to the desk and stared down at the notes he'd made for the two broadcasts he wanted to record. The finished sentences began to take shape in his mind. The writing was simple. It was the living that could be so hard, the living and the dying. He scraped the chair back, sat down, and began pounding away at the battered Underwood, shaping the piece as he typed. He was conscious of how noisy it was, odd in a cave so far below London, below Regent Street. The Bakerloo underground rattled through the early morning. The sound of the ventilation system. Boilers. Generators. All the fallback systems in case a bomb knocked out the primary power sources. Toilets flushed, water coursed hissing through the pipes overhead. Beth Kilbane had always said the sewage system made for the perfect metaphor. When the war finally ended, they'd all be washed away in a torrent of shit. And the world would be clean again. Godwin said that Vera Lynn's bluebirds over the white cliffs of Dover made for a more graceful image, was more poetic. "Poetry, my sweet romantic, is irrelevant," she'd said, and there was no arguing with her. In any case, it all made a hell of a racket. And now, of course, the relevancy of any of it mattered not a bit to Beth Kilbane, who was gone, gone.

He looked at his watch. The engineer would be waiting, washing down flat, dry oatcakes with gulps of lukewarm tea, and time was flying, the galleys awaited his attention. So many things awaited his attention.

"We've had the Phoney War," he wrote, slowly speaking the words as he put them on paper, hearing the familiar clatter of the old portable he'd taken to Paris with him when he'd set off to make his name and his fortune fourteen years before, in 1927. "And we here in London have had the real thing, too, a bit of business called the Blitz and the Battle of

Britain, and now while most of us on this side of the Atlantic have turned our eyes east to the voracious, marauding beast marching across the steppes of Russia, we've got another war that for the moment nobody's paying all that much attention to. We might as well call it the Forgotten War since there's not much shooting going on at the moment—but it's a war, it's a heck of a war, unlike any other, and it's going on out there in the North African desert . . . in places called Cyrenaica and Libya and Egypt. Right now it's a War in Waiting, a war having a lull, but when it heats up, when, as they say over here, the balloon goes up, then brace yourselves, my friends . . . it's going to be something. . . . But let's take a look at it. Let's ask the question—what is it we're waiting for?"

When he'd finished the piece he sat back and reread it, timing it, cutting a line here and there, tightening it up, and sighed at the vagueness and inaccuracy and incompleteness of detail when you were trying to sum up several months of war in the desert or anywhere else; you were left with a child's portion at best, half a plate, but you did the best you could and tried to get the sense of it right. You tried to get the outline right. That was all you could ask for, really, settling for the right outline, so your listeners wouldn't mistake a camel for an elephant. That was the best you could do when you were in the broad-generalization and uplift business.

The second piece took almost no thought at all. It was a lighter thing altogether, one of his "War Is Heck" stories. He had to keep doing them. The researchers back on Madison Avenue had the numbers to prove his audience liked them most among all his pieces. So there he was, stuck with them, somewhere between Fred Allen and Bill Shirer, trying to be wry in a half-assed kind of way. It made him nervous. The network boys were adamant, however, and it was tough to change a network boy's mind from London because the network boys were heavily involved in numbers over their lunches at Jack and Charlie's or over at the Taft or swapping bullshit stories with Winchell in the chairs at the Dawn Patrol Barber Shop. The network boys wouldn't let him do a piece about finding Beth Kilbane's arm with the charm bracelet, in the dust and smoke and rubble at Broad-casting House. A question of taste, they'd said, and when he'd reminded them that war was always a little short in the taste department they'd said that while that might indeed be true and in fact probably was, they knew his audience better than he did and that audience didn't want to hear about pretty young women blown to body parts just as they were sitting down to supper in Westport and Cedar Rapids and Anaheim. On the other hand, they argued, stroking him long distance, "War Is Heck" made a nice appetizer, let the folks know that things weren't so bad after all, no matter how bad things really were. So Godwin began to do an Astaire on the typewriter keys and pretty soon he was working up a wry smile and a worldly grin which was what "War Is Heck" was all about when you gave it some thought.

```
BBC NEWS                         BROADCASTING HOUSE
USA NY Transmis sion                      GODWIN
6 pm 17 October 1941            ''Duke of Bedford''
```

Symbols are importan t during wartime. Everybody says so, so it must be tru. Some might even say that wars are primarily about symbols. Herr Hitler's mustache is a sykmbolfor our side. Something we can make fun of. Like Il Duce's pugnacious jaw and toy soldier stance with his tiny fistz on his hips. One supposes the Death's Head and that twisted cross, the swastika, and the lightning flashes of the SS insignia all somexxx how lift the spirits of xxx Nazis everywhre. Symbols.

We found ourselves with a xxx good one a few weeks ago when Churchill returned form lhis meeting with FDR in Newfoundland. When the old boy got back to London he ws chomping on a cigar and carying a gold-knobbed cane and he made a certain gesture which has, as they say, caught on. At King's Cross Sta-tion he turned to the asembled crowd and made a 'V' sign with his forefinger and middle finger. The cowd cheered. A new symbol was born.

Now comes news of a somewhat more elaborate sym-bol with some teeth in it, some actual firepoer. Workmen using oxyacetylene torches have xxxx begun dismantling the railings at Buck House—Buckingham Palace to us Yanks. It's a large-ish chunk of rail-ing. About twenty tons of iron which is a lot of railing in any man's language. So what's the big deal you ask, what's the point? Well, they're going to make a tank—yes, you heard me, a tank—which will be christened the Buckingham Palace. It is a mighty fine idea for a symbol, one more reason among a great many why the man in the street so reveres his king. And further reason why so many of these same men in the street are calling for the Duke of Bedford's

hide . . . or at least for lhis internment for the
duration of this war.

How did the new Duke of Bedford get into this
railings-into-tanks dust-up? Well, as it turns
out, he has a great many railings of his own in London and he has, God help him, refused to have his
railings gurned into a tank of two—presumably to be
named after him. The Home Secretary Mr. Herbert
Morrison has taken an exceedingly dim view of the
Duke's refusal to play up and play the game, ov-
serving that he is ''interested in the Duke's activities.'' Anonymous observers have taken a less
circumspect view, painting the word ''traitor'' on
the statue of a previous Duke of Bedford in Russell
Square. Spreaking from his Wigtownshire home the
Duke announced, ''I am no Quisling.'' Whch was a
great weight off all our minds. And proof in the
eyes of some that not only will there always be an
England but as well the insitution of English Ec-
centricity and Bloody-Mindedness, as my bootblack
puts it. Which adds up to the kindest interpreta-
tion of the Duke's behavior as you're likely to
hear these days. Yes, War is Heck, and I am Rodger G . . .

Once he'd finished recording it was nearly eight o'clock and the
building had come to life and somewhere up above, on the crust of the
planet, the sun or a reasonable facsimile was trying to shine. Monica
Knowles, who had taken over for Beth Kilbane, popped her head out of a
former mop cupboard which now housed a tickertape machine and said
someone was waiting for him in his office. "A priest, I think he said. A
vicar maybe?" She made a face and shrugged, then grinned. "Not going
RC on us, are you?" Her tone said that nothing could surprise her anymore. She cocked a foot on a pile of sandbags, obviously once intended for
another place, which had sat outside her doorway for nearly a year. She
ducked into her cubbyhole when the phone rang. Godwin headed down to
his own office. A priest? A vicar? What the hell was she talking about? Oh,
Christ, it was Cilla's mother—the stroke had killed her and the priest was
calling. Cilla must have asked him to. But when he rounded the corner it
wasn't a priest. It was Monk Vardan.

"Rodger, old stoat. Bit of luck I finally caught you. I've been ringing the flat." Monk was talking, walking around the small room, staring up at the photos on the walls. Godwin with FDR, Godwin with Churchill, Godwin with Hemingway, Godwin with Priestley, Godwin in Paris with Rommel, the Arc de Triomphe rising behind them.

But Godwin wasn't paying attention. He kept thinking about Cilla, wondering about her mother, wondering if she were hanging on, waiting in vain to hear more from Cornwall. Maybe Max was there by now. Maybe he'd flown down from Stillgraves. Max had access to the very heart of her life, a husband's access. At times it nearly drove Godwin mad, having to settle for what he had of her.

"Not a priest," Godwin murmured. "A *monk*. The mind is a messy business . . . so, what's up? What are you doing here? I thought the PM was at Chartwell—why aren't you off emptying his ashtrays?"

"You have been misinformed. He's safe as houses at Number 10 and I'm off for Cambridge this afternoon. I was hoping to lure you down to my precincts tomorrow. We'll have lunch. I'll dredge up an admittedly indifferent claret. Give you dinner, as well, if you can get out of your late broadcast. High table, mutton, upturned faces of eager young chaps in search of an education, their shining faces full of hope—"

"Hoping that the war will be over before it's their turn."

"You slander the flower of British manhood. I shall overlook that, however. There'll be a prize for telling the mutton from the young chaps. Followed by port, walnuts, the dear old combination room. Later still, a pipe in my rooms, blazing coal fire, the sound of the rats in my walls— Well, then, can you get free?"

"Why the hell not? I deserve it."

Monk was staring up at the pictures again. "Good, that's good." He pointed at the photograph of Godwin and Rommel in Paris. "You've never told me the story that goes with this one. You and the Desert Fox—"

"He wasn't the Desert Fox then."

"No, he was the conqueror of France. What did you think of him? Oh, I read the story. Everyone in the world must have read that interview —one of your great coups, I daresay. But what sort of chap was he?"

"Good enough chap. It was a rather heady time for him. I think he truly thought the war was over. He believed the fall of France had ended it."

"He's a Nazi, though, isn't he?"

"Yes. He seemed to feel it was much like a glorified organization of Boy Scouts. He seemed uninterested in politics—he wouldn't really talk about that."

"Well." Monk harrumphed. "He's handing us our lunch pails in the desert, wily devil. But that's neither here nor there. Enough woolgathering —good show, then, your coming down." For just an instant he sounded uncharacteristically unsure of himself. He sighed. "Actually, if you'd been unable to get away . . . I'd have had to insist. Matter of life and death." He laughed too loudly. Self-consciously. And he was the least self-conscious of men, the centuries having bred doubt out of his genes. "Yes, there's something I have to lay at your feet. There's a chap who needs to have a chat with you. So, you come. Chop-chop. And we'll have a good talk."

CHAPTER 3

Godwin drove a little red Sunbeam-Talbot, a drophead coupe with a dent in the off-side fender and the beginning of a small crack in the windscreen. It had seen him through most of Europe, from the North Sea to Hitler's Berlin and Franco's Madrid and Seville during the civil war and Pamplona and Lisbon and beyond to the jumping-off place for Gibraltar and Africa. It suited him. It reminded him of Paris, of being young and beginning to learn about life and waiting for the promises the future whispered, everything stretching before him, an endless field.

The weather was fine at the start. Vivid blue sky, mountains of white clouds rimmed in dark purple like a child's drawing with an outline around everything. A chilly breeze creased the stark shafts of sunshine, October's illusions. Driving into the Fenlands was always vaguely ominous, made him think of Ely Cathedral up ahead, damp and chilly and haunted, somehow always cold and echoing with the clang and smash of holy statues put to the sword and pike so long ago by Cromwell's followers.

He shifted down as a spotted dog minding ten or twelve sheep across the road turned and began barking at him. Then he was pushing the gear box through its paces, slowly gathering speed. The top would have to go up soon. The wind was picking up and it was getting colder.

Funny how Monk had stopped by on a morning so infected by the way things were going with Cilla. Monk was still the only person who knew about them, and Rodger had told him nothing in months. Not the complicated nature of their triangular relationship, her ever shifting states of mind, the instability and the sudden warmth and the black depressions and the gaiety of her laughter when the clouds lifted and guilt and fear and anger took a holiday; on the road to Cambridge he couldn't quite imagine how he was going to deal with it all. Sometimes the cry would well up within one of them, *End it, leave me, give me some peace!* But never in both at the same time. And even if they had come to it simultaneously, reached their emotional flashpoint in a dead heat, and agreed, and stormed away from each other, even if all that happened, would the denial have lasted? Was theirs the equivalent of the Phoney War? Or was it the real thing? Guns going off and blood on the walls? Alone in the darkness of a bomb-shaken night, months ago, they had gotten the giggles beneath the blankets, laughing at their own private agonies and frustrations. She'd called their strife "the real Battle of Britain." It had seemed terribly amusing at the time. On the road to Cambridge, as it began to rain, it struck him as markedly less so.

He was drawing in on Monk Vardan, who wanted to feed him and talk about women and something that was life-and-death. There was no rushing Monk Vardan, though. He was a great one for following the forms. But sooner or later he'd get around to this life-and-death matter. So what was so damned important? Godwin had no idea. But Monk Vardan, though he might at first seem a silly old ass, was the sort of fellow you underestimated at your peril.

When you said Monk Vardan was an old Etonian you'd said a mouthful. Englishmen had a quaint tendency to take their old schools pretty seriously, but none more so than Vardan, who felt he had a larger than average stake in Eton. Godwin found the habit both amusing and confounding, perhaps because he'd attended a public high school devoid of tradition, had gone on to Harvard only because a rich uncle known as "Pus" Godwin—due to his immense girth—thought he might someday make a banker. Pus Godwin was a childless banker himself who had the good sense to pretty much own the small Iowa town where he lived and loaned out the money. It might have been Rodger Godwin's way to great riches but banking was not for him. In any case, the fascination with the old school struck Godwin as difficult to understand. Maybe if he'd been a Groton or an Exeter or a St. Paul's man, he'd have gotten the point of it. As it was, Harvard or Oxford or Cambridge made more sense in his view. Still, Vardan never had much to say about Cambridge, but Eton was always there, always lurking in the shadows of his mind.

Vardans had attended Eton in an unbroken male line since the early eighteenth century, from the Jacobite Rebellion onward, and when Vardan once mentioned that fact while standing Godwin drinks and dinner at one of his London clubs—White's it was—Godwin's first reaction was to wonder what the hell the Jacobite Rebellion had actually been. Whatever the history, Vardan actually did epitomize what Godwin had learned Eton stood for: The exact rightness of anything and everything you did simply because it was *you* who did it; and everything you said, wore, thought, or became was included in the same law. It was an attitude of utter confidence, and it went far beyond the possession of a mere family fortune. You might not be very bright, nor even very rich, but by God you were an Eton man and you were going to run the country. There was really no American equivalent. American boys had for generations left their prep schools thinking they had it, but what they had was mere snottiness, which completely missed the point. It was all rather mystical and Godwin was sure he'd never gotten it quite right. There was, in fact, something of the mystic in Monk Vardan.

Godwin found him curled up on the window seat in his college rooms, a coal fire sputtering in the sooty grate, a book open, an immensely long gray scarf wrapped many times round his long, scrawny neck. "Old stoat, old snail, where ye been? Highwaymen set upon ye in the forest?"

Rain was streaking the casement sunk deep in the thick wall behind him. The college was one of the older, grayer specimens among the thirty-one that composed the university called Cambridge. The staircase—he was on the second floor—was damp, smelled of mold and disintegration which had been creeping about for centuries. Vardan's rooms were comfortable, heavy armchairs flanking the fire, yellow-shaded floor lamps, an expensive old rug that was showing some perfect English tattiness, dark smoke-blackened beams crossing the low ceiling, an ornate old drinks cabinet, a heavy coal scuttle, bookcases overflowing, a nondescript old desk, framed maps, a Victrola with a lot of recordings stacked beside it.

"Monk," Godwin said. "Sorry I'm late. You're right, of course. Highwaymen in the forest."

Vardan nodded sagely as he unwound himself from the windowseat. "I thought as much. Well, shall we totter?" He withdrew an umbrella from a boot by the door and they set off across the wet green quad splotched with sodden leaves, beneath a tolling bell, out to the street and the welter of bookshops, tailors, chemists, and grocers. The rain was slackening but fell steady and cold, though the sky seemed to be lightening in the direction of the fens.

They lunched at a restaurant looking out on a busy square where a market was in progress. Hot game pie with chutney, hard rolls, tankards of ale on scarred tabletops. Students gathered around a couple of tables in the back, arguing about a production of *Richard III* that they seemed to be staging quite soon. "Well, I must say I am most perturbed," Vardan said, showing a countenance of utter tranquility. "I've written to *The Times* as well as to the old school. Severe steps. My blood is up, damn it."

"Do I hear an Eton story approaching on tiny cat feet?" Godwin was amused by the predictability of it.

"It's the gas-mask thing." Vardan spoke as if any civilized man was sure to know the subject to which he was warming.

"Ah. The gas-mask thing."

"Well, it all comes down to tradition, doesn't it? We cannot let this reptile Hitler shake the very foundations of our way of life. The Blitz business is behind us. And still the toppers have not—I repeat, have not— reappeared. It's a shame and a crime and a disgrace and I say bring the toppers back where they belong. On the heads of Eton's tousled-haired lads. I had to make my feelings known." He was in dead earnest but a smile played across his lips.

Godwin nodded, remembering. He'd done a "War Is Heck" about the crisis at Eton when the invasion threat was at its worst. The students had worn top hats as a standard part of required dress. When things looked darkest, gas masks had been issued, but there wasn't sufficient room on the cloakroom shelves for both the top hats and the gas masks. Thus, the end of the top hat at Eton, though it was promised to be a temporary measure, for the duration of hostilities. But Monk Vardan had his suspicions. Evil forces were at work, a small triumph for Herr Hitler: The top hat, he feared, was gone for good. "I wore one, my father wore one, my grandfather wore one—"

"I get the idea, Monk."

"Reminds me that I need a son," Vardan said suddenly.

"According to you he won't be wearing one anyway. So you could save yourself a lot of trouble."

"Point well taken. Boy would need a mother." He made a face. "And Monk a wife. Now there's a thought to put you off your feed."

Vardan made no mention at lunch of his own involvement in the war, nothing of Churchill and that great world where decisions were being made over brandies and cigars. He knew Vardan had frequently been a visitor to the War Room in the basement at Number 10, but of that there was not a word. In its place, Vardan insisted on hearing Godwin's views of the war, what he thought would develop on the eastern front and in North Africa and the Mediterranean, what if anything he'd heard about the chance of getting a "super bomb." Godwin made it clear and brief. It wasn't all that complicated.

"Yes," Vardan said, "things have been rather grisly in the desert."

"Ah, would that be British understatement? Wavell got a raw deal."

"Two views of that, old fox, two views. Pretty disastrous out there once Rommel went to the whip. Pretty bad. Had us on the run. Pudding?" Godwin declined the offer of dessert and had what turned out to be boiling water with a hint of coffee flavoring. "Yes, bad out there in the sandblown precincts. Saw poor old Puffy Blacklands at the War Office the other day; he's bearing up. His son Stringer bought it in one of those damned desert retreats. Rommel just shot them to pieces." He lit a cigarette, coughed. "We put up a bad show out there, Rodger. The PM felt Wavell had to go—*something* had to be done, and we couldn't just call in another army to take over, y'see. Poor Stringer. Sorry to say he was a bit of a tart at school. Very pretty boy. *Very* pretty. Can't imagine how he landed himself in the middle of the desert during a war. Should have been behind a desk buggering the occasional complaisant aide. Well, that's all behind him now, pardon the expression. He's dead now, Stringer, dead, dead, dead."

"It's going around these days," Godwin said.

"Ah, like a bad cold, you mean? Good for you, old weasel. Humor in all things, that's the ticket. Let's go for a walk. It's clearing up out there."

There was still no hint of why Vardan had summoned him to Cambridge.

The rain had gone and the puddles shone golden in the afternoon sun. They passed back through the portals of the college and across the quad. Men in their black gowns hurried, late for appointments. Virginia creeper blazed like flame on the ancient walls, and the bright red leaves blew helter-skelter across the grass. The place was drunk with color, lavish and opulent.

Vardan stopped to speak with a couple of passing undergraduates, stooping slightly to hear, then chuckled and came back, set off toward the river Cam. He was, Godwin thought, a perfect specimen of breed: several inches past six feet, all bones, narrow-shouldered, slouchy when he stood, loping when he strolled, his movements jerky and apparently uncoordinated. He was equally and carelessly at home in a Huntsman suit or corduroys or tweeds or, presumably, riding pinks. This day he was very rumpled in an aged suit with frayed sleeves and trouser cuffs; his boots were muddy, as was the ferrule of the Brigg umbrella he'd inherited from his grandfather.

They walked along the Backs above the Cam, the great colleges spread out behind them; in the slanting sunshine the whole picture gilded like something from a vast, imagined Camelot. Autumn bonfires smoked, filling the damp afternoon with the rich scent of burning leaves, potent in its nostalgic power as Proust's bit of pastry. Sun glinted on the water. The sounds of the city were lost as they strolled, kicking leaves.

"Puffy Blacklands, now I think of it," Vardan drawled, "mentioned he ran into you and Kim Philby and Chips Gannon and that Murrow fellow at one of Lady Astor's dinner parties the other night. What a cast! Said you were on your best behavior, nearly as bright as Philby and not half so drunk." Vardan was smiling, stabbing at leaves with the umbrella.

"I'm surprised he could tell. About Kim, I mean. The man must have a hollow leg. He just pours it down but never gets more than a little tiddly."

"Puffy said Kim had a skinful and threw up in a potted palm. Maybe you'd left by then."

"I always miss the cabaret at those parties. Must have had a midnight broadcast."

"Puffy also reports that Murrow nearly went home in tears. Some person unknown criticized his tailor and then a fat woman sat on his new hat. Puffy thinks Murrow's a fine fellow and all but insists that no real chap should take his clothes quite so seriously."

"Philby told me a good one that night. Swore it was true. Apparently von Ribbentrop was over here a while back and had a meeting with Churchill, before he was called to Number 10, of course. And von Ribbentrop was trying to convince Churchill how pointless it would be for the English to risk a war with the Nazis. He was going on about the immense Nazi war machine, the Luftwaffe, the Wehrmacht, the panzers, all of it, and Churchill just puffed on his cigar and listened. Finally, to clinch the point, von Ribbentrop announced that Germany *also had the Italians*. Churchill puffed a while longer, then took the cigar out of his mouth and said, 'Seems only fair. We were stuck with them last time.' "

Vardan laughed appreciatively, covering his mouth with his huge clawlike hand. "I must admit it sounds like Winston."

"Philby said it's true, he was there. Von Ribbentrop was a little slow on the uptake but finally got to laughing, couldn't help himself."

"Vicious little *poseur*. He's not entitled to the *von*, you know."

"So I understand."

"He's a swine. Goering may be said to have his points but he's a swine, too. They all are. Give swine a bad name, actually." The wind was coming up cold again, and there were clouds gathering on the horizon slicing through the sun. "Murrow thinks he's Beau bloody Brummell, that's his problem. Symptom of an underlying psychological problem."

"Maybe he just likes being well dressed."

"But that's the point, isn't it? He cares too much. Now you, Rodger, you'd have done the old school proud. You get the point."

"It's just that I can't seem to find a decent cleaning establishment. My old reliable got bombed out and never reopened."

"I'll tell you this, I'd have seen you made Pop at Eton. I've said that to damn few men."

"Kind of you, Monk."

"I still have my Pop waistcoat. Brocade thing. Went down very well in its day. Still fits as it did then, Squire Godwin, and I'm as old as the century."

They stopped to watch the river. Smoke drifted past bearing a load of memories. Vardan cupped his hands and lit a cigarette. His long blond hair was thinning. The wind caught it and he brushed it back with a palm. "You're wondering why I asked you down here."

"Life and death. The question crossed my mind."

"There's someone coming to town tonight, he wants to see you. Asked me to set it up. He's a busy man, as are you—it's been a bear getting it arranged. You're a good lad to come like this."

"Is there a story in it?"

"I rather think there may be." He smiled secretively.

"He doesn't have a name, I take it."

"Why take the fun out of it? He'll have a name by tonight." He clapped his hand on Godwin's shoulder. Vardan was a sly, sardonic man who loved his secrets. He enjoyed making a joke at another man's expense, all the better if the subject were present. He had fewer stars in his eyes than most men, had less respect for others. He liked to believe he saw things as they were. But a curious quirk in his nature had emerged when he met Winston Churchill: As much as he'd seen men with a harsh and penetrating stare, so had he been searching for someone worthy of his faith. In Churchill he'd found the hero to worship. There were those who said Monk Vardan had been transformed by his love for Churchill. Others said Monk Vardan had found his Hitler.

Godwin was happy with the slow-motion quality of the time in Cambridge. But Monk was growing less easy by the time they dined. He said that on reflection he couldn't stand the academic dithering at high table, so they went to a small dark restaurant that smelled of beer and port and beef and potatoes, full of smoke and commercial travelers and the occasional party of dons or students with parents.

As they walked back to the quad Monk was consulting his gold hunter, stuffing it back in his waistcoat. Life and death matters were drawing closer. The night had turned bitterly cold for October and the rain was slashing at the ancient Gothic buildings on every side. Godwin followed Vardan through the archway of his staircase, up the narrow, damp steps to his rooms. It was cold inside, draughts playing at the deeply recessed windows but Vardan was used to that. Within ten minutes the coal fire was blazing, giving off a warmth that drew them to the armchairs grouped on the ancient rug which bore the scars of occasional showers of sparks. There were three chairs. The two of them sat facing each other with the third chair between them and facing the fire. Clearly it was for their visitor. There was a drinks tray between them on a campaign table, its brass hinges warmed by the fire. Scotch, gin, brandy, a soda siphon, fat heavy glasses of lead crystal and ashtrays big enough to kill a man in one of Agatha Christie's novels. Vardan dropped into the chair, draped his long legs over the arm with his feet near the fire.

"All right, Monk—how much longer?"

Vardan checked the gold hunter again. "Half an hour. He's coming from London. He's a very important chap, you know."

Godwin nodded. The mysterious guest would not be arriving until nearly eleven o'clock. Vardan stared into the fire, said, "Tell me, are you still thick with Cilla these days? It's not an idle question, actually. I rather need to know."

"Whatever for?"

"I'll have to ask you to trust me for a few hours. You'll understand before you leave here."

"Isn't all this mysterious hinting and lurking in the shadows just a bit sophomoric?"

"No, as it happens, it isn't. As you will see. So humor me—what is the situation with you and Mrs. Hood?"

"All right." Godwin sighed and rubbed his eyes. "It's not the simplest thing in the world, is it?"

"I must assume that General Sir Max Hood knows nothing about it."

Godwin smiled at the memory of Vardan's prediction, a year before, that Max was headed for high honors. Close as he was to the Prime Minister, his information had not been far wrong. It was after Hood's experience in Cairo in the winter months of early '41, some eight months ago, that he'd gotten his knighthood and the rank of general, if not field marshal.

"Max doesn't know."

"Rather a rotten situation for all concerned."

Godwin shrugged. "Ignorance can be bliss."

"It's a lucky thing," Vardan suggested, "that she's an actress. All this must be quite a test for her."

"I suppose. I try not to spend too much time thinking in exactly those terms."

"No, one wouldn't. She makes you miserable, doesn't she?"

"That's the way it is with love, isn't it, Monk? Keeps the songwriters in business."

"I thought love was all about June, moon, spoon—"

"Call it sexual obsession, if you like. Whatever it is, sometimes it seems to be the only thing that matters . . . *having her*. Let's call it love for the sake of the tone of the discussion."

Vardan grinned wolfishly. "I'm not the one to talk about love—never been much on love. Lots of work, not much dividend if my circle is any way to judge. Did you know, I've been accused of being rather remote when it comes to personal relationships." The grin turned sly around the eyes. "Beggars the imagination, doesn't it?"

"If you say so, Monk."

"Have you ever loved anyone else?"

"Yes, I guess I have. Once."

"What became of her?"

"It was a him," Godwin said. "Not sexual love, of course. But love. Devotion. Admiration. Whatever love is."

"Yes," Vardan mused. "I wonder what it does mean in the end."

"I can boil it down to this. If you would go over the top, if you would quite literally die for someone, die to save them, die in their place—then, in my simple, childlike way, I'd say that's love, whether it's a man or a woman or a child, whether there's sex involved or not. I repeat, I'm a child when it comes to philosophy and morality." The fire was warm on his face. The coal crackled and the chill wind prodded the heavy curtains and scurried along the stone floor.

"May I ask who this male paragon was?"

"You may."

"Who was it, then? You interest me strangely." His mouth was curled into its amiable, cynical smile.

"Max Hood."

There was a flicker in Vardan's eye, a tic, which was about as much loss of composure as he ever exhibited. "I'm not sure you haven't lost me, old boy."

"I expect I have. No one on the face of the earth knows about Max and me but Max and me . . . except, well, it's not important—"

"How extraordinary. You are full of surprises. Except for whom? Cilla, one assumes."

"I've never told her and I'm sure Max never has."

"Well, who then?"

"Monk, what the hell is this?"

"I need to know. I didn't have you come here on a whim. . . . Everything in this room tonight is confidential, but you must be open with me."

"You sly bastard! You've got Max coming here! But what for? I can see Max anytime."

"Just tell me who knows about whatever went on with you and Max Hood."

"Clyde Rasmussen."

"What? Clyde? The bandleader?"

"Same one."

"For heaven's sake . . ." His tone was one of theatrical incredulity. "Clyde Rasmussen? *Our* Clyde? You, Max Hood, and Clyde Rasmussen."

"It was a long time ago."

"And you all know something that no one else knows." He stroked the side of his imposing nose. "What could it be? It's like trying to break a Hittite cipher. . . . Perhaps you could see your way clear to telling me."

"Not a chance. None. And if this meeting tonight depends on my telling you, I'd say you've got a social flop of major proportions on your hands. Ask Max when he gets here. But drop it with me, Monk."

In the silence that followed, footfalls were heard on the stairway beyond the door.

"At last," Vardan said cheerily. "Our guest."

He went to the door and stepped outside, a blast of cold damp air filling the room. Godwin stared into the fire, wishing he'd told Monk what he might do with his big meeting. Low voices could be heard but none of it was intelligible. Then a pair of feet descending the stairs. Someone's driver? The door behind Godwin swung open, creaking on its hinges. Pungent cigar smoke gusted in with the smell of rain.

"Godwin! Good of you to come!"

He recognized the voice. He would have even if he hadn't met the man half a dozen times. Instinctively he heaved himself up out of the deep chair and turned to look through the haze of cigar smoke into the eyes of Winston Churchill.

It was Monk Vardan's fervor that had, as much as anything else, formed Godwin's early opinion of Winston Churchill. Now, portly and seeming larger than he actually was, he came swiftly into the room, sixty-seven years old but full of energy, smoking a long, plump cigar, wearing a Royal Navy peacoat. His face was pink and smooth, his head bald, his lower lip thrust forward to form a rubbery ledge on which the cigar rested. He put the naval cap on a table, shrugged out of the coat which Vardan hastened to hold, and rubbed his hands together as he went to stand by the fire. He wore a long navy blue cardigan sweater that hung below his small pot belly, a white shirt with a navy-and-white bow tie in polka dots. There was an air of heightened reality about him: He might have been on stage somewhere, impersonating Churchill.

He made small talk easily with both Godwin and Vardan, noting mordantly the deadly dull nature of the dinner he'd just endured, grousing contentedly about the increasing nastiness of the weather as he and his driver had drawn near Cambridge. He made a small joke at Godwin's expense, remembering their last meeting, and chided Vardan for his spartan college surroundings.

"You have wealth, Monckton," he said, "and may I remind you that you can't take it with you? Push some of it about, there's a good fellow. We won't have to feel sorry for you and take up a collection. Monckton," he said, turning to Godwin, "thinks I'm an old ass much of the time but, as I point out to him with great regularity, when it comes to saving the world I'm the only old ass he's got!"

He looked ageless rather than old, but in fact Stalin was four years younger, FDR eight, Mussolini nine, and Hitler was fifteen years his junior, the representative not merely of another kind of men but another generation. Godwin thought that those two, Hitler and Churchill, left in a room together, would have had little to talk about. Drawing and painting perhaps—they were both artists—but otherwise they might have come from different planets.

Vardan had once remarked, years before, that Churchill was the last great man of the Empire, the last Victorian hero, cast by history into what was bound to be both a triumphant and a tragic role. "He's the only damn one of them, the only public figure of his class," Vardan had told him then, "who hasn't betrayed old England. You Americans have a tough time grasping that one, but you'd better take up the study. The Establishment and the bloody BBC are selling appeasement to the people like confidence men unloading damaged goods from the back of a lorry in Limehouse—they've had themselves a damn good laugh at Winston, trying to warn them about Hitler. Before it's over, Rodger, mark what I say, we'll all be knee-deep in blood and they'll come whining to him and he'll have to save them. Just watch it happen." Not many men had agreed with

Vardan back then but he'd had it just about right. Over the years of Hitler's rise and Churchill's vindication Godwin had come to agree with Vardan's assessment of the man. Morally and politically he seemed to tower over what was left of the civilization he'd vowed to defend, so huge that he nearly blotted out the sun and cast a shadow into every corner of the realm.

Churchill had spoken so eloquently in the seventeen months since he'd become prime minister in May of 1940 that his words had lodged themselves, like bullets in a wall, in the collective consciousness of the people. Godwin knew a great many of them by heart, had repeated them over the air and in his columns, and as he chatted so casually with their author in the glow of the fire, he remembered a speech Churchill had delivered the day after France fell. It scanned like poetry, which made it easy to recall.

But if we fail, then the whole world, including the United States, including all we have known and cared for, will sink into the abyss of a new Dark Age, made more sinister, and perhaps more protracted, by the lights of perverted science.

Let us therefore brace ourselves to our duties, and so bear ourselves that if the British Empire and its Commonwealth last for a thousand years, men will still say, "This was their finest hour."

Godwin had come to believe that the simple fact was, if fate had not provided Churchill, the British Empire would by now be only a rather grand memory.

Churchill was rolling a fresh cigar between his fingers, sniffing it with a look of satisfaction. Vardan handed him a box of matches. "White men go mad in the desert, you know," Churchill said out of the blue. "We used to call it going native, going bush. Like that song of Noel's. 'Mad dogs and Englishmen going out in the midday sun.' You recall. It's pointless to deny it. Bakes the brains or something. I've been near it myself in the old days. Quite beastly days, occasionally. The desert is a problem for the European. Always has been. You've spent some time in Cairo, Godwin. Did you get out into the desert?" He blinked and lit the cigar, puffed quickly, vast clouds of smoke circling his head. His jaw thrust forward and he bent one arm up against the back of the chair as if bracing himself for the worst anyone could do.

"Not long enough to go seriously mad. Momentary hysteria, perhaps," Godwin said.

Churchill nodded, chuckling. "Well, that's a relief. We can deal with a spot of hysteria, can't we?" A slow smile played across his lips, making his face rounder, more babylike. "Did you ever come across Lawrence?"

"I met Lawrence once. Not long before his accident. You knew him well, I believe."

"Quite. We went out to the Middle East in '21. I was the Colonial Adviser and I took him as my guide and friend. He was officially my adviser on Arab affairs. Later on we used to have him visit the house." The house was the magnificent family seat, Chartwell. "Remarkably interesting man. Very fond of him. Sad end, of course. It's been said that Lawrence himself went round the twist out there—well, who's to say? He was noticeably uncommunicative on the state of his own psychology, which was good taste on his part, I should think. But the Arabs looked upon him as a god. One man's god, another man's maniac." He shrugged. "The desert is much on my mind these days." He puffed. "Did you know some chappies call me a half-breed American? I tell them Groucho Marx is an American—there's not much they can say to that! You're an American." He paused. "I'm half-American, of course." He spoke as if Godwin might somehow have missed this bit of biography, that Churchill's mother was the American heiress Jennie Jerome.

"Yes," Godwin said at last. What exactly was going on? Had he missed a paragraph or two?

"The desert," Churchill said softly. "And America. Those are the reasons we're here tonight. . . . Monk, would you be good enough to make use of the brandy and soda? Some of us have a thirst."

CHAPTER 4

"The difficulties of our adventures in North Africa," Churchill continued, his voice soft and all the familiar theatricality drained off, "stem from two problems. The Greece card, which set the ground rules for the entire enterprise, and the personalities of Archie Wavell and Erwin Rommel."

He blew smoke across the table and the draft sucked it away into a dark corner of the room, a blue plume disappearing. "The Greece card was bound to be played once Mussolini invaded Greece a year ago. He was trying to impress Herr Hitler, who wasn't, he felt, treating him with the respect due him—so off he went, sending his army in Albania marching into Greece next door. The problem for me was one of honor. You see, poor old Neville had pledged in April '39 to come to Greece's aid if they were attacked, aid with both men and arms. There was never the slightest question as to my duty toward the Greeks. . . ."

Godwin settled in, closer to the fire, with a tumbler of scotch in hand. He knew the story, but hearing it from the Prime Minister's lips was an experience of an altogether different order.

"Everyone advising me," Churchill continued, "said that I was mad to keep our word. The government here had undergone a crisis, Chamberlain was gone, I wasn't bound by his policies, forget our commitment—imagine that. They argued, too, that the only forces we could send to Greece's aid would have to come from Wavell's Middle East army. True enough but they missed the point—we were *committed*, we had given our word. Eden told me it was folly—his word, *folly.* And Wavell began chewing the draperies, I'm afraid. He told his chaps I was balmy, said I didn't understand the situation he faced vis-à-vis the Italian army in North Africa. He said the situation in Greece had turned the enemy into Time rather than the Italians. Jolly good, I told him—then shake a leg! Bloody the Italian nose before I need your forces for Greece, I told him. In short, make haste, rid the desert of the Italians!

"The great problem with Archie Wavell, of course, is that he's an introverted sort of chap, kept to himself, hated politicians—and everyone who didn't agree with him was nothing but a damn politician. Not a well-conceived attitude in a military man at war, working for politicians. Politicians sack generals, not the other way round. Wavell is a difficult chap—had this habit of answering perfectly reasonable questions with cryptic, unhelpful replies, or with no replies at all. He is master of the ten-minute silence. The lull in the conversation, you might say. No, Archie is a good enough colonel decked out in a general's kit.

"All through the autumn of '40 he kept telling people I was barracking him, ragging on him, bedeviling him—I rather suppose I was, Godwin"—he laughed, tapping ash away—"from his point of view. I found him irresolute. I wanted him to giddap after the Italians—I began to wonder if he'd ever get on with the fighting, the bloody *winning*! So, I shipped Eden off to chat him up—ha, like talking to a wooden Indian—and damned if he didn't charm Eden nearly out of his underwear! Anthony told me Wavell and General O'Connor had a remarkable plan. And by jove, they did. Anthony left me purring like six cats. Perhaps Wavell and O'Connor would win through in the end. In short, Godwin, I was overwhelmed with hope.

"In December, O'Connor—a brave, determined little man, I promise you—struck like a fer-de-lance. Vastly outnumbered, he came like Attila, he devastated the Italians at Sollum and Halfaya Pass, he burned onward like a torch into Libya and captured Fort Capuzzo and Sidi Omar. The fighting was fierce but O'Connor was the man for the job, a British man-o'-war. In a week the victories were beyond our imagination. And what's more he salvaged Italian guns and trucks which we could send to Greece . . . and he swept onward, took Bardia, followed that with the great victory at Tobruk. It was a great campaign, Wavell and O'Connor had won through . . . but Wavell inevitably reverted to form, went beyond himself. We *had* to face the situation in Greece. But Archie went back to grousing and bitching and making a nuisance of himself. The man insisted on telling me how to do my job—so tiresome.

"O'Connor wasn't finished, however. Remember how he pushed a hundred miles to the west past Tobruk and took Derna, Godwin, then set off in pursuit of the remainder of the Italian army? Then it was over—7 February, the Italians surrendered. By God, they were surrendering! Four hundred of them came to Colonel Combe of the Eleventh Hussars, pre-sented themselves for the purpose of being taken prisoner—and Combe was so exhausted he told them, 'Come back in the morning!' " His stom-ach shook with laughter, his cheeks reddening and his eyes watering. "He told them . . . to come back in the morning . . . *and they did!*" He wiped his eyes with a stubby finger. "Godwin, what does that story remind you of? What?"

Godwin smiled, shook his head. "What should it remind me of, Prime Minister?"

" 'War Is Heck!' " He began to chuckle again. "You should use it, Godwin, so help me, you should! Take it from an old newspaperman!"

"With your permission, I will. May I attribute it to you?"

"Absolutely. Colonel Combe's family will be very proud." Churchill shifted his bulk in the chair. "Monk, attend to the fire, will you? There's a good chap." He regarded the remains of his cigar and took another from a pigskin case in the pocket of his sweater, sniffed it, and carefully clipped it. He applied a match. "Now, O'Connor was ready to push on to Tripoli. Marshal Graziani had holed up there. Wavell and O'Connor smelt blood. O'Connor had advanced five hundred miles and taken 130,000 prisoners, four hundred tanks, a thousand guns, and the fortresses at Bardia and Tobruk . . . and here I must tell you that we ran afoul of a great irony— if I didn't know perfectly well that God is an Englishman, I might have begun to doubt. O'Connor had been too successful, too expeditious!"

Godwin nodded. "But he was in a race with time—because of Greece. Wasn't he?"

Churchill ignored the interruption, the irritating truth. "If he'd taken a bit longer, four months longer, Hitler would have committed all his resources to the invasion of Russia . . . but, alas, the Italians weren't up to much in the last resolve.

"Two events now opened the doorway to our destruction, Godwin. The Greeks finally played their card, the new Prime Minister asked for our help . . . and for our sins Herr Hitler sent Erwin Rommel to fight us in the desert."

The rain was blowing harder still against the windows. It trickled down the chimney and hissed into steam against the slabs of coal. Rodger Godwin had been chased across the desert by Rommel's army; he knew the story. But hearing the PM tell it was something else altogether.

"The British lion might have been roaring and feasting in the desert but Erwin Rommel, it could reasonably be said, came to North Africa with a whip and a chair, intent on taming the lion. A whip and a chair and a sense of daring and a willingness to run great risks—he chose to control the war in the desert with the power of his will. If Lawrence was the first desert god of our time, then the second was about to be born, for that is what this great warrior has become, Godwin, nothing less than a god of the desert . . . but you were in Cairo, you know what happened.

"Our expedition to Greece began last March. Seven months ago. Inevitably our defenses were reduced. And Rommel caught us unaware. Blitzkrieg! He didn't wait for more panzers, he went directly for our throats."

Godwin was fascinated by the crucial shadings Churchill gave the tale. It was all basically true, all he said. But it wasn't necessarily the whole truth. The fact was he'd stripped British defenses nearly naked when Rommel went to the whip. And Godwin would have bet that the utter failure of the mission to Greece which culminated in the evacuation of over fifty thousand British troops and the swastika raised over the Acropolis in less than two months—Godwin would have bet that this detail wouldn't make its way into the telling.

"Al-Agheila, Mersa Brega, Benghazi—all fell before his fury." Churchill's voice rumbled like the thunder rolling across the fens beyond Cambridge. "Neame and O'Connor and Wavell couldn't stop him. For a week of pure hell and damnation, for five hundred blistering miles, we British fell back in disarray trying to escape Rommel's charge. . . . It was a ghastly joke. They called it the Benghazi Handicap and the Tobruk Derby! Well, by God, I for one am not amused! We were disgraced!" His face had darkened, his rock hard jaw had clamped down on the wet stump of cigar. "Neame and O'Connor were both captured by the Hun and are now in Italy in a prison camp—British generals!" He stared grimly at Godwin. "Rommel is a great general but he is on the wrong side. And he failed at Tobruk. . . . My blessed Desert Rats held out, besieged, and hold out still . . .

"I managed to get Wavell two hundred more tanks by convoy through Gibraltar and across the Mediterranean but still Rommel was too much for us. He outfought us, outmaneuvered us, and when Wavell was finally ready to fight, finally, *finally*, we launched our great counteroffensive. BATTLEAXE. And Rommel made mince out of it! Mince! Why bother to recount the disaster? We failed. Wavell failed. Horribly. Alex Cadogan said it best. 'Wavell and suchlike,' he told me, 'are no good against Rommel. It's like putting me up to play Bobby Jones over thirty-six holes.' I had no choice, you see. Wavell *had* to be sacked. I've put Auchinleck in his place. Now, nothing has changed over the summer. But Hitler has attacked Russia and stayed Rommel's hand. Auchinleck has put Cunningham in command of the Western Desert Force—he could be the right man, he whipped the Italians to jelly in East Africa. . . ." He shrugged his rounded shoulders, the polka-dot bow tie bobbing.

It was past midnight but he showed no sign of fatigue. Godwin knew it was the effect of his well-known afternoon naps. The Prime Minister could work all night, and frequently did. This had the earmarks of such a night. Vardan stifled a yawn, got up and stretched his long legs. Churchill was regarding Godwin closely. Godwin had the uncomfortable sensation that he was being measured for a task of some kind which was going to prove much too large. Surely, the Prime Minister wouldn't have come to Cambridge in the middle of the night to summarize the desert campaign, which both of them already knew in some detail. Beyond providing Godwin with something to tell his grandchildren in some far distant, possibly unlikely future, there had to be a point. Churchill fidgeted in his chair, trying to find a comfortable spot for his backside. His forehead, massive and shiny, seemed to glow in the firelight. They were all perspiring. Vardan swung a casement window open to the storm.

"We are now poised for another great adventure," Churchill said. "A great offensive, less than a month off. I should hate to see it fail. And I shall do what I can to see that it doesn't fail . . . everything within my power. Operation CRUSADER. We will destroy Rommel's armor, we will relieve the gallant Rats of Tobruk, we will take back all of Cyrenaica, and we will take Tripoli. . . . We will do all these things if we can prove to the British fighting man that Erwin Rommel *is not a god!* The British fighting man has engaged in the most humiliating retreat in British history —and must be made to see that Rommel can be beaten. Which is why you are here, my young friend. I want you to do something for me—two things, in fact." He grinned humorlessly, the famous jowls and outthrust jaw more formidable than ever. "You're in a hell of a spot, young Godwin. I want you to help get America into this damnable war and I want you to help prove that Rommel's as human as the next chap. It will be a good day's work, all in all. But first—"

He leaned forward, the tip of his cigar glowing like hellfire, tapped Godwin's knee with his forefinger, and fixed him with his stare. "But first, I want the benefit of your special knowledge. . . . I am curious about this man Rommel. And you know him. I read what you wrote about him last year. But I want more. I want you to *tell* me about him. Tell me how you came to meet him, tell me what you thought of him, how you sized him up." He smiled. "You have my undivided attention."

It was the summer of 1940. France had fallen by the end of June, as if it had been run down by a speeding freight train. The Nazis held dominion on the Continent. England stood alone and the air war called the Battle of Britain had begun. Goering had proclaimed that a bloody invasion was unnecessary: His Luftwaffe would have the English suing for peace by early autumn.

Rodger Godwin had watched France collapse like an egg crate in a tornado. He had, like everyone else, been fascinated by the arrival on the world stage of a new player, General Erwin Rommel, who had commanded what the press and politicians had christened "the Spook Division." Rommel's Seventh Panzer Division had moved like "a ghost fleet," striking with unbelievable swiftness from out of the rain and fog, wrapping up the enemy, then drifting away only to circle and ensnare from behind more bits and pieces of the French army. Never had an army in European combat moved so fast, so decisively. The French believed they were up against a force of nature. And Rommel was the man of the hour. He had put into action the brilliant theories laid out in his already classic book, *Infanterie greift an* (Infantry Attacks), which had been published in 1937.

Godwin wanted a scoop. The newspaper syndicate wanted something big and new, something no one else had. Godwin decided to get his hands on this General Rommel for an interview. He mentioned it one day to Max Hood, who was either just back from or just off to Cairo, you never knew for sure in those days.

"But why Rommel?" Max asked. "Why not go to Berlin and let Goebbels set you up with the whole damn general staff? Or with Goering —he loves to talk."

"They're old news, comparatively speaking. Rommel's the new glamour boy."

"Doesn't sound like you, glorifying a Nazi hero."

"Look, everybody's writing about how sad it is, Paris in the hands of the godless Hun. We feel the sadness, you and I, Max. But the story isn't the French. The story is the Germans. I'm afraid the world is starting to look at them as some goddamn master race, just as Hitler says! Unbeatable. And that's the worst thing that can happen. And old England is next on the menu—"

"Your point is well taken. I know him, actually."

"You *know* Rommel? How? When?"

"Remember when we all left Paris back in '27? You took off for God knows where in that little car you were so proud of. Well, I bought a motorcycle and went off on a tour. Found myself in the Italian Alps one day. Saw this chap pulled off to the side of the road—bloody marvelous view it was, but this bloke was working on his motorcycle, a two-seater, bloody big machine compared to mine. Engine was misfiring and dying on him. Dangerous on those mountain roads. I stopped to give him a hand and we got to talking. He said he was showing his wife the venues where he'd fought during the war, and one thing led to another, we were comparing war stories . . . then his wife came over, she'd been enjoying the vistas. So I met Erwin and Lucie Rommel. We got together that night in the next town for dinner, spent a long evening together. Lucie was pregnant and they were having their outing early enough in her term for it to be quite safe. Rather nice people. I'll never forget the way he looked at her —he was mad about her. Not that I blame him. Lovely, dark, rather exotic creature. Polish and Italian blood, I think, though she was German through and through. We stayed in touch, and I saw him again in '34. . . . By then their son Manfred was six or seven. Nice boy. Very funny—Rommel was trying to teach him to be brave and learn to swim and young Manfred wasn't buying it . . . and Rommel had this way of being enslaved by Lucie. He'd look at her, she'd be wearing some great hat, looking like an advert, and he'd say, 'Whatever you say, dear.' It was rather comical. And Lucie knew she had him absolutely in thrall."

"And you're still in touch?"

"Well, the war makes it less convenient, but I always say never let a thing like a war stand between friends. There are channels of communication." Max Hood grinned like a boy proud of a conjuring trick. "You want to meet him?"

"Hell yes. America's not in this war yet. I'm a neutral. Can you set it up?"

"I wouldn't be surprised, old boy."

A few weeks later Godwin was met at the Franco-Swiss border by a fresh-faced young officer of the Seventh Panzer Division. He greeted Godwin with a click of heels and an earnest smile and a flood of English as he led the way to the unmarked Daimler-Benz sedan.

"My name's Henry Harte. Heinrich, I guess. But I grew up out on Long Island—you know *The Great Gatsby*? Well, I spent my summers in what Fitzgerald called East Egg. Remember the lights Nick could see from the dock? Well, I saw those lights every summer. Then my father, he's the German, Mom's an American, he moved us back to Germany. He's an executive at I. G. Farben. He got me this assignment, pulled some strings. Don't hesitate to tell me to shut up, sir. I just don't get to speak English much—and you can imagine I don't see many Americans anymore. But being a New Yorker gets me some interesting jobs. Like this one, sir. And I got to spend some time with Lindbergh when he came to see Goering. . . . They like to use me to relax visitors, I guess. I'm not all that scary—not exactly anybody's idea of the Nazi monster. It's all propaganda, of course. I don't know any Nazi monsters. You can just tell me to shut up if I talk too much. I guess I said that. Call me Hank, by the way."

"Well, Hank, it's nice to make your acquaintance."

"Thanks," he said, incongruous in his dress gray with the high-peaked visored cap. He smiled like the Long Island high-school kid he'd once been.

By the time they'd lunched and hit the flatlands, the clouds of a summer storm had gathered. And Hank Harte had turned into a fine traveling companion and a remarkable source of background information.

"Look, sir," he said, "I'll be glad to put you in the picture about the General but I've got to ask you to promise me it's off the record. I don't want to get in dutch—it's really something, the way the army is over here, it's real strict . . . I mean, *strict*. And if I get in dutch, well, being an American, you know, some guys are jealous of me and my job—"

"No problem with that," Godwin said, "but don't carry this naive routine too far, son. You know that I know that your job is to tell me just what your boss wants me to know. Okay? And if you want to tell me anything just between two innocents abroad, fine. My lips are sealed."

"Well, I guess there's no slipping a curve ball past you."

"Just tell me what he's like," Godwin said. "Your impressions."

"Pretty demanding, that above all. Keeps me hopping. I guess that's pretty common among great men. At least my dad says it is. But he's hardest on himself. I'm telling you, sir, I've never seen anything like him . . . I've seen him leading his men, standing on top of a railroad embankment, shouting orders, directing fire, while these snipers—I'm told they were *Scottish* snipers fighting for the French and, boy, that was a new one on me—anyway, they were picking our guys off like flies. Darnedest thing I ever saw—he just took no notice of them! And another time, we were in the middle of a tank battle—I mean I was scared to death, wishing my father had never come back to Germany—and the General sees that one of our tanks isn't firing. So he shakes his head, there's gunfire everywhere, I'm afraid he's going to ask me to do something and I'm about ready to call a retreat or dig a hole or something, I'm just paralytic—but no, he just stands up and walks sort of angrily through all the bullets whipping around and when he gets to the tank he starts banging on the turret and swearing at the guys inside. He wants to know why the heck they're not returning fire! The man leads a charmed life—*Gott mit uns!* Wow." He went on to recount the story of Rommel's proudest moment, the winning of the Pour le Mérite during the Great War. It was a harrowing tale. Godwin thought every general should be so lucky as to have a Hank Harte on his staff. A one-man publicity machine.

Rain was beating on the windshield and the hood, bouncing as they nosed through the countryside toward Paris. It all looked so normal but for the occasional truckloads of soldiers. Farmers, cows, dogs yapping in the fields. How was it different from what it had been before the Germans came? It wasn't. They made no difference to this scene.

"He's very humane. That surprised me. The less fighting, the better. Don't kill anybody you don't have to. He's a great one for trickery, for getting the enemy to surrender by making them think they've no chance." Harte smiled.

"Is he political?" Godwin asked.

Harte shrugged. "I don't think so. Not really. I hear he was pretty much a socialist at one time but then Hitler came along . . . he's pretty close to Hitler. The first six months I was on his staff, that's before this business in Belgium and France got started, he was part of the Führer's circle, spent a lot of time with him—"

"So how do you like Hitler?"

Harte shrugged again. "He pulled the country out of the Depression. He gave the country back its pride and belief in itself. So . . . Heil Hitler!" He smiled. "Rommel thinks he's okay. Hitler doesn't get along very well with the general staff either, so Rommel likes him for that. Don't worry, Mr. Godwin, you're going to get along with him just swell."

It was a heavy, sultry night in Paris, and Harte insisted on entertaining him, compliments of the Seventh Panzer Division. As they made their way through the narrow crowded streets, Godwin suggested that perhaps the German occupiers might be pretty unpopular with the natives.

"I'm not so sure," Harte said. "People tell me it's not much different now that we're actually here and the war proper is over for the French. It's not as bad as they thought it would be. They've discovered that we're well behaved, we appreciate French culture. After all, sir, it'll always be France, won't it? We're not going to make them all speak German or something. Really, sir, they don't seem to mind us all that much."

"Give 'em time, Hank. Let 'em get to know you."

"Very funny, sir."

Godwin was tired from the long day but he didn't want to reject Harte's determined hospitality. When he looked around, paying attention to the *quartier*, he realized he knew where he was. He'd been there before. "Where are we going, Hank?"

"Le Jazz Hot. You're going to love it."

And so it was that Hank Harte introduced Rodger Godwin to Django Reinhardt, the great gypsy guitarist. Through the smoke and the music, past the mixture of Parisians and Germans in uniform, listening to "Out of Nowhere" and "In a Sentimental Mood" and "Sweet Georgia Brown" and "Sweet Sue" and "Lady Be Good" and "Bugle Call Rag," he might have been back in Paris at Clyde's place thirteen years before. It all seemed somehow the same. He drank too much wine and stayed too late and thank God, Hank was there to see him back to the Ritz. Once he'd been installed in his suite he ran the tub full of cold water, peeled off his traveling clothes, and lay in the water with the window open, praying for a breeze, and fell asleep. It was, for the moment, as far from a world at war as it was from Paris in 1927.

Rommel was standing at a window in his Paris HQ, looking out at the Arc de Triomphe. Sounds of traffic, the grinding of gears and the beeping of horns, came through the open window which was down to the floor and swung open. Bouquets of flowers filled several vases, the blossoms twitching slightly in the morning breeze.

Rommel wore a gray tunic without decoration, riding boots, and held a scarred old riding crop which was clearly a prop, something for his hands to do. He was slowly flicking it against his trouser leg. He was on the smallish side, five-six or -seven. A strong straight nose, crows' feet carved into the corners of his eyes, the eyes themselves dark and probing and curious, a very firm wide mouth, and a strong chin. His hair was parted on the left and combed back close to his skull, gray above his ears. He looked like a successful businessman, direct, no nonsense, sure of himself. Which was what he was, the business being war.

Hank Harte introduced them, Rommel coming away from the window, shaking hands. The first words out of his mouth: "Tell me, how is Max Hood?"

"He's very well," Godwin said. "Sends his regards, of course. Tells me you should try to convince Goering to pull the Luftwaffe back. It's pointless."

"Well, he's quite right about it being pointless. If we come to blows with England, it won't mean a thing until we face each other on land. English land, I should add. And you might tell him that if the RAF would stop bombing Berlin, Goering might be made to see the wisdom of his proposal. Max has seen enough of that to last his lifetime surely?"

"I'm sure he has, sir. But on the other hand, I'm certain he'd tell you the English didn't start it."

"No, they didn't. Not exactly. But do you know who did start it? Not

Hitler . . . no, the man who murdered Archduke Franz Ferdinand at Sarajevo, he started it. This is just act two of the Great War. We're in the clutches of history, playing out our fates. At least that's what I think this morning. And so . . . is Harte taking good care of you? I thought you might find him a pleasant surprise."

"He's taking very good care of me. He took me to hear Django Reinhardt last night."

"Harte's favorite diversion." Rommel smiled thinly at the young officer. "He's been trying to get me to go hear him. The man's a gypsy, Harte tells me. Something about his left hand being badly burned in a fire —he's had to invent a new way of playing the guitar and has thus invented a new music. Do I have that approximately correct, Harte?"

"The General is precisely correct."

"My wife would enjoy it more than I. She's the one with the musical inclinations." His gaze turned to a grouping of framed photographs on the escritoire that was serving as his desk. "Max tells me I am to be the subject of your pen, Mr. Godwin. I am familiar with your name, of course. You and Mr. Priestley and the older gentleman with the German name"— he snapped his fingers as if commanding a memory to shape up, "Hans Kaltenborn. Sounds like a member of the general staff. Von Kaltenborn. Do I have that right, Harte?"

"Exactly, sir."

"Harte keeps me up to the mark on these matters. Kaltenborn was the man who made his name covering the Munich crisis from New York back in '38. Very tense days, believe me. I got orders several times to prepare to strike. But I do apologize, I have not read your books."

"Well, we're even then," Godwin said. "I haven't read your book either."

Rommel's eyes snapped wide. "Just so, just so." A smile crossed his face. "You know, I discovered there is a surprising amount of money in books. Even tedious military treatises like mine. I find I have tax problems, something a simple soldier never anticipates. Harte, coffee and croissants, *bitte*. Come, sit down, Mr. Godwin. I will talk with you. Let us begin."

"We've already begun."

"Yes, I suppose we have. I must watch what I say."

Godwin sat down and turned the framed photographs toward him. There was a striking studio shot of a lithe, slender woman with dark hair and skin, luminous eyes. Another of her in a straw hat, a provocative Mona Lisa smile on her lips, head slightly cocked. Another in a garden with her arm on the shoulder of a boy with blond hair.

Rommel indicated the first picture with a flick of his riding crop. "That was taken when she'd won a tango competition. My wife is a wonderful dancer."

"She's beautiful. Exotic."

"Polish and Italian bloodlines. She dances and I don't—not if I can avoid it. I am an indifferent dancer at best. Always feel foolish. But I met her at a cadet dance in Danzig a long time ago. I was smitten, as you can imagine. The first time we talked we discovered that our fathers shared the same profession—they were schoolmasters. So we had a subject for discussion at the outset." He gazed fondly at the photograph. "I couldn't take my eyes away from her. Like all young fellows in love, I made a point of making a great fool of myself. Max Hood told me the same thing once —that he'd made a fool of himself over a girl in Paris. In my case, I believed that though I was still a cadet in training, my appearance and manner were miraculously enhanced by the wearing of a monocle—and I wore it with Lucie whenever I could. But one of the rules for cadets was that we were forbidden to wear monocles at any time! So, we'd be sitting having coffee or a sweet in a café and one of my officers would pass by— and I'd be struggling to get the glass out of my eye and into my pocket so I wouldn't be found out and reprimanded. What an idiot I must have seemed to her—"

"She married you."

Harte reappeared with a silver tray and coffee service and croissants. He poured the coffee and served.

"There you see her," Rommel continued, "in her Red Cross uniform during the war, and I'm looking very fierce with my Iron Cross. And there she is with our son, Manfred. He's a good boy. But I don't hold out much hope that he'll make a soldier. Not that I want him to, actually. I'm forty-eight, I'll be forty-nine in November, and war has been too much of my life. It's no way for a man to live his life, Mr. Godwin. But one cannot control these matters. I spent two years in the charnel house we soldiers and politicians managed to make of France—so I have every reason to hate war. That's something Max Hood and I have never quite agreed upon —but we had entirely different wars. France scarred me and the desert scarred Max. But I don't know quite how—well, it's beyond me." He shrugged. "My son once asked me what war was like and I found that words failed me. So I sat down with him and I drew him a picture of dying horses and broken buildings and dead cows with their feet in the air and men being blown into bits, arms and legs and heads flying off, and I told him that that was war. I believe he took it to heart. It was impossible to convey the rich and powerful men who always benefit from war—I must wait until he is older for that lesson." Rommel sipped the steaming coffee and nodded approval to Harte. "Tell Rifleman Gertzbach his coffee is improving."

"My readers are going to want to know," Godwin said, "what you make of this man Hitler. Whatever you choose to say, I'll report accurately. You can trust me."

"Before Hitler my own political inclinations, such as they were—I am not a political man, I assure you—but back then I might have passed for a socialist. I was certainly at odds with the moneyed classes, the old aristocracy—these are not secrets, Mr. Godwin. But then Hitler came . . . I'm at a loss to describe the flood of energy that flowed through an entire people. Perhaps your Roosevelt had the same effect on Americans—Hitler is a political genius, the first political figure I have ever followed. . . . He instituted radical reforms, quite revolutionary plans. He solved Germany's economic problems. There is simply no denying it . . . and no one else could have done it. No one I've seen, in any case. Yes, he and Franklin Roosevelt, they must share some magic. Hitler is a gigantic presence in a room. Then he begins to talk—very softly if it's personal, very powerfully if he's addressing a great audience, and he is somehow irresistible. I say this not because you will write it but because I believe every word of it."

Godwin nodded. "How long have you known him?"

"I met him at Goslar in '34, at Kaiserpfalz castle, but only in passing. I got to know him a bit at the Nuremberg rally in '36. I am a skeptic, Mr. Godwin, but it was at Nuremberg that I began to fully realize the personal power of this man. I am frequently called arrogant, and I am a proud man —but I was humbled by what I saw and heard at Nuremberg. A year later my book came to his attention and he wrote me a very kind letter which showed he'd read it. He also sent me a personally inscribed copy of *Mein Kampf*. In sum, he has saved Germany from the trash heap . . ."

"But all we hear about the treatment of the Jews? You say you hate war. Yet these people are unarmed civilians."

Rommel stared at Godwin for a long time. Then he finally said, very slowly, "What you may have heard is quite untrue. I was in Warsaw, in the ghetto, and I can tell you we simply evacuated people, shipped them off to work in labor camps . . . nothing in the least inhuman. I am not that kind of man, Mr. Godwin. We did nothing that any other army in our position would not have done. They fought us to the last bullet and we overcame them, took them prisoner—I'm talking about Poles, not just Jews—and put them to work. If you've heard anything else, you are misinformed. As for me personally, I am not involved in any policy decisions

. . . I am merely a tool of the government, like any other soldier. Like Max, for instance. I have my job, I do it."

Godwin said, "But I've heard that you had your tanks fire on ambulances here in France—"

"I am guilty of that and I can never forgive myself. A ghastly mistake. I saw that it had happened, I rectified it as soon as possible but the damage was done. It is sometimes very confusing in the field . . . but it is pointless to apologize for such a thing. All one can do is not let it happen again. One more reason to hate war."

There was a knock at the door and Harte ushered in a pair of photographers in uniform. They began to snap away, moving quietly around the two men. "You may continue, Mr. Godwin." He winked at one of the photographers. "Pretend they are not here. They are invisible. I am a camera devotee myself so I sympathize with their job. Please, continue."

"I have heard that the proudest possession you have is the medal, the Pour—"

"—le Mérite. Yes, you are correctly informed as to that."

"How did you get it?"

"Oh, good Lord . . . such a long time ago." He tilted his head back, collecting his memories. Then he began to talk, his voice changing, a storyteller who was in his métier.

November of 1917. The Italian Alps. The Italians were on the run and nothing was going to stop Rommel and the men he led. Not the cold and the avalanches of snow and the sheer rock faces he pushed his men to scale. Not being outnumbered—least of all being outnumbered, because numbers meant nothing when you were always attacking at the least expected point, at the least expected moment. Circle, ensnare, then surprise with a torrent of machine-gun fire calculated to break the spirit of even the very best of the enemy troops.

They were working their way along a deep, narrow ravine toward the town of Longarone, which was the linchpin of the whole Italian mountain defense network. The road snaked along first one side of the ravine, then by means of a dangerous, swaying bridge reached over to the other side. Lieutenant Rommel led his men in a dash across the bridge, ripping out all the demolitions mining the structure as they went. Leaving the valley, they came under brutal fire from the general direction of Longarone which was now within only half a mile. But the river Piave lay between them and the town. While Rommel scanned the streams of Italian troops running away on the other side of the river, explosions demolished the only bridge. Through his glasses he could see the town, the streets clogged with troops and military trucks and guns.

There was nothing to do but cross the river under the raking of the enemy guns. Rommel led one of his companies and a machine-gun platoon downstream and across the river. Then another followed and another. "Brave men," he recalled nearly a quarter of a century later. "Useful soldiers." By late afternoon they had established themselves near Longarone, blocking the road and the railway lines leading out of town. As nearly a thousand Italian troops tried to escape down the road during the next couple of hours, Rommel's men wrapped them up, accepted their surrender. But as night fell, Rommel led a band of twenty-five of his men to have a look at the fortifications and defensive positions within the town. He knew there were about ten thousand troops in Longarone, but he needed more information.

Suddenly they were confronted by a street barricade and machine guns. Rommel retreated in some haste, but in the rain of enemy fire all of his men were killed, wounded, or captured . . . but not Rommel. He slipped into the shadows, escaped back to the main body of his men. He organized them anew and six times the Italians stormed his position and six times Rommel directed the machine-gun fire that drove them back into the cover of town. Knowing that they might try to outflank him, he set fire to the houses lining the road, flooding the battlefield with the lights of the blazing buildings. During the night, reinforcements arrived to supplement his small band and Rommel decided to attack at dawn. But by dawn the Italians had surrendered. On that day Rommel took more than eight thousand prisoners.

One month later the Kaiser awarded Lieutenant Erwin Rommel the Pour le Mérite . . . a Maltese cross of brilliant electric blue enamel, trimmed in gold, on a black and silver ribbon. Few men ever won it, and it was often said that to win it was to become a legend in your own lifetime.

"But I am not a legend, Mr. Godwin. I am what I have always been. A useful soldier for my country."

"I am a coward," Godwin said. "I don't understand quite how men do things like that . . . wading across a river with machine guns firing down on them—I don't understand that kind of bravery—"

"Nonsense. Most men feel that way. But when the test comes things often turn out differently. I've told my son as well as the men who serve under me: Courage is easy. You simply must overcome fear *the first time.* Remember that, Mr. Godwin. It will serve you well."

Later they went outside and the photographers followed along and

Henry Harte arranged pictures at the Arc de Triomphe. Paris was truly the city of light that day. And Godwin gave in to it. He was in the grip of a man who had seen so much more than he, Godwin, ever would. Rommel had cast a spell, he supposed. He was the only man Godwin had ever known who put him in mind of Max Hood. The only one.

In the afternoon they drove to the country place Rommel was using as his primary HQ. A shooting party had been arranged by some of Rommel's new neighbors, a variety of rich and titled aristocrats, le duc this and the marquis that, and they'd obviously taken happily to the German conqueror. The shotguns were elegant and the birds behaved perfectly and died on cue and the aides and the dogs were the essence of obsequious devotion. Clouds pressed down on them in the late afternoon and the humidity grew oppressive and when the shooting was done Godwin found himself strolling back to Rommel's house with an elongated, slope-shouldered old Frenchman with sad, world-weary eyes and a wicked smile. He owned the next estate: it had been in his family for several hundred years with minor interruptions for revolutions and other unpleasantnesses.

"The Germans." He sighed, lighting a cigarette, stuffing the extinguished match into his pocket. "The Germans. One hopes they put some backbone into my countrymen. The average Frenchman has an inclination toward anarchy and rebellion. Laziness. Self-indulgence. They are easy prey for the Communists, you see. The average Frenchman harbors the illusion that he is equal to his betters. The Germans will impose a little order on their lives. Frenchmen are like children, they can be mindlessly destructive, they can wallow in fear and despair . . . the Germans will solve those problems. Take a baby out of his playpen, he is confused and overcome by his freedom and he will end up crying and breaking things. Put him back in his enclosed space, give him his toys, give him something to do, let him know what your expectations are, and the baby will behave. It is the same with Frenchmen. A dose of German discipline will instill some character in my countrymen and will serve as a deterrent to the greatest evil—Communism. In all, Mr. Godwin, General Rommel is not only a fine chap—he may well be the savior of France. A German! One appreciates the irony, is it not so?"

That evening Godwin and Rommel dined alone with his staff bustling about in the kitchen and throughout the house. The windows were thrown open and candles flickered and insects buzzed about. A table was set up outdoors and the food brought to them by Harte and his helpers. The wine was good. Owls hooted in the trees and from where they sat at table the house seemed to glow from within like a very old space ship settling down in the field. Godwin thanked his host for a remarkably memorable day, then said: "It's a shame that sooner or later my country and yours will be at war again."

"I sincerely hope that you are mistaken." Rommel was lighting a cigar. The sound of Brahms came faintly from the house. "This is not America's war and we certainly have no quarrel with America. We are not monsters—you must help the Americans see that. We are carrying out European destiny, nothing more. The history of Europe is the history of the wars we've fought. We are a bellicose family, we Europeans. This tragedy between us and the English—it's preposterous, on the face of it! Look at the connections between us . . . including the English royal family! It's nearly a civil war, brother against brother. And if that's not bad enough, the thought of adding America to the conflict—it's intolerable. We Germans helped build America! We came as mercenaries and fought in your war for independence. We settled there. . . . And now we must fight another war? No, it must not come to that."

"I believe it's inevitable. It's not the Germans, you know. It's Hitler."

"But men pass from the scene. Why should thousands, maybe millions of men die over the policies of one man you do not care for? No, it would be a tragedy. Most of all, Mr. Godwin, it would be a tragedy for Germany." He leaned forward, tapping the tablecloth with his forefinger, ash dropping from his cigar. "If America is galvanized economically and industrially and morally, then no other nation can possibly defeat it. In truth, if the Americans have the will, they are simply too big to pick a fight with—we want no war with America. We might win a round or two, it would have to be done with seapower, the U-boats and the battleships, but it could not be sustained. We could not defeat America, nor could anyone else, not in the end. You must make your readers see that we have no quarrel with America. . . . We can occupy France. But imagine occupying America—it would be like occupying Mars! It cannot be done. If you leave here with one idea about General Erwin Rommel, let it be this —he is a realist, he is a useful soldier, and he knows the limits of what can be done . . ."

When the cigars and the cognac were finished Rommel walked back to the house with his guest. "You've had a long day, Mr. Godwin. And tomorrow I have a bit of a surprise for you. So get a good night's sleep. Tomorrow is the comedy—something you didn't expect."

Heat shimmered off the dusty road, giving the scene something of a mirage quality. Clouds of dust hung in the heat waves and dust lay like

frosting on the trees and the uniforms of the German troops just edging
into view around the curving strip of road. Horseflies buzzed, butterflies
fluttered above the long grass in the fields. A herd of cows across the road
stared off into space, chewing their cuds while some farmers stood talking,
smoking pipes, wearing straw hats. The cows took no notice of the neigh-
boring fields where the panzers were clanking into view. The cows were
out of harm's way.

The village that lay a few hundred yards away was being defended by
a battalion of smartly dressed Negro soldiers, French Colonials. They were
shouting and urging one another on, waving rifles and crouching behind
machine guns. Suddenly one of them was shouting and pointing dramati-
cally from a church tower, giving the alarm—the panzers were coming.

Then the lead tank swung around and began trundling straight at the
village, a flood of tanks following in its wake. Standing in a staff car
running beside the lead tank was Rommel, directing the attack. At his
command the tank's cannon belched flame and after a pause the bell
tower of the village church exploded, debris filling the air.

On the road the German troops were double-timing toward the village, then threw themselves off the road into the ditches and onto em-
bankments as machine-gun bursts riddled the road. The troops began
returning fire and from the village there was plenty of fire, puffs of smoke,
the battle had begun . . .

A flare went up, a siren whined to life, and the tanks ground to a halt;
the German troops sat up and lit cigarettes and wiped their dripping faces.
Their uniforms were soaked through with sweat.

The camera crews went about the process of arranging lights and
reflectors, summoned individual soldiers for makeup so they could get
their close-ups. Another staff car sped across the field toward Rommel,
who'd left his perch and was stretching his legs. A man wearing a beret
and jodhpurs began speaking to him, and more lights and reflectors were
arranged around the General's car. Finally Rommel nodded and climbed
back into the car, standing with his leather-gloved hands on top of the
windshield, staring determinedly past the camera which had begun to roll,
staring toward his and Germany's great destiny. Or more specifically, at
the mildly interested cows.

Hank Harte shook his head at the bizarre scene, turned to Godwin.
"It's all Dr. Goebbels's idea. Thousands of soldiers, tanks, the works. *Victory in the West*. Rommel takes to it like a duck to water. He's a natural.
He loves getting into directing the soldiers, how they should walk and
what expressions they should have." The caterers came by with coffee.

Lunch was laid out on tables for special guests. Godwin and Harte drifted over and had their plates filled. German journalists and a few Frenchmen were gathered in groups, laughing and joking at the bizarre spectacle.

Harte said: "So, how do you like my boss?"

"He's quite a guy."

"Boy, you can say that again. It looks like he's going to be pretty tied up all day." He looked at his watch. "We're going to have to move out pretty soon. Anything else you want to do before we go?"

Godwin shook his head. He was looking forward to getting back to what passed for reality. "I've got plenty. I made the poor devil tell me his whole life story last night. From his sickly boyhood on . . . he's been very generous with his time."

"He's no fool," Harte said. "I've got a packet of pictures for you. He went through them before you got up this morning. Signed them for you. He's had a good time with you, sir." He handed Godwin a small envelope. "He gave me this for you, too."

Godwin unfolded the sheet of notepaper and read it. Just three words.

> *Godwin—*
> *Danke!*
> *Rommel*

"He told me to tell you he looks forward to meeting you again when all this is over. He thought it would be most enjoyable to meet again, you and Max Hood and Rommel. He said you could all tell war stories. Then he laughed."

"Tell him I'll see he gets a copy of what I write. Max says he has ways."

"He'll be very interested, I promise you. Oh, something else . . . he told me to tell you if this were a Hollywood movie he knows who should play Rommel. Humphrey Bogart! If you think about it, it's not a bad idea."

"He's right. It's good casting."

The last time Godwin saw Rommel cameras were rolling, guns were firing, the black soldiers were running out of the village on cue, waving their arms in a pantomime of surrender, giving up in the face of Rommel's army. From where Godwin was watching it all had an absurd quality.

When the attack rolled to a halt and prepared for a retake, Rommel caught sight of Godwin getting ready to leave. They were too far apart to speak but Rommel made a huge gesture, throwing up his hands in confusion at the world of movie making. Then he took off his high-peaked general's hat and waved it in farewell.

Winston Churchill sat quietly like a great frog, slowly puffing his cigar. Monk poked about in the fireplace, threw more coal into the flames. Godwin waited, took a long drink, trying to bring himself all the way back to the present. Finally Churchill spoke.

"Nothing quite like being with a man to take a reading of his character. So you liked the chap." He paused, chewed on the cigar. "He'd just overrun France and Belgium, he'd helped smash Poland, he represents the most inhuman power of our lifetimes and admires the most demonic man on earth—and, still, you liked him." Clouds of smoke wreathed his pink face.

"Look, I make no apology. I liked him. He's an impressive man. It's a fact."

"And this Henry Harte—he was devoted to him?"

"Worshiped him is more like it."

"Is that your impression of the men who serve under him?"

"I'd say his men respect him, are awed by him, and, and . . ."

"Don't be shy," Churchill rumbled.

"Well, I'd say they think he's the luckiest man alive. Harte told me he's like their good luck charm. You said the British fighting man has come to believe Rommel's a god. That may be, Prime Minister, but I suspect there's something more important than that . . . *his own men think he's a god.*"

Churchill nodded. "And you like him," he mused. "That makes the job I want you to do more . . . uncomfortable for me. But, war is war, that's the point, I daresay."

"Isn't it about time you just tell me what you want me to do?"

Churchill glanced at Monk, raised his eyebrows, then spoke with deliberate cool.

"I want you to kill Erwin Rommel for me."

Godwin felt his mouth go dry and drop open at the same time. He couldn't possibly have heard correctly—

"Let me tell you," Churchill said, "about a little surprise we've cooked up for your friend the invincible Herr Rommel. Let me tell you about PRAETORIAN. As I said, some of our British fighting men are going bush. Do you know what I mean, Godwin?"

"I think you'd better explain everything very carefully."

"I mean that they are beginning to think like the desert nomads, not like Britons. They've begun to say that Rommel cannot be defeated. And why not? Because it is written! Do you understand? *Because it is written* . . . Lawrence told me a story once, told me that the chieftains he rode with believed that everything was 'written.' Fate, *kismet*, whatever it was, there was no escaping it. What do you think of that, Godwin?"

"I guess it leaves out free will. I think a man can control events to some extent. But, of course, if he does, then they'll say that that was what was written. It's not worth arguing about. I know a man who rode with Lawrence. He says Lawrence taught the chieftains that nothing is written—"

"Not exactly," Churchill interrupted. "He taught them that there are men who can do the writing. He showed them that T. E. Lawrence, for one, could write what was to be written. Well, young Godwin, I'm going to show the British soldier what's written and what isn't and who's doing the writing. Nowhere is it written that Rommel owns the desert. I intend to make that point with perfect clarity. Furthermore I intend to reveal exactly who is doing the writing these days. It is written that Rommel will be destroyed and the Hun swept from the desert as if by the plague itself. They may ask how I know that this is written . . . well, I have written it, Mr. Godwin, and so it shall be! The sands of the western desert will bury the Hun. *It is written.*"

"And what is it," Godwin said, "that you have written about me?"

"Let us look at your position. You are already famous and you must be very rich, as well. Books and radio and lectures when this is all over. The world will be your oyster. So, fame and riches are already yours. With what can I reward you? Tempt you? Ahhh . . . I know—I'm going to make you a great hero, Rodger Godwin. How do you like that? Godwin of North Africa!"

"It scares the hell out of me. Heroes have a habit of getting killed. Not my kind of thing at all."

"You're far too modest. Great strapping fellow like you, carrying your weight pretty well. Do you have a temper, Godwin?"

"I have a sense of evening the score and a lot of patience. Temper? I'm a rather phlegmatic chap—"

Vardan spoke up. "He's a tenacious lout. No braver than the next man unless, of course, the next man is me. Good man in a scrum, I should think."

"Well, I'm about to make you a part of the history of this war." Churchill leaned forward, hands on knees, cigar burning low, ash about to drop. "I'm going to give you the exclusive of a lifetime. You, an American. You are going to be the only correspondent covering PRAETORIAN. And PRAETORIAN is one of the most daring moves of the war. The stuff of which legends are made. And important—important to America, important to Franklin Roosevelt."

"All right, fine. Now let's get back to Rommel and me. The scary part."

"We're going to take Rommel out of this war. And get America into it. Is that important enough for you?"

"How?"

"I'm sending a commando team to North Africa. Their orders are to kill Rommel." He waited, his face bland.

Godwin swallowed hard. "And what about America?"

"You will tell the astonishing story to your countrymen. The story of British heroism and determination and derring-do. Franklin wants to get into this war but he needs a willing public, a mighty wave of public opinion to convince Congress . . . and PRAETORIAN is the kind of thing he can use. He needs all the reasons he can lay his hands on. We need more than American ships and guns—we need an American fighting army. Your story will light the fuse . . . and America will be blown right into this war. After PRAETORIAN you'll go stateside, meet with Franklin, give some speeches and join with him in a 'Fireside Chat,' you'll brief prominent members of Congress—talk with your own congressmen. Where are you from? What state?"

"Iowa."

"Well, there you are, then. You'll meet with the senators and whatnot from Iowa—right in the heart of the nation. You'll be selling the British and their lonely struggle to save the world from the bloody anti-Christ! Believe me, Godwin, it will help. More than you know. Franklin is almost ready. While you're in Washington, we'll be launching our huge offensive, CRUSADER. We'll bury the Germans—the time will be right." Churchill beamed at him, eyes bright, full of delight at the plot he'd constructed. "My God, I wish I were your age again—you see, it's an eyewitness report I want, from the man who was on the team when we went in after Rommel."

"Let me get this straight. Are you suggesting that I actually take part in the mission?"

"All the way, in and out. It's the chance of a lifetime, is it not?"

Godwin began to grin. He was seeing Homer Teasdale's frantic face. He was thinking about Hector Crichton and all the rest of the network boys. Suddenly the bombing mission over Berlin didn't seem like such a big deal. Not compared to this.

"You seem pleased by the idea," Churchill said.

"More than you can imagine," Godwin replied. "On the other hand, I have several allergies, my eyes could be better, my arches while not completely fallen have seen better days—and the idea of joining a commando unit scares hell out of me."

"Remember what Rommel told you. All you have to do is conquer fear the first time. You're the sort of chap who'll do what he has to do. Won't he, Monk? He's just the man for the job, isn't he?"

"The one and only," Monk said.

"I'm no commando," Godwin observed.

Churchill shook his head. "Don't give it a second thought." He slowly swirled the dark amber fluid around the glass, watching it seep back down the sides. "You'll be in extraordinarily good hands. The best man in the world is leading the mission. You will be safe as houses. You have my word."

Godwin nodded. The whole idea, in its immensity, was beginning to sink in. He felt as if the heat from the fireplace were melting him. "The best man in the world. Bulldog Drummond?"

"Altogether more incomparable," Churchill said.

"Who is it?"

"Why, Max Hood, of course."

Vardan was smiling at Godwin. Churchill was smiling at Godwin.

Everybody was smiling but Rodger Godwin.

CHAPTER 5

In the week that followed his visit with the Prime Minister and Monk Vardan, Godwin slept badly. Was he about to throw his life away trying to murder a German tank commander whom he actually liked? And who fought like a god? Was he just plain nuts? What had he been thinking, going along with it?

Was he doing it to confound and irritate the network boys? Because he enjoyed imagining Hector Crichton going off like a rocket? Was that worth dying for? What were the chances of getting out alive?

There was always ambition. His career. Make it better, make it bigger, there was going to be a hell of a world after the war and it would be good to have a running start. There was going to be a lot of money around and it was going to be closer to one big world than most people had ever dreamed. He had seen the future and it was called television, and as soon as the war was over, whammo, climb on board or it would run over you. It would be a good thing to have gone into the desert with Max Hood and have come out with Rommel's scalp. Unless, of course, he got killed trying to do it.

Ambition had him in its grip, at least in the middle of the night. Maybe it had always had him, holding him tight, never letting him go. Well, so be it.

Maybe it was written.

And then there was the war. Winning the war. It didn't depend on Rodger Godwin, but it sure as hell depended on America. PRAETORIAN would give him the chance to take action against what was evil. And it was evil. He'd looked it in the eye and he knew.

In September of 1938, at the Hotel Dreesen in Godesberg, during what came to be known as the Munich Crisis, while Neville Chamberlain was handing Czechoslovakia to the Nazis, Godwin had run into Adolf Hitler in the lobby. The Nazi leader was staying there, and after breakfast one morning Godwin had come through the entrance and suddenly there he was. Wearing a gray double-breasted suit, hands in the pocket of his jacket, Hitler walked across the carpet with almost mincing steps. He was alone, seemed lost in thought. When he looked up his eyes widened, as if surprised to find another human being in his path. His arm jerked and he stopped, his leg twitching slightly as if taken by a cramp. He brushed the dark hair from across his pale forehead and his eyes darted across Godwin's face. "You," he said in a pleasantly conversational tone, so unlike the shrieking and ranting Godwin had witnessed at party rallies. "I know you. Don't tell me. Your face. Ahhhh . . ." He slowly began to shake his forefinger in Godwin's face. "A journalist. Ahh . . . American! Correct?"

"Yes, sir. Rodger Godwin."

"Of course, Godwin. Well, do you think these English will let us all live in peace? You are a judge of such matters." Hitler's eyes were lit with curiosity, lit by a fire from deep within his skull. He was a caricaturist's dream, the mustache like Chaplin's tramp, the flopping hair. For that matter, he bore a striking resemblance to Karl Nesheim, who'd been sports editor on the old paper back home, the *Clarion Eagle*. But Karl's eyes were soft and emotional, a beer drinker's eyes, nothing like Hitler's. You had to see Hitler's eyes for yourself. They burned like torches. His question seemed utterly sincere. Waiting for Godwin's answer, he placed one hand on his hip, almost the pose of a boulevardier, turned to look out the window at the Rhine. A group of aides had appeared in the lobby behind them. The official Mercedes waited.

"I think," Godwin said, "they will give you what you want." His German, he was sure, was hopelessly ungrammatical.

Hitler stared at him for a moment, getting the meaning clear. Then he smiled. "As I said, peace. The English are a reasonable people. We have many ties to the English. We all want peace. The German people know suffering better than anyone else. So we want peace more than anyone else, I assure you." At that instant he seemed a middle-aged, middle-class German. "If we have peace, then it will be a good day's work, Mr. Godwin. Good luck to you, good luck to all of us." Hitler then extended his hand and shook Godwin's warmly, in both of his, the feverish eyes glimmering by themselves, utterly unrelated to the small smile beneath the brush mustache. Then his aides reached him, gave Godwin questioning glances, and they were gone down the stairway and into the Mercedes.

Until then Godwin had seen Hitler only once close up when he'd answered reporters' questions. Godwin had been one of maybe ten men with notebooks, yet Hitler had remembered him. The man was superbly banal, on the surface a kind of Sinclair Lewis creation from *Main Street*, a booster; but in his eyes you saw Old Nick, the spirit of madness and evil, and the banality was gone. Something horrible was living in the body of a man. The meeting had clarified and defined Hitler for him. He never forgot it and never tried to describe it to anyone else. It was quite enough that he knew, and that knowing gave him a stake in the war, in the fate of civilization. Sometimes he wondered if anyone would remember in fifty years what all the fuss had been about. That an entire civilization had been at stake. Fifty years hence, would they still be able to think such large thoughts?

Max Hood would be leading the charge. That thought would turn him around in those midnight fits of fear. Into the fray with Max—the thought buoyed him. Nothing would go wrong with Max Hood in command. Max Hood always got through and he always came back. . . . Godwin supposed he'd follow Max Hood anywhere.

Godwin was still waiting to hear from Max Hood the night he had dinner with Anne Collister and her brother Edward. Anne was a tall, elegant, stately English girl, blue-eyed and with a shimmering golden pageboy, who represented the ideal of a county family, landed gentry from the old days, far more accurately than the dark, compact Cilla. Anne looked as if she'd stepped out of an advertisement for the latest miracle shampoo or a holiday in the Lake District. She was, with her V-shaped face and intelligent, curious eyes, always steady and serene. Or, as her father, a financial source in the City, might have said, Anne was *sound*. She was thirty years old, her complexion was English perfect, her accent and view of life as impeccable as all those generations of Collisters could make it, her voice on the flutey side but very soft, and she was in love with Rodger Godwin.

For his part Godwin was very fond of Anne, enjoyed her company immensely, and felt a good deal of guilt about the whole relationship. Anne was by nature independent and undemanding but she had come late to sexual passion and, in her shy way, she needed Godwin's attention to satisfy her various desires. He did what he could to make it clear that he wasn't marriage material and she would smile knowingly, in her mind writing off his attitude as part of the romantic mystique she saw in the aura surrounding the famous foreign correspondent. He would, she believed, come round in time if only she didn't push it. When a man is a loner, her mother had told her, the best thing to do is forget him entirely and move on. But if you simply couldn't behave sensibly, if you had to have him, then never hem him in. Anne wasn't at all sure her mother knew what she was talking about but, still, her words had the ring of good advice. She gave Godwin plenty of room. When she let herself think about it, she assumed he must have other women from time to time—after all, wasn't that more or less a part of being a trench-coated foreign correspondent?

Some hints of Anne's views on such matters as his aura or mystique occasionally seeped through to Godwin and he felt that for such an intelligent woman she certainly had it well within her power to be quite dim. What she was, of course, was an extremely sheltered, well-bred young woman of taste and integrity trying to seem worldly. Godwin was very fond of the woman she really was, respected and admired the taste and integrity, found the self-conscious acceptance of her own passion touching and appealing; indeed, he might very well have fallen in love with her if he had not been obsessed by everything that was Cilla Hood.

As it was, he took what measures were available to him to avoid hurting Anne while at the same time trying to project an attitude of detachment which might one day cool her ardor and finally turn her away. The irony was not lost on him: He wanted with all his heart to be a warm, giving, adoring man, which was precisely what Anne Collister deserved. But all his warmth and concern and adoration were spent in the course of battering away at whatever he and Cilla managed to have between them.

Cilla knew, of course, about his relationship with Anne and it set differently with her on different days. Cilla looked upon life as a complicated board game along the lines of chess, "but lots more fun," as she'd pointed out to Godwin. He couldn't imagine reducing life to a game status. Anne Collister, like everyone else, knew nothing of Godwin's involvement with Cilla beyond passing friendship. When Godwin thought about it the whole business gave him something like a gin headache. So he tried not to think about it.

Edward Collister was slumped forward over his drink, elbows on the table, chin in palms when Godwin escorted Anne into the Ritz dining room. He was a few years older than his sister and a few inches shorter, a thick, chunky man with a delicately chiseled face, deeply lined by overwork. His thick dark brown hair looked as if it had been combed with a rake and some of it hung down across the creases in his forehead. Godwin hadn't seen him since somebody's wedding in midsummer. The intervening months had taken a considerable toll. He'd come down from Cambridge in the mid-Thirties, leaving the world of academic science for a ministry job in Whitehall. He'd had a hand overseeing or advising or administering the development of radar which had given the RAF one of its critical advantages in the air war of summer 1940.

Across her sherry Anne Collister gave her brother a worried, appraising look. "You're half dead, Ned."

"Please, no poetry," Collister said.

"Doesn't he look half dead, Rodger? Oh, I'm so worried about you. Mother's beside herself."

"I'd like a picture of that." He grinned past the rim of his martini and glanced beseechingly at Godwin. "Tell her, Rodge. Everybody I know looks the same way."

"I don't and you know me," she said. "Rodger doesn't."

"You know what I mean."

"You need to get away. You need a nice holiday—"

"Rodger, explain to her, there's this war thing—"

"Ned! I'm serious!"

"Well, I've been away. Cambridge, actually."

"Cambridge," she said, "is not *away*. And I meant to say abroad, anyway."

"Annie, Annie, Annie . . . listen to her, Rodger. *Abroad*."

"Bermuda—"

"But I'm not the Duke of bloody Windsor! The war is abroad, look around you, little sister. There's no nipping off to anywhere, not anymore—"

"You know damn well what *I* mean, Ned!" She flared at him, her face suddenly flushed, first with anger, then with regret. "Please don't play games with me, Ned. You'll make yourself ill, the way you're going."

Edward ignored her, drained his glass, motioned to the waiter for another, and grinned at Godwin. "Women," he said. "Pretty women. Remember this, Rodge. Every pretty woman you meet, just remember, somebody, somewhere has had her up to here. That's the next law, right after the old one about gravity. Say, speaking of scientific laws, I ran into a scientist who thinks you're just swell. A swell fellow."

"You don't say. I don't know many scientists."

"Really? Well, I don't blame you. I have reference to L. W. Winship. Said he listens to you on the radio in his laboratory. Can't imagine how your name came up but it's a fact. I wouldn't lie to you." His fresh martini arrived and he nodded to the waiter. "God bless you, Antonio. Won't you join me, Rodge? Anne? Go on, have some more of those simpering little sherries."

"No, thank you," Anne said. "And you've had quite enough, too. Antonio, we'll order now."

Once Antonio had departed Edward turned back to Godwin. "What would I do without a little sister to pester me? No, I can't imagine it." He sighed. "Yes, L. W. Winship. The man has a great future." He yawned involuntarily.

Godwin said: "Is he working for you?"

"For. With. He's one of the best men in England. It's all very secret, you know. But he's one of the best and brightest of his generation. I think I'm safe in saying L. W. Winship is one of the men who will remake this world after the war. If there's anything left to remake."

"Wasn't he in on the radar thing?" Godwin was probing gently. Edward Collister was the kind of man who put great stock in knowing more than anyone else. It was always best to reinforce his confidence in himself.

"Yes, yes. But only peripherally. He's on to something else now. Much bigger. Just the earliest of opening moves but . . . let's put it this way, the bombing of Coventry will belong to another era altogether if everything goes right for Winship."

"Coventry," Godwin said softly. He felt Anne's hand closing over his on the table. It was an almost unconscious gesture, proprietary.

"Yes, we're coming up on the first anniversary."

Anne shook her head angrily. "Ghastly. Bombing unarmed civilians . . . how can people do such things?"

"Well, the RAF is giving it back in kind," Godwin said. "Precision bombing of military targets has been proven a fiasco. If you come in low enough, in daylight, to know what you're hitting—well, it becomes a suicide mission. That's simply a fact. There's no choice but to simply level cities—"

Edward coughed, lit another cigarette, said: "Terror bombing—"

"Well, that's jolly good by me," Anne said. "Fine! Think of all the terror they've inflicted on us! If we destroy all of German culture, I wouldn't shed a tear. Would you?"

Her brother's bloodshot eyes blinked at the smoke. "It's not German culture that concerns some of us, Anne. It's the women and the children and the old, noncombatants . . . our policy now is to make no distinctions, we're killing everyone—"

Godwin said: "It's the nature of war, isn't it? What else is there to do? Stop bombing Germany?"

"You may know," Edward mused, "that we're losing planes at an unfeasibly high rate."

"Yes, I know," Godwin said.

"But the Germans must be made to *feel* this war," Anne insisted. "They must accept the consequences of their acts, surely. I'm not ashamed to be biblical, are you? An eye for an eye."

"Yes, yes, of course," Edward said. Dinner had arrived but he was only managing to pick at some sorry boiled vegetables. "That's all very easy to say, the Germans are no damned good, let's kill them all—but it's not the real world. Rodger says there's no other choice but bombing the civilian population but that's not quite the case, is it, Rodger? Some of us question the efficacy of terror bombing—leaving morality out of it utterly. Break their spirit, I hear some people say. But did the Germans break our spirit with the Blitz? Of course not. Why should the Germans be any different? I can't think of a single reason. So why not transfer our bombers to the Middle East, the Far East, to the battle going on every day in the North Atlantic? Our bombers would be more useful in any of these theaters. That's the way we might best hurt the Nazis and aid the Russians, for instance . . . while maintaining some honor, some of the RAF's *amour propre*. Unlike our enemies." Edward brushed hair out of his eyes only to have it fall back again. He gave up on it.

Anne, finishing her sole and neatly putting her cutlery down, said: "You worry too much, Ned. You always worry about making a better world. I say start making it better by bombing the Germans to dust and have done with it. Don't you, Rodger?"

Godwin shrugged. "I don't know. I always want to have it both ways. My head tells me one thing, my emotions tell me something else."

She smiled indulgently. "You mean you'd like to bomb them to dust while being a great humanitarian."

"I suppose. Something like that."

"Sooner or later," Edward said, "you'll have to choose. Morality or the reverse. What you know to be right or what you know to be wrong."

"But it never seems clear-cut, Edward. That's the problem—I don't mean Hitler, obviously. That's not a choice. No sane man could think it over and choose a world made by Hitler. No sane man would want America to stay on the sidelines. That's not a choice either. But the *choices*, there are always so many sides—"

Edward Collister chuckled softly behind his hand, then trailed off coughing. "Anyone can make the decision when it's clear-cut, Rodger. When it's clear-cut, it means absolutely nothing."

Anne defended him. "But Rodger's a journalist, Ned. Be fair. He has to see both sides—he's not an advocate. You must see that, surely."

Edward smiled wanly. "Is that it, Rodger?"

"Well, all I'm advocating at the moment is getting America into the war."

Edward nodded. "That's right. We've got to get some help for the Russians, for God's sake. Let's face it—they're fighting the war for us. We haven't even glimpsed this war—"

"Oh, Ned! That's preposterous!" Anne shook her head.

"Oh, we've seen it out in the desert, but otherwise it's true," he insisted. "We've seen nothing of it compared to the Russians. If Moscow is lost, history will lay it at our doorstep, you know that. The Russians needed a second front in the West to help them out and we were useless. This old country had decayed and we were useless, toothless—"

"There wasn't much the English could do," Godwin said.

"Ah," Edward said, "is that what we must put on our tombstone? 'There Wasn't Much the English Could Do. Rest in Peace.' No, this is a society that committed suicide, choked on its own fat. 'Dead of the Gout'—that's the epitaph." He sank back in his chair, trembling, face white.

Anne looked worried. "Will Moscow fall? It does look that way, doesn't it?"

Edward threw up his hands, spoke impatiently. "If Moscow falls there will be a massacre like the world has never seen before. The stench of the bodies will reach us here. At the bloody Ritz!" He lit another cigarette and stared off into space. His nearly full plate was pushed away. Anne waited a long time and then in her very well-bred way tried to lighten the conversation.

"Mummy was telling me about what Mary—our ancient cook, Rodger, such a grumpy old wonder—what Mary did last spring. She just doesn't think the Germans are *serious* people. For instance—"

"Who doesn't think the Germans are serious?" Edward muttered.

"Mary, our cook."

"I've always said she was insane. This proves it if that pudding—what was it?—"

"Spotted Dick," Anne said.

"Yes, Spotted Dick. No sane person could have served that to impressionable children. She was mad then and is mad now."

"Well, Mary was making one of her famous breakfasts for Daddy, everything from hot scones to kippers and that awful kidney dish he dotes on—"

"Oh my God, worse than the Spotted Dick!"

"—when the Germans dropped some unexpected incendiaries in our street. One bounced off our roof, fell right past the kitchen window where she was working, and came to rest against the side of the house. Burning like mad, you see. Well, Mary was very irritated by the interruption. So she took the great pot of newly made oatmeal and dumped it out the window on the bomb—and put it out! She didn't think much of it as a fearful weapon of destruction! And she told Daddy he was going to have to make do without his porridge—can you believe it, she never told Daddy about the bomb! Thought it would put him off his feed!"

Edward seemed cheered. "Take more than that to put the old bugger off his feed!"

Godwin wished he'd heard the story at the time. It would have made a perfect "War Is Heck." Not much later they left the dining room. Edward was heading back to his office, intending to clear up just a few more odds and ends before going home.

Godwin and Anne returned to Hay Hill with the mist thickening, dripping from the rainspouts. It was eleven o'clock and in an hour Godwin had a broadcast to make.

Anne smiled as they stood under the eaves. "Thanks for being so helpful with poor Ned."

"It's easy, I like him."

"I know you're dying to be off, Rodger. You always get that hunted, shifty look, like a fox hearing the baying. Are you coming back here after the broadcast?"

"Would you like me to?"

"Well, you know what kind of naughty girl I am. I always *want* you to. But Mummy is coming by practically at dawn on some mission or other— so perhaps I should get my eight hours." She smiled and kissed him softly, squeezing him.

"You should, by all means. I'm whipped myself. Just watching Edward is enough to wear anyone out."

"I'm worried sick over him." She fit her key in the lock. "And don't forget the party at the Dorchester, sweet."

"What?"

"The movie party—oh, you have forgotten! Rodger, really! Greer Fantasia. Your publisher. The party he's giving for your friend Mrs. Hood's new picture? Oh, shame on you, Rodger! Think how she'd feel if you didn't show up?" She was smiling indulgently again. She seemed to do a lot of that.

"Yes, of course, yes. Her little heart would break. But I didn't forget, not really."

"You promised we could go."

"Of course. Incidentally, his name is pronounced *Fan-ta-see-ya*. Not *Fan-tazh-ah*. He's sensitive."

"I'll call him Greer."

"Well, no, he's sensitive about that, too. He thinks it makes him sound like a girl."

"The man is simply too, too sensitive for this brutal world."

"Tell him that."

She came to him and kissed him again but she knew he was leaving, she didn't try to turn it into anything.

At Broadcasting House he went over his script. He hadn't needed Edward Collister to remind him of Coventry. Tonight he was talking to America about the bombing of the undefended city almost a year before, reminding them of what had happened, how the British, without warning, had suffered at the hands of the Luftwaffe. Coventry had not been an unlikely target when you thought about it. On the fourteenth of November the Luftwaffe carpet-bombed the city, hitting twenty-seven war factories, in the course of which a firestorm was begun. Sixty thousand buildings had been left in ruins, nearly six hundred people had been killed. Men, women, children. Most of them, burned beyond any possible recognition, were buried in a common grave. The next day the King had gone to Coventry to see his subjects, to share their grief and suffering. Godwin had gone there the same day and reported on what he believed to be George V's finest hour. He had intended to devote his broadcast to Coventry one year to the day after it had happened. But by then he would be on his way to kill Rommel. PRAETORIAN would have begun.

So, tonight he told them about Coventry.

He got back to Berkeley Square at half past one. He was thinking about PRAETORIAN and Max Hood and Monk Vardan and Erwin Rommel and he was very tired.

There was a plain envelope with his name on it propped against his front door. He picked it up, went into the flat, and turned on the lights. He threw his trench coat onto the back of a chair and made himself a gin and tonic.

He sipped the drink, took the envelope, and slowly tore it open. He yawned and unfolded the sheet of paper.

End things with the Hood woman or I will tell her husband. If he doesn't kill you, I will.

CHAPTER 6

It was cold enough to turn the rain to ice on the blackened tree trunks in Sloane Square. The trees were cold and slick and the wet chill sank through his clothing, making him curl inward on himself. Godwin's hat was pulled low, rain dripping from the brim. It was well past one o'clock. Sloane Square was quiet, dark, deserted. Across the way in Sloane Street a Bentley limousine from the studio sat purring, glistening in the wet.

Cilla was in the Bentley with Stefan Lieberman, and Godwin was freezing his ass off in the rain. She had looked exquisite, every inch the movie star at the party Lily and Greer Fantasia had given earlier to celebrate the opening of the film. The party, to which he had as promised escorted Anne Collister, had proven to be the strain he'd expected. The problem had been Lily Fantasia herself, though it was impossible to be angry with her. She was just being Lily Fantasia, going on in her own fashion about her "Matrimonial Bureau."

She had an unusually puckish sense of humor for so beautiful and young a woman. Perhaps she was so sure of her looks and status that she could play the clown, knowing that she became only more appealing. She was rumored to be just twenty-three: she had married her publisher husband Greer, who was by now closing in on sixty, five years before, and her hairdresser had said he believed she was definitely eighteen at the time— her hair told him so. Her age was only part of her mystery. In fact, she was nearly all mystery. There was her dark, petite beauty, the way she wore her hair coiled, the exotic, almost Egyptian eyes, the way she wore—with such ease—the fabulous Fantasia emeralds. Not all of them at once, of course, but enough to get your attention. This evening she wore a huge pendant set in diamonds, brilliant against the dark flesh between her high, plump little breasts. The emeralds were said to have inspired one of the famous Victorian novelists, Thackeray or Trollope.

Nothing was more discussed, though in particularly hushed tones, than her background, and Greer Fantasia seemed to enjoy leaving it all rather unclear. She was Portuguese, and it was said that Fantasia had found her performing a variety of extraordinary acts in the very fancy establishment Kate Outerbridge ran down Elephant and Castle way. It was said that he had paid only two visits to Kate's house before deciding that Lily must be his. He was supposed to have made a handsome settlement with Kate. After all, he was spiriting away one of her most valuable assets. Godwin knew much of this to be true because as it happened he himself had paid a few visits to Mrs. Outerbridge's and had on two or three occasions taken the good woman's advice and spent some time with the sixteen-year-old Portuguese girl about whom Kate felt particularly protective. Later on Kate had assured Godwin that she took a very maternal pride in Lily's marriage to the fine gentleman. She considered that she had arranged the whole thing. One time, shortly after the marriage, Lily had told Godwin that he, Rodger, was the only man in Greer's circle for whom she had "performed," as she put it. She was a girl of great charm and discretion. She had never asked Godwin to pledge his secrecy. She had too much dignity and tone. She knew such a request was hardly called for.

Lily had dragged him onto the dance floor. She was only a shade over five feet tall and as she nestled into his arms, he looked out over the crowd, saw Greer Fantasia chatting with Alaric Mottersby who had directed the picture Cilla had starred in and Greer had financed. Mottersby was wearing a bottle-green velvet lounge suit and smoking a pipe, proving that he was a creative artist, not bound by evening clothes convention but much too successful to be thought a bohemian. Anne Collister was sipping champagne with Homer Teasdale and Homer's date, a tall busty girl Godwin didn't know. Homer never kept them long enough for anyone to get to know them. Anne smiled dazzlingly across the crowd at Godwin. He was struck by a sudden shaft of happiness at having brought her, made her happy.

"Anne is such a lovely creature," Lily Fantasia said. "Much too nice for you, of course."

"Nice to know I'm appreciated."

"You're getting on, you know, Rodger. You're no longer in the first blush of youth, are you?"

"Gosh. That's exactly what I thought I was in. And what do you know about it anyway? You're barely out of rompers yourself."

"My soul," she said, scowling up at him, "is a thousand years old."

"Well, keep it out of sight and no one will notice."

"Don't try to slither away from my point, Rodger. You are such a . . . a *man!* What you need is a good—"

"Lily!"

"A good wife! Then you'd be perfectly fine. Someone to take care of you. Someone to come home to at night. You should try it, Rodger, I'm quite serious. It would do you a world of good." The music ended and he released her but she wasn't about to be deterred. "And, to be frank, you have the perfect girl ready and waiting, absolutely dying to marry you—"

"Lily, I'm busy. There's a war on."

"Which has precisely nothing to do with anything—men, of course, will use any excuse . . . we all know that. I knew a man who wouldn't consider marriage as long as he owed a very large tax debt. His excuse was going to last a lifetime. Well, I settled his hash." There were those in London who thought Lily Fantasia's love of idiom was the single most charming thing about her. Greer had once told Godwin that she brought him such happiness that he'd end his life if anything were to happen to her. The bombing had driven him half mad for fear of losing Lily.

"How did you settle his hash, Lily?"

"I found him a very rich wife to pay his debt. I made him the most devoted husband in England. Possibly Europe."

"Lily Fantasia's Matrimonial Bureau."

"Laugh if you will. Make your excuses. But Anne Collister is a gem and I, as you can see, am an expert on gems."

There was no arguing with Lily.

But the note slipped to him by Cilla nearly at party's end had saved the evening.

My love,

Come to Sloane Square after your broadcast and after disposing of Miss Collister. I'll be waiting.

Love, C.

But now, in the cold and damp, it was Godwin who was doing the waiting. He was getting pretty damned tired of it. Too bad the Nazis had let the bastard Lieberman slip through their fingers. Personal frustration, he reflected, could turn you into a real shit, and he supposed he didn't mean he wanted Lieberman in the hands of the Nazis, but still—well, he might be a bit jealous, too. Lieberman had written the screenplay of *Primrose Crescent*, which they'd celebrated tonight; he'd also written a play, *The Widow Weeds*, that Cilla was in rehearsal for now. He was always at Cilla's side these days, hovering over her like a shroud. . . . Besides, just because a man was persecuted, a refugee from Hitler's monstrous crimes, didn't mean you had to like him.

At last the driver got out of the car with a huge black umbrella and opened the rear door. Cilla emerged in her long fur coat to stand beneath it. She leaned back down out of his line of vision where he supposed she was planting a show business kiss on the writer.

He waited a few more minutes after the Bentley had whispered away. He wanted to give her time to go upstairs to the nursery and kiss the sleeping Chloe and make sure the nanny was asleep in her own quarters. Then he crossed the street and found she'd left the door off the latch for him. He went in, draped his trench coat across the back of the bench in the foyer, and went into Max Hood's study, booklined and smelling of furniture polish and the old leather bindings. There was a huge globe that turned into a bar if you knew the magic word. Cilla was waiting for him and she knew the magic word. The globe was tipped open behind her, a siphon gleamed. She smiled slowly, splashed water in on the scotch, reached out with the glass in her hand and let her fingers touch his. "Rodger," she whispered, in her trademark breathy voice, "it feels like a hundred years." He felt his heart leap in his chest at the sight of her, the sound of her voice. It would happen, time and time again, yet it always surprised him. "God, I've had a rotten time," she said. "And I've missed you every minute of it." Her eyes shone, enormous, slightly slanted, fawn-like. She dropped the jacket, heavy with brocade, from her shoulders. She wore gold serpents which twined around her upper arms. "Hold me, for heaven's sake."

He put his arms around her, felt her warmth compressing as she nestled against him, and he supposed this was what people meant when they talked about time standing still. He felt her trembling against him and there was no war, no dying, no secret commando mission, no Rommel, no Max, no betrayal, just Cilla. He tilted her head up, saw tears of relief on her cheeks, kissed her. Maybe this would be one of the good nights, when she loved and needed affection from him, needed to give warmth and ease and simple affection herself. Maybe she was feeling the click within that relaxed her and made her reachable. He never knew which Cilla he would find and he dreaded the uncertainty, the way it poisoned his mind. But just when he felt he couldn't go on, something clicked inside her, and she was his, entirely his again.

They made love in the study on the carpet and then she finished undressing and he watched her as she climbed the stairway. She was naked with her underclothes and slip hung over her shoulder. Her back was so delicate and fragile, her hips firm and broad, her legs solid and strong. He picked up his things, made two more drinks, and followed her up the stairs to the bedroom. Her bedroom. Max's was on the other side of the stairway, overlooking Sloane Street. The nursery was at the other end of the hall, and across from it was the nanny's room. He got into her bed and turned off the light and waited for her to come out of her bathroom. When she did she was silhouetted in the light for a moment. She said something to tease him, came and stood beside the bed. She put her hands down and turned his face and pulled him against her flat belly, pushing his mouth down between her thighs toward her lips. He began kissing her, sinking slowly into her, and eventually lifted her onto the bed and when they finally lay exhausted, coated with sweat, he opened his eyes and lay studying her profile, the tilt of her nose, the jut of her lower lip, the damp hair plastered across her flat forehead.

She stared at the ceiling. "What are we going to do?" The question, so simple on the surface, was bending under the weight of the implications.

"Divorce, that's one option, isn't it?"

"But would you still want to marry me?"

"Yes. But even if I didn't, what difference—"

"You know I'd only be divorcing him for you. To be with you. To marry you, Rodger."

"All right."

"But, of course, I don't know . . . I don't know if I could divorce him. I don't know what it would do to Chloe. That terrifies me. And Max would die if I took her away from him—and somehow that's what it would amount to. One way or another. It would never be the same for Max." She wiped at one eye, he wasn't sure why.

"What about you? He loves you—"

"I'm not easy to love, Rodger. Chloe is. If I were gone?" She shrugged her naked shoulders and drew the sheet up around her neck. "I suspect he'd be relieved. Once he got used to it." Again she said: "I am not a good wife."

"Stop saying that. It doesn't mean anything."

"Of course it does. What are you talking about? It's true. It's simply true."

"You're too hard on yourself. It's not good advertising."

"I'm not advertising for a husband. If someone chooses to apply for the position, I may give it some consideration."

"Well, just stop saying you're not a good wife."

"Look, you're in a position to know the truth. So what are you complaining about?"

"I don't see what's so awful about your wifely performance."

"Oh? Well, there's *this*. I'm sleeping with his dearest friend—"

"I don't know that to be true. I am his friend. He is much more than a friend to me."

"I'm an unfaithful wife. You're an unfaithful friend. Which is worse? Do you know?" She twisted inside the sheet, clamping it between her thighs. "My mother says I'm an unfaithful bitch, simply a whore, and she suggests I admit it to myself."

"Oh, Jesus, spare me your mother's wit and wisdom."

"She says I am permanently in heat, she says in another age I'd have been the village whore, dead of pox at twenty-two."

"Do drop it, Cilla. She thinks that since you're her daughter, you must be made in her image. Exactly like Lady Pamela."

"But sometimes I think she may just be right. She often is, you know. Sometimes it seems to me that I have always been a little whore." She paused, looking at him, then shut her eyes. "What if I am? You've known me for such a long time. And you know how I am, Rodger. You know . . . I *do* always seem to be in heat, don't I? I can't seem to help myself. I hate it sometimes. And sometimes I don't hate it."

"There's nothing wrong with you. Don't be overly dramatic."

She caught her breath. "Lord, I hope you're right. You don't know everything about me . . . I've never been faithful to Max, I told you that . . . not after the first six months."

"Don't talk about it, Cilla. That was then, this is now."

"Why should it ever change? You *know* me, Rodger." She waited, shifted gears. "You know I never deny Max anything, not now, not ever."

"I know."

"And I don't deny you."

"I know. Deny only what you want to deny. You're in charge of what you do. It's your business. It's in your control."

"But Pamela says that's the point, she says I *can't* control myself, even if I want to." She wiped at her eyes again.

"Well, bless her poor old soul," Godwin said, hoping to deflect the conversation. "How is she?"

"Oh, she's making yet another recovery. The doctor says she'll come back less far each time, with more impairments, and then one day"—she snapped her fingers beneath the sheet. "She refuses to die—it's just to spite me, I'm sure of that."

"She'll go one day soon."

"You know, there was a moment when she lay there on the path, when it happened, and it was I—this is very odd—it was *I* who saw *her* life passing before my eyes, and . . . and it was so goddamn sad, Rodger. In my mind she was a girl in a pinafore, then a young woman, she was wide-eyed and innocent and discovering the world, there was so much hope for her, and I saw her on the path and Chloe had run up and I thought of the three of us frozen in that moment, three generations of Legend women, and one was passing on, and only a wink ago she'd been a young girl with her life before her . . . and I didn't want her to die! *Me!* I didn't want Pamela Legend to die!" She sniffled and finally he knew she was crying but it was softly, it wasn't going to get awful. "Bloody hell, sometimes I think I'm losing my mind, Rodger—I bloody well hate the passing of time, darling, it just won't ever stand still to be savored or enjoyed or understood . . . everything's always rushing forward, knocking over the furniture, to get to the next stupid damn event and maybe you don't want to go just yet . . . I hate the *brutality* of time . . . time is a fucking bully, darling, and Cilla wants it to slow down a moment." She sighed. "Pamela must have thought it would never end once. Think—she was twenty-nine once and now I'm twenty-nine. It seems as if I'll always be twenty-nine . . . but I won't, will I? Everything only lasts for a moment and if you miss something, then it's gone and you can't get it back . . . Max always said that in the desert there was no time, no past or future, only an endless present where nothing ever changes . . ." A sob escaped her and he soothed her cheek with his hand, stroked her hair, and she brushed the tears away. "There'll be a wink in the eye of time, I can feel it starting that goddamn wink, and everything we know now will be gone. It's 1941 . . . in twenty-nine years I'll be fifty-eight . . . it will be something quite unimaginable, won't it? It'll be what? 1970. Rodger, can you begin to imagine 1970?"

"Well, with any luck this war will be over."

"Yes, Rodger, I daresay it will be over and several others will have been fought in the interim. 1970, Roger . . . You'll be sixty-five!" He laughed. "What if I'm dying, sick and dying and maybe little Chloe will be fed up with me and maybe she'll have a husband and a daughter of her own who has seen pictures of my mother, her great-grandmother, and maybe Chloe will be impatient with the trouble I'm making while I die and maybe she'll have a lover of her own . . . Oh, God, make me stop this, Rodger. I want you inside me, make me feel alive, Rodger, I need that, I need to feel alive and immortal, just for a little while . . ."

Later Godwin was trying to pin down something Cilla had said about her mother and it kept eluding him. Whatever it was, even the faint memory of it was suddenly sending a cold chill down his spine. "Are you still awake?"

"Of course, you fool." The mischievous smile was still detectable in her voice.

"You said something tonight that made me think Lady Pamela knows about us. Tell me I'm crazy."

"Rodger, must we? Now?"

"Put my mind at ease."

"Ah, well, I'm afraid I can't. I think, yes, I think she does know, actually."

"You think? Why wouldn't you know?"

"That's what I mean. Yes, I know that she knows."

"You told her? I don't understand—you told her about us? Practically a state secret and you told a woman who has only one-fourth the normal complement of marbles left?"

"I didn't *tell* her. Obviously."

"You don't seem very upset . . . it is *your* marriage—"

"And the man you—I never know what to say—idolize? Revere? I wonder which of us is more concerned with secrecy? I could live without Max—"

"There's the matter of your career, as well. England's sweetheart mustn't run out on her husband. But that's another issue. My point is just this, aren't you afraid she'll just blurt it out to Max? Just to hurt you?"

"Oh, impossible! Don't worry yourself, she'd never tell *him*. He's a man, my love, one of the enemy, and you do not share the dirt with the enemy. Seriously, my love, she hates men, which is why she has always persisted in making their lives such beastly bloody utter hell."

"But she knows. If you didn't tell her, how the devil did she find out? We've always agreed, for Max's sake, for *our* sakes—"

"If you must know she simply guessed. I was talking about you one day and her eyes lit up in that fiendish way she has . . . she knew. That's all."

"My God, when did all this happen?"

"What difference does it make? She *knew*. Besides, she's quite mad—"

"All right, all right. But what if somebody—not your blessed mother —what if somebody told Max about us? What then?"

She shuddered, her flesh suddenly reaching out, touching him. "We'd have to deal with it, wouldn't we? Maybe it would even serve us right. We'd have to accept the consequences of our acts." She buried her face in the pillow, then looked up at him, curious about his reaction.

"Well, I'm not just raising a hypothetical question."

"What is that supposed to mean? Are you trying to scare me?"

"You see, I've been told very clearly what will happen to me unless I stop seeing you . . . Somebody's going to kill me."

She slowly grew still. Godwin could hear the clock ticking on the bureau. "You could use a coach on your line reading, Rodger, but your sense of timing is impeccable. What in the world are you talking about?"

Watching her, once he'd told her about the note, had in fact shown her the note, and described how he'd received it, watching her was like seeing her withdraw into a movie for which she has been insufficiently prepared. She didn't seem to know her lines and wasn't too sure about the story so all she had to fall back on was her face, her tricks, her technique. He watched her compose her face, keep the awkwardness and surprise out of it because they were the enemies of the way "Cilla Hood" looked. He noted the familiar planes, the shadows from the bedside lamp defining the face like a scene in the movies. She slid her tongue across her lips. She was almost ready for the close-up. She was slipping away from him, she was thinking her way through the problem and out by way of some hidden exit, always assuming the writers had put one in the script where it was supposed to be. "You don't think it could be some terrible joke, do you?"

"I hardly think so," he said.

"But to whom can it matter? That's the crazy part! Who could possibly think it worth killing over? Except . . . oh, darling, except . . . Max, of course . . ."

"That's what I've been asking myself since I got it. Who? It's obviously not Max . . . so who? The one inescapable conclusion is that somebody knows and doesn't like it . . . somebody is watching us, Cilla."

She slowly slid out from under the sheet and got up, stood naked beside the bed, covered with gooseflesh, gnawing on a fingernail. Slowly, with deliberate movements like an amnesiac struggling to remember the simplest actions from the past, she put on her robe. Her head was cocked to one side as she thought, checking in her mind through all the possible authors of the note. "It could ruin my career," she said as if the idea were becoming palpable for the first time. "It could destroy my marriage. And kill you."

"Glad I made it there at the end. I thought you were going to leave me out altogether."

"Who? Who could it be? Nobody knows," and she turned abruptly toward him and shook a forefinger in his face, "and don't mention Pamela or I'll scream and throw myself through the goddamn window." She was standing by the window, staring down into the rainswept street. "I know," she said softly. "It's simple . . . it's someone who wants me. *Wants* me. Someone—a movie fan, a coworker, one of the crew people, maybe an actor, more likely just a fan . . . someone who has watched me, someone who is *jealous*. . . . Think, Rodger. Isn't that logical? What else is anything like as logical? I've known other actresses who've been stalked by crazy admirers. . . . Merle had a problem like that, Alex made sure it was hushed up . . . crazy people. It's all sex, isn't it? I've gotten letters over the years, men who imagine sexual things about me—you just toss them away and forget them. They're harmless. But now we've got one who's gone the next step. He's followed me, somehow he's seen us together and now he's in our lives . . ."

He was out of bed, going toward her, when he saw her stiffen. "Oh, my God," she whispered. He looked past her shoulder.

In the street below, a Jaguar moved slowly out of the square, down Sloane Street. It eased up to the curb like an old Cunard liner nosing up to the pier. "It's Max," she said breathlessly. "It's Max."

She was a blur of economic motion. He almost forgot to move. But she pointed to his clothing, his dinner jacket and formal shirt and the black trousers with the black braces dangling over the back of a chair. As he scooped them up she said: "I can keep him out of my bedroom but in case I can't, you've got to get to the priest's hole right away." In an instant the bed was straightened, the cover thrown back and the pillows plumped and a book thrown on the sheet as if she'd been reading. "Hurry, darling," and it seemed that she was almost giggling. "It's like a bedroom farce, isn't it?" she said, catching her breath.

She pushed him ahead of her down the darkened hallway, past the occasional tables and little chairs and bowls of flowers toward the void. Between a high cabinet with a narrow mirror and carvings on the door and the corner meeting of walls there was a width of several feet. "It's been here for centuries—well, since the place was built in Victoria's day, anyway. They called it a priest's hole but it was just another Victorian folly, I suppose—they loved secret passages—"

"We don't have time for a history lesson, Cilla—" He dropped a shoe and struggled to pick it up without dropping everything else. He strained to hear the door opening downstairs, the step in the hallway. Cilla was pressing the wall, something concealed in the pattern of the floral wallpaper, and suddenly the section of wall next to the cabinet swung open.

"I wish I had a snap of you, darling."

"Cilla, so help me—"

"Let's see, there's a candle somewhere." She was feeling her way in the darkness. There was a stale, peculiar smell which might have been there from the day the foundation was laid. "Ah, here."

"Fucking cobwebs," Godwin sputtered, feeling the wisps against his face.

"No doubt a mouse or two, as well." She struck a match and applied it to the curled wick of a candle in a pewter holder with a curling handle. "Now just wait here until you hear him come up. You can leave the door ajar. If I can I'll come to you when the all-clear sounds. Just listen. You can hear very well from here. I don't know why he's suddenly appeared but I'll try to get him to bed—he's bound to be exhausted—"

"Cilla—"

The door slammed shut in the foyer. Max Hood was home.

"I must dash, my love. Look, there's a nice book for you to read. Trollope."

She pecked his cheek and the next thing he knew the door was swinging shut. The candle flickered, made him feel as if he were trapped in a gingerbread house. The bricks were loose and crumbly with ancient dollops of mortar squeezing out between them like cake frosting. It was cold as a crypt, and the stale smell bothered him. His sense of adventure was failing him. It was odd, how it all seemed rather funny, like a bedroom farce as she'd said, yet so sad, so serious, so laden with pain for everyone involved. He pushed that aspect out of his thoughts. The bottoms of his feet were coated with ancient grit. She was right, a bedroom farce. Or one of Fielding's novels. Tom Jones caught in milady's boudoir when soldier husband bustles through the door. Dignity—never robust—was dying a slow, agonizing death. Only Max Hood could come out of this episode having behaved well.

He pushed the door open again, strained to hear voices. At first it was hers, barely audible, then something deeper, Max, and she seemed to be maneuvering them closer to the long curved staircase which rose from the parquet. Then her voice was clearer, the tone indicating it followed their greeting, the embrace, the kiss. "Max, you must be worn to a frazzle. Why don't you come up now?"

"In a moment. You know the trouble I've been having trying to sleep. It doesn't seem to be improving. Not to worry, though. How was your party?"

Godwin imagined him standing at the foot of the stairs, a glass of scotch in his hand, a stack of mail in the other, looking up at his wife, who stood on the third step with her hand on the banister. His mind was full of PRAETORIAN, full of his wife, full of his daughter, full of the war, wondering if he were cracking because he couldn't sleep . . .

"As such things go, it went. Everyone was very sweet about the picture, which is, let's face it, rather dim. I was desolate when you couldn't come."

"Couldn't be helped. Which reminds me—I may be out of touch for a week or two. Commencing sometime next week."

"Oh, Max. Tell me it's nothing dangerous—"

"No, no, of course not. Just maneuvers, training some youngish chaps. I'm much too old for danger."

"You'll always be dangerous," she said. "I always say that, you know—my husband Max Hood is a damn dangerous man."

He laughed. "And so I am."

"And you won't tell me any more about your maneuvers?"

"You know I can't, old girl. It's nothing. Really."

"When you talk like that it always means just the opposite."

"Oh, I wouldn't say that."

"Well, I missed you at the party and Lily and Greer missed you. Everyone missed you. Rodger came and looked about like a lost soul when he discovered you were missing."

"Did he indeed? Well, he's a grand fella. In fact, I must see Rodger in the next few days."

"Oh? Why? Can I come? Or is it boy talk?"

"Very boring talk, I expect. Public relations. Yes, that's exactly what it's all about, public relations. How was our Rodger, then? Beyond looking like a lost soul?"

"Fine, I suppose. He brought his lady friend, Anne Collister. She of the very long teeth and the very large feet. An English beauty, that is. Lily said she thought they should get married."

"And what do you say?"

"I doubt that Rodger is the marrying kind. And, furthermore, I say you should get some sleep."

"Cilla?"

"Yes?"

"I was thinking I might come to your room tonight."

"Max! I said you were dangerous. But better yet, why don't I come to you? We can have a fire—I'll light it. The flue thing isn't drawing properly in my room. Do hurry, though."

"All right. I'll be along shortly."

"Would you like a hot bath first?"

"I'd love one."

"Bring your drink, then, and I'll wash your back and tell you about the party . . ."

Godwin hated listening, hated all of it, wondered how she could traverse the high wire. It was the next thing to listening while people made love. Maybe Monk was right. Maybe it was something about women that men could never hope to understand.

He was fully dressed when the door swung all the way open. She stood before him in her robe. "Could you hear?"

He nodded.

"When he comes up I'll close the door to his bedroom to keep the warmth in. He'll be in the tub. Then you can beat a decorous retreat. There was an anxious moment." She was breathless, whispering.

"What do you mean?"

"Your trench coat, it's in the hallway, over the bench."

"Oh, Christ have mercy—"

"I was going to tell him I asked you back for a drink and you must have left it behind. But then I thought, what if it's gone in the morning?" She giggled. "But it was dark in the foyer and he didn't seem to have noticed so I said nothing."

"But what if he did notice?"

"He didn't. Now I must go run the bath and get the fire lit. Did you hear that he's going away for a week or two?"

"Yes."

"Well, that will give us some time, won't it?"

"Don't you think you'd better go attend to business?"

"Are you all right, Rodger?"

"Cilla, Cilla—what a question."

"All I need now is to have Chloe come wandering out of her room. She's taken to sleepwalking. I'm off. I'll call you, my love."

She disappeared down the hall. He could taste her mouth on his while he waited for Max to climb the stairs, waited for the door to close.

He gave it plenty of time. Then he went downstairs. Moonlight had fought its way through the clouds, casting shadows across the parquet floor. It looked like a huge chessboard. Cilla was the queen. What was Max? King or knight or rook? As he picked up his raincoat and slipped it on over his rumpled dinner jacket with the tie hanging loose, he felt very much like a pawn which, he supposed, was just his tough luck.

It was raining when he passed through Sloane Square.

"Rodger? Is that you, old chap? Godwin?"

He turned and saw the round, dumpy figure beneath the umbrella. For a moment he didn't recognize him.

"It's me. Sam. Sam Balderston, for Christ's sake." *The Times* reporter stepped forward.

"Sam. Sorry, I couldn't see you beneath that great awful bumber-shoot. What's brought you out?"

"Visiting the crumpet, old chap, what else? And you?"

"Just out for a walk. Couldn't sleep."

"You got out of bed and put on your dinner jacket?" He laughed. He was chewing on a cigar. "I'll believe you. Thousands wouldn't."

"Well, you're a trusting old soul. I'm headed up Sloane Street."

"Then we'll go together. Whereabouts do you live?"

"Berkeley Square."

"You must have felt like a *long* walk, old chap." He grinned through the smoke, a jolly fat man, a bulldog with a story in reach. "You're up to something, Rodger. I can smell it. I saw you at the Dorchester tonight but you were engaged with Mrs. Fantasia. Lucky dog. Corblimey, she's a beauty!"

They'd crossed the empty square into upper Sloane Street.

"I'd hoped to say hello to Sir Max Hood but he stood his wife up on her big night. Must have had a good reason, what? Wouldn't you agree, Rodger?"

"You're probably right," Godwin said. Of all the people he might have met, why Sam Balderston? Sam Balderston, who could never leave a loose end alone.

"Sloane Square," Sam mused. "I used to live in Blacklands Terrace. Very nice little flat. You know, now I think of it, Max Hood lives just back there." He jerked his thumb back over his shoulder. "Did you know that, Rodger?"

"Yes, I believe you're right, Sam. Just the other side of the square if I'm not mistaken."

"Well, ain't that a coincidence?"

"Is it, Sam? I don't see it."

"Of course it is. Don't you see? We were just talking about him, weren't we? And didn't you and I just happen to run into each other? Practically in the man's front hall? Well, I call that a coincidence."

Rodger sighed. It was going to be a long walk back to Berkeley

Square. Maybe he could strangle Sam Balderston and leave him in an alleyway for the dustman to find. It seemed an unlikely turn of events, however.

"At the end of the day, I think we might well get out of this with our hides intact and one big chief's scalp on our belt. Of course, one knocks on wood. But our chances are rather good." Max Hood was sitting in a brass-studded club chair. A fire blazed, warming the study. The globe that was a bar was tipped open. He'd urged his guests to build their drinks as they liked them. For himself he had a tumbler that had been full of single malt he sipped like Napoleon brandy.

Lieutenant Colonel Martin Jellicoe of Middle East Commando Force would be Hood's second in command on the mission. He was a stocky, compact man in his early forties, not unlike Hood in shape and size. His nose was red with permanent sunburn, and beneath it a thick mustache bristled. He wore a lounge suit and slouched near the globe. It was a practiced stance as if when out of uniform he was determined to enjoy himself, whatever it took, up to and including lounging about like a gig-olo. He smelled of lime cologne. Beneath the suit, behind the slouch, he was made primarily of iron. He bore six bullet wounds, according to Monk Vardan who knew about such things and was now sitting on a leather couch facing the fire.

Godwin sat at the other end of the couch. As he had in North Africa, in the desert with Hood, he now felt the mingled anticipation and fear that came with being on the inside of the war, a participant rather than a reporter. Jellicoe looked up from a consideration of the fire's reflection in his highly polished shoes and said: "I bloody well tell you there'd *better* be a good chance we're coming back out. I've made a very serious vow not to get myself shot anymore. And suicide missions are definite non-starters."

Monk Vardan shifted his long, bony frame to look at Godwin. "They're just trying to put the wind up you, Rodger. Old military twits at play. Isn't that right, Martin? Max?"

"Don't worry so much about Godwin." Hood produced a steely smile, not overly comforting. "Rodger and I have heard the chimes at midnight. Rodger will be fine."

"Nothing against Godwin," Martin Jellicoe said, sweeping a knuckle across his mustache, "but I'm not utterly enchanted by risking the old monkey's brass balls on what is apparently a publicity stunt. Like Teddy Roosevelt charging up San Juan Hill for William Randolph Hearst. There I'll be, burnt cork all over my face, in my eyes and up my nose and in my mouth, walking through cold water trying not to drown, with Rommel's personal bloody bodyguard ready to start shooting and heaving those great awful potato mashers at me—and at the rest of the lads, of course, but most importantly at me . . . all for a story in the Daily Blatt. I ask myself, is it all worth it?"

"I believe I was a late addition," Godwin said. "The publicity part of this is nothing but a by-product."

"Let me address this once and for all," Monk Vardan said. "You may be sure I represent the PM here. CRUSADER's primary aim is to relieve Tobruk and knock Rommel's army back on its heels, set them running. It's their turn, after all. As CRUSADER nears, a variety of operations are being effected with the aim of disrupting and confusing the enemy—both the Italians who are headquartered at Cyrene and the Germans headquartered down the road at Beda Littoria. Brigadier Reid and the nimble Stirling with his paratroops are doing their part. The idea is to keep Rommel off balance, keep him looking behind him and keep him seeing things in the shadows. Our purpose—PRAETORIAN's purpose—is to remove the head of the beast—the brain, if you will. Rommel himself. The shock of losing their leader, the architect of their triumphs, will send them into disarray . . . and before they know what's happening CRUSADER will be upon them with every bit of firepower we've got. The best publicity will be the relief of the Desert Rats at Tobruk and the defeat of Rommel's army. *That* is what we are about. The idea to include an American war correspondent was added on. It is a good idea—and Rodger has his particular role. He has a huge audience both here and in the States. We want to pull this thing off and we want our success to be told to the widest possible audience by the most widely heard voice . . . we want to use Godwin to weld us ever tighter to the Yanks, it's that simple . . . because Britain and America must stand united to win this war . . . we must get America off its duff and into the field . . ."

Max Hood spoke softly. "We don't really require a speech, Monk. You may number us among the converted. I suspect all of us in this room want Hitler to lose the war."

"Carried away, was I? It happens."

"Martin's fault for bringing it up in the first place. Martin always enjoys prying into matters that are none of his business. Such as whys and wherefores. He forgets he is but a simple soldier. It is part of his limited charm."

Jellicoe laughed, suddenly beaming. "All right, all right. Take that as read, Monk. Returning to the point, how the dickens do we pull off this bit of larceny once we get to Beda-fucking-Littoria?"

"Indeed," Max Hood said. "How do we pull it off? You'll be relieved to hear, Martin, that I have a plan. Come over here." He had gone to a long library table that stretched before a wall of books. "It's show-and-tell time."

Godwin tried to make sense of the maps and the recce photographs, some of which Max had taken six weeks before when the plan was coming together. Godwin tried but eventually they all became meaningless, the photos blurring together in his mind. From somewhere in the house came the sound of a phonograph playing and he had a hard time keeping his mind off Cilla. Somewhere above him she was bathing or reading or playing the records and the music was eating him alive. It was as if she were doing it on purpose, playing a stack of records by Hutch, their favorite, records they'd made love to, because she knew Godwin was there. They'd all heard him first at that little club in Paris back in '27, Joselli's in the Place Clichy, where he'd played the piano and sung Cole Porter songs and wiped his handsome black gleaming face with the white handkerchief. Leslie Hutchinson, everybody had called him Hutch even then, and he'd sung like an angel and they'd all been getting to know one another and never having a clue where it would lead, not a clue. Now she was upstairs playing his recordings of "Mist on the River" and "Star Dust" and "All the Things You Are" and Godwin was downstairs knocking back the scotch and her husband was telling them just how they were going to charge off and kill the god of the desert war.

Godwin had thought the attack would involve a simple dash up across the beach, the demolition of Rommel's HQ and the murder—or kidnapping, he'd hoped in his innocence—and a dash back down to the waiting rubber rafts and then a quick paddle back to the submarine. Well, he'd had the wrong end of the stick on that one.

The maps had been carefully executed by hand, indicating the primary route inland and the fallback approaches available in case of problems. First there was the narrow North African beach. Then the first escarpment. Then a rough trek of fifteen miles across a rocky hillside honeycombed with caves where goats and goatherds sheltered in bad weather of which there was, apparently, a great plenitude. In one of the caves they would find "stores" and Godwin was too befuddled by his growing awareness of the operation's complexity that he didn't bother to ask about the stores. Then there was another nasty escarpment to be dealt with. And then, all in due time, the town. A group of several whitewashed buildings, a grain tower, a police barracks, Rommel's HQ, Rommel's villa, an electrical station noted on the map as "dynamo." There was also a carpark but unfortunately they wouldn't be driving to town. A few miles down the main road leading eventually to Tobruk there was a communications pylon which would have to be put out of commission. Of course there were also routes of retreat which would take them back to the beach. Christ. It looked to Godwin as complicated as a full-scale invasion of Europe to open the fabled Second Front.

Max Hood filled a pipe from a tobacco humidor in the shape of Merlin the Magician's head, lit it, and pointed at the X marking the spot of Rommel's HQ, tapping it with the toothmarked black stem. "This is a rather formal building, three stories, an outhouse in back, and it will probably be closed up when we arrive. My guess is the villa's the place. If we're lucky he'll be in bed, a skeleton guard on duty. They won't be expecting us, obviously. In we go, then the work of a few minutes—"

Jellicoe spoke, almost as if thinking aloud: "We used to call that part 'dirty work at the crossroads.' That's what any mission was all about. The dirty work at the crossroads. Sorry, Max, go on."

"If we're good, and if we're lucky, there'll be no survivors to summon help. The communications center will be out of business. The dynamo, ditto. No electric light. It should take them some time to figure out just what's been done to them. And by then we'll be back in the hills, getting as far away as possible."

Godwin said: "Sorry if this is a stupid question but how long is all this supposed to take? It looks like about a six-week campaign to me."

"It's a two-day job. We come in about midnight and get as far inland as we can by dawn. Then we lay up for the day in the caves. Come nightfall we do the work on the communications center. I'm betting they'll look at it as British deviltry, quite isolated from any danger to Rommel. Then the dynamo. One group will take it out while the others hit the villa. We'll coordinate. When the lights go out, we go in. This will happen to our German friends about twenty-four hours following our disembarking the subs. We spend the rest of the night getting back to the caves, lay up the second day, and that night we get back to the beach for the pickup." Max puffed his pipe, applied another match, and nodded to Godwin. "Sound like fun, Rodger?" He smiled fondly.

"Not exactly a day at the beach."

"Ah. Well, look at it this way. You'll be on land, you'll be able to *do* something . . . I've always liked that aspect of commando work. Pity the poor devils in the bombers over the Reich. They can't do a damned thing about the flak. They're just out there in the wind and the cold and their fate is out of their hands. A very bad feeling, I should think. You'll be fine, Rodger. I promise you that. And don't forget—I *know* you."

Jellicoe said: "Just remember this, Godwin. Do as you're told. You're along for the ride. You're a fine fellow, I'm sure, but if you misbehave and somehow endanger my survival I'll shoot you dead without blinking an eye. Nothing personal, you understand. Just my way of doing business." He smiled behind the mustache and having spoken his piece he sipped his drink, turned to Hood. "Now, Max, tell us about this cave again. I, for one, hate caves. I particularly hate caves full of goat dung. How can you be sure we'll find the right one?"

"Believe it or not, Jelly, I've actually thought of handling this little problem. But let's run through this again, maps and pictures. We'll have plenty of time to go over it on our way out to Alex but once more tonight will help place it in your minds."

"If I know you," Jellicoe said, "you'll still be drilling it into us as we leave the sub in those lethal little dinghies—"

"Not this time, I'm afraid."

"And why not, if I may ask?"

"I won't be on the sub."

"Swimming? A bit showy, old chap."

"No, I'm going overland. A bit ahead of you chaps. Long Range Desert Group will get me as close as they can, then I turn myself into an Arab. Or maybe an Italian officer. I'll find the cave, I'll signal the sub for the drop-off and bring you in."

"Damn," Jellicoe said. "You have all the fun! We're cooped up in the steaming sub, you're out having a holiday. Godwin, you must watch this man every minute. Always the soft duty for himself. Fancy dress, mixing with the natives, some decent Italian cuisine. All right, Max, take us through the pictures and maps again. Monk, can you top this off for me? Deserts give me a thirst."

From the upper reaches of the house Godwin heard Leslie Hutchinson singing "You Keep Coming Back Like a Song." It was such a sad, beautiful song. He was beginning to wonder if he'd ever see Cilla again.

They were walking up Sloane Street, along where Sam Balderston had stopped him that other evening, when he'd barely escaped Max's detection, but now the large black Rover from Number 10 was trailing along behind them, at Monk Vardan's disposal.

"There's still the blood sheet for you to sign. It simply absolves His Majesty's government from being liable in any way in case of your death. We're blameless if you get your head shot off. Your network can't sue us. That's the point."

"I understand. Where is it?"

"In the car. Sorry for leaving it so late."

"This is all rather sobering, Monk."

"War often has that effect on people, I daresay. I hope I never have to face any of it. Still, what an adventure you'll have had once it's over. You'll dine out on it for the rest of your life. Godwin, the man who made the raid on Rommel. I'll never have such a story to tell. I envy you that."

"You'll have Churchill stories. You'll doubtless write a book in your dotage."

They strolled on, heels clicking on the damp paving stones. Godwin couldn't get the thought of Cilla upstairs memorizing lines in the bath, Hutch's voice coming from the other room. He'd never been so acutely aware of not wanting to die.

Godwin tried to sound casual when he spoke again. "How does Max look to you, Monk?"

"How do you mean exactly?"

"He's changed."

"Pressure. Tension. Travel. This war. Put them all together, they take their toll. He's not a boy anymore. Who among us is?"

"I was thinking he didn't look well this evening."

"Really?" The word came out in three articulated syllables. "Seemed the same old Max to me. Oh, he says he's been suffering a spot of insomnia. Not surprising in light of all he's been up to these past two months. Back and forth to Alex, infiltrating Rommel's lines. Getting ready to raise the curtain on this particular show. I'd say he's on edge . . . which means he's ready to fight. Ready to kill. That's what we're using him for, after all." His umbrella was tapping along beside them like a blind man's cane. "That's what war does, I've learned. It uses people up. But Max—he seems an endless resource. He is kind of a killing machine once he gets started, isn't he?"

"That's a bit heavy," Godwin said.

"Really? He told me you had reason to agree. Ah, well. He told me something else . . . he said it was harder to get ready for a show like this nowadays. I told him not to worry about it."

"That must have been a great help to him."

"I told him everything was getting harder for everybody. I wouldn't lie to Max Hood."

"I suppose that's true. We're getting on."

"And Max more so. That's why his preparations are so thorough. As a young man he could improvise, depend on his instincts and his agility to get him through. As a young man he was fearless. That's dangerous. Give me a man who has a healthy complement of fear when it comes to playing Hood's kind of game."

"Well, I'm certainly your man in that case."

"But his fear will get everybody through this. It's your ace in the hole."

"I'm glad you think so. I still think he looks pretty ragged around the edges."

"Jellicoe's been down this road with Hood before. He seems quite confident. That's a good sign."

They were standing at the corner of the Brompton Road. Harrods loomed off to the left. The Rover purred behind them in the darkened, naked street.

"Monk, do you think it's possible that—"

"Don't be shy, my man."

"Do you think Max could possibly know about Cilla and me?"

"Isn't that what I'm always asking you?"

"I know, I know. I only wondered if . . . maybe that's what's been weighing on his mind. Keeping him awake nights. . . . Has he said anything that might make you think—"

"Relax, old boy. You'd know if Max had found out."

"How, for God's sake?"

"How? Why, because Max would kill you, obviously."

"But would he?"

"You doubt it?"

"No. I suppose he would."

"So, nothing to worry about. Now get in the car and sign the blood sheet. You're setting off for Alexandria in six hours."

CHAPTER 7

The first man died in the water before they even got to the beach, and at the time Godwin counted him the lucky one. They had already been through hell. Death was a relief.

Anything would have been a relief. Anything but what they were doing. Anything to get out of the submarine—*Kismet* was its name, and it was his fate, his destiny, no goddamn doubt about that—anything, even to give yourself to the sea, embrace it, anything to get out of the heat and the smell of sweat and the sound of the sweat, his own, everybody else's, the actual sound of sweat dripping from their bodies, regular as a metronome, dripping onto the metal underfoot as they lay in their tiny bunks or curled in cramped painful balls on the floor under the torpedo tubes or huddled in the wardroom sick and exhausted, ready to puke the linings from their stomachs because they couldn't get away from the smell of their own vomit, anything to get away from the heat and the smell and the lurching and pitching and rolling and the bruises and cuts from banging into sharp edges and falling against metal because they had no sea legs and didn't give a shit anyway because what difference did any of that make when you wanted to die, when you couldn't breathe the stale air, when you couldn't have a smoke during the day when they were submerged because there was no way to clean the air, when you couldn't smoke during the night when they surfaced because the Mediterranean was in a rotten mood, the winds ranging from force four to force eight, when you couldn't stop vomiting, and when there was nothing left in your belly and you couldn't stop retching and were too dead on your feet and too weak and too dehydrated, so when the first man finally died, drowned in the water when the time came to land, he was the lucky one. The first of the lucky but not the last.

Jellicoe came to him the second night out of the Alexandria sub pens. "Have you been topside?"

"I can't stop throwing up long enough. Legs won't hold me up."

"Well, on one hand, the fresh air would do you good."

"And on the other hand?" Godwin felt his stomach heave. He could hear the echo, the rumbles in his intestines.

"On the other hand you'd sure as hell be washed overboard and never seen again."

"Ah, the easy way out."

Jellicoe chuckled bleakly. "This is what I meant about Max. Remember what I said? Pulls the soft duty . . . wily old scout. Think of him now, Godwin. Lolling along on the back of a camel . . . veiled dancing girls attending to his every whim . . . figs, grapes, that sort of thing . . . ah, Max . . . you look rather unwell, old man." He looked away from his mental picture of Max and the easy life, regarded Godwin. "Bit of gyppy tummy, I expect."

"What the hell is gyppy tummy?"

"Well, it's like this. Gyppy tummy is the nether end of things while what you've been doing these past twenty-four hours is simple puking. Gyppy tummy opens the other end. Either one can throw you off your stroke. You don't want to encounter both at the same time. Word to the wise." He laid his finger beside his nose, then tweaked it. "How do you like being a commando? Think your listeners and readers will enjoy the unexpurgated story?" The bristly mustache jerked, a smile, and he turned away without waiting for an answer.

That night Jellicoe told the raiding party—thirteen men, most of whom were holding their stomachs, trying to keep things under control— that they were going to kill Rommel. No prevarications about kidnapping. They'd have thought he was insane. "It will be a nasty business, gentlemen. A shooting gallery. We are the last thing on earth they expect. The idea—if you need telling—is to check your merciful instinct as you leave the sub and collect it when you return. Understood? No prisoners, no survivors."

"Dirty work at the crossroads, what, Colonel?"

"We've been there a time or two, Pinkham."

"That we have, sir."

"Gentlemen, a formal word. Should I fall before we reach the crossroads, and if General Hood should fall as well, Pinkham will lead you. Hood and I have arranged this between us. Pinky is a bit of a bounder but—" he waited for the round of laughter to subside, "but you'll be in good hands. None better, if it comes to that."

"Kind of you to say so, sir," Pinkham said.

Cyril Pinkham, Bert Penrose, Brian Qualley, Alf Dexter, Reginald Smythe-Haven, Bill Cox, Anthony Jones, Jim Steele, Boyd Malvern, Ox Bester, Lad Holbrook, Jellicoe. And Godwin.

Godwin wedged himself beneath a torpedo tube and closed his eyes and let himself drift off, not quite asleep but surely not awake. Thirteen men, strangers to one another for the most part, drawn from Middle East Commando Force largely, skilled at what they were being asked to do, off on a great adventure, off to kill a man, off to take them by surprise and kill them all.

They had trained in Alexandria. The main body of them had been working for two weeks. It was assumed Jellicoe knew what he was doing. Hood was on land. Godwin was little more than cargo, like the stores they would be bringing ashore from *Kismet*. The stores consisted mainly of bully beef to avert excessive hunger and gelignite to blow everything to hell and gone. The idea was to keep the gelignite from getting wet. The bully beef didn't matter.

Godwin and Jellicoe had joined in the tail end of the training, spending two days working with the rubber dinghies and folbots, getting used to wearing the Mae Wests, learning the use of the foot-pedal pump to inflate the dinghies and how to maneuver the cumbersome things once they were inflated. It was very wet work. They all kept falling out of the dinghies, laughing in the sunshine like kids with sandbuckets and spades on holiday at Brighton, splashing and horsing around, the water beading on their arms like crystal baubles. All they needed, Boyd Malvern observed, were the girls and the sticks of Brighton rock candy.

That last day in Alex they made a practice landing on a beach near the city and it went off without a hitch. Bill Cox said it showed what a commando could do once he put his mind to it. Aside from Steele getting entangled in one of the grass lines holding the dinghies together like beads on a string—that might have counted as a hitch but on the whole Jellicoe thought not. It was a job well done and they were ready for Rommel.

Twenty-four hours later the weather, the terrible seas, had undone them. The ship's captain, Stanley Wardour, said it was unusually bad. Pressed, he admitted he'd never seen anything much more rotten in these particular waters. A pleasure cruise was what it should have been, or so he said.

That second night while *Kismet* lay on the surface airing itself out, recharging its batteries, and being hammered by the waves which fell on it as if from a mountaintop—that night Bert Penrose was sitting next to Godwin, gingerly pulling on a cigarette, hoping it wouldn't make him sicker, telling him what he thought about when the going was particularly bad. He was a skinny guy, looked like the cartoon man with the fat wife. Pale, receding chin, stray bits of black hair plastered with sweat across his forehead, a beaky nose, big ears. He was, according to Jellicoe, "a fucking dab hand with the gelignite. He could blow out your molars and your bicuspids would never know it."

He confided to Godwin that when things got bad—"like it musta been for me dad down the pits, that night o' the big explosion, the cave-in, they ne'r bothered to dig 'em out, ne'r saw me dad again"—the thing to do was to think of the moving pictures, preferably the funny ones. "I was just thinking of one. Lifted my spirits right up. Took me out of meself. That Jean Harlow, now there's a right tasty bit, what, Rodge? There's Myrna Loy, William Powell, one of my favorites Spencer Tracy, y'see. And Jean finds out that Powell, who's married to her, has also just married Myrna Loy. Our Jean looks at 'em, then she looks at Tracy . . . are you ready for this, Rodge? She looks at Tracy and she says . . . 'That's arson!' She's real indignant like but thickish, y'know. 'That's *arson!*' I larfed my head nearly off, Rodge, I swear I did. Our Jean! 'That's arson!' I find it helps me to think of that sort of thing. If you wish, lad, you have my permish to try it. It gets you out of yourself when things are bad."

"Out of myself," Godwin said. "Sounds like a fine place to be."

"Y'know, I been thinking about this Rommel business of ours. They'll make a movie about us someday. Think of it, Rodge. A movie about us. The lads who went out and died for Rommel. Did it for king and country. And you're a Yank! I don't suppose it'll be a humorous picture, though. It's not suitable for comedy, going off to kill a chap. But still, it'll be a movie. A talkie! Makes a chap feel humble."

"Don't forget, Bert—you're the real hero. The other guy is just some overpaid actor with makeup getting in his eyes."

"But still . . . who do you want to play you?"

"Robert Montgomery." Godwin laughed, forgetting his guts for a moment. Bert Penrose was right. It was getting himself out of himself. "Or Gary Cooper. Or Joel McCrea. Or Gable. Maybe Gable."

"You be Gable. I want to be Gary Cooper."

"Just so I'm not Mickey Mouse," Godwin said.

Bert clapped him on the back and went over to play cards with Smythe-Haven and Lad Holbrook and Alf Dexter. Holbrook was systematically turning everyone on board into paupers. When poker got boring he'd suggest a change of pace, a few rounds of Persian monarchs. He'd win at that very simple game, as well. Then, eventually, everybody would have to go throw up.

That last day, before nightfall and the coming landing, Jellicoe brought a cup of coffee and sat down beside Godwin at the wardroom table. "You've never been part of this kind of thing, have you?"

"If I had, I sure as hell wouldn't have come along on this one."

Jellicoe chuckled. "You're an honest sort of fella, Godwin. I'll say that for you. Being a bit green, then, you may not know about the letter. Am I right?"

"I have no idea what you're—"

"I thought not. Well, it's customary for chaps in our position to write a letter to someone—wife, girlfriend, mother or father, whomever, that's up to you—to be delivered in case we run into some difficulty. In case things go wrong. You understand?"

"In case we get killed."

"Well, that, yes. Or captured. Or wounded . . . but mainly in case we get shot to pieces. Yes. If you have someone you'd like a final word with, fine, you write the letter, give it to the captain, and he'll see that it's delivered." He coughed self-consciously, drew his knuckle across his mustache in the gesture Godwin had grown accustomed to. "Of course, we'll make it all right. I always write the letter, just like all these lads, and it's never once been delivered. But, just in case, you never know. Here's some paper . . . It's not obligatory, mind you. Well, I'll leave you to it, old man."

My darling, my dearest Cilla

Well, I've finally gotten my wish to see some more of this war first hand. If at first you don't succeed, as I did not succeed in getting the network to okay the bombing mission, you naturally persist—only the next time you don't discuss it with the network dimwits.

I can't tell you where I am or what we're about to do but sufficeth to say that these rather wonderful colleagues of mine call it what it is— "dirty work at the crossroads." I'm hopelessly out of place and scared to death but they're all good guys and if anyone can get me through it they can.

Of course, if you receive this letter it means that the outlook is decidedly grim for the Mudville Nine but you don't know what that means, do you, my love? Well, if you get this it means that I am now numbered among the missing. That will be a bad break because now that I've found you I'd hoped for a hell of a long life.

I regret the whole thing about Max. I regret it with all my heart and soul; but there it is. Somehow I must have you, whatever the cost. Perhaps everyone in love feels this way, but I doubt it. We are passionate souls, Cilla, capable of anything, and not everyone is so constructed. We are not comfortable people, you and I, and I think we need each other. Maybe we deserve each other, as well. Maybe it is in our natures to betray—not lightly, not in a trivial way, but for love, for obsession. The truth—sad or otherwise—is that I would have committed any act imaginable to have you. Paid any price. It turned out that Max was the price. I'd do it every time, too, which is a fact I must live with. Or die with, as the case may be.

Well, as you read this, you know that I am gone. You are young, your life stretches magnificently before you. You have your exquisite daughter, a brilliant career. And you have certain memories. A memory of Paris long ago. A memory of Cairo. A memory of London. Memories of me and what we were together. Let them be good, loving memories, my enchanting Cilla. And then, my darling, let them go, let them fade until it seems as if they all happened to someone else, as if you'd read them in a book. You will change as time goes by and that is as it should be. Never worry about it if you discover one day that you have forgotten Rodger Godwin.

For I will have died with you in my heart and some fine day in Paradise I will find you again and we will be together forever.

Rodger

He put the letter into an envelope with her name on it; then he wrote a short note and slipped both envelope and the note into another envelope addressed to Homer Teasdale. He gave the sealed packet to Captain Wardour.

The weather worsened, turning colder, as they closed on the beach.

Standing on deck, frozen with wet and cold, braced against the waves, listening to the wind howling, Godwin barely picked out the dark line of coast ahead. The submarine had become a kind of reptile underfoot: a slithering, skittering, trembling black tube in the night, slipping down among the swells, as slippery as if it had been lathered with Vaseline, treacherously shifting in every direction at once, as they struggled to blow up the dinghies and avoid drowning. Each dinghy was designed to carry two men and supplies, the bully beef and the gelignite and the ammunition. It wasn't just the waves slamming across the plunging deck, it was the slashing icy rain driving at them, down their turtlenecks, soaking inside their oilskins. Every time you took a breath you inhaled a good deal of the Mediterranean. There was no way to stop choking and coughing.

Somewhere out there in the darkness Max Hood was supposed to be waiting for them, giving them the signal with a torch, guiding them in. Without that signal the landing would be hopeless, blind, doomed to founder on unseen rocks. "Don't worry, gentlemen, Max Hood will be there. Our job is to be ready for him. Now get a move on." Jellicoe set to work himself, as if to show them what work actually was.

The stores were lashed to the dinghies before they were inflated. Godwin worked a foot pump, holding with one hand to the single wire stay which ran fore and aft while trying to hold the dinghy steady with the other. The men were lined up in pairs holding on for dear life, the wire cutting at them, desperately fighting to prevent their dinghies from being swept overboard, struggling to keep from going into the black sea themselves.

Bill Cox, a fleshy young man with a beard and the muscles of Goliath, was fed up with the effort to do it all with only one hand free. Finally he sat down in his inflated dinghy and began tightening the straps on the mound of stores. A wave hit him in the chest like a wrecking ball. He went over backwards, slamming his head on the deck. He was gone as if a trap door had opened. In a moment the men had trained several torches on the frothing sea and were calling to him. In a moment, out of the blackness, his white face rose for an instant like a blanched leaf in the torrent.

Jellicoe howled at him: "Get into the dinghy, man, get in, hang on, use the fucking paddle," but the sea was carrying him away.

Cox and forty pounds of vital ammunition wrapped in oilskins were drifting away on the dinghy, his hand waving to them in a kind of pathetic farewell, his mouth working soundlessly in the gale.

Godwin barely heard, barely recognized, his own voice as he yelled into Jellicoe's ear. "Let me go get him. The waves will bring him closer in a minute, they're bound to. Tie a line around my waist, I'll get to the dinghy . . . then you haul us back in—"

"Waves, man! Bloody waves'll smash you to bits against the hull of the sub—"

"I'm a pretty strong swimmer. If anyone's going to be lost, best it's me. Let me bring Cox back. Come on, dammit. Tie the rope around me—"

"Godwin, you're mad!"

"Get the goddamn rope!" He was screaming at Jellicoe. He saw Cox's face again, darting toward him, bouncing among the towering waves. He felt the rope being cinched tight and then they were lowering him down the slippery hull into the water.

I die as I have lived, he thought, a fucking idiot. . . .

He braced his feet against the hull and kicked off with all the strength he had. He felt the waves closing over him, felt as if a hammer were driving him deeper and deeper into the total infinite blackness, like the inside of an eternal black ice cube, and his lungs were collapsing inward and his brain was threatening to burst like a grenade, and then when it was a second or two from being too late he bobbed up, the rope sliding like a huge noose up his chest, chewing at his armpits, cutting into flesh, but the pain didn't last because the water was so cold he was losing sensation of any kind very quickly, and he saw the torchlight playing across him and the roiling waves and blinking furiously at the water he glimpsed the dinghy, saw Cox waving to him, and he began swimming. At best guess, it took him a month of hard swimming, lungs bursting, brain starved of oxygen and easing well into the red line, to reach the dinghy. Cox grabbed him by one arm and nearly fell out but finally hauled him up high enough so that Godwin found himself hanging on the rim, gasping, locking his arm beneath the ridge.

"Good of you to come, sir," Cox called. He was grinning. "I'm not much of a swimmer, I'm afraid."

"That makes . . . two of us . . . afraid." Godwin felt the first stiff tug on the rope. "Hold me tight. They'll . . . haul us . . . in."

Jellicoe was laughing back on deck. The rest of the men seemed equally lifted by the incident. The gathering tension had been broken. They were slapping Godwin on the back. It was all oddly miraculous. They were inexplicably acting as if he were a hero rather than a half-drowned imbecile who'd merely known he was the most expendable of the lot. Jellicoe grabbed him by the shoulders, shook him. "You'll be mentioned in dispatches, old chap. See if we can get you a VC or something. Whatever we give civilians. Damn fine work." He was laughing. Godwin couldn't stop shaking. It was the cold. It was shock. Whatever it was he couldn't stop shaking. "Come on, lads," Jellicoe called down the line. "Back to work, blow these blasted things up and make 'em secure."

The rescue of Bill Cox was, as it turned out, the easy part. The hard part was yet to come. It began when Cyril Pinkham pointed to the distant shore.

"The signal, sir," he yelled to Jellicoe. "It's Hood. He's made it, sir!"

Each one of the dinghies capsized at least twice on the way from *Kismet* to the beach but Godwin wasn't counting, not even paying attention to how many times he went in the water, he was just trying to survive so they wouldn't have to deliver that letter to Cilla, so he could get back to London and find out who was threatening to kill him, so he could get back to the relative sanity of murder instead of this water-logged, freezing madness. He'd feel himself being pitched back into the water, feel the envelope of cold fold around him, squeezing his heart in a vise, and he'd begin to struggle to right the dinghy and keep the magazines of ammunition from slipping their moorings and get back into the godawful thing and wait for it to overturn again and send him back into the water and while he waited for the inevitable he paddled in what seemed like an utterly hopeless attempt to reach the light swinging in the darkness on the beach.

Kismet was drifting, which made it all the more difficult. One moment it was there, a benchmark, the next it was gone and you were lost, diving down between swells where you couldn't see the shoreline, couldn't see Max Hood's beacon, couldn't see the submarine. The other dinghies were going through the same drill. He could hear the occasional screams of frustration and anger and fear; he could see the odd body tossed up on a wave and then buried. The water was full of commandos and everybody was shouting and trying to get hold of the dinghies and it was a mess. The last time Godwin went into the drink he knew it had to be the last time; he just might get back into the little rubber coffin one more time but then the game was over: The thought flashed through his mind as he went in headfirst, down, down into the thick, suffocating, crushing depths. He kicked weakly, righting himself, struggling upward, feeling the water pushing him back to the surface, the dark and cold and oily water. He broke the surface and saw Jellicoe fifteen feet away. His face had lost its color. He was shouting and struggling to swim back to the dinghy. Jellicoe didn't look so hot. Godwin made a few strokes trying to get to him, then realized that if he didn't get hold of the dinghy it would be lost altogether. He fought the swells until he'd reached it. He heaved himself back in with what he knew was the last of his strength, barely made it, weighed a thousand pounds as he dragged his legs up over the side. He was damn near all the way back into the dinghy when the ammunition broke loose and coldcocked him. He felt the skin of his scalp pop like an overripe plum and when he could see through the pain he expected to find his head floating along like a grapefruit, just out of reach. At last he felt warmth, the pain tracing down the back of his head and neck and along his spine like fire, and something else warm, blood, running down his neck. A swell caught the dinghy, lifted it up, tipped the box of ammunition all the way out into the water. Jellicoe saw it go, began beating the water trying to get to it, gave up, turned back to Godwin, waving to him.

He was calling for help. Godwin began paddling, inching closer to Jellicoe. Godwin could see, but vision was the only sense left him. He was numb, even the heat of the pain was gone. The howling of the wind and the roar of the crashing, tumbling, exploding waves made it impossible to hear, but he didn't think Jellicoe was saying much he didn't already know. His face was gray blue. Hanging out of the raft Godwin finally got hold of Jellicoe's frantically waving hand, tried to squeeze it but couldn't feel his own hand let alone Jellicoe's. He tugged, trying to draw Jellicoe against the rubber, he heard Jellicoe's voice, *bloody bad luck, touch of gyppy tummy, stomach cramps, bloody hell* . . . Jellicoe's eyes kept rolling back in his head, blinking, trying to focus, then rolling back so that only the whites showed, his mouth was open and the black water rushed in, a wave smashed down. It was like having a four-storey building collapsing on your head and back. Godwin felt the strength go out of his legs, felt his mouth slammed down into the rubber, tasted blood, and when the wave had blown itself out Martin Jellicoe was gone.

An hour later he lay on the cement-hard, water-packed beach, blood in his eyes, gasping for breath like some newly evolved creature feeling its way onto dry land for the first time, and not knowing quite what to make of it. He was hoping that what he felt in his extremities was life. Then he saw Cyril Pinkham on his knees, tugging the dinghy out of the surf with the help of Boyd Malvern. They were five hundred yards down the beach from the beacon. But they were alive.

"Pinkie," Godwin said, croaking, coughing up sea water.

"Mr. Godwin," Pinkham said, staggering toward him. "Everyone accounted for, sir?"

"I hate this," Godwin said, pushing himself up onto his knees so he was face-to-face with the crouching figure of Cyril Pinkham. "Pinkie, I gotta tell you . . . you're in command now."

They huddled as close to the roaring blaze as they could, close enough to feel it scorching the water off your face and drying out your eyelashes. Max Hood had shepherded them down the beach, past the hammering surf, to a ruined, burnt-out fort which dated from well back into the nineteenth century. He had the huge fire laid and a single match had set it going. It burned the clinging wet and chill away, drew the dazed commandos like a magnet. The cold rain slanted through ragged holes overhead. Ox Bester passed around a bottle of rum Hood had provided. The wind shrieked in the ancient stones. The men spoke in whispers, exhausted men who couldn't raise their voices.

Max Hood hunkered down next to Godwin and passed him a second bottle of rum. "Tell me about Jelly. You were in the dinghy together. What happened?"

"It was bad. We couldn't stay in the damn thing, we kept falling out. He wasn't feeling up to par. Said it was gyppy tummy—"

"Him and his gyppy tummy," Hood said softly.

"I tried to reach him, Max. I got back in the dinghy and paddled and tried to reach him, I had his hand, I was so close—"

"It's not your fault, old man. Relax. It's over now."

"I had his hand, I was pulling him back to the dinghy, then there was a helluva wave and he was gone. He was weak at the end, Max, he couldn't really grab hold of my hand . . ."

Hood patted Godwin on the back. "He had a good innings, all told. He did some damage in his day."

"How old was he?"

"Forty-five, forty-six. Too bloody old for this kind of fun and games. That's the problem, Rodger. Some of us old bastards don't know when we're licked."

"Anybody could have drowned out there. We're lucky we didn't all drown. It was crazy."

Hood nodded. "Difficult sort of night, all around. I'm awfully sorry about all this, old man. It wasn't supposed to be quite such an ordeal. Best laid plans and all. How's your head?"

"Still attached."

"Same old Rodger." Hood chuckled under his breath and swigged at the rum.

"Give 'em irony and pity when they're feeling shitty."

"Hemingway. Remember the time we met him playing tennis in the Luxembourg Gardens? Seems like yesterday. Irony and pity. How true, how true. Feel up to a little walk, old man?"

"I don't want to think about it."

Hood clapped him on the back again, moved on to the next shivering figure.

They stored the deflated dinghies and pumps and made ready to carry the stores. Godwin was having trouble believing the night's work wasn't over. But, of course, it wasn't.

Once they'd had an hour to soak up the heat and recover some small sense of equilibrium, Hood got their attention by tapping the barrel of a tommy gun on the stone wall.

"Now that you've had a good rest and gotten your land legs back—"

Groans, good-natured, heartfelt.

"—we have a wee hike ahead of us. Nothing much, about five miles.

Divide up the stores as best you can. There are time constraints. It's past midnight and we can't be moving around once day breaks. So, finish off the rum, gentlemen, and forget that you're tired. In a few hours you'll be sleeping like babies."

"Absolutely, sir," Smythe-Haven drawled. "Waking up and crying every quarter hour."

The hill country as it was called began immediately after they'd slogged across the beach. Somehow Hood knew the way, though it was a trackless waste of rock and scrub and grit leading steadily upward until it finally reached an escarpment of two thousand feet. It wasn't sheer but the grade was steep, the outcroppings of rock sharp and slippery. The rain and wind were steady and the temperature was dropping and the clothes on your back clung and rubbed and your feet were raw and everything was wrong. Godwin carried a package of gelignite. They had to walk within an arm's length of each other or they'd lose touch, lose their way, and the darkness would pick them off like a hidden sniper. The wall of rock was seamed with gullies and ravines, some of which were choked with scrub, others already turning into rushing streams of rainwater gurgling and swelling all around them. On top of the escarpment the tableland would turn abruptly into desert and the desert went on forever. Insofar as he could think at all, Godwin thought this was hell, the worst, no matter where you looked. He wasn't throwing up, yet if given the choice he'd have picked the submarine. Maybe he'd forgotten how bad it was. Maybe he was just plain losing his marbles. Anyone who could have been in London having a drink at Dogsbody's but was here—well, any such person was ready for Bedlam.

They were halfway up the escarpment, two and a half hours into the little hike, when he fell.

Christ. It was the wind and the rain and the mud underfoot and the exhaustion, it was clumsiness, it was stupidity, and whatever it was it didn't matter once you fell. Then it was too late. He was reaching for a handhold, a root or a crevice, his face nearly touching the trouser leg of the man ahead of him, mud squeezing out between his fingers, but he found a smooth protruding finger of stone, and he slipped off, felt himself going backward like the cop on top of the ladder in one of the Keystone Kops movies, teetering back and forward, only he was sliding in the muddy sand and for an instant he thought he might not fall, and then he heard Ox Bester behind him grunt as they collided, felt Bester's arm around him, trying to hold him or break the fall, but it was hopeless and he was blind in the darkness and he was tumbling, holding the gelignite, smashing against more rocks and feeling the scrub scraping his face, sliding, desperately trying to get any kind of foothold and failing, rolling with the gelignite held tight to his chest, down, down, until with a sudden cry he slammed into something hard, felt a pain streaking across his kidneys and the wind leaving him in a hurry like blood from a sliced artery, lay there gasping, feeling life slipping away.

He blinked in the sudden glare of light. It shone down on him from a hundred feet above, shadows spilling down the rockface.

"He's dead!" The voiced cried out involuntarily and Godwin shook his head, achingly raised his hand.

"I'm all right," he called back into the wind, the wind whipping the rain across his face.

The light moved away, met another finger of torchlight which was shining at something off to the left.

"Not you," another voice came faintly.

"See if he's dead." That was the first voice again, coming from light years away.

Godwin fought the mud and the rock, finally got up on his knees, panting, looking for a handful of something to bring himself upright. When he stood up with his foot braced against the boulder he saw the other man caught in the glare of torchlight. He worked his way across the width of the huge stone to where the body lay. It was bent backward over a sharp edge of rock shelf thrust out beneath a clump of gorse. The head was twisted sideways, the eyes staring. The back and neck were surely snapped. It was Ox Bester, who had once been a Glasgow iron worker, a shipbuilder, and was now the second man to die for PRAETORIAN.

"Rodger." It was Max Hood calmly calling his name. "Rodger, can you hear me?"

Godwin waved.

"Bring the ammunition pack he was carrying. I can see it from here. Ahead of you. Twenty feet above you."

Godwin saw it, looked again at the body of Ox Bester. He wanted to say something, some kind of farewell, but what?

"Leave him, Rodger. He can't hear you." Hood's voice cut through the wind, the oily darkness of the night, as if he'd read his mind. He'd seen it all before. He knew how men thought. He knew they wanted to say good-bye. "We need the ammo. Get a move on, old boy. We've got to get these lights off."

Max Hood kept talking to him until he'd made the climb and was back among them.

CHAPTER 8

The morning came hot and sunny and still, and they woke slowly, groggy, only half-aware of their surroundings until reality set in. The smell of goat seemed to rise like steam from the floor of the cave and Godwin coughed, blinking as if that too would do some good in keeping the stink out of his body, and staring wildly at the brightness beyond the cave entrance. Jim Steele and Brian Qualley had gone through similar exercises in the scruffy edge of desert and knew the flora and fauna. They sneaked out before the others were awake, found Hood brewing tea over a fire in the mouth of his cave, and went on to harvest a ration of arbutus berries which were nearly identical to strawberries. They brought tea in tin cups and the berries back to Godwin's cave and along with Penrose they sat cross-legged and tried to ignore the goat smell while breakfasting.

"Arabs call these berries the fruit of God," Qualley said. "Beats eating grubworms unless, of course, you're really hungry and then a grubworm isn't half bad. Right, Jamey?" Steele nodded, grinning. They both grinned about almost anything that happened. As the day progressed Godwin never heard any of the remaining men mention either Jellicoe or Ox Bester again. It was as if the memory of them, given life in speech, would somehow queer the deal, doom the operation. They might never have existed.

Careful to hurry and hug the trees and shrubs for cover, Godwin and Penrose and Alf Dexter were detailed to go with Max back to the lip of the escarpment. There they found in ancient Roman tombs, still bearing Roman insignia, wooden crates of Thompson submachine guns. Stone doorways to the tombs had been loosened. He saw the Roman carvings and shook his head to brush the cobwebs and fantasies away. He felt one with time and it wasn't a bad feeling. You could live or die in a place like this. It didn't really seem to make much difference. Men had been living and dying here for centuries and it hadn't changed anything. The tommy guns were stored in one tomb along with a couple of sheltering goats who belonged to the brother-in-law of the Sanusi guide Hood had engaged to give them a hand. He stood shyly petting one of the goats while they inspected the tommy guns, then pitched in to help carry them back to the caves on the tableland. Hood explained to Godwin that the Sanusi guide, who wore an incongruous lounge suit with a belt in back and shoes made of pieces of tire track, was an exceedingly brave man. The Italians normally dealt with Sanusi who aided the British in a prompt and decisive manner. A meat hook was driven up through the underside of the jaw and they were strung up in the town squares, left to hang until they died in the sun. The Sanusi hated the Italians with a deep, savage passion. Forced to join the Italian army when Mussolini had attempted to conquer North Africa, before requiring German assistance, the Sanusi tribesmen had deserted in large numbers to Wavell's army, then to Auchinleck's. Mussolini had tried to effect a vast fantasy for Cyrenaica; he had been engaged in an occupation and more or less constant warfare with the Sanusi for almost twenty years. To keep them from deserting their native land for Egypt, Mussolini had built a barbed wire fence along the entire length of Cyrenaica's eastern frontier. In the present series of brutalities, the Sanusi were kept in subjugation by the iron fist of Marshal Graziani. When given the chance to aid the British, those not broken by fear were quick to answer the call. Hood moved among them with ease. They were loyal to him. They would never betray him. For the past week he had lived among them, disguised as an Arab merchant, moving at will behind German and Italian lines. Now the job was nearly done.

About noon an Italian ambulance plane flew over at eight hundred feet but didn't spot them. Other than that there were no intrusions. It was hot and still and Godwin had the impression that nothing was moving. Occasionally there was a sound or a flicker in the scrub but he ignored it. He wondered if he would ever get home. The past twenty-four hours had made him care both more and less than he'd ever cared before. He felt as if he were becoming one with something huge and indifferent and vastly encompassing: was it history? or time? or some kind of blinding infinity which was sucking them toward a core, toward the emptiness of space? He knew that he no longer mattered at all and it was a powerful revelation. Here nothing seemed to matter: not Cilla, not Churchill, not Monk

Vardan, not Homer Teasdale, not Dogsbody's, not someone who was writing him threatening letters. Nothing mattered here. It was rather pleasant. Maybe it was like being very sick or very old and just feeling it all slip away. He felt as if he just might be letting go. He wondered what it would all be like if he got back to London. Would it all seem important still?

The guide prepared them a late lunch of goat stew. It was a little bland but quite edible. Lad Holbrook said: "I've just dined on a linseed poultice." They were all glad, however, to be able to eat without vomiting. Hood thanked the guide and sent him back to the real world. If he were caught, or killed, in the presence of British soldiers, the retribution taken on the Sanusi would be general and terrible.

Late in the afternoon Hood assembled the team in the largest of three caves. Some of the men were smoking pipes and some cigarettes and some chewing on bully beef. Godwin looked around him, making sure their names and faces were locked in his memory. Boyd Malvern, Jim Steele, Bert Penrose, Reggie Smythe-Haven, Tony Jones, Cyril Pinkham, Alf Dexter, Bill Cox, Lad Holbrook, Brian Qualley, Max Hood. And himself. If he got back on schedule he'd be telling their story, turning them into the stuff of legend. The men who got Rommel.

"There have been some changes of plan, gentlemen," Hood said quietly. "We'll be moving out as soon as it's dark. Once the mission is accomplished we'll have the advantage of extreme confusion in the enemy camp. We will be met by our guide at a place I will show you on the way to town and he will lead us down an easily managed *wadi* to the beach, back to the fort, where *Kismet* will be waiting to take us away. Twelve hours from now we'll be gone. Now there's the matter of the next twelve hours." He leaned back against the wall of the cave and crossed his legs before him. He began, slowly, to apply the burnt cork to his face, and as he talked the others followed his lead.

"The day before yesterday while you lads were enjoying your Mediterranean cruise," Hood went on, "I gathered a couple of my Sanusi friends and had a go at the communications pylon twelve miles down the road to Tobruk. We didn't quite knock it down but it will be pretty useless until they take delivery on some supplies—and Auchinleck's Eighth Army may delay those spare parts for the millennium."

"Well done, sir," Pinkham said. "There'll be no need to spread us too thin."

"Exactly. I have also determined that Rommel spends most of his time at the villa. And certainly the evenings. So we can pretty much forget the big HQ building. We'll form two detachments. One for the dynamo— it's a concrete block building at the foot of the grain tower. Gelignite, tommy guns. The rest of us will take the villa. Grenades, tommy guns, handguns. We'll cut the phone lines. Everybody should be asleep except a very minimal guard. Two men at most. When we hear the explosions and the lights go out . . ." He shrugged. "We do it." His face was black. Night was falling quickly. "Now the detachments. Penrose, obviously you do the gelignite at the dynamo. Pinkham, you lead it, Malvern and Jones —the four of you should enjoy the job. I'll lead on the villa with Dexter, Qualley, Smythe-Haven, Holbrook, Steele, Cox, and Godwin. Now we might as well load up. Grenades for the latter bunch. Gelignite for the former. Rodger, there's a Colt .45 for you, grenades, but not a tommy gun, I think. They take a bit of getting used to. You worked with grenades in Alex, am I right?" Godwin nodded. "Good. Stick with me—you and I go as a single entry, understood?" Godwin nodded again. His face was disappearing under the cork. He made sure his light brown hair was secure under the watch cap. They all wore dark trousers, turtleneck sweaters in midnight blue. For an hour they opened, checked, repacked explosives, distributed arms and ammunition.

The sunny day had gone long ago and as the afternoon wore on the weather had steadily worsened. Hood couldn't believe it. It was utterly wrong, against all the forecasts. Rain began heavily about seven o'clock and the temperature had dropped. It was no different from the night before. As bad as it could be for the operation.

Godwin was standing alone by the cave's entrance, watching the rain turn the clearing to a quagmire, when Max Hood came to stand beside him. "You're right," he said, reading the look on Godwin's blackened face. "If CRUSADER weren't kicking off tomorrow morning I wouldn't dream of going tonight. It makes no difference to Rommel when we come. But everything hinges on CRUSADER. Rommel must be dead. The Afrika Korps must be confused, demoralized. Auchinleck's Eighth Army will be rolling. The lads at Tobruk need relieving." He stared at the remorseless rain, the mud deepening, and lit a cigarette. "That's what Jellicoe and Ox Bester died for—to keep this thing on schedule. We have to go, Rodger, like it or not."

"One thing's bothering me," Godwin said. "I don't know quite how to say it . . . I feel like a bad omen. Two men are dead and I've been involved in both deaths." It was a relief to speak about it. The refusal of the men even to acknowledge what had happened to Jellicoe and Bester had spooked him. "I'm bad luck, Max. And now you want me close to you tonight. It worries me. I don't want you taking care of me when you should be thinking about the job—I don't like it. This whole thing is so different from what Monk told me it would be—"

"Look, Rodger, you can't carry around any guilt about Jelly and Bester. This is a war. Things do happen, things go wrong. If I felt responsible for all the men who've died under my command—well, I can't and I don't. There is one lesson about war. People are always getting hurt. Now, you stick close to me. We go together. We come back together. We go home."

Godwin's legs ached from the previous night's exercise. Now, in the sucking mud, they weighed him down, made every step an eternity filled with pain and torrential rain and the same bloody darkness. At least he wasn't climbing a rocky hillside. Pinkham's detachment were too heavily laden with explosives. The load was redistributed for the hike. The darkness was made palpable by the rain, the sliding and slipping in the mud, the muffled curses, the occasional sound of a gun barrel clicking against a buckle or a strap clamp. They had to stay well clear of the road which left them a narrow path that had become a river of mud. Each man held on to the bayonet scabbard of the man ahead of him. Otherwise the line would collapse, disaster ensue. It was another version of the night before, the ditch rushing with water and mud and mined with hidden rocks yawning like a chasm only a couple of feet away. If he'd had any idea Rommel would be this difficult to kill . . . well, it was too late for that now.

Suddenly Steele slipped or tripped, fell forward with a muffled shout and slid off into the ditch. The rest of the line froze, waited.

A dog began barking, a hacking sound, as if he were a hound who should cut back to a pack a day. Steele knelt in the muddy water, afraid to move. The dog yanked at a chain. Fifty yards away.

A light came on in a hut. The door slammed open, light spilled in a wedge from the doorway. Nobody breathed. The man stared into the darkness, grumbled to the dog. The dog barked again, defiantly, and the bark ended in a yelp as the man swatted it with a pole or board of some kind. He hit it again, yelled at it, then stamped back into the house, the stillness and the sound of the rain reverberating with the slamming of the door. Slowly, exhaling a long sigh, Steele grabbed a hand and was pulled up onto the track, and they set off again. Hood stopped them as they reached a cart track, rutted, wider.

"This track leads directly into Beda Littoria. We're half a mile from target. We'll stop now for a cigarette. Final weapons check. Pinkie, get your lot together. About a hundred yards along this track there's a branch off to the left. It'll take you to the grain tower and the dynamo. We'll go on ahead into the main square."

Everything changed as they moved down the cart track. Godwin realized that these were now, had suddenly become, men going to work.

Everything was different: the way they walked, the pattern of their breathing, the way they looked from side to side as they came within the spreading, penumbral light of the village. Godwin felt his own heart rate increasing, the sense of energy that came with the squirting of adrenaline. The tension had replaced the rain and cold as the central fact of the evening. The rain didn't matter anymore. It was there, harder, colder, but it didn't matter. All Godwin felt was the tension, the rawness of his nerves. The pounding of his heart. Odd, how it occurred to him: His heart felt now as it did when he glimpsed Cilla. Another reason why war was like love.

Pinkham detached his group and set off toward the grain tower, the highest building in the cluster that made up Beda Littoria, or Sidi Rafa as the Arabs called it. The low concrete block house squatted at the foot of the tower. It looked from a distance to be undefended. Pinkham turned to Hood and Godwin, a smile splitting his blackened face, teeth shining. "Candy from a baby, sir," he said. "See you at the villa."

They moved on, hugging the line of cedars and cypresses and eucalyptus trees marking the road. They had moved off the cart track, joined the main road as they passed the Arab market of hovels and shops sheltering in the shadow of the grain tower. The rain blew in rippling sheets. The wind snatched at bits of paper and cloth spilling from the deserted market.

The four-storey *prefettura*, which housed the local courthouse and police station and local offices, faced out on to the square. It also was the German HQ. And it was dark. A fountain stood like a rainswept derelict in the middle of the square, overflowing, splashing. Across the square stood the rostrum from which Mussolini had once spoken. His main road to Egypt ran directly through the square. The white Chapel of Our Lady reposed darkly. The priest was gone, the verger left in charge. Hood had been thorough in his recce. The villas were widely spaced as they moved quietly in the shadows, leaving the square. The villas were all modern concrete buildings built by the Italian invaders.

"Right there," Hood said. The men gathered around him. It was nineteen minutes past midnight. "That's the villa. Rommel is in there, gentlemen. Let's make it his last resting place."

Hood led his men to the wire fence surrounding the villa, motioned to Cox who quickly cut it with clippers. They filtered quietly through onto the grass surrounding the villa on three sides: Grass which clung hopelessly to life and had become mud. In front of the villa was a gravel carpark. They moved like black ghosts, as if they were floating.

The villa was dark, quiet, almost supernaturally quiet. There was only the sound of the rain: being driven into the earth, against the walls, pelting the deserted bell-tent where a guard would normally have been stationed. The tent was straining against the pegs in the wind and the canvas was soaked through, bits of it flapping. The guard had presumably found it too wet and been forced inside by the storm.

Cox went to cut the telephone wires.

Lad Holbrook spoke briefly to Hood and then slipped away in the shadows at the front of the building.

A single guard stood sentry by the front gate at the foot of the driveway leading up to the carpark. He was looking outward into the rain and darkness, occasionally, listlessly, crossing the driveway, then returning to the gatehouse which was only about the size of a telephone box. An electric light hung over the entry to the driveway. It swung furiously in the wind and the hinge needed oil. The shadows played like goblins in the street. Rain pounded and danced on the steel helmet of the sentry as Holbrook moved along the cypress trees lining the driveway. It was mesmerizing, watching the rain hit the helmet, bounce, arc brightly in the light.

The scene might have come from a movie. Holbrook stood poised in shadows behind the sentry as if he were listening for something. Then he moved into the light, knife out. It was done quickly, economically, left arm jerked tight around the windpipe, the knife sliding through the overcoat, pushing between the ribs, then the sentry, now just a carcass, going limp. Holbrook let him fall back into the shadow of the gatehouse. Then he disappeared back into the shadow of the tree line and presently appeared next to Hood. Godwin tore his gaze away from the crumpled bundle beside the gatehouse.

Hood whispered: "I'm not sure I like this. Too bloody quiet."

Smythe-Haven pushed his way next to Hood. "Don't look for trouble, sir. It couldn't be better. It's just that everybody's asleep and like you said, we're the last people on earth they're expecting."

Hood nodded, but he didn't look convinced. "Let's go round back." He moved on, leather grenade belt squeaking in the darkness.

They circled to the rear of the house, checked the outhouse which was attached, gently tried the back door which was locked. "Qualley. Take a position behind the two trucks and cover the back door. We may have chaps running for their lives. Kill 'em." Qualley arranged himself with two tommy guns, a belt of grenades, two magazines for the guns. The trucks bore the palm tree and swastika markings of the Afrika Korps. A dim light bulb burned over the back door to the house. Target practice.

Hood led the way around the other side of the house, through a hedge, until they stood at the rim of the gravel. There were three staff cars parked before the steps up to the porch. "Quiet now," Hood said and ventured out onto the gravel, stood looking up at the house from beside the cars. The ground-floor windows were both barred with iron and tightly shuttered against the rain. Rain was pouring off the roof, dropping three stories to hit the ground in staccato spurts. A shallow porch ran across the middle third of the frontage. Stone steps led to the porch and the door was perhaps eight feet across the porch.

Hood looked at his watch. "They ought to have blown the dynamo by now."

"Well, they haven't run into trouble," Steele whispered. "We'd have heard any gunfire."

Rain swept in gusts across the front of the house. Godwin looked back down at the gatehouse. The sentry was still dead.

At last Hood said: "All right, I've got to tell you. My belly tells me there's something wrong here. Too quiet. It may be deserted for all I know. We could be raiding an empty house. Or it could be something else. But I'm not prepared to wait around until inspiration strikes. We're going in now. Dexter, give the door a knock."

They all followed Alf Dexter up the steps to the door. Dexter spoke perfect German. He pounded on the door, impatiently, like a kraut officer ready to tear a strip off somebody. Godwin felt the heavy Colt .45 in his hand. He should have been focused but he wasn't. He was half-drunk with it: he was part of it. It was what he'd wanted and in that instant the realization of the truth swept him away. He was with Max Hood again. He was at war at last. He felt he was completing a journey begun so long ago.

Alf Dexter kept shouting. He said he was soaking wet and wanted the door opened without delay or he'd personally tear somebody a new asshole.

The door was opened by a German soldier in steel helmet and overcoat.

Dexter slammed through to secure the door against the wall. Hood lunged past Dexter, pile-driving into the German, thrusting his .45 into the man's chest. "Where is Rommel?" Dexter growled in German. The German's eyes were round behind his wire-rimmed spectacles. He was very tall and thick, six feet four, towering over Hood. The sight of the commandos with their guns and blackened faces seemed to have frightened him. Godwin couldn't blame him.

Quite unexpectedly the German responded to the question by engulfing Hood's gun barrel in a huge hand and jamming it aside with enormous strength. He slammed Hood across the narrow hallway, pinned him to the wall with such force that the plaster gave a crack all the way to the ceiling. A dim light burned at the far end of the hallway. Dexter tried to pull the German off Hood but there wasn't enough space to get sufficient leverage. The German was huge, like an all-in wrestler, and he was fighting for his life. He swung one arm, heavy as a ham, following a brief arc that ended with Dexter's face. Dexter fell. His nose was spurting blood onto the floor as he gasped for breath. Hood was trying to get at his knife but his arm was being crushed against the wall. Godwin took it all in in three or four ticks of the second hand, furious, desperate struggling. The German soldier had drawn his own knife and was overpowering Max Hood. Godwin leveled the .45 at the German's face, red and contorted with exertion and fury and terror, eyes bulging, nose red like a clown, and pulled the trigger. The face was blown completely off. There was a pink explosion of blood and bone and brains that seemed to float off in a cloud toward the light at the end of the hallway. The body, dead on its feet, swayed backward and fell over. The body was blocking the hallway.

Hood swung around and motioned the rest of the men inside. Hood's left arm which had been against the wall hung unnaturally limp at his side. The floor was stone and slippery with blood. They flooded the hallway. Dexter, Smythe-Haven, Holbrook, Steele, Cox, Hood, and Godwin. Too many men already. At the far end of the hallway, by the light, stone steps led upstairs. Several doorways, closed, led off the hall where they stood. Hood gestured to Godwin to follow him toward the stair at the back. The commandos, having filled the hallway, looked to Hood for instructions. The building had returned to utter stillness but for Dexter's breath whistling through his broken nose. They waited in suspended animation, white eyes flickering this way and that, waiting for their fates to be decided. What was going on? Hood turned to Godwin. "I don't like this a goddamn bit . . ." Explosions began going off not far away. The dynamo. But the light stayed on over the stairway. The villa had its own generator.

Hood turned abruptly to Godwin. "They knew we were coming, old chap. They're ready for us."

As if on cue, the hallway doors flew open and soldiers spewed out, guns drawn, mouths open, guttural shouts spraying like shrapnel. The front door was blocked. Ten seconds of surprise and confusion and bawling Germans and Max Hood said aloud: "Fuck all this," and shot somebody. A German fell back in midcry and utter, complete hell ensued. The close quarters seemed to burst apart with gunfire, shouts, screams, a total insanity of noise and pushing and shoving and things Godwin had never dreamed of. Cox was backing toward him, his body jerking as he fired the tommy gun, Godwin saw bullets plucking at Cox's back, like fingers picking lint from his dark sweater, as they went through him, all the way through him. Cox tumbled backward, dead. Hood pushed the falling body aside and fired point-blank into a German chest. Bullets were ripping the walls to shreds, plaster dust filling the narrow space like poison gas. Godwin felt a searing pain, looked down, saw a nail protruding from broken plaster slice across his calf. Then he was slammed to the floor, felt another pain, like a poker straight from the fire laid across his right side below the armpit. He turned his head which was almost touching the bottom step of the rear stairway. He was trying to breathe in something but plaster dust. He knew he was going to die. Somewhere deep in the reptile portion of his brain he knew it was the time, that it would all be over in a minute or two. It didn't bother him because it wasn't registering properly. They weren't thoughts. They were merely things he knew. Life was over. His side hurt. He'd killed a man. Hood was firing his automatic. The noise would be over soon. He wouldn't be worrying about breathing or anything else very soon. He blinked at the dust. Heavy boots were coming down the back stairs. He had a good view of the boots, the stone stairs. Hobnailed boots, very Teutonic, the rest of the man clumped into view, knees, heavy thighs, hand at his side. The hand held one of the long-handled potato-masher grenades. There was nothing to do but kill him. Godwin raised the .45 and fired twice. The kick made his side hurt like blazes. The first slug caught the man in the crotch, the second in the chest. He fell backward on the steps. The grenade bounced down to land beside Godwin. He had no idea whatsoever how the damn things worked. He grabbed the handle and threw it back up the stairs. More feet and legs and boots had come into view. At the sight of the grenade flying upward toward them they turned and started to climb back up but the stairway was narrow and the men in back didn't understand what the men in front were playing at and it was more Keystone Kops. It was funny to watch. The grenade exploded, bringing down a massive cascade of plaster and blowing a hole in the back wall. The blast was deafening in the confined space. Godwin felt the heat and the stinging bits of plaster on his face, then rain blowing in through the hole.

He got up and was trying to figure out what was going on in the forty feet of hallway which was a seething mass of bodies, knives flashing, guns firing, fists flailing. The fighting was hand-to-hand. He saw Hood in front of him withdraw his dagger from a man's chest. Grunts and groans rumbled like something in a cage at the zoo. Hood turned abruptly, brought his gun up, and shot out the light bulb over Godwin's head.

. . .

Godwin felt the crush of bodies, smelled sweat and blood and plaster dust and the unique acrid smell of guns going off. He pushed his way along the wall, scrambling against other men. Who were they? Friend or foe? It was impossible to know what was going on in the dark. He heard machine-gun fire from out behind the house, men shouting. He fell to his knees, began crawling among the legs and boots. An electric torch was snapped on, then another, raking the hallway like spotlights searching the night sky for bombers. Guns began going off again, quick bursts, single shots, and a body slid down in front of him among the scuffling boots. A bullet had blown a hole in the man's throat and shattered the jaw, the eyes were blinking. False teeth were halfway out of the remainder of the mouth. It was Smythe-Haven. Godwin crawled across the body, knowing it was too late to help him. He felt Smythe-Haven's fingers clawing at his legs but the man was dying, the blood was gushing from his throat.

He was thirty feet along the corridor toward the front door, on hands and knees, his palms slipping and sliding in the blood on the floor. Plaster cut holes in the fleshy palms. It seemed he'd been in the hallway all his life but he knew it had been perhaps two, maybe three minutes since Alf Dexter had pounded on the door and they'd gone in ready to raise hell and kill Rommel. Now how many of them were already dead? He'd seen Cox and Smythe-Haven die with his own eyes. He'd plucked Cox out of the sea and brought him back to die in the noisy, exploding hallway. He was out of breath but the front doorway couldn't be far ahead.

Without warning there was an explosion out front. Flames leapt into the stormy night. One of the cars had blown up, orange and red against the blackness. It had to be Bert Penrose and the boys from the dynamo. There was a crush at the door. The Germans were confused and some were trying to get outside. Godwin lay still, felt boots jamming down on his back, digging into his kidneys. He saw figures outside by the cars. The good guys, he thought. The Afrika Korps seemed to be in brigade strength, everywhere. The commandos outside opened up with tommy guns as Germans poured through the doorway, across the porch only to die on the steps and in the gravel. Another explosion, another car engulfed in flame, burning debris twirling through the night trailing sparks like the Fourth of July.

Godwin felt the prick of a bayonet in his back, lay still, heard muttering in German, saw the glow of a flashlight shining on his face. He struggled to keep his eyes shut. A boot prodded him. He lay lifeless. The man moved away. Godwin leaned up on his elbows and shot him twice in the back.

The hallway was quiet, the battle had moved outside where firing—lit by the burning cars—was furious. Cries punctuated the rattle and bang. Godwin felt a hand on his shoulder. He'd thought he was the only man left alive in the dark hallway. Max Hood said: "You haven't lost the killing instinct. Damn good thing, too. Well done. The grenade on the stairs gave you the high score."

"Are we going to get out of this?" His mouth was so dry he could hardly speak.

"Looks a bit dicey at the moment, doesn't it? We've lost a fair number. Dexter and Qualley out back are dead."

"Cox and Smythe-Haven, too."

"Holbrook's going to lose an arm, I'm afraid."

A figure crawled through the wreckage of the walls and bodies. It was Lad Holbrook. "I'm shot up, sir." He spoke in a monotone to Hood. Shock was taking over. "Have we found Rommel yet?"

"Forget Rommel, Lad," Hood said softly.

"I got a peek through the door over there. They've opened the shutters and have got a heavy machine gun covering the park. I propose to take the bastards out with grenades. I only need one arm to throw them . . ."

"Be my guest," Hood said softly.

The third car blew up in the carpark.

"Penrose is having a jolly time of it." Hood turned back to watch Holbrook crawling along in the dusty, smoking gloom, his arm dragging.

Holbrook was on his knees by the door leading to one of the front rooms. He struggled to his feet and unhooked two grenades from the belt. He was having trouble with the lame arm. Godwin made a move to crawl back to help him but Hood clamped a hand down on his shoulder. "Leave him to it," he said. "He wants to go out alone."

Holbrook got both pins pulled, kicked the door open, and flipped the grenades into the room. There was a scuffling sound, feet moving in the room, shouts of alarm, Holbrook turned to come back up the hallway. Heavy machine-gun fire ripped through the wall as he went and he was lifted, blown sideways, fell through the open door on the opposite wall. The grenades exploded blowing out the front wall of the house on that side and reducing the plaster wall in the hallway to rubble. By the time the wall collapsed Godwin and Hood were through the front door, onto the porch, then diving low down the stone steps onto the gravel. Two bodies were hanging out the hole where the bars and window had been on the side of the house looking over the burning staff cars. The cars were red hot and the rain hissed loudly. Godwin could hear it over the continuing gunfire and the bellowed orders.

They crouched beside the steps trying to see what was going on. Clouds of steam rose like balloons from the burning cars. Figures darted in the flickering light from the fires. Machine guns were squirting tongues of flame from the window on the other side of the porch: a big one mounted on the floor, two hand-held. A man—for some reason Godwin thought it was Bert Penrose, heading for home, heading for the movie of his dreams, forever—burst from behind one of the burning cars and the big machine gun burped and he spun around and fell.

Blindingly, like a dozen phosphorous flares, light flooded the forecourt. It shone down from the roof, silvery, like the lights on a movie set. Commandos and German soldiers froze for a moment, blinking, blinded by the light. The machine gun opened up again. Cyril Pinkham and Boyd Malvern were caught in the open. The machine gun mounted in the window chewed through them, turning them into raw rag dolls, jerking, twisting, their dancing shadows stretching deep beyond them and then they were down and still.

Jones moved out from behind one of the burning cars which provided the only cover. He had his tommy gun ready and began firing at the roof lights. A German lying on the ground shot him with a rifle. He fell into the burning shell of the staff car, sending up a shower of sparks made all the more visible by the extinction of both spotlights.

Steele was kneeling by Hood, Godwin on the other side. In the darkness they were for the moment invisible. Steele whispered: "We're all that's left, sir. My legs took some hits, sir. I can't run. I can't make it out, sir. Sorry."

"They may not find us for a minute or two. We've got to get that second machine gun." Hood nodded at the barrel poking through the iron bars.

"Let me make some noise," Steele said. "Bit of a diversion, you might say. You chaps do the other job. Might as well take as many of them with us as we can, right, sir? And, sir?"

"Steele?"

"I'll see you walking the streets of glory, sir."

"I'm looking forward to it, old chap," Hood said.

Steele slipped away, back across the length of the porch, into the darkness.

"Fine men," Hood whispered, "one and all. Heroes, every fucking one of them." He turned to Rodger Godwin. "Stay with me. It's just possible he's going to die saving our lives. Do you care, Rodger? Do you care if you ever leave this place?"

"Not much, Max."

"Odd, isn't it? One rather hates to leave the men. Fact is, I don't care whether I live or die at all. This is a good death, isn't it? King and country and all. One thing, though. Rankles."

"What's that?" Godwin asked. He heard the Germans getting up from the gravel, their belts and weapons making the customary little sounds.

"They knew we were coming."

"But that's impossible. How—"

"There's a spy somewhere, old boy. Don't you see? That's the bloody thing about spies. Good men always wind up dying. Well, that's not our concern, is it? Not for the moment."

Godwin felt Hood pressing a grenade into his hand.

The metal continued to hiss in the rain. A man moaned with the pain. The soldiers were moving across the gravel, coming closer, coming to check out the house. Occasionally they would stop at the bodies strewn across the scene. The flames were dropping in the cars. The soldiers called to one another, prodded a body with a foot. An isolated coup de grâce cracked. The rain continued blowing.

There were fifteen or twenty soldiers moving slowly.

Steele's voice came loud and clear. "Over here, chaps! Bloody fucking krauts!" And in quick succession three grenades landed and exploded among the Germans. Everything began again. Germans were being chopped down by shrapnel and concussed and were firing at the sound of the voice.

Hood crouched, dashed around the corner of the porch. Godwin followed, hugging the wall, until he stopped beside the window. Hood nodded toward the window and pulled the pin on a grenade. Godwin pulled the pin on his.

Hood counted off the ticks, then moved underneath the window and threw the grenade between the bars. Godwin's clicked against a bar but dropped through into the room. The explosions followed immediately, filled the air with bits and pieces of the front wall and soldiers. Hood dashed across the space toward the line of cypresses. Godwin took off in his wake, dodging and weaving.

They almost made it.

It was the men on the roof. They were sharpshooters intended to pick off the strays. The shots sounded like firecrackers.

Hood grunted and pitched forward as if he'd tripped.

He had his Colt out but there was nothing he could do with it. No point in returning fire. Slugs were ripping at the mud. "Leg," Hood said. He was sprawled on the muddy edge of what was once grass. His body jerked as he was hit again. The bullet shredded the lower back of his heavy sweater. "Damn," he sighed. The gun was shaking in his hand. "Always knew this was going to happen. Sooner or later." He coughed.

"Max . . ." Godwin knelt beside him. It was pointless but he couldn't leave him. He couldn't lift him out of the mud. He couldn't have carried him far enough to make any difference.

He leaned down, felt something like a sledgehammer hit his shoulder, and he went over backward. He knew he'd been hit. He saw Cilla's face for a split second and it was gone.

"Bloody rotten business," Hood gasped. "They were . . . waiting for us . . . come closer, Rodger . . . I want to . . ."

Godwin gritted his teeth against the pain, pushed himself forward. There was no feeling in his shoulder. It was the rest of his body that hurt. He began to drag Max Hood toward the tree line. He looked down at Max.

Max Hood was smiling. "Not a bad death, though . . ." He raised his hand.

Godwin saw a blinding flash and knew that it was coming toward him, that he was being swallowed by the light. . . .

CHAPTER 9

LONDON

Cilla Hood was having an evening at home while her director conducted a tech rehearsal for *The Widow Weeds*. She had dinner with Chloe in the warm, fragrant kitchen with Nanny bustling in the background. Then they had crowded into a big chair by the fire in the study, just the two of them, and Cilla had read to her daughter from Beatrix Potter and the little girl had chortled over the illustrations while she listened, occasionally interjecting a comment. Then they had chatted for a bit until Chloe was yawning and ready for bed.

Now Cilla lay in a steaming tub thinking about the list of calls Nanny had taken for her during the day. Stefan Lieberman, Homer Teasdale, Patricia Smith . . . who in the world was Patricia Smith? Was the name ringing a faint bell? Yes, she'd heard it somewhere before but now it meant nothing and the appended telephone number meant nothing. There had been no answer when she'd rung Teasdale. And Stefan could wait; she'd see him tomorrow at rehearsal. She'd sooner or later get around to calling Patricia Smith but she'd feel better about it if she could place the name. . . .

She was dripping with sweat in the hot bath. She licked it from her upper lip. The hair was clinging wetly to her forehead. Her eyelids grew heavy, fluttered closed. What could Homer want? She was afraid to hope it might be word from Rodger. But why else would he call? She hadn't eaten properly, or slept properly, or been able to concentrate worth a damn for the past three weeks, ever since the last time she'd spoken with Homer, the night he'd phoned hoping to catch her before she went to bed, hoping he could stop round for a moment. He'd shown up, rather self-conscious, hating to disturb her but it really was rather urgent, though he clearly had no idea why it was necessary in the first place, but, you see, he'd had a note delivered by messenger from Rodger Godwin. . . . Godwin, you see, had wanted him to tell Mrs. Hood personally and at once that he was going to be out of touch for a couple of weeks. . . . While he'd stammered along, she'd urged him on with a drink. What in the world is going on, Homer? she'd wanted to know.

That was the first she'd heard of it—"Rodger's gone off on a special assignment and he wanted me to let you know." It must have been a spur of the moment thing since he'd not hinted a word to her? "Well, a couple of weeks and he said I should tell you not, under any circumstances, to worry—"

"But where?" she'd asked. "He must have given you some hint—"

"No, actually, he didn't. I'm in the dark and I'm trying to calm his employers, not an enviable task, I promise you—"

"But it's bound to be the war, isn't it? It's something dangerous and secret—"

"Let's hope it's not too dangerous," Homer said fervently.

"He told me about that cockeyed idea he had about going on a bombing mission just because some other nitwit did—"

"Reynolds. Quentin Reynolds."

"It's not that, is it? Not a bombing mission? But, no, it couldn't be, not for two weeks—"

"No, it couldn't be that, could it?"

Homer had finished his drink and been eager to go. She guessed he was curious but knew nothing of her relationship with Rodger. She'd thanked him and had heard nothing since and it had been three weeks. Rodger was a week overdue and she was handling it badly. She was used to Max's unexplained absences but this was different. A bombing mission, one day and it was over. What could be taking so long? What might have happened?

Had she lost him? Had he gone to some desolate grave? When she thought like that she began to shake. The war was touching her as it never had before, even during the Blitz.

She was out of the bath and sleepy and sitting in the study before the fire when she heard a car pull up outside. From the window she saw Homer Teasdale get out and she was waiting at the open front door when he'd come up the walk. "Homer, come in, I've been trying to get hold of you—"

"Cilla. Hate to drop by unannounced like this."

"Don't be silly. Come and get warm by the fire. Have you heard from Rodger? Tell me, for heaven's sake, what's going on?"

"No, no, I haven't." She was pouring him a scotch and at the word *no* the decanter struck the lead crystal a glancing blow. It was just like being on stage. He said: "I was hoping maybe you'd had some word. Damn!"

"I suppose we'll just keep waiting, then."

There was nothing else to say. He asked how the show was coming, and she was about to tell him when she heard steps on the walk outside, a knock at the door.

It was Stefan Lieberman. "Oh, dear lady, a drink for a dying man. Saint Cilla, your reward will come in heaven—what is it about tech rehearsals that drives men to strong drink? Did I wake you? Oh, God in heaven, I'm blundering in on you—"

"Stefan, stop babbling. I'm up. As a matter of fact, Homer Teasdale just dropped by for a nightcap. Come in, please, join us."

Teasdale was on his feet, standing by the fireplace. "Lieberman, how are you? Look, you two, am I interrupting anything? Is this theater business?"

Lieberman calmed him with the wave of a meaty hand. He was stripping off his gloves and muffler, slipping out of his fur-collared overcoat. "Not at all, I'm quite unexpected. I thought I might throw myself on Cilla's mercy. I was planning to bore her with theatrical whimsy and a list of complaints." He accepted a glass of scotch from Cilla.

She curled herself on the end of the couch, tucked her robe up under her feet. "Homer's worried about Rodger Godwin."

Lieberman's eyes widened. "Has something happened to him? On the BBC they say he's on assignment, which sounds as if it could mean anything. Where is he?" He looked expectantly from Cilla to the huge rumpled shape of Homer.

Teasdale frowned into his glass. "He left three weeks ago saying he'd be back in two weeks. Some military adventure. Wouldn't tell me. Not a word. I'll be back in two weeks, that's all he said. I've been trying to keep the network boys calm. It's turning into a full-time job."

Cilla said: "I haven't heard anything from Max either—they must have gone off about the same time—"

Lieberman said: "Wait, darling. Are they together?"

Cilla shrugged. "Not that I know of. In any case, I'm used to Max being gone for long periods." She was trying to keep her concern for Rodger from showing. "Rodger's case is rather more worrying, I'm afraid. He's such a civilian."

Lieberman gave one of his sorrowful chuckles, deep in his chest. "In time of war, there are no civilians. Believe me, I know."

Teasdale said: "You had a tough time, did you?"

"Me? No, no, I got out . . . or rather, I was out—it was my family. All my relatives. Men, women, children. The Nazis make no distinctions of age or sex. No, I had it very easy—"

"Stefan, you know that isn't true. They interrogated him, Homer—"

"Cilla tries to make me a hero. They wanted me to write some nonsense for them. I told them hell yes, I'd do whatever they wanted. I had to go to Italy to work on the libretto for an opera. Things got very bad at home and the composer I was working with, a very brave Italian nobleman, smuggled me out of the country to Lisbon. I've never been able to go back. My name is on a list, you see."

"What a hell of a world we've made." Teasdale finished his drink and said he'd be going. But the conversation dragged on and Cilla looked at her watch and Lieberman yawned and said he'd talk to her tomorrow at rehearsal and finally the men left together and she was alone again.

She took the glasses and ashtrays to the kitchen, turned out the lights and went upstairs. Pausing at the end of the hall, she heard Nanny snoring softly in her room. She went in to look at Chloe, who had scrunched her rear end up in the air and was sleeping on all fours, surrounded by a menagerie of her stuffed animals.

As she did every night, she lay in bed, listening to the wind in the chimneys, staring out the window at the moonlight in the trees. Rodger, you dear sweet fool, why have you done this remarkably stupid thing? Are you still alive? Or are you dead somewhere, and I don't even know it. . . . Tears soaking her pillow. Why wipe them away? What difference did it make? Please, speak to me, Rodger, tell me you are alive. . . . Her body arched and trembled with the sobs until there were no tears left. She sniffed, got out of bed, stood at the window staring at the familiar view, the street, the corner of the square. Rotten, bloody, war. . . .

Rodger. Max.

Maybe they were both dead in the goddamn war!

How would she put her life back together?

Damn you, Rodger! What are you thinking of? Max is a soldier— that's his excuse. But what's yours, Rodger? How dare you choose to go get yourself killed?

She was crying again, in anger and frustration.

For no reason Patricia Smith's name and identity popped into her mind.

She was the nurse to whom she'd handed little Dilys Allenby over a year ago, the night they bombed Dogsbody's.

What could she possibly want?

But the question slipped from her mind and, finally, she fell asleep, missing and loving and cursing Rodger Godwin, who was either dead or alive, remembering the summer in Paris when he'd wandered into all their lives. . . .

An hour later she heard a footfall on the stairway.

Oh, bloody hell. . . . She swam back toward consciousness.

She'd hoped he wouldn't come but she'd known he would. He wouldn't miss the chance. Perhaps it was for the best. This way she wouldn't be worrying, at least not for the darkest hours of the night.

He was standing in the doorway. He cleared his throat.

"*Liebling?* Are you awake?"

"Of course, you poor darling. Hurry, come to bed, Stefan."

There would be time later to dream of what once had been, long ago in Paris.

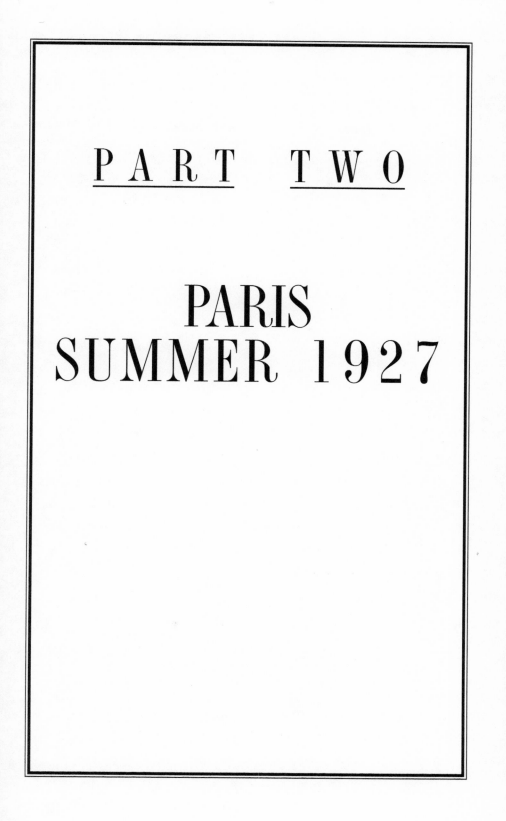

PART TWO

PARIS
SUMMER 1927

CHAPTER 10

EXCERPT FROM UNPUBLISHED, FIRST DRAFT OF
YOU CAN TAKE THE BOY OUT OF IOWA
BY RODGER GODWIN,
FIRST VOLUME OF HIS *PARIS TRILOGY*,
PUBLISHED BY BONI AND LIVERIGHT
NEW YORK, 1930

Clyde Rasmussen used to say to me that you just never knew, you never could tell. For a man who was uneasy with words, he had a habit of saying things that stuck in my mind.

Clyde was a trumpet player and not a philosopher, though the longer I live, the more sensible Clyde's point of view seems. Still, it was unlikely that a grateful world was ever going to turn its eyes on Clyde Rasmussen of Toledo, Ohio, home of *The Blade* and the Mudhens, and thank him for providing any of the really big answers. But he did play the trumpet like the angel Gabriel. And he had beaten me to Paris by nearly a decade.

Somehow—maybe because he was an oddity among the sleek, sophisticated expatriates—Clodbuster Clyde, as Hemingway called him quite approvingly, knew just about everyone in Paris. He was tall, pink and lanky and instantaneously recognizable as an American. He was all sharp, bony, inconvenient edges where the people he knew, the people who took him up, were all rounded and smooth and calculating. He possessed, at the most, a barely rudimentary grasp of sophistication. The top of his head always seemed to have just exploded with spikey red hair which began well above his ears, which themselves turned deep pink at the slightest provocation. No, he wasn't at all like the people he knew, at least not on the surface, and perhaps they looked upon him as slightly jokey, but I don't really think so: They seemed genuinely to like him. Maybe it was the way he played the trumpet. That was what brought them back again and again to the club on the Left Bank. And he was all they hoped for in an American, a kind of perfect cartoon. He was even born on the fourth of February, the same day as Charles Lindbergh, but several years before.

If I hadn't known Swaine and if Swaine hadn't been slightly crazy, I'd never have met Clyde, which only goes to show you that, as Clyde would have said, you never know.

I was twenty-two at the time and I'd come to Paris because a Harvard friend of mine had sworn that his father had connections which would ensure a warm welcome for me at the Paris *Herald*. As it happened, his father was prone to exaggeration. His connections were apparently that he went out and bought the paper on a daily basis when in Paris. His son had been too trusting and I had been hopelessly naive. There was little warmth in the welcome and certainly no job. But I persevered, hounded this one and that one as they went out for lunch or left the newspaper offices for a drink in the late afternoon. I generously provided them with copies of things I'd written at college, scurried along, willing to stand them drinks for the chance to chat them up, give a sales pitch.

After a few weeks of this nonsense, with my money running low and my spirits on the road to collapse, my earnest and increasingly desperate pleading produced a miracle; like a lucky bough in a roaring flood tide, it kept me afloat, saved me from what might surely have turned out to be another life altogether. A writer had run off with a Folies dancer, left a hole in the *Herald*'s coverage. A kind—if crusty—editor was sitting in a wicker chair at the Dome drinking a cocktail I'd paid for when he was brought the news. Swaine was his name. When the breathless messenger was sent on his way Swaine looked up from his glass, lit a cigarette, and looked me in the eye, man to man, like someone in a movie.

"Well, Godwin," he said in a sort of newspaperman's growl which it occurs to me now he'd doubtless taken pains to perfect, "can this be opportunity I hear knocking at your door?"

"Sounds like it to me, sir," I said. I turned my straw boater around and around in my hands, offering up a silent prayer. At breakfast that morning I'd broken up with a girl I'd been sleeping with: It was only a minor emotional squall, neither of us cared much. In practical terms it was more than that because it was her apartment in which I'd been living. A job, an advance against salary from Swaine, could save the day.

"If I take you on I don't want you writing any of that hotsy-totsy Harvard crap," he said. "I'm up to my knees in that stuff. But make it, you know . . . pithy. You hear what I'm saying, Godwin? Pith. They seem to like that."

"I can do it," I said. "I may be young but everyone says I'm very pithy. But tell me, ah, what was this fellow covering?"

"Music mainly. Newman does the rest of the culture crap." He gave me a fishy look. "You know about music?"

"Me? Music? Sure, backwards, forwards. Love music, always have, since I was a—"

"Well, it's all bullshit, of course. That's understood. Bullshit. Remember that, Godwin, and Merle Swaine says you'll never go far wrong. Come to think of it, maybe some of that Harvard crap will come in handy. Now, f'rinstance, tonight—" he fumbled in his pocket for a scrap of paper, assignments scribbled in soft, smudged black pencil, "some damn ballet. I can tell you one thing—Merle Swaine hates the ballet. People paying good money to watch a bunch of queers jump. It's a goddamn mystery to Merle Swaine." He sighed, mystified by the state of the human psyche. "Ballet just your thing, I suppose?"

"An uncle of mine's one of your worst jumping queers—"

He reached across the small table and punched my arm. "You're really full of crap, Godwin. Now I think of it, I like culture guys who are full of crap. But don't misunderstand me . . . go to the ballet and write something for the ponces, something I can't quite figure out. If I can understand ballet crap, it's not worth a damn. Laugh if you will, my lad, but it's a rule that's never been known to fail Merle B. Swaine."

It would be nice to relate that in this moderately unlikely manner a music critic was born. Not so, however. The ballet was, as I recall, *Swan Lake*, and it had been performed the night before as well. Between leaving Swaine after extracting a loan of a few francs and showing up at the theater in my new role as critic, I managed to find two reviews which had appeared that day in the French press. I translated them as best I could, noting crucial critical evaluations, and stopped for half an hour at a used bookshop where I found two battered volumes which addressed themselves to the subject of Russian ballet. It was a frantic few hours. In fact, by the time the ballet actually began, I had already written my review while sitting over an omelette in a small, hot, and smokey café. To be on the safe side, remembering the classic instance of the critic who faked a review of a play which was in fact canceled due to the destruction of the theater by fire, I attended the ballet. My first. When it was over I judged the review sufficiently poncey and incomprehensible to please Merle B. Swaine.

I was aware that this sort of thing could not go on indefinitely. A few days later I reviewed a concert of two Schubert symphonies. Then an opera. Incredible: I was an imposter. My nerves were frazzled: At any moment I was bound to be exposed, given the sack, deported, God only knew what the French authorities might do to a fake music critic who also happened to be an American.

The most important thing in my life just then was staying in Paris, whatever the means, but being a music critic was pretty well off the edge of possibility. It was like trying to convince my fellow man that the world was flat after all.

Depressed and in the grip of an increasingly icy terror, I found myself sitting on a bench in the Luxembourg Gardens, well within shouting distance of the evening's divertissement, something which promised to involve massed woodwinds and a large number of Hungarians. The combination struck me as peculiarly ominous. Before me the old men played bowls and sucked at cigarette butts no longer than their thumbnails. Their blue berets and worn tweed jackets struck me as quintessentially Parisian, foreign, somehow touching. The sky had gone cloudy, softly gray, and the breeze in the green treetops matched it as if it had all been artfully stage-managed to complement my melancholia.

I had wandered to the gardens following a luncheon with Swaine, whom I was beginning to see less as my savior, and more as a uniquely subtle tormentor. He had been full of questions about music: By some ugly twist of personality he had begun seeing me as a kind of cultural mentor, someone he said he could ask questions of without feeling a complete idiot. My only hope was to guide the discussion insistently to the few areas I'd boned up on during the past couple of weeks and, though he occasionally sent me a fishy glance at a deflection even he thought oddly abrupt, he seemed to take my comments seriously. In short, we had become the stars of a rude intellectual farce.

Over coffee, with the traffic tootling by in the narrow street and the birds chirping in the plane trees, he drummed his stubby fingers on the tabletop, as if calling for attention. I thankfully dropped the subject of Diaghilev. "Yes, Mr. Swaine?"

"Jazz," he said.

"Ah. Jazz. Yes, jazz." I tried to sound as if I were recalling many a happy hour spent at Armstrong's knee back at the whorehouse in New Orleans. Self-destructively I led myself deeper into the morass. "King Oliver," I said, nodding, weighted down by the implication that I knew what I was talking about. "Jelly Roll and his Red Hot Peppers . . ." I had exhausted, quite literally, everything I knew of the subject as I recited a few names.

"You've actually heard this stuff? In Chicago?"

"Summer vacations from college. My parents had a summer place near Chicago . . ." That was true, though all I ever heard then was society dance bands at one suburban country club or another. I watched the girls in their summer frocks, nodded at Swaine, lied.

"Good man, good man," he growled, watching me like a lumpy hawk circling its prey. "By God, this is working out damned well. Newman said something about what you've been turning out . . . took notice of it—"

"He did?" Newman, the primary culture man, full of experience and inside knowledge, was the one I feared. He would see through me first.

"Yeah. Said what you're writing is absolute shit."

"Absolute? I see."

"No, no, you don't see at all. That's *good*. Critics, culture men, they always hate other culture men. First rule of being a culture man. You listen to Merle Swaine." He hooked his thumbs into his vest pocket and looked pleased with himself. "No, no, you're my man, Godwin, and jazz is next. All these little ratholes on the Left Bank. Add 'em to your beat." He punched me on the arm and told me to ignore Merle Swaine at my peril and we parted.

With a sense of gathering doom I'd stopped by my bookshop, picked up a volume promising to unravel the mysteries of jazz, and found some recordings by Armstrong imported from America. Now I had to find someone with a gramophone. And so I came to the bench where I sat watching the old men at their games.

Eventually a long shadow fell across the path, stopped above me. I pulled myself out of a disconsolate reverie involving jazz and Swaine and the industrious, many-legged bug I'd found in bed with me that morning —I'd moved to a cheap hotel with a fetching view of a drainpipe and the sound of water rushing in a sewer—and looked up to find the perfect vision of a hayseed. He took me by surprise, reminded me of the cartoon figure who always sprouted stalks of hay from his hair and wore trousers that were too short and revealed hightopped shoes and hairy ankles. This fellow looming above me didn't actually look like the cartoon character, who was found in a series of roguish pornographic booklets; rather, he caught the essence sufficiently well to bring the fictional bumpkin to mind.

"You look like an American," he said affably. "Mind if I take a pew?" He sat down at the far end of the bench. "An American with something on his mind—"

It was remarkably irritating to be recognized so easily as an American.

"Say, you're not one of these idiots who dashes about from bridge to bridge, interrupting and bothering potential suicides?"

"Not me," he said, smiling quietly. "I'm one of those idiots who blows the trumpet for a living . . . trumpet, cornet, a little piano on the side." He crossed his long, spidery legs at the knee, picked up the stack of recordings from the bench. "Saw these, they naturally caught my eye. Figured an American in Paris with a bunch of gramophone records was somebody I ought to know." He looked at the labels, nodded, grinned widely revealing teeth that somehow managed not to touch one another. His smile looked like a ragged ear of corn but his teeth were very white. "Clyde Rasmussen," he said, stuck out his hand which protruded a good deal too far from the sleeve of his plaid Norfolk jacket. The jacket wasn't quite right, nor were the brown-and-white striped shirt and the trousers too rumpled to be a casual artistic affectation. The scuffed brown high shoes had bulbous toes where the leather lay peeled back in odd patches. Still, he didn't look destitute or disreputable. Perhaps he just didn't care. We must have looked a strange pair, me in my black French suit looking like an apprentice in a banking firm and Clyde looking like Clyde.

"Rodger Godwin," I said, and we shook hands.

In a quarter of an hour we knew the essentials of one another's backgrounds. He was a shade older than the century, had come to France as a doughboy with the American Expeditionary Force, had been surprised by the way he took to the country and the people. Back in the States, mustered out, he had bounced from one band to another, spent some time in the Midwest learning what kind of music he had inside himself. That was the way he put it, as if the music were already there and you had to track through the maze of art and technique until you learned how to set it free.

"It's the same for a writer," he said with a curious mixture of laziness, in the pose he struck leaning back on the bench, and enthusiasm which you could see at work behind his eyes and hear in his voice. "There's something pretty well formed inside you but you don't know what it is, you haven't lived enough to find the key to it. I knew guys in the trenches, wanted to be writers, poets and such, and the war turned it loose inside them—the talent, the way of seeing things—and, golly, it was great to watch . . . 'course most of them died. But not all of them. Paris is crawling with the ones who didn't die, the good writers and the bad, seems to me most of 'em feel pretty bad about not dying themselves." He rapped his chest. "It's in here—there's no guarantee of what you'll find in here, it might even be empty—" He laughed quickly. "You just never know." He smiled, gap-toothed, a little self-conscious. "The simple fact is, you don't know anything about music. And even less about jazz."

I nodded, watching him touch the thick discs with his broad fingertips, almost lovingly.

"Louis Armstrong, now there's a good start. I don't see any reason why we can't educate you pretty quick. You never know, you might take to it like a duck to. . . . Look, you game, Godwin? For some boning up?" His head was cocked just slightly off center. His hair was sticking out but his eyes weren't funny at all. Inquiring, taking my measure. Would we be student and teacher?

"Sure, Clyde," I said. "I'm game but I hope you'll be patient with me."

"Now you're sounding like a girl back in Dubuque."

As we walked toward his flat, he began my education. "What do you know about jazz?" He took a hard roll from his pocket and broke off a piece, began munching. He handed it to me and I brushed a bit of pocket lint away, ripped off a tiny corner. He jammed the remainder back in his pocket.

"Nothing," I said. "Paul Whiteman . . ."

"Jean Goldkette?"

I shook my head.

"Frank Trumbauer? Mezz Mezzrow?"

"Sorry."

"Well, you must have heard of Bix."

"What?"

"Bix Beiderbecke. You've heard of Bix Beiderbecke, I assume."

"Never assume, Clyde."

We were standing under the chestnut trees, feeling the wind cooling off as the sky darkened, purple clouds piling up over Montmartre. I chewed laboriously on the dry, rather stale bread.

"Pretty sheltered life you've been leading, sport. I'd think Harvard would be a little more . . . au courant." He grinned at the French expression. "Well, to begin with," he said, resuming his walking, then stopping to buy hot chestnuts from a vendor, then walking on kicking a pebble before him until he tired of the game, "as far as you're concerned, jazz begins when they closed down Storyville in New Orleans and the musicians moved north to Chicago—"

"What do you mean, closed down Storyville?"

"New Orleans became an important wartime port," he explained patiently, "and the Secretary of War took a close look at what was going on in Storyville, that's part of New Orleans, and he figured it wasn't going to do his troops much good. . . . You get my drift? So, slam! They shut old Storyville down tight and the musicians, black they were, and the girls headed up the Mississippi for Chicago . . . and they began to play their music in Chi town.

"The white musicians in Chicago were fascinated by this jig music. Naturally they began to tinker with it, tried playing it for themselves. Well, they kind of got the hang of it, y'know, but they couldn't get it quite right . . . those New Orleans boys were damn good, fact was they could just plain do stuff the Chicago boys couldn't touch—they could keep several melodic lines in balance simultaneously, a whole lot of music going on all at one time. I'll let you hear it on records . . . anyway, the white boys couldn't handle that. I still can't.

"So what the white boys did with the melody was something different. *They let everybody take turns.* Do you get it, Rodger? *Take turns . . ."*

"Like solos," I said timorously.

Clyde sighed, nodded. "Solos—that was the key point where New Orleans jazz became Chicago jazz. A man can carve out something for himself with a solo, do you see that? When I go to work tonight, I'm going to enjoy the ensemble playing, everybody fitting together, but something happens to you in a solo . . . you're looking for that groove that puts you in touch with the other you that lives inside you. Then the key fits in the lock and the music that's inside you, why hell, Rodger, it's free, you've liberated it, and you know it!" He peeled the shell off the last chestnut and popped it into his mouth. "You're letting it free and hoping to God it's good."

We went on to his place, a fifth-floor garret which he referred to as "the penthouse," and in fact it was a surprisingly pretty place. It had been done by a lady friend who had passed loudly through his life a year or so before. Pillows, deep mauve chairs and couches, a couple of beaded curtains, mirrors with etching along the edges, a variety of Bakelite objects with a sleekness which contrasted mightily with Clyde himself. He seemed a stranger in the room, yet he took a good-natured pleasure in pointing out particular items he liked especially: a gleaming cocktail shaker, a lamp, a bamboo frame around a picture of a young girl on a beach with palm trees behind her, a long low coffee table in gleaming black. There was a huge, free-standing gramophone.

He went to pour us glasses of wine and I sat down in one of the two mauve chairs. There was a stack of seven books on the table, Hemingway and Fitzgerald and Wodehouse. I wondered whose taste they reflected. He was talking to me from the kitchen.

"Margaret was too old for me," he said, "but I didn't mind her most of the time. She was what they call a decent, God-fearing woman back in Ohio. Damned strange she wound up in Paris as a decorator, but then you never know. I think she was Sapphic, deep down in her heart. She worships Natalie Barney, so I wasn't surprised when I heard she'd gone off to keep company with a lady friend in Clichy."

He came back in, handing me a squat thick glass with a thick rim. "Cheers and absent friends." We drank and the young wine puckered my mouth. "I'm afraid it's pretty awful, but it was free. Fella gave it to me so we'd better drink it. Course you'd never recognize Natalie Barney now, pretty ghastly considering how gorgeous she once was . . . Margaret made her come to a party once in these rooms—she stayed about ten minutes and couldn't seem to think of anything to say, grabbed her great lump of a pal and left."

"Who else has been here?" I was beginning to see Clyde Rasmussen in a new light.

"Josephine Baker, I guess, though I was sick in the bathroom during most of her visit. Leslie Hutchinson—do you know him? Well, Hutch is the best singer I've ever heard. Got a number called 'Murder in the Moonlight' that's just tops. You really should write about him, but we'll get to that, we've got the time. Look, we can eat at the club, if you don't mind. Take a look in my kitchen. You wouldn't want to eat anything that came from there. I'm going to have a bath."

I went to the window and sat on the ledge, leaned into the alcove and stuck my head outside. The sky was deep purple now and a light rain had begun. It made soft noises when it splattered on the roof tiles beside my head. It cleared the dust from the air and left that perfect summer smell in its place. An automobile passed like a beetle in the narrow street below, its yellow headlamps picking out the umbrella vendor at his stand near the corner. Across the way was a pretty girl with short reddish hair, wearing only a chemise. She leaned out of the window toward me and smiled as the rain hit her face. She waved at me, leaned farther out, and called: "Are you a burglar? Or a friend of Clyde's?" She spoke English with a thick French accent.

"Both," I said. "Clyde's friend, the burglar." She had a long neck and one of those small French heads with huge eyes and a mouth from here to there.

She laughed and ducked back inside. I sat staring out at the rain streaking the chimney pots, hearing the sounds of the street muffled by the rain, thinking that it was quite possible that I'd never been happier than at just that moment, within that moist, sweet-smelling bubble of time.

Clyde came back eventually, wearing an exceedingly well tailored tuxedo which hung from his square shoulders much as it might have from a hanger in the closet. He'd attempted with no great success to slick down the red hair, but still, he had a new, almost handsome sense of sophistication. I was taken aback and it must have showed.

"Not a word about this get-up, sport. It adds a little class to the joint and if I can stand wearing it, you can stand watching me." He unlatched his horn case, had a look at the gleaming golden cornet, and closed it. Then from the closet he got another case, opened it, showed me another burnished instrument. "Trumpet. I play both of them but the cornet won't be around much longer. The trumpet's the thing. Sharper sound." He closed it back up and got an umbrella from a crockery stand in the shape of an owl which stood by the door. "Grab an umbrella for yourself. Have enough people over and eventually you collect plenty of umbrellas. No, Bix is the only guy I know who won't give up on the cornet . . . but then he plays the cornet better than God ever imagined it could be played. I'll tell you, Bix Beiderbecke's cornet sounds more like a trumpet than my trumpet does, if you get my drift. But God only made one of him . . . and he made him in Davenport, Iowa—hell, you're practically neighbors, sport!"

We reached the Club Toledo, its name illuminated by red and blue light bulbs and featuring badly peeling paint and a primitive drawing of a roadster cornering on two wheels with a man in a raccoon coat at the wheel.

"This is it," he said, stepping into a narrow doorway. Above us, the building, which was very old, listed toward the street, threatening an imminent collapse that had somehow not come in several centuries.

A gendarme passed within arm's reach, saluted us, but there was a hint of mockery in his voice. "Monsieur Clyde," he said, inclining his head. His head was too large for his height and his arms too long. His eyes burned from far behind and beneath two thick black eyebrows, eyes like fires in a cave. He caressed his *baton*. I was reminded of a villain in a melodrama. "How is M'sieur Clyde this fine rainy night?"

"Getting wet, Henri," he said and inside the doorway he murmured to me: "Everything a *flic* shouldn't be, the bastard. Likes to roust old men, the *poules* out looking for customers, anybody weaker than he is . . . he's got a partner, Jacques. Bad cess, damn bad cess . . ."

There were Dubonnet stains on the marble-topped tables and a fan was going in a corner. The shutters on the windows were open and it seemed to be raining inside as well as out. The *flic* Henri stood in the street, tapping the nightstick into the palm of his left hand, watching us through the window, expressionless. Clyde shook out his umbrella and sat down close to a window. Every few minutes there was a little freshet of wind and a few drops of rain would hit my face. It was dim and very pleasant. I took off my boater and laid it on an extra chair. Clyde lit a cigarette. The smoke clung to the low ceiling, then left by way of the window, like a rumor or a bagman. Henri had finally moved on.

The waiter came over to the table, a swarthy fellow with a cleaver for a nose. The light caught him for a moment: His Adam's apple was green where the brass stud, which would have held his collar in place had he been wearing one, had rubbed against his skin. There were wine stains on his white shirt. He wore a long apron that tied at his waist. "M'sieur Clyde," he said, glancing at a group of four snappy dressers who had just entered and were shaking off the rain.

"Whatever looks best to you, Jean. We are at your mercy."

"You are in my hands. I prefer that, if you please. I shall find something acceptable, M'sieur Clyde. Have no fear." He moved stealthily away, past the new arrivals.

For dinner Jean brought us bowls of hare stew with the taste of mustard sauce soaked clear through to the bone, a platter of green beans cooked with bacon, some fried potatoes, a glistening salad of greens doused with oil and vinegar, crusty bread still hot and soft Brie, a bottle of unlabeled table wine. I congratulated Clyde on the dinner.

"I was talking to the chef one day, just sitting in the kitchen shootin' the breeze, and every half hour or so he'd get up and go to the window—it was a bright sunny day—and he'd stand there at the window for a minute, then come back and go on with the conversation. I finally asked him what he was doing—he had a big container of rabbit pieces soaking in mustard sauce, sitting in the sun. Said that was the way his mother had done it and he'd never tasted better rabbit stew. So on sunny days, the rabbit in this joint can't be beat. I know, wasn't too sunny today but yesterday was a beaut." We mopped up the last of the stew with jagged chunks of bread, sipped the anonymous wine to wash it down. When we'd finished he patted his mouth with his napkin and slid his chair back from the table.

"Give yourself an hour, then follow the arrows and tell anybody at the door you're to sit at my table. Dinner's on me. You'll do the same for me another time." I watched him walk away, tall and awkward but something more than that. Whatever the hell it was, movie stars had it and Clyde had it. You just never could tell about people.

At the door he stopped to speak to three people just coming in: a heavyset man in acres of dark gray suiting, about fifty with a rather florid face; a girl I judged to be in her early teens wearing what looked like a school uniform of some sort; and a hard-looking, compact man, dark hair combed straight back from a rectangular face, somewhere in his thirties although the hardness made him look older, remote. I watched Clyde lift the girl's hand to his lips and click his heels. They all laughed and smiled at the ritual, presumably a joke. While the fat man spoke to Clyde the other man listened, his eyes moving back to the girl. They came to sit down at the table next to mine and Clyde disappeared through the doorway.

"Jolly good," I heard the girl say in a low, dark-tinted voice, an English accent. "I fancy the window, don't you?" The men nodded and the girl looked happily out the window at the rain.

They scraped their chairs, sat down, went on speaking but too softly for me to overhear. I opened my book and began reading about ragtime but my attention kept drifting back to my neighbors. The older man was speaking animatedly, wheezing slightly, and the other man was listening, his face enigmatic. From time to time he shrugged, interjected a word or two, frowned. Once he leaned over and helped the girl pull her sweater up around her shoulders. Her face still carried a final reminder of childish fullness but she was at the beginning of the coltish stage, getting taller, leaving childhood behind. She listened, played discreetly with her napkin, let her gaze float this way and that. She caught me watching her once, smiled at me unself-consciously, and I, like a dunce, quickly looked away.

They were obviously acquainted with the restaurant: They all ordered the hare, the girl proclaiming the aroma divine when it arrived. Jean smiled broadly, calling her "the mademoiselle."

During the meal, the fat man dropped his spoon with mock astonishment and I heard him say: "Colonel, damn me if you're not just the sort of man who should see its importance! Instead you . . . well, you . . . I don't know, old chap, I simply don't know."

"I am merely saying," the hard man replied, his voice flat yet agreeable, "that fixed positions, fixed gun placements, are too blasted risky for my blood. Mobility, hitting and running to hit another day, that's the thing, Anthony." His back was to me, I couldn't see his face.

I heard no more of their conversation.

The hallway was dark and smelled seductively of the falling rain. The plaster was bubbled and brown rust stains ran in wayward rivulets from ceiling to floor. Someone had painted in black the words *Le Club Toledo*. The arrows looked as if they'd been painted during the Revolution. At the back of the long hallway a bulb burned nakedly over a narrow black door which opened onto the top step of a clammy stone stairway spiraling down into what appeared to be pitch darkness until you caught the hint of a reddish glow somewhere below. At the bottom of the stairs the wine cellar with dusty half-filled racks stretched away beneath the Byzantine archways. The floor of small, smooth river pebbles crunched and gave slightly underfoot. Where the hell were the other patrons of *le jazz?* Incredibly, at the other end of the pathway between the racks, there was yet another doorway, a massive studded and banded oak affair with brutally large iron drift pins driven into it to make an odd, abstract design. Through the door there were several more steps down into a long, low room apparently carved out of stone, candles guttering on perhaps twenty marble-topped tables stained with the messes of thousands of drinkers. The floor was the same fine gravel and a zinc bar ran thirty or forty feet along one wall; overhead, rafters a foot thick supported the entire Left Bank for all I knew. A Turk in a business suit and tasseled fez greeted me in an obscure language and I told him I was a guest of Clyde Rasmussen. The name worked a small miracle with the Turk, who flung a golden smile at my feet as he bowed and took me to a table opposite the bar, seated me with my back to the stone wall and the bandstand to my left about a third of the way down the length of the room.

"Bourbon or scotch for Monsieur Clyde's friend?"

"Bourbon? You're joking!"

"Yes, of course," he said with a prideful grin, "the very best bourbon from before the war. Monsieur Clyde's drink."

"Bourbon it is, then," I said.

I catalogued the arrivals as the tables began to fill up. The men looked very handsome and gaily doomed, acting out the popular fantasies of the day, while the women wore clinging dresses in very pale shades of champagne and peach, bare shoulders, little wraps. Apparently, as Clyde had said, the right people knew how to find it. And the bourbon was excellent.

The threesome from the table next to mine upstairs reappeared and were brought to yet another table near mine. In the candlelight the fat man's face was dappled with perspiration and his eyes seemed moist in their sockets, small, busy eyes. He seemed still to be amazed at the Colonel's refusal to follow what he deemed a logical course. The girl looked over at me as she sat down: This time, prepared, I smiled in recognition and she looked away as if she hadn't noticed. She was paying me back.

I was just taking my second bourbon to hand and wondering when things were going to start happening when a familiar-looking woman approached my table. She was short and slender and walked like a dancer: Her auburn hair was bobbed, fetchingly disheveled as it lay on the nape of her long neck. I grinned stupidly, half recognizing her, wondering who she was, and she asked if she might sit down.

"My distinct pleasure," I said, holding her chair.

"Merci, Monsieur Burglar." She smiled mischievously.

"You're the girl in the rain across the street . . ."

"Clothilde." She extended her small pale hand.

"Rodger," I said, taking it in mine.

"I wondered if you'd be here at Clyde's table. He sometimes has a guest or two . . . those people, for instance, the three English. I've seen them sitting here but I did not find them so sympathetic." She shrugged. "Much is explained by their being English, of course."

"What a very French thing to say."

"And what do the English say about us, eh? So, we are not natural allies. Out of necessity, *oui*, but of course. Fate makes strange bedfellows." She smiled primly. Her face, small and heart-shaped and animated, kept changing. Her shoulders, narrow and sloping, moved this way and that, her hands fluttered and swooped. "Anyway, I am half-French and half-Austrian, so I have two personalities myself. Sort of Boche . . . and sort of Frog, as Clyde calls us. Mainly Frog. Are you an old friend of Clyde's from this Toledo place he keeps talking about? Toledo is in Ohoho, is that right? Oh, well, close enough, agreed? May I have some bourbon of my own?"

"Yes and no."

"*Pardonez-moi?*"

"*Oui*, you may certainly have some bourbon of your very own, and *non*, I met Clyde today in the Luxembourg Gardens." The Turk caught my hand signal and fetched her some bourbon. While she sipped and grinned at me boldly, I told her about my predicament, how Clyde had set about helping me.

"I adore Clyde," she said at last. "He makes sex with me, you know. But not love, eh? But nice, very nice. Generous man. I adore him."

I tried to get past the unexpected sex part. "How long has he worked here?"

"He is not employed here, Rodger," she said, making a slight move as if she were shyly being kissed, pronouncing my name *Roge-air*. "Clyde owns this place. It is all his, the club, the restaurant, everything." She tapped her forehead, then rubbed her fingers together as if counting money, and winked. "He is a very smart fella, eh? That's what he says, 'fella.' What kind of fella are you, Rodger?"

"You can't outlaw war, Tony old boy, however much you might wish to. It just won't wash." It was the Colonel with his slicked-back hair at the next table, shaking his head. He was facing me now, a bitter smile hooking upward almost imperceptibly at the corners of his mouth. His lean face was leathery tan, as if it had been weathered long ago in some other place. There was a white, three-inch scar on his forehead over his left eye, a furrow of stitched tissue disappearing back into his low hairline. You still saw the scars all over Europe. Shrapnel from a war that had been over nearly a decade. A remnant.

"I am sorry," I said to Clothilde, turning back. She had gone on speaking. "I missed that."

"I said, Clyde has talked to you about this Beiderbecke?"

"A little, actually. Yes."

She nodded. "That's good. It means he likes you." She put her hand on mine. "I like you, too."

"You're a dancer, aren't you? A ballerina?"

"Does it show? How can you know this?"

"I always know a dancer."

"I am a model, too, you know."

"I'm not at all surprised. You're very pretty."

She smiled at me a little crookedly, squeezed my hand.

"They say six new warships will be authorized by the end of the summer . . ." It was the fat man again. Tony. "You may be quite right, old boy, come to think of it. Outlaw war on one side, build great hulking warships on the other . . . makes one long for simpler days, what?"

"They never were, Tony."

"What? What's that?"

"Simpler days. They never were."

"Ah, well then, that's all right, then. Spare me the cryptic commentary, lad."

"They're going to start. Look." That was the young girl. She was clapping excitedly as the band congregated at the end of the room. A spotlight caught Clyde in the eyes and he shielded them with the shining cornet, squinted out across the crowd. *He owns the place* . . . Well, you never knew, did you?

With no prelude at all, he nodded to the band and the music played . . .

No one ever recorded Clyde and the Club Toledo band in those days and that's a shame because they were very good, an excellent example of the Chicago style. Hearing him that night changed my life because it set me to thinking about my first impressions of the scene in Paris, the Left Bank in particular. It was my first real look at the Paris I'd heard about, my first sighting of the reasons I'd come. Clyde's music and the *cave* where he played and Clothilde and the hare stew and the Englishmen talking about gun emplacements and Merle B. Swaine and the fellow who'd gone off with the Folies dancer and all the rest of it. All this was running helter-skelter through my mind as I listened to the band and Clyde's roaring solos. What we heard, of course, was directly traceable to Bix Beiderbecke, the one god in Clyde's life and, ironically, the reason that Clyde would always be more of an interpreter than a creative genius like his master. Clyde always insisted that it didn't bother him, that his own genius was for living in the real world.

In any case, what I heard that night came as a revelation and I can still hear that first number, "Way Down Yonder in New Orleans," the first solo going to the clarinet after a trombone introduction, then Clyde's cornet rising on its own, swinging and lilting and driving, the cymbals exploding like toy gunfire toward the end when there was a positive wail from all the horns, Clyde bending like a reed in a strong breeze at times, leaning into the music at others.

The women caught the rhythms first, their heads and shoulders moving, fingertips rattling on the marble, lips parted and then touching spasmodically. The sense of movement spread and the men were into it as well: I was drumming on my thigh, head bobbing, but there was more to it than that. It wasn't a society band and this wasn't a prom. I suppose what I recognized in my egglike innocence was the presence of art, not merely the spirit of letting down your hair though that was by no means absent.

Perhaps most remarkable was the lid Clyde put on the proceedings toward the end of the first set. The haunting, lonely melancholy of "I'm Coming Virginia" brought conversation and drinking to a halt. The mournful cornet solo came soon, bordered on a kind of elegant dirge, and it was as if he were alone in the low-ceilinged room with the pebble floor, wishing he had told us to scale down our dreams while there was still time . . . wishing he had but knowing he'd failed, had only given us a fine time and not prepared us for what he seemed to know lay ahead. It was a kind of intimacy I was almost too shy to watch: I might have believed just then that Clyde truly knew what was in store for all of us that summer and was regretting that he hadn't the nerve to tell us, to warn us. But in fact we were all in the room, we did hear it, and I for one got a glimmering of the sorrow behind the music.

Clothilde looked at me once, between numbers, and smiled in a slightly knowing way. It didn't quite work because she had one of the sweetest, gentlest faces I'd ever seen. I took her hand.

"He likes me to dress up like a young girl of twelve," she said slowly, shyly. Her tongue wetted her lips. She looked at the band, Clyde talking to one of his sidemen. "I wear kneesocks and a pinafore . . . nothing else . . . he says I have the figure for it . . . and we do sex. Would you like to be in bed with me, M'sieur Burglar?"

"You should be a fortune teller."

"That means *oui?*"

"*Oui.*"

"*Très bon.*" She grinned impishly. "Clyde won't mind. Clyde is very generous, you know?"

I wasn't at all sure that I knew anything at all. The more I found out about M'sieur Clyde the less I seemed to know. But I had no doubts about Clothilde.

CHAPTER 11

Late April was uncharacteristically warm that year and everyone always remembered the period as summer, it all happened that summer. When Rodger Godwin met Clothilde Devereaux then, he was an innocent. When he left her and Paris behind several months later he was . . . well, he would never be innocent again. People might sometimes think he was but they were wrong as well as frequently sorry. Clothilde was part of the process of change, his metamorphosis. And really there was nothing to it. She merely did what she did best. She let him fall in love with her. She wasn't yet twenty but she was much older than Godwin in what people used to call the ways of the world. Clothilde was a crash course in sophistication. She gave him no choice but to grow up.

He was inexperienced sexually. She set about repairing his various deficiencies with the energy and enthusiasm of an Olympic athlete. Within a week or so, he was a new man. He was quite sure he'd fallen in love. He was feeling quite liberated, quite a Bohemian as they used to say back in Dubuque. That she was a "model" as well as a singer and dancer made the whole business all the more intriguing. Not every guy was man enough to fall in love with a beautiful young prostitute: Damn, if he wasn't a rakish devil. It made him feel as if he belonged in Paris, with these people in this strange new place. He was enchanted when Clothilde would take him to the *bal musette* for dancing and then on to the Dingo and the Jockey and the Dome and La Coupole where they would stay up all night and walk to the Senate or past Notre Dame as the pink and gray dawn came up. She made him feel it was his city, too. One night she pointed out most of the characters from Hemingway's celebrated novel of the year before, *The Sun Also Rises:* Lady Duff Twysden who was Brett Ashley, Pat Guthrie who was Mike Campbell, Kitty Cannell who was Frances, and Harold Loeb who was Robert Cohn. A man called Donald Ogden Stewart was said to be Jake Barnes's friend Bill. And the writer Ford Madox Ford was clearly Braddocks, who in the novel gave the parties at the *bal musette* up behind the Pantheon. Jake Barnes was, of course, Jake Barnes. Meeting them, seeing them come to life, made Godwin feel for the first time that he was on the inside of something, that he'd moved onto a new stage where things truly happened, and he loved it.

In the mornings, if he stayed the night in Clothilde's room, he would wake after only a few hours of sleep and listen to the city as it too began the new day. He would be too excited by each new day to waste any more time asleep. He would watch Clothilde sleeping, her small head on the pillow, a little fist clenched beneath her chin, her mouth slightly open, her face young and sweet and vulnerable. He wondered how she could look so peaceful while at the same time having such a complicated life. He had no idea that what he was observing was the miracle of resilience called youth. How could he know? He was so young himself.

He was intrigued by the scar on her cheek, midway between her ear and the high, prominent cheekbone: there was a cross—like a Christian cross—carved into her skin. He'd never seen anything like it. It didn't disfigure her. There was actually a kind of allure in it, like a peculiar beauty mark. It must have hurt like hell when she got it though. Something from childhood maybe. But there was something about it that kept him from inquiring as to its origin. It seemed, somehow, very private. And he didn't want her to think he found it ugly.

He would get up as quietly as he could, get dressed, and before leaving he would lean down and gently kiss the cross on her cheek.

The mornings seemed always the same. The streets were usually rain-washed from early showers, the air was clean as a whistle and sweet. There were window boxes and tubs of flowers, tulips and geraniums and all sorts of colored blurs he couldn't name. Old men were sweeping the sidewalks with brooms that looked very worn, nothing more than bundles of twigs lashed together at the end of a pole. The cafés they'd visited on their rounds the night before were open for breakfast, the aroma of dark-roasted coffee wafting outside where waiters were arranging tables, hosing and sweeping and pouring buckets of water across the pavement.

Godwin would head for the Dome, a notebook in his pocket, newspapers under his arm, and settle in at one of the tables commanding a view of both the corner and the Rotonde in the first blush of sunshine across the street. The waiter would bring croissants and coffee and Godwin would uncap his big orange Parker Duofold fountain pen and begin jotting down his impressions of the previous night. If he had something for Swaine, that's what he'd write before going into the office to type it up. If not, he tried to capture the people and places he was seeing for the first time. The Negro bands at certain popular clubs, the astronomical prices being paid for Impressionist paintings, the sporting figures he met at Clyde's and what people were saying about politicians and Isadora Duncan and writers and painters. He wrote a sketch of Jimmy Charters, the best barman in Paris, the essence of Paris for so many people he was meeting, and Swaine thought they weren't bad pieces and ran them and people talked about them and the fellow who wrote them. He wrote about Kiki herself, not having a clue that one day she would be known everywhere as Kiki of Montparnasse and would write her famous memoirs. Of course no one knew Rodger Godwin would be famous one day either, which only went to show you that you just never knew.

Occasionally Clyde would come wandering down the street, past La Coupole, and fold himself into a chair across the table from Godwin. He would have brought his own newspapers and together they would sit, neither impinging on the other, until Clyde had poured down sufficient coffee to get himself started. Godwin was toying with the idea of writing a piece about Clyde, though he hadn't discussed it with either Swaine or the subject himself. Thing was, Clyde Rasmussen was quite a fellow. His band had caught on and the restaurant upstairs was doing good business. He was making, it dawned on Godwin, a lot of money. More than the writers and painters and remittance men who were his friends—and an interesting lot they were, too. Everybody seemed to know him and he knew everybody. He had told Godwin about an apartment in "his" building, had wondered if Godwin might want to move in. There was furniture, there were dishes, some linen that went with it. Godwin doubted he could afford it. Clyde thought he shouldn't worry about that too much, he was sure they could work out something. Godwin wondered to whom he should speak about it. The landlord would probably be the fella, Clyde figures. And where would I find him? Godwin inquired. You're talking to him, Clyde had said, one of his big gap-toothed grins breaking across the hayseed's face. "I own the place. And because you're gonna get tired of sleeping over at Clothilde's, you're gonna need a place of your own." Clyde thought four dollars a week might be about right and if some weeks he couldn't make it, it didn't matter. Godwin was moving in at the end of the week.

One night Clothilde had lain moistly in Godwin's arms, her back to him, and had said she wanted him to know about Clyde, how it was between them. Godwin nodded, smelling her hair and the soap she used. He wasn't feeling any jealousy about Clothilde and Clyde obviously wasn't in the least concerned about her private life and the part Godwin was playing in it.

"He is very dear to me, Monsieur Clyde is," she whispered, "do you understand? He is like my father and my brother because I have no father or brother. You see? I love him that way. And I do whatever I can to please him . . . Clyde saved my life. No, he truly did. He found me . . . in an alley . . . I was bleeding. And he took me home and saved my life and kept me in his bed while he slept on the couch until I was all right again. Understand? I can never repay him. He takes care of my dance classes. He feeds me at the club. He owns the building I live in, he gives me my place, he buys my clothing . . . He is very dear to me. I love him but it is not like you and me. Tell me you understand . . ."

Godwin told her he understood and he believed he did, more or less. It was a brave new world, everybody kept saying it, and what the hell, they did things differently in Paris.

When Clyde had polished off his first two or three cups of coffee they would begin to talk. About music, about what Godwin was writing, about Paris. Clyde would say, "Jeez, Rodger, you really oughta talk to Hemingway about all this. He's got the concession on Paris these days." They seldom spoke of Clothilde, but one morning with Godwin thinking about how he'd kissed the cross on her cheek, Clyde mentioned that he hadn't seen much of her the past week or so. "How are the two of you getting along, sport? She being good to you?"

"Fine, we're both getting along just fine."

Clyde nodded. "You're probably cutting into her business, if you know what I mean. You make yourself scarce when she's, ah, entertaining?"

Godwin shrugged. He didn't want to talk about that. Instead he changed the subject. "She worships you. I guess you know that. It's kind of sad in a way. She sounds as if she's Sisyphus, like she knows she'll never be able to get the job done but just has to keep doing it anyway."

"Well, she's sort of melodramatic. You know how women can be. Everything's a big drama. She'll get over it. She may not realize yet that I'll be her friend forever, no matter what. People don't see that lots of times. Particularly people who've been hurt and forsaken a lot."

"She said you saved her life."

"Well, you never know, do you? Maybe I did." He smiled crookedly. They were still in the shade while across the way the Rotonde was gleaming in the soft morning sun. Yet the Dome was beginning to fill up and the Rotonde was almost empty. The Rotonde had once been equally pop-ular, maybe more so. Then the management had made a crucial error. An American girl had been sitting in the sun one morning having coffee, reading the papers, smoking a cigarette. She wore no hat. The manager and captain had watched with mingled dismay and horror. A lady did not venture out in Paris without her hat. And even if she did, she most cer-tainly didn't smoke. It was not the done thing. Given the Gallic obsession with the exercise of insect authority, the manager and the captain marched out to tell the American girl that she must cease and desist at once. The girl had been astounded by the effrontery of these two imbe-ciles, had objected. The conversation had grown increasingly heated, even bellicose. A crowd had gathered, almost entirely in support of the young woman. The two French refused to reconsider. The girl, however, was no quitter. Finally she gathered up her bits and pieces and marched across the street to the Dome, her newly formed entourage at her heels. Would the Dome welcome her custom? Absolutely, mademoiselle. And so the history of the *quartier* was changed irrevocably. From then on the Ameri-cans and English were always seen at the Dome, leaving the Scandinavi-ans, Russians, and Germans and whatever else might turn up to the Rotonde. Hemingway himself had written that the scummiest of the Greenwich Village scum sometimes showed up at the Rotonde but every-one else knew better. Clyde had told Godwin the story and he'd turned it into a small Parisian sketch for Swaine and Swaine had said he should write stuff like that whenever he came across it and they'd use a new heading called Paris Nights.

One morning Godwin said: "What's that mark on her face?"

"Mark?"

"The cross that's cut into her cheek. What's the story?"

"Oh, I guess that's what she means about old Clyde saving her life. Just one of those things, not much to say—"

"What? Are you crazy? What happened?"

"Well, the cross thing on her face is called a *croix de vache*. You've seen the apaches, they think they're tough, wear black and look pretty damn silly to me which they aren't because they're pretty mean . . . they get sorta violent, like Apache Indians, I guess. When an apache or some-body who thinks like one anyway figures a woman has done him, y'know, wrong, like with another fella, been disloyal you could say, then he'll beat her up and then take his knife and brand her with the cross . . . that's what happened to little Clothilde one night, coupla years ago, she was seventeen, eighteen, I guess. Anyway, I found her in an alley, she'd been given a pretty good whipping, some guy had cut her . . . I helped her out. Hell, she's a sweet little thing . . . not a bad singer, chantoosie. I'm teaching her some phrasing tricks with the trumpet." He grinned. "That's the story, no big deal, sport."

"Do you know who did it to her?"

"She'd never say. She was scared for a while, that's why I made her my 'property' in an obvious way. I mean, hell, she's free as the breeze. You know that. But I let people know she was a damn good friend of mine. The way to hurt her again led right through me. The apache never showed up again and she's never said who it was."

"I'd like to kill him," Godwin said. She was so fragile: He saw her curled in the bed, tiny, sleeping.

"Now don't get your hair in the butter, sport. It's all over and done with. Forget it. She's all right. Say, you're not in love with her, are you?"

"Why shouldn't I be?"

"Well, God love her, she is a whore, y'know. Dearest little thing in the world, I won't have anyone say a word against her and I'd fight to the death for her, but you probably haven't had a lot of experience with girls like that . . . selling themselves does something to these girls, it makes some of them a little too hard and it makes some of them a little too sad deep inside. Clothilde is of the latter persuasion. She's had a tough time —she could break is what I'm saying. I don't think you want to be the one who has to pick up the pieces. But you do what you think best, sport. I'm just thinking out loud here, that's all."

"Don't worry about me," Godwin said. He knew Clyde was telling him the simple truth but he was damned if he wanted to hear it. "I can handle it."

"I don't doubt it for a minute, sport."

But the problem, of course, was that Godwin was beginning to handle it less well. It wasn't the business of Clothilde's sex-for-pay shenanigans: He was able to fit that into the new framework of his life, as if they were all characters in one of those Paris novels. It was, rather, the mixture of his growing emotional attachment and Clothilde's almost slavish devotion to Clyde. Godwin wanted to tell her that she was overdoing it, that Clyde didn't expect it, but he'd look at her, at her solemn little face with the cross carved in the cheek and the look of concern—concern for him, for Clyde, for everyone it seemed but herself—and he couldn't open it all up again. She felt as she did about Clyde and maybe she was right. You just never knew. But it was Godwin who was the latecomer. And it was Godwin she said she loved, in a different way than she loved Clyde.

Some nights, fairly frequently, Godwin would notice Clyde disappearing after the last set, a wave and a smile and he was gone, and it was said he had a secret girlfriend stashed somewhere, something scandalous. Presumably she was somebody's wife. No one asked. There was, after all, a code in such matters. There were rules.

Clothilde would spend the late evenings at the club with Godwin, once he'd arrived from some other venue where he'd witnessed an opera or a ballet or a concert. While he was off at work, she too would work, servicing a client or two between dinner and Clyde's last set when she met Godwin. When he saw her in the dim light of the cavernous club, when she came to kiss him, he could taste the toothpowder in her mouth, feel the slight grittiness against her tongue, and he knew why she'd been careful to brush her teeth for him. Her body would also be freshly bathed and powdered and perfumed and the sheets on the bed would have been changed. It was part of her life, part of the deal they'd struck, and Godwin tried not to let it bother him. For the most part he was successful.

Clyde.

Clothilde loved him and Godwin sure as hell liked the guy and was thankful for all the aid and comfort he'd provided. But it was getting to him in the funniest ways.

For one thing, Clothilde was too concerned about Clyde's late night disappearances, the rumor of the mystery woman. She didn't say much but Godwin could see it in her face. The look of slight distraction, the knitting of her perfectly penciled eyebrows. Was she jealous? Or was she, for some inexplicable reason, worried by his nocturnal wanderings?

For another, he seemed part of their life in bed. She had coquettishly shown him some of the clothing Clyde liked her to wear when they were alone. Godwin had tried to laugh it off but it had all turned oddly exciting. It was a schoolgirl's clothing. A long white middy blouse with navy trim over a pleated navy skirt. White kneesocks. She became a child of twelve, slim and boyish, but the body yielded and was a woman's. She would step out of the skirt and wearing only the long blouse and the knee-high stockings she would pose for him, smiling shyly, and she would methodically seduce him and Godwin would lose all track of what was happening, love, lust, desire, adoration. Did it make any difference? He thought that maybe it should but pleasure was pleasure, how were you supposed to *think* about it? Whatever it was, it was a hell of a long way from the Methodism of his youth.

One night Clyde had wanted her after the last set. Godwin marveled at the subtlety of it, how smoothly it all went, as if Clyde didn't want any hurt feelings. If Godwin had worked himself up he'd be breaking the code. You had to know how to behave. Godwin always had. He'd kissed

Clothilde before she left and she'd whispered that she'd wake him when she got back.

But Godwin hadn't been able to let it go at that. Alone in her darkened room, sitting on the edge of their bed, he stared across the alley at the lit window of Clyde's apartment. It was warm, and down the street someone was playing an accordion. Clothilde was standing in the window, her elbows resting on the window box with its bright red geraniums looking black in the night with the light behind them. He was almost sure she could see him. She was smoking. Clyde moved in behind her, began kissing her hair. She laughed, pulled away and turned. She was wearing some kind of dark school blazer with a crest on the breast pocket. Clyde reached for her and she skittered out of view and Clyde went after her. It was a game. A little later the light went out. It made no difference to Godwin. He knew exactly what was happening over there.

When he finally fell asleep she hadn't returned. When he awoke she was curled beside him, almost as if he'd dreamed the whole thing.

One afternoon following a meeting with Swaine and before he would have to think about setting off to review a provincial ballet company, Godwin came puffing up the sharply raked flights of stairs to Clothilde's apartment. He was living in his own place across the way but he continued to center much of his daily life on Clothilde. Because she cared about him and because she wanted to spend as much happy, carefree time with him as possible, she'd cut back what she sometimes referred to as her "modeling hours." Godwin was thankful for small blessings. On this day, however, his timing was imperfect if not exactly unfortunate.

As he crested the final few steps he saw the door of her place fly open, bang against the wall, and a large man, tall, stout and perspiring in the warmest time of the day, come rushing into the hallway. His suspenders were in place but his shirt clung to him in damp patches and his suit coat was draped over one arm. His hair was somehow out of kilter. His small eyes focused briefly on Godwin, there was a faint flicker of something, then he was brushing past, head turned away. He descended the stairs heavily, as if his brakes had gone out and he had lost control.

Clothilde was standing in the kitchen gargling, spitting into the sink. She wore a Chinese wrapper featuring red dragons, unbelted. It hung open. When she'd finished at the sink she turned and he saw her small pointed breasts, the flush on her skin, the round thighs. "You scared me," she said, breathless. Her face dissolved into a pricelessly French, toothy smile. "I'm so glad it is you." There was money on the table, next to a vase of cut flowers. She took a towel from the rack and turned partially away. He went to stand behind her, pressing himself against her high round hips, feeling the excitement he couldn't have stopped if he'd wished to.

She was wiping the towel between her legs. "Tell me you're not angry with me . . ."

"I'm not," he whispered. He was cupping the tiny breasts in his hands. "Your life is up to you." She was stroking him with her hips. She finished with the towel.

"I didn't know he was coming. He was just here, out of the blue. He was most insistent. He has been . . . a very steady client. You understand, Rodger?"

"I want you. Right now."

"You are very droll, Rodger. It excites you, doesn't it." She was whispering, suddenly breathing hard. She pulled the wrapper up around her waist. Her hips were pink. "He spanks me," she sighed. "It does no harm, does it? He has to spank me first or he doesn't get ready, he isn't able to . . . he is like a naughty little boy . . ." She leaned forward across the table, her fingers toying with the franc notes. She spread her feet, bracing herself against the table. When he began, her arms stretched out before her, her fingers tightening on the far edge of the table, her breath coming in deep groans as he began driving rhythmically against her. She moaned certain words, again and again, until it was over. Then he picked her up, a helpless bundle, and they spilled kisses from mouth to mouth, and he cradled her against his chest and gently carried her to the bed. He lay down beside her and she smiled with her eyes closed as he brushed his mouth across the *croix de vache*.

Later they went out to a café and drank bowls of *café au lait* and munched on bread. She felt safe and secure and he knew she wouldn't worry if he mentioned the man in the hallway. He couldn't bear hurting her. Maybe that was love. He knew he was too young to be sure.

"He looked familiar," he said. "I've seen him before. I think he may have felt the same about me."

"Yes, you have seen him. He comes to the Toledo. He brings his friend and the young girl. The three English."

"Of course, that's it. He's Tony something or other. And the other man is the Major or the Colonel—"

"Colonel," she said. "I don't know him or the girl. Only Tony Dew-Brittain. He is a—what do they call it, it is so insufferably English . . ." She tapped her mouth with a dark red fingernail. "Landed gentry." She shrugged. "I suppose that means he owns land. It's an old family. He's very proud of that. No one but the Chinese put such great faith in their

ancestors, I think. Or is it the Japanese? Shintoism." She was always saying things that took him by surprise. Shintoism, for God's sake. He'd have
to look that up. "I have known him for a year. Nearly. He is not a friend
but he is what? Sad, I think. He is unfortunate in his choice of a wife. So
many men are, is it not so? He pays me well. He is very quick. He is easy to
please. The other two, the Colonel and the schoolgirl . . . He does not
speak of them. From what I have seen"—she shrugged—"they are not
sympathetic."

When he was about to leave for the ballet she took his hand. "Rodger
. . . do you want me not to see him again? Do you want me to change?
Tell me what you want, Rodger."

He touched her scarred cheek.

"I want you to be my Clothilde. Any way you are, any way you ever
change . . . it's all one to me."

"I do love you, Rodger."

That evening his mind wouldn't grapple with the ballet. But he
wasn't worrying about Tony DewBrittain. He was thinking about Clyde.
He was wondering if she would go to Clyde in the night.

Swaine was sitting in the café, leaning back in a wicker embrace, his
Panama straw on an empty chair, his pale forehead growing pink in the
midday sun. The sleeves of his striped shirt were rolled up, revealing
white, nearly hairless forearms that seemed stuffed to the stretching point.
He was squinting up at a tall owlish-looking man wearing glasses and a
bemused expression who peered more than stared down at the editor. The
tall man then peered curiously at Godwin, who turned in off the sidewalk,
checked his wristwatch, and pulled up at tableside. Swaine mumbled
some kind of introduction, something about Iowa, meet Ohio, and the
owlish-peering fellow shook hands and excused himself, backing away,
bumping into a waiter, then hurrying off.

"What was that Ohio stuff? Who was that bird?"

"Just the best rewrite man in Paris, that's who. Jim Thurber by name.
I keep trying to hire him away from Colonel McCormick's rag, the Chicago Trib's Paris edition. Jeez, they're an arty-farty bunch over there. Mc-
Cormick must never read the damn thing, he'd fire 'em all. Elliot Paul,
he's a novelist, Eugene Jolas, he's a poet . . . arty-farty but not bad, not
bad. But this Thurber guy, he's a genius at rewrite. Just makes stuff up if
he has to. Siddown, siddown. Did you know what you were talking about
in your art piece?"

"Certainly not. I eavesdropped on people at the opening and wrote
down what they were saying. They seemed to know what was going on."

"Just so you don't, sonny. We've got other fish to fry. Merle Swaine has been thinking and when Merle Swaine thinks strong men cower. Mark my words." Swaine was probably only forty but his lank hair was long and gray and his face was lined and he was twenty pounds overweight and he cultivated the role of curmudgeon. To Godwin he seemed old as Methuselah. Old and smart.

"What have you been thinking about?"

"Merle Swaine has been thinking about Rodger Godwin and Rodger Godwin's future. Do you have ambition? Would you like to be somebody? These are the questions on Merle Swaine's mind. Have you ever been tested?"

"Yes, yes, and I don't suppose so. I'm only twenty-two."

"Well, quite a few fellas your age got the shit tested out of them a few years back." He blinked in the sun. "Aw hell, that was ten years ago. Ancient history. Well, you've got some kind of bullshitty flair. I don't know what it is exactly but your writing sort of pops when I read it. People like it because it's the way they talk—"

"Maybe it's because I don't know much and am always writing down what other people say—"

"Doesn't matter. It's fun to read. It touches a chord in the breast of Merle Swaine. So I'm giving you the go-ahead to do this piece on your friend Rasmussen. I asked around, a coupla people, he's real is what they tell me, got a certain cachet according to these assholes—and cachet is very big these days. I'm getting pressure to load up on cultural crap because McCormick's boys don't do a goddamn thing but cultural crap." He shook a French cigarette out of a pack and lit it. The waiter brought Godwin's coffee. "Go ahead, kid, have the omelette *fines herbes*. Merle Swaine's got plans for you. You'll be doing a lot of listening."

As he ate the omelette and the *pommes frites* and the crusty *baguette*, he listened with growing wonder as Swaine grew expansive and the sun crossed the dome of blue sky dragging fluffy thunderheads behind it. It was dawning on him that he'd done something right because the fact was Swaine was announcing that he was going to make something of Godwin who was, let's face it, a good old Iowa rube and bullshit artist and feather merchant and damn proud of it, thanks.

"Let me tell you where you are, sonny, and you can take this as gospel. It doesn't matter if it's true. Truth is, shall we say, relative. Forget true. There's no such thing. What's true is what we say is true because we write what's in the paper and everybody knows it must be true if you read it in the paper. Always remember, sonny, that's the law, the first law of this business. Now, to my point—let me tell you where you are. You're in

Paris, it's 1927, inflation is out of control and the French are fed up and over in Germany the Germans are fed up and the Eyties have got this dipshit Mussolini running things . . . but nobody cares because this is Paris, and it's the most exciting city in the world. And I'm giving you, somebody new and fresh seeing it for the first time, the chance to write it all down and make yourself famous. Of course it will also destroy you, as well, but that's your lookout." He took a huge red bandanna from his rear pocket and blew his nose loudly.

"Merle Swaine is betting on Paris. Merle Swaine is betting that we happen to be sitting on a keg of nitro, culturally speaking, you understand. For one thing, we've got all these nuts and drunks and womanizers over here, all writing and talking about each other, they've got a whole goddamn industry in high gear over here devoted entirely to making each other famous . . . my thinking is, you've got enough bullshit in you to join the party. You missed the war but most of these nitwits missed it, too. That's why Hemingway makes such a big deal out of it: He was in it and they weren't and by God he's gonna make them pay. So don't worry about the war. You're not one of the goddamn Lost Generation I'm so sick and tired of hearing about. You're the next generation. We'll call you the Found Generation . . . you can be the one who finds the Lost Generation, that's an idea, 'they were lost but now they're found and our man Godwin's the one who found them.' See, that's an idea. We can use that. See how it starts to come together when you put your mind to it?"

That night Rodger Godwin got down to some serious writing. About Paris and Clyde and Clothilde and the *flic* Henri who liked to beat up on the poor panhandlers and Swaine turned out to be right again. It all started to come together when he put his mind to it.

Swaine was beginning to develop positively mythical proportions. His personality filled Godwin's mind as if it were a balloon inflating within a telephone booth. He encouraged, he berated, he edited, he suggested, he applauded, he scorned, he viewed with alarm and he held in contempt and he demanded and he sometimes said not bad, you're catching on, all as Godwin worked on the piece about Clyde and the world of the Club Toledo. "Find your voice," Swaine would say. "You're feeling around for it, you're almost there. Find your own distinctive voice and you will find your fortune, sonny."

One day Swaine was pacing his office, his manner distracted. When Godwin stuck his head in to ask him why the long face, Swaine pulled him in and closed the door with a frame-rattling slam. "Nungesser and Coli have disappeared."

"Friends of yours?" The names rang a faint bell.

"Friends of mine? Jesus H. Christ, yes, they're friends of mine! But that's hardly the point. Jesus, you are one ignorant son of a bitch." He stared at Godwin's blank face and threw a box of paperclips past his head into the corner where they spattered everywhere like bullets ricocheting. "Merle Swaine is looking at an ostrich with his head in the sand! Or, better, a wet-behind-the-ears know-nothing with his head up his rosy red rectum! So you've got yourself a little French girlfriend and you're writing a big story about your pal—well, so what? That give you the right to depart the human race? You must . . . you *must* . . . be interested in every goddamn thing! That's the first lesson—you can't afford to miss a goddamn thing! You must pay attention to the whole fucking world! Nungesser and Coli! Welcome to planet Earth, sonny. Now Merle B. Swaine is going to tell you a thing or two and you'd better listen . . ."

All through the winter and spring public interest had been growing, snowballing, about the possibility of a New York–to–Paris nonstop transatlantic aeroplane flight. On the face of it the idea seemed preposterous and the attempts seemed to bear out the doubters. In 1919, almost a decade earlier, a British pilot and his American navigator had in fact made a nonstop flight but it had been the shortest way—Newfoundland to Ireland, just under two thousand miles, in sixteen hours. They crash-landed in a peat bog and informed the world that it had been a nightmarish experience of ice, fog, and awful turbulence. The hell with it.

The New York–Paris flight would be nearly twice the distance and was bound to take thirty-five to forty hours. Advances in design seemed not to have produced the aeroplane capable of such a flight. Yet men kept trying.

Captain Charles Nungesser and Captain Francois Coli were ready to make their attempt in a Levasseur biplane, *L'Oiseau Blanc*, which had a five-hundred-horsepower engine, the most powerful ever built. They had calculated their chances and remained undaunted, even though they intended to fly in what most pilots and engineers said was the wrong direction, Paris to New York, against the strong winds rather than with them. Their only worry was weight: eleven thousand pounds. If they could get *L'Oiseau Blanc* off the ground, they were certain they could make it to New York. They intended to jettison their heavy wind-resisting landing gear over water. They wouldn't need it to land in New York. They'd had the aeroplane built water-tight. They intended to land in New York harbor, right in front of another gift from the French . . . the Statue of Liberty.

While Godwin had been consumed by his own pursuits Swaine had become obsessed with the chances of Nungesser and Coli. He liked them personally, he admired them as fearless adventurers, he saw them as men he could admire which was a nearly new experience for Merle B. Swaine. He had spent all day Saturday with them in the hangar at deserted, wind-blown Le Bourget aerodrome while they made their last-minute preparations.

Swaine found himself half weeping, another first, as he watched in the gray murk, the huge engine at full throttle. The heavy-laden plane bouncing on the soft, spongy grass. He gasped as it lifted six or seven feet off the grass, then settled back, bounced again. The plane was too heavy. They weren't going to make it. Swaine wiped his eyes, waited for the sickening crash, the plane side-slipping into a ditch . . . but at the last second, against all logic, Nungesser pulled the nose up. Swaine watched until the speck they'd become disappeared in the gray northwest sky.

"At noon Sunday," Swaine said, slumping behind his cluttered desk, "they were seen leaving the coast of Ireland, heading for the open sea. Monday, yesterday, we had a report they'd been sighted over Newfound-land on the way to New York." He looked at Godwin, said sarcastically: "You may have noticed the snake-dancing in the streets last night? Champagne flowing like . . . like . . . champagne? Well, that was because a couple of Frenchmen had apparently done the impossible . . . but no, you were too busy to notice, I forgot." He stood and went to the open window, trying to catch a breeze. He patted his sunburned forehead with his red bandanna. "Now Merle Swaine's calendar says it's Tuesday and there's no sign of them . . . they're out of fuel by now. All we can do is wait and see if anybody finds the wreckage . . . It's a helluva thing, God-win. Merle Swaine lays a hundred to one the boys are goners." He sighed heavily, staring out the window.

His anger at Godwin's uninformed state had faded as he thought about the lost airmen and a foolish American named Lindbergh who was about to follow their example.

Sensing the opportunity Godwin stood up, began edging toward the door. Swaine was apparently lost in thought. In the distance the Eiffel Tower caught a torrent of sunshine pouring from between purple clouds. As Godwin reached for the doorknob Swaine said, still staring at Paris: "Your Rasmussen piece, it's too good for this rag. And too damn long. So I sent it on to Arthur Honan. He likes it. You know Arthur?"

"Well . . . no. And if he's about to fly the Atlantic I don't want to hear about it."

"Jesus, Godwin, you worry me. I'm trying to make you a . . . look, Arthur Honan is editor-in-chief of *europa* magazine. New York, London, Rome, Paris. The *big* little magazine—"

"I know, I get it. But Honan is used to . . . well, real writers . . . Gide, Cocteau, Fitzgerald, Gertrude herself, Ford—well, I—"

"He likes it. What you've got done. The first half."

"He does? He likes—"

"He wants you to finish it. He thinks you've caught 'the light and spirit of the time and place.' He talks like that. He's so full of shit he can't move out of that apartment of his, all the perfume and the astrologers and the drawn curtains, he's a first-class nutjob in Merle Swaine's opinion. He has to be rolled from place to place. Or carried on that throne. I mean, it's a horrifying show. But he's smart and I can't help liking him. He'll make you famous if you let him. He wants you to finish the piece. He doesn't care how long it is. That's the kind of asshole he is. Don't ask me . . . it's beyond me. He was born rich, maybe that explains it."

"Well . . . do I meet him? Does he want to talk about the piece?"

"Mon Dieu! He never meets the writers he publishes unless he's buggering them. He absolutely hates writers. Won't have them around. It's the writing itself he likes."

He came back to the desk, fumbled through papers, until he found an envelope. "He sent this over for you."

Godwin took the envelope. He cut his finger opening it and the check fell to the floor.

"He calls that one of his Honan Traveling Fellowships."

"Do I still work for you?"

"Of course, Godwin, of course."

The check was for five hundred dollars in francs.

"This is sort of hard to take in all at once." He was discovering the meaning of the expression "tears of joy."

"Indeed it is. But you know how it is, sonny. Every so often—contrary to God's plan for the universe—something good happens. Now go finish the piece and you'll get another check just like that one. And, Godwin—Merle Swaine congratulates you."

"Rodger Godwin thanks you."

"Get outa here. Get lost. I'm busy."

Godwin worked in a white-hot fury, day and night, writing, rewriting, thinking, walking along the Seine in the hours before dawn, working the material over and over until it felt right, until he could hear his voice in it. Not since the days when he was trying to work his way onto the Harvard

Crimson and had spent similar middle-of-the-night hours packing along the Charles in Cambridge had he applied himself with such determination. He forgot to shave and he saw little of Clothilde, who was always smiling at his furious activity, urging him on. He saw little more of Clyde, at least once he stopped interviewing him. Once he'd gotten a fix on the piece, then it was time to be alone, to do the work, to face the blank pages.

Clyde's schedule was erratic. He had a habit of disappearing after lunch with a wink and a grin which meant there was a girl involved. All Godwin knew about it was that the girl wasn't Clothilde, who—though she didn't know it—was playing an ever growing role in the piece about Clyde and the world of the Club Toledo. He only hinted at her sexual conduct: A knowing reader would draw his own conclusion. But her solemn face with its impish smile and its scar, her dance classes and the way she would suddenly pirouette as she walked through the tangled streets of the Left Bank and the care she took with her toe shoes, the occasional songs she sang with the band, the delightfully accented English, her fragile exterior and the steely resolve within, the way Clyde found her in the alley after the beating and the branding of her face. . . . It was all real. As he wrote he could hear the music in the crowded *cave* in his mind, he could close his eyes and there was Clyde bending and swaying as he blew his horn into the thick blue smoke, he could smell Clothilde's perfume and taste her mouth, and sometimes he'd rub his tired eyes and think of the heavyset, red-faced Englishman Tony spanking her until he was ready. . . .

He wondered briefly if any of his subjects might object to his portraits of them—well, Henri the *flic* could not be pleased but then he would never know, one way or the other—but if they didn't like it, the hell with them. He was writing about real people in a real place and he had no choice, he would write about them because they were there, the way a painter used his models, dammit, he *owned* them artistically, he had claimed them like an explorer claimed virgin territory, the way Hemingway had taken possession of Lady Duff Twysden and her circle. Somehow, by leading their lives within Godwin's view his friends had forfeited their privacy. And, anyway, he was making them famous. Well, maybe not famous, but people in Paris and London and New York were going to be reading about them . . . and they would be reading the work of Rodger Godwin. He was, in an odd way, their creator. It was an idea, in the years ahead, he never discarded. On paper, for his readers, he had created them. Breathed life into them. He liked the feeling. Whatever they might think about the use he'd put them to simply didn't concern him.

.   .   .

Godwin finished it on the night of Thursday, 19 May, and went by the terrace at the Dome where he found Swaine sitting with Thurber and a man called Nesterby who wrote sports for Swaine. Obviously the campaign to land Thurber continued. Swaine insisted that Godwin join them. While he ordered the superb Alsatian beer, Nesterby went on about the tennis championships being contested at Saint-Cloud. When Nesterby pulled up stakes Thurber sat quietly, content not to talk at all. Godwin pressed the envelope into Swaine's hand. "I wish you'd read this, Mr. Swaine. Tell me what you think. It's up to you what we do with it. If you think it's ready for Honan, ship it off to him."

Thurber murmured: "You look as tired as I feel. Don't spill that beer."

Godwin nodded. His hand was shaking and his eyes burned from the lack of sleep but he also felt as if he belonged at the table with men who actually knew what they were doing. They were treating him as an equal and Swaine was saying that *europa* had just taken a helluva piece that was going to put Godwin on the map. They ordered another round to toast his success and finally, half asleep, Godwin tottered happily back home.

In the morning, while he was still deeply asleep, there was a pounding at the door. It was Hélène, the sturdy old woman with a white mustache whom Clyde employed as concierge for the building. There was an urgent call from Mr. Swaine. Godwin slipped into his seersucker robe, staggered downstairs barefoot, to the telephone at Hélène's desk inside the front door. She went back to her watering can and the tubs of geraniums on the sidewalk.

"Godwin here," he muttered, yawning.

"The news just came through from New York," Swaine shouted. "He's just left from Roosevelt Field. He's airborne, the crazy bastard! He's on his way!"

"Who's left? What are you talking about?" Did this somehow have something to do with Honan?

"Who? Who, for chrissakes? Charlie Lindbergh in the *Spirit of St. Louis*, that's who! He's coming to Paris and you know what? Merle Swaine's got a feeling the son of a bitch just might make it. And if he does, sonny, we've got the biggest story of our lives. Man bites dog. Man does the impossible. The Yank is coming, sonny boy, the Yank is coming!"

When Swaine ran down Godwin said: "Did you read my piece?"

"Jesus," Swaine sighed. "Actors and writers! Yeah, sure, I read it. It's great, full of light and magic and the temper of the times. All that crap. I had a kid take it over to Honan's office first thing this morning."

"You really think he'll make it?"

"I don't know why the hell not. Honan's office is only about six blocks from here."

"No. Lindbergh. Will he make it?"

"All I can say is, Merle B. Swaine's got this feeling."

Godwin went back to bed.

He figured nobody would ever hear of this Lindbergh again.

At noon somebody was pounding on his door again.

What was a fella to do?

"Godwin!" Someone was yelling at him. "Time to get up! We got ourselves a damn big day! Rise and shine!" It was Clyde feeling mighty chipper.

CHAPTER 12

Clyde had planned an outing and there was no way of avoiding it. It had all the makings of an event.

The French tennis championships had reached the semifinals out at Saint-Cloud and the great match of the whole tournament might be the one Clyde didn't want to miss—the American, Big Bill Tilden, versus the diminutive, darting Frenchman, René Lacoste. Could the smaller man withstand Tilden's service, the likes of which had never been seen before? Clyde had a fistful of tickets and Godwin, while he bathed and shaved, was already thinking about the match as a colorful piece on Americans in Paris gathering to support their idol.

It turned out that Clyde had put together an elaborate party for the day, centered on their means of conveyance—a large, open, capacious yellow Rolls Royce which had been custom-built for his friend Anthony DewBrittain, the hefty, red-faced Englishman Godwin had first glimpsed the night he met Clyde and subsequently run into outside Clothilde's door. The car, its picnic hampers, its jump seats, was the key to the enterprise because it held so many passengers. DewBrittain's man drove and arrayed throughout the car were DewBrittain himself, Clyde, Godwin, Clothilde—whose presence obviously came as a surprise to DewBrittain who seemed to blush deeply when he saw her with Godwin and Clyde— the young girl and the compact man with the shrapnel scar who had been at the club that first night.

The yellow Rolls drew up to Clyde's street door beneath a bright sun in a luminous sky. Clyde introduced Godwin and Clothilde to everyone. DewBrittain looked momentarily as if he might pass out. Clothilde was very demure, ladylike, not quite distant. The young girl was called Prissy and was DewBrittain's daughter. The other man was Colonel Max Hood.

The drive to St. Cloud was a slow process. The conversation twittered around Godwin's ears like birds skittering from shrub to gutter to flower, and he kept trying to isolate it, capture it in his mind for later transcription.

"What's the point of art today?" DewBrittain was beginning to sweat as he looked from face to face. "To irritate the bourgeois. Not to be pretty, but to bloody irritate, irritate, irritate. Dada. Surrealism . . . Our civilization is dying, at least culturally . . . surrealism isn't the cause but, damn all, it's a symptom . . ." No one seemed able to think of a cogent comment. DewBrittain's expression was floundering between chagrin and vague despair. "It's the Impressionists, the last of the great innovators. Prices are out of sight, of course. Glad I bought them up when I did. Manet, the first Impressionist—when he died my dear wife thought she remembered something to do with Manet, couldn't recall what . . . turned up a picture in the back of a closet under the stairs, brought it out, showed it to me, 'It's a Manet,' she said. 'Manet gave it to me' . . . well, she had it slightly wrong—that's your mother, what, Prissy? It was a Monet that Manet had given her sister and the sister had left it at our place. But you see my point. Lovely picture, ain't it, Prissy?"

Godwin was rather unsure as to what the point had been.

"You've mixed them up, Papa," the young girl said. Her face was framed by thick dark hair cut short along the line of her jaw. She leaned her head forward to reach into the hamper for a jar of lemonade. There was a perfect arrow of faint down on the nape of her neck. She wore a white dress, sleeveless, collarless, with lace cut out of the material at the throat. "It was Claude Monet who died recently. Manet inspired Monet, Monet inspired Zola . . . It was a *Manet* that *Monet* gave Mother's sister . . ." She smiled very slowly at no one in particular. "My father always confuses the two of them, you see."

"Well, the point is," DewBrittain said with good nature and pride in his daughter's knowledge, "they were a couple of damn fine painters."

The girl said: "Monet was a great friend of Clemenceau's. When Monet died his very simple coffin was carried on a village handcart and two peasants from his village, dressed in their very best, pushed it to his grave in Giverny. Clemenceau walked alone behind the coffin." She was very grave, befitting her story.

Clothilde gave her a fresh appraising glance. "That is a very nice thing to know and to tell. I congratulate you."

"It makes Monet seem real," the girl said, "doesn't it? Sometimes people forget that the great artists and such are really just people. I think we must keep that in mind, don't you?"

"I agree with you completely," Clothilde said, won over. "It is also a great pity that Monet was not a better painter." Together the two girls, only a few years apart in age, giggled.

"Well, money comes into it, too," DewBrittain said.

The girl caught Clothilde's eye and together they sighed. Godwin felt as if, somehow, they were all part of the same family, on an outing for the day.

"A Rousseau—picture of a gypsy fella—went for half a million francs the other day." DewBrittain wiped his forehead with a huge linen handkerchief. "Art, I'm sorry to tell you, is no longer art. Art is now commerce and don't forget it." He snorted. "The chap who figures out this art game is in clover! Agreed, Max?"

"I don't know a damned thing about art, Tony. And neither do you. You know about commerce. I'll trust to Prissy's judgment when it comes to the pictures."

"Mother likes Modigliani and Braque and Picasso," the girl said.

"Do you?"

"Yes, rather. Particularly Modigliani."

"Well, that's good enough for me, Prissy," Max Hood said.

DewBrittain offered round a dish of pâté and another dish of tiny pickles, cornichons. There was also a mustard pot and bread as they rode along under the heavy, spreading chestnut trees. "Belgian pâté," he said, "very fine, Mr. Godwin. Try it."

As Godwin spread pâté on bread and decorated it with a pickle, Prissy made a face and said, "Oh, Papa!"

"Now, now," her father said, suppressing a laugh.

"I shall tell him," she said, turning to Godwin. Her eyes were so large, the color so mysteriously brown and velvety, that Godwin felt slightly taken aback, as if he'd been caught spying on her. Perhaps everyone was struck the same way the first time she made eye contact. "Mr. Godwin—"

"Call me Rodger. Please."

"All right then. Rodger. Belgian pâté is one of Papa's little jokes. He likes it, you see. But I believe people should be told the truth. It's half horsemeat and half rabbit. Do you know what that means?"

"What?"

"One horse to one rabbit." A small smile played at the corners of her mouth. Her face was heart-shaped, eyebrows heavy and dark, cheekbones high. She'd be a great beauty one day. She was beautiful even now.

"Should I try it?" he asked.

"Well, I suppose you must, mustn't you?" She sat very quietly, hands folded in her lap. A white dress, suntanned arms. "Or you'll be thought a terrible coward. I admit it is quite tasty. Pistachio nuts in it. But it is horse because," she gave a small Gallic shrug, "we must face the fact that we are in France."

Clyde and Hood were talking about the tennis match, munching on bread and pâté. Clothilde winked at the girl, then looked at DewBrittain. "I can see that you are familiar with all your father's little tricks." She smiled sweetly at her client who looked away, fumbled for something in the hamper.

Godwin ate his pâté. He had eaten plenty of horsemeat since arriving in Paris. As the girl said, he'd found himself in France.

"When we get to the tennis," DewBrittain said, "I want us all to concentrate on this great match. There will be an immense crowd. Five thousand they say. Max's money is on Tilden. What do you say, Mr. Godwin?"

"Tilden. He's like Babe Ruth . . ."

"I am leaning toward Lacoste. Craft, speed, tactics."

Hood said: "Tilden's service will wear him down. Of course, anything can happen in France."

The crowd was a glare of white in the bright sunshine. The two players moved like well-oiled clockwork figures. Godwin had played a bit of tennis but had never seen a bigtime match. He soaked it up, mentally making notes, wishing he'd brought pen and paper. He sat with Colonel Hood on his left and the girl Prissy on his right, Clothilde beyond her, then Clyde and Tony DewBrittain.

Hood told Godwin he'd read some of his things in the *Herald*. "What do you make of Paris, Mr. Godwin? How does it set with you?"

"It's all new to me. It's like living in a novel. To tell you the truth, I'd never imagined there were people like the people I've met here. They live in a world where art and writing is something to talk about, argue about . . . it's like being at the center of the world. What do you make of it, Colonel?"

"Nice enough place, I suppose. I come from up north, up by Hadrian's Wall, near the border of Scotland. Don't take naturally to a place like this . . . it all seems a bit frivolous to a dour chap like myself. But I'm learning . . . the City of Light, yes, it's something you get used to."

"How long have you been here?"

"I came over a month ago. Been here before, of course."

"Where are you living?"

"Lucky enough to be a guest of Tony's, actually. He has a few houses not too far from the Luxembourg Gardens. Gave me one for my stay. Quite comfortable. Tony's a good sort of chap. The daughter's a treat. Very grown up for a child—I expect you noticed that on the way out here. She gets a certain worldliness from her mother, I suppose."

Hood drifted into silence, concentrating on the match which was a grudging, hard-fought business. In the relative stillness they were close enough to the court to hear the serve whistling through the air as it came off Tilden's racquet. Godwin heard five thousand people gasp in unison when Tilden smote the ball. But Lacoste handled it more often than not, scampering this way and that, lobbing and lacing crosscourt volleys and placing drop shots just over the net and firing backhands toward Tilden's feet. It was a battle between power and guile. Lacoste was finally unable to crack through and the first set went to Tilden, 6-4.

"Excuse me, Rodger." It was Prissy, who had waited until Hood set off up the aisle to rendezvous with an old friend who'd caught his eye. "Which *journaux* do you write for?"

"Paris *Herald*. Do you read it?"

"I shall start tomorrow. What do you write about?"

"I review music, ballet, art stuff. The first night I ever saw you was—"

"At Clyde's. I remember. We all like Clyde's music ever so much. Even my mother when we can find her."

"Clyde was the person who rescued me. Started teaching me about jazz. He's the one who got me really interested in Paris."

"*Moi, aussi.* He's an excellent teacher. Do you know a lot about the violin?"

"All I know is that I like the sound it makes. Very emotional."

"Do you really?" Her face brightened, the light brown eyes grew enormous again. "I'm glad. I play the violin. My father and Madame Javert think I'm a prodigy. I'm not, of course. A prodigy is what they want me to be but I'm already too old for that. Much too old. But if I work very hard for four more years I'll be able to play . . . well enough, I suppose. Papa has made sure—with the aid of Madame Javert—that I have had tea with some of the composers. Milhaud, Satie, Poulenc . . ." She caught his blank stare, which had fixed on her enormous eyes, the green-flecked irises. "You've never heard of them, have you? I'm sorry, I'm talking too much. Papa calls me Chatterbox when I go on so."

"Well, I'm sure I should know about all of them."

"I could tell you about them someday. Would that be nice?"

"If you can put up with my ignorance."

She nodded. "And do you like to fish?"

"I've never done much, I'm afraid."

"But I could tell you about the composers while we fish, you see. Clyde takes me fishing along the Seine sometimes. It's jolly good fun. He talks to me about music and fishing and all sorts of things. Would you like to come sometime?"

"Well, sure, I'll fish."

"Some days we go to the book and print stalls along the river, too. I tell him my favorites. Daumier's lawyers . . . How about tennis? Do you play?"

"My gosh, you're full of questions."

"I'm sorry. Chatterbox."

"I've played some tennis, yes. College." He shrugged.

"Where?"

"Massachusetts."

"What school?"

"Harvard."

"Clyde says you can always tell a Harvard man but you can't tell him much." She grinned at this bit of knowledge she might never otherwise have had the chance to use.

Godwin laughed, enchanted somehow. She wanted so much to be friends. "I guess Clyde's right about that."

Hood had returned to his seat beside Godwin. Tony DewBrittain leaned forward and called to his daughter. "Watch the tennis, Priss. That's what we're here for. Don't distract Mr. Godwin. You may never see Tilden again, so watch him. See how he serves. Try to learn something." His face was terra cotta, burning in the sun.

"Yes, Papa." She nudged Godwin with her arm, murmured: "I'll *never* be able to serve like Tilden, no matter how hard I watch." She leaned forward, elbow on knee, chin in hand, watching as hard as she could.

With craft and extraordinary reflexes and daring placements, Lacoste evened the second set at five all. It was enough to make Godwin wish he were a sportswriter like Bill Shirer at the *Tribune*.

Hood said: "Rather a good match, what? Hot work down there. Do you play? One's always looking for a game. Tony's not up to it. Ticker's not what it was."

"I play a bit."

Prissy leaned over eagerly: "Shall he play with us? The Colonel gives me lessons. Say you will, Rodger."

"Well . . ."

"Just a friendly hit," Hood said. His face was burning over his tan. The shrapnel scar seemed to have whitened.

"Please, Rodger," Prissy said, looking up at him from beneath the broad-brimmed straw hat with the blue ribbon at the back like the tail of a kite.

"Well, thank you. Sure. I'd like to."

Hood nodded. "Good chap."

Tilden powered his way through the eleventh game to go up 6-5. The booming serves were taking their toll. Lacoste's returns had lost their crispness. The placements were less accurate and Tilden attacked with cannonading forehands, finished it out with shots exploding off the reddish clay, won 7-5 to take the match in two straight sets.

On the way out of the stadium, in the pushing and shoving of the crowd, with the sun slanting in their eyes, Tony DewBrittain had a heart attack.

Godwin was walking with Clyde and Clothilde a few feet behind the others when DewBrittain staggered against Hood, his face losing its red blush and turning the gray of wet cement. He clutched at Hood's sleeve, knees buckling. His mouth was opening and closing like a fish on a pier. Hood helped him to a bench, eased him down. He slumped back as if his strength were utterly gone. Prissy was kneeling on the grass beside him. She was calmly searching the pockets of his jacket. Godwin stood looking down at the man wondering if he was going to die. He was dripping sweat, soaking his shirt. Hood had loosened his collar and tie. Prissy found the vial of pills and pressed one into her father's mouth, spoke to him softly. He nodded. The crowd surging past was slowing, staring in that appraising manner so common among the French, as if they were about to announce odds on his survival. Prissy turned to them, her temper flared out for a moment, "*Allez, allez!*" She waved at them like a woman shooing chickens away from the farmhouse door. They gave a collective shrug, and moved away, as if to say let him die, then, it is nothing to us. She turned back to her father. He was blinking in the slanting sunshine but he looked better, his eyes were focusing. Prissy turned and looked up at Godwin. "He'll be all right. It happens sometimes but he has his medicine with him always. Feeling better, Papa?"

"Feeling like a bloody damn fool," he said, suddenly hoarse and weak-voiced. "It just took me all of a sudden." He moved his arm very slowly, shading his eyes. "I've ruined your day. Feeling damn foolish."

Clothilde said: "Can we get you anything? To drink? Should we summon a doctor?" She was gazing down at him, her expression one of affection. She knew him quite differently from anyone else there and he smiled up at her. He trusted her. He was a good customer and that mattered.

"No, no, really, I'm quite all right. The old ticker, y'know. Really ought to get back to base camp, eh, bwana?" He looked at Hood.

"We'll go together," Hood said. "See you tucked in." He looked around, saw Claude, the driver, across the street by the yellow Rolls. "Godwin, could you have him bring the car over here? Be a great help."

Godwin loped over, delivered the message, and when he came back Prissy was smiling radiantly, giving her father a large kiss on the cheek.

Clyde grinned at Godwin. "She's got old Tony wrapped around her little finger. He has a heart attack, she sticks a pill under his tongue . . . and she's Florence Nightingale. Her wish is his command. Women, sports, women. Fella really should learn not to trifle with 'em."

"Imagine when she grows up."

"She'll be *giving* heart attacks, sport."

She came away from her father, hands behind her back, smiling in a very collected way as if she were managing things according to plan. "Papa has said we can take the *bateau-mouche* back and the Colonel will go with him in the car. Have you gone on the *bateau-mouche*, Rodger? It's so lovely. Isn't it, Mademoiselle Devereaux? You see all the lights of Paris and they have music and dancing—please, say you'll come with us." She looked up expectantly, anxious, as if there were any doubt. It was so important to her. She was still a little girl.

"I wouldn't miss it," Godwin said. "If your father doesn't need you, Prissy."

Clyde put his arm around her shoulders, gave her a shake. "I told you he was our kind of fella. Old Rodger, game for anything."

They stood at the rail watching Paris drift by as evening came on. Familiar landmarks glimpsed over the rooftops, fishermen with poles and their lines drifting in the dark Seine, lovers strolling and embracing, the sound of the accordion and the violin coming from the dance floor. Colored lights were strung on wires outlining the ship. They reminded him of the Japanese lanterns at the country club's summer dances outside Chicago when he'd been a kid. Well, last summer, for that matter. Clyde was smoking a cigar, beating rhythm on the railing. "Let's have a dance," he said, looking from Clothilde to Prissy DewBrittain. "Who's game?"

Clothilde finally said: "You promise to look out for this dancer's feet?"

"I'll do my level best." He steered her away from the railing toward more colored lights where people were dancing and it was smokey. Clyde and his stogey would fit right in, like remnants of Lautrec's days at the Moulin Rouge.

"Do you want to go inside?" Godwin looked sideways at the girl.

She shook her head. "I like it out here. This," she waved at the night, "is perfect. Look at the crescent of moon. Isn't Paris beautiful? I feel old here, almost grown up. My father says I have an old soul. I wonder what that means?" She leaned forward, looking down at the reflection of the moon in the black water.

"Your father, he'll be all right?"

"Oh, yes. Don't worry. One day one of these attacks will kill him, though, won't it? But not for a while."

"You sure knew how to take care of it."

She shrugged. "Not much to it, really."

"The way you handled the gawkers—*allez, allez!*—now that was very good. The voice of command. I was impressed. Look, how old are you, anyway? If you don't mind my asking, Prissy. I mean, it's none of my business."

"Fourteen. I don't mind. You see, I'm much too old to be a prodigy. Five years ago, yes, but not now."

"But you enjoy playing the violin."

"Mmm. It's easy to enjoy something you're rather good at, isn't it? I enjoy almost anything, if it doesn't mean I have to skim along the surface. I hate that." She grinned, eyes sparkling, reflecting the colored lights. When he looked away he saw the lights dancing in the water near the moon. "I take everything rather seriously, I'm afraid." Her face had grown pensive but she shook it off. "Tennis, *par example*. Don't believe Colonel Hood, either. He's serious about his tennis. He's serious about everything —he's quite sad, actually. He's a lonely man . . ." She smiled brightly, a somewhat false smile, he thought, as if she were trying to rise above some dark side of her nature. How had she come to seem so ambiguous, partly a child and partly not?

"Tell me about Colonel Hood," he said.

She cocked her head at him. "Well, he's a great war hero. My father enjoys his company and trusts him. Sometimes they talk about my mother. Do you know what my father says about Colonel Hood? I think it's quite significant, actually."

"What does he say?"

"He says that Colonel Hood is lost without a war! That he's just waiting for the next one to break out somewhere and he'll be off! What do you think of that?"

"You're right. That sounds pretty sad."

"He says that Colonel Hood is by nature a hero. A professional hero without a war. And he says there is nothing sadder than a hero with nothing to be heroic about. It's like being unemployed and pointless. I don't know quite what to make of it myself. It's too bad for Colonel Hood, I suppose, but there is nothing worse than a war, surely . . . it doesn't seem there's a very nice answer for Colonel Hood's problem, does it?"

Clothilde and Clyde eventually came back and Clyde talked to the girl and the young woman—that was how Godwin saw them in his mind —and checked his watch because he had to be at the club soon. Godwin watched them, Clyde's vitality enveloping them, lighting their faces. Notre Dame loomed ahead, the Ile de la Cité with its sparkling of lights, the cafés on the Left Bank.

Clothilde kissed the girl on both cheeks, her original opinion of her apparently drastically revised. She was going off to the club with Clyde, and Godwin said he might be by later, then he was standing with the girl across the water from Notre Dame.

"What would you like to do now?"

"Oh, I really must go home and make sure Papa is resting."

"Where do you live?"

She pointed. "Not far from the Luxembourg Gardens."

"Well, I'll see you home, Miss DewBrittain."

"You are very kind, Mr. Godwin." She smiled as if she were flirting. She was so dark, so much like a little animal with her immense velvety eyes.

Godwin found a taxi and they rode in silence, watching the life swirling around the cafés and in the streets. Godwin had never known a girl of her type before. Her physical type, he supposed was what he meant, but he meant all the rest of her, too. And she was so damn young. A kid, just a child, when you thought about it. Still, she had this *quality*. When, several years later, he met Anne Lindbergh he was quite struck— almost painfully—by her beauty, the small, fine-featured darkness which gave her the look of an exquisite, restrained little animal, and then he realized that Anne Morrow Lindbergh reminded him of Priscilla DewBrittain and was very nearly as beautiful.

When they reached the walled enclosure of the house she shook his hand and said, "Good night, Rodger, and thank you so much."

"Good night, Prissy."

"Oh, if you only knew how much I hate that name—Prissy! Sounds like an adjective, not a name! Isn't it simply unutterably horrible?"

"Not at all—"

"You're just too kind to admit it. Well, I've been thinking about it. Priscilla. It is an absolutely calamitous name. Why are you laughing?"

"The way you talk. Unutterably horrible! Calamitous!"

"It comes from being with adults all the time. I'm not at all good with children. Clothilde, now she would be a nice friend . . . but . . . *my name*. I think I have the answer. What do you think of Cilla? I rather like the sound of it. Cilla DewBrittain? Is it all right?" She looked up at him from beneath the straw brim. "Tell me you like it . . ."

"I think it's beautiful," Godwin said.

"Oh, I'm so glad you like it! You are such a very nice new friend!" Impulsively she stood on her tiptoes and kissed his cheek, one hand holding her hat in place.

"You're not so bad yourself," he said.

"And listen to how well it goes with other names." She was going to tease him, he knew it. "Let's see . . . Cilla Godwin? Or Cilla . . . Hood? Or Cilla . . . Rasmussen?" She dissolved in laughter. "Oh no, that one will never do!"

She giggled and he watched her disappear through the doorway, heard the bolt slide shut behind her.

He felt lighthearted and foolish and happy as he walked home from the DewBrittain house, whistling, vaguely contemplating what seemed to be a future rosy as the pink glow over the rooftops and the thick, dark treetops. Alone with his prospects he decided against joining the group at the Club Toledo: He didn't want the underground heat and smoke and the reverberating music and, he had to face it, he didn't want to see Clothilde and run the risk of not going home with her. He wanted no risks that night; the day had been perfect and he wanted to keep the feeling inviolate through another night.

His hopes were, as it turned out, doomed.

He was thinking about how Clothilde had changed her mind and had quite taken to the DewBrittain girl, he was wondering just how anyone could quite resist the girl's charm and solemn beauty. There was something indefinable about the way she seemed to balance the solemnity and the apparent desire to be girlish and happy. She held both impulses in her face: that was what made her dark, heart-shaped face so compelling—it seemed to quietly demand your attention but more than that, your sympathy, quite unlike any other face he'd ever seen before. How would she handle life? Of course, he knew so damn little about life himself. Still she had that highstrung look, those haunting eyes, the desire to please struggling to coexist with the need to have things her own way.

Godwin heard an odd, moaning sound, half gargle and half sob. He heard it again as he turned the corner beneath the green-and-white striped awning of Corre, the Breton who was the horse butcher for the neighborhood. The cool night breeze ruffled the awning with its golden horse's head against the stripes. He was still whistling "You Do Something to Me" and he stopped, heard someone retching in the shadows. There was a figure slumped between a trash bin and a heavy tub of geraniums.

The man was kneeling, probably drunk but as he looked up from the flowers where he'd been vomiting the light picked out the blood and bruises and swollen, split skin. His face bulged like a ripe tomato that had burst. His nose was flattened, the skin stretched over the cheekbones split, one eyebrow cloven, his left ear bloody, and when Godwin approached he cowered back into the shadows, arms feebly raised to fend off any more blows.

Godwin recognized him. He was a crippled chestnut vendor who worked a few of the corners nearby. He was missing half of one leg and wore a peculiar device strapped to the stump with a small wheel resting on the pavement. Godwin was never sure how a wheel improved on a peg or an artificial foot, but it was an oddity he'd noticed and included in a piece he was doing on a typical morning's stroll through the *quartier*. Now the wheel and its apparatus lay beside the tub of flowers. Someone had beaten him severely, ripped off the wheel and its shaft—the man was miming this as he struggled to speak through bloody lips—and had robbed him. Godwin helped him to his feet, retrieved the wheel and helped him strap it on. When Godwin offered to get the police or accompany him to the *préfecture* the man cowered again, violently shaking his head, muttering the name *Henri* again and again. Godwin got the picture. It was the *flic* Henri, the *gendarme*, who had beaten and robbed him. Henri's reputation was widely known in the *quartier* but Godwin had never seen an example of his handiwork up close before.

He helped the man up, steadied him, saw that he was crying, tears mixing with the blood on his face. There was, however, nothing more he would allow Godwin to do. He asked if he could see the poor bastard to a hospital or home but the man kept shaking his head, sniffling. Through bruised, split lips he kept repeating the single word, *merci, merci,* and slowly hobbled down the street staying in the shadows, moaning only infrequently.

Someone in the neighborhood had told Godwin that the vendor had lost the leg in Flanders during the Great War.

He climbed the stairway, suddenly exhausted and dispirited by the vendor's condition and how he'd got that way. Maybe he should devote an entire piece to Henri . . .

A heavy buff envelope had been slipped under his door. Tiredly he tore it open.

20 v 27

Rodger Godwin

Your Clyde Rasmussen piece superb! You are old beyond your years. Your champion, Merle B. Swaine (and what could that "B" stand for?), tells me you are but a pup. However, you see Paris as I wish I could—but don't now and never did. I was born jaded and you, I will pray, will never become jaded or blasé or sophisticated. Writers often do, you know.

I want more of your work. Keep the personal tone—surely you must realize that in your case the writing is your personality.

Marshall Hacker of Boni & Liveright, Publishers, New York, is in Paris for a month or so. He shares my opinion of your work and wants to do a book of your Paris pieces. He suggests BOULEVARDIER or the more prosaic PARIS SKETCHES as possible titles for you to consider.

He will be in touch with you.

Young man—play your cards properly and you are made!

A. Honan

<u>europa</u> *magazine*

He read it through several times. The great thing was to grasp its importance. It was, he supposed, the turning point in his life. Maybe it would take him years to understand what the devil was going on, how the entire remainder of his life was being shaped—but he was going to try to keep the memory clear.

When Godwin was coming out of the bath there was someone knocking on his door. He put his robe on and padded across the small living room, rubbing his hair with a towel.

Colonel Hood stood in the doorway: tennis flannels, baggy whites, tennis sweater flung over his shoulders, sleeves of his white shirt rolled halfway up his forearms, carrying two tennis racquets and a bag of tennis balls. "We were talking about playing a bit of tennis. I always play on Saturday . . . *voilà*, this is Saturday morning. Prissy said no time like the present. So, what do you say?"

"*Bonjour, m'sieur!*" This came brightly from Priscilla, who had followed Hood up the stairs. She was laden with a paper bag and a bottle of cream. "I've brought freshly baked croissants and brioches. Cream for the coffee. All in a kind of bribe to make you say yes. Mmmm, you don't seem to be dressed yet. I can make coffee of course. Shall I? Do you have *sucre?*"

"Well, sure, I guess I do. Come on in. Ah, you've brought your violin, too." He was shaking Hood's hand, leading them into his privacy, glad that Clothilde wasn't there.

"I know," she said patiently.

"Sorry to take you by surprise," Hood said, putting the two racquets in a cheap pressed tin umbrella stand. "Seemed like too good a chance to pass up. Fine morning."

"And you," Godwin said, turning to the girl, "are you going to favor us with a violin accompaniment?"

"You're really quite lucky—I'm not. I have a Saturday lesson with Madame Javert. I always walk the Colonel to the Luxembourg Gardens and then I go off to my lesson." She was already arranging the coffee things in the tiny kitchen, boiling water, spooning coffee into the infusion maker. He watched the pleats of her white skirt swinging from her round little fourteen-year-old rump and smiled, shook his head when Hood caught his eye. She was only, what? seven, eight years younger than he, but he felt both older and younger. She was going to be the sort of woman who took over and got a fella whipped into a lather wanting her and she'd have him jumping through hoops. He didn't know much about females but he'd seen the type.

By the time he was dressed in something approaching tennis kit, she had the coffee made, the little table set with plates, cups, flatware, and decorated with cut flowers she'd brought from home. She'd even found the napkins. The Colonel was nibbling at a brioche. She had also produced some fruit from a bag and put it in a bowl. She handed Godwin a steaming cup of coffee, added cream. *"Sucre? Oui?"*

"Sure, you bet. How's your father?"

"He's fine. He slept like a log—woke up all covered in bark. That's one of his jokes. He's terribly embarrassed."

"He's lucky," Godwin said.

Her eyes were still enormous, plush brown in the morning light at the window. She looked from Godwin to Hood, a huge smile on her wide mouth, looking her age, holding her coffee cup in two hands. "We're all lucky, aren't we? We must be the luckiest people in the world. Don't you think so? Well, I do, I think so."

They watched her walk away. The sun was baking the tennis courts at the Luxembourg Gardens.

"Pretty little thing, isn't she?" Hood was bouncing a ball on his strings, his shrapnel scar crinkling.

"She's about a thousand years old," Godwin said. "The wisdom of the ages resides in that girl."

"You've had a lot of experience with women, have you? That's what they say about Americans. Lots of experience when it comes to women."

"Only a very little, speaking for this American."

"Are you pulling my leg, old boy?"

"Not even a little."

"Well, I'm not much of a ladies' man myself. Always been too busy with one damn thing or another. A soldier's life—well, the class of woman one meets in that line of country can be, well, dubious is probably the word I'm looking for. Then," he chuckled, "there is the renowned British public school system. But I'm not a victim of the English disease as it's called over here. Shall we hit a few, Mr. Godwin?"

"Call me Rodger."

"All right, Rodger. Let's see, my friends seem to call me Colonel. Or Max, they call me Max sometimes." He shrugged, walking to the far side of the net. "Call me whatever you like, Rodger. It really doesn't make any difference, does it?"

Hood played an economical, compact game, striking the ball briskly, moving about quickly but almost stiffly. Once they'd gotten the feel of the dusty court and Godwin had felt the tension of the strings, once they'd warmed up, Hood began to return the ball to Godwin's feet, the worst possible place for a large man trying to return it. Lacoste had done the same to Tilden. Then Hood switched tactics, working the ball around the court, testing first the backhand, then the forehand, never seeming to exert himself. Godwin knew within ten minutes that he was badly overmatched. He had to decide if he'd play hard, try to stay competitive. Oh, what the hell, why not? His only hope was brute strength which could never win against Colonel Hood. But it turned out to be fun, occasionally rifling a line drive into the corner, too much pace on it for Hood to get his racquet in play. Those were infrequent moments, however, just enough to keep Godwin's dignity intact. When they got around to keeping score it was 6-2, 6-1, 6-2 for Colonel Hood. Still, there had been good rallies and they were both winded when it was over. Their tennis clothes were tinted with reddish dust, as if they'd been rouged.

They sagged down on a bench in the shade. Hood flipped him a towel from his bag. "Well done, Godwin. I'll have to keep my eye on you. You've got the tools, all you need is a bit of grit. You need a bit of blood in your eye."

"I'm impatient. I overswing."

"Errors of youth. Wanting to win all at once, at the beginning. It's like life, isn't it? It's the young who are impatient but paradoxically it's the old who are running out of time. And you lack the killer instinct. You treat tennis like a game. I could see it when you'd run me into the corner and then let me recover. Fair play and what not." From his lips it sounded like a sad accusation. Treating tennis like a game was not Hood's way. But what is war, if not a game?

"Well, we must play again." Somehow he felt as if he'd failed in Hood's estimation. "I need the exercise."

Hood nodded.

"Prissy tells me you had quite a war. Do you mind my bringing it up?"

"Mind? No, I don't mind. You were too young for that show, I daresay."

"Yes. I was nine years old when it began."

"Really? Nine years old. Well, you're damn lucky out of it. Still, I expect you'll get a good taste of the next one. Shan't be too terribly long. Ten years maybe." He half smiled at the thought.

"The next one? It was supposed to be the war to end wars."

"Yes, it was, wasn't it? Well, the next one will really be the second half of the Great War. Everyone needed a good rest period by '18. But the Germans are a resourceful lot, you know, and we, the victors, fixed it so they'll have nothing to lose by starting it up again. We should have treated them humanely or put them to the sword. Basic rule of warfare. As it is we have made their life a miserable one. No, they'll have nothing to lose. And everyone else will have *something* to lose, surely. So the Germans will start it up again and we'll all have to fight them again."

"But the Germans can't raise any army," Godwin said. "It's forbidden. So how can they ever hope to begin a war?"

"As I said, they're a resourceful bunch. Much too serious about everything. Of course, the kind of beating they took—particularly at the conference table—can play hell with anybody's sense of humor." He wiped his face with a towel, held it up to his eyes. "They'll find a way. It'll be up to us—will we have the guts and good sense to stop them? We shall see."

"Prissy says you were a hero."

Hood laughed into the towel, then wiped his face a last time and tossed the towel aside. "She is a beautiful girl but very young and highly impressionable. She thinks she understands adults and sometimes one assumes she does but the fact is she's a girl with much to learn."

"I had an uncle, came over with the AEF."

"A doughboy. What did he make of the war?"

"I don't know."

"He didn't want to talk about it?"

"Couldn't. Killed in September of '18."

"Rotten damn shame."

"Where did you spend your war?"

"Riding a camel, old man, most of the time."

"What do you mean?"

"Well, you know . . . big dirty bad smelling evil beasts, bad dispositions, they can go great distances without water, always appear to be grinning . . . leg at each corner, in short a camel."

"But where is what I mean—"

"Oh, the desert. I was out there with T. E. Lawrence." He stood up. "Come on. I always wait for Prissy at the Medici Fountain. Have you seen it?"

"I'm afraid not."

"Well, you must. Most beautiful thing in Paris."

The fountain's water was still as glass, leaves of yellow and green resting on it, moss growing like velvet, Paris quite still as if collectively holding its breath.

Priscilla DewBrittain was staring into the fountain. Her violin case resting on a stone bench. Clyde Rasmussen was standing quietly on the other side of the fountain. Her back was to Hood and Godwin as they approached. Sunlight streaked through high clouds. Children were playing some sort of game that involved skipping in a circle and singing, high piping voices. Two nuns stood watch. Clyde and Priscilla seemed to have nothing to say to each other. Clyde moodily chewed on a blade of grass.

"Clyde," Godwin said. "What a coincidence. You should have come for tennis. Together we just might have given the Colonel a decent game."

"It's not exactly a coincidence, sport," Clyde said. "I often meet little old Prissy here after her lesson and conduct a kind of seminar."

"A tutorial," she said. "So I brought him along. He says he knows the only man in Paris who can make decent ice cream. I've just about got him talked into taking us, haven't I, Clyde?"

"Honest to God, it's just like back home," Clyde said.

But as they set off to find the ice-cream man Godwin knew that something was wrong. Maybe it was what he'd sensed as they approached the fountain, something about Clyde and Prissy. A chill. Had they argued?

Had Clyde treated her like a child, squelched some enthusiasm or other? He'd never seen either of them so restrained. Or maybe it was all in his head. Maybe everything was fine. But he was absolutely sure it wasn't just like back home.

They left Priscilla at home with her father, who was having a few friends in, just possibly including his wife, Lady Pamela Legend, the girl's mother. Priscilla thanked Clyde for the ice cream, thanked them all for seeing her home. Godwin watched her shut the courtyard door behind her, wondering if she were really just a girl, after all, just another adolescent girl who wasn't trying to control anybody. She was so solemn in repose, so sweet, so pleased by little things like the ice cream.

"Ain't she something?" Clyde beamed from Hood to Godwin. There was a little dab of ice cream in the corner of his mouth. "She's got all them female wiles my old mama warned me about when I was just a little fella."

Hood said: "It's so colorful when he talks like a rustic. What's the American equivalent?"

"Hillbilly," Godwin said. "Redneck."

"I'm never quite sure what he means when he talks hillbilly."

"I'll tell you what I mean, Colonel. I mean here we got us a fourteen-year-old girl. And she's got three grown men escortin' her around Paris lookin' for ice cream . . . and then she leaves 'em outside the gate moonin' over her, waitin' on her. Now if that ain't the result of female wiles, my name ain't Clyde Rasmussen."

"I've been wondering about her," Godwin said. "Sometimes I think I've got her number—"

Hood said: "Really, old boy, you only met her yesterday."

"But she grows on you real quick," Godwin said.

"Rodger," Clyde said, "you're gonna find out she's the quickest little grower-onner you ever did see. World class."

Hood was laughing. "You two! She's a child! Just a very sweet child growing up in a world of adults." He was shaking his head. "You two make her sound like Kiki!"

"No, that's not possible," Godwin said, beginning to laugh at himself. "Because as we all know Clothilde is Kiki."

"Damn!" Clyde slapped him on the back. "Ain't it great? Ain't life just great? What a day, what a day!"

The courtyard door swung open upon this scene of hilarity, creaking on its hinges.

She stood smiling at them.

She was holding a camera.

"Look handsome," she said.

Godwin thought: She is the most beautiful thing I have ever seen. Better than the Medici Fountain.

Click.

CHAPTER 13

Godwin wanted to swing past the office to check for any Saturday evening assignment Swaine might have dreamed up for him. Clyde and Colonel Hood went with him just to see the offices of the Paris *Herald* which Godwin assured them were nothing special. But it was a warm Saturday afternoon and Paris smelled of chestnut trees and flowers.

In the office the windows were thrown wide open and great black oscillating fans blew hot air back and forth across the half-deserted newsroom. The man working the rewrite desk was not the Thurber fellow, and Godwin doubted that he ever would be.

Swaine's office was at the far end of the cavernous room. The door was open and through the pebble glass wall Swaine's shadow was pacing back and forth. A few typewriters clattered away. A couple of reporters with sleeve garters stared out the window and smoked cigarettes and wished they were at Saint-Cloud for the doubles championship.

"Come on," Godwin said. "Meet my boss."

When he stuck his head in the open doorway Swaine was standing by the window, a thick, stumpy figure, round-shouldered, wearing his vest, tie pulled askew from an old collar that was coming loose from the shirt. He was talking on the telephone.

"Merle Swaine doesn't give a good goddamn, Hercule. You got that, boy? I've got five hundred dollars American that says he'll make it." He nodded impatiently at the telephone and motioned Godwin to come in, raising his eyebrows as the other two men followed. "That's right, you fornicating Frog *imbécile!* Merle Swaine is good for it, always has been, always will be. Merle Swaine only bets on a sure thing! What? *Oui, oui,*

oui, you miserable little man. *Couchon!*" He laughed abruptly. "And the same to you, Hercule!" He slammed the earpiece back into the pronged cradle and looked at his guests. "My Paris bookie. Five hundred simoleons at ten-to-three. I've got a lock on five grand. The first rule of wagering on games of chance is to remove the chance. That's what screws up every sound wager—chance! Go for the sure thing. That's Merle Swaine's rule. Who the hell are these bozos, Godwin?"

Godwin introduced them and Swaine's lower lip jutted out and he nodded appreciatively. "Well, let me down slowly, Mother! Rasmussen, I feel like I know you already. Young Godwin here has, against all the laws of probability, turned out to be a writer—and he has written something fairly decent about you." He presented his guests with a dour smile. "What did you think of it?"

"Lordy," Clyde said, determinedly doing his hayseed routine, all but shuffling his feet. "I didn't read it. Old Rodger's just a trustworthy sorta fella. I put myself in his hands. Long as he spells my name right."

"And Colonel Max Hood—Merle Swaine's proud to shake the hand of the man who—"

"Pleased to meet you, as well, old man. You're a wagering man—tell me, is it horseflesh?"

"Not this time, Colonel." Sweat was running down Swaine's face, his shirt was damp and clung to his rounded shoulders. He brushed the lank gray hair off his forehead. "I put down my sou or two on the tide of history." He smiled slyly.

"You don't say. You must have considerable foresight."

"Merle Swaine will ride the tide of history—because if you don't ride it, you will be swept away by it, swept away without a trace left behind."

"What the hell are these fellas talking about?" Clyde was grinning.

"Mr. C. A. Lindbergh, otherwise known as the Tide of History. Which is, of course, air travel. I was telling Godwin the other day— actually I was screaming at you, wasn't I, Rodger?—I was telling him that C. A. Lindbergh was going to make it. And he is, he's coming."

"Ah, the flyer," Colonel said. "Do you have word of him?"

"You feel a kinship, do you, Colonel?" Swaine eyed him carefully. "Out there alone in the night sky, must be a little like the desert, makes a man feel very small and pretty damn lonely."

"You're not alone out there," Hood said. "You've got the desert and your camel." He smiled, tight-lipped. "Mr. Lindbergh has the night sky and his plane and the stars. No, he isn't alone. He's someplace else alto-gether. Outside of time—I know, I've been there. And you're not alone."

"Well, alone or not, they've sighted him! I got the cables, they started coming in this morning and this one just got here." He waved the sheets of cable paper. "He's made landfall in Ireland! They've spotted him over Valentia, Ireland . . . hell, he's made it—it's just a matter of steering now! And Lloyd's is still quoting ten-to-three against his making it to Paris! Can you believe it? Jesus H. Christ, they *deserve* to lose their shirts!" He went to a map spread out across his long table. He rapped a forefinger on a dot. "Valentia here." With his other forefinger he reached out, tapping Paris. "Paris here. A lousy six hundred miles. If he's got the fuel . . . well, he's a cinch, Colonel. Hundred miles an hour." He pulled out his pocket watch and unsnapped the lid. "It's four o'clock. He'll be here about ten o'clock. Do you boys drink scotch whiskey? Come on, pull up chairs and join me in a toast to C. A. Lindbergh of Minnesota. We'll get word as he flies the length of England. He should cross from right about here." He pointed at Plymouth. "Godwin, see if you can make that goddamn fan work, willya? I'm about to have a touch of the vapors."

Godwin followed the cord. "It's unplugged, sir."

"Well, Jesus, sonny, plug it in and have a drink. The tide of history is rising beneath us. We must be ready!" He grinned and stuck a cigarette to his lower lip. "Rich, gentlemen. I'm going to be rich . . ."

At six o'clock a cable came through.

Lindbergh had been seen over Plymouth, heading out across the Channel toward Cherbourg, toward France.

They had done justice to the bottle of scotch.

"Time we were going," Swaine said. He stood up, pushed his squeaky swivel chair back against the windowsill.

"Whoa there, Bessie," Clyde said. "Hold on—where are we going? I got a nightclub dependin' on me tonight."

"Not you," Swaine barked, buttoning his vest, rolling down his shirt sleeves. "Don't mean to be brutal but the last thing I need is a cornet player. Godwin, you ready to roll?"

"Am I ready for what?"

"Like I been telling you, the biggest damn story of your life. The story of the century! C. A. Lindbergh is on his way to Le Bourget and so are we! He oughta set that baby down in about four hours—we want to be out there in plenty of time. You want to join us, Colonel?"

"My pleasure," he said.

"All right then." Swaine went to the doorway. "Mallory! Get us a couple of taxis. You and Philpot take one and see if you can get him to remember his camera! Destination Le Bourget. Dickens, you stay here for rewrite and work the wires. Make sure we get time on them. Godwin and I will be back if we can, otherwise we'll telephone. Keep the lines clear. We've got to get the story for ourselves but we've got to get it to New York first."

"Press Wireless Service? Western Union Cable?"

"Yeah, both of 'em. And Mallory, I want you to do an end run and use Commercial Cable, maybe nobody else will think of that. Now get those taxis!"

They clambered out of the office, down the stairs, and into the street where Mallory had hailed two large noisy taxis. Philpot was there with his cameras.

"What wrecks," Swaine muttered. "The Taxis of the fucking Marne! Get in, get in, we want to get there, get set up, get a good seat. I want to get a good look at this bird. Bird? Now that's a good one. Kind of Lindbergh dropping out of the sky, a bird."

It was stifling in the backseat. Hood shifted against the door and yanked the window down. Swaine mopped his brow. "Step on it," he shouted to the driver, who shrugged expressively and moved off into traffic.

They crossed the Porte de la Villette and ran smack into a solid mass of vehicles. Godwin swung the door open, climbed onto the running board. The two-lane road to Le Bourget had disappeared, as if it had been replaced by a peculiarly long, narrow parking lot. As far as he could see, cars bumper to bumper, only infrequently lurching forward, then grinding, Klaxons sounding, to a halt. The word on Lindbergh was out. Cars, trucks, three-wheeled motorcarts. It was four miles to the little ramshackled airfield that served Paris. So far as Godwin could tell it might just as well have been four thousand miles.

"Hell's bells," Swaine said.

"I didn't know there were this many cars in Paris," Hood said.

"Maybe it'll ease up. Maybe there's an accident up ahead—"

Swaine looked at Godwin. "Ah, you've got a helluva lot to learn, rookie. When you speak, the voice of goddamn youthful optimism. Always remember, accident or not, it never, ever gets easier up ahead. We call that life, sonny. It's always worse up ahead. You listen to Merle Swaine." He sighed, wiped his face. Dispensing wisdom was hot work. "Jesus, we might as well wait it out for a while." He didn't sound hopeful. "Sunny Jim, you stay out on the running board and keep an eye peeled." His collar had wilted like a piece of lettuce.

Two hours of waiting and they had advanced about two miles. The crowd milling around the cars was constantly growing.

Colonel Hood had had enough. "Let me tell you what T. E. Lawrence once said to me, Mr. Swaine. We were looking out across approximately four million miles of burning desert sand."

"Migod," Swaine said.

"He fixed me with those eyes of his, you know about Lawrence's eyes, I suppose—"

"I met him once here in Paris after the war when he came to talk to that commission. I'll never forget those eyes, never . . . Y'know, I had no idea until then he was such a little squirt, only came up to about here—"

"Small of stature," Hood said, "but he was no squirt, Mr. Swaine."

The Klaxons were howling, impatience boiling over, men wandering along the roadside with bottles of wine.

"No disrespect, I assure you. Just surprised me, his size. So what did he say to you, looking out across all that burning sand?"

"To any mortal man, the desert was impassable. It was hopeless. And he fixed me with those eyes and he said, Max, let's go for a walk. And we did. We walked across the desert."

"Let's go for a walk," Swaine repeated in hushed tones. "I'm not sure I get what you mean, Colonel . . ."

"Let's go for a walk, man," Hood said, getting out of the taxi. "Pay the driver and let's go for a walk. That is, if you want to get to Le Bourget before C. A. Lindbergh does. Come on, Godwin, old chap, we're going overland."

Thousands of people had the same idea, pouring like a human wave toward the airfield, much as if they were Swaine's tide of history. Godwin had never seen so many people, crowding and pushing and yelling and laughing, like a vast population setting off on their annual holiday at precisely the same moment. By the time they got to the airfield another hour had passed. It was just after nine o'clock. The next day Godwin learned that the police had estimated the crowd at half a million and he didn't doubt it. Being in it, struggling against it, you couldn't see anything like the whole of it, but it was a mess, a hot, sticky, unruly mess. The *gendarmerie* was out in force with *batons* ready, joining in the shouting and pushing, trying vainly to control the ebb and flow, finally being swept aside by its rush. In the end, when a kind of panic was bubbling in his guts, he saw the soldiers surging from the side of the airport devoted to the military. They came on the double, bayonets fixed, and for a moment held the crowd at bay as it began to leak across the grass airstrip where the *Spirit of St. Louis* would be landing.

Swaine was puffing and bedraggled, waving his press credentials at the guards cordoning off the oversize hut that was the terminal. They were grudgingly shoved on through the doorway into a packed, smoke-filled, overheated room that was noisier than the madness boiling over outside. Swaine bulled his way with a fine indifference to wounding his fellow man and fetched up at the bar which was manned by a couple of angry types dispensing carafes of *vin ordinaire* and sandwiches. Isadora Duncan was drinking champagne and talking to Shirer of the *Tribune.* Swaine stopped to ask Shirer what the hell a sportswriter was doing covering a real story and Shirer said a man did not live by Bill Tilden alone and then they got to talking about the Yankees and Babe Ruth and things back in the States and Swaine bragged about his bet on Lindbergh.

It was almost dark outside and everybody was jumpy, running to peer into the sky whenever a plane was heard. The floodlights outlining the runway would come on. But it wasn't Lindbergh, only a military craft coming back from patrol.

Mallory had arrived, leaving Philpot at the edge of the grass landing strip with three cameras slung around his neck. Mallory, a man of forty with bushy hair and a worried expression, was shaking his head. "No word for hours, boss. Y'know what I think? I think we're getting bullshat, that's what I think. It's Nungesser and Coli all over again. False reports. Lindbergh's probably asleep in the deep right now . . . I hate to say it but that's the way it looks."

Swaine said: "Mallory, so help me God, you're an idiot! Merle B. Swaine's savings are on C. A. Lindbergh's nose. Merle B. Swaine has a sure thing. The issue is not in doubt. Merle B. Swaine cannot, repeat cannot, afford to lose."

Mallory cast a baleful glance at Godwin and Hood.

Having left the terminal, they were pushing their way through the crowd, then standing at the edge of the strip.

Suddenly the crowd began to quiet down. The sound of yet another airplane in the navy blue, almost black, darkness above. The floodlights flicked on. The beam of a searchlight poked into the darkness, wavering, searching for the sound. Someone gasped nearby. "There! There it is! My God, what a tiny plane!"

It swooped in a great arc, reflecting like a floating silver coin in the finger of light, lower, lower, banking slowly, coming in over the trees at the far end of the runway, Swaine's fingers were crossed, then it was gracefully setting down between the rows of hissing, smoking floodlights.

The crowd started surging onto the runway while the plane was still a hundred yards away. The *Spirit of St. Louis* was bearing down on them. They waved, cheered, screamed, and Godwin began moving with them, felt a viselike grip on his arm. Flashbulbs were beginning to pop like firecrackers. Godwin turned. It was Colonel Hood. "Be careful," he shouted. "The propeller could turn you to mince . . . these fools, they could be killed."

"But he sees them, he'll stop the plane."

"He can't," Hood said. "There are no brakes on planes. It's not like a car. It has to roll to a stop."

Godwin spotted Philpot with Swaine and Mallory, edging toward the center of the field.

Men were running wildly toward the plane, toward the flashing propeller.

Miraculously the propeller cut out in time and the small silver craft rolled to a halt within ten yards of Godwin and Hood. The crowd had reached the plane, was swarming over it like locusts, plucking, picking, rampaging past the soldiers and *gendarmes*. Chaos.

Finally Lindbergh stuck his head out of the cockpit's side window, beneath the wing. His hair was mussed and he was grinning, surprised, stunned by the reception.

The images in Godwin's head began blurring together, he was having trouble keeping it all straight, the noise, the lights, the urgency of the crowd's excitement, the boyish face in the light.

Swaine had been right about everything and Godwin hadn't quite believed him. Lindbergh had made it. It was the story of the century.

The long night of the flyer's arrival had just begun. There had never been anything quite like it before. But the moment, the shred of time, that stuck in Godwin's mind for the rest of his life was not of Lindbergh but of Colonel Max Hood.

From the corner of his eye Godwin saw him smiling and turned to face him.

Colonel Hood was smiling at Lindbergh as if it were a private communication that crossed over the heads of the screaming, leaping, totally insane crowd. The smile seemed to be directed into the brain, into the essential nature of the man Lindbergh.

And there were tears streaming slowly down Hood's face.

Godwin must have looked curious, for Hood turned to him and said: "It's something about a hero, old boy, just something about a hero."

Years later Godwin said that many different accounts of Lindbergh's arrival had been written and, speaking as an eyewitness, so far as he could tell they were all accurate. Anything could have happened and most of it probably did that night at Le Bourget. The half million on hand were unruly and confused and jubilant and Lindbergh was lucky to get out of it alive and with his little plane more or less intact. There was a curious comic opera turn when a young man by the name of Wheeler was unwillingly escorted to Ambassador Herrick, who was on hand to receive him. Herrick insisted that the young man was Lindbergh but the fellow was adamant about his identity. Harry Wheeler, he kept insisting was his name. Herrick was finally convinced, but if Wheeler was Wheeler, where was Lindbergh?

Escorted to another hangar by an armed guard, Lindbergh had been swept away to safety.

By eleven o'clock Swaine was anxious to get back to Paris and start filing their stories. The transportation situation was impossible. Half a million people had to get back to town. Swaine hated it but they had to set out on foot. In the event, a taxi was found about two miles from Le Bourget. Swaine peeled off a thousand francs, waved them at the driver with the message that speed was everything.

Miraculously they were back in Paris at the office by midnight. Colonel Hood volunteered to take a thermos to the corner café for coffee. Swaine took Godwin's arm. "When Mallory gets here, *if* Mallory gets here, he's going to write a factual sidebar, hours of the flight compared to weeks taken by the Pilgrims, shit like that. And maybe some human interest stuff, the traffic jam in terms of numbers and cop interviews. I'm going to do the lead straight news piece. You—sonny, I want you to write about *what it was like.* Y'understand? How it felt, what you were thinking, what the sandwiches tasted like, seeing Isadora Duncan, those crazy bastards running right at the goddamn propeller, the Wheeler kid, the look on Lindbergh's face—it's the kind of bullshit you've got a gift for. We'll use it here in Paris and Dickens will feed it on to New York and they'll probably use it too. You've got about half an hour . . . and look, kid, give it all you've got. You'll never get another chance like this."

Up until last night at 10:24 it had often been said that Paris, the City of Light, belonged to the world.

Now it belongs to a tousle-haired, lanky young Minnesotan with an infectious grin and the guts of a human cannonball. And he, my friends, belongs to the ages. They used to sing that the Yanks were coming, the Yanks were coming. . . . Well, one Yank is here and there's never been anything quite like him. They gave us the Statue of Liberty. Now we've

`repaid them with interest. Believe me, I know, I`
`was there.`

That was the lead to Rodger Godwin's Lindbergh piece. Swaine was right again, of course. It put him on the map, journalistically speaking. When it appeared in New York, as well as in Paris, he became a name to be reckoned with. Honan and Marshall Hacker smacked their lips; they were on the scene, they could get to him first. And when the same byline appeared for a piece about another midwesterner, the one whose music had captured Paris, then Clyde Rasmussen's name was on the lips that counted, as well.

Swaine read the Lindbergh piece as it was going out on the wire and couldn't stifle a grin. It could have been pride at having picked another winner but he'd never have admitted it. What he said was: "This will be read by millions of people." He let that much sink in. "It will set you on the road to fame." He paused again. "Try not to be a complete asshole about it."

It was one-thirty when Swaine shooed them out of the *Herald*'s offices. Swaine was waiting for Mallory, who had come in with Philpot, written the sidebar, and gone back out to Ambassador Herrick's place in the Place d'Iene where Lindbergh was sequestered. Philpot struggled along in his wake, having dropped off his film with Swaine personally. "You've done a fair day's work," Swaine said to Godwin. "Listen to them in the streets—you might as well go out and join them. It'll go on all night. Migod, think of it! Five thousand bucks! Gentlemen," he said with a dismissive wave, "Merle Swaine thanks you for joining him on this day of days. Off with you. Merle Swaine will be at the helm through the watches of the night. There is nothing to fear."

After leaving him, Godwin and Hood strolled aimlessly, unwinding, not talking much, listening to the celebrants making the rounds after straggling back from Le Bourget, watching them drinking and horsing around in the bars of Montparnasse. The Dingo was overflowing but Hood suggested they crowd in for a cognac. Then they moved on past the street washers and the flower girls going home, the cheap jewelry merchants. The man who stood on the corner chewed bits of broken glass for tips. There was pink foam in the corners of his mouth.

Godwin said: "He's a German. I interviewed him. He said eating glass is his life."

They moved off the busy main thoroughfares and found a deserted café, still open, a puddle of light in the darkness. A few wirebacked chairs on the sidewalk, the coffee machine hissing inside and clouds of steam rising past the wooden rack of cigarettes, the counterman with weary eyes. You could smell the fresh, hot croissants he was baking for the morning trade only a few hours away. They sank into chairs and ordered coffee and two plates of croissants and jam made of *framboise*. The rolls were hot enough to burn your fingers, flaky, butter melting. They ate them like doughnuts. Godwin was bone weary, yawned mightily, but the coffee was bringing him back to life. Colonel Hood lit a cigarette and leaned back in the chair. "A day to remember," he said.

"Tennis, the Medici Fountain, Cilla making us coffee, Cilla and her ice cream, the good scotch in Swaine's office—"

"What did you call her?" Hood watched him through the smoke.

"Oh—Cilla. She said that she doesn't much care for Prissy or Priss or Priscilla . . . she thought Cilla was a pretty good version of her given name. I'd appreciate your not mentioning it. It might embarrass her."

"Don't worry. I like her very much and she's had rather a bad time of it with Mummy and Daddy, one way and another. Particularly Mummy. She's taken quite a shine to you. I'm very glad of that—you seem a decent sort of a chap. She's a lonely creature. She's got me and Clyde but—well, she needs friends. She's caught at that awkward age, no longer a child in every way but certainly not a woman. Her mother either ignores her entirely or sets a very bad example. Her father, a good enough chap, mind you, is a rather weak man who would not be much noticed at all were it not for his definitely gaudy wife. She's made him a mess, y'know. She has robbed him of his masculinity. He has responded to her provocations by becoming a chaser of women, a client of every manner of prostitute, all in the attempt—one must assume—to convince himself that he is still a man. Somewhere along the way his search for self-respect is going to kill him." He sighed softly, his cool gray eyes opaque, impenetrable. A hero's eyes, Godwin supposed, giving away little. Had Hood's face and eyes ever been boyish like Lindbergh's? Had he ever known anything like the joy they glimpsed on the pilot's face as he'd peered from the cockpit? Maybe not. Maybe that was what had brought him to tears. "Priscilla works so hard at making the best of things. She wants to be happy, she wants to make everyone else happy. As you can imagine, it's very hard work. So . . . I'm glad you like her. You do like her?"

"Yes. There's something about her—how could anyone not like her? She makes herself so vulnerable. It's that she tries so hard. It makes your heart go out to her."

"Exactly. You are to be congratulated on your sensitivity." He sipped the last of his coffee. "It's odd but . . . well, this is indeed late-night talk, isn't it? I was about to say it's odd but sometimes I half think I love her. I'm a fool, of course. Comes from an underdeveloped set of emotions, I daresay."

"Well, you will have to wait a while, won't you?"

"The waiting is no problem. I'm a very patient man. The hard part will come when the waiting's done and it's time for action, time to declare myself . . . then it's a question of nerve, isn't it? When the time has come to act it's always a question of nerve."

"Surely nerve is no problem for you."

"Your friend Merle B. Swaine was right. You have all the optimism of youth. The reality, of course, is that I can have all the nerve in the world and it won't make her say yes."

Godwin was somewhat surprised by his own ease in the face of what Hood was saying. It didn't seem all that peculiar to be discussing her in such terms, even though she was only fourteen years old. Maybe it was just that Hood was giving voice to the thoughts that had been poking around in Godwin's mind since he'd met the girl. Of course Hood knew her, really knew her, and they were a couple of fellas sitting around in the middle of the night talking about a beautiful woman. Young girl, that was.

Oh well, it was just middle of the night talk anyway.

Didn't mean a damn thing.

They were friends rather than acquaintances when they left the little café on the dark, quiet street smelling of coffee and hot croissants. A night breeze played in the trees, whispering like a gossip among the leaves. They were friends suddenly, despite the difference in their ages: Hood had to be in his mid-thirties, maybe even thirty-six or thirty-seven. Fourteen or fifteen years Godwin's senior. Yet he could feel it, they were friends.

That was what talking about women could do for you. It was something you shared with another man. War stories. Woman stories. They drew men together. He supposed that ought to tell you something but he didn't want to think of it that way. And, anyway, he didn't know a damn thing about women. Everybody seemed to think he was full of youthful optimism and maybe he was, maybe they were absolutely right. But he knew for sure there could not possibly be anything on earth less like a war than Cilla DewBrittain.

They had passed the turning that would have taken Hood to his house but he'd shaken his head, said he wasn't ready to go home just yet.

Godwin saw the horse butcher's shop with the green-and-white awning and the gold horse's head and remembered the night before, the beating. "You wouldn't believe what I saw right here last night—"

Hood put his finger to his lips. "Wait, listen . . ."

Godwin heard nothing.

Hood moved quickly around the corner, into the shadows by the trash bin. Godwin followed him into the shadows along the wall. Something skittered away; a cat was flushed out into the narrow street where it stopped and stared back at them, slowly, insolently licking its paw. A faint yellowish light burned deep in the alley across the way. The cat sauntered toward it, peeked in, then disappeared.

There was a strangled cry, more of a moan, a sob.

Hood nodded toward the entrance to the alleyway. "Stay over here in the shadows," he whispered. "Somebody's getting killed in that alley."

"What are you talking about?"

"You can tell by the sound. It's a wet sound. It's dying."

They moved on, drew opposite the alley.

At the back of the narrow cobblestoned cul-de-sac, the walls narrowed and buckled as if they might collapse inward at any moment. Two men with clubs, *batons*, were beating what seemed to be a lump of old clothes huddled on the stones. It was methodical, the thick thudding of the *batons* pounding on the fallen figure. The moaning had stopped but the two men kept hammering away as if they were engines and couldn't stop, had to keep hammering. They kept at it until they sagged back against the wall, exhausted.

Godwin whispered: "We've got to stop them."

"No."

"We've got to!"

"It's too late. Be quiet."

The taller of the two men prodded the lump with his boot, then kicked savagely, and the other man laughed.

"Jesus. I know them."

"So do I," Hood said. "Just wait."

"We've got to help him." Godwin's mouth was so dry he could barely form the words. He could taste bile, felt his stomach churning. "We can't let them—"

"Do be quiet."

The two men turned away from the lifeless lump and carefully placed the high round hats with the short visors squarely on their heads. They straightened their uniforms, shadowmen in the dim, half-light of the alleyway. Quite calmly they walked away from the body to the intersection with the street. They gave their hats a final squaring. The light from the corner fell softly across their faces. Sweat glistened. One head was massive, like an Olmec sculpture, and the man wiped his face with a wrinkled

handkerchief. His arms were too long, like a gorilla's. The other man was
shorter, stocky and wide. Godwin was staring from the shadows into
the face of the man with the huge head. Eyebrows like crowbars, deepset
eyes.

"It's Henri," Godwin whispered.

"And Jacques. Coppers." Hood sounded as if the sadness of man's
condition was for the moment overwhelming him.

The two *flics* stood in the alley entrance, casting casual glances up
and down the narrow street. Behind them the cat had begun an inspection
of the pile of rags at the back of the alley.

"We can't let them just walk away—"

Hood said nothing, shook his head.

What was going on? What kind of hero was this guy? Godwin started
to move forward but Hood's grip held him back.

Henri and Jacques turned and walked up past the horse butcher's
shop, their shadows stretching the length of the street. At the corner they
turned and were gone.

"We had them red-handed, caught in the act—"

"You've got to stay calm. Let's take a look at the victim."

"Stay *calm?*" Godwin's knees were shaking.

The lump of clothes wasn't moving. The cat had gone a few feet away
and was staring back at them.

Godwin tripped over something, caught himself against the wall. He
looked down. The peg leg with the wheel on the end lay at his feet. He'd
gotten entangled in the harness.

Hood was kneeling beside the body. He looked up as Godwin approached. "Mind the blood. The cat stepped in it. See, little footprints . . ." The cat was licking a paw. "I don't think you want to look
too closely here, old boy."

"He's dead."

Hood nodded.

Godwin leaned down, had trouble making out what he was seeing.
Then he saw an eye in a dark puddle near the wall. He staggered back,
feeling faint. The alley was spinning. He got four or five feet away, pressed
his forehead against the rough wall and vomited.

Hood took his arm, led him back to the street.

"Why would they . . ." Godwin heard himself croaking. The taste in
his mouth was disgusting. Scotch and wine and ham and coffee. "Just
because . . . he wouldn't pay them off?" He was gulping fresh air, felt a
cool breeze that saved him.

"They killed him for sport," Hood said softly. "Are you all right?"

"Sport?"

"Or for practice."

"Christ, we should have done something!" Godwin felt hot tears of rage, wiped his eyes roughly, angrily. He straightened up and swallowed hard. "Why didn't you—"

"They might have killed us. I've seen it often enough. Blood lust. They were in a killing mood. We weren't. They were drunk with it."

"Jesus, don't you care?"

"I've seen a lot of men killing and a lot of men dying. Killing feeds on itself. They were doped up on killing . . ."

Godwin yanked away from Hood.

"I know all about it, old man. It's the sort of thing you have to learn. You've got to keep your emotions under control. Watch. Wait. Be patient."

"You did nothing! You—*you* could have done something! How the hell can you live with yourself!"

Hood—surprisingly—laughed, a brittle sound in the stillness. "Sometimes I wonder. Now come on."

Godwin staggered forward. His head was spinning, his balance was going. Out of control, smelling himself and the soiled stench of the corpse's greasy, bloody clothing, knowing he was going to vomit again soon, he took a roundhouse swing at Hood. "Bastard!" He fell. He looked up. What did he think he was doing?

Hood was lifting him up. "Come on, laddie. It's all over. You'll be all right. You're not cut out for this sort of thing. So forget it. Just forget it."

"Some goddamn hero you are!"

Hood laughed again from far away.

"Come on, puss," Hood called over his shoulder. "Puss, puss, come on, kitty . . ."

Hood and Godwin and the cat with the bloody paws set off up the quiet street.

The next day Godwin turned the murder into a piece of journalism. He titled it "Acquiring a Pet the Hard Way." It ran in America but Swaine said it was too close to the fire for Paris. Swaine said: "I run that story and the next thing you know, you wake up dead in the same alley."

Years later, when it was published in the first volume of the *Paris Trilogy*, Ernest Hemingway, whom he'd never known at all well, wrote him a very brief note: "*The thing about the cat with the bloody feet isn't too bad. Too often you over-write. Stay away from the adjectives and the adverbs. If the cat is still alive, give him a sardine from Ernie.*" He didn't bother to sign it.

CHAPTER 14

Following the night he witnessed the murder of the crippled vendor, Rodger Godwin learned about the taste of ashes. The glorious, thrilling night of Lindbergh's arrival, the race to the aerodrome and the way the plane had swooped out of the night and come in above the stand of trees, the frantic dash back to Paris and the office, pounding out the story at top speed and under pressure, relaxing at the little out-of-the-way café with Max Hood: it all turned to ashes with the murder and the taste was bitter and foul, the joy and pleasure of the night ruined forever. Unlike the fabled phoenix, the glories of the night were not about to rise anew.

And it wasn't only the murder that Godwin was trying—with a marked lack of success—to forget. Equally unsettling in a rather subtler sense was Max Hood's refusal to take action against the killers, the two *flics*. It was another new experience for Godwin: disillusionment with a hero's behavior. In the first place, he'd never come within hailing distance of a hero of any kind before, certainly not a hero of the Great War who had been with Lawrence in the desert. In the second place, although he had no idea just what Hood should actually have done that night, he had been shocked by the hero's lack of involvement in what they had watched. Max Hood was a cold fish. That was what it came down to.

So Godwin tried to lose himself in his new work, dashing about Paris with the *Herald*'s imprimatur giving him access for interviews, lingering in the shadows of the great city watching and thinking about how he might capture it on paper, observing his friends and storing away bits and pieces of their lives for future reference. He was eavesdropping on life: He couldn't keep from hearing and seeing and building his inventory. Like a shopkeeper, he needed his inventory, stories to tell.

Years later, however, it was neither Lindbergh nor the murder of the vendor that he remembered about that day. Rather it was the ice cream they all had as they traipsed about Paris with Priscilla DewBrittain, it was the three of them—Hood and Clyde and Godwin—standing in the street outside the courtyard door when it swung open and she was snapping them with her little camera; it was sitting at the little café in the middle of the night with the smell of strong coffee and fresh baking bread and Max Hood admitting that damned if he wasn't half in love with that girl Prissy, just fourteen years old. They were good memories and in time they drove out the bad, which was enough to make you thankful for small blessings.

What he remembered perhaps most of all was the radiance of the girl's smile, the half-nervous, half-hopeful glitter in her huge dark eyes, the way her mouth would quiver or curl up at the ends, revealing her inner self in an instant, how vulnerable she was yet how she controlled all of them, controlled their actions and their moods and at times their lives, all of them, as if she'd set them spinning and then she had had to keep them going, like the plates twirling feverishly atop the slender poles in the old circus trick.

As the warm weather settled over Paris for good that summer, she took to serving afternoon tea in the garden courtyard. She was the woman of the house for her father, dependable and calm and reassuring, a welcome relief for DewBrittain who, according to Max Hood, was accustomed to being victimized and tormented and humiliated by his wife who was apparently content to remain absent. There was, at least superficially, nothing in the daughter to remind the father of the mother, and DewBrittain seemed to flourish under the girl's attentions. She took all of her responsibilities very seriously. She took everything very seriously. Playing tennis with Godwin and Hood whom she pestered for lessons and which he willingly gave; her violin lessons, the long discussions with Clyde about music . . . everything.

But it was Clothilde, not Priscilla DewBrittain, who occupied the forefront of Godwin's thoughts. He was in love for the first time, and even the unique complexities involved in loving Clothilde in particular were enchanting, not quite real. For instance, her job, which continued to bedevil him when he let himself think about it. He made sure he didn't burst up the stairway to her place unexpectedly: he didn't want to risk meeting another client, let alone Tony DewBrittain in a state of passion. The job aside, however, Clothilde was taking on new dimensions the longer he knew her. She remained elusive about much of her past, particularly the cross cut into her cheek, but her present held surprises of its own. She really was a promising young dancer and her small, breathless, very French voice possessed a timbre he'd never heard before. She had talent.

She also knew a hell of a lot more about life than Godwin despite being three or four years his junior. He smiled at her all the time. She kept him from taking his sudden success too seriously. She was better at that than Swaine, yet he never minded. She was a blessing. When he told her he loved her she giggled, and when he touched the cross on her cheek she shut her eyes and turned away and grew still, mute. And she too, like Godwin, had become fascinated with Priscilla and her life in the big house tucked behind the wall, beneath the huge chestnut trees.

Priscilla had warmed to Clothilde, too, made a point of inviting her to the house for tea or coffee when the two of them could be alone and talk. Priscilla was very discreet but couldn't help asking questions about a subject that was beginning to dominate her imagination. Men. She asked about Clyde and Godwin and any other men Clothilde had ever known. She never hinted that she knew Clothilde was a prostitute. Clothilde doubted if she actually knew. It was just that Clothilde was young enough to talk to and old enough to have done some practical research into the subject at hand.

When Clothilde told Godwin about one of her early chats with Priscilla they were sitting on the terrace at Le Dome drinking coffee late one afternoon, watching the passing parade. Godwin had written all night, gotten up a little after noon, and had spent the balance of the past few hours with Swaine at the office. He interrupted Clothilde's story with a shake of his head. "Wait a minute—I hope you don't start revealing intimate little secrets about us. And by that I mean *me*. Tell her whatever you want about yourself, but leave me out of it. Fella likes to have his little secrets." He grinned at her over the top of the newspaper he'd been scouring for the latest baseball scores from the States. Lindbergh wasn't dominating the papers quite so thoroughly of late and it was a relief to get back to wondering how the Cubs and Yankees and Red Sox were doing.

"You wish to have secrets from little Priscilla? Why is that? You are so silly! What do you think I would tell her?" She was teasing him about sex and he enjoyed it. "You should be ashamed of yourself! Truly, my sweet! And I must say, she adores you—simply adores you."

"Oh, come on," he said, remembered the way the girl had said *Cilla Godwin*, and was flattered by the memory. "Kids go through these phases. A crush. Just leave me out of it."

"But I like her so much," Clothilde said. "Am I foolish to feel sorry for her, too?"

"I don't know, I've felt the same way sometimes . . . I think maybe she wants us to feel that way. It's crazy, my feeling that way about a kid . . . but I wonder, the way we all think about her and do what she wants." He shrugged. "Okay, so I'm nuts. But she has some funny quality . . ."

"Men always romanticize women, even very young women." She laughed softly. "Especially very young ones."

"Young? You're practically a kid yourself."

"That's how I know, you silly boy."

"And listen to us—what are we talking about? Priscilla . . . Cilla . . ."

"She's lonely, Rodger. She has no older woman to speak with . . . no one to learn from. She turns to me. It is natural."

"Older? You're barely five years older than she is, and you didn't have a mother to turn to anyway. Where is her mother? Does anybody know?"

"You mustn't confuse the two of us, Clothilde and little Priscilla. I am very different. I hardly noticed a mother was missing because everything else was missing as well. And I only had one way to start filling up the nothingness so that's what I did. Now this one, our Cilla—yes, she told me about her idea for a name, pain of death if I reveal it to anyone— she has everything, at least everything money can buy. And some of the things money cannot buy, things that come only from God . . . she's going to be stunningly beautiful someday—"

"From where I'm sitting on Tuesday it looks to me like Thursday is the day—"

"Be careful, you make me jealous."

"Her beauty is not exactly a secret." He signaled to the waiter for another coffee. The stack of saucers grew.

"And she has the great talent for the violin. And she is very brainy, in case you hadn't noticed."

"And she's fond of ice cream, tennis, and flirting with a bunch of grown men. A hoyden."

"She flirts, it is true. Do you understand why?"

"I have the feeling you don't think I do—"

"She wants desperately to be grown up. She *needs* to be grown up, she needs someone to help her . . . her father is not much good to her . . . when she began her monthly time, her period, she told me how frightened she was—you can imagine, she felt so alone. She has no one to guide her and hug her, she's trying so hard to understand it all by herself . . . so she asks me questions about life, about men, about you and Max Hood and Clyde—"

"Tell me, does she know about you and her father?"

"Certainly not. Sometimes you are such an idiot! She is not ready for that kind of serious disillusionment. She does not yet know that the story of men is the story of disillusionment."

"No kidding. Well, maybe you should sort of just let that dawn on her slowly."

"Perhaps she will never have to learn. One must never give up hope. But she is curious about life. Who can blame her?"

"Agreed. So what's the story with this mother, Lady What's-her-name?"

"I don't know much but her mother has what Tony calls 'a gaudy and shocking history which she takes great pains to cultivate.' Little Cilla doesn't know if she's expected to be just like her mother . . . glamorous and quite bad . . . and she has a difficult time playing that role. She doesn't really understand any of it, least of all what's expected of her. So there she is, the center of Tony's life, trying to take her mother's place one way or another, trying to shield her father's feelings—"

"Aw hell," Godwin said with a sigh, "I still think she's rigged it so she's the center of all of our lives . . ." But, of course, he didn't know any more about it than anyone else and didn't feel anything like as tough as he was trying to sound. Later it occurred to him that, for the first time, he might have been striking a pose. Much later he knew that one pose or another had become his career, had grown to define what he'd become. When the ad boys got into it, they called it an image. Whatever they called it, it was just the way things worked.

All those reflections came a good deal later on. At the time the fact was they were all just a bunch of kids riding on top of the most remarkable bubble, quite unaware that it was bound to burst at any moment. Later Godwin would write about all of that, how Hitler was already at work dispensing his poison and the Crash of '29 was just about to come down and bring the planet to its knees. The boom was already pretty much gorged at the trough. But it was tough to see the downside with Lindbergh and Babe Ruth and with Merle B. Swaine giving you the chance of a lifetime.

Clothilde was also worried about Clyde Rasmussen. Her early life had been so difficult, so brutal, that she might understandably have gone either way herself. Mistreated by a variety of monsters, it would have surprised no one had she become a monster herself. Godwin thought it was reasonable evidence that there was indeed a God.

When she wasn't trying to be mother and older sister to Priscilla DewBrittain, she was wondering just what she might do to keep Clyde

Rasmussen from making a mess of things again. She wanted to confide her concern in Godwin but the subject of Clyde was a sensitive one. The first thing she'd noticed was that Clyde no longer seemed interested in going to bed with her: she liked that because she knew Godwin was bothered by Clyde's attentions to her, try as he might to pretend he wasn't, but the implications—based on Clyde's past performance—produced the worry. If Clyde wasn't having sex with her, then whom was he having sex with? It was a matter of presentation: If she were going to discuss it with Godwin, who loved Clyde like a brother, she'd have to bring it up while leaving herself out of it. So she waited until she had some evidence rather than merely an uneasy intuition.

Neither did she have any idea of what Godwin knew about Clyde's past troubles with his little weakness. Was it the sort of thing men discussed? Well, how was she to know? She couldn't know *everything* about men. She was only nineteen, after all.

Her opportunity arose one night at the Club Toledo. She and Godwin had left her stifling room in search of a breath of fresh, cool air. Clouds sagged on the rooftops and chimney pots and there was nothing fresh to be found. Everything smelled of inevitable rain. The lights from the cafés were diffused and multiplied by the humidity. It was, on the streets, like walking under water. Sometimes the deep, cavelike Club Toledo acted as a kind of natural icebox, staying cool, saving your sanity as you descended into the noisy darkness beneath the Left Bank. The rain had begun to patter in the trees just as they came in off the street. They could feel the first draughts of cool air in the long hallway.

Downstairs there was something approaching a full house, several parties of Americans and English who had read Godwin's pieces about Clyde and the Club Toledo in the *Herald*. As Swaine had urged him to write more and more autobiographically, Godwin had included references to the club more frequently, featuring it as a regular stop on his rounds of Paris nightlife. The effect had been to attract a disproportionate number of tourists, but that was fine by Clyde. They spent money lavishly and were enthusiastic about the American bandleader. There was talk in the air about a new deal to make recordings on an American label. A famous New York hotel was sending a representative to bring Clyde Rasmussen home alive. Clyde was beginning to realize the power of Godwin's writing, not only in Paris but in the *New York Herald* as well. "Power of the press," he would say with one of his great toothy grins. "The pen is mightier than the sword." He was well on his way to the top of the world.

"There she is," Clothilde whispered. "*L'Africaine.*"

The black girl sat at a table near the bandstand. Two men sat with her though she was quiet, almost ignoring them. They may well have been the recording people. Or maybe one of them had come on behalf of the New York hotel. It was Clyde's table, reserved for his special guests. The girl was thin, wore a very tight, very simple black dress. Her hair was cropped close to her skull. Her arms were long and thin, the shiny black skin, like polished ebony, drawn tight across her particularly high cheekbones. Her forehead was high and rounded, her lips in profile full and pouting. She seemed to have no breasts at all. Seated as she was, glanced at quickly, all that revealed her as female were gold earrings, a beaded and gold appointed necklace, and a gold band circling her upper arm.

Clothilde whispered conspiratorially: "She's the one I've seen him with. Several times. Walking along the Seine by the stalls. At cafés. It's as if he's showing her off. You've been too busy to notice."

"She must be somebody's daughter," Godwin said. "Maybe some musician or other has a daughter. She can't be more than twelve years old. I mean, look at her. She has no shape . . . she could be a boy."

"But she is a she. And she is Clyde's new girl."

"A Negro? I don't get it—"

"This is not Ohoho, Rodger."

"Nor is it Iowa."

She shrugged. "Negresses are very highly prized by many men. Particularly in Paris. *Exotique*. You know about Clyde . . ." She searched his eyes questioningly. She had lit a cigarette, leaned forward with one elbow on the tabletop. She was wearing a beret at a rakish angle. The cross on her cheek was in shadow.

"Negresses, you mean?"

"Young girls," she said softly.

"Sure. He likes them to *look* young."

"You are such an innocent." Impulsively she leaned over and kissed his cheek. "Looks young is all right for Clyde. But young, the real thing, is better. It is a weakness. A kind of illness." She sighed and exhaled a cloud of blue smoke. "Do you understand what I am saying?"

He nodded. He didn't like thinking about it. "But a girl can be too young. This girl here, gosh, she could be a boy—right? I mean, well, what would he see in her in the first place? No, you're mistaken. You must be."

"Twelve, thirteen. She's old enough."

"Maybe she works in one of the houses," he said.

"She would be very expensive. She could be a model, I suppose."

"Well, Clyde could afford it. Afford *her*."

"But if she doesn't work at one of the houses . . . if she is some-one's daughter . . ." She bit her lip. "I'm afraid for Clyde. I'm afraid he'll get into trouble again."

"What are you talking about? What trouble?"

"Oh, I don't know—"

"Clothilde," he said.

"Well, last year—there was some trouble. If this girl works in one of the houses, then there won't be trouble. But if she truly is someone's daughter"—she made a pistol with her hand, pointing the forefinger at him—"bang-bang, like last year."

"Bang-bang, like last year! What the hell *are* you talking about?"

"You mustn't tell him that I told you. Promise."

"Okay, okay."

"When he gets like this he goes out of his head. Last year there was the daughter of an American businessman, he met her here at the club, they all became friends . . . he said the girl seduced him to punish her father. Maybe she did, who knows? It doesn't matter. She was a child. The father found out. The girl was a wicked little thing—" She shrugged expressively with a lift of her eyebrows. "Or not—perhaps she had her own reasons. But she taunted her father with what she had done . . . the father quite naturally got a gun and went after Clyde, fired at him twice, causing a good deal of damage to a doorjamb and scaring several people half to death. He then turned the problem over to those two *flics*—"

"Henri and Jacques?" He felt a tingle of surprise mingled with dread.

"The same. He told them what Clyde had done to his daughter. Rape. Kidnapping." She nervously lit another cigarette. Her fingers trembled as she told the story. "You know Henri and Jacques? You know the kind of men they are?"

Godwin nodded. He knew better than she could imagine. But it was his secret. His and Max Hood's.

"They waited for him one night. They gave him a beating. They broke his nose. They split his lip open. He couldn't play for months, that was what scared him . . . he came to me when they were through with him, I thought he was vomiting blood but it was all from his lip." She shivered at the memory. "They told him he was lucky. They told him they would castrate him if he saw the girl again. They do not engage in idle threats. So . . ." She sighed deeply. "Who knows about this little Ne-gress? Maybe she belongs to another man . . . a jealous man who takes care of her . . ." She hugged her chest, as if holding herself safe in a dangerous world. "He's seeing this girl, he's slipping back into it. Rodger, he saved my life, and now I'm so afraid for him. But I don't know what to do. What can I say to him? He'd hate me, of all people, for reminding him of his weakness . . ."

Later on, once Clyde had worked his way through the first half of the second set, Godwin and Clothilde slipped away, went back upstairs where it was raining hard and everything was sticking to everything else. The heat was syrupy, hung in the night like an evil perfume. The awnings overhead bulged as if they were pregnant, about to burst.

Godwin sent Clothilde on her way alone, her little pink umbrella bobbing like a flower in the night. Rain drummed on the deserted tables in the café terraces and crowds all but spilled through the doorways out into the downpour. Cigarette smoke billowed from every aperture and Godwin heard some accordion dance music from on down the street. A *bal musette.* Sweaty bodies dancing, fingers clutching. He ducked his head and dashed across the narrow street to stand in the shadowy doorway of a tobacconist where a ripped awning dripped steadily in front of him. There was no traffic in the street. The water rushed and gurgled in the gutters. A deserted *pissoir* stood down the block like a determined sentry. There would be taxis soon to pick up the crowd leaving the Club Toledo. The taxi drivers always knew what was going on, knew Hemingway and Kiki and Josephine Baker and Fitzgerald and—believe it or not—a member of the *Académie* had visited the cellar, *le cave,* the Club Toledo within the past couple of weeks. Godwin watched the doorway through the rain and wondered exactly what he was waiting for.

Once the crowd began to bubble up, the taxies swept down like birds of prey and Godwin walked a few feet back toward the *pissoir* and got into one driven by a very fat man with a walrus mustache. Godwin told him to wait and the man grumbled, sank back in the seat which let out a desperate sigh, and belched. He smelled as if *vin ordinaire* had soaked through his skin and clothing from deep within.

Godwin watched the door. Finally Clyde appeared, tall and broad-shouldered in a double-breasted white tuxedo jacket. In the crook of his arm, almost like a doll, he seemed to be carrying the young girl, about to drop her into his pocket. She was looking up at him as he spoke with the last of the well-wishers who wanted to be able to say they'd spoken to Monsieur Clyde and had been close enough to that little colored girl of his to touch her, damn near.

A taxi glided up in front of the doorway and stopped. Clyde stepped out into the rain, opened the door, and followed her inside.

"Follow that one," Godwin said. The driver made a dismissive noise but yanked the gearshift and clanked away from the curb.

Clyde's taxi headed down toward the river, then across past Notre

Dame to the Right Bank where Godwin eventually lost his bearings. He knew l'Etoile and l'Arc de Triomphe, slick with rain, but otherwise it was a welter of dark sidestreets until the taxi up ahead pulled over to a massive eighteenth-century building, now a block of apartments. Godwin's driver pulled over with a mighty sigh, sat sucking his teeth while Godwin watched. Would Clyde go inside to spend the night? What was going on?

Finally the door opened, Clyde got out, reached back in for the girl and followed her up to the entry. They stood talking for just a moment under the foreshortened overhang. Then the girl put out her hand, Clyde kissed it briefly, and she went inside.

Clyde returned to the taxi and went home.

Godwin got out of his taxi a couple of blocks away and walked back to his apartment through the rain, hoping he didn't run into his landlord.

He doubted if anyone—not even Henri and Jacques—would castrate Clyde for kissing the girl's hand so chastely. Beyond that, Godwin wasn't sure his detective work had proven much of anything.

Godwin met Hood one morning at a small café not far from the Luxembourg Gardens. They had each brought their tennis racquets and there was a string bag of scuffed balls resting in a third chair. Hood was reading the *Herald*, turned to Godwin's new piece about an American heiress visiting Paris. She'd danced naked on a tabletop at some bar where she'd gone slumming with several boyfriends of the moment, French, Spanish, English, and Greek, though she had in fact gone off into the night with a sailor from Marseilles. She'd hired a Negro band to follow her around town on her escapades. Paris was under her spell. The night, people said, belonged to Amanda the American.

She'd been introduced one evening to Godwin, she had taken him up for a few days, and he'd gone along with it, joining her procession, one of the courtiers. It was wonderful material. She was so vulgar, so trashy, yet so genuinely what she was, so candid and in moments at rest so sweet. "If you can't have fun," she remarked after kissing him in a darkened taxi, "and behave disgracefully when you're eighteen, Rodger, then when can you?" Godwin had finally staggered off the merry-go-round and written the chronicle of her adventures in a series of three pieces, "The Girl Who Wasn't Cinderella."

Hood looked up as Godwin's coffee arrived. "Reading about your friend Amanda. You must be very tired."

Rodger nodded. "She's a natural subject for me. Young, American, too much money. I've known dozens of girls who liked to pretend they were Amandas but this one has the guts to say the hell with it and do it."

"I take it you liked her."

"She's all right. No brains, all instincts. Zest for living, you could say."

"You're at a turning point, of course. Take a word of advice—don't do anything foolish." Max flipped the folded paper onto the table.

"Such as?" Godwin felt himself bristling.

"At your best, your writing is intelligent. Young, full of life, eager to see things fresh . . . because you *are* seeing it all for the first time. You're making choices for your readers, you're creating yourself as they'll see you. You want them to have the right idea. So you have to see things the right way round."

"You think I don't?"

"I remember how I was when I went out to the desert for the first time, met my first camel, met Lawrence . . . it was all new and clear and bright. I saw what happened to me . . . before I knew it I was thinking the camel was God's worst mistake, I hated the desert, I thought Lawrence was quite mad, a man who exulted in pain inflicted and pain received, everything I saw became evil and cruel, drenched in blood . . ." His voice was very low and without emotion. He sipped his coffee, slowly pushed the newspaper away. Only Godwin's story was visible. "Then it all changed again. I began to see it realistically, for what it was. A camel was a camel. Lawrence was a brave man on a mission, somewhat obsessive, of course. And what we did out there was worthwhile, needed to be done, it was a part of a much bigger picture—I'm sorry, I'm not good at talking about all this. But I look at you, I see the way your life is suddenly changing, and I don't want you to do something foolish . . . like getting things all wrong—"

"I'm doing okay," Godwin said. "Far as I can tell."

"Not with *this*, I'm afraid." He held up the Amanda story. "It's rubbish."

Godwin felt himself flushing, as if he'd been slapped. "You're a critic? I didn't know—"

"Everybody's a critic—get used to it. And lots of them are going to be telling you how wonderful and colorful all this nonsense about Amanda is. If you listen to them, you're not only a fool . . . you're lost, almost before you begin."

"I'd put my writing up against anybody's. I got the Amanda story exactly right, it's dead on—"

"Well, bloody good for you! One might ask, so what? What's it all in aid of? Why waste good writing on a subject beneath you? You come across as one of them, Rodger. You were impressed by this idiotic if harmless girl who should bloody well be sent to her room without dinner. Good lord, where are her parents? Counting their dividends? Buying up South America? The girl is dancing naked and drunk and playing this string of thin-blooded princelets as if she were mounting polo ponies . . . and Rodger Godwin, wide-eyed and simple-minded, is agog—"

"You're not being fair—"

"Bloody hell! I'm being accurate and you know it. You're not a reporter sent out to cover something stupid. You're not a stenographer of events. Swaine has let you stake out a different territory—he's let you write what you think and feel. You're the luckiest man on earth—you have an audience for whatever you choose to write about. You're certainly not a newspaperman, not by any stretch of the imagination."

"If I'm not, then just what do you think I am?"

"Look around you, man. Wake up. You're a writer! Out of nowhere, out of some mysterious wellspring deep inside your soul and your background, you have emerged a writer. That doesn't mean you're overly bright, or, God knows, wise, or anything but lucky and talented. You were the right chap at the right time, and you'll never be so lucky again, not in your whole life—"

"So what the hell is eating you?"

"You. I don't want you to waste it. I don't want to see you become some bleary-eyed chronicler of the smart set. *Book of the Dead*—is that your aim?" He smiled slowly at Godwin's flushed, stricken face. "It's no place for a man. You know that as well as I do. Don't be seduced by it."

"You've got a hell of a lot of nerve."

"Not really, old boy. What have I got to lose? If you're the sort to go yapping after every little nitwit passing out free champagne and handing her titties around—well, then, you're no great loss. If you've got real bottom, if you're a man, then you'll be able to handle what I'm telling you. But it's time for you to make a choice. I'm just pointing out your options." He tapped the newspaper with his fingers. "Shit like this . . . or personal views of Paris, the real Paris. The piece on Lindbergh—now there was work a man could be proud of. This crap—well, you'd be well advised to leave it alone. Really, you would."

"I wonder about you, Max. I really do. You know what you are? You're a cowboy."

"A cowboy?"

"All this about what's right and proper for a man. You've got to be a man. A man does this and that." He thought to himself: A man would have taken care of Henri and Jacques the night they killed that old man in the alley.

"Well, it's a matter of honor, a matter of pride. A matter of the mission that makes you what you are. Certainly, you can settle for being something else. But then you won't ride with me, cowboy."

"Who the hell said I wanted to ride with you? I came all the way to Paris for an Englishman to teach me the code of the West? It's crazy."

"No, it's life, old man. Shall we go hit a few?"

Godwin never remembered the tennis that day but he never forgot getting told off by Max Hood. It took some getting used to.

It seemed that he was meeting someone new every day, writing constantly, sitting in the bar below the newspaper offices turning his notes into coherent sentences, sleeping as little as possible, as if he were hooked on some drug that made sleep unnecessary.

One night the group—Tony and Priscilla and Clothilde and Merle B. Swaine and another reporter, a guy from *The Times* called Sam Balderston —went along with him to Joselli's in the Place Clichy to hear Leslie Hutchinson play the piano and sing in that unbelievably silky voice. They listened to him do some of the new numbers, "Among My Souvenirs," "My Heart Stood Still," "My One and Only," the tango "Jalousie," " 'Swonderful," "Thou Swell," "Side by Side," "Strike Up the Band" . . . Godwin had never seen or heard anything quite like him, quite so immaculate and mysterious.

On the way home, after stopping briefly at a café, Priscilla managed to get Godwin to herself with Clothilde walking in front of them with Tony.

"I think my father rather fancies Clothilde," Priscilla said. "Would that be an unwise liaison for him?"

"Honest to God, the stuff you come up with—"

"Well, I know Clothilde and you are friends—I'm not an utter child, you know. But you're not serious about her, and it would be so good for him—"

"Who says I'm not serious about Clothilde?"

Priscilla giggled, whispered: "You're only really serious about yourself!"

"Oh, is that right? And who told you that?"

"You'd be amazed at how many things I figure out for myself. But we're talking about my father. Getting out tonight was good for him, you saw how much he enjoyed her. It's because of my mother, of course, she's such a millstone round his neck. Have you heard much about my mother?"

"Not much. 'Gaudy' is the word somebody used."

"Mmm. Sounds like me," she said. At the door in the wall she held him back for a moment. "Tea again tomorrow, Rodger?"

"If I can make it."

She smiled slowly. A breeze played in the trees. "You can make it. Tea with me and billiards with Daddy." She turned to Clothilde. "Good night, Clothilde."

Tony DewBrittain was smiling at his daughter's grown-up ways. He winked indulgently at Godwin. He seemed to have forgotten entirely the unfortunate chance meeting outside Clothilde's door. It might have been two other men. Godwin wondered how often they were together now but then brushed the question aside. What did it matter, anyway?

Godwin was a frequent afternoon visitor to the DewBrittain house that summer. The house always seemed cool and dark and calm whatever Paris was up to outside the walls. Hood was often there, as well, and they would play billiards or sit and talk, smoking cigars and sipping brandy and soda or lemonade and listening to the buzzing of insects in the garden. In the background they would hear Priscilla practicing the violin and thank God she played wonderfully well. Perhaps somewhere another group of idlers heard Fritz Kreisler going through the same drills. There was a warmth to Priscilla's tone that was quite unlikely in one so young. And when she wasn't playing there was a sense of her moving about the polished, dim rooms in her summer frocks, replacing bowls of flowers, occasionally checking on the men to inquire if they were in need of any little comforts. Godwin would watch Hood, the way his eyes followed her, the look of something verging on despair moving across his face. Or was it longing? Max Hood, he knew perfectly well, was quite unlike anyone he'd ever known in a great many ways.

DewBrittain and Hood would sometimes go off together to see their brokers and go to the races or to meet unexplained men on business, and Godwin and Priscilla would go to the garden with its splashing fountain and settle down in canvas chairs to read. Godwin was reading *The Red and the Black*, but, of course, she'd already read that and was now working her way through *Middlemarch* and Trollope and Thackeray. Several house cats lazed about as if staying awake were a terrible trial. They moved only enough to stay in the sun and stretch and yawn. Dust rose slowly from around the base of the crumbling fountain. Little birds flickered in and out of the shadows. Much of the time Godwin was writing, and Stendhal was put aside. He was always aware of it when she began watching him work but he didn't mind.

He watched her, too, couldn't keep his eyes off her at times. Partly because he knew what Hood thought about her, partly because he was trying himself to figure out just exactly what it was about her that seemed to make her so potent a force in their lives, and partly because he found her more beautiful with each passing day. She brought him iced tea and she'd catch him watching her and she'd smile as if she were giving him permission to look as long as he wanted. Sometimes it would be her eyelashes, how long they were. Sometimes it would be the wave in her newly bobbed hair, the angle of dark hair cutting past her ear and across her cheek like a scimitar's point. Sometimes the sight of her coming through the light and shadow from the house was just about enough to make a man do anything . . . write poetry, even.

She always wanted him to read her what he was writing, and she would sit, head cocked, listening carefully, nodding or frowning as he read about Hemingway or Hutch or Chevalier or about a bunch of Americans playing baseball in the park with a statue of Victor Hugo overseeing their exertions.

One afternoon, following a particularly late night, with the day very hot and still, he sat nearly asleep, *The Red and the Black* in his lap where it had slipped from his fingers, and he was drawn back to the surface by the sound of her voice. She was talking about her mother. There was no particular reason. She just began.

"My mother is called Lady Pamela Legend. A very old Bucks family. She pretends to scorn it but she never forgets it, it's all part of a game we English have."

"Bucks? What does that mean?"

"Buckinghamshire. The Buckinghamshire Legends are, well, a bit legendary. It's a very tedious joke but Lady Pamela, deep in her heart, takes it all very seriously. There was a Legend with Wellington and a Legend with Nelson and a Legend led his men into the valley of death with the six hundred and who knows where else—there was even a Legend at the War of Jenkins's Ear. Lady Pamela's legend is not quite so distinguished . . . she refuses to acknowledge the distinction between fame and notoriety. *I* know that much and I'm only fourteen. She is very beautiful and given to what people call 'indiscretions,' which makes things rather trying for my father. Poor man. He can be quite sweet . . . Someone said once that 'old Tony's blood is so thin he don't give a bloody damn who's poking his wife just so he don't have to.' I wasn't supposed to hear that but it was some old county friend of the family's. I wasn't sure what it meant until I got a little older."

"It must not be very nice either for you or your father."

"Oh, people always make excuses for Lady Pamela . . . One indiscretion is a tragedy, two are a disgrace, but commit dozens and it becomes your style. Max Hood told me that—it's funny, isn't it? Is it true, Rodger?"

"Sounds like it might be. But I'm no expert."

"Do you hold things against people?"

"I'm pretty much a live-and-let-live kind of guy. Easygoing."

"A year ago Tony came home one night and found Lady Pamela 'at it' —we know what that means, don't we—with her cousin Marc Legend on the billiard table, this was at our Belgravia House. Well, Tony blew a gasket that time . . . I was asleep upstairs and heard all the noise and looked out the window and I saw him throw her and Marc out into Eaton Square. He was standing in the doorway and he shouted at her, he said she was 'a slut, no better than the commonest, cheapest whore' . . . I couldn't keep myself from looking. Mother was standing on the sidewalk crying—out of anger, I'm sure—and her dress was torn and Marc had a bloody nose and kept yelling that Father had broken his glasses . . ." Priscilla's voice was soft and not overly involved, as if she were reciting at last something she'd been practicing for a long time. The story was so sad, however, coming from a daughter, that Godwin had been unable to continue watching her, was instead following the exaggeratedly careful movements of one of the cats stalking a bird in the shadows. "Finally, when she stopped crying, she stared up at my father and said, 'Not cheap, Tony darling, believe me, not cheap—and I'm the best you'll ever have!' Then she looked up and saw me at the bedroom window watching, and she began waving at me like some royal, as if nothing were wrong or out of the ordinary. But some of the lights were beginning to come on in Eaton Square, people were noticing the noise . . . and she got into Marc's Bentley and away they went. Last I saw of them."

Finally, once she fell silent, he looked at her again. There, on her cheek, were two tears, untouched, as if she hadn't noticed them. Impulsively he reached out and wiped them away with his fingertips. She clutched his hand, held her face against it, and he felt the flood of warm tears. She came and knelt beside his chair and rested her head against his chest and sobbed. He stroked her thick hair and whispered again and again that it would be all right, everything would be all right.

CHAPTER 15

Rodger Godwin was pretty sure he'd begun figuring things out by the end of the Bastille Day party at the DewBrittain's. Everything changed that night. There was Before the Party, there was After the Party. And while it was going on everyone agreed that it was the best night of the summer. Bar none.

Certainly it was Priscilla's great triumph. Not only was she Tony Dew-Brittain's hostess, the lady of the house; she had also planned the party, sent the invitations which she'd written by hand, she'd ordered all the decorations and the flowers and supervised the menu and seen to the staff that would serve it. She was glorious, radiant. Godwin found her astonishing, as if she'd emerged from childhood and become a woman, the product—the exquisite product—of a mysterious rite of passage.

She was standing by the doorway into the garden when Godwin came through from the street. Japanese lanterns were strung through the trees and the interior of the house, seen through the open shutters, glowed with the light of candles. She was silhouetted against the glow, her short hair cropped against the graceful neck, and she waved hesitantly in greeting. Someone was playing the piano. The soft warm breeze wafted the sound toward him. The lanterns swayed gently as if to the music. She held out her hand. It was damp with anxiety. "Oh, I'm so glad you're here. Tell me it's going to be fine, Rodger. Oh, I wish I'd never gone ahead with this . . . will it be all right?"

She wore a very short, silky mauve dress with shoulder straps like pieces of string. Her broadening female hips pulled the dress tight so it clung to her flat belly and moulded itself to her thighs. But she was still only fourteen, not entirely sure of herself, still one of those enchanting creatures caught between playing at and actually being a grown-up.

"It's going to be wonderful," Godwin said. "Bank on it."

"I'm too nervous to stand still. Why don't you go in and introduce yourself to the piano player?" She smiled and went off to meet someone else newly arrived.

She'd really pulled it off; he had to give her credit. Hutch was sitting at the grand piano; with his smooth face and easy smile and English accent, he seemed the personification of style and wit and sophistication. How many Parisians must have wanted him for parties this particular night—yet it was Cilla who'd gotten him. He winked at Godwin when she brought him a glass of champagne. "The lovely Miss DewBrittain," Hutch said, "surely does know how to throw a party. She *launches* a party. I tell you, Raj, they're gonna say what a girl . . ."

"I hope they do," she said, blushing.

Later, once the place had begun to fill up, Tony DewBrittain joined Godwin, who was leaning on a railing just beyond some french doors, looking back in at people dancing to the ripple of the piano. "Enjoying yourself, Godwin? Where's your lady friend? Clothilde?"

"She'll be along presently. She had to have a holiday drink with some old friends."

"Well, I'm about to burst with pride in my daughter."

"I can't blame you. This is all quite wonderful."

"Her mother and I have made such a cock-up of things . . . who'd have thought Priscilla would be the one who'd make all the nonsense worthwhile? Life is full of surprises. And occasionally there's a nice one. You're fond of Prissy, aren't you?"

"Very fond."

"I worry sometimes, you know."

"About Priscilla?"

"In a way, yes. It's this ticker of mine. I want to hold on until she's grown and out on her own. She'll have a great deal of money then. Won't need her old dad. Then, pfffft, what difference does it make? But I don't want to leave her while she's still a child. So I worry a bit. But tonight, tonight is a wonderful night. She's brought it off, hasn't she?"

Many of the guests were unknown to Godwin but he was glad to see Merle Swaine, who had the round-faced, bespectacled fat man from *The Times*—Sam Balderston—in tow. Balderston's face was both cherubic and sly, oddly foxlike, and his glasses were smudged and he'd got something sticky on his necktie. He reminded Godwin of an insurance salesman from back home. Balderston knew Paris well and always referred to Frenchmen disparagingly as Frogs. He was fond of talking about politics, a subject which at the time held little interest for Godwin. Between them, as they came toward Godwin, was Clothilde. "Look what we found," Balderston grinned slyly. "Your frog queen!" She looked at Balderston as if she had no grasp of English and took Godwin's arm, kissed him warmly on the mouth.

"Just met her outside," Swaine said. He was perspiring profusely. "Quite a do," he said, taking in the party, "those colored lights in the trees. Sam's usually under a barstool this time of night. I thought he should see how English society bloody comports itself abroad. The man's nothing but an ink-stained wretch."

Balderston was staring across the room. "Good Christ, is that the DewBrittain girl?"

"Our hostess," Godwin said.

Clothilde nodded matter-of-factly. "Exquisite, isn't she?"

"Knock your socks off, in a manner of speaking. She ought to be in pictures, that's what comes to mind." Balderston was grinning widely. "Must go have a word with the young lady. Somebody should be photographing her."

They watched him trundle off and Swaine sighed heavily. "There goes Merle Swaine's burden," he said.

Clothilde sang with Hutch as the evening wore on, and when she dragged Godwin out to dance she was so good she made him feel nearly human on the floor. "Just the slow ones," he said. "No Charlestons for me."

She laughed at him. "You worry too much about your dignity, m'sieur."

Godwin was standing in the shadows on the stairway with people sitting on the steps at his feet when he saw Max Hood come in and stand quietly at the edge of things, watching the party. In the glow of candles, protected as he was by the distance between them and the guests at his feet and Hood's not seeing him, Godwin had the feeling that he might be seeing The Hero for the first time.

Hood was almost supernaturally handsome at just that moment. Perfectly tailored in the close-fitting dinner jacket and black tie; smoothly tanned from lots of tennis and fishing and riding in the Bois de Boulogne. Something made Godwin grin at the picture: Max Hood was perfect but, in the end, he had problems. When Godwin came down the stairs he went to Hood with a feeling of something he could only call brotherhood —he knew it sounded sappy, it *was* sappy, but he couldn't help it and he was damned if he knew why.

Hood was an enigma: He was so quiet, so silent at the center, that he drew you in, made you powerless, made you a conspirator in his secret, enigmatic plot. The effect on Godwin was to make him want Max Hood's approval for its own sake. He wanted to be worthy of Hood's friendship. He wanted to *reach* the man. And while none of this seemed possible, Hood seemed to consider Godwin a friend. Godwin hadn't earned it; it had been conferred upon him, unearned. He wanted to earn it, wanted Max to see it happen. But how?

They fell into conversation and drank champagne and talked more freely than they ever had before. And when they moved apart Godwin couldn't quite get him out of sight or out of mind. Through the evening Hood seemed to be standing alone, an observer, or playing with the cats in the garden, his face an impenetrable mask. There was something preying on the man's mind.

At one point from the corner of his eye, he saw Hood approach Priscilla and engage her in ordinary pleasantries, undoubtedly congratulating her on the party. She listened intently. His smile was as unrevealing as ever, and then he asked her to dance and she nodded. They moved very slowly, following the basic box-step, and they didn't seem to be saying much of anything. He looked resolutely over her shoulder, his expression never changing, but he held her firmly, not *too* close—she was just a chit of a girl after all, not a woman—and when the dance was over she smiled shyly at him and he thanked her with a slight bow and as if removing a spell he released her attention and she was able to be the hostess again.

Godwin was listening to Swaine and Sam Balderston debate the merits of baseball and cricket when he felt a tug on his arm and Priscilla was pulling him away. It was nearly midnight and the party was just in full swing. Her eyes shone. He saw candlelight in them. She was happy, she was still anxious and nervous but in a good way. She'd pulled it off. The party was all she could have asked for and more.

"Is it all too horrible? Tell me, Rodger." Her eyes were wide.

"It's a sensation, Miss DewBrittain, and you know it."

"It *is* nice, isn't it?" She hunched her shoulders and looked gleefully about her, suddenly a little girl staying up late. "Everyone is having a good time and I'm feeling quite jolly about it myself. I'm so glad for Father . . . he even allowed me a glass of champagne."

"Cilla—"

"Thank you for calling me Cilla tonight." Her huge eyes glistened.

"Cilla, right at this moment I have to tell you something—no, just let me say it. You are so, so . . . you are beautiful. You are . . . like no one I've ever known. In fact, I'm a little awestruck looking at you—" He was out of breath and realized how clumsy he was being.

"You are so sweet to tell me that. A little tipsy and very sweet. But if I'm so . . . presentable . . . why don't you like to dance with me?"

"Well, I'm not much of a dancer—"

"I'm terrible, I know nothing about dancing. We'll fake it, Rodger. Please, dance with me again."

She led him out into the garden, beneath the Japanese lanterns, and they danced for a while on the dusty tiles near the splashing fountain where they so often read their books in the afternoon. Hutch was playing one of her favorites of the day, caressing the words.

> *Murder in the moonlight*
> *Another mystery*
> *Cupid will find us guilty*
> *Of love in the first degree . . .*

"Max Hood is quite taken with you."

"I know."

"You know?"

"Well, a girl can tell these things."

"Does this happen to you often?"

"Of course not, Rodger. I'm only fourteen, silly. But I think it's just one of those things."

"Which things?"

"One of those things you're born with if you're a girl."

"He told me . . . well, I don't suppose I should say . . ." He wasn't sure why he was telling her any of it. Maybe to warn her. But he wasn't sure of that either. Maybe he wanted to keep her from hurting Max Hood. Maybe it was just the champagne talking.

"I understand. He's shy. He hasn't had much to do with women. Have you met his wife?"

"His *wife?* What wife? Did you say *wife?* Hood?"

"She's sick, I think. She's been in a sanitarium in Switzerland."

"Tuberculosis?"

"Not much hope, I've heard."

"Well, that's a shame . . . still, Max has certain feelings about you."

"It's all right, Rodger. You look so worried."

"He's old enough to be your father."

"But he's not my father. And, really, what difference does age make? You're not very romantic, that's my opinion. He's not even forty yet—" She was half teasing him.

"It's not *his* age that worries me, Cilla—"

"Well, then—"

"It's *your* age."

"Oh, Rodger, don't worry. I'm fine. And Max Hood is a perfect gentleman. You can trust him." Then she was humming with her head on his chest.

Murder in the moonlight
Another mystery . . .

An hour or so later, past one o'clock, Max Hood appeared from the back garden, an uncharacteristically worried look on his face. There was a pinched expression dragging at the corners of his eyes and mouth, and his face was damp with perspiration. Seeing Godwin he self-consciously smoothed his hair with his palms and wiped his forehead. With an effort of will, he forced his face back to its normal configuration and offered one of his perfect, studied smiles. The enigma was just barely back in place.

"I say, old chap, have you seen our hostess? Prissy? I was thinking about calling it a night and went to find her and thank her for this remarkable party . . . but I can't seem to find her. I've looked everywhere. Fact is, old man . . ." He shook his head, licked his lips. "She is not to be found."

"Well, she must be somewhere. Did you check the kitchen?"

"Never thought of that—"

"That must be it. Let's have a look."

Following Hood down the hallway to the kitchen all Godwin was really thinking was, Hood's got a wife! The idea seemed quite impossible . . . Max Hood had a wife, a sick wife, a tubercular wife in Switzerland and she was going to die. . . . Well, you never knew. But why had he never mentioned her? And what the hell was he doing falling half in love with Priscilla if he had a wife, dying or not? Godwin thought he might just take it up with Clyde, who was familiar with the way they did things in this part of the world. He might have an insight or two.

They couldn't find Priscilla in the kitchen, nor in the upstairs bedrooms, nor in the wine cellar. Tony was having a game of billiards and drinking brandy with Sam Balderston and suggested quite reasonably that she was probably powdering her nose. Or maybe the champagne had gone to her head and she'd lain down for a nap somewhere they hadn't looked.

Godwin followed Max Hood back up the stairs to the second floor, then to the narrow, darkened stairway to the third floor. "Wait a minute," Godwin said, out of breath, leaning against the wall. Above there was nothing but darkness. "She's not up here. It's hot enough to roast a turkey." Sweat was suddenly running into the corners of his eyes, stinging. His shirt was wilting and clinging to his back. He grabbed Max Hood's arm. It was like ramming your hand into a crowbar. "She's not up here, Max."

He couldn't see Max Hood's face in the darkness but he thought he heard something. He strained to hear. "What is it, Max?"

Max Hood sobbed, a muffled, damp sound, choked. His voice whispered in the darkness. "I've done a bad thing, Rodger. I've done a god-damn bloody rude thing. I don't know quite what to do, you see. Do you understand what I'm saying, old chap?"

"I can't say I do." He wanted to escape from the cramped darkness. He smelled camphor and old dried flowers and the scent of mouse he recognized from the attic back home, a hot summery smell. "Let's get out of here, Max. I can't breathe." He started back down the narrow, shallow steps.

A vise clamped down on his shoulder.

"Dammit, Max! I can't see a damn thing!"

"That's the point, old man." Hood was still whispering in the stillness. Very far away the piano was playing.

"What are you talking about, Max? What happened? What's the point?"

"The darkness is the point. I've made a fool of myself. Don't want to discuss it in the light." He swallowed half a chuckle. "I'm no coward, you'll have to take my word for that. I'll do what needs to be done. I'll never flinch from my duty. But this . . . this is, is . . . I've done a terri-ble thing . . . really must apologize . . . the joke is, I don't quite know how . . . bloody fool, lost control of myself . . . damn!" He coughed. "Damn sorry now I'm dragging you into it. You must try to forgive me, old chap . . . feel a perfect fool. I've seen men who couldn't face the officers' mess, y'know. Feel the same way now."

"Look, I don't know what you're talking about and, honest to God, Max, I'm not staying here any longer—now you've got to come down these steps, pull yourself together, and—"

"For God's sake, Rodger . . . I kissed her. I *kissed* her!"

"Who? You don't mean . . . oh, Max—"

"Priscilla. I walked out into the garden with her, we were playing with the kittens, she was holding one of them up to her face, it was licking her face . . . I seemed to go momentarily mad. Never happened to me before. I can't explain it." He was calming down and Godwin led him back down the stairway to the second-floor hallway. Moonlight was filtering through windows at either end of the long hall. Hood's face bore the look of someone almost in shock. Dazed, uncomprehending. "I took the kitten and dropped it onto the little bench and she looked at me rather curiously and I took her face in my hands and kissed her mouth . . . it was like a bolt of lightning going through me . . . I was suddenly tremendously excited by her and she knew it . . . then I stopped kissing her, stepped back, I must have looked like the bloody phantom of the opera, I was speechless at what I'd done . . . she just looked at me and I was saying I was sorry, terribly sorry, and d'you know what she said, Rodger? You won't believe what she said . . . she said, 'It's all right, Max, don't be upset.' I mean, what a creature!" Hood was leaning against a high pine cabinet, shaking his head.

"Well, then," Godwin said. "Let it go. She understood. She isn't upset with you. . . . It's the champagne, that's it, Max. Summer night, dancing, a party, champagne—"

"But I didn't want to stop," Hood said softly. "She felt like a woman, her mouth was a woman's mouth, I held myself against her . . . I *wanted* her. She's a child!" The last came hoarsely. He was at the end of his tether. At least for the moment.

Godwin couldn't quite cope with it. But it was true. Max had done it and he was terribly shaken by his actions. Maybe his mind had turned to his wife, as well. But the worst part of it was, Cilla was a child.

"And now I can't find her," Hood said. "What has she done? Where has she gone? I've got to find her—"

"Listen to me, Max, I don't think that's such a hot idea. You're pretty upset right now. You're not yourself. If I were you, I'd steer clear of her. For tonight, I mean. She knows you felt bad, that's enough. To tell you the truth, I think our little Priscilla is more grown up than we realize. I'm sure she understands. I'll bet she won't hold this against you for a minute. It's a party for God's sake. Don't make too much of it, Max. It's not so terrible."

"But it *is* terrible, Rodger. You don't understand. She may, but *you* don't." He was getting a cigarette lit, the flame flaring against his face, reflecting in his flat gaze. "I can't be alone with her again. It's that simple. I'd do it again, I would do more . . . I can't run that risk. Don't you see? If I'm ever to have hopes of her I can't ruin it now. You see?"

Godwin nodded, wondering if he did understand at all. But, yes, perhaps he did. What it came down to was that Max Hood was a good deal more than "half in love" with Cilla DewBrittain.

In a way you couldn't blame the poor bastard.

For some reason Godwin couldn't tear himself away from the party. Maybe he sensed that there was some kind of magic raining down.

A great many of the other guests found themselves equally unable to leave that night, so seductive were the music and the champagne and the company and the guttering candles flickering in the night's breezes. Godwin was sitting alone in the garden beneath the brightly colored lanterns dimmed by the tree branches, running his fingers through the fur of a couple of soft kittens, when he saw Cilla again. It must have been three o'clock and he was sleepy, his eyelids drooping. The fountain provided a soporific sound. His mind wandered. He heard the doorway to the street click and squeak softly as it swung open.

She came in, her face pale in the creamy moonlight. She stroked an errant strand of hair away from the corner of her eye. She saw Godwin and smiled brightly, then covered her mouth as she suddenly yawned. She leaned against the fountain, facing him. "You were asleep," she said.

"Are you all right?"

"Of course. What do you mean?"

"Max and I looked all over for you a while ago."

"Whatever for?"

He shrugged. "Max wanted to say good night and thank you for the festivities. He got worried when we couldn't find you."

"Oh." Her fingers tightened on the rim of the old fountain.

"Are you sure you feel all right? You're white."

"I got a bit light-headed." She lowered her eyes. "All the excitement . . . I haven't had a great deal of experience with this sort of thing."

"So where were you?" He kept thinking of Max kissing her, kept seeing her face in his hands. He didn't know what to think of it. It was just one of those things.

"I was so hot. All the candles, smelling the melting wax . . . the champagne. I had to get out so I slipped away. There were so many people, I didn't think anyone would notice. I went for a walk, sat in the park . . ."

"Well, you earned it," Godwin said. He got up and gave her a hug. "I'm calling it a night myself."

She turned and walked with him to the doorway into the street. She was standing with him when they saw a familiar figure coming toward them.

It was Clyde Rasmussen.

He waved a big hand. "Hi, sport. How's your big shebang, darlin'? Am I too late?" He slapped Godwin on the back and pecked Priscilla's forehead.

"It's such a success," Godwin said, "we're both about done in."

"Well, keep it goin' a little longer. I'm a workin' man, y'know."

"You're in plenty of time," she said. "Come in and have a glass of champagne. Hutch is still here."

"That devil." The wide gap-toothed grin.

"You two go to it," Godwin said.

"Rodger, is that you? I thought you were asleep." It was Clothilde passing the fountain. "You're leaving without me."

"I came without you."

"Well, you're not getting off so easy." She kissed his cheek. "What a triumph!" she said to Priscilla.

"None of us will ever forget it," Godwin said.

"Well, let me have a crack at it before it's history," Clyde said. "Lead me to the good times, young lady."

She did and then Clothilde took Rodger Godwin's hand and led him home to bed. But when it came time at last to sleep, his last thoughts were of Max Hood.

After that night Godwin believed he'd seen it all but, the fact was, he hadn't seen anything yet.

In a peculiar way, he was weary of the whole bunch of them. They really were wearing him down and he didn't know just what to make of any of them. There was Max Hood and his longing and his sense of shame and despair, all for the sake of Cilla; there was Clyde with the passion for young ladies, at the moment the mysterious little *Africaine* who might or might not lead him by his prick into big trouble. He was even oddly weary of Cilla, who was so central, too damn central, to their lives: her ambiguous role of girl/woman was exhausting him because he didn't know what to make of it, didn't know what toll it was taking on her. So, he stayed away from the whole bunch of them and the elegant house with the kittens and the fountain and the stacks of books by the canvas chairs. He saw only Clothilde, concentrated on his work, writing thousands of words a day about Paris and its inhabitants and the way he saw them.

Lunch with Marshall Hacker of Boni & Liveright Publishers took nearly four hours. Signing the contract left Godwin in a highly celebratory state.

He took the long walk home, turned into the familiar doorway after making sure that Clothilde wasn't available across the way, and decided to take Clyde out for a drink. The story of Marshall Hacker and Fouquet's and Boni & Liveright and the contracts simply couldn't wait. It was the evidence, the proof, that his summer had not been a prolonged hallucination.

He gave Clyde's door a peremptory knock, then burst in and called his name. "Clyde! Clyde, where are—"

He felt his knees buckle as if he'd been hit by a two-by-four, or had a heart attack, or seen the worst thing in the world. His heart had stopped, he knew the blood was draining out of his face. Then a flush of embarrassment spread through him and he wanted to run but he was rooted to the floor. His stomach was slipping away, like an elevator in a free fall. A cold sweat began soaking him. It was all happening at once.

Clyde was naked, kneeling on the floor with his back to Godwin. His face was buried between a woman's legs, her thighs squeezing his face, her fingers buried in his spikey hair pulling him tight against her, the only sound her breathing, a hard, throaty sound as she pushed and strained, flinging herself against the back of the couch, then thrusting against him.

Godwin felt as if he watched for a long time. The heat of the day billowed in, the curtains moved, drifted, the room was dim and smelled of flowers.

Her eyes looked into Godwin's. They were only partially focused, glazed with desire, her cheeks flushed, her naked little breasts with large, hard nipples, were blotchy with the heat of what she was doing. She was at the verge of her climax, working her way to it, and while he watched she finally released his eyes, before he could run away, before anyone could do anything, she was at the peak, then over with a quiet little moan, biting her lip to keep from crying out as her body bucked frantically, as if she were eager to get it all over with, but she couldn't slow it down or ignore it, she moaned past ragged gulps of air, her huge eyes slowly returning to Godwin's as the spasms slowed and stopped and she pulled away, pulled a wrapper across herself and pushed up against the back of the couch, said something softly to Clyde, covered the wet dark triangle of pubic hair as she pulled her legs up under her so she was sitting on them, suddenly demure, and Clyde sank back, sitting on the floor, a towel clutched to his groin, his mouth and face glistening, and he saw Godwin and he groaned, swore, his eyes rolling upward as if pleading with the Almighty for mercy. "*Merde*," he whispered, "goddammit . . ." Words failed him. He sat oddly askew, like a huge broken doll.

Godwin looked back at the woman on the couch, praying for magic, praying she wouldn't be there, praying she wouldn't be Priscilla DewBrittain.

They sat in the darkening room, each staring into space, each in his own envelope of shock, as if a terrible explosion had blinded and deafened them and left them helpless. Godwin's mind was almost entirely blank. To his credit, he never for a moment felt as if his two friends had betrayed him. What had happened between Priscilla and Clyde had nothing to do with him. Not until he came through that door. But he did feel alone. He wasn't entirely sure he knew these people. He supposed he'd find out soon but until then he wasn't quite sure.

Eventually Priscilla went into the kitchen, squeezed lemons, and brought back a pitcher of lemonade with glasses on a tray. They heard her back in the kitchen chipping with a knife at a block of ice. Godwin almost drained his first glass straight off, then sat sipping, trying to organize his thoughts . . . trying to *have* a thought. Sooner or later someone was going to have to say something but for the moment they all sat sweating, doubtful. When she spoke it still jarred him out of his sense of solitude.

"Don't be angry with Clyde, Rodger. You must understand that first of all. It's my fault. There really is something wrong with me. Or something . . . different. I must be like my mother. I don't know. Sometimes I'm so hopeful . . . then it all gets dark and I'm lost."

Clyde had put on his trousers and shirt. He was running his fingers through his unruly hair. "Oh, hell, Rodger, you know better than that. She's trying to get me off the hook. Well, I've been on the hook a long time. Just don't listen to her. My God, she's an angel, an innocent, trusting angel. It's me. You know that, well as I do, for Christ's sake. You know about me. I can't help myself. Look at her, Rodger. She's an exquisite child. It's me, it's always me, don't listen to her . . ."

Priscilla was calmly shaking her head. Her eyes were dark hollows. Godwin couldn't see those huge café-au-lait eyes but he saw the graceful slope of the back of her neck as she turned toward him. "The literal truth is that I led him on . . . he was a perfect gentleman, whatever he says now. I was crazy, I wanted it to happen . . . you must believe me. And then I couldn't stop. Listen to me, Rodger. *I won't stop now.* I won't . . . I *can't.* And now Clyde can't stop, either. Can you, Clyde? Can you stop? Do you really want to stop?" There was a little tremor in her voice but not much. She was so composed it made Godwin shiver.

Clyde said: "Somebody should stop me. Somebody ought to put a slug in me and get it over with . . . hell, the way I'm headed, they'd be doing me a favor—"

Godwin said: "If Max Hood found out, he'd sure as hell stop you."

Clyde laughed, high pitched. "He'd kill me and get a good night's sleep. I heard about him, the way he was in the desert."

"Well, he'd stop you. He's quite taken with Priscilla."

"Stop it!" she cried. "Please, just do stop it! Nobody's going to find out and nobody's going to kill anyone. Nobody's found out yet and now we've got—"

"What are you saying, *yet?* You mean this isn't the first . . ." Godwin stopped. You catch somebody at something bad, it's never the first time, is it? "How long has this been going on?"

"Months," she said. "Since shortly after we met . . . some considerable time before you turned up."

"I took one look at her, sport. Try to understand—try to put yourself in my shoes . . . with my weakness. There's one big difference this time, though . . . this time I'm in love. I love her. She's not too young to love . . . and I'll wait for her, old man. Do you hear what I'm saying?"

"Jesus, Cilla," Godwin said. "Everybody's going to wait for you. Max, Clyde, there's going to be quite a line . . . still, I guess Clyde didn't exactly wait."

Clyde turned to Priscilla. "You said now we've got something. Got what?"

"Well, we're not alone with our secret anymore. We've got an ally. Someone to help us. We've got Rodger . . . it makes all the difference."

Godwin sighed. What was there to say?

Priscilla was having a bath. Clyde was getting into his tuxedo to go to the club.

"Help me with these studs, willya, sport? So, listen, where do you stand on this? I mean, do you hate me for this? Doing this to her?"

"Aw, Clyde. How can I hate you? I can't even blame you. All I have to do is look at her. . . . But God knows you're a fool. You're going to wreck your life for damn sure and maybe hers—"

"Not hers, sport. Definitely not hers. You can't imagine . . . she can take care of herself. She may not know it yet but she's built by the same firm that did Stonehedge."

"Henge. It's Stonehenge." Godwin stood back, now the studs were taken care of. He could smell brandy on Clyde's breath. "Okay, so you wreck your own life. That's bad enough."

"I know, I know. I could wind up dead. Tony . . . I don't know what he'd do to me if he found out. And Hood. Makes my flesh crawl. I can't even stand to *think* what he'd do. Damn fool, doesn't know whether he's the girl's father or brother or suitor . . . And—I'm not joshing with you sport—if she cuts me off I swear to God I'll kill myself. I'm not crazy, Rodger, but without her I'd be better off dead. I love the girl. I'm good to her, sport, I . . . I—"

"What about the black girl you're always with?"

"A decoy. She was Prissy's idea. She said we ought to have a decoy. It would make us all the safer if I was known to have a new girl."

"She thinks of everything."

"She *cares* about me, Rodger. Whattaya make of that?" He was having a second go at his black tie. "She's the best thing that ever happened to this old country boy." He sighed at their two faces in the mirror. "What are you going to do about us, pal?"

"Do? I don't know what I'm going to do—"

"Well, you're for us or agin' us. Which is it gwine to be?"

It was bad for her, it was bad for Clyde, but what were you supposed to do? Her life, his life: Surely they had the right to live their own lives. Clyde was on his own; he could face the consequences. He knew damn well what he was doing. But Priscilla—she was obviously a child playing at being naughty in a very grown-up way. What could he, Godwin, do to help her, to make her see how destructively she was behaving, the harm she could do herself?

"Clyde, I don't honestly know."

"Well, old sport, we're depending on you. But I guess you know that. You get her home, will you? Tony and Max went off to play golf way to hell and gone out at Versailles or Saint-Cloud or some damn place. They won't be home 'til late."

"Clyde, how can you do this? She's just a kid—"

"Well, she is and she isn't. And when it comes to girls—I mean *girls* —I'm like one of those opium eaters, a hophead, it's under my skin, it's in my blood. It's going to ruin me, Rodger. Anyway, don't be too hard on her, all right? She took it all pretty well, you seeing her like that and all . . . She may act like it's all very simple, but she's just putting a good face on it. She's pretty cut up inside. Just do your best with it, champ. We'll talk later. Do what you have to do." He slapped Godwin on the back. "I'm in no position to ask favors."

Godwin and Cilla went for a long walk along the Seine, saying next to nothing, crossing over to the Île de la Cité where they walked out to the point and sat on a bench beneath the trees. The leaves were painted with summer's dust. Men in work shirts or smocks or vests were sitting at the water fishing, smoking, waiting and tending their poles as if time had no meaning. She stared clear-eyed at a passing *bateau-mouche*, its lights reflected in the dark water like a sprinkling of gigantic diamonds.

"Remember the night coming back from the tennis?" She smiled at the boat, the memory. "You and I, we had our very first talk . . ." Her voice was very small. "I feel as though I've known you for the longest time, Rodger. Do you feel that way about me?"

"Of course I do. I feel like I've known you all my life."

"Would you mind if I were terribly frank?"

"At this point, anything less would be ridiculous."

"Well . . . it could have been you. Or it could have been Max Hood. I was going to pick someone. And if I'd waited a bit longer it might have been—"

"Max or I might have had better sense than Clyde."

"Do you think so? I don't. At a certain point, having sense probably doesn't matter much. I was bound to do what I did. Best that it was Clyde —he's the one I care least about. He doesn't love me, you must realize that, and he's certainly not going to kill himself." She was wearing a pinafore and a straw hat with a ribbon hanging down the back. He was watching her in profile, watching the finely chiseled lips, the tilt of her nose. She was right, of course. If she'd picked him, he'd have gone with her eagerly. He saw in his mind Clyde kneeling between her legs, her firm thighs holding him, he heard the rasp of her breathing, the insistent desire in it. He wanted to kiss her. He was only human.

"Clyde doesn't know I have a mind or a soul or even a sense of humor. He's simply driven quite mad by my age and my body, the way I look . . . I mean nothing to him. That's why it had to be Clyde. Deep inside, he's nothing to me and I'm nothing to him—not truly. And I knew he wouldn't be shocked or confused at what I wanted to do; I knew he'd had experience at all this . . ."

"Why do you say it *had* to be Clyde?"

"Well, it *had* to be someone. I told you, Rodger, there's something *wrong* with me. Oh, dear, don't make me explain it to you. Sometimes I think if I had some girlfriends to talk things over with, I'd have discovered some other way to handle all this . . . I mean, maybe I wouldn't have just gone ahead with it . . . Clyde's not the first, you see."

"Cilla, please—"

"No, I have to tell someone. I've never been able to talk about it with anyone. At school, when I was twelve, the French master . . . I suppose I was quite shameless. He had a wife and a sickly little baby. He was so sad all the time. He seemed doomed. He just wanted to look at me in the beginning . . . he couldn't believe what was happening to him . . ." She smiled to herself. "He said I was proof that there must be a God. And there was my music master in Switzerland last summer. He was quite rude at times and made me work frightfully hard with my violin but I had to have him . . . it always starts when I know they can't stop looking at me . . . at first I couldn't understand why that was, I wanted to find out . . ."

Godwin said: "How old were you then?"

"Thirteen. About that time there was an older girl at school, eighteen, I had to see what it was that men wanted so. Everything she and I did was very sweet, very gentle—it wasn't nasty, Rodger. She told me not to worry, that we weren't hurting anyone . . . she was very sweet to me, she taught me so much, much more than the men. So, Rodger, please don't blame poor Clyde . . . even if it makes you hate me, even if you can't look at me without being disgusted, I beg you, don't blame this on Clyde. If you think it's horrible—well, that's your business. But I'm not a horrible person, nor is Clyde, and none of this is Clyde's fault."

"Even if it is your fault, he should have stopped you. You obviously don't know what the hell you're doing."

She laughed softly at his earnest concern. "But I do know. That's the point. I must have my way. That's all. There's no good reason for me not to have my way."

The acrid smell of the fishermen's cigarettes blew back across them, a harsh, grating scent. Something jumped and splashed in the water.

"The real point is you've got to stop. It's not too late, you're not pregnant—"

"Don't be vulgar!"

"Oh, don't be such an idiot! Vulgar—good lord. My point is, nobody knows . . . so don't push your luck. Otherwise you're going to destroy yourself."

"I don't mean to be disrespectful to my elders, but aren't you being awfully melodramatic? I mean, really, what's so awful? Why do you say I'll destroy myself? I'm not some backward, illiterate peasant girl who really doesn't know what she's doing . . . he's not making me do anything against my will. I am what I am, he is what he is. You can't change us. I don't want it to stop . . . it doesn't *mean* anything . . . it's something very interesting to do. I'm still the same person I was the day we met."

"Well, I'm just a country boy from Iowa and I don't get it. Any girl

I've ever known back home would be screaming and crying and begging for mercy—"

"Well, that's just not me. Is that what you want me to do?"

"I guess not."

"Everything's all right. You're our friend. My emotions aren't really so involved. Clyde and I, we're like playmates, don't you see?"

"You don't seem to get it, Cilla. He's not your playmate. Clyde is in love with you."

"Oh, you can't believe *that*. It's so silly. He likes my body, that's all. He likes something that belongs to me. Oh, Rodger, I'm trying to make you see . . . I wish you of all people wouldn't be silly about this. I want you to be our ally, our friend. You can help us . . . you can help us spend time together, you can be the third person—someone we can trust and talk to about it, you can try to keep Clyde from working himself into a fit when it ends . . . In September I'm going back to school in Geneva or back to England, perhaps. Another year will begin, new friends, old friends, hard work with my violin . . . Clyde will have to get on with things. You can help him. He'll think he needs a friend—"

"Oh, you can be sure of that. He will need a friend. He loves you, like it or not, little girl."

She smiled wistfully. The breeze tugged at the ribbon and she put her palm on top of her hat for a moment, anchoring it. "Well, if he does . . ." She shrugged. "Love is some kind of awful trap, isn't it, Rodger? It comes and goes and I don't trust it. It's never done anyone I know a bit of good. Look at my poor father . . . But then, I want to be in love, I want to believe in love. Don't you?" She grinned. "But what can I possibly know? I'm only fourteen . . ."

"Out of the mouths of babes . . ."

"How very wise of you to realize that."

He smiled back at her and felt like a grinning idiot.

"When you came into the room?"

"Yes?"

"When you saw us . . . did you think I was pretty? Doing that? Or was it ugly and horrible?"

"For God's sake, Cilla—"

"Did you think I was pretty?"

"Yes, yes, of course."

"Did it excite you?"

"Shut up, Cilla."

"Well, men are a mystery. But you *would* like to do that with me, wouldn't you?" She was looking at the edge of the moon sneaking up into view.

Godwin stared at her then looked away, anywhere.

She said: "I like knowing that you would. Don't worry. I'm much too fond of you. We couldn't be close friends anymore. I think all that ruins friendship. I'm already terribly, horribly tired of poor Clyde in every imaginable way but one. And even that . . . I want the summer to be over. At least this part of it. The Clyde part of it. But I want to do it with him . . . you know what I like most? When he watches me . . . well, please help us and then . . ."

Godwin shook his head. "After all, what's all this to me? I'll never see any of you again after this summer."

"Now you're being silly again. It seems to me that men are always making big, awfully dire statements. The truth is we'll all know each other for the rest of our lives—"

"I don't think life works that way. We'll part, we'll go our own ways and that'll be that."

"Oh? You think you know how life works? Why, you're not even ten years older than I and you're supposed to be an authority on how life works? Just because you're a writer, you know so much?" She was teasing him. "Well, that's you being silly again. I'm sure I've thought about all this much more than you have."

"I'm not going to argue with you, Cilla."

"Well, that's good. Believe me, we'll know each other all our lives, it'll be like a dance or a dream, a recurring dream, we'll keep seeing each other, we'll pass through all the stages of our lives and we'll still know each other. Read your Dickens, read Tolstoy and Trollope and Thackeray. It's all there. And don't think it's over then, when we die, because it's not . . ."

They were walking along the bank, seeing the lamps floating among the waves.

"Cilla, I give up. I don't even know where to begin thinking about it. Or about you."

"Just remember, I am what I am. I always will be. We never really change. You are a perpetual innocent, decent, honest, like someone from *Barchester Towers*. Max Hood is a hero, dealing with this great burden of character and honor and responsibility—it all weighs him down. Max thinks about things like God and honor and his code . . . He's pure Tolstoy. Clyde is a victim of weakness . . . his 'weakness.' It's how he defines himself—young girls, they'll always be his excuse. Later on he'll drink—he likes hauling his doom around within himself. He stepped out of something by Fitzgerald, don't you think? And I am what I am."

"A spiritual descendant of Hemingway's Lady Brett, I suppose."

"Oh, I don't think so. Read *Vanity Fair*. You'll find me there, that's my suspicion."

"Becky Sharp?" He had to smile at the quality of her perception. You had to hand it to Cilla. He'd found her having sex with Clyde and she'd pulled herself together and now she was giving him literary insights into their own lives.

She shrugged playfully. "Well, think about it. Mischief. Temptation. Curiosity. The center of attention. Don't look so surprised, Rodger. I know myself. I know who and what I am. I just have to watch out for the Lady Pamela in me, that's all."

They had stopped at the railing, leaning on it, looking at each other. Godwin thought, God help me. He said: "I've never known anyone so alive." It was clumsy but it was, after all, exactly what he meant.

"We're all terribly alive, I think."

"It's hard, talking about things tonight, hard to believe we'll ever die and be gone. I look at you, Cilla, I don't see how you can ever cease to be . . . not you, somehow not you . . . it scares me, but I think I'd die right now if it meant you could go on living . . ."

"Well, it's my firm belief that we never actually cease to be."

"What do you mean?"

She took his hand, looked up into his eyes.

"Try to remember what I'm going to tell you now, Rodger. I don't know where it comes from but it seems to me as if I've always known it. The secret of the universe and I will make it yours. Listen to me . . .

Life is eternal and
Love is immortal and
What we call Death
Is only the Horizon
Beyond which we cannot see.

Now that's all you need to know and if you find true love—if such a thing exists—then all the better."

Godwin was overcome by a wave of emotion. "Why do I feel so damn sad?" He wanted to hold her in his arms and kiss her and smell her hair and what the hell was going on?

"Because you're an incurable romantic."

As if she knew every thought in his mind, she kissed him then, her mouth soft and warm and moist, and her arms were around his neck as she let the kiss linger. Then she whispered: "Don't be sad."

He had never imagined that life—or another person—could be quite so complicated and magical and alluring.

Many years later he would reflect on it and know that, standing in the warmth of the Paris evening, being kissed by a fourteen-year-old girl, was the moment that his real life, the life of imagined possibilities, his manhood, had really begun.

CHAPTER 16

As August approached, with the heat and humidity preceding it, Godwin tried hard to keep from thinking about Clyde and Priscilla.

They used him but he'd known they would and he had no complaints. He could have said no. And he didn't really mind. It was all too deep for him, or too troubled, or too corrupt, or too irrelevant to his own life. But they used him. He conspired with them. He betrayed them. He made it possible for them to continue. He let them know when the coast was clear. What the hell.

He spent more time with Max Hood, or with Hood and Tony Dew-Brittain, who enjoyed staying in town when so many Parisians headed for the Atlantic beaches or the countryside. They played golf. They went to the races at Longchamps and Godwin bought a pipe, a very handsome item, the briar covered with stretched leather, with a leaping horse stamped in gold on the stem. They played tennis at the Luxembourg Gardens.

And all the time they were occupied with these various pursuits, Godwin knew Clyde and Priscilla were at it together, making the eventual conclusion of the affair all the worse for poor Clyde.

It was a damn hard thing, keeping his mind off what they were doing, keeping his mind on business while he was haunted by the image of the girl opening her body and taking the man inside.

The heat was getting to everyone with the possible exception of Max Hood. The desert had made him immune. He never seemed to exert himself. He was compact and fluid and when he hit a golf ball his swing was flat and quick and his accuracy unnerving. Godwin, six inches taller, had a longer, more upright swing and had been taught early on to shift his weight properly, getting his considerable heft into mashing the ball. He consistently outdrove Hood but the smaller man made up for it around the greens. They were evenly matched when you considered the whole golf course. Though Godwin was drenched and exhausted at the end of a round, Hood looked like a man who'd merely been out for a stroll. His composure was becoming an affront to Rodger Godwin.

His composure and the memory of the dressing down Hood had given him about his writing a few weeks before. It seemed like a lot had happened since then but Godwin couldn't get that morning out of his mind. The keeper of the Book of the Dead. Make a choice, he'd said, be a man. . . . But Godwin kept remembering how together they'd watched the two *flics*, Henri and Jacques, kill a man and then stand preening themselves when it was over. He remembered how Max Hood had held him back, had let the murderers walk away.

And yet Max Hood was the one riding him about being a man.

It put him in a lousy mood when he thought about it and he was thinking about it one afternoon when he went to play tennis with Max Hood at the Luxembourg Gardens. It was hot and humid and dusty on the courts. Not even the *boules* players were in their usual spot. Insects hovered over the Medici Fountain. The courts were empty. Max was waiting for him. "Bloody hot, Godwin. We needn't play, y'know."

"It's okay. Let's hit a few." His white shirt was already stuck to his back. He had a headache from the heat and sun. He might as well die on the dusty tennis court.

The first set went quickly. Hood was playing like LaCoste. Godwin was not doing much of a Tilden. What would Max Hood have done if he'd known about Cilla and Clyde? Godwin backed away from that one and squinted into the sun, saw the black dots before his eyes. Frustration was building in him. What had happened to the simple life?

The first three games were replays of the first set but then Godwin got into a rhythm and felt as if the sweet spot on his racquet had grown to the size of a bass drum. The ball was finding it again, again, again, coming off it heavy and true.

"Well played!" Hood called as the ball hit the court at his feet, spraying dust. "You're hitting your stride, old boy."

Then Hood had gone ahead.

"Now's your chance, Max," Godwin called to him. "One more game and you've got me. You bastard."

Hood laughed. His shirt was soaked, his hair matted, his face caked with dust and sweat. "Godwin, you're wearing me out."

"Remember the desert, pal. It'll pull you through."

At deuce Hood went one up.

The ensuing rally went on approximately forever. Godwin's legs had turned to jelly. His arm felt like a sledgehammer. But Max Hood was feeling it, too, moving like a man trapped on flypaper. The court was sucking at his shoes. He always smiled between points. "Well stroked for America," he'd shout, grinning through the waves of heat at Rodger Godwin.

The rally was lasting so long because both men had been finished for a long time. Godwin wasn't altogether sure why he was staying with it. But he couldn't stop. It had become important. *Life and death* . . .

He wasn't going to last much longer. He knew it and Hood could doubtless see it, too.

Then, suddenly, the ball was floating up before him, hovering like a hummingbird mirage, as if it were dangling on a string, and he thought he might have just one more forehand left. One more real forehand.

The ball floated up, he could see it spinning, it was bald and scuffed with dust, a black hole moving through the sunshine, and Hood was charging the net to finish him off. He was smiling across the net, in love with the struggle, with the effort, with the smell of the kill.

Rodger Godwin drew his arm back, squared the racquet, drove the head through the ball, felt the breath leave his chest with a mighty gasp, saw the strings collide with the ball—

He blinked, sweat stinging his eye, and the next thing he saw was really too fast to see, he saw the splintered fractions of a second, the ball smashing into Hood's face, the blood exploding from his nose, saw the racquet fall from Hood's hand and bounce slowly in the dust, then Hood was draping himself across the net with blood dripping into the dust . . .

When Godwin reached the net he saw the blood splattering at his feet. He felt like a man at the far end of a long dark tunnel, seeing only pinpoints of light. His head was swimming. He was afraid he was going to fall on his face. He just didn't give a damn.

Slowly Hood looked up. The blood had run into his mouth and his teeth were red and white. He was grinning.

"Best damn shot you ever hit," he said. His tongue flicked out at the blood. He wiped his hand across his upper lip and held it out, bloody, to shake hands. Godwin took it and they sealed the game. "That's it for me," Hood said. "Shall we call it a draw?"

"Call it whatever you like." Godwin could barely speak.

"I'll tell you what it was," Hood said, wiping at the blood. "Men only. That's what it damn well was." He slapped Godwin on the back as they slowly trailed along the net. He left a bloody handprint on the wet shirt.

"I'm learning, Max, I'm learning."

They sat on a bench looking out at the deserted courts baking in the late afternoon sun.

"Life and death," Godwin went on. His legs were shaking and he couldn't stop them.

"Exactly," Hood said. "And when we've left the little balls and things behind, the game is still going on. You do see what I mean, don't you, old boy?"

Godwin knew exactly what he meant.

You learned something new every damned day, that summer in Paris.

When August came Merle Swaine surprisingly arranged for a farmhouse in Brittany, not far from the wild rocky coast. He told Godwin to go there to have a rest . . . and write a couple of long pieces he'd been preparing. Take your little girlfriend, the dancer or the singer or whatever she is, take her and make a holiday of it.

Godwin went, took Clothilde, and wrote and lay in the sun and went for cold midnight walks on the cliffs above the pounding surf. He forgot to blot out images of what was going on back in Paris. He almost told Clothilde the story, then thought better of it. What was the point? She didn't need to know.

Swaine drove down to visit them the second week. He'd acquired a new car, an open model, and wanted to break it in. They'd only been gone for ten days but Godwin was out of touch. Swaine said he was apparently not "a rusticating kind of man." He brought news and Godwin devoured it, as if he'd been exiled to another planet, not merely to Brittany. Babe Ruth was continuing to swat home runs at an alarming pace and Godwin wondered if Marshall Hacker was in Monte yet with Willie and was keeping tabs on George H. Ruth from across the ocean.

The three of them were sitting outside in the moonlight hearing the waves cannonading against the rocks and drinking wine when Clothilde mentioned Max Hood.

"The penny drops," Swaine said, dribbling wine down his shirtfront. "I have news of Max. A shadowy man, our Max, I hear things about Max Hood."

"For instance," Godwin prompted.

"Seems Brother Hood is some sort of British agent. Acting as liaison with the French on new armaments, gun emplacements, airships with heavy bomb loads, new tanks, artillery . . . all very hush-hush and, frankly, who knows if it's important? Any war is years away, the way things are. But, still, hush-hush. And, oh, by the way, it transpires there's also a Mrs. Hood! What say you to that?"

"I'd heard the rumor," Godwin said.

"Well, she's shown up from somewhere, either the Dordogne or Deauville, I get my *D*'s mixed up. Max apparently isn't overjoyed about it. You'll have to meet her. Both of you. She has the eyes of a jackdaw and the talons of a vulture."

"How enchanting," Clothilde murmured.

"She's a novelist," Swaine said, oozing contempt. "One of those lady novelists. Name of Euterpe or Eulalie. Something astonishingly irritating. Esmé, that's it. Christ. *Esmé.* You have to hate her. Hood must have been drunk that day. People say she draws the characters in her novels from real life, or so says our culture man, what's-his-name, Newman. He says she has a following. Lesbians," he winked broadly, "are much devoted to her. And what else? ah yes, she travels with a Spanish woman, titled and very la-di-da, and Newman swears they're widely known to be lovers . . ." Swaine beamed in the moonlight and held out his glass for a refill. He laughed aloud. "Max seems appalled by the whole thing but he keeps such a damned stiff upper lip you can never be quite sure. Esmé Hood. He picked a real winner there, kids, did our Max!"

"Tell me," Godwin said, "is she sick? I heard she had consumption and was in a sanitarium in the mountains."

Swaine shrugged. "Sounds more like one of her horrible books, the way you describe it. She's not what you'd call exactly robust but she doesn't look like a lunger."

Back in Paris Godwin got a call from Hood to meet him late one night at the Dingo for a drink.

Hood looked tired, eyes red-rimmed and bloodshot, and he drank more eagerly than was his custom. He told Godwin about Esmé and Carmen and his voice was a little shaky. Not with anger as much as with frustration and anxiety.

"Bloody woman," Hood said, stroking his mustache as if he'd doubted for a moment that it was still there. "I've been trying to get her to agree to a divorce. I've been trying for years. She teases me, she taunts me. It's simply not acceptable but there's only one way I can think of to put a stop to it and I'm not ready for that yet."

"No children, I take it."

"Children! She'd have drowned them like cats. I hate to imagine what her issue might be . . . Oh, my young friend, be vigilant when it comes to youthful indiscretions. In my own defense, I can only say she didn't seem a monster at the time." A grin flickered across his handsome face. "One of my secrets, that's Esmé. Most of the time it's as if I never met her, let alone married her."

"Tell me, is she ill?"

He laughed harshly. "Tony say that?"

"Priscilla, actually. Something she'd heard—"

"Poor Prissy. Well, I told Tony and she must have been there. Esmé *told* me she was dying . . . it was her idea of a dandy leg-pull."

"Sounds crazy," Godwin said.

"And, to make matters worse, I think about Prissy all the time. Damned if I know what to do. I should never have kissed her."

"If I were you, I wouldn't give it another thought."

"But you," Hood said, "don't know her like I do."

"Perhaps not," Godwin said.

Clyde Rasmussen also turned to Godwin for aid and comfort.

"You know how much Cilla and I appreciate everything you've done for us. But it's been hell since you left for the country. This goddamn heat, for one thing. Pardon my French, but some days it's too hot to fuck. Never thought I'd hear myself say that. Tony's been staying closer to home. And there's that godawful wife of Hood's! He must have been crazy as a flea!" He sighed. "So Tony hasn't had Max to play with. The problem is, I get the feeling that Hood's suspicious about, you know, Prissy and me . . ."

"You're imagining things. He's got his hands full."

Clyde looked doubtful. "No, he's up to something. Every time I see him he asks me if I've seen Priscilla. He's got this cold look in his eyes. I don't trust him."

"Wait a minute. You're the one who's not trustworthy—"

"You know what I mean. The man scares the shit out of me." He paused, staring into Godwin's face. "It's been hell since you left, sport. Prissy would tell you the same thing. Have you seen her?"

"No."

"You're not punishing her for my sins, I hope." He blinked at Godwin, the hayseed face sorrowful.

"I just haven't seen her."

"Well, listen, can you stop in and see Tony tomorrow afternoon? She's got a lesson and we may be able to have an hour together . . . if you can keep old Tony's mind occupied. Can you do that for us, sport?"

The next afternoon Godwin dropped by to see Tony DewBrittain, found him sitting out-of-doors in the shade, half dozing. He didn't look terribly well but then nobody did with the heat and the humidity and the oppressive stillness. Shortly after Godwin's arrival, Max Hood appeared and joined them. He alone seemed to have some reserve of energy. His shirt collar was crisp, his white linen suit spotless and fresh, his white perforated wing tips without a blemish. He no longer looked tired.

DewBrittain noted Hood's general spiffiness and said, with reference to Mrs. Hood and her friend, "The girls leave town?"

Hood smiled wanly. "Would that it were so. But, alas, no. I've decided to rise above it."

The conversation moved slowly and once Hood went into the house and came back with a tall glass of clear liquid. Godwin got a whiff as he passed. Hood was drinking gin at a remarkable clip. His hands couldn't seem to stay still but otherwise he showed no ill effects.

Eventually the afternoon dwindled away; shadows groped their way toward the middle of the garden and insects began yelling about things. Godwin reckoned he'd given the lovers—his guts rebelled at the idea but there was no point in denying it to himself—time enough. When he finally extricated himself from the deck chair he heard the squeaking hinge of the courtyard door to the street. Priscilla was home, looking flushed from the heat, a pink-and-white skirt and blouse against her tanned, healthy face and arms. She was carrying her violin and the music folder and waved happily, called something over her shoulder as she dashed up the few crumbling steps and into the darkness of the house. Tony DewBrittain, still reclining in his chair, looked up at Godwin and Hood. "I don't know what I'd do without that girl. She makes me a happy man."

Moving slowly along the quiet street Godwin made some mention of Priscilla, and Hood said: "You know, you were quite right about that spot of trouble I had with her. I finally tried to apologize and the funny thing is, I'm not even sure she remembered it. She just gave me a sort of vague look, and said something about what a wonderful night it had been and started reminiscing about the party. Women. Well, who knows what's going on in there, eh?"

"I'm beginning to think it's better we don't."

"Daresay you're right. You know she's not quite herself at the moment."

"Really?" He reflexively wondered: Is this going to be something about Clyde? Is he suspicious?

"Well, a couple of things, actually. You know how Clyde has rather taken her under his wing, like an older brother. Always talks to her about music, about the commitment to daily practicing, about the intimacy of the musician and his instrument. Rather like a soldier and his weapon, I gather. You become one, so to speak. She says he's really quite sophisticated about music theory and whatnot. Well, I have the feeling he's let her down rather badly of late. He doesn't seem to come over to the house anymore. I realize the man has his own life, there's the black girl one sees him with, he has the demands of the club, I'm not saying I blame him, not by any means, but frankly I think she misses those chats about music . . . that's one thing bothering her and then there's this business with her mother, Lady Pamela—she seems to be threatening to put in an appearance . . . about as welcome, I expect, as an adder in one's underwear. As welcome as my wife, for that matter. There is, in any case, the news that Lady Pamela may return to Tony this summer to try and make things up. I told him he ought to give her the boot but he always thinks she might mend her ways and make a decent mother to Priscilla. Amazing how blind a man can be about a woman, isn't it? Pamela's a bad 'un, make no mistake about it. Why can't he see that? People are what they are. Have you ever noticed that? They don't change much, not after they've got a bit of personality on them."

Godwin nodded. He might have been listening to Priscilla. "Things any better at your house?" It was strange, feeling sorry for Max Hood.

Hood laughed. "No, it's all rather trying. Putting up with Esmé makes a chap long for the blood and screaming of the trenches. Add the Spanish creature . . . But I won't bother you about that, old man, it's my spilt milk and there's no use my crying over it. With any luck you won't be required to encounter them."

The Eiffel Tower brooded in the heat haze that August. The city seemed half-asleep in the heat, trapped in a kind of languid torpor, then it would flare up emotionally and the cause was frequently a demonstration in support of Sacco and Vanzetti, who were running out of time in far off Boston. Parisians were firm in their belief that the two Italians were being railroaded for armed robbery and murder because they were foreigners and anarchists. They were probably right. As the execution date approached, demonstrations broke out across Europe. In Paris, relatively deserted at the moment, you could occasionally stumble across a raucous, placard-waving group of demonstrators without the slightest warning. Godwin found it all rather amazing. It was by way of an introduction to the fervor of European political emotion.

It was that time of year in Paris. Heat waves, everything partially paralyzed, shopkeepers more surly than usual. Flowers wilted and drooped and dried up in untended window boxes. Dogs panted in the shade. The cafés were still full but the babble was in English. The same was true of the Club Toledo: Business was good but it wasn't quite Paris.

Rodger Godwin felt the edginess. It was like catching a fever that bubbled in your blood but wouldn't burst out and drop you into bed. He got a check from Marshall Hacker so there was some real money in the bank. He began thinking about buying a little car. He had his eye on a red two-seater, English made. He thought about how much better it would be when the heat wave broke and you could get some halfway decent sleep at night.

Clothilde was unhappy for the first time since he'd known her. She wanted out of the life of the occasional prostitute. She was trying to get a job singing and dancing in the clubs with shows but it wasn't easy. It wasn't going well. At night she lay in Godwin's arms and cried. The heat was too heavy and thick; he could barely move. He offered to help her with money and that made her cry harder. She said that when the summer ended she wasn't going to go with men for money anymore. She asked Godwin what he was going to do. He felt her eyelashes flutter against his chest. He had no idea, no answer, and that bothered him.

The boxing match was Clyde Rasmussen's idea.

The tickets came from a local promoter who was a jazz fan and a regular at the club. Clyde gave himself a night off, booked a "darkie" band in his place, and asked Hood and Godwin to join him for a boys' night out. He reckoned they could all use some time together, without the various women.

The fight was held in a converted *bal musette* where a ring had been hastily set up under a large low-hanging light similar to those seen above billiard tables, only larger. There were twenty rows of chairs on each side and behind that there was crowded standing room. Insects hung in a cloud around the light, occasionally snapping and popping as they drew too close and were fried. The room was thick with blue cigarette and pipe smoke and stank of sweat and warm wine. They found their seats by pushing through the crowd to ringside right next to the man who rang the bell.

Godwin was busily taking mental notes, registering everything he saw. The bugs sizzling on the lights, the bottle of Alsatian beer in the bell ringer's hand, the long wet droop of the referee's mustache, the three-legged stool that sat unevenly when a fighter sank down between rounds, the sweat-soaked trunks that clung like bathing suits, the battered bucket to spit in, the sponge dripping pink water, the short black socks rolled down over the canvas shoes, the hairless legs, the sodden boxing gloves heavy as sacks of wet cement, the spray of sweat and blood when one of the gloves smashed into a face, the bloody water squirted from between broken teeth . . .

The main event featured lightweights, a swarthy little Monagasque and a sailor from Marseilles with a shining, shaved head. The sailor, who had the body of a young man and the scowling, disappointed face of a fifty-year-old stoker, cornered the Monagasque against the ropes above them in the third round, broke a rib with a left uppercut, and as the poor bastard gasped and lurched forward split his nose with a straight right. Blood sprayed through the air like an end-of-the-world rainbow, splashing Godwin's face, tracking across Hood's shirt like a burst of machine-gun fire. The Monagasque sunk to his knees, buckled forward on his face, blood smearing the stained, slippery canvas while the crowd shouted and stamped their feet. The sponge came flying through the ropes, landed like a dead mackerel at the referee's feet.

Sweat was running through the blood on Godwin's face as they pushed back up through the crowded aisle, back out into the sweltering night.

Godwin felt vaguely sick to his stomach but he was damned if he hadn't enjoyed every minute of it.

They stopped briefly for a nightcap, then strolled down toward the river in hopes of encountering a cooling breeze off the water. Their hopes were dashed, of course, but they made the best of it. Godwin had tried to wipe the blood from his face but felt the remaining bits drying, flaking, tightening. They kept on along the embankment, the sound of the music from the dance halls fading behind them. Eventually they struck off through the little streets angling away from the river, through the odd pools of light at the corners, then back into the darkness where the bats fluttered from the bell towers of ancient churches.

Without warning a bit of the recent past came hurtling like an express train out of a dark pit of alleyway.

A cry for help, a sob. A faint scuttling sound.

Hood stopped, raised his hand, cupped it to his ear, listening intently.

The wet moan came again, a wordless sound like something from a dying animal.

There was a shape on the ground toward the far end of the short, narrow alleyway. It was a man. Godwin had seen it all before in another shadowy passage. He felt as if events, the memory and now this, were pinning him to the spot.

The man was trying to pull himself along the ragged bricks away from the glow of blue light which seemed for the moment a thousand miles away.

Hood was running toward the huddled, convulsed shape. Clyde followed him at a distance, not quite knowing what was going on.

The man was dead but didn't know it yet.

Godwin came even with the body but stood well to one side. He couldn't face going any closer.

The man had squirmed over onto his back. Hood was kneeling beside him. There was a terrible smell, like a slaughterhouse. Clyde suddenly gagged, turned away with a stifled cry, leaned against the wall and vomited until he was empty and still retching.

Hood stepped away at last, stood looking down at the body. "Go back," he said to Godwin. "He's dead. There's nothing to be done." He walked slowly toward the blue light.

From where he stood Godwin saw steam rising from the body. Even in the heat of the night there was steam.

He went closer, stared down into the swollen face, the sightless staring eyes. The cheeks bulged. One outflung arm looked like a sausage jammed too tightly into its casing. He gave the impression of being a balloon overstretched. Finally the shirt had split open, his chest bulging outward, buttons ripped off.

He had been beaten until he'd burst.

The steam. It took Godwin a moment to realize what had happened. He stared at the middle of the body, the source of the steam.

The swollen body had come apart.

He had been beaten to death, beaten until his distended wino's belly had burst, spilling his entrails, everything, spilling it all like a long writhing snake hanging from his gut.

Godwin backed away from the body, heard Hood whisper his name. He joined him at the end of the alley across from the blue light.

Hood pointed at the smear of blood on the cobblestones at the entrance to the bricked alley. He raised his eyes toward the blue light.

It shone over the rear door to the *préfecture de police*.

The police station.

CHAPTER 17

The morning of August 24 brought the official confirmation that Sacco and Vanzetti had been put to death. Passions flared, there was talk of more anti-American riots. Everyone seemed to be planning one, looking forward to joining one, or at the very least making arrangements for a good spot from which to watch one. Godwin tried to imagine something happening in Paris which could produce such a reaction in the United States. The very idea was laughable.

As chance would have it, it was the evening of the same day that the DewBrittain household was entertaining again, a reward for those who'd lingered through August in the city. The occasion was a violin recital by Priscilla.

The idea, however, was Lady Pamela Legend's. Shedding her role as *femme fatale*, Priscilla's mother had appeared from somewhere beginning with a *D* determined to resume her more domestic role, that of wife and mother. People were not altogether sure why she had adopted this particular stratagem, though it was commonly thought that money came into it somewhere. Either the money was Tony's and she was back because she'd run out, or the money was hers and she was using it to buy her way back into the family circle. Money, it was agreed, was involved.

There was a scent of danger in the air that night. The streets were full, there was an unusual amount of milling about, lots of placards and banners all protesting the fates of Sacco and Vanzetti. There was a warm mist falling with the promise of rain to come. Rumors seemed to ride on the warmth, breed in it.

The party was the sort that glitters and coruscates and sometimes almost blinds you. Many of the women wore long gowns and most of the men were in evening clothes and the lights were bright and they all seemed to exist, suspended, in a giant, fragile bubble. Esmé Hood was peculiarly elongated, almost starved, with vast eyes outlined in black, her skin pale as parchment. She clung to the arm of the stern Spanish woman, Carmen. Hood was frequently seen on his wife's other side though she did not seem to notice. Godwin decided Esmé Hood *was* sick, maybe dying. Lady Pamela was altogether different: a small woman with a wide mouth, a pouting lower lip, the same brown eyes and level gaze you saw in Priscilla, her shiny dark hair cropped short and seemingly polished. She was very quick, very charming, impressively alert. With Godwin she was brightly intimate, quick to establish a relationship, thanking him for having such a good effect on her daughter.

"It's a relief for her to have someone to talk with about books and writers, she's such a precocious little thing, and both Tony and I are virtually illiterate. Country families, you know. Ignorance is our birthright and we cling to it for dear life." Diamonds caught the light. She had a wonderful silvery laugh.

Godwin tried to imagine what it must have been like for Priscilla the night her mother went off with Marc, her cousin or whatever, while Tony screamed after her into the stillness of a Belgravia night. How did people ever come back together after that sort of rift? It was foreign to Godwin, impossible to understand. Yet he was a writer, suddenly successful, money in the bank. Of all the people he'd met in Paris that summer, it was Lady Pamela who'd made him unsure of himself and the flurry of acclaim he was experiencing. It was Lady Pamela on whom he knew damn well he had no line at all.

Priscilla played beautifully. Astonishingly. She stood at the foot of the stairs, acknowledging the crowd with a fleeting smile, and then disappearing into the music. She was accompanied on the piano by a young man who looked like one's idea of D'Artagnan. It was a romantic programme, Tchaikovsky, Paganini, something else full of yearning. Godwin had to be reminded by Swaine to close his mouth when the performance was over. Godwin had never known anyone who could do anything like what Priscilla DewBrittain had just done.

Swaine was grinning at him, his jowls flooding his collar. "So, the kid's not bad." He began to chuckle. "You oughta see yourself. Relax. The kid's a fiddler."

Her teacher, an elderly woman in a high-necked black dress from the previous century, a cameo choker at her throat, a white mustache, said: "She plays as if she is very old and has seen so much and is yet very forgiving of life, of fate. She seems to understand life . . . I sometimes fear for her. Perhaps she will never again be so wise as she is now, a dear child . . ."

Priscilla found Godwin, only for a moment, her eyes huge and liquid and shining. They did not speak. He took her in his arms and held her, and when she broke away he reached out and wiped tears from her face. He didn't know what she must be feeling. He only knew that whatever it was he would never feel it, he would only know it as it was reflected from her that night. Then, in an instant, she was gone, swept away by her mother and father and their friends and he was quite sure that he would never again be alone with her, never again enjoy her undivided attention.

Clyde had to leave early, not long after Priscilla's performance, because the club was booked solid and some recording people were on hand. He was perspiring heavily and his eyes were bloodshot. Godwin was looking a trifle anxiously for Clothilde, who once again was having to arrive late. It was a client and she had faced the appointment grimly, swearing she was all but done with "the life." She had had an excellent audition for a singing job at a fancy Right Bank nightclub: If it came through, she'd put all that behind her. Then he felt Clyde's hand on his shoulder and got the sweet, sick whiff of absinthe. Clyde was urgently pulling at him. "Come on, sport, walk out with me. I'm heartsick, goddammit, that's what my old mother used to say . . . 'I'm heartsick, Clyde, you're breaking my heart.' Well, I know what she meant now . . ."

A couple of blocks from the walled house Clyde suddenly began to sob and sank back against a tree. He ground his palms against his eyes, swallowing against the tears. "I'm in bad shape, fella, you know all about it . . . she's in my blood, I can't do anything about it and . . . and . . . well, you know all the things Clothilde does for you? Well, I'm teaching Priscilla all those things. Can you imagine what that does to a man? A girl like Prissy? Aw, hell . . ." He sniffled and ran his huge hand through the spikey red hair, then tried to smooth it down, gave up. "What am I going to do, pal? I can't give her up . . ."

"What is it? She's going back to school?"

"I could deal with that, I'd find a way . . ." He sucked some damp warm air deep into his lungs. It was thundering again with cascades of heat lightning picking out landmarks on the skyline. "I'd see her, no school could keep me away from her. No, it's me . . . I've been offered a helluva lot of money to go to New York. They're saying they'll name the Roof Garden at the Hotel Cleveland the same as the club here . . . Clyde's Toledo Club at the Cleveland; they think that's cute. Big hotel, sport, on Lexington . . . lots of money, recordings, every goddamn thing I could want. Except Prissy. So there's only one thing for me to do . . ." He was pulling himself together, straightening his jacket, wiping his face with the incongruous red bandanna.

Godwin had to ask because he couldn't imagine the answer. "What *can* you do?"

"I want her to come with me!"

"Cilla?" He heard the amazement in his own voice. "You want Cilla to go to New York? Clyde, she's only fourteen. She's not some barefoot girl from the Ozarks. How are you going to pull this off?"

He shook his head. "Got to figure out a way. Hell, I'd kidnap her . . . but Hood, oh God, I know what he'd do. He'd come after me, he'd kill me, that bastard has murder in him—I can't believe you don't see it, pal—"

"Clyde, it's not going to work. She's not going to New York with you. Look, have you talked to her about it? You've got to do that, you've got to see what she thinks. And Hood isn't all you've got to worry about. There's Tony and God help you if you run afoul of this Lady Pamela. You don't want her for an enemy."

"I don't need to hear all this from you, sport. What I need from you is some help—"

"I've already helped you a damn sight more than I should have." Immediately, he regretted saying it, but he didn't need a lecture from Clyde Rasmussen. "I don't need to hear you tell me you need some help from me. You've *had* some help from me, my friend. I've got no obligation to help you in another chapter of this craziness—"

"Is that the way you feel about things, then?"

"I think taking her to New York is an insane idea, it's insane even to think about—"

"And I thought you were my friend . . . *our* friend."

"I am, I'm trying to give you some good advice."

"And you not wet behind your ears, for chrissake! You know what I think, sport? I think you want her over here . . . you want a crack at her yourself!" He was staring hard, face white.

"Well, Clyde, I don't give a good goddamn what you think. You're drunk on absinthe and you're out of your mind and—"

Clyde looped a right hand at Godwin's head. Godwin caught it like a fly ball and pushed the hand down. "Don't bite off more than you can chew. That's fair warning, Clyde. You don't want to have an honest-to-god fight with me, I promise you . . ."

Clyde looked down, rubbed his hand. "Jesus, Rodger, you've turned out to be a son of a bitch . . ."

"You don't know what you're talking about. I'll see you tomorrow." Godwin turned his back on Clyde and walked away.

From a block behind him he heard Clyde Rasmussen, his first friend in Paris, calling to him through the sudden warm, sodden wind rushing through the trees.

"Godwin . . . you're a son of a bitch . . . you know that? Godwin . . . you're a lying traitor, you bastard . . . Godwin . . ."

The thunder finally drowned him out.

When he returned to the party, Clyde's taunts still burning in his ears, Godwin found Swaine sweating like one very hot porker and waving to him from across the room. "Come on, there's all hell breaking loose over at the American embassy. The Frogs are rioting! Very excitable people." He smirked happily. "Barricades going up. I've got a photographer on the way. Let's get over there."

"Sacco and Vanzetti?" Godwin asked as they dashed out into the street.

"Sure as hell ain't Babe Ruth, sonny," Swaine said. "We've got to get a taxi—ah, there's Hood, he's got one, he's coming with us!"

Two and a half hours later, nerves frazzled from the hysteria swirling around the embassy, the three of them were back in their own *quartier* at a nondescript café from the terrace of which you could just, by craning your neck, see the doorway of the Club Toledo. They were drinking cold beer and Godwin couldn't seem to reduce the rate at which his heart was pounding. He felt as if he'd been injected with something that had upset his equilibrium.

They were all soaked with sweat, out of breath, legs trembling from running. Everywhere you looked, you saw the mixture of high spirits and burgeoning rage and too much wine. Normally calm individuals expressed their feelings that an injustice had been committed across the sea and before you knew it, before they understood it themselves, they were yelling and getting ready to punch somebody.

The rain finally came as they sat on the terrace, splattering on the tables and in their hair and bouncing in the street and puddling up, a warm dirty rain but a rain nonetheless, and it felt like school was out. People had been talking edgily before and with the rain the noise rose and music came from a couple of horn players and a drummer on the corner and some of the crowd on the terrace began to dance and shout and they were joined by the crowd from across the street and before you knew it there was an impromptu street dance going on and it grew in size as if it were more liquid spilling endlessly out into the wet, rainy streets.

The music grew ever louder and Godwin found himself swept out into the street on a tide of shouting, singing revelers. Hood stood impassively near the corner, watching, and Swaine was laughing, surrounded by pretty girls dancing and shouting and lifting their skirts.

Hood seemed to be the only man in the street who wasn't having any fun. He was somewhere else. Maybe he was angry with Esmé. Maybe he was in love with Cilla. Maybe Clyde was right, and Max had come to suspect something about Clyde and Cilla. Godwin watched him, wondered what was going on behind that remote, chiseled face. He was thinking about Max Hood and his secrets when something at the corner of his eye, something out of place, caught his attention.

A woman was standing in the shadows at the corner, leaning against a plane tree, one hand covering her face. She wore only a pale blue slip. She was clinging to the tree, her wild eyes raking the scene with desperation. At first he thought her lipstick had smeared across her face. But there was too much of it. It was in her hair and it was on her chest and on her slip and no one was paying any attention to her. She was smeared with blood. The rain streaked through the blood as she stood, alone and hurt, washing it down her body as if she were wax and melting.

It was Clothilde.

They took her to Godwin's place because his hot water was more dependable and she said she was afraid to go back to her room. Her lips were swollen and split and the cheek bearing the carved cross was bruised, the skin scraped raw. She had trouble speaking. One front tooth was loose and she'd bitten her tongue. There was blood between her legs and the crotch of her underpants was ripped and stained. Godwin gently undressed her and bathed her. She lay in the tub, didn't protest. She moaned with pain sometimes and he leaned over the tub, kissed her hair, whispered to her.

Swaine stopped short of the doorway to the bathroom, decorous, a gentleman. "Rodger, she's got to see a doctor. Don't give me any bullshit about that. I know a good man in the rue de Rennes. He'll come."

Godwin helped her out of the tub and gently toweled her off. The sounds of the party in the street below floated through the open window. Thunder rumbled and rain blew across the sill. He wrapped her in his robe and led her to the bed. Her eyes were purple and black and swelling tight.

He helped her to lie down, watched helplessly as she drew herself up, knees tucked toward her chest.

Max Hood had been smoking, standing at the window, staring down into the street. Once she was on the bed, he slowly turned away and came over to stand beside her. He reached down and carefully turned her face to him. Tears squeezed out between her eyelids. Godwin knelt beside her, took her hand.

"Somebody," Hood said, "knew what he was doing."

Godwin looked at him. "What do you mean?"

"The man who did this to her was not simply a client. Isn't that right, Clothilde?"

She nodded almost imperceptibly.

"You'd finished with the client," Hood said. "You were alone . . . then what?"

She shook her head, touched her split lip, murmured something indecipherable. Her eyes were puffy slits. Godwin was still so shaken he couldn't pay much attention to anything but her pain. He pointed the fan so that it blew across her face from the top of the bureau.

Hood went on insistently, calmly. "This is very important, Clothilde. The client didn't do this—"

"No," she whispered.

"Someone came here afterward . . ."

"Two of them, they hurt me . . ."

"They raped you."

She nodded. Godwin held her hand, stroked her hair.

Swaine said: "I don't think we should wait much longer for the doctor, gents."

. "In a minute," Hood said softly. "These men, did you know them?"

She nodded again, wincing at the slight movement of her head.

"You must tell me who they were."

"No . . . they will come back . . . he cut my face . . . long ago . . ."

"Your face? With a knife?"

She touched the cross on her face with her fingertips. "He owned me . . . he bought me from one of the houses four years ago . . . he cut me to show I belonged to him . . . I left two years ago, I had a man to protect me . . . Clyde . . . but he watches me all the time . . . then tonight . . ." She sobbed, trying to turn away, crying out in pain. Blood from her face stained the pillow.

"Don't be afraid," Hood said. "Tell me . . . who are these men?"

"I can't . . . they'll kill me next time—"

"I assure you they will do nothing of the kind, my dear. Just tell me their names."

Her eyes shone between the swollen lids. She looked at Godwin.

"Go ahead. Tell him." Godwin squeezed her hand.

"Jacques . . . and Henri . . ."

"The police?" Godwin said. "They did this to you?"

"Jacques owned me." Her tears were soaking the bloodstains, spreading them.

Hood reached down and stroked her hair. "Don't worry. I'm going to have a word with Jacques and Henri." He stood up from the bedside. "Rodger, stay with her. Swaine, get that doctor. She's going to be all right. But get the doctor."

Godwin said: "Use the telephone downstairs, Merle. I'm going with you, Max."

Hood looked into his face. "You're quite sure, old boy? There'll be dirty work at the crossroads, I'm afraid."

Godwin had never heard the expression before.

Hood added: "I'm rather more experienced at this sort of thing."

"Then I'll be learning from an expert."

Hood smiled slowly. "Yes. Now I think about it, Rodger, you're right. You're just the man for the job, after all."

Hood leaned against the black iron fence circling the small churchyard cemetery, inclined his head toward the lights at the end of the block. An out-of-the-way café was spilling its last customers out into the street, into the rain. Standing under the awning with the steady drumbeat of rain, with their uniform jackets unbuttoned, were Jacques and Henri, surveying their little domain. They were smoking cigarettes, occasionally laughing, nodding good night to weaving patrons. Both Jacques and Henri were drinking from small glasses, an empty wine bottle on the dark green metal table between them.

Rain slanted across the street, lashed the church tower, rippled in the light of the street lamps. It looked like a hail of bullets in the light. It was in fact a warm soaking rain. Hood climbed the fence into the graveyard, then gave Godwin, much the larger and more cumbersome man, a helping hand. "Mind the points," Hood said. "Chap could hurt himself."

Godwin dropped to the ground. The grass was wet, needed cutting. The graveyard smelled like a golf course back home. An open grave, a mound of dirt running to mud, the hole awaiting its new resident. Behind the pile of dirt the grave digger's wheelbarrow, filling with muddy rainwater, a spade leaning.

They stood staring at each other across the grave, faces dripping, hair matted, thoroughly soaked.

Hood picked up the spade, ran his thumb along the edge. A ghost of a smile may have flickered across his thin lips.

Hood strode to the head of the grave and began banging the spade on the new gravestone. It made an absolute hell of a racket. Godwin watched in amazement. Then, in an earsplitting baritone, Max Hood began to sing "Danny Boy." Then "Champagne Charlie." "Come on, old boy. Let's have a song . . ." Godwin's mind went blank and then he began singing "The Battle Hymn of the Republic." Then he sang "Pop Goes the Weasel." He sang until he thought his head would burst. He sang it until Henri and Jacques were standing at the fence, watching them, muttering to each other. Jacques was draining the dregs from the wine bottle.

Hood staggered drunkenly through the mud to face them, nose to nose, bawling some barrack ballad at them. Jacques made a sudden grab but Hood backed away and fell down, laughing, singing, swearing at them in French and blowing raspberries their way. Hood picked up the spade and hobbled back to the gravestone and began pounding again.

Jacques held the wine bottle by its throat and smashed it against the fence.

The two *flics* found the gate and came inside, came looking for more sport. They were grinning. They knew what they were doing.

Hood waved drunkenly at Jacques, who was in the lead, called him a fat pig, challenged him.

When Jacques was close enough, broken bottle waving before him, thinking about killing another drunk, when Henri was stumping along behind him, when Godwin was watching the scene across the pile of mud and the open grave—something happened.

Jacques lunged with the bottle at Hood's face. Blood spurted in the rain.

Suddenly Hood braced himself against the headstone and swung the spade upward.

Jacques's hat flew off. For a moment Godwin thought it was the man's head. The bottle described an arc and finished with a splash in a puddle.

Jacques staggered back clutching his face, clawing at the collar of his jacket. Before he could fall the spade flashed again. The blade chopped through the fingers. They flew away like chips of wood. Blood was spraying into the air as if from tiny geysers. His fingers were gone and his throat was slashed open. He pitched over sideways onto the mound of mud.

Hood took a step toward Henri, slipped and went to his knees. Henri lunged forward, clubbing with his heavy truncheon.

Godwin leapt across the yawning grave pit, grabbed at Henri's head, slipped off into the mud. Hood rolled away, slammed up against the headstone, pinned. Henri went for him, hit him square in the back, folding him forward over the gravestone. Henri was driving his heavy boots into Hood's kidneys, grunting with each kick. Hood slid sideways gasping, Henri falling forward. Godwin reached over the stone and sank his fingers into Henri's wet greasy hair, began smashing his face into the wet marble. He'd never known he was quite so strong. It was easy. He kept doing it until Hood's muddy face rose in front of him. Hood shook his head, put his hand on Godwin's shoulder.

Godwin stepped back and the body remained draped over the stone, still, the warm rain pelting down.

"He's dead, old boy. Well done."

"No, no, he's knocked out . . . he's unconscious—"

"Quite dead. You see, what happened was you drove all the bones in his face, the front of his skull, you drove all that into what served him for a brain. About the size of a walnut, I'd say. Damn good work."

Godwin poked at the body, head swimming, dazed. He watched the shape slide off the stone and flop onto its back. The man had no face. Godwin's stomach revolted but he fought it off. Blood mixed with the mud on Hood's face. The broken bottle had caught him beneath his eye.

"Saved my life," Hood said. "Cry havoc, as the Bard said, and loose the dogs of war, or words to that effect. You've done a good night's work. You're one of us now."

"One of whom? Jesus, I killed him—"

"One of the dogs of war. All in a good cause."

"It's murder." Godwin wiped the rain out of his eyes. It was coming down harder now. Occasional flickers of lightning lit up the low skyline, the chimney pots. "We've just murdered two men."

"We know they've killed two men at the very least. We know what they did to Clothilde. We've done the only honorable thing." Hood was staring down at the body of Jacques. He picked up the spade with one hand, wiped blood from beneath his eye with the other.

"Max, we *murdered* them!"

"Rubbish, old man. We executed them. World of difference. We were the instruments of a just, albeit vengeful, God. If that makes you feel any better." He had begun doing something with the spade. "Now I'll hear no more about it. You thought I was a gutless bastard not long ago because I didn't do this. Well, now it's done. The time was right, they'd had a go at one of ours. We presented the bill." He was digging with the spade, his foot driving the blade down like a man in his flower bed. As Godwin went closer, Hood lifted the spade. Jacques's head, eyes wide open, lay on the blade. "His head was almost off anyway. It's a question of sending a message, you see. You learn things like that, symbols you might call them, in the desert." He pitched the head into the wheelbarrow. It landed with a thud and a splash.

Together they hauled and struggled and lifted the two corpses into the wheelbarrow. The mud sucked at everything, at their shoes, at the bodies as if the graveyard were clinging to them, coveting them. Finally the two bodies were lumped in the barrow. At one point the head rolled out into a puddle. Hood pointed, waited. Godwin picked it up by the right ear and wedged it between the bodies. The ragged throat where the head was removed gaped darkly. Hood yanked a bit of uniform over the raw bloodiness.

They took turns wheeling the barrow through the narrow streets. The rain pounded down. Four in the morning and everyone driven inside. Gutters flooded. The barrow weighed a ton. And the wooden handles were slippery. Godwin was light-headed.

Hood stopped and pointed up the short alleyway.

At the far end of the passage a blue light glowed through the rain.

They pushed their load on up past the place where the old drunk had been left to die.

Together they dumped the bodies of the two *flics* beneath the blue light.

"Killing a man is never just killing a man." Hood put his hand on Godwin's shoulder as they moved away into the shadows. "Killing a man always stands for something else. The world is all symbols, Rodger. Take tonight . . . take Cilla and her mother and father and you and me and Sacco and Vanzetti and Clothilde and Jacques and Henri . . . tonight was all symbols. Someday you'll read the story of your life in symbols. I learned that from Lawrence. It's true."

Neither of them looked back at the pile of bodies in the rain. The head had rolled a few feet away and a curious cat was advancing out of the shadows, chancing the rain, intent on such a remarkable specimen. But Godwin and Hood missed that.

"Feeling all right?"

Godwin nodded. "I'm feeling fine."

"Often affects a chap that way, a good killing. Oh, primitive, I'll grant. But good for one's soul on occasion. After all, we're a primitive bunch."

. . .

Rodger Godwin had a hell of a time dealing with the truth of having helped kill the two *flics*. He was slogging his way through an undiscovered country of guilt and fear and he couldn't eat or sleep, he couldn't see people, he holed up for a few days, wondering just what had happened that night, trying to remember every detail. But the details weren't there —no, that was a lie, he kept seeing the eye stuck open and soiled by mud, staring at him, dead as a mackerel, the eye of one of them, who cared which one?

The police naturally wanted to solve the murders of two of their own, yet there was among them no great affection for the departed. Everyone in the *quartier* was questioned, all of the regulars. That included Clyde and Godwin and Max Hood and all their nodding chums from the restaurants and bars. Godwin tried to lie as convincingly as possible. No, he hadn't seen them, yes, he and Max Hood had been in the vicinity, yes, they knew the prostitute Clothilde, yes, Godwin more than knew her, yes, she'd been badly beaten, no, he didn't know by whom, no, he didn't know that she'd had some previous relationship with one or both of the *flics*, on and on. He tried to keep it simple. He tried to play the American from Iowa, the yokel, the innocent, but it was a hard sell: The police knew he was a newspaper writer, not a fool. But no one had seen the murders committed, or if they had they weren't talking. They were glad the bastards were dead. After a week, the investigation began to blow itself out. The *quartier* became a better place to live. Everybody said so.

But Rodger Godwin still saw the eye staring at him from the wheelbarrow, still would come awake in the hot midnights and wonder what had happened to him, what had driven him to join in the blood-letting.

He turned to Max Hood, who was preternaturally calm, his mind already turned toward planning for the autumn. He was contemplating a motorcycle trip in the Alps but he wasn't sure. The summer was coming toward its end. There was a kind of sadness, wispy and insubstantial but still identifiable, in the air. And there was the panic and fear and guilt nibbling away at Rodger Godwin.

He and Max Hood went for a stroll along the Seine late one afternoon when the police questions had died down. They browsed through the book and print stalls and then stood, watching the river flowing past Notre Dame.

"You're fine," Hood said. "You're not insensitive to what happened, but you can't tell me you regret it. Can you?"

Godwin shook his head. "They were rotten bastards. I'm glad we killed them. But I can't sleep, I can't stop thinking about them—I hear them, how wet and heavy they were when we moved them, and I don't know, were they wet with rain or with blood? I smell the blood."

"But you don't regret it."

"I don't regret it. Somebody had to do it."

"You'll get over it. Most people do. When it comes to killing, it's best to have a personal reason . . . that's what makes war such a waste. Decent chaps mindlessly killing one another. These chaps—our chaps—got what was coming to them." He draped an arm around Godwin's shoulder. "Cheer up. It's like one of those African blooding rituals, sort of thing I saw among the desert tribes. Kill one of the enemy and you become a man. Much of my life has been too bloody primitive by half, I reckon."

"I'll never forget it." Godwin was staring at the shadows on the face of Notre Dame. The church seemed half-alive.

"You're not supposed to forget it. You mustn't forget it. Hope you never have to do it again. But know that you're capable of it." He smiled and gave Godwin a pat on the back, took his arm away. "You're one of the tribe now, Rodger. One of Hood's Boys. That's what they called the fellas I led in France. Hood's Boys. It was silly but we took a certain pride. We did what needed to be done. It was muddy there, too, slithering about in no-man's-land, wondering if we'd ever get back. Sometimes we did it. Got back."

"Hood's Boys." Godwin looked at Max. "Is that what I am?"

" 'Fraid so, old chap. Resignation's not allowed. You're in the tribe forever. Baptized with blood." He turned his back on the river.

Watching him, Godwin felt a kind of childish pride. One of Hood's Boys. Now and forever. In the moment it seemed that maybe this had been the point of the summer. Max Hood. Swaine and Clyde and Priscilla and Tony and Clothilde. He'd come fully alive for the first time, but maybe it had all come down to Max Hood. Maybe Hood was the one who'd claimed him. It sounded right to him, the way it was supposed to be. They all had their claims on him but now he knew, in the end he was one of Hood's Boys.

"Come on, Rodger, let's go have a drink."

"We'll drink to Hood's Boys," Godwin said.

"If you like, " Max Hood said. "Past and present."

"And future," Godwin added.

They had spilled the blood together, Hood's Boys, and there was no getting it back into the vessel.

. . .

Tony and Pamela and Priscilla packed up and went off to a château in the Loire Valley. It was owned by English friends, according to Priscilla, who stopped by Godwin's place one day to say good-bye. Tony had left the great open Rolls by the front door and gone off to pick up something for his wife after bidding Godwin farewell. When they were alone Priscilla walked through his rooms, touching things, smiling at the memory of the summer.

Finally he took her by the shoulders and stopped her and looked into the warm brown eyes. "If I don't see you again, I want you to have a wonderful life. I want you to do all the things you long to do. Cilla . . . I want you to be happy." He felt so much older than she and yet he was so much younger in so many ways.

"Oh, Rodger," she said in that matter-of-fact way of hers, "don't be melodramatic. Of course we'll see each other again. You'll come to England and see us there—it's been decided that I'm to go to school there, now that Lady Pamela and Father have negotiated a truce of sorts. Let's see—I'll bet you a fiver that you'll be in England by Christmas and we can all see the dawn of 1928! Or you'll be with us for a visit next summer at the latest and we'll tell stories about our wonderful summer in Paris and you and I'll go to the theater or punting on the river 'neath Oxford's dreaming spires—" she was grinning, conjuring up the future—"and we can sit in the garden and I'll play something horrid on my violin and you'll tell me it's beautiful and you can read me what you've just written and . . . and . . . so, don't be silly now and make me sad . . ." She gave him a piece of paper with the address, a house near Sloane Square, a place he'd never heard of. "Now you must promise you'll write and let me know all the wonderful places you've gone and people you've met and tell me where you get your mail—promise me, Rodger."

"I promise, Cilla."

She kissed him in a very womanly way. He felt her in his arms and was suddenly filled with a longing that brought tears to his eyes. He couldn't have said what she made him long for—for the force and tides of life, he supposed, and whatever it was she was part of it. There was something about Cilla, almost exactly the way there was something about Max Hood. He'd never felt such claims on his heart, his soul, and he whispered her name near her ear. *Cilla DewBrittain.* He spoke as if remembering an incantation.

Then she was gone down the stairs and he watched from the window as the Rolls pulled away and for the moment he was sure that Cilla DewBrittain was taking life and excitement with her, wherever she would go in all the years ahead. Later, he realized he hadn't remembered to ask her about poor Clyde. But it didn't matter.

Clothilde's sister came to Paris from Marseilles to stay with her and Clothilde got the singing job she'd wanted so desperately. She and her sister found other quarters and it was harder for Godwin to see her once she'd left the little neighborhood and was so busy with her work.

She was out of the life of prostitution and he thanked God for that.

Esmé Hood and her Spanish lady-friend went off to Madrid and Max was relieved. The last time Godwin saw him he was getting ready to spend a couple of weeks with the DewBrittains at the château in the Loire Valley.

"Go boating," Hood mused, "tramping about in the hills. Play some tennis with the young lady. Try not to make a fool of myself over her." He smiled. "Will of steel, that's Max Hood."

"Good luck," Godwin said.

"I'll see you later, Rodger."

"I hope so."

"Count on it, old man. Just when you least expect it."

"Hood to the rescue."

"It's been known," Max Hood said, and they shook hands and that was it.

Merle Swaine, the sanest of the lot, told Godwin to take more time off because he'd been working hard and Swaine had a very big job for him when he got back.

Godwin used some of his publisher's money and bought the little red car and went to Biarritz in September. It was cool and storms blew in off the Atlantic and when he went to lie on the beach below the casino the skies were usually the color of old pewter. He drank too much, though it wasn't his style. In his room while the storms tore the nights to shreds he reread *Vanity Fair* and thought about the way Cilla had compared herself to Becky Sharp. He supposed by now she was back in school. A schoolgirl.

When he finally got back to Paris he learned that Clyde had tried to shoot himself late one night at the club and had instead blown a hole in the back of his bandstand. He'd all but missed his head and after a night in the hospital he'd returned, leased the club to someone else, and set sail for New York and the Cleveland Hotel and the big time.

Swaine told him that story and told him, too, that Max Hood had passed back through Paris and had asked about Godwin. "Said he was sorry he missed you. Said he'd be in touch. I told him he could always get hold of you through the *Herald.*"

Where had he gone?

"He said something about a safari." Swaine grinned. "Heart of darkest Africa. Maybe he was pulling my leg. Merle B. Swaine told him . . ."

But it didn't matter what Merle B. Swaine said. *Heart of darkest Africa . . . the hunt . . . more blood rituals. . . .* One of Hood's Boys wished he could have gone with him.

The big job turned out to be a series of pieces from the great European capitals, and from "out there on the road," as Swaine put it. Which was what brought Godwin to Lisbon. It was late afternoon, clouds scudding in over the Tagus River from which Magellan had set off to circumnavigate the globe for the very first time. He'd just come from drinking coffee at a little place behind some columns in Rossio Square, feeling forlorn without all his friends. He saw their faces and wondered what they were doing and he wanted to speak with them but of course he couldn't and he felt lonely as hell.

From Lisbon he was going on to Madrid, Rome, Vienna, Berlin, and then on into Central Europe. He didn't know what he was looking for so he wrote about what he saw and heard and smelled and felt, almost as if he were writing to the folks back home in Iowa. His ignorance was manifest to him but he made a point of presenting himself as what he was—a wide-eyed young fellow, listening to whatever he could hear, never pretending to know things he didn't. He mentioned to Swaine that he was worried he'd be found out for the uninformed fool he was. Swaine said he ought to stop worrying about it and stop thinking about himself and pay attention to what was going on all around him. "Trust your instincts, Godwin. Stop thinking you'll be found out. There's nothing to find out, for chrissakes." That was what Merle B. Swaine had to say about it. Godwin figured that maybe if he paid attention for a long enough time he really might figure out what was going on over there and then, only then, would he be what he wanted to be . . . the man in the trench coat, the foreign correspondent.

On the night of 16 October 1927 he unpacked his biggest suitcase, which he had tied shut with a rope and strapped to the back of his little red car. He unfolded his bathrobe and later slipped it on and sat by the window overlooking the tiles of Rossio Square with the old town rising in the shadowy distance.

He heard the crinkle of paper and found a folded sheet in the pocket.

It was from Cilla. She'd left it there the last time, when she came to his room to say good-bye.

R—

Until we meet again, remember me. And remember this.
Life is eternal and
Love is immortal and
What we call Death
Is only the horizon
Beyond which we cannot see.

Love, Cilla

Rodger Godwin sat at the window as darkness fell and the cool wind came up from the river. He could smell the smoke from the fires the tramps built in trash cans by the river to warm themselves and to gather around, telling stories.

He read Cilla's note again and again. He had never missed anyone so much in his life. It had never occurred to him that it was possible to miss anyone so much. You learned something new every day. You just never knew. And you never could tell.

PART THREE

ENGLAND
1942

CHAPTER 18

Cilla Hood, widow of the hero, widow of General Sir Max Hood, the recipient of the Victoria Cross, was surprised, that bitterly cold February morning, when the call came through from Monk Vardan at Number 10 Downing Street. It was still quite dark outside and she was tired, some of the timing in the previous night's show had been off, some lines dropped, Roddy beset by a bout of wind, all too tiresome to dwell on the morning after but still there it was, stuck in her mind. The lamps glowed in Sloane Square and in the house a fire was already burning in the brick kitchen grate. Nanny Jane was preparing breakfast and the toast was burning. Cilla Hood sat at the scrubbed oak table sipping tea, reading *The Times*, listening to something innocuous on the radio—the *brrrr* of the telephone startled her and when she picked it up it took her a moment to get it straight that it was Monk Vardan.

"Sleeping Beauty may be waking up," he said. "The doctors have been on to me this morning. I know it's not your day to traipse all the way down but I was wondering if you mightn't see your way clear to visit him today. I can lay on a staff car from some ministry or other . . ."

"Wait a moment—you say he's waking up?" Vardan had a way of getting under her skin. There was something insinuating in his nature, something about that vulpine ridge of nose or maybe it was the large rock of Adam's apple that seemed to bob around like a buoy in heavy seas. "What do you mean? *How* is he waking up?"

"They tell me he's muttering something. Sounds like gibberish but then you never know in cases like this. He's been out a long time. On the one hand his brain may have become rather turniplike. But the sawbones tells me it's just as likely he'll be up chasing nurses and taking nourishment tomorrow. The contraption they stuck in his head—"

"Mr. Vardan, it's not a contraption. The horseless carriage was a contraption, the wireless was a contraption. What they put in his head was a plate—not a contraption." She shivered at the thought. "Very common in head wounds these days."

"Well, the jolly old thing is working, that's the good news. No brains running out, at any rate."

His flippancy made her want to strangle him. "Yes, I can go down. However, I don't want to poach on Miss Collister's time with him."

"Don't worry. Taken care of. Shipshape."

"All right, then. There's no need for a car. The train will do perfectly well. I'm very familiar with the schedule." Vardan interrupted but she was only half listening. Vardan, like the war, was something to be endured.

"Good show. I'll accompany you."

"Don't bother, please."

"No bother. I'll pick you up, and I won't take no for an answer."

In the event, Cilla hardly noticed Monk Vardan during the train ride to Salisbury. She discreetly rebuffed his attempts at conversation and he took no offense, lost himself in buff folders and closely typed reports. She kept thinking about poor Rodger.

There was so much he didn't know. He didn't know how the world had changed since he'd gone away on his secret mission with Max. He didn't know how all their lives had changed.

Three and a half months since he'd gone away.

She'd had one daughter when he left and now she had another. Would he remember little Dilys Allenby? Would he remember the night Dogsbody's was bombed, Dilys's mother dying in the bombed-out building down the street?

Did he know Max was dead? How would he take it all?

The questions made her break out in a cold sweat.

Was his mind intact? Would he ever be all right again?

Would he know her?

Would he love her?

She stood at the window in the stone turret of the manor house. The view was familiar by now, across the snow-patched landscape toward the ominous mound of the Roman hill fort Old Sarum to the left, across the black leafless stands of trees to the right with the great spire of Salisbury Cathedral just visible through the clouds of blowing snow. The snow was dry, rattled like tiny peas thrown against the thick glass. It was collecting in the parkland below. Large dogs roamed, shaking their massive heads, tongues out. The owner of the manor was said to have kept lions in the park some time ago.

The sprawling four-story gabled and turreted house had been converted to serve as a hospital for "special cases" when the Battle of Britain had begun spewing out casualties. RAF burn cases, nervous breakdowns, the newly blinded or legless. There were also security risks and captured spies. The German spies occupied a wing of their own to keep them isolated and safe from other patients. Some of the spies were recovering from the effects of rather intense interrogations. There was a fair amount of armed security around the place. From her window she saw several soldiers guarding the gate, manning a machine-gun emplacement commanding the lawn sweeping down to the road, more soldiers marching in a detachment in the car park.

Godwin lay quietly beneath the starched, stiff sheets, face in repose, breathing regularly, still wrapped in the coma. She had been coming down to Salisbury three or four times a week since just before Christmas when it had been heavy odds against his making it at all. He'd had rather a lot of one side of his head shot away and for weeks had been cared for in a makeshift way on board a submarine and in Alexandria and Cairo until finally being shipped back to England. He had been her Christmas present from the great beyond. At first she had dealt with the loss of both husband and lover. Then one of them—or at least what was left of him—had turned up, compliments of Monk Vardan, who'd broken the news in that special way of his.

The nurse was finishing trimming his beard, scissors snipping. Vardan was visiting with one of the administrators downstairs. The doctor, whose name was Arbuthnot, bustled in and stood beside Cilla, arms folded over a clipboard, hugging it to his chest. "Well, this is the situation, Mrs. Hood. The work on his cranium is just fine. No point in being technical but there's nothing but good news in re the old noggin. You know there's no paralysis. He simply won't wake up . . . he went through quite a lot. He seems to have been sleeping it off. But . . . he's begun to talk. He hasn't opened his eyes, so far as we know, but there is a repetition of words—"

"What words? What does he say?"

Arbuthnot shook his head. "Can't quite tell. But it's the same thing again and again. Like a bit of poetry. We're all quite hopeful. Come, take a good close gander at your boy."

Monk Vardan had slipped in. She ignored him, sat on the chair near Godwin's head.

"Rodger, darling, can you hear me? It's Cilla . . ." She took his hand which lay on top of the sheets. "Anyone at home in there? I'm sure you can hear me . . . it's time to wake up, isn't it? Why don't you speak to me, Rodger?" She squeezed his hand and felt him squeeze back. "That's it, you *are* there, aren't you? It's time to wake up, darling . . ."

His lips moved, she saw them moving, forming words. "Your beard is very neatly trimmed," she whispered near his ear, wishing they were alone. The bandage on his head had gotten smaller and smaller through the weeks since the last surgery. "I'll bet you've never had a beard before . . . Don't you want to see it? I'll hold a mirror for you. Oh, please open your eyes and wake up, Rodger . . ."

He said something. Monk Vardan leaned forward. She leaned down close to his mouth, felt his warm breath on her ear. He said it again, squeezed her fingers again. She smiled. He whispered again into her ear.

Arbuthnot could contain himself no longer. "What is it?"

She said: "Life is eternal and love is immortal . . ."

"I beg your pardon?"

"It's just an old scrap of something . . . long ago." She brushed her hand across her eyes, trying to stop the tears. They clung in her lashes, blurring her vision.

Rodger Godwin smiled. "Life is eternal . . . and love is immortal . . . and death—"

She leaned down and kissed his mouth, felt him smiling against her lips.

"Cilla," he said softly. "I knew it was you, I smelled your perfume. Had to be you." He opened his eyes very slowly, squinting. "For the love of God . . . there's old Monk . . . the angel of death perched at the foot of my bed. . . . What's going on here? Who's this other bird? Where the hell am I? Jesus, I'm stiff." He spoke with great deliberation as if he were unfamiliar with his tongue.

She held a glass of water to his mouth and he sipped thankfully.

"Cilla . . . I've been dreaming . . . it was all so real, I didn't think it was a dream at all . . ."

"What have you been dreaming about?" She felt him tighten on her fingers again.

"About Paris . . . the old days . . . you and Tony and . . . Max and Clyde . . . remember Merle B. Swaine?"

"Of course," she said, crying with happiness and relief, recognition. He was all right.

"It was so real," he murmured. "It was all there, Cilla, we were all there again . . ." He blinked hard as if he were struggling to remember something. "Max is dead . . . oh, my God, they're all dead . . ." She kissed him softly. "I'm sorry, I'm so sorry. They're all gone. . . . Where the hell am I, Cilla? What's going on here? Monk, is that you? What are you doing here?" He tried to lift himself up on his elbows but didn't have the strength. "Hell of a headache . . ." He sank back. His eyes were deep in the sockets. The beard made Cilla forget how much weight he'd lost, 50 pounds gone from his 225.

He was asleep again.

He woke next a couple of hours later.

Cilla was sitting by the bed drinking tea and he fluttered one eye open. "Smells good. I'm hungry. Starving."

Dr. Arbuthnot looked up from notes he was taking. "Well, Mr. Godwin, it's so good of you to join us at long last." He was smiling encouragingly. He had unruly black hair which made him look like a teenager. He was stocky and radiated good humor.

"Anything to oblige," Godwin said softly. "I'm a bit hazy. Sorry if I've been a bother."

"Spoken like a hero, old man." That was Vardan, puffing on a slender, red, highly polished Dunhill. Between puffs he rubbed the bowl against his beak.

"How are you keeping, then?"

Godwin turned his head carefully to look at Arbuthnot. "I've been better. Hell of a headache. And my scalp keeps itching. Anybody going to tell me where I am?"

"You're home. Back in England. Salisbury. You've been rather badly banged up but you're going to be tip-top now that you're awake. Don't fret about the headache and the itching—"

"Easy for you to say."

"Your head hasn't fallen off, that's the good news." He was beaming at his patient like a man admiring his prize cabbage.

"How long have I been asleep?"

"Roughly ten weeks."

"Ten weeks! Are you serious? Well, of course you are. But it's a hell of a note, isn't it?" He moved his eyes from face to face while holding his aching head still. "I can't seem to remember things . . . I get hints . . . they come and go—"

"They're all there in your head. It'll all come back to you. You've been shot in the old bean so the machinery may not work quite like a Jaguar straightaway—"

Godwin smiled. "You mean it *will* work like a Jaguar for a while."

"Jolly good," Vardan said.

"All the fellows I was with, they're all dead, aren't they?"

"Yes, Rodger," Vardan said, "I'm afraid they are." He struck a wooden match, sucked the flame into the bowl of the pipe. "We'll talk about all that later. In good time, never fear."

"Cilla, I am so terribly sorry about Max—"

"It's all right, Rodger. You mustn't think about it, you mustn't upset yourself. You're back, you're the only one who got back. It's a kind of miracle. I'm handling everything all right . . . we'll sort it all out later."

"Max is dead. Dammit, dammit . . . I was with him right at the end . . . we were almost clear . . . then the bullets started hitting him, they kept hitting him . . ."

"Please, darling, don't, don't—"

"And then there was this awful flash." He sighed deeply, his fingers rubbing the bandage on his head. "How the hell did I get here?" His voice was trailing away. "I'm so bloody tired . . . my head is killing me . . ."

When he was asleep again Cilla kissed him.

Vardan told her he had to stay on in Salisbury. "I'll want to talk with our boy. We've got to find out what actually happened out there."

He saw her to the train station, put her aboard.

She had a curtain to make.

Alone in his room Godwin slept a great deal, sleep interrupted by the ministrations of nurses and doctors, the arrival of meals on trays, the signs of returning strength. Sometimes he would gently tap on the metal plate in the left side of his head. There was a noticeable scar, several inches long, at the temple where the bullet had hit him; then the plate beneath some skin and the thin layer of bandages. The tapping sound was hollow and sounded as if it were coming from within his skull. He would smile at the thought, whisper, "Help! Help! I'm trapped inside this man's head . . ." At the time that struck him as terribly funny. When he told Cilla she gave him an odd, quizzical look and the faintest of smiles.

Godwin wanted to know what had happened but he just didn't have the strength or energy to insist on getting it all at once. What strength he could muster was spent on Monk Vardan.

Monk had taken up temporary residence at the Red Lion in Salisbury. When he wasn't sleeping he was at Godwin's bedside. He was always there, smoking cigarettes or puffing his pipe, slouching by the window or draped in a chair with his long spidery legs crossed. Godwin showed him the head-tapping trick and Vardan leaned close to hear, a wide grin on his narrow face. "A parlor trick," he said. "You'll be dining out on that one, old boy."

"You told me it would be a piece of cake," Godwin said the first day he had the green light for a real talk. "Turned out you were mistaken."

"Too true, too true. Do you feel up to talking about it? It's necessary, you know, sooner or later."

"It's all jumbled up. I'll do what I can. What have you been able to find out at this end? How did I get out of there?"

"How's your headache? Are you up to this?"

"It's been worse."

"Actually we had a devilish time finding out what did happen. No radio contact. No one there when the sub came back to pick you up. Damn lucky they came back the next night, damn lucky they saw you . . . do you recall starting the fire on the rocks? Well, you did it. Somehow. It's an everlasting mystery how you found the raft to get back to the sub . . . you were sinking so they sent two chaps off in their own raft to get you, pluck you from the sea." Vardan shook his head. "I'm not surprised you don't remember. You were delirious, more dead than alive. They took one look at you and nearly threw you back . . . godawful head wound . . . some of the lads reportedly threw up at the sight of you—"

"So glad you chose to tell me."

"You had a hellish story to tell but nobody knew how reliable it was. Everybody dead, nobody even saw Rommel let alone killed him, a total balls-up, a massacre. They were sure you'd die on the sub . . . they said they could see your brain, old chap . . . not a pretty sight . . . they kept packing your wound with bandages, thank Jehovah there was a doctor on board and supplies, they'd always assumed there might be some casualties coming off the shore, otherwise they swore your brains would have run out on the floor, or should I say deck?"

"Could we have a bit less about my brain? I get the idea. Hard to realize it's me you're talking about."

"Well, they got you to the hospital in Alex, then on to more elaborate facilities in Cairo. By then you were comatose. In the end you were shipped back here, a bit of an ordeal but you made it. And here you are in the bosom of a grateful nation, more or less. You got back to old Blighty on Christmas Eve. Quite a treat for your newly widowed lady-love. I was pleased to give her the news myself. I felt like Father Christmas."

"I appreciate that, Monk. You're the only one who could have done that for her. Nobody knows about Cilla and me, I mean. That's still the case?" For the first time it occurred to him that it no longer mattered quite so much. Max Hood was dead. "And the mission, what about that? What do people know? What story did you give out? And the war—how's the war going?"

"Slow down, my child, and Uncle Monk will reveal all." He lit his pipe and stood looking out at the gray afternoon beyond the turret window. "You and Cilla are still a secret, of course. That's all your private affair." He puffed ruminatively.

A thought flew up like a startled grouse from the underbrush that was Godwin's mind and memory. A thought swooped about and came home to roost. *You and Cilla are still a secret.* . . . But they weren't, were they? He remembered the threatening note delivered to his flat. Someone was going to kill him if he kept on with Cilla.

"I say, are you feeling all right?"

"Sometimes I get a little woozy. The real world keeps taking me by surprise. I'm okay."

"Perhaps I should mention that while you two *are* still a secret, so far as I know, there is one small disclaimer. Nothing to worry about, I'm sure, but Anne Collister did run into Cilla here at the hospital one day. I just brushed it off, said you and Max went back to year one and a courtesy call was the least she could do. Words to that effect. Not a problem, I should think."

"So the mission is sort of general knowledge, is that what you're saying?"

"Hardly, old boy, hardly. Quite the contrary. Oh, by the way, I've discouraged Miss Collister from any more visits on the grounds that sawbones says no."

"Fine, fine. The mission?"

"There's damn little point in publicizing a nightmare."

"And what about me?"

"Special assignment."

"That must be making Homer's day. Explaining that to the network boys."

"Well, actually I've had a placating word with them myself. Secret mission. The reward for their cooperation will come in heaven."

"You're joking."

"Indeed, not. I think I went down rather well with your Hector Crichton but check with Brother Teasdale. Chaps like that are always impressed by limeys, aren't they? I mean Madison Avenue network boys." He smiled self-satisfiedly. "Now, the mission. Here's the bit we've pieced together. Rommel wasn't there, he wasn't even in North Africa . . . he was in

Rome celebrating his birthday!" Monk seemed to think that was pretty rare.

"How did you find that out?"

"Cheeky fellow dropped us a line—no, seriously, we got a letter from bloody Rommel." Vardan was chuckling. "What a fella he is! A letter. However, the point is, our intelligence turned out to be worthless, so there you—"

"Wait. The intelligence . . . that was Max's work—"

"Well, yes, he was certainly key . . . and he was mistaken, as it turned out. Or was he? Perhaps he wasn't. In any case, Rommel came back in the next day or so. Very well planned, what? The curious thing is what he did then. He honored the fallen, you see. He saw to it that both our lads and his were buried with full military honors. He had crosses made from fresh young cypress for each grave. You know he's a camera buff, well, he sent snaps of the graves for the families . . . and he wrote letters to them, assuring them that their men died heroes. Dashed decent, don't you agree, considering what we were attempting?"

"What a story that'll make." Godwin sighed, forgetting for a moment everything else.

"You see, you're sounding like your old self already."

"The photos, the letters, where—"

"Well, yes, all in his own hand, too. He sent them on through to Number 10 and I was put in charge, I delivered Cilla's to her under the lips-are-sealed proviso. The families of the other chaps will have to wait till war's end, I expect. They'd be bound to take the packet round to the Bull and Daffodil and sound off to the regulars about young Dan's exploits. But we'll make a nice ceremony of it after the shooting's stopped. Ask Cilla to show you hers. Quite a souvenir."

"Rather a steep price to pay, Monk."

"Yes, well, there is that of course. Still, a cloud not without a silver lining. Think of the chaps who die and are just left to rot anonymously into the mud. And, then, on a more personal level, it's an ill wind, isn't it?"

"What the hell are you talking about?"

"Well, it's simple arithmetic, isn't it? You, Mrs. Hood, Max . . . take away one from three and you have a couple."

"Hell of a thing to say, Monk." Godwin felt his face burn, another sign of life. "Sometimes you're not a very likable man."

"No offense intended, I'm sure. One loses one's sense of delicacy in time of war."

"I loved Max, too. I loved both of them."

"Life grows simpler. You love only one now."

"Drop it. Just drop it. Get on with the story. What happened with CRUSADER? Did we disrupt things enough to do any good? Or was it all a waste?"

"Not for me to judge, is it? I mean, PRAETORIAN was a bit of a clanger, wasn't it? Who knows what might have happened if Rommel had been killed . . . still, CRUSADER." He rubbed the bowl of the pipe against his nose, making the briar gleam. "The start was bad. Do you really want to hear all this?"

"I almost died for CRUSADER, and all the rest of them did die. Yes, I want to know."

General Sir Claude Auchinleck picked Lieutenant General Sir Alan Gordon Cunningham to lead the Eighth Army—the renamed Western Desert Force—in CRUSADER. Cunningham was optimistic on the eve of this greatest British desert offensive but he was badly troubled by his doctor's orders to give up smoking his pipe. It was, Vardan pointed out, the fulcrum on which Cunningham's career, and nearly the fate of the operation itself, would turn.

At the outset the British optimism seemed well founded. The Eighth Army consisted of 118,000 men, more than 700 tanks, 600 field guns, and 200 antitank guns. It was supported by the Desert Air Force of 650 planes.

Rommel, on the other hand, had received no reinforcements since June, though his army also had a new name: Panzer Group Africa. He had as many men as the British, but only 400 tanks including more than 100 obsolete Italian jobs, and 50 of them were being repaired as the British offensive began. He had about 500 aircraft. Because the German campaign in Russia was bogging down horribly after its blazing June beginning, Rommel could expect no help from home.

Still, the British confidence suffered a bloody nose, almost a knockout punch. On Saturday, 22 November, 70 tanks of 21st Panzer Division had engaged the British at Sidi-Rezegh. The British Seventh, Twenty-second, and Fourth Armored Brigades were shredded. By the time the Fifteenth Panzer Division had joined the fray, the Fourth Armored Brigade HQ had been overrun and the brigade commander taken prisoner. The British airfield was taken, 100 British tanks and 300 men were lost.

Sunday was worse. Rommel's massed tanks took on the British units in the vicinity of Sidi-Rezegh and destroyed them one by one. It was a movable panzer feast. By nightfall the desert was ablaze with the shells of hundreds of burning tanks. The Fifth South African Brigade alone lost 3,400 of 5,700 men.

At the outset, CRUSADER was in ruins.

"Cunningham was a wreck," Vardan said. "Some of the men around him reported that he was on the verge of a nervous breakdown without his damned pipe! I'd have jammed the bloody thing into his mouth and made him smoke it. The fact is, the man was broken by the magnitude of the disaster. He wanted to count CRUSADER a defeat, pull his army back into Egypt and regroup. Finally he sent a call for help to Auchinleck, who immediately flew out from Cairo. The Auk took a look around and told Cunningham to pull up his socks and press the attack . . . 'Down to the last tank,' were his words, I believe."

But true to his nature Rommel went to the whip on Monday, driving the entire Afrika Korps and a couple of Italian divisions like a stake through the British lines, hoping to turn on them from the rear and cut them to pieces.

Instead the British, confronted with such a terrifying thrust, broke ranks in panic and lit out in disorganized retreat. It was Rommel's first Cyrenaican offensive all over again, a carbon copy of the infamous Tobruk Derby, which had so enraged Churchill a few months before. Throughout the day both armies raced eastward, hopelessly intermingled in the blowing sand.

"Our reports said if it weren't so ghastly, it would have been uproarious," Vardan observed wryly. "When dusk fell one of our chaps was directing traffic, trying to keep us from banging into one another, when he suddenly realized the trucks and tanks he was directing were German! And the Germans never even noticed—he said he actually shit his pants. We found out later that Rommel himself spent the night in the absolute midst of British troops and no one realized it."

Fifteen miles inside Egypt, Rommel reached the end of his supply lines. It was 26 November and he was out of petrol. He had overreached himself and it was then that the tide of CRUSADER turned.

The day Rodger Godwin was taken off the sub in Alexandria and carted to a hospital, more dead than alive, was the day Auchinleck relieved Cunningham, who was shipped off to a hospital in Cairo where he was diagnosed as suffering from both mental and physical fatigue. "And needing a smoke in the worst possible way," Vardan said.

Auchinleck picked, in Vardan's words, "a little rosebud called Ritchie to replace poor old Cunners. Ritchie was a sort of shirt model type, a millionaire who didn't really seem to grasp what the dickens he was doing.

But the fact of the matter was that the Auk was running the show by then. By the first of December the Eighth Army was itself again and ready to hold the Desert Fox's feet to the fire. Now it was Rommel in retreat, Rommel taking the losses, though—giving him his due—the withdrawal was orderly and hard fought. As late as 28 December—you were back in England by then, Rodger—he destroyed thirty-seven of our tanks while losing only seven of his own, but he was done, at least for the moment. For the first time we'd well and truly slipped him the mitten. By mid-January we had taken thirty-three thousand prisoners and destroyed three hundred of his tanks. We had to pack it in and return to Cyrenaica. After all the fighting and dying we had pushed him back to exactly the same place where he'd begun when he got to Africa in March of '41.

"And that, old sot, is where we stand now. I gather that everyone out there in the desert is a bit winded at the moment."

Monk was knocking the dottle from his pipe, which was a sign that he was preparing to leave.

Godwin said: "What does Churchill think?"

"About what?"

"Any of it. All of it. PRAETORIAN, I guess that's what I mean . . ."

"Well, he thinks what I think. He thinks Max Hood's intelligence was good."

"But how can that be?"

"It was good when he got it. Then things changed."

"Things changed," Godwin said numbly.

"Tell me what happened. Go back to that last night at Rommel's villa or HQ where everybody got it . . . try to remember what happened . . ."

Godwin tried but it was a jumble of sounds and images and smells, rain and gunfire and burning vehicles, bullets smacking into Max. . . . Godwin was out of breath, he felt as if his memory had sprung a leak and was bleeding. . . . He saw Max Hood down in the mud, hand reaching out to him . . . Max saying something, what did Max say, when did he say it?

"Max told me . . . he said they knew we were coming . . . or they were waiting for us, something like that . . ."

"Exactly," Vardan said. "He was an old campaigner and he saw it for what it was. A sellout. They were waiting for you. What does that tell you, I wonder?"

"I don't know," Godwin said, impatient, not up for any games. He was too tired. "You tell me."

"They *knew* you were coming. How could they know?"

"Somebody told them."

"Bingo. We have a spy among us."

"But that's simply impossible. Nobody knew but . . . well, *us*."

Vardan shrugged. He was putting on his long black overcoat, arranging his scarf. "So it would seem. Nobody knew but us. Therefore we must look at the problem all the more closely." He buttoned up the coat, held his slouch hat in his hands. The wind whined at the window. "Think on it, will you, Rodger? Who told the Nazis about PRAETORIAN?" He stopped in the doorway and looked back at Godwin. "Who murdered all the lads?"

CHAPTER 19

Homer Teasdale came down with a couple of suitcases crammed with newspapers covering the period Godwin had been, as he said in his horn-rimmed, Indiana way, "out of touch." He told Godwin it was gratifying to see him so well.

"What about getting back to work, Homer?"

"Up to you. Crichton and the rest screamed bloody murder, of course, but I explained things and, frankly, Monk Vardan lent a hand. So, they're waiting to see if you're planning to come back soon. What do you want me to tell them?"

"I've been thinking that maybe I'd better ease back into things. A couple of pieces a week. Who do they have in my place?"

"A stopgap. They're using Desmond Nickerson from the Beeb. They like his accent."

"Good. He's no threat."

"They never intended him to be. Easing back into it sounds like the right thing to do. What about the newspapers?"

"Will they go for a Sunday thing? Weekly column for a while?"

"Damn right they will. We'll play up the secret mission thing, cannot be told while there's a war on, nearly gave his life for freedom—who could resist? You do a think piece, bits and pieces of what you pick up, the story inside the story. Shouldn't strain you. You can do all your research over lunch at the Savoy."

"I'm going to write a book about what happened to me."

"Touchy. Secrets and all. What actually did happen to you, by the way? Are the bits I hear anything like the truth?"

"What do you hear?"

"Rommel. Commando attack. Disaster."

"So much for secrets."

"Really? True?"

"Where did you hear all this?"

"It'll surprise you."

"I can use a good larf."

"Jolly Jack Priestley."

"Well . . . he has tremendously good connections."

"Poll just came out showing that after Churchill he's the most famous man in England."

"I wonder who his sources really are."

Homer shrugged dismissively. "You want me to make these suggestions to your various employers?" Godwin nodded. "Then I might as well be on my way. I'm satisfied you're back, now I've seen you in the flesh. From here on it's only a question of time until you're back in place. Keep well, my friend. As always, you may rely on me."

Godwin read the newspapers like a man discovering an unknown country. The events of 7 December 1941 struck him with a cannonball of irony. The Japanese—the *Japanese*—had brought America into the war! Hitler had successfully kept the Americans on the sidelines for two years; he had even speculated that America's aims and Germany's might in time coincide. Well, the Japanese had changed all that. Godwin reflected with grim pleasure on what a rotten winter Herr Hitler was having, with Russia on one side and the sleeping giant across the sea roused to anger by his allies, the Japanese. It seemed to Godwin in his room in Salisbury, regaining his strength, that the outcome of this war was no longer in doubt. With the entry of America, the Empire of the Rising Sun and the disease that was Nazism were hopelessly doomed. All that mattered now was how long it would take and how much of the world would be in flames and how many people would die.

The irony was simply that he need never have gone to North Africa to kill Rommel at all. Godwin's role had been to tell the story of the heroic raid to his American audience, to sell the Americans on getting into the struggle with the Nazis. There was no other reason. Sure, it was a great story. Maybe he'd have gone anyway. But it was the appeal to patriotism and his fear that America might choose to sit it out that had made his decision for him.

The mission had failed, he hadn't told the story, and America was in the war anyway. You just never knew and you never could tell how things would turn out.

The news from the Pacific, however, was a litany of catastrophe as the Japanese attacked, invaded, occupied. The names were Tarawa, Guam, Wake Island, and the Philippines—Luzon, Manila, Bataan. The Japanese drove MacArthur to Corregidor at the mouth of Manila Bay. The Japanese laid siege to Hong Kong and on Christmas Day the British garrison surrendered. The Japanese fury was unleashed in Burma, in a furious attack on Singapore, struck at Malaya and Borneo, sank the *Prince of Wales* and *Repulse*, occupied Bangkok, and in China the American garrison at Peking fell to the armies of Emperor Hirohito.

But things were going horribly for the German armies in Russia. They were freezing to death, they were eating frozen horses and their own dead comrades. The Russians, having waited for the arrival of General Winter, were counterattacking with bloody revenge in their eyes, and Churchill told the House of Commons: "In Hitler's launching of the Nazi campaign on Russia we can already see, after less than six months of fighting, that he has made one of the outstanding blunders of history."

There was, however, little good war news during February outside the Russian front.

"Oh, darling, the play is a great success. Are you proud of me?"

They were sitting in the sun room of the hospital manor house, which saw precious little sun that winter. A couple of patients in bathrobes and wheelchairs were drawn up before a stone fireplace where heavy logs smoked and burned fitfully. The man who had decreed a fireplace for the sun room had been a genius.

Godwin was up and dressed in heavy gray slacks and a navy blue cashmere sweater. He'd been out for a walk around the parkland that morning with Dr. Arbuthnot for company. His legs were still shaky from all the weeks in bed and he used a cane. Cilla had just arrived and had kissed him, told him it was good to see color in his face again. Now they were sitting by a window looking across the lawn to the machine-gun emplacement. She was holding his hand, her eyes wonderfully alight. "Are you proud of me?"

"I'm very proud of you. You should have seen me reading through the war news and finding the review of the show. That critic said you were wonderful and seductive and beautiful and funny. I was drunk with pride."

"Yes, it was a very fair notice, I thought. And quite typical of the others."

"Said you were the glue that held it all together."

"Glue. Yes. I could have done without that actually." She leaned back in the deep chintz-covered chair and sighed. "We're in for a long run. Which makes Greer happiest of all. He'll make a mint."

She told him about Dilys Allenby coming to live with her.

He was stunned. "Cilla, what a huge responsibility."

"Not if you already have one Chloe. Another added to the mix is minimal. Do you remember little Dilys?"

"Yes, of course. I remember her poor mother even better. What a night that was. Little Dilys . . . as I recall she slept through most of it. That was the night you insisted on telling me you loved me. And a few days later I got the gate by way of the mail. Charming, Cilla."

"Let's not go over all that. It's too dreadful and it's over. Dilys is nearly two now. Her father was RAF. A Hurricane pilot. He was killed in the B. of B. The grandparents are old and unwell. The nurse from the night at Dogsbody's remembered my concern about Dilys and when she got wind of Dilys being put into a home of some sort she decided to call me. She thought I might help with money to ensure Dilys a marginally better life. She's quite a remarkable woman, this nurse. I told her that fate had placed the child in my path—so I said I'd do more than a bit of money, I'd provide a home, a whole way of life for this little creature who had everything taken away from her before she could even put up a fight."

She was kneeling beside Godwin's chair, watching the fire. The other patients had gone away. She looked up at him, touched each of his fingers with hers. "She and Chloe took to each other like mad from the first moment on. Rodger, they're sisters now. I'll have it no other way."

"It is written," he said.

"Bloody right it's written. I wrote it."

Later when she was preparing to leave to get back to London for her curtain in The Widow Weeds, she stood close enough so he felt her warm breath on his cheek. "When will we be able to be alone? I'm frantic without you. It wasn't so bad when you were in the coma. I concentrated on wanting you simply to survive. I pretended I was a nun and lost in prayer. But now," she sighed deeply, "it's different. You're all right. You are alive and I'm on fire. Give me some hope, Rodger, please."

"Soon. Can you arrange to come down for a night?"

"Here? To the hospital?"

"No. The Red Lion is somewhat more inviting."

"Will they let you out?"

"I'm not a prisoner, you know."

"I'll see when I can get away. I'll come down on our dark day and stay overnight. I'm positively wild for you." She kissed him and ran her tongue along his lips.

"I love you," he said.

"I'll bet you do," she whispered.

He watched her go, watched her wave from the back of the beetling black taxi as it pulled away down the drive. He waved, wondering what was going on in her mind which was, of course, something he'd spent a fair amount of his life doing. But this was different. He'd come back from the dead and her husband was going to stay dead, he was sure of that. Thus, everything had changed. For the first time in their lives there was no barrier between them. What would they do?

For all he knew, this too was written.

J. B. Priestley was a very busy man. In fact, he considered himself the busiest man in England. He was also extraordinarily famous for his radio talks, bestselling novels and collections of essays, his lectures, and his running battle with the Establishment. He belonged to the public at large, like the British Museum or the Nelson column. At least the public felt he belonged to them.

J. B. Priestley was not too busy, however, to come to the aid of a chum, and Rodger Godwin was a chum in need whether he knew it or not. And so Priestley took a run to Salisbury late on an afternoon when cold sleet was falling. Godwin was waiting for him in the bar of the Red Lion Inn.

Priestley was cordial, but quick in dispensing with the amenities.

"I hear things and I know things. I know men. Now I'm hearing there's going to be fiery hell to pay over this PRAETORIAN fuck-up."

"I thought PRAETORIAN was still a very dark secret."

Priestley harrumphed that away and, taking scotch in hand, said, "I came down here to warn you, boy-o. They're looking for a spy and they'll find one. They've been ordered to find one, so they must. When dealing with Vardan, stick to your story."

"Jack, what are you talking about? I don't have a story. I only know what happened. That's all I can tell."

"Who do you think did it? Betrayed the mission?"

"Nobody. I think nobody betrayed the mission. It was bad luck. Very bad luck."

"Well forget that. They think somebody did it." Priestley flashed a sour, weary smile. "They're the ruling class, Rodger. They can be fine fellows right up to the minute they decide not to be. Then they ram a red-hot poker up your arse just to show you who's boss. You are not one of them. You're a Yank, the perfect example of what they've always said about Yanks—oversexed, overpaid, and over here! Keep your guard up."

"What are you telling me, Jack?"

"Never turn your back on 'em, that's all. And remember who your friends are." He repeated these words later while climbing into the backseat of the great dark car that would return him to London.

Godwin was sitting in the uniquely misnamed sun room having his breakfast tea and reading the papers. The news was uniformly awful. The Ministry of Food announced the end of white bread for the duration, to be replaced with the more healthful "wheatmeal loaf." There were reflections on the fall of Singapore. There was a long piece about the Japanese atrocities committed on the British garrison at Hong Kong. Foreign Secretary Eden and Viscount Cranborne, Colonial Secretary, had addressed both houses of Parliament on the subject. It made gruesome reading.

"Rather lowers the esteem one may have had for Japanese culture."

Godwin looked up. Monk Vardan was staring down at the open newspaper, balancing a cup of tea in a saucer in the palm of one hand.

"Never thought much about the Japanese."

"Well, the little yellow devils have been telling us that their soldiers are guided by the chivalric code of Bushido, compassionate regard for the honor of the enemy. Apparently all this honor involves the bayoneting of bound British officers, the refusal to bury the dead, the systematic rape and murder of an entire district of Chinese women . . . I would personally like to push a button and eradicate the whole nasty race. Genocide, old chap, is not always a bad thing. Feel like continuing our chat?"

"Sure. Why not?"

"Let's drive into town. Do us good to get outside."

They went for a walk in the narrow streets. There was a chilly wind whipping through the blackened trees.

"I'm just doing my job, old boy. I hope you keep that in mind."

"I know, Monk. It's just your job." He glanced sideways at him, remembering Jack Priestley's warning.

"Well, this is all terribly difficult for me. We've known each other for dog's years, of course—"

"Not all that long, Monk."

"Well, I wouldn't want you to think that our friendship doesn't count with me. But still, my job's my job, my masters are not to be trifled with . . . the point is, my job's not always easy, not what I would choose it to be—"

"For God's sake, Monk, what are you going on about? You're making my head hurt. Get to the point."

"Well, you seem willing to agree that someone betrayed PRAETO-

RIAN. Only a handful of people knew about the plan's existence. The idea came from Number 10, you know. There were no written records that mention its purpose in any way. Everything was conducted on a very personal level, just the way you were brought into it. The sad fact is, most of the men who knew are dead, died on the mission itself." He sighed, pulled his muffler tighter around his huge Adam's apple. He sounded as if his nasal passages were blocked and a cold was coming on. "Now a great deal of pressure is being brought to bear on the PM. . . . What went wrong? Why did all these men die? What the hell were we playing at and who mucked it up?"

"But how do they even know something went wrong? If it was so secret—"

"It's impossible to keep the lid on a disaster. Particularly on a disaster that claims the life of General Sir Max Hood . . . and every gallant lad who went with him. Word leaks out. Rumors began flying about . . . and then Rommel sends these photos of heroes' graves back to England. . . . There's no 'official' announcement but a lot of the rumors are pretty close to the bone. What the PM is doing now is twisting all the arms he can get hold of to keep the whole business from being raised in the Commons— that's the lid that must be kept in place. Once the good member from East Grinstead or Gurney Slade starts raising hell the lid will come off . . . mucked-up plot to murder Rommel, bad intelligence, a national hero and all his men dead for no good reason . . . it's the sort of blot the PM will not allow to soil his copybook."

"But how can he keep the good member from Chipping Sudbury from raising the issue? What pressure?"

"Patriotism. Security in time of war. But it'll only work if he drops the other shoe."

"And which shoe would that be?"

"The rumors insist there was a traitor. The PM must play the traitor card, take the trick. And, to be frank, the PM can't see it any other way himself. The problem is that so few people knew—"

"Then somebody else must know. If you're right, if the Germans knew we were coming—"

"Oh, they knew, they had to know—"

"I still say it could have been a coincidence."

"But that *is* what you'd say, isn't it?"

"Just what does that mean? Spell it out for one of the slower boys, Monk—"

"Well, it's the other-shoe business, old boy."

"Yes?"

"The traitor. The PM can keep the lid on if he finds the bloody traitor. Now, though, now it's hot to the touch and it will burn the man who grabs hold . . . we must go after the traitor, we must be *known* to be going after the traitor. A word must be placed in the right ears . . . and then it will be forgotten."

"That's very cynical," Godwin said. "Good men died."

Vardan ignored Godwin's comment. "The PM thinks we've got our man, actually."

"You don't say . . ."

"Well, we have to face one possibility, however unpleasant, mustn't we? Wasn't it the tiresome, immortal Holmes of Baker Street who said something to the effect that if there is only one possibility remaining, however unlikely it may be, it must be the truth? You see, Rodger, the PM thinks it's you."

Godwin's laughter exploded like the gasp of a man dealt a blow to the solar plexus by Joe Louis.

"Well," Monk Vardan said, "at least I've found the man who sees a shred of humor in this rather shabby tale. I was worried about how you might take it."

"Oh, you were, were you? Well, it's not so much shabby as it is preposterous. Insane. I can see the headlines now. 'America's Most Famous Foreign Correspondent Unmasked! A Nazi Spy!' It's really a doozie, Monk. It'll be the making of you, all right. You'll have a knighthood and a funeral at Westminster Abbey, all in the same week. Let's see a smile on that long face, pal."

"Sorry. I can't do it. This is serious."

"Well, Monk, let me say this just once . . . I am not a Nazi spy. For the record."

"No one is saying that. At least not exactly."

"What a relief. I must write my folks."

"It's no joke. I assure you of that."

"It's utter bullshit and you know it and if Churchill thinks I'm a traitor then he's nuts and the future of civilization as we've come to know and love it is in the hands of a drooling lunatic."

Vardan steered Godwin back toward the car park. It was raining again. Black umbrellas blossomed along the walks. Godwin stared at Vardan, oblivious to the wind and rain.

"You're acting like you believe this. Answer me straight, Monk, do you believe this bullshit?"

"You know me, Rodger, I'm a careful man, covering all the exits. What do I think? I think we have to take a long look at it."

"Monk! Jesus!"

"We have to start somewhere, don't we? I thought you might want to talk to me about what happened in Cairo a couple of years ago. 1940. That's all clear in your memory, surely . . ."

Godwin spun away from the hand Vardan had placed on his sleeve. "Not now, you bastard, the hell with Cairo in '40." Godwin stumbled. "I'll be goddamned if I'll talk to you about Cairo. . . . Fuck it, Monk. There's a traitor here all right but it's sure as hell not me!" Rain was pouring all of a sudden, running in his eyes, tapping like fingers on his damaged head. He felt as if his brain was pounding to get out from behind the metal plate. He had to get back to the hospital. He had to get to his medicine . . . now everything was spinning, his head felt as if it were about to burst . . . then he felt himself falling . . .

"Are you sure you can do this? Are you strong enough? Are you all right?"

She was whispering in his ear, her lips brushing against him. Then she shifted so she could look down into his eyes.

"I think I'm doing okay," Godwin whispered back, "considering the shape I'm in."

"I'm not complaining," she murmured, pushing down on him. He lay on his back, arms extended back above his head, holding tight to the headboard. She was straddling him, leaning forward, rocking against him, working him deep inside her. Her hair was plastered across her forehead. He opened his mouth and she slipped one taut nipple into his mouth and he sucked the sweat from her, heard her moan and felt her clamping herself on him. The taste of her breast flickered through his brain, a memory of Cairo, and he pushed it away and she said, gasped, "Just a little longer." He held back as long as he could but finally she made it impossible and then she was kissing him and making little sounds against his mouth and he let go of the creaking headboard and held her tight, felt her back slippery with sweat.

She lay on him, tugging the covers up across her back, her body holding him down as if she were afraid he might try to get away. In a little while she began contracting on him and it all started again. He could hear the wind blowing the sign outside, heard the squeaking, saw the glow of the courtyard lamp through the rain-spattered window. She was pulling him along with her but he was remembering something, a lamp blowing in the rain and wind, a lone sentry standing beneath it . . .

An hour later they stood side by side, wrapped in wool blankets, staring out into the rain-swept courtyard of the Red Lion. In the wind the naked vines seemed to writhe on the walls, the odd little branch tapping at a window. The stones below shone like pebbles in a streambed.

Cilla was nursing flat champagne from a bottle she'd brought for the occasion. They'd opened it before bed and now it was on the downhill side. The joy, the possessive, erotic delight they'd found in resuming their sexual relationship had also cooled off and now they were perhaps even closer, but not in quite so enjoyable a way.

Unwisely, trying to set the tone, Godwin told her he loved her.

She smiled fleetingly, tugged her wool plaid blanket tighter, shivered. "Think how much more comfortable it would be here if word of fire—the warm, bright red thing we city dwellers depend on—if word of fire had reached the dark interior of England."

"You're cold."

"Right the first time."

"I have a sixth sense that way."

She sat down on the bed, leaned against the pillow and pulled the blanket around her knees and feet. "What happened after you fell down? Did you hurt your head?" She took his hand.

"Hardly. That's the part that's metal."

"What a fool you are. You'll be making stupid jokes the rest of your life."

"Better get used to them, then."

"Monk Vardan wasn't actually serious, he couldn't have been. A Nazi! What a thought . . ."

"Well, that wasn't quite the way it turned out."

"I might as well tell you my little problem," she said.

He felt his heart jerk in his chest, as if he'd crossed a tripwire. "What problem?"

"Look, I know how silly this is going to sound but . . . do you remember the letter you got at your flat? The one about us and what the sender was going—"

"I try never to forget murder threats—"

"Darling, do try to stop sounding like a play that closes on opening night. I love you dearly, really I do, but forced levity wears thin so quickly—"

"In that case, I'm going to kill myself. Everything is rotten and humor is dead and that's the only way out. Better?"

"Somewhat. But I've been thinking about that letter."

"And?"

"I'm being followed. Watched. It's not my imagination. I've seen a

man watching the house at night. I'm sure I've seen him outside the
theater after the show . . . I *know*. So please don't tell me I'm seeing
things."

"How long ago did you notice?"

"Three weeks roughly."

"About the time I showed signs of coming to life?"

She nodded. "That's what set me thinking about the letter. While
you were in your coma . . . well, you weren't likely to come back to me
in that condition. But when you'd come out of it . . . well, you follow
my train of thought. It was only a question of time."

"But who would know of my condition? That I was coming out of it?"

"People always seem to know things." She shrugged helplessly.

"There's someone who knew, of course. Monk knew."

"But what's it to him if you and I are—"

"Well, more than you might at first think, actually."

"Oh, I don't see any of it!"

"Look, Cilla, listen to me. They think I'm responsible for getting
everybody on the mission killed. Most particularly Max."

"You're mad! Somebody's mad . . . the awful Vardan, he must be
round the twist! They can't be serious, Rodger!"

"Well, they've begun scaring the hell out of me. Jack Priestley warned
me. As much as told me. They need a scapegoat. As I told you, Monk says
it's politics . . ."

"But why you?"

"I'm the only one left alive. They're sure the Germans were tipped
off. So there *must* be a spy. They're being pressured to find the spy. It's
going to be me."

"Just because you were lucky enough to survive?"

"That's not all, darling."

"What do you mean?"

"Monk knows I had a motive for wanting Max to die—"

"Oh no—"

"You."

"Oh no, Rodger! He's serious isn't he? It's monstrous—"

"Yes, it is."

"Are you sure?"

"He wants to talk to me about Cairo. He wants to get back to the
beginning."

She held out her arms to him.

·   ·   ·

The thin watery sunlight, gray as a fluke's belly, trickled through the tall windows. The room had apparently been some sort of grand parlor. It was known around the hospital as the Interrogation Room. Once Godwin had been up and walking about the place he'd learned about the Interrogation Room. It was all very civilized. Sometimes tea was served from a silver service. The German spies—not necessarily Germans, by any means, but spies, according to hospital gossip—were brought there and given tea or cigars and brandy, in hopes of softening them up, getting them to relax and lower their guards and spill the beans. No one was quite sure if it worked or not but at least there were never any screams coming from the parlor.

"All right if young Prestonbury joins us, Rodger? Prestonbury the Scribe, the keeper of the scrolls, he'll just be taking down a note or two. Keep the records straight through all this nastiness—"

"I couldn't care less about young Prestonbury. Go, stay, who cares?"

"Fine, fine. Good. Well, are you quite comfortable? The old head stop its banging? We don't want another little episode, my son. Are we ready, then?"

Godwin stared at him. It was the same old Monk but he felt as if he'd never seen him before. Well, trick of the light, as the man said. He kept thinking about Priestley. Whenever he had trouble believing what was happening, he thought about Jolly Jack Priestley. "Quite ready, Monk."

"Now if memory serves," Monk Vardan said, "you went to Cairo twice. The first time was the late spring or early summer of 1940. The war hadn't really got going yet, had it? But you knew it was coming. It was in the air. It was Symonds who met you at the airport, have I got that right? Derek Symonds, the Reuters stringer, with those bright, eager little eyes . . . like a very alert dog's eyes . . ."

CHAPTER 20

It was Cairo, it was quite unlike any other place, and it seemed serenely uninterested in the possibility of an impending desert war. The censors had decided that they didn't want Cairo to learn just how badly things were going for the British in the opening moves of the war with Hitler and Derek Symonds was frantic to hear the real news from home because Cairo was a city subsisting on rumor. Godwin was glad to comply over a long lunch in the dining room of Shepheard's Hotel, where he was staying.

As he was leaving, Symonds said, "Drinks in the bar at six, if that's all right?"

"The bar at Shepheard's . . ." Godwin mused. "Yes, that'll be fine."

"Won't be there myself. I'm arranging it for a fellow who wants to see you."

"Who's that?"

"He asked me to keep it secret, sir, even if you went after my finger-nails with red-hot pincers."

"Well, that won't be necessary, Symonds."

It was frequently said in those days that it was possible that the pyramids were more famous than the bar at Shepheard's Hotel, but you could get a damn fine drink at Shepheard's. It had been built in 1841 and its fame stemmed from its service as base camp for Thomas Cook's expeditions of tourists in the 1870s. Every visitor had his favorite bit of Shepheard's. There was the Terrace Bar with all the wicker furniture and the piano playing and the palms swaying in the breeze and Ibrahim Pasha Street just beyond. There was the Moorish Hall, cool and lofty beneath the dome of colored glass, outfitted below with terrifically discreet octagonal tables and overstuffed antimacassared chairs. And in the ballroom there were the famous pillars copied from those at Karnak with the lotus tops, which had moved someone to characterize the hotel's style as Eighteenth-Dynasty Edwardian. And there was no forgetting the sweeping staircase from the Moorish Hall with the pair of tall ebony caryatids with spectacular breasts, not infrequently decorated in provocative fashion by the rowdier guests.

And, of course, there was the Long Bar to which Godwin repaired at six o'clock.

"Well, I'll be damned. It is you, after all. Young Symonds will be mentioned in dispatches."

Godwin looked up, almost recognizing the voice he hadn't heard in thirteen years.

"How are you, Rodger? Keeping well?" The face was deeply tanned, etched with some ridges at the corners of the mouth and eyebrows; there were streaks of gray at the temples and in the wings combed back over the ears. Under his eye, the scar tissue from one night in Paris. He wore a perfect suit, a perfect tan with a pale blue silk shirt and a deep burgundy tie. His compact body wasn't a pound heavier.

"Max," Godwin said. "You set me up, you son of a gun!" They shook hands warmly and Godwin remembered he was one of Hood's Boys. Max Hood was the only man on earth with whom Rodger Godwin had in fact "seen action," as certain kinds of men used to say. They had killed together.

"Yes, young Symonds mentioned he was meeting the famous Rodger Godwin—I impressed him immensely by telling him that you and I were old campaigners. I told him we'd heard the chimes at midnight."

"It's been a long time since that rainy graveyard."

"Seems like yesterday. A good night's work that." He gestured to a chair. "Mind if I sit? Let's have a drink and tell each other lies about the years between. I want to hear what brings your august self out to our dusty corner of the world."

"And I want to know what's going on out here. Something tells me you're the man to ask."

"Why, Rodger, you're the famous writer. You tell me. Gin and tonic?" He waved to one of the waiters. "It's fine to see you, Rodger." His gray eyes clung to Godwin's for a moment.

"I thought about you the day war was declared. You finally had a war, Max."

"Rather sad, isn't it? But it's what I do best. It's the tragedy of my life but I try not to let it get me down. It'll be good business for you. You've certainly come to the right place to pick up any stray bits of intelligence."

"Cairo?"

"The bar at Shepheard's," Max Hood said. "Just get close to Joe. The barman. He's Swiss, collects information the way his countrymen collect money. Women aren't allowed here either so you'll discover that chaps unbutton a bit. Keep your ears open and you'll hear everything that's going. Place is full of spies." He lowered his voice. "I rather suppose I'm one myself."

"If you're a spy why don't you tell me what the hell's going on here? When's the shooting going to start?"

"Any day now. Mussolini's working himself up to move against Britain. It's as close as your whiskers. He's jealous of Hitler getting all the press coverage. Hitler's having his way all across Europe, there's never been anything quite like it. Mussolini has Libya, Eritrea, Somaliland, and Ethiopia. He figures England's got her hands full with Hitler. So now's the time to swoop down on England's interests hereabouts. If he pulls it off he'll triple the size of his empire here on the African continent. He figures it'll be easy pickings. He may be right, actually. It remains to be seen. Egypt is on the menu, I'm afraid. There are fewer than forty thousand British troops here and Mussolini has a quarter of a million men just in Libya, ready to come."

"Is it really that bad, Max?"

"Oh yes, I'm afraid it is. Of course," he added with a small smile, "they *are* Italians. Good chaps, easy going, I like 'em. I've done some recce in Libya—man of a thousand faces, y'know—and when they come there'll be hell to pay." The ice in his glass tinkled. The bar was filling up. "Shall we adjourn to the Terrace?" He got up and led the way.

The dark wicker chairs were deep, clustered around small wooden tables, ashtrays filling up, waiters wearing tarbooshes and long white skirts. Nearly half the men wore military kit and sat studying notebooks and stapled sheets of paper and newspapers. The level of talk was low but incessant and determined and striving to convince or extract a nugget of fresh information. It was a hothouse world, all right, and he might have been watching a roomful of orchids, trying to survive.

They sat at one of the little brown tables beside the railing and Hood made sure they had fresh drinks. "Now it's your turn to tell me how bad things are in Europe. We get garbled information here, even at the garrison. What's going on at Dunkirk? We get hints—none of us can figure out why the Germans don't just finish off the BEF. When's Hitler coming across the Channel? Is there any way to stop him?" He grinned sheepishly, looking the way he had in Paris when he'd told Godwin he was half in love with Cilla DewBrittain. In the bar, when he'd first seen Max Hood, Godwin had thought of her at once, as if she were there beside them. It had been more than a little disconcerting. He wondered if he should mention her or if it was one of those memories better left alone. But Max was asking questions about the faraway war and maybe it was better that way.

"Dunkirk isn't easy to explain," Godwin said. "Quite impossible on the face of it. Impossible to know why they didn't come on and finish us off. They could have driven the whole damn lot of us into the sea. But they didn't." He shrugged at the vagaries of the military mind. "There shouldn't have been a way in the world to get those men off the beach. But they seem to be doing it. RAF providing air cover like you've never seen. When I left London they'd been evacuating for three, four days. I talked to men who'd gotten out. They said there are three hundred thousand troops yet to come, maybe more. Dunkirk is being bombed to bits by the Luftwaffe. When the Brit ships get out of the harbor they run into heavy fire from the German batteries at Calais and then there are the U-boats coming down from the North Sea.

"I flew into Paris on 31 May, the same day Churchill arrived with Attlee, Dill, and Ismay—"

"Aren't they cutting it just a little close? Hitler has to pull the trigger on Paris at any moment."

"That's what I thought. Paris is just waiting for the end."

"Did you see any of the old crowd?"

Godwin smiled. "Merle B. Swaine says he'll be surprised if the Frogs hold out two more weeks. He never did think much of the French."

"What are his plans?"

"I think he'll try to get out in the nick of time. Or maybe he'll stay. He's nearly sixty now. The Nazis may not bother him if he stays."

"He'll probably try to find the same cab driver that we caught coming back from Le Bourget that night."

Godwin laughed. "What a night that was.

"I lit out for Lisbon and caught the first flight out to Cairo."

"Things look a trifle bleak," Hood said. "But, of course, we will endure and prevail."

"If we don't believe that, what's the point?"

"It would help if you Yanks got on board."

"We will, sooner or later."

"Let's hope it's in time."

"Well, bless my rather tatty soul." Someone was standing behind Godwin. "The things that do turn up in the most peculiar places. Welcome to our little home away from home."

Godwin stood up, turned around. "Monk! What a treat, you miserable git! How long have you been here? Max, do you know this person?"

"Know me?" Monk sighed down his long nose. "Comrade Hood and I come as a set. By the way, I bring gloomy tidings. Herr Goering's intrepid flyboys bombed Paris only a few hours ago. Word just came through."

The announcement was greeted with silence. Then Hood said: "Any news of Dunkirk?"

"Dunkirk is over. The last British soldiers were taken off yesterday. The Germans should have reached the beach by now. Dicey. I have word the PM will address the Commons tomorrow." Monk Vardan had folded himself into a chair. He was holding a glass of beer. "It's a bit tricky on the home front, I'm afraid. If Hitler crosses the Channel now the next generation of Englishmen will speak very fluent German. It's just a fact of life."

Godwin said: "It's my understanding that there are about five hundred guns left on British soil for the defense—"

"And a good many of them," Hood said softly, "are museum pieces. Pray God he doesn't come."

"We left just about everything on French soil," Vardan said. "Roughly two thousand guns, sixty thousand trucks, seventy-five thousand tons of ammunition . . . six hundred tons of fuel—we had to get the troops out. There was no choice."

"Our Monk knows all," Hood said.

Vardan smiled slowly. "I would only say that my information is, as a rule, fairly accurate."

Godwin lifted his glass. "Our Monk," he said and they all drank.

The evening had been a long one and when he woke the next morning Godwin felt every minute of it in every bone and muscle. Through more drinks and dinner and cigars and some lavish port they had trekked back and forth over the years.

Max Hood said that he'd gotten a divorce in '28, and they drank to that while Max smiled quietly to himself. Tony DewBrittain's heart had given out while shooting grouse in Scotland and he'd had a rather good bag his last day. Clyde Rasmussen had gone on to be famous, had appeared in several movies involving places like Sun Valley and Palm Beach, seemed to divide his time between Los Angeles and New York, and led the band on the weekly radio show starring Mickey Hopewell, the comedian.

Even with a bit of a snootful, Godwin couldn't bring himself to mention Cilla DewBrittain for fear of opening an old wound of Max Hood's.

A clearer picture of the Hood and Vardan linkage emerged as well. Both men were Churchill's, body and soul. Before he had been asked to form a government, Churchill had asked Max Hood to become his eyes and ears in Egypt. With Churchill at Number 10, Vardan served as a kind of roving representative of the PM. He'd come to Egypt to connect with Commander-in-Chief, Middle East, General Sir Archibald Wavell and Lieutenant-General Sir Henry Maitland Wilson, better known as Jumbo. Monk Vardan was reporting back on the rebuilding of the British military infrastructure which had fallen into ruin once the war had ended in 1918. The job was overwhelming. Roads, airstrips, water-purifying plants, training schools, field hospitals, communication lines, pipes to bring water from the Nile into the desert, canteens. They were scouring Palestine and Egypt for vehicles which might be made desert worthy. And something had to be done about the tanks which were built for the mud of Europe and didn't seem to work worth a damn in all the bloody damn sand. The engines seized up, the tracks ripped off on the rocks, and the air filters choked and died on the blowing sand. "It's simply a nightmare, old boy," Vardan said happily. "Jumbo's doing his best. We'll be fine at the end of the day."

Lordy, it had been a long night and Derek Symonds was looking so bright and youthful that Godwin winced on first sight of him. Thick, industrial-strength coffee helped. A little.

Vardan had arranged for Godwin to have an hour with Wavell himself. "Simple, old chap," he'd said. "You're famous. Archie wanted to meet you. I can't swear he's read your books, mind you."

From Wavell he went to see the memorable Thomas Russell Pasha for an elaborate lunch at the Gezira Sporting Club on its island in the Nile. In the afternoon there was a briefing with Miles Lampson at the British embassy. By the time Symonds deposited him back at Shepheard's Godwin felt dragged out and no better informed than he'd been when Vardan had finished with him the previous night.

He was working at the desk in his room, roughing out newspaper columns and radio broadcasts, when he heard a knock at the door. It was one of the boys from the lobby.

Max Hood was requesting his company at a small gathering on a Nile houseboat.

Godwin stood at the railing of the houseboat sipping champagne. The reflection of the huge candles and lanterns shimmered in the gently lapping waves. Behind him, around him, the conversations of Cairo's daily life hung in the warmth like a new species of barrage balloon. He'd briefly played the role of visiting celebrity, promised to have drinks at the Turf Club with one fellow and sign a woman's copies of his latest book over cocktails before he left for London. Vardan had passed him around and then gone off with a couple of hussars to talk about Dunkirk. And Godwin had finally slipped through the wildly elaborate golden doors to the outside deck. Cairo had a glow of its own and the wind wasn't warm. It was hot. He turned away from the water, looked back in through the open shutters, smelled the burning candle wax, saw the bowls of white ostrich feathers.

It was an hour after Godwin's arrival that Max Hood and his wife appeared. A man called Algernon Nesbitt from the foreign office was standing beside Godwin discussing Cairo's brothels, then said suddenly, "Ah, there they are, the guests of honor. I say, she is rather dishy, isn't she?"

They were surrounded by the other guests for a moment, and the woman had her back turned. She wore a beige-and-white dress with a fetching amount of tanned shoulder blades showing. Her hair was thick and dark brown and cut rather short at the nape of the neck. And then she turned, first in profile, then facing him.

She was a woman now; she must be twenty-seven. Cilla DewBrittain.

"I know her," Godwin said. His mouth was suddenly dry.

"You *know* her?"

"I knew her when she was a girl in Paris. Years ago."

"Well, better go say hello, what? You can introduce her to your old chum Algie."

Max Hood wasn't the sort of man given to a great deal of social levity but he positively twinkled when he spotted Godwin heading through the crowd. "Surprise, Rodger! Meet Mrs. Hood!"

Cilla was smiling at Godwin, her café au lait eyes with their chips of green wide, expectant. She threw her arms around him, standing on tiptoe to press her cheek to his. "Oh, Rodger, you're so huge! And famous! And wonderful to behold! And this rotter of a husband of mine didn't tell me you'd be here either—Max, shame on you! I might have been looking forward to this all day!"

Max shrugged, smiling at both of them. "I thought a happy surprise was in order. It's good to be together again." He took Cilla's hand.

"Well, how long have you two been married? Why wasn't I informed?"

"You were probably off in Indochina or up the Amazon." Hood

clapped him on the back. "We knew we were bound to run across you sooner or later."

"And you were not a good correspondent," Cilla said. "It's entirely your fault."

"So how long has this been going on behind my back?"

"Oh," she said gaily, "years and years and years."

Max said: "Since '35, Rodger. She's not so good with figures."

"We were married at the Hood family monstrosity up in Northumberland! It's called Stillgraves and it's a fine name for it. Dragged everyone up there. All very daunting."

"It *is* a bit of a hike," Max said. "Old Victorian pile."

"Damp is the word," she said, "very damp," and Max gave her arm an affectionate squeeze. "And so began four years of relentless bliss."

"My wife is a world-class violinist, Rodger. Concerts all over the world. And she's just finished two movies—"

"Look at him, Max! This all comes as news to him! Oh, Rodger, you started out as a *music* critic in Paris."

"Of course I know about your career," Godwin lied. "But my career as a music critic was deservedly brief. Swaine called it the blind leading the preposterous. Clyde was my teacher."

"She's just back from a tour. Buenos Aires, Rio, Mexico City—where else?"

"Max, please, don't bore poor Rodger—"

"Nonsense, Cilla. She's going to the States for a month, New York, Boston, Philadelphia—" Max's pride was disarming, innocent. "But the movies, that looks like the future. Dammit, Rodger, she can *act*. Life's full of miracles, old boy. Chap who should know says she'll wind up in the West End . . . says she's a natural. Miracles, Rodger."

"It's so good to see you, you were just a girl when I last saw you—"

"But I was very grown-up for my age."

"Yes, that's true, you were."

Max said: "Say, Rodger, she's had a bit of very good news—another face from the past. You recall Clyde? Well, she tells me he's forming a new band in London of all places. Isn't that extraordinary—what a sight for sore eyes he'll be. He was a good enough chap, old Clyde. Given to tastes that weren't mine but still, live and let live. Rodger and I were speaking of Clyde only last night."

"Can you believe it, Rodger?" she said. "Clyde Rasmussen and His Society Boys. Something on that order."

"I'm amazed. I thought he was too successful in the States ever to leave."

"I understand there's a story behind it," she said. "He's represented by the same management as I. Apparently he has a wonderful new recording contract. Won't it be fun to see him again?" Diamonds sparkled as she took a glass of champagne.

"We're both looking forward to it," Max said. "He was a great help to Cilla in Paris. He taught her how to grasp the music personally. Apparently that's the key to performing. Do I have that approximately right?"

"Approximately," she said.

Their host came by and detached Max, led him away, and Cilla turned to Godwin with an elusive smile playing across her mouth, barely reflected in her eyes. "Don't worry about Clyde and me, dear old Rodger. You looked positively stricken. I thought you were going to give it all away, lo these many years later." Something moved in her eyes. "I do have my secrets from Max."

"I'm sorry. It was just that the memories all came back so fast—"

"I know, I know, but I am glad you weren't indiscreet. I wish I could have a long chat, but I really must mingle with these people."

"Yes, I suppose you must. Well, it's been good to see you after all these years." He looked away. He felt as if he'd been brushed off by an expert, and the hot blood was rushing to his face.

"I was just wondering—is there any chance I can see you again?" She looked up at him, like a girl once more. "When do you leave Cairo?"

"The day after tomorrow. Or the day after that."

"Do you have any time for me tomorrow? Late afternoon?"

"I could arrange it, Cilla."

"Where are you stopping?"

"Shepheard's."

"Of course," she said, mocking him. "Where else would the great Godwin bed down? Silly me."

"I'm so glad your career has gone well. I once told you to get your priorities straight and you could go wherever you wanted. Maybe you were listening after all."

"Max wasn't joking, you know . . . I'm going to be a movie star . . . it's quite absurd but they think I can act."

"I think they're right. I've seen you act, you know, and you were very good under pressure."

"Greer Fantasia introduced me to some of Korda's people and some of the Gainsborough people and it happened before I took it seriously."

"You know Greer? He's my publisher."

"I know. He was very sweet and helpful. They say the camera loves me—isn't that jolly? And this American tour Max was talking about?

Well, I've backed out of it. He doesn't know it yet. There's another picture for me to do this summer . . . I'm not doing any more concerts. My future is in films. If it turns out I'm any good they've even mentioned the stage, the West End, someday. It all seems too preposterous but one never knows. I'm working with a good teacher. I think they're releasing one of the pictures this week in London—promise you'll go?" Talking about her career she'd come vibrantly alive. He could see how the camera would love her. Max Hood was a lucky man.

"Cilla—I'll try, all right? There's this war on, you know. Things are busy for me at the moment, too."

"Don't be silly, Rodger. You can take a couple of hours. I'll take you myself if it's the only way. We could have a date and things. It'll be like Paris . . ."

"I meant to ask you something—"

"Yes?"

"You put something in the pocket of my dressing gown when I last saw you. I didn't find it until some time later. Do you recall it?"

"I'm afraid not, dear Rodger. It was a very long time ago, wasn't it? What a very girlish thing to do. Perhaps I had some kind of pash about you." She shrugged coolly and smiled.

"I just wondered. Not important. I thought you might remember where you'd heard it. A scrap of poetry."

"Well then," she said, "until tomorrow afternoon. Now I must rejoin my husband. He has that trapped look in his eye." She looked back at him sharply as she turned away. "Are you surprised I married Max?"

"I suppose, the way things take one by surprise—"

"He was very patient. He waited and he put up with me."

He watched her cross the room and then someone was saying that the Prime Minister was about to speak on the radio. He was addressing the Commons. Monk Vardan drew close to him and said: "My master's voice. He's not going to be very cheering, I'm afraid. Time for the stiff u.l. and all."

Algie Nesbitt was fiddling with the dial. The static crackled and somebody called out that he'd better learn how to operate a simple wireless or was that beyond the ken of the foreign office and there was a flutter of laughter. Nesbitt stuck out his tongue at the speaker. Sweat was glistening on his pink face.

The familiar voice cut through the static and the room was utterly quiet. It was as if somebody had dropped a hood over a bird cage. Godwin was still thinking about grown-up Cilla Hood, trying to relate her to the provocative girl he'd known in Paris. She'd been a handful then and that hadn't changed. She hadn't been afraid to bring up the past. Godwin doubted if he'd have been able to do that so casually; she behaved as if the thirteen years had slipped past in the wink of an eye. She'd been sending out a variety of signals but he hadn't the key to the code. He supposed Churchill was speaking in a kind of code, too, knowing that throughout the world he was being heard by the great leaders as well as by the commonfolk. But coded or not, the overt message couldn't have been clearer. He spoke of Hitler crossing the Channel and invading England and he vowed to carry on the fight if necessary from the outposts of the Empire. But first they would fight tooth and nail in the homeland.

"We shall fight on the beaches," he growled, "we shall fight in the fields. . . ." Static sliced through the voice and they next heard him say: "We shall never surrender."

Godwin was standing with Vardan preparing to leave when Nesbitt tottered up. He wiped his face with a white handkerchief.

"You ought to have introduced me to the lady. I'm a devoted admirer. And now I'm told she's making movies. The name going round the bars is Greer Fantasia—I had no idea he was interested in movies. In fact, the story seems to be that he wasn't until he met Mrs. Hood. From what I hear about the lady I was hoping they might be movies of the blue variety. Apparently she demonstrated the joys of the casting couch for Fantasia. Some people say Korda himself has had her. And Jacob Epstein. Personally my money's on Fantasia. No actual corroborations, though I've been told there are some very hard-to-find photos of her having it off with what's his name, the actor, Sam Townes. I've never seen them either, I regret to say."

Vardan said: "One mustn't believe all one hears. She's beautiful and well known. I venture to say one wouldn't want to get on Max Hood's bad side. It would take a braver man than I."

"Oh, don't be so sure," Nesbitt said. "I hear he's so besotted by her he'll turn a blind eye. Thinks it's a phase she'll get through."

Godwin was staring at Nesbitt. "I expect it's all bullshit. I've heard stories about myself . . . not a word of truth. Pure wishful thinking on the part of dirty-minded buggers. People love to think the very worst of others, don't you agree? Max Hood's no fool. No blind eye there."

"Know him well, do you?"

"In the old days I did. He's a great man, you know."

"You don't say, old chap?" Nesbitt raised an eyebrow. "All I've heard about is the desert stuff with Lawrence. All a long time ago. Perhaps not as tough a customer as he once was, now the girl's got her teeth in him."

"I knew Mrs. Hood back then, too. She was only a child of fourteen. I knew her and her family."

"Ah, that mother of hers, Pamela Legend. I hear young Cilla gets her hot blood from that old rip. Quite an item in the old days, Lady Pamela."

Godwin said: "I'd say you're damn lucky Max isn't within hearing distance now."

"Well, give me some credit. I'd hardly be saying it to Max Hood, would I?"

"Crossing Max is ill advised," Vardan said, "at best."

"Well, I know for a fact that Sidney Jacobs had Cilla Hood one night in The Hague, or was it Amsterdam, after one of their concerts. Old Sid met her at a party and before the night was out she was playing a tune on his flute. And Bertie Wilberforce—you chaps know Bertie, surely, damn near had his century at Lord's—well, Bertie was in his cups one night at Brat's and bet young Poole he would find a small heart-shaped mole, a beauty mark, at a certain spot between Cilla Hood's legs should he ever be in a posish to conduct a thorough search."

"Monk," Godwin said, "I've heard about all of this I can take—"

"I say, old man," Nesbitt said, grinning, "don't get all chuffed. What's she to you, anyway? I'm merely making conversation, telling you what I've heard. Sorry if I've cut a bit close to the bone."

Godwin put his hand heavily on Nesbitt's shoulder. "I'm asking you to drop it or you'll find I'm a lot more *chuffed* than you could imagine in a million years. I've never hesitated to hit a man because he was small and stupid and drunk."

"You'll only hurt him, you know," Vardan observed sagely. "Still, defending the lady's honor might do you a world of good. Now, Algie, you're an absolute disgrace. You're supposed to be some sort of diplomat but at this rate your future is not an encouraging prospect. Ignore him, Rodger. He's had too much to drink and—"

"I'm getting out of here," Godwin said to Vardan. "I suggest you throw this guy into the Nile, feed him to the first really large thing that slithers past."

She came to his room at Shepheard's the next day. She was wearing a French silk suit the color of her eyes. There was a tortoiseshell bracelet, a matching necklace against the cream silk blouse, a cameo ring on one hand, diamonds on the other. Her short hair was combed back on the sides, parted like a man's. She wore a version of a man's panama hat and when she'd stepped into the dim room she plucked it from her head and sailed it into an occasional chair.

Godwin wasn't sure how to greet her. Somewhere in the back of his mind she was still a little girl. But he heard Algie Nesbitt's voice going on and on about her and he didn't know what to think. She smiled at him quickly, nervously, and kissed him in passing on the lips. He stood in the doorway, watching her swagger past, wondering at how she made him feel so big and clumsy and uncertain. She was so compact and tightly wound.

She turned back as if she knew he'd been watching the promise of her swaying rump in the perfectly cut suit. "So, how do you like it?"

"What? The view? Well, you've grown up shall we say?"

"Shepheard's, silly. How do you like it?"

"It's fine. I haven't spent much time here. Discovered my room has no phone."

"No, only fourteen rooms have phones. Didn't anyone tell you?"

"No, no one told me."

"You need someone looking after you. There is the Terrace. You know what they say about the Terrace at Shepheard's."

"No, I don't think I do."

"If you sit there long enough the most boring people you've ever known will eventually show up. It's quite true, you know." She cocked her head at him, wearing a kind of evaluating smile. "You've changed, Rodger. I think you've gotten older. Could that be it?"

"You've changed, too."

"How?"

"Well, you know."

"Tell me. How have I changed?"

"Filled out a bit in certain crucial places . . ."

"Really? I've been told I have the smallest tits on the concert stage today. Oh, now, have I said something impolite? I was quoting, Rodger, so don't think I'm unduly vulgar—"

"I want to hear about your life, Cilla. Gin and it?" He'd had gin and quinine water and ice brought up. He'd put one away while waiting for her and trying not to remember what that idiot Nesbitt had said the night before. He handed her a drink. She sat in one of the upholstered armchairs, he in the other, two not entirely comfortable people in a hotel room in Cairo.

She didn't seem forthcoming so he said: "So, where's Max? How does he spend his days? And what brings you to Cairo, anyway?"

"Oh, Rodger, who cares, really? Max is off being a soldier somewhere, plotting with Monk Vardan what they'll do when the big show begins in the desert. It's only going to be the Italians so I don't know what they're so worried about. They'll be put to rout. How can anyone get angry enough to fight the poor Italians? I came to visit . . . I don't know, to show him I cared enough about him to come. Cairo is a moderately awful place, isn't it? So much of it is so poor . . . it's all so sad, really, and the rich are so very rich." She smiled brightly. "Sounds exactly like England, doesn't it? But you know what I mean. Everything always seems so much more awful when it's hot, don't you think?"

"You and Max," he said. "He was certainly stuck on you when you were fourteen. But it never really occurred to me that you two would—"

"We're not terribly happy, Rodger. I mean, a lot of people aren't terribly happy these days. And it's going to get worse with this war. I haven't been good for Max; he's had a bad time of it. Sometimes I rather wish he'd be allowed his fondest hope . . . to die for his country, a hero. Because that's what he is. A hero. And that's the only end for a hero."

"I'm sorry to hear that. Maybe things will get better—"

"Oh, yes, probably. And I heard only the other day that pigs are beginning to fly in Surrey. Don't be trite, Rodger. Things won't get any better for Max and me." She sighed. The window shutters were closed to keep out the heat and a large ceiling fan was rotating slowly. It sliced the sunshine coming through the shutters. A strip of light fell across her lap and the rise and fall of her belly. "I'm afraid I'm rather too *vivid* for poor Max. Sometimes we're like two colors that clash. Obviously wrong for each other. It's just one of those things."

"How did it all happen, you two? I had no idea, I'd never heard. I just went off and never looked back."

"Yes, you went off in your little red car and I knew you were lying last night about following my career. You're such a transparent oaf. I actually have read your books and liked them very much, though why I'm admitting it to you I don't know. I cried when I read the ones about Paris."

He smiled at her. "I cried some when I wrote it. Paris was . . . what? Youth, I guess. People are always bawling about their lost youth. And you're quite right about my lying—God knows, I'm culturally deprived."

She laughed edgily. "I was never a prodigy but they treated me like one. It was all because of my looks, as my mother points out at every opportunity. She used to say that every man and half the women who heard me play wanted to get my knickers off. She assumes I slept with all the important conductors and booking agents. What a woman! I had quite a success in Berlin. I'll tell my grandchildren I played for that fat Mr. Goering and his wife and drank champagne with them afterward and danced with him. I've been apart from Max a good deal. Our lives are not exactly congruent. He likes that place of his family's way up on the back-side of beyond. He likes to lurk about up there like Quasimodo in the cold and rain—maybe because it's not like the desert, who knows? But now he's quite excited about the war." She wet her lips with the drink, then rested the beaded glass on the pillow of her full lower lip that had begun to pout more than it had in her girlish face. "I'm glad he has the war at last. He's waited for one so long. He's not a boy anymore; he's nearly fifty. It came just in time. They need him for all this desert business. He hasn't been needed in a long time."

"But how did you come to marry him?"

She stood up, complaining of the warmth. She slipped out of her jacket and threw it on the bed. She went to the window and worked the lever that opened the slats in the shutters, stared out for several moments as if making some sort of decision.

"We were married in America, in Boston. Red tape and all. I was on my first American tour. It made very good publicity. I thought at the time that surely you would see it written up somewhere and get in touch. Apparently you didn't."

"But . . . well, why? Had he been after you to marry him for a long time?"

"Oh, Rodger, he's been in love with me from the day we met. In Paris. Or it's important for him to believe that. He never gave up. He kept asking me and I said yes in the end. He knew I would. He knew my faults." She shrugged. "He wanted me anyway. Not that I've told him . . . all I told you." She turned back from the window. "What about that old crowd from Paris? Do you ever see any of them now?"

"No. I thought I would when I left Paris . . . no, I lie, I didn't actually think I would. But later on I kept remembering them, thinking they'd turn up sooner or later. Somewhere or other."

"When I saw Clyde in New York he was terribly successful and quite dissipated. The girls seem to get younger and younger. I felt quite *emeritus*." She flashed the smile again, the lower lip jutting forward.

"Didn't he try to kill himself over you in Paris?"

"Did he? Yes, I suppose he did. But he mucked it up." She sighed, paced across the room, turned on her heel, took a deep breath. "I shouldn't have come here. It was a bad idea. I thought it would be like Paris but it's not, it's all very different. I'm different, I guess. Anyway, I should go. I really should go, Rodger—"

"What's the matter? You're a nervous wreck. Is it Max?"

"You wrote to me, Rodger. I got your letter that autumn. Thirteen years ago. I still have it, hidden in a very special place. I was in England in school and you wrote me a very sweet letter."

"You never answered it, as I recall."

"Oh but I did, yes I did. You just don't want to remember. You're too embarrassed. I sent it to you at some bank office in Vienna. That's where you said you'd be—"

"I never got it."

"And so," she teased, "the fates of men and women are decided."

"Why do you say that?"

"Look," she was breathless, "this is why I came to see you . . . the letter I wrote, and it's why I should go now. It was a stupid idea in every possible way and I can still cancel the performance, so to speak. Please, let me just go—"

"But why, Cilla? It was so long ago—"

"Because I told you in my letter all the things I couldn't dare tell you face-to-face."

"Listen, you were fourteen—"

"But you know what I was like. I'd told you everything, almost all my secrets." She poured gin and quinine into her glass, swirled it, took a drink. "This wasn't supposed to be so difficult. But suddenly I feel fourteen again. I told you in the letter that it was you I'd fallen in love with that summer. From the first day . . . it was terrible. I was doing all those things with Clyde and I thought it didn't make any difference, nobody knew. Then I met you and you were so nice to me, and spent so much time talking to me and listening to me and treating me like a real person . . . so then you found Clyde and me and I thought by telling you everything I could be somehow intimate with you . . . it excited me to tell you and I kept hoping it might excite you, too . . . but I thought if I told you I loved you you'd think I was simply a stupid, oversexed, wild girl who knew nothing and cared about nothing but sex . . . but all I could think of was how I wanted to have you inside me and see me naked . . . I put it all in the letter. I asked you to come back to England and marry me or have me for your mistress. . . . All these years I've thought you got my letter, read it, ignored it—now you see why I should never have come here, never have brought it up, but I had to ask you why you never answered me—I poured my heart out in that letter and I never heard a word—"

"I don't know if I believe you," he said.

"My God, you *are* a bastard!"

"Cilla, if I'd gotten the letter, I'd have answered you—"

"I told you how glad I was that you caught me in bed with Clyde—I wanted you to see my little breasts. I had always thought I was so sophisticated, having those men I told you about, but when I met you I felt like a child again, I was trying so hard to make you like me. It was all in the letter, Rodger. You should believe me. And I told you all the things you could do to me, the most private things I'd ever thought or written down." She came toward him, sat on the edge of the bed leaning toward him. "I could never have spoken them to you while you could look at me . . ." Her face was damp, her eyes not entirely focused as if she were about to faint. "But you never answered the letter and it was Max who waited for me to grow up, Max who followed me and visited me at school and took me out for tea and biscuits and a meal at the hotel dining room and brought me presents I could show to the other girls and encouraged me and finally I married him because no one had ever cared about me for so long. Oh my, yes, I married Max for better or worse and it's been an agony for him. Would you possibly consider kissing me, Rodger?"

"For old times' sake?"

"For my sake, my darling beast," and she leaned against him and took his face in her hands and pressed her mouth to his for a long time. When she pulled away at last she was gasping and out of breath. Her lips glistened. "Was it really such a chore?"

"Cilla, try to be sensible—"

"Don't you see? This isn't about being sensible. I'm not anything to do with being sensible!"

"You're another man's wife. You're caught up in memory. You didn't love me in Paris. You were discovering your extraordinary power over men. Your sexual power. I was aware of it, awed by it, we all were . . . it was in the air, like a scent, you were so ripe and so gifted and so bright . . . and so very young . . ."

"I have been rather unstable in recent years." She snapped her head up at him, ready to defend herself against accusations. "It's true. I was in a loony bin for a bit . . . well, not Bedlam, actually. But a convalescent home. I had doctors from Vienna."

"Whatever for? Were you chewing the rug and barking?"

She ignored him. "Have you heard stories about me?"

"What sort of stories?"

"Don't be disingenuous, Rodger. If you haven't heard them, you will. And if you've already heard them, you may as well believe them." She opened her eyes wide. They seemed to lap against him like a sea, engulf him. They were so huge and the color so unforgettable. At the moment they were the eyes of a supplicant, an innocent, a girl. "Poor Max, he's been very loyal to me through some pretty disgusting times. It hasn't been easy for him. I'm very bad marriage material. I suppose I ought to have known that . . . I got off to a pretty scandalous start, didn't I?

"Precocious, at least."

"You were very lucky you didn't get my letter and come back for me, Rodger. I'd have led you a hell of a chase." She set her chin at him. "I may still."

"Impossible. You're Max Hood's wife."

"We shall see. I will have to be going quite soon so I have one favor to ask."

"Which is?"

"Kiss me again. You do it this time. Just once. I won't bite."

He took her shoulders, kissed her firmly but with curiosity, not passion. He knew it was a mistake. It was the simple truth: She was Max Hood's wife.

"You're afraid of me, aren't you, Rodger? You think if you give in you'll be lost for good. Frankly, I think you are almost certainly right about that. I've been told I can be comparatively irresistible when I put my mind to it."

"I don't doubt it for a moment."

"Do you love me? Do you love me at all?"

"Cilla, what a hell of a question. I haven't seen you in thirteen years and you were a child then."

"I'm not arguing with you, Rodger. I'm just asking a question."

"I don't know—how can I love you? I'm afraid I'm not quite with you . . . you're so beautiful, so desirable . . . you're married and not just to anyone, to Max Hood! What do you expect me to say?"

"I rather hoped you would just admit it. But this is just the start—"

"It's the end. You may betray Max . . . you do betray him with every hint and implication, but I'll be damned if I will!"

"But, Rodger, you great oaf, you haven't seen him in thirteen years either." There was triumph in her voice. "So why should you be more loyal to him than to me?"

"Surely you can see that's quite different."

"These thirteen years, have you thought about me?" She was standing again, unable to stay still. Her hips had broadened from the days when she was a girl. You could see the power in her hips and thighs and he couldn't take his eyes off her.

"Not for a long time."

"Liar. Have you had lots of women?"

"Tons. Thousands. All beautiful. Far more beautiful than you, each and every one of them."

"You are such a terrible liar." She went to the shutters with her back to him. When she turned around she had unbuttoned her blouse. She was looking in his eyes and her face was solemn. "How in the world to get your attention," she said softly. "That's the question . . . well." She pulled her loose slip down far enough to expose her small round breasts. Her nipples were very large and dark and erect.

"Cilla, for God's sake . . ."

She came toward him and took his hands and lifted them to her mouth where she pressed the fingertips to her lips. She carefully pressed the fingertips, moist from her tongue, to her nipples. "You must realize I am not a child anymore. You must pay attention to me. You must listen to me and take me seriously. Can you do that?" She squeezed her nipples tight between his fingers. "Can you?"

"Cilla, you don't know what you're doing."

"But I do, Rodger, that would seem to be the entire point, wouldn't it? I have thought about you for so long. I tell the truth." She pulled his head down and he let her. She put one of her nipples into his mouth. "Suck me," she said. "Taste just a little of me. Suck me, I want to feel your teeth biting me. I hate you for not thinking of me. So many years of not thinking about me. I thought about you every day. I'll never forgive you for that, for not coming to find me. The things I'd have done for you, you'd never have left me." She moaned sharply and he took his mouth from her flesh. "You bit me. Look at the teeth marks." She slapped him. "That hurt."

"I'm sorry."

"I liked it. You're so slow, Rodger. And you are such an almighty bastard. Everything about you says I'm independent, proclaims your independence, says I don't need you. Well, you only think so. Your free ride through this life is over, darling. You've escaped all the entanglements of life these past thirteen years. You were alive there in Paris and you may be sure you're going to come alive again. You've had it all your way while the rest of us have been struggling with each other, trying to survive. Somebody really should teach you about real life and pain, dear Rodger." She had dropped her hand and was stroking him. "I've grown up. Now it's your turn. Maybe you'll remember this, today, what's happened between us. Do you think so? You're excited now, aren't you, Rodger, you're almost there, I can feel it . . . well, hold the thought, darling." She backed away, they were both panting in the heat. She pulled the slip up and stood in the doorway to the bathroom patting her face with a thick towel. Then she threw it to him. "Max wants you to join us for dinner tonight. Nine o'clock. Don't be late. And don't even think of staying away. Max expects you." She was buttoning her blouse. She slid into her jacket and stood watching him. She wrote the address on a pad of notepaper.

Finally he spoke. "Cilla, none of this just happened."

"Oh, Rodger." She laughed. "Such a dreamer. You don't even know what it is that has happened, do you?" She smiled crookedly. "You've just run headlong into your future. You've had a peek at the rest of your life, until your dying day. I expect you're a little dazed, I understand. Try not to worry so. We'll all survive or we won't. It's life. You'll have to get used to it, I'm afraid."

CHAPTER 21

Godwin yawned, stared out at Salisbury's afternoon gloom. It was drizzling. The dogs loping about the parkland had a dispirited air. He'd edited the story for Monk. He didn't have to know the details, only the outline. And there was no point in telling Monk to take a walk because they were going to ask the questions, get the answers, and build their idiotic little case, and doing it here and now was the easy way. There were interrogations and there were interrogations.

The aide, Prestonbury, had gone to fetch tea and biscuits. Godwin groaned. Biscuits. Why couldn't they call them cookies, like everybody else? Monk said, "Some of us like biscuits, I like the sugary ones myself. Sometimes they have little faces made of currants or sultanas. I enjoy those particularly."

Godwin ignored him. The question was: What was the point of this exercise, what were Monk and his boys really trying to prove?

"So, let's see what we have thus far, old boy," Monk said. "After thirteen years you and Mrs. Hood were reunited in June of '40 in Cairo."

"We had known each other when she was fourteen. Max and I were friends, Max and I were reunited in Cairo and she happened to be there."

"Well, yes, all comes down to the same thing, doesn't it? Very nicely fortuitous." He was smiling, staring off toward a very large and not very distinguished painting of a fox hunt that was looking pretty decent for the wily fox. Was he remembering happy outings in his pinks, riding to the pounding hooves and the baying hounds? Where did his mind wander? It was a mystery to Godwin.

Vardan swung his leg over the other knee, like a metronome. "You and I attended that party on the boat and then you saw her again the next day at Shepheard's for a brief chat of no great consequence. And in the evening you had dinner with both General and Mrs. Hood."

"That's what I just told you."

"Of course, old boy, I only want to be very specific. My masters are very precise."

"Three cheers for them, Monk. They must also adore a nice game of charades. Like this one."

"Merely following my brief, old man. Now let's see— Ah, Prestonbury, like a faithful Saint Bernard, in the nick of time. Oh, Rodger, have a look at these . . . the little currant faces. Well done, Prestonbury. Well, are we ready to press on? No rest for the wicked." He chewed half of one of the little faces and smiled contentedly. "You and Mrs. Hood both returned to London, June '40. You were preparing to cover the expected invasion of England and when the time came, after you'd fought them on the beaches and in the fields, run for your life."

Godwin had to laugh. It was the old Monk. "You read me like a book."

"I'd been running right beside you, dear boy. And you didn't see her again, at least not the two of you alone, until you had lunch one day and you subsequently suggested a picnic on the south coast where you'd have a good view of the fighter action. Indeed, you had a delightful day out, saw the war, and—just like one of her movies—you fell in love. Chaste, but love nonetheless. You knew you were in love, both of you, when you and I dined together . . . that was at Dogsbody's, the night we got bombed. It was that evening that you told me you were in love with Mrs. Hood. Am I right?"

"More or less, Monk."

"Now let's see, what next?"

"It had been an intense, troubled relationship. We were both torn to pieces by it. Guilt about Max, frustration over the secrecy—"

"Guilt," Vardan interrupted. "Over your betrayal of Max Hood. Lovers have been pleading about their sufferings of guilt for dog's years but in the end the urge to betrayal seems always the stronger. Human beings—all of us—are an astonishingly dishonorable lot."

"I loved the man, respected him, admired him—"

"What is the saying? With friends like you he hardly needed enemies."

"Monk, you're being such a prick. You're not making this easy for me—"

"Strictly speaking, I'm not here to make it easy for you. We believe you committed an act of treason. Or possibly a murder. I'm sorry, old man, but there it is."

"For God's sake, Monk, it's ludicrous! Somebody's either pulling your leg or setting you up. I haven't quite figured out which yet. Anyway, I can't explain this very well, Monk, but Max *made* me, he taught me how to behave, taught me the code. . . . Unfortunately, I was also in love with his wife."

"If I may be hypothetical for a moment—would you have married her if she were free?"

"I would have asked her to marry me. Speaking for Cilla is never a very good idea."

"But of course it was impossible since she would not leave Max Hood."

"We were in love but she felt a great deal of loyalty to Max Hood."

"Ah, life's complexities. But your relationship was ended by Mrs. Hood."

"That's right."

"But now we come to your *second* trip to Cairo almost a year later. It's March of '41, there's a hell of a war going on out there. Through December and January we've beaten the pants off the Italians and it looks like a good time for Rodger Godwin to go back and have another look—"

"It was the only good news coming out of the war. I wanted to write and broadcast about something that was going right for a change."

"So you let Max Hood know you were coming. You hoped he might be your guide to the war in the western desert."

"You were out there, too, Monk. Checking on the size of the victory, getting Wavell braced for the inevitability of coming to the aid of Greece —my God, how Wavell, O'Connor, and Neame must have dreaded the sight of you flapping into view! Observing, judging, running off to tattle to the PM—"

"Yes. I rather think they did. However, such is the unhappy nature of war. Now let's go back to Cairo for the second time, the last time . . . let's see, it was just about a year ago, wasn't it, Rodger? March of '41?"

"Seems a thousand years ago . . ."

"Yes, old chap, I suppose it must."

Max Hood was waiting for him on the terrace at Shepheard's. Nine months had passed since the party on the houseboat in the Nile, nine months during which London had been blitzed and Rodger Godwin and Cilla Hood had fallen in love. Christmas had seen the enormous British victories in the desert. Max Hood had been shuttling back and forth between England and North Africa, had gone back to Cairo at New Year's to be in on the last stages of the rout of the Italians.

Hood looked thinner, tireder, but his smile was brilliantly white in his dark, sunburned face. He was excited by what was going on in the desert and had, indeed, come back to Cairo from some distant outpost only because Godwin was coming in.

"You've got to get the timing clear in your mind," Hood said. "On 4 March poor Wavell gets the word that he's got to strip his command clean to send sixty thousand men to Greece with Jumbo Wilson in charge. That means the desert army that rolled back and destroyed the Italians—it *no longer existed.* Three weeks before Wavell got his orders, Rommel arrived to salvage the North African situation for Hitler . . . and it was a dog's breakfast, I assure you. Wavell had been denuded of his army, Rommel had only the ruins of his army, and it wasn't even his but the Italians'. Rommel had to wait for Hitler to supply him with an army . . ."

"From what I gather," Godwin said, "nobody's really ready to do any attacking for a while. It's a lull, nobody spoiling for a fight. Is that about it?"

Max Hood nodded. "Well, I wanted to take a look for myself at this German general. I knew a bit about our friend Rommel. He led the Seventh Panzer Division which entered France last May. They called it the Ghost Division . . ." Hood's face was alight with the story he was telling. Godwin saw what he must have looked like as a little boy playing with toy soldiers. "So I got into my fancy dress, put on my Arab face, and set out looking for him. It was great fun. He was hard to pin down, always on the move, but I finally found him in Tripoli on 12 March. That's about fifteen hundred miles due west of where we're sitting, damn near to Tunisia, about 250 or 300 miles due south of Malta. Anyway, there I was in Tripoli, looking like an Arab businessman, a used-camel dealer, so to speak, and there was Rommel. Rodger, the sky was blue, the palm trees were perfect, and you wouldn't believe the display he was putting on. I'm sure he was doing it for the benefit of however many British spies might be in the crowd. He knew the spies were there . . . he wanted to play a game with them . . .

"In the main piazza he had what must have been a thousand mint-condition panzer III and IV tanks, twenty-five tons apiece, each of them painted sand yellow. Desert camouflage. The tanks rumbled past, the whole piazza was shaking, and in the turret of each tank was the tank commander, each wearing tropical uniforms to match the yellow of the tanks . . . they each wore the death's-head badge in the lapel. It was a bloody awesome sight, all the bloody panzers in the world—it looked like

Wavell was hopelessly doomed . . . but then I noticed a tank with a floppy tread, very distinctive, and I thought I'd seen one like it before. Not much later I saw it again and I had to laugh out loud—there stood Rommel on the reviewing stand taking the salute, stern-faced, pale blue eyes straight ahead, and the crafty bugger was having the tanks go out one end of the square, circle round, and come back in the other end! It was magic —he'd turned a regiment into an armored corps." Max Hood was smiling broadly. "This man will be a worthy adversary. You really should use this story, Rodger. It's always good to know your enemy. This one is an arrogant bastard who thinks we're fools he can trick . . . colorful chap. Why don't you come with me, Rodger? We'll go out there and see how things stand in the desert. We'll have some fun, Rodger—"

"That's what I'm here for," Godwin said. "To have some fun."

Max Hood's enthusiasm for what he was doing was contagious. His will seemed to infuse Godwin with a certain spirit quite unlike Godwin's own. When Hood was done selling him on the opportunity, Godwin couldn't wait to get out into the desert with him. To have a look-see, or a "dekko" as the Brits say. And logic, Godwin figured, was on his side. Wavell had just come back to Cairo from a visit to Al-Agheila, which was the British front line. Tripoli was several hundred miles west along the Mediterranean coastline; halfway between was Sirte, another dot on the map where Rommel had set up some sort of HQ. Wavell was worried when Hood and Godwin met with him for an hour or so on the twenty-first of March. He wasn't happy with Neame's defenses from Benghazi on south to Al-Agheila; in fact, while holding Neame in high regard as a fighting man, Wavell called the defenses he'd set up "just crazy." To make matters worse, half of the big cruiser tanks of the Second Armored Division were in various states of disrepair. But as he put it at the end of their chat, "I've done what I can. There are no more clubs left in the bag. Greece takes first priority and there's nothing I can do to change that."

Hood, who was as familiar with German strength as any man in the British command, tried to calm Wavell's concerns. Hood had seen for himself that half the apparent German tank strength was phoney: wooden and cardboard tank bodies—life-size models, in fact—set onto Volkswagen auto bodies. Window dressing intended to intimidate the faint of heart. "Rommel will use them mainly to raise dust," Hood said. "It's a damn impressive sight. I was impressed the first time I saw them and I knew they were quite harmless."

They took off for Benghazi on the twenty-second, hitching a ride with an RAF courier, firm in the belief that nobody was about to start shooting anytime soon. Godwin believed he'd lucked into perfect timing.

. . .

After lunch and a thermos of tea and a general tour of the encampment at Benghazi, he and Hood caught a ride in a truck making a run down the coast road to the forwardmost British outpost at Al-Agheila. The defenses were hardly elaborate. It was hot, flies everywhere, and the troops seemed unworried for the moment. Godwin went to sleep in a tent in the outer perimeter of the defenses, listening to the curious, comforting sound of sand sifting against the canvas, of the night breeze. It was odd, thinking how Rommel and his army were out there in the blasted desert, probably up near Sirte, which was roughly two hundred miles away. They were out there waiting, waiting for more tanks, more arms, more men, waiting for the time to fight. As he fell asleep it occurred to him that all of them were sleeping that night in the desert, as the stars looked down, friend and foe, enemies to the death, men who had no reason to hate each other. . . . It all seemed so mindless, so desperately unnecessary were it not for a single man. Adolf Hitler. The stars looked down and he wondered what someone out there, lost in the reaches of space, noting their existence might make of such wanton idiocy? How could the world be held at knifepoint by the evil residing in one twisted soul?

He heard the noise as he lay shivering in the cold dawn and thought perhaps it was a dream or something in his head. It was as much a vibration as it was a distinguishable sound. Then Hood was tapping his shoulder, grinning down. "Slight miscalculation, old man. They're coming. Rommel will be here for breakfast."

They came like a sandstorm, vast clouds rising from the desert, the very desert itself shifting underfoot as if it were trembling in fear. Hood had told him about the phoney tanks, how they were supposed to raise dust, creating the illusion of a huge attack, but he was in no mood to shrug off what he saw when he first glimpsed the tanks of Rommel.

They came across a front of a thousand yards. It was like watching a tidal wave bearing down on you. He looked at Max Hood.

"Looks like they're gonna run us out of Dodge," he said, gleeful at the reference from American westerns. "They've got the drop on us, pardner."

Those in command of the garrison at Al-Agheila shared Hood's opinion. Thus, Godwin's first personal experience of war was a harried retreat under fire. It looked to him like the end of the world. He heard the sharp, cracking cough of the panzer guns and each shell had his name on it. And he wouldn't have believed how much worse it could get over the next couple of weeks. He wouldn't have believed he was going to be part of what came to be known as the "Tobruk Derby" as the days of panic swept past. He wouldn't have believed any of it.

They came to rest thirty miles northeast at a place called Mersa Brega. And then the attack stopped. They had no idea why, no idea when or if it would start again. The Luftwaffe flew over every so often but nothing came of their sorties. Apparently there was a good chance that Rommel himself was having a look at the situation from the sky. He loved flying over the battlefield, snapping photographs.

Mersa Brega was by its location and topography a natural strongpoint, primarily because it was comparatively easy to defend. The defile an attacker had to breach from the coast road was a natural aid to the defender, a kind of lethal bowling alley.

They dug in anticipating further shenanigans from Rommel but for a week none came. Godwin could have caught one of the occasional flights out but he was in no hurry, particularly since Rommel seemed to have stopped for the time being. Accompanying Max Hood was an education. He was a creature of the desert. He was more at home in dusty khakis and aviator's sunglasses, his eyebrows bleached, his face darkening almost to the hue of an American Indian's—more at home there than Godwin had ever seen him. He knew the desert like Captain Ahab must have known the ocean and the white whale, an old, implacable adversary. What the desert could do to you, however horrible, he would remind Godwin, was nothing personal. He never romanticized the desert, never swore at it. He said it was important to understand it. It wasn't out to get you. It wished you no particular harm. But on the other hand you weren't an invited guest, you came at your own risk. The desert really didn't care what happened to you, one way or the other, and it certainly wasn't going to change itself for you.

The spotters came back with the news that Rommel was coming up the coast road, then turning back inland and making ready to attack. It had been a week. Godwin recognized he should have taken one of those planes out when he had the chance.

They were standing on a hard, sandy rock shelf about a mile long, looking down as the panzers came across the desert toward them. At first it looked like a vast sandstorm, but then you saw the tanks out front.

Captain Colin Torrey, a chartered accountant in the City back in real life, turned to Godwin, tight-lipped. "Sorry about this, sir, but I'm afraid there's about to be a bit of a free-for-all."

•　　•　　•

The battle that followed was the most terrifying experience in Rodger Godwin's life. It concentrated on the breaching of the defile and the defense was spirited, stubborn, and bloody. Several German tanks were knocked out of commission, left spewing flame and black smoke rising in columns from the desert floor. Godwin ventured into the defile himself and came under intense fire. As daylight faded the muzzle flashes of the tanks guns pointed at him became sharp golden flashes followed by lazy puffs of white smoke. He had the feeling that if only you paid closer attention you might be able to see the shell, follow its flight until it reached you and blew you to smithereens. When one of the German tanks was hit, the yells and cheers of the British soldiers reminded him of boys at a football game back home in Iowa, a stark contrast to his own sorrow at the sounds of men—Germans and British—dying all around him.

The day's battle had gone reasonably well for the British, but late that night Rommel dispatched a machine-gun battalion to circle away through some sandy hills which gave them a fresh angle to attack the defenders of the defile. After the bitter struggle of the day, this nighttime thrust dislodged the British and they hastily withdrew, leaving behind the town of shell-blasted white houses for the victorious Afrika Korps. Godwin's legs were cut by shrapnel and bits of flying rock; Max Hood disinfected them by drenching them in brandy; he also suffered a brain concussion when a sixty-pounder exploded nearby and hurled him headfirst into a boulder. He figured he got off easy.

He looked back on the mad scramble out of Mersa Brega, the utter confusion, the darkness, trucks, tanks, men on foot, armored cars, the rattle and bark of gunfire, flares following them like demons into the night—he looked back on that and none of it made any sense at all. He had a hellish headache, he vomited several times during the race into the darkness, his cut-up legs hurt like the devil and his trousers were stiff with what he hoped was blood rather than anything less noble.

He was in a truck with Hood and several others, bouncing violently on the wooden benches, and he gathered that, since they had no idea what Rommel would do next, they were heading for the coast road and Benghazi. Nothing mattered anymore. Fear and chaos do that to a man. By rights you should be dead so, at the end of the day, you just no longer give a damn.

On 2 April, Rommel's march continued as he took Agedabia and the port of Zuetina. He then split his forces into three parts, one thrusting northward up the coast road to Benghazi, another more directly east, and a third between these two aimed at Antelat and Mechili. Benghazi fell on the sixth and the nightmare of the Tobruk Derby was in full swing. Rodger Godwin, with his leg wounds receiving minimal but efficient care, was caught in the inglorious panic of the unseemly retreat. The men were at the end of their tether, exhausted, beaten, sleepless, wounded, befuddled, men being attacked by an army—a man, really, Rommel, his reputation growing huge—which gave them no time to regroup, to stand and organize themselves and fight. Godwin saw the haggard, haunted faces of the men bouncing along in the trucks, the faces caked with yellow dust, their eyes empty and staring. "It was as if the dead had risen from the earth and decided they needed to hitch a ride somewhere, anywhere." He saw a panicking British soldier running madly in circles in the sand, screaming that Rommel had come to his tent in person during the night and told him to surrender unless he wanted to die; an officer couldn't make the man stop his tirade and finally shot him dead where he stood.

By the time Benghazi fell, Godwin and Hood had moved on fifty miles along the coast to Barce, where Neame had his HQ. Wavell had just visited Neame, concluded that he'd lost control of his army, and summoned O'Connor to take over. In the event, it was too late to salvage the situation. It was during the night of 6 April that Neame and O'Connor finally withdrew from Barce, leaving it to the Germans. At the same time Godwin and Hood were looking for transport out. Later it was all but impossible to make sense of the chaos and confusion and heart-stopping panic of a mass retreat. Order was the first victim of sheer fright. Hood simply disappeared in the madness, having told Godwin to latch on to transport, *any* transport, going *anywhere*, if they were split up.

Godwin had his own ideas about how to get out of Rommel's huge net. The trucks he found seemed to have plans of their own and he wasn't eager to go to his fate on the wheels of somebody else's bad idea. He knew it was hopeless to look for Hood. Night was falling. Rommel was closing in. He was standing in a small, palm-lined square, wondering if perhaps the game was up. He was very tired. His legs hurt. So he sat down at a lonely table outside some sort of café or tavern that seemed quite deserted. Everything, all around him, seemed deserted. He decided to wait and see what happened. Maybe the Germans would find him and take him prisoner. Maybe they just wouldn't care about a journalist. Maybe he'd be able to reach Rommel himself. His old pal. And maybe he was simply delirious from exhaustion and fear. So he sat and waited.

Though he had no way of knowing it, only a few hours later that evening, Neame and O'Connor, themselves utterly frazzled, pulled off the road in Neame's staff car to get some sleep. They were awakened at three in the morning by Rommel's army and spent the next three years as prisoners of war in Italy.

But Godwin only knew that he was out of ideas and down to the last reserves of hope. So he sat in the empty square waiting for the Germans and stared into space until he heard someone calling his name.

He supposed salvation takes many forms during the course of something as chancey as a war. Fate wears many faces, and some of them are bound to be rather absurd, though nonetheless decisive for that. When Godwin heard his name called a second time he tiredly raised his head and looked about.

"I say, Godwin, is that you? You there, at the table? Better get a move on!"

It was Sam Balderston of *The Times*. His fat, foolish face was staring out from the window of a Ford station wagon, wooden side panels bullet chipped and sandblasted. But it was beautiful, just as Balderston himself was a rather more welcome sight than he might normally have been.

"Sam, you're the last man but one out of this lovely oasis. Going my way, by any chance?" He was trying so hard to sound devil-may-care.

"Where would that be?"

"Across the bloody desert."

"I hear tell it's full of Krauts."

"Unfounded rumor, my good man. It's a very big desert with a smattering of Germans in it. Shortest way home. That's in its favor."

"I was thinking of Tobruk—"

"Nonsense. Everyone goes to Tobruk this time of year."

"Let me see if I have you straight on this. You're saying not Tobruk?"

"It's the done thing," Godwin said. "Not for the likes of us. I have a map you know. Bought it off an Arab. I can find the way home."

"Home, old man? Iowa?"

"Well, Cairo."

"Let me see if I grasp your point—you suggest we *drive* to Cairo? Of course the back of this crate is full of petrol cans . . ."

"It's been done, you know. But we'll see if we can get a ride on a plane somewhere. Are you up for it, Sam?"

"Oh, what the hell," he said and they got into the pockmarked Ford and set off on the Barce-to-Cairo run. Godwin didn't know what had happened to Max Hood. He could only hope to God he was all right.

Mechilil, which lay roughly in the path Godwin and Balderston had embarked upon, fell to Rommel on 8 April. It was on that day, in that place, that Rommel first laid eyes on the extralarge sand goggles among the effects of the British general he'd just captured, Michael Gambier-Parry. They caught his eye and he claimed them as booty. He adjusted them over the gold braid of his cap and his photograph was taken. Now, he was the Desert Fox.

It was also on that same day that Wavell, in Tobruk at a hotel down on the water's edge, announced that the city must be held. Henceforth, in song and story, Tobruk, like Leningrad, would become a synonym for endurance, determination, and courage. The Germans might have their Fox of the desert; the British would have their Rats of Tobruk. Wavell knew that holding Tobruk would offer immense problems; it would have to be supplied entirely by sea, under Luftwaffe attack. But as Wavell told his men at Tobruk, there really wasn't much choice: "There is nothing between you and Cairo."

The problem for Rommel, who wanted to conquer Egypt and take the Suez Canal, was that he couldn't do it with the abscess that was Tobruk festering on his flank. There were thirty-five thousand men holed up at Tobruk and Rommel could not simply bypass them, turn his back on them. But at the time, Godwin knew none of that. He and Sam Balderston were trying to find their way out of the war. They didn't know that Max Hood was among the missing.

They took turns. When Sam drove, Godwin prayed. When Godwin drove, Sam bitched about his driving and the idiocy of the plan.

The map was fairly detailed. Godwin judged their progress partly by the wreckage they spotted from other battles. More often than not they were British tanks and trucks and bodies, all of recent vintage because the desert had not yet reclaimed them. The wind came and went. They found tiny outposts where they filled their canteens with water and cadged some kind of food and filled the petrol cans. Sometimes there were clouds of sand in the distance, the Afrika Korps. Sometimes they were on the right, at other times on the left. Godwin and Balderston were always in the middle of them.

Once they drove into a bomb crater and had to push the Ford out. At one point on the third or fourth day, they went over a ridge and, half-deafened by the howling wind, stumbled quite unaware into a tank battle. It was night, the stars were out, more stars than Godwin had ever imagined there could be. The wind was sifting the sand everywhere and when the flares went up it was as if someone had flipped a switch and extinguished the moon and stars. The flares would blossom a couple of hundred yards overhead and sort of hang there, shedding an unreal light over maybe a square quarter of a mile. Then another flare would be added to it, then another, and from behind the ridges and dunes firing would begin, then fade away.

They waited, shivering, completely visible between a plateau on one side where they saw muzzle flashes from tanks and a series of rolling, cement-hard dunes on the other where the opposing tanks stood, blazing away.

"What the hell should we do?" Sam's eyes were as big as the head-lamps on an old Rolls.

"Well, hiding is out of the question."

"Firm grasp of the obvious," he groused.

"Well, let's just push on."

"We'll be right between them, Godwin!"

"But well below the line of fire. Maybe they can't see us from inside the tanks. I can't think of anything else."

Balderston screwed his face into an expression of great passion. "I *hate* this."

They heard shells whistling overhead but none came near them. It was entirely surreal.

As they drove out of the immediate fire zone and darkness enveloped them, Godwin saw something burning ahead. There were three British tanks scorched and burning in the night. There were several dead soldiers in the sand and hanging out of the turret hatches . . .

The next night they came upon a group of eight Afrika Korps tanks drawn up in a circle. The remains of a cooking fire glowed in the sand. There wasn't a soldier in sight. It was a cold night. They must have been huddling inside the tanks, staying out of the wind. They must have been just as tired as Godwin and Balderston.

In the end, having struggled into Mersa Matrûh out of water and in bad humor, they caught a flight to Cairo which, thank God, was still in British hands.

Godwin supposed the trembling would stop soon.

It was Easter Sunday when they landed back in Cairo. Word of their reappearance after the confusion of the retreat had filtered back, and gangly, windblown Monk Vardan was waiting for them on the tarmac as they taxied toward the hangar. He gave them the once-over, said: "What a remarkably bedraggled pair! Still, it is Easter and you *are* in a sense risen, but hold on—where's Hood? I thought Hood would be with you . . ."

That, of course, was the question on all their minds, though less so on that of Sam Balderston, who didn't know Hood well and could take him or leave him. Godwin was worried about an old friend. Monk Vardan was concerned on an official basis. He was the connecting rod tying Hood to Churchill. Together they all feared the worst but as Sam Balderston said on the drive into the city, Hood was a resilient and wily bastard and a hell of a lot of people could get lost out there and then turn up later on. After all, it was a big desert.

Vardan had booked them both into Shepheard's. At dinner, he leaned forward on his bony elbows, his long face in the long palms of his hands, and cast a doleful eye at the two correspondents. "Actually, I am very glad you two specimens got back alive. The news we've been getting is spotty and disastrous. Did you really see any action? Was it bad?"

"See action?" Balderston laughed, chins shaking. "Did we not! Bloody miracle we're here! Jerries to the right of us, Jerries to the left of us, bloody Rommel breathing down our necks!"

They told Vardan what they could of the retreat, from Godwin's waking up to the onslaught of tanks at Al-Agheila that first morning on through the escape from Barce. Since then, Godwin pointed out, they'd been operating in a vacuum themselves.

"All I know is this," Vardan said. "They've driven us back into Tobruk. Now Rommel's throwing everything he's got at those trapped bastards. It's a coin toss at this point. He needs Tobruk. It's the only port east of Benghazi that can supply his army. We reckon he needs fifteen hundred tons of water and rations each and every day. If he can't bring it in through Tobruk, the stuff will have to be landed at Benghazi or Tripoli and trucked the rest of the way across the desert. So, as I say, he'll do everything he can to take Tobruk. He must have Tobruk. And we must deny it to him."

Godwin was sleeping when the telephone rang. He couldn't imagine where he was when he opened his eyes. He listened for the sounds of the desert, the wind in the sand. He heard shuffling feet, laughter, and smelled the unique aroma of a lot of camels. It came from the street below his shuttered window or was borne on the night's breeze from another quarter of the city. The telephone kept chirping and he finally realized what it was. He was on his feet, heart pounding. He picked it up, swallowed in his dry throat. It might be news of Hood. "Yes? Godwin here?"

"So you have one of the fourteen rooms with phones! Congratulations—you *are* important." It was a woman, speaking softly.

He was shaking the cobwebs out of his head. "Who the hell is this?"

"Oh, darling. Is this my punishment? Well, you are a forgetful swine.

It's me, Rodger. I just got in and I heard two chaps discussing your return in the bar. You've become the stuff of legend—'Leave it to that fucking Godwin,' was the verbatim quote. So I thought I'd give you a ring—"

"Cilla, for God's sake . . ."

The last time he'd seen her had been the night they bombed Dogsbody's. There had been the smell of the bombing and the burning buildings and the sound of the water spraying into the flames and hissing, turning to scalding steam. It all came back to him with the sound of her voice.

"Yes, it's bad penny me—"

"But they're not allowing wives out here anymore. So how did you wangle this trip?"

"As an entertainer. I'm here with Bea Lillie and Vivien Leigh. Spent today at a hospital joining in the Easter services and then behaving like naughty schoolgirls for the wounded chaps—I had no idea you were here, darling, and now I discover that you were busy being brave out in the desert—how are you, my darling? It's been so terribly, terribly dreary without you."

"You don't say."

She sighed. "I suppose I deserve that."

"I suppose you do."

"Was I really so beastly to write that letter? It seemed the right thing to do—"

"Yes, you were beastly to write the letter, beastly and cowardly and, I guess, quite right. But I hated it."

"Would you describe it as feeling like cold steel in your heart?" There was a faint tinge of mockery in her voice. She'd spoken the line in a film.

"That pretty well covers it."

"So, darling, how was the war?"

"Not one of Britain's finest hours."

"Godawful Germans," she said with sudden feeling. "Ever since the day you took me to the downs to see the war . . ."

"It's not the Germans. It's just the war."

"Have you—have you seen Max?"

"Oh, yes, he's the one who took me out there—"

But she seemed to have forgotten Max. "When can I see you, darling? Can I come see you now?"

When she got to his room he told her about Max, how he'd gone missing in Barce when everyone was looking for an escape.

"Are you telling me no one knows where he is?" Disbelief registered on her face. Her hair was still cut short, framing her face, wide across the cheekbones and pointed at the tip of her chin. Her coffee-colored eyes, flecked with green, enveloped him as if the earth were giving way beneath him.

"I think he may have had some plans of his own. He probably didn't want to put me at risk. I'd have been a drag on him anyway."

"But where could he be now?"

"Maybe he got to Tobruk. Maybe he's out raising hell in the desert. Sabotaging Rommel—"

"Maybe he's dead," she whispered.

"He'll turn up."

She sagged into a chair. Her silk blouse clung to her, her breasts heaved a sigh. "Oh, Rodger, I wish he just wouldn't turn up. If he never came back, it would all be so much easier. You and I . . . we could be together, no guilt, nothing . . ."

His mind turned back almost a year, to their meeting in Cairo after not having seen each other since Paris. He thought about how she'd come to his room then, too, and shown him her breasts and told him the easy part of his life was over, that now he'd met his destiny and it wouldn't be easy. She was as good as her word. It hadn't been easy. He'd had no idea what turmoil and longing and frustrated desire and betrayal could do to you.

"I don't want to play games with you, Cilla, and I don't want to join you in wishing Max wouldn't come back. He'd be dead, then, and I don't want that—"

"If you truly loved me—this is why I can never quite trust you, your feelings—then I'd be worth *any*thing, worth more even than Max—"

"Shut up, Cilla."

"It's true, though," she said defiantly, closing her face against his. "You always *say* you love me but—"

"You wrote the goddamn good-bye letter after Dogsbody's. Not me. You wrote it and so be it. Max is your husband. Why not just let it go at that? I won't play your games . . ."

"Wait. You don't seem to understand—I'm back, Rodger. That's why I came to your room. I'm back. I want you. I *fancy* you. There's no point in being mean to me . . . I'll only make you pay for it later. You do love me, you know you do—"

"*Are* you back? How do I know? Am I supposed to take your word for it?"

"But I'll convince you, darling. I promise you. And don't try to be a tough guy with me. I'm coming back because I hated living without you, because I like how you make me feel, because I've been in love with you for half of my life—"

"Then don't be a bitch, Cilla. You weren't a bitch half your lifetime ago."

"I am what I am. I've told you that before. I may be a bitch but I'm willing to be *your* bitch. And *your* bitch seems to be in heat—"

"You're on probation."

"And you're addicted to me. So be quiet and get on with it. And, Rodger, hurt me a little. You know what I mean . . . Oh, Rodger, I've been such a naughty, beastly girl . . ."

"Well, Tobruk has held. They've biffed Rommel on the nose, in fact." Monk Vardan lifted his glass an inch or two from the tabletop. They were dining at Shepheard's, Vardan and Balderston and Godwin. "To the chaps at Tobruk."

"Pray God they hold out," Balderston said dabbing at the soup stains on his shirt. "Otherwise that cool bastard will be sitting down to dinner across this very room in a week's time. I hear they caught him in a trap yesterday. Is that the true gen, Monk?"

"Yes, that's about it. Morshead let them come inside the perimeter, panzers and infantry bearing down on Tobruk proper, then let him have it from behind and in front both. Jerries lost seventeen tanks. When they tried to retreat they had to fight their way back out. He'll think twice before he gets in a gunfight with Morshead again."

"Tough Aussie," Balderston said. "You know what his men call him? Ming the Merciless—you know, the Yanks' comic strip, *Flash Gordon.* He's commanding thirty-five thousand men, Brits, Anzacs, Indians, and you know what he says? 'There'll be no Dunkirk here. If we have to get out, we will fight our way out. No surrender, no retreat.' I wonder if Rommel has ever gone to the dance with an Aussie son of a bitch. . . . If Morshead's his first, he's just begun to get a taste of it."

Godwin said: "Carson Earle briefed me today. Stuff for my broadcasts. Derek Symonds sets all these things up for me. Once you get used to him, he's all right, he's an ambitious kid. Anyway, Earle tells me that Morshead's sending out these patrols every night. They're raising holy hell. He's got one patrol of warrior-caste Hindus who specialize in never taking a prisoner."

"How are the broadcasts going?" Vardan signaled for three brandies.

"Fine. I've been telling the folks at home about my war in the desert."

"Nothing too humiliating about the retreat, I hope."

"More about the confusion, my own fear, Sam and me running hell for leather across the desert—Max. Max will get back, I know it."

Vardan shrugged. "Lots of chaps haven't."

For four more days Cilla entertained the troops in Cairo and Alexandria and spent the nights with Godwin at Shepheard's. During that time they grew closer than they had ever been before. They lay together making jokes about little things, remembering Paris, remembering youth. Cilla told him of her marriage. She talked of Hood and how formal and shy he could be, how undemonstrative, how haunted he was by his youth in the desert with Lawrence and how glad he was to be back in it . . . and they made love violently and desperately and she worked very hard to convince him that she was his, that somehow the issue of Max Hood would be resolved.

"Given his own way, he'll get himself killed in this war," she whispered. She leaned back on the sweat-dampened pillows.

"You don't want that, not really."

"Don't be so sure. But it's not me we're discussing, Rodger. It's what would make him happiest, I think. He has no life but me. And Chloe. He's seldom with us. He's lost me, Rodger. Sometimes I think he knows it. He has a—a kind of emptiness at the middle. He went to war too early and after that nothing else seemed important. He tries to live like other people but it's hollow, there's an echo inside him . . . *he* is an echo, a reverberation, a shadow of the life he's trying to live or might have lived in some parallel universe. He doesn't know how to have a life . . . he is really only alive when death is at hand . . ."

Godwin thought: the rain, the mud in the graveyard in Paris, death.

"Now," she went on, "I think he finally accepts the need for death." She lit a cigarette, watched the smoke curl up. "He has no idea how to deal with me—I'm a wild animal he's somehow gotten hold of and he works hard to keep me under control. He knows it's hopeless. So . . . he'd just as soon die in some heroic, selfless way, so that chaps in the mess or over a pipe in some distant outpost or before the fire at the club would tell great stories of Max Hood. . . . It's true, Rodger, he says as long as the chaps remember you and draw on the memory for strength, then you never really die, you're always there at the ready when they need you . . ."

It was dark in the room, somewhere in the middle of the night; they were far away from where they'd started out, and it felt as if Max were somehow there with them, as if he would always be with them. Max

Hood, who just wanted to be remembered by the chaps in the mess, was always going to be with them.

Godwin held her, felt the flutter of her heart, the slightly irregular beat she'd always had. She said: "He's the saddest man in the world, Rodger. All he wants is a good death."

Max Hood walked into the bar at Shepheard's the next afternoon about four o'clock just as all the regulars were gathering for the daily skinful.

He'd been a bit of a legend before, but this was the sort of thing men who had never been near Shepheard's would claim to have seen with their own eyes. He was dusty and sandy, his face wind-bitten, and he was standing at the bar before Tubby Cadwallader, the last man in the room to see him, looked up from an afternoon sulk noticing the sudden stillness, looked sideways, rubbed his bloodshot eyes, and let out a warwhoop. "Crikey lads, look who just walked in!"

Godwin only heard about the actual moment of arrival. He had stopped in, quite innocent of the news, about half an hour later, and there was Max drinking pink gin with all the chaps gathering around him hearing the story. Monk Vardan was standing alone, off to the side, watching in a prideful way, almost as if he'd stage-managed the whole thing.

Hood looked up and saw Godwin and interrupted the tale to call him over. "Thank God you made it. I've felt like merry hell, losing you that way. Probably just as well you weren't with me. Got through all right, did you?"

"Sam Balderston and I drove across the desert."

"Damn good show! Let me see you—all in one piece?"

"You're the one everybody's been worried about."

"Well, I wound up at Tobruk. I was just telling these blokes—"

"But how did you get out?"

"Shank's mare. I just walked out one night, had a look about, and kept on going."

In the laughter, someone repeated that line. "Hear that? He just walked out. . . . Max Hood's just walked home from Tobruk!"

Godwin sat down at the table and listened to the story, how Hood had gone out with the raiding parties every night, how he'd been with the Hindus and watched them cut the ears off thirty-two German soldiers to prove their success. He'd also gone out with stretcher bearers into no-man's-land beneath the blistering sun, looking for any surviving wounded. They'd come upon a party of Germans doing the same thing. The German officer ordered his men to help the Tommies with their wounded and then they'd all stood around chatting for a few minutes, drinking lemonade the Germans had brought with them and willingly shared. They commiserated with each other about the wretched drinking water they all had to endure. "It looked like coffee," Hood said, "and tasted like sulphur. But the lemonade was grand. The Jerries were damn fine about things. Good chaps. Meet 'em after the war and you'll like 'em and be swapping yarns. That's the way it is." The Afrika Korps officer remarked to Hood that the tinned meat they were having to eat was so awful they'd nicknamed it "Mussolini's ass." And when the lemonade was gone and the wounded safely on stretchers, the German officer had kindly told them that the wounded British soldiers they had found were being given the best care available. "Like our own men," he'd said, and shrugged. Then both groups had set off for their own lines singing, amateurishly, discordantly, the song that had become the anthem of all the soldiers in the desert, "Lili Marlene." "There were brave men there that day," Hood said softly in the bar at Shepheard's.

Godwin listened to the stories and smiled at Max Hood, a happy man. These were the stories that would be told, through war and peace, by the old soldiers, the stories that would keep Max Hood alive forever.

When they finally broke up, Max and Vardan and Godwin were left alone, finishing their drinks.

Max looked up tiredly and said, almost shyly, "Now what's this I hear about my wife being in the vicinity? Can such things be? Have either of you seen her?" He grinned at Godwin. "Let's go surprise her . . ."

PART FOUR

STILLGRAVES
WINTER/SPRING
1942

CHAPTER 22

Godwin stood at the window of the study in the great house called Still-graves where he knew Max Hood must have stood for countless restless, lonely northern hours. It was just past noon but the clouds had darkened as if night were already falling, as if this particular day deserved a quick coup de grâce. There was a wintry draft coming from some hidden chink. He warmed his hands on a mug of coffee he'd fetched from the kitchen where Mrs. Morecambe seemed to scrub and polish and stir and clatter endlessly onward. She was an apple-cheeked old soul who must have been born in a fragrant, slightly flour-dusted apron. She gave the impression of singlehandedly holding the grim, dour climate at bay. Her coffee was always ready and hot, and in the week Godwin had been staying at Still-graves they had grown used to each other. She made cinnamon toast that reminded him of his mother's and kippers that didn't but were delicious.

His image was reflected in the square panes of window glass. He looked much more like himself. He'd put on weight, and the brown tweed suit gave him a familiar bulky look. He'd been up since dawn, prowling around the vast, creaking house, had walked for two hours in the stubbly frozen fields and along the cliffs above the airstrip constructed for Max.

He had to get things straight in his mind. That was why he'd agreed so readily when Cilla had insisted he complete his recuperation at the great old house. She knew he wasn't ready to return to London and she knew he needed time to think things through. Sometimes he believed she knew everything in his mind. Yet he never seemed to know what was in hers.

His thoughts always seemed to begin and end with Max Hood. It was

Max Hood's house, his *home*, and he pervaded every room. It would hardly have surprised Godwin to hear a footfall in the hallway and look up to find him standing in the doorway. *It's all a mistake, Rodger, I wasn't killed after all, I lived, I escaped and made it back and how's that for a war story, Rodger? You'd better use it, Rodger, it's a damn fine story . . .*

But, of course, Max was dead and that was that, he wasn't coming back anymore . . .

Someone had betrayed him, had betrayed them all, and there was no one who gave a damn, no one who wanted to find out the truth. Monk and the PM wanted a scapegoat, an early, easy solution, an angle that would allow them to keep the lid on and the politicians quiet, tame, and Godwin was perfect for the role. *Don't you see, chaps, he was at it with Hood's wife, let slip a word, fell into the wrong ears, hell of a mess, but what can we do? Prosecute a famous American journalist just when our lives depend on the Yanks? Well, hardly! You do see why we've got to keep it all just between us surely . . .* In time it would all blow over, some new crisis or scandal or triumph would replace it, all would be forgotten, in the end no one would have the energy to pursue it anymore. By then the war would be over, the file on PRAETORIAN would be buried, Rodger Godwin would be gone, an ocean away, and time would eventually lose them all.

Godwin couldn't accept that.

He would take the place of Max Hood. Hood would have found the traitor, hounded him to death, but Hood was gone, and someone else would have to do the hounding. Only Godwin was left, so Godwin would have to do it. Godwin was the only one who cared.

In the week at Stillgraves, he had thought it through.

Cilla had taken two days off in addition to the days the show was dark and they'd come north by train. Mr. Morecambe, who had been born at Stillgraves and served the Hoods all his life, had met them at the station with the old Rolls which dated back to the days of Max's father. He had met them with the long sheepskin coats the weather along Hadrian's Wall required and he'd taken their bags and secured them with belts and seen the two of them safely into the deep backseat. Cilla had installed Godwin in his unfamiliar surroundings, in a guest room where he would stay out of deference to the Morecambes' sensibilities, their reverence for the Hoods. For the first time since the Old Master's day when they'd built the place, Stillgraves belonged to someone other than a Hood. Max had had no son, no brothers or sisters. Never again would a true Hood live at Stillgraves. "We must tread carefully," Cilla had said. "This is the Morecambes' home, too. And they've only approved of me because of Max. The Young Master." While she was there Godwin came to her at night in the master bedroom. When she left he was the guest, in the guest room. Though she made it clear to the Morecambes that she needed them, depended on them, she left no doubt that she was not to be crossed.

There was, however, remarkably little of her in the house, no sense of her having put her stamp on the long draughty corridors, the dark panelled rooms, the places where Max Hood had been a boy. Only in the master bedroom did he smell her perfume. When she returned to London he would furtively enter the chamber just to smell her pillow and her nightgown and underthings, yearning for her all the time.

Sitting in the deep chair before the fire with the snow rattling at the window, he sorted through the mess.

So far as finding out who had betrayed the mission went, there was little he could do up north. But as he worked on getting his strength up and accustoming himself to the plate in his head, he set about getting his ducks in a row.

Where did he truly stand with Vardan and the PM? What plans did they have for pursuing the issue?

What about the threat he'd received just before embarking on PRAE-TORIAN? Who was going to kill him if he didn't stop seeing Cilla Hood? Did Hood's death make a difference to the killer? Dare he trust the darkness?

Was Cilla still being watched? In fact, could the watcher have been her imagination? Say she'd been right: then, why? What did a man watching Cilla have to do with anything?

What more did Priestley know? He had to sit down and ask some specific questions because he knew Jack was full of all sorts of surprising things.

How should he start looking for the traitor?

He was by nature and profession an observer. Taking a stab at action, adventure, had resulted in PRAETORIAN. Still, the men of action hadn't survived. Now he was dashing back into the fray—if only he could read the signs, find a path. Maybe you were expected to find your own way. . . . How the hell should he know?

He wrestled with all these questions and dozens more, he dreamt the questions, never the answers. He came awake in the night, shaking, sweating, trying to remember what had just flickered through his mind, his sleep. He relived the mission, saw it all again up to the blinding flash, and there was something he knew he should remember . . . something terribly important . . .

Max Hood was there in his dreams, sometimes in the shadowland at the edges, moving like a ghost, taking center stage for only two events. The night in the storm-swept graveyard in Paris, the mud, the bodies . . . and at almost the moment of his death, once again in the rain, kneeling in the bloody North African mud, looking up, holding out his hand to Godwin as the bullets ripped at his body, Max Hood's voice coming to him . . . *they knew we were coming* . . .

But who might have told them?

That was the question.

Where did you start looking for the answer?

One day he was looking at the silver-framed photographs in the study and stood for a long time staring at the one Cilla had taken when she was fourteen, that summer in Paris. He remembered the moment as if he'd been flung backward through time, the way she'd surprised them and snapped it . . . Max, Clyde, and Rodger . . . fifteen years ago in another country. My God she'd been so young and dewy and so indescribably lovely. . . .

There was another snapshot someone had taken in the garden of the Paris house, sunlight filtering through the trees, Godwin asleep in his canvas deckchair, a book open on his chest, wearing a white shirt with his sleeves rolled up, Cilla curled on the ground beside him, sitting on a cushion, leaning against the arm of his chair, engrossed in a book of her own, oblivious to the photographer, perhaps her late father.

Yes, of course, he'd loved her even then. Why could he see it so clearly now when he hadn't seen it then?

He supposed it was the sort of thing that turned some men into poets.

For himself he felt only the desire to weep at the passage of time, at love, but he fought off the impulse.

John Morecambe had known Max Hood for Max's entire life. If Godwin wanted to find out who might have wished Max Hood's death, if he wanted to look deep into the life of the man he had loved and subsequently cuckolded and nearly died with—then Morecambe was as good a place to start as any.

He made the approach over a chessboard. John Morecambe was a friendly bloke once you got past the reserve of a lifelong servant. Mrs.

Morecambe had once passed a stray remark in the kitchen to the effect that he was not only a keen player of chess but even a founder of the chess club in the nearby village.

Once they were settled in the study one evening Godwin found himself badly overmatched. After a couple of moderately hard-fought games that concluded with Godwin's withdrawing, he had gained Morecambe's confidence. Together they were sipping twenty-year-old single malt whisky, chatting about strategy, at which time Godwin led the conversation to Max Hood, who, Morecambe said rather proudly, had learned the great game at Morecambe's knee. Max by the age of twelve was a competent player on an adult level and at the age of thirteen he won his first game from his teacher.

Reminiscing about his late master seemed to please the old man. He didn't grow misty in the course of recollection but he clearly enjoyed talking about Hood, sifting through memories stretching across fifty years.

Godwin said: "I didn't meet him until 1927. I'd never known anyone like him. A hero, a man who'd been with Lawrence—"

"Yes, well he never really got over that. By the time you met him his best years were behind him." Morecambe stroked his short, wiry close-cropped mustache of salt and pepper. He was a spare man who enjoyed the cigar Godwin had offered from Max's storage. "He peaked early. Men often do in war. He went off from here a boy, really, came back a hero, but something had gone out of him. He'd seen too much, done too much. Odd to say so now but he'd lost his edge in the desert, lost it in the war and never found it again. He couldn't concentrate the way he had as a boy. Couldn't beat me at a game of chess anymore—he'd lost the ability to focus properly. The twenties were a lost decade for him but then they were for a lot of people."

"I got started on my life in those days."

"You were lucky to miss the Great War."

"In a way, I'm missing this one, too."

"Not entirely, sir. I'm quite an avid reader of yours, you tell a good story. Made me feel like I'd been in Paris with you. The Young Master loved your books. Still, you may have peaked too early yourself," he added thoughtfully.

"Let's hope not. For Max, I guess you might say he got back on track when he married Cilla."

Morecambe stuck out his lower lip, struck a judicial pose. "You might, sir. Others might disagree with you."

"Really? Why would they do that?"

"As my good wife says, the Young Master has not been lucky in love. His first wife was quite extraordinary, sir—like nothing I'd ever seen. My wife says Esmé was a postwar impulse and I daresay she's right. A mistake, of course. None of us took it seriously. Then the Master got a divorce. But the second Mrs. Hood—well, he became allover smitten by her, didn't he? Lost his mind, like. She was only a child. Aye, and there's some would say she's never grown up. Some would say she's what ruined his life, she's what killed him in the end. Me, I make no judgments, but we're far from a consensus on Mrs. Hood. She's always treated me and Mrs. Morecambe all right, but her husband couldn't have said the same. There was always someone to spread a nasty rumor about her—other men, always other men. They were apart so much of the time, weren't they? He'd be up here, she'd be off in London or Paris or America, not my idea of a good marriage. Hoods have never run to sophistication and she was one of those sophisticated whatchamacallems—Mrs. Morecambe would know . . . bright young things! She was one of them and it was hard on the Young Master. He wasn't bred to that, was he? No. A simple man. Marrying her was the end of his hopes. So some would tell you." He puffed the cigar contentedly. He was satisfied, perhaps relieved to be speaking so frankly. "Then, of all things, he killed that young chap, and I said to Mrs. Morecambe it was like killing himself, I said it was like putting a bullet in his own head. I told her then he wouldn't last much longer—"

"Wait a moment, just hold on. Who got killed? What chap did he kill? I've never heard about any of this—"

"But Mrs. Hood said you were an old friend of the Young Master's—"

"Yes, but there were years in between when we never saw each other."

"Then you missed out on the killing."

"That's what I'm saying." Godwin poured a generous dram into each squat glass. "What happened?"

"Well, you see, it was the wife again, wasn't it? It was more than the poor man could bear, though I don't for a minute say it turned out the way he wanted, no sir, not for a minute. But what happened, happened. It was right in plain sight, that was the thing."

"Tell me. He was my friend."

"As you say, as you say. Well, after the marriage, he spent more and more time here at Stillgraves, a very solitary way of life, too solitary for a man with a beautiful—Lord, she *is* that—with a beautiful young wife. She was always off playing the fiddle, South America even, then acting. Well, I'd never known the Young Master to be much of a drinker, mind you, but after the marriage he took to the Highland malt and it weren't the water of life for him, no sir. I've seen men who had no purpose in their lives and that's what he was, a man without purpose. Then he killed the fellow, just a young fellow, little more than an overgrown boy, and it was worse after that. . . . Then the war gave him a way out . . . a way to die with honor, you see."

"Who did he kill? Was it some sort of accident?"

"Colin Devitt. He killed young Colin Devitt. Let's see, it was about two years after he and Mrs. Hood were married. People said young Devitt took a fancy to Mrs. Hood while he was doing some work about the house here—"

"You must have known him, then—seen him with Cilla—"

"Oh, yes, he was about, working on the lawn, cleaning away some undergrowth on the cliff face. Big strapping fellow, twenty or twenty-one, quite a lad with the local girls, everyone knew young Colin—"

"Was there anything between him and Mrs. Hood?"

"Now there you have me, sir. I really couldn't say. But she was friendly toward him that summer and the Young Master was off at Sandhurst lecturing, he enjoyed that, he did. Now Colin was not the lad to hide his light under a bushel. Which is to say that a smile from Mrs. Hood might grow into something rather raw in the retelling over a game of darts and a pint or two. . . . The rumors were all over the county. I turned a deaf ear, but there they were and when the Young Master—"

"Why don't you call him Max, Morecambe?"

"Yes, of course. It's just that he was always the Young Master, his father the Master, *his* father the Old Master."

"All right, okay. So how did Devitt die?"

"Sir Max was at the pub one night, I think he must have been with the doctor, an old chum of his, and he was one or two over the limit. As I said, he was drinking a good deal . . . well, Colin and some of his chums were there and one thing led to another, Colin and the boys were looking at him and laughing . . . eventually blows were exchanged . . . a nasty scene, I understand. . . . A few weeks later Max shot him."

"I thought it was an accident?"

"Absolutely. A hundred people, more than a hundred, saw it. There was a shooting party, all the best county families, the flower of Northumberland you might say . . ." Morecambe's cigar had burned low and he regarded what was bound to be the final segment of ash. The clock on the mantelpiece was striking eleven. "Young Colin was one of the beaters . . . got in the way of Sir Max's shot . . . he fell where he stood, great hullabaloo, but he was dead. Some said he was too close to the line of fire, others said Sir Max should have been more careful. Everyone seemed to know there'd been bad blood between them and why. . . . Some people said Sir Max had caught them at it in the greenhouse . . . nonsense, of course . . . and none dared call it murder, not aloud, not to Sir Max's face *or* to mine . . . oh, those were sad days."

"It was just left at that?"

"Well, sir, what would you have had them do? It *was* a tragic accident. All those witnesses." He placed the cigar in the heavy ashtray and withdrew his handkerchief from the sleeve of his heavy gray cardigan, gave his thin nose a severe rubbing. "My bedtime, sir. I greatly enjoyed the game."

"I need a good bit of practice before I can give you any competition. But tell me . . . was there no ending to the story of Sir Max, Colin Devitt, and Mrs. Hood?"

"Ah, the Young Master—that is, Sir Max—got worse . . . depression, terrible headaches, days in bed. But he came round in the end. The war, you know, the war saved him, sir. And did him in. But as I said, the inner man had died long before . . ."

Godwin sat alone, late into the night as the fire slowly died. Poor, poor Max. And Cilla, the rose, but was there the canker within? Now he was lost within her, lost in the labyrinthine ways of her mind and soul and desires. Would he ever drive himself to know the truth of her? Did he dare? Could he take it?

And why had she never mentioned the killing of Colin Devitt?

When Cilla realized that Godwin's recuperation was just about completed, that it was nearly time for his return to the London Life, she issued invitations to a weekend house party at Stillgraves. Getting people to traipse all the way to distant Northumberland required more than a social whim. Therefore, she gave them plenty of notice, managed to get herself and Roddy Bascomb excused from the Friday and Saturday performances of *The Widow Weeds*—a blessing for their understudies—and made sure that the guests, a smallish and select group, were all able and determined to attend.

She arrived in time for cocktails and a simple buffet supper Friday, coming out of the cold and into Godwin's arms, trailing the playwright Stefan Lieberman, looking very middle-European and impresario-ish in a fur coat, as well as Roddy Bascomb and Greer and Lily Fantasia, all disgorged like a conjuror's trick from the vast Rolls.

"Oh, darling," she whispered as she took his arm and led the way into the house where logs burned in all twelve fireplaces, "we were all on the same train. *Quel* shock! I thought I'd be all by myself but there was Stefan at the station and along came Roddy and Greer and Lily . . . well, I suppose I oughtn't to have been taken by surprise. So there we all were and we made the best of it, quite a gay little party." She shuddered. "Exhausting. Stefan got into a brown study over the war, not that one blames him . . . and Lily wanted to have a heart-to-heart with me for some desperately inexplicable reason, and Greer, bless him, had a manuscript he wanted to read but it was impossible and he was being so urbane it gave me the most frightful headache—oh, you do look wonderful, darling!" She squeezed his arm against her body and they were all inside and sorting out their room arrangements and hugging and kissing and exclaiming over how fit Godwin looked.

After supper Cilla, Lieberman, and Greer Fantasia settled on the floor before the fire in the study to read through the first act of Lieberman's new comedy, in which Cilla might be persuaded to star. Lily was sifting through the records. Sinatra's recording of "All or Nothing at All" had caught her fancy. Godwin stood near her, watching the extraordinary delicacy, the fragility, of her hands and face, her every movement. "Half a love never appealed to me," she hummed softly. Greer called down the length of the room wondering if she could dim the racket a bit.

"How very Greer he is," Lily said with a smile. "Thinks Sinatra is a racket. He once called "Ode to Joy" a racket. Nothing to be done with him, I'm afraid."

"Come with me. I want to be somewhere else. And make it snappy, Lily."

"Well, you have surely recovered." She followed him down a cold corridor and into the billiard room.

She stood sipping brandy, watching him stroke the balls across the green field. "Cilla tells me you have a plate in your head."

"Spode," he said.

"You must always make a joke."

"That's me. Always ready for a picnic. Bring my own plate."

"Ah, if only you were funny—everything would be complete. Seriously, Rodger, you look very fit. Any problems?"

"I'm fine. Quite used to the plate. I suppose I might use it to scare inquisitive children. It sounds like a bigger deal than it is."

"Small price to pay to come home a hero."

"Me? You must be joking. A survivor."

"People are saying there was a secret mission. Greer said he heard someone at White's say Max was killed on the same mission."

"Lily, I can't talk about it. I'll find my balls on top of Nelson's column if I do."

"Well, we wouldn't want that. Greer says he heard at Brat's that there's talk of a spy."

"Well, I don't know anything about that. Now, Lily, you've asked all the questions you're allowed."

"But, Rodger, there's no one else to ask—"

"Ask Greer, he seems to be in the know—you're out of luck with me."

"Men always take their secrets so seriously. If women did there'd be so little to talk about. But I'll be good. So, what now for the intrepid Godwin? Back to work?"

"Homer will be here tomorrow. I suppose we'll discuss that sort of thing. A lot has happened since I was working last."

"And then there's your nonprofessional future."

"Oh, Lily," he sighed, straightening up from the table, leaning on his cue. He smiled at her. "Torquemada missed a bet when he didn't sign you up as interrogator. What exactly is on your mind under the heading of my future?"

"Well, with Max having gone to his reward, my first concern is for the living—that is, Cilla. I know that she is very fond of you and I suspect that you have strong feelings about her—"

"Now, Lily," he said. He couldn't be absolutely certain that Cilla had never confided the truth in Lily Fantasia. After all, he'd told Monk Vardan. You almost had to have someone to tell, someone with whom you could think aloud. "I sense Lily's Matrimonial Bureau at work."

"Don't shush me, Rodger Godwin. I shall have my say, whether you like it or not. Cilla is a warm and deeply passionate woman. She is passionate by nature; she doesn't need to be brought to life—do you understand what I am saying? The passion is there. She needs to find an object for it. In all truth, I must say there hasn't been much of that in her life with Max, not for a long time, maybe never. . . . The problem was, he worshiped her and she's not really built for worship. Worship is too cool for her. Now she's free . . . she needs a steady hand to guide her, to inflame her, to fill her needs, but to keep her in line, someone to cling to and depend on—"

"What you're really saying, Lily, is simple—someone who'll put up with her."

She ignored him. "You understand Cilla. Now what you must realize is this—if you're feeling up to the job, and if you are so inclined . . . may I be absolutely frank, Rodger?"

"Lily, you've never been absolutely frank in your life."

"You know perfectly well what I mean." She was moving slowly around the table, running a finger along the dark polished wood. "You won't want Cilla to get tired of waiting for you—"

"Lily, for God's sake, Max just died—"

"Almost five months ago . . . and who knows how long ago he died for Cilla? The point is, you don't want her to grow weary of waiting for you to state your intentions—"

"You sound like Jane Austen and besides I was in a coma! What do you women expect from a fellow, anyway?"

"—and turn to one of her other suitors." She flashed him a dazzling smile by way of punctuation.

He tried not to show the effect, which was much like a blow deep to the solar plexus. He never seriously thought of the situation as anything other than a triangle. Max, Cilla, and Rodger. It was always the three of them. "How in the world can she have suitors? She may be a widow but the wrapping paper's hardly off."

"Be reasonable, dear. For a woman like Cilla there are always suitors. Max had to get used to that, anyone who chooses her will have to get used to it."

"You make it sound an appealing post. Good luck to the poor bastard."

"Don't be silly and small-minded. Because a woman has suitors, it doesn't logically follow that she responds to them. You must realize that marriage does not render other men uninterested and impotent. Men are always ready for new sport, Rodger. It's just a fact of life."

"You're obsessed by intrigue and romance," he argued weakly. "Everything doesn't have to be so complicated."

"Oh, it usually works out to the plan I've sketched for you. And a certain amount of unnerving complication is the price one must pay for a woman like Cilla. Really, Rodger, it's written all over her. She has so much energy. Look at her life, would you? The music, the theater, the movies, the children—how many women do you know who would have made little Dilys their own? She is simply a remarkable woman. She follows her own lights, she hears her own voices. Her sexual life is the same way . . . she needs to use it, don't you see? She needs a man who can—well, you know?"

"So people keep telling me," he murmured.

Lily cocked her head like an exquisite bird. "Well, there you are. Where there's smoke, there's fire. I'm so happy we could have this little talk."

"Lily, why are you making such a point of this?"

"Because I am so inordinately fond of both of you. And I know Cilla has a soft spot for you. I'm doing my duty as a woman and a friend. Rodger, the truth is, I want you to win the race for Cilla's hand. But the stampede is on."

"Well, I'm not joining any race."

She laughed and leaned up on tiptoe to kiss his cheek. "You'd better. If she has to choose one, it's you she wants."

"I'm not in the field, Lily. Any picking needs to be done, I'll do it. Sometimes I think I should pick you."

"Oh, I know, dear, I know. Men always think they do the choosing, don't they? That's one reason they're so lovable. The last time one actually did, Hadrian had just started his bloody wall. In any case I'm betting my shirt on you."

Once Cilla and Lily Fantasia had gone off to bed the three men sat in the study having a nightcap. Godwin was comfortable with Greer Fantasia and had revised his original opinion of Lieberman: Now the man had grown on him; he had even visited Godwin one day at the hospital in Salisbury. He was a thick-chested, powerfully built man who might have seemed many things before you'd guessed he was a writer. Until you saw his huge dark eyes, hypnotic, compelling, and deeply sorrowful. Maybe that was what women saw in him. His reputation had preceded him when he'd come from France to write films for Korda. His play for Cilla was a huge success. Yet he seemed exhausted, pained, unhappy. He slouched his heavy shoulders when he walked, thrust his massive head with its curly hair forward. Now he sat before the fire, smoking a thick cigar, his silence dimly morose.

Fantasia assured Godwin that Lieberman's new play was a masterpiece. "Very, *very* funny," he said, tapping a cigarette he had made up in quantity in Jermyn Street on the back of a gold case, "but with a very serious core. That's what will put it over the top."

Lieberman snorted at Fantasia's description. "I'm disgusted with myself. It's the frothy, frivolous treatment of a tragic reality, but Greer keeps telling me that laughter is the best medicine. There is no medicine for what ails us, all of us, no hope and no medicine. We're no better than anyone else when it comes to the common man . . . the world has become a great toilet and we're all being flushed away . . . I was born with sorrow and doubts, and even I could never have imagined how bad it would all become—"

"You were also born with a jolly good sense of humor," Fantasia said, lighting his cigarette, crossing his legs before him. Somehow his trousers had retained the perfect crease through the day's travels. "Humor always saves the day. Or should I say . . . 'saves the play'?" He chuckled to himself.

"You see, Godwin? He is perfectly English. No sense of tragedy, always waiting for the clouds to blow away and the sun to shine again. Well, the sun is an illusion, a lull between the bouts of murdering. I am nothing more than that ancient cliché, the wandering Jew, leaving one place, going toward the unknown in the full knowledge that it will be no better, that eventually I shall have to run again . . . I wonder what makes us go on . . . it is our fate, perhaps, we are driven to survive."

"Maybe it is written," Godwin said.

"He will go on like this, Rodger. It's his style. Then he sits down and dashes off ten of the funniest pages you'll ever read. It's a gift."

"Greer's simple belief in an English God can cheer me up if anything can. He is my Candide. All actually *is* for the best in this best of all possible worlds. Fantasia's world. My spirits are lifted for as much as thirty seconds at a time. For Fantasia tragedy is always a passing inconvenience but comedy is perpetual and eternal. Every Jew with a tragic point of view —that is, every Jew afflicted with reality—should have a Fantasia nipping at his heels. Fantasia. It's all a fantasy but he believes it, this good man believes it. How do you see life, Godwin? Comedy or tragedy?"

"I suppose I see life as an adventure."

"But you're an American," Lieberman said. "That explains it. A philosophy of life is quite unnecessary. To be an American is to invent the airplane and the motorcar and always to know what is right. To be an American is enough. Optimistic. Immortal."

"Well, the war is turning our way," Fantasia said, decisively turning the conversation toward something sensible. "The eastern front is using up Germans at a terrific rate. The Luftwaffe is tied up fighting Russians. The RAF has won the air war in the west, the Krupp works in Essen is being bombed flat . . . the tide has turned. It's only a matter of time now. You Yanks are in with both feet now . . . the war will be won. There'll be bluebirds, by God, over the white cliffs of Dover . . . and all the world will be free."

"There's a long way to go," Godwin said. "A hell of a long way in the Pacific. Americans have just begun to die. Try to keep your high spirits under some semblance of control."

"Listen to him, Greer," Lieberman intoned from deep in the leather wingback chair. The fire had burned down. "There is a long way to go and my people are being expunged from the face of the earth. So I am disgusted with myself and my comedic gift. No one should be laughing, no one anywhere. . . . My people are being crammed into cattle cars and sealed up in ovens and half the world doesn't believe it and the other half doesn't really give a damn—and I write my little comedies." He shook his head defiantly. "What a sad fellow I am. Forgive me. I had word the other day that my uncle and aunt have been taken by the Gestapo in Paris . . . oh yes, word gets smuggled out one way and another."

"No need to apologize," Fantasia said. "It's absolute hell, of course. But be thankful for your gift, Stefan, and try not to dwell on the tragedies all around us. Each of us fights in his own way, you know."

"Good advice, I'm sure," he said. "I shall do my best to abide by it. Godwin, it's so good to see you've come through your ordeal so well. Cilla has spoken of you so much these past few months that I feel I know you well." He stood up, thick and bulky, built for power. "I'll see you chaps in the morning. Unless I'm lucky enough to sleep until noon."

"Sleep well, old man. Pip-pip."

Godwin said. "Tinkerty-tonk."

Lieberman laughed. "A pair of Bertie Woosters sitting before the fire."

When Lieberman had climbed the stairs and could be heard only vaguely in the upper reaches, Fantasia sighed and poured himself another finger of brandy. "Poor devil, his family's had a bad time of it. Art collectors, bankers, artists, in Poland, France, Germany, for the better part of two centuries. I don't know how many are left alive."

"He broods," Godwin said. "Can't blame him. At least he got out in time."

"I think he feels terribly guilty, y'know, being safe and sound across the Channel—well, you see the point. He's not a bad cove, really. Women, y'know, they seem to find him devilish attractive."

"It's the brooding. Has the damnedest effect on women. Seems to make women weak in the knees. They seem to think it reflects well on them if they hang around with brooders. Makes them feel serious."

"You've given this some thought, Rodger."

"I've known a brooder or two in my time. I tried it myself once."

"How did you fare?"

"Not well. I was seen through right away. Lieberman's something else."

"The real thing?"

"Absolutely."

"Yes, I'm afraid he is," Fantasia said. "Poor devil's done his share of suffering."

. . .

Godwin lay in bed unable to sleep, hearing the wind and all the noises the house made. His mind was wrestling with the issue of Cilla and her other men, her suitors, her affairs, and he knew the struggle would end undecided, unsatisfactorily. How nice it would have been if Lily had just kept her trap shut and her advice to herself. She's mine, damn it, Lily . . . he'd wanted to yell at her, lay his claim. You're all wrong, Lily, she loves me and I love her, and it's been going on for a long time, it's all settled, Lily . . .

But now he lay in the guest room, maintaining the fiction so that their relationship might be seen to develop over time after Max's passing. It was all a matter of respect for the memory of Max Hood, for the sake of appearances, so no one would whisper that she'd been betraying her husband with his old friend. Fine. It was the right thing to do. But that didn't stop Godwin from remembering all the things Cilla had said about herself, her immorality, her hints at her corrupt soul, and all she'd said about her mother's influence, or the way she'd made Max Hood's life utter hell. . . . He remembered what that son of a bitch in Cairo had said about all the men who'd had Cilla, including Greer Fantasia. Preposterous, entirely preposterous! Wasn't it?

Finally he got out from beneath the heavy comforter and stood staring out the window at the latest snowstorm blowing up. Through the darkness he glimpsed the headlamps of a car rounding a turn, the yellow lights poking, probing at the snowy darkness. It was coming up the long road to Stillgraves, the long road that led nowhere else.

As it drew nearer he wondered who could be arriving so late. Slowly, slowly, pushing through the snow, huge tires grinding, the car swaying like a train in the wind and snow. It was the Rolls and Morecambe was getting out from behind the wheel. He had met the last train which had obviously been held up by the storm. It was three o'clock.

The new arrival was wrapped in an enormous belted mac, collar turned up, a heavy scarf wrapped round and round, a slouch hat pulled low, but in the light from the coach house Godwin saw the long hooked beak and it wasn't Sherlock Holmes.

Monk Vardan had arrived from out of the darkness.

The bedroom door behind him opened. Turning, startled from long thoughts, he saw Cilla in her robe.

"I couldn't stay away. I've been frantic to be alone with you ever since we all descended on you." She jumped girlishly into bed, pulling the covers up to her chin. "You look better and better, Rodger. So fit. Do you realize what's happened? You are *alive* . . . and we are *together*. Come to bed, darling. Warm me up." She giggled. She had the power to make his cares fall away, to make him feel like a boy. "I feel so naughty . . ."

He slid into bed beside her and she pushed him down and herself ducked under the covers. For an instant her head reappeared, smiling at him in the darkness. She kissed him and went back down under the bedclothes. He lay back, for the moment free of worry, consumed by her desire.

They made love almost by way of greeting each other, then she lay in his arms, the heat beneath the covers drawing them damply together. The tension that normally fueled her had ebbed. She was in a loving mood and he sighed with relief. She asked him what he'd been doing since she'd last visited and he told him this and that, making no mention of what Morecambe had told him about Max and Colin Devitt. Neither did he tell her of his decision to find out just what had happened to PRAETORIAN, who had betrayed it. But he did say in passing that he'd been looking at the collected photos of their past lives, that he'd been moved by pictures of the time when they'd all met in Paris, moved by pictures of Max through the years.

She listened, turning her head on the pillow to face him, nodding at the memories, but then gave a perplexed sigh. "Max's death is like finishing a book, closing it, putting it back on the shelf. I simply don't think about him much these days. He's gone, he's part of the past. That's where I think of him . . . in the past. It's always that summer in Paris . . . I was a girl then. I inspired men, didn't I? It was so easy . . . all I had to do was *be* . . . I must have been rather magical, mustn't I?" She spoke wistfully. He never knew if she was acting, if she'd rehearsed the lines before. He didn't want her to be acting.

"Magical," he said. "Yes, you were that. It was the popular opinion."

"Is that lost forever, darling? It is, isn't it? It always goes and one never quite knows when—one knows only that it's gone. Is Time the villain?"

"Don't be silly. I still see you that way, magical and fresh and—"

She nuzzled his shoulder. "You're sweet to lie. Men can be so nice. But the truth is, a woman is only fresh and new and magical for a man once—"

"Sometimes it lasts. I believe that."

She was quiet so long he thought she'd fallen asleep. But she hadn't. "The only moments of real honest-to-God triumph I've ever known—not in concerts, not on stage, none of that—they've been when a man was with me for the first time and I saw in his eyes that he was lost . . . lost in me, he believed he had somehow gotten the point of it all, that I was the reward and the point . . . that is a moment of pure, perfect triumph . . . you have become someone's answer and they love you for it. But it quickly goes—"

"Have you seen that look in my eyes, how lost in you I become?"

"No, darling, I never have. It's not your fault."

"Listen to me, Cilla—"

"It's my fault, I robbed you of that moment, I took it from *both* of us, it was a terrible mistake—"

"What are you talking about?"

"When you saw me with Clyde, when you found us that way. Clyde between my legs. . . . It was a pity, really, it made those moments of triumph impossible. . . . Entirely my fault. Wanton little slut. Don't look so sad, my love. It took me years to realize I'd never see that look in your eyes. In fact, Rodger, you're altogether perfect but for that . . ."

CHAPTER 23

It was a house-party weekend, a bit of a quiet chaos, walks outside in the snow when the wind died down, constant talk of the war; theatrical gossip primed mainly by Roddy Bascomb, discussions of the publishing and broadcasting worlds fueled by Homer Teasdale's arrival with a previously unseen, very buxom beauty who was fair and perfectly English. Monk Vardan was his usual self, ironic, sought after as an inside source on war doings: When he was with Godwin, aware of his stare, he shook his head and said blandly, "Now this is social. No shop talk, old boy."

"Social. Yes, by all means. So let me say socially, who the hell invited you here this weekend?"

Monk Vardan shrugged, all bony shoulders and wounded innocence. "Why, I thought it was you, old boy."

"Not me."

"Well, Cilla then. Must have been, by process of elimination."

"Funny. She's the one who asked me if I'd invited you . . ."

"Well, it's a mystery then, isn't it? But I'm sure you'll agree, the important thing is I'm having a fine time. I've always loved this house." He lit a cigarette and smiled happily.

"We can't have just anyone showing up here. It's a private home, Monckton, not feeding time at the zoo."

"Yes, by Jove, and it's a hell of a long way off the beaten track as well. But your hospitality is worth the inconvenience. Look, old boy, you know how I've always valued your friendship—"

"Does that mean that you and your masters have come to your senses?"

"I do beg your pardon?"

"Am I off the suspect list?"

"We don't have a list, Rodger. Just the one name. Who knows? Perhaps it will all be forgotten." He smiled across the silver dishes at the sideboard where he was loading his plate. "I think I'll have another scone." He placed one on top of the other. He was a hungry man. "I just remembered . . . it was Lieberman actually. Ran into him in the Strand one day; he mentioned coming up here this weekend. Naturally I assumed my invitation had merely gone astray. I mean, what else was I to think, old boy? The old Monk's always a good man for a house-party weekend. Perhaps, if I'm properly encouraged, I'll do my magic tricks this evening. Would that be nice?"

"Why don't you make yourself disappear, Monk?"

"I'm Bernard MacIntyre." He was stocky, wore a hairy tweed suit and carried a knobbed walking stick liberally pitted by the teeth marks of hounds. Straight out of Sherlock Holmes. "The local vet. Or that was how your predecessor Max Hood liked to think of me. Actually, I attend mostly to the bipedal inhabitants of our desolate little corner of the world."

"Rodger Godwin. Would that I *were* the successor to Max, but rather I'm merely an old friend of both Max and his wife. And at the moment I'm the resident guest and convalescent. Did you know Max a long time?"

"All our lives. Friends, all our lives. I've read your books, heard you on the air. Feel I know you, in a way. You must get a lot of that."

"It's the radio that does it. I'm a professional innocent. People kept telling me that for so long I finally believed them."

"Well, less innocent since your recent adventure, I understand."

"I don't know what you've heard."

"Oh, very little. Gossip in the village. Don't know where it comes from. You're supposed to have gone on some sort of commando raid. We figure it's the same business that got Max killed."

"Well, I'm sorry I can't elaborate. I'm not supposed to talk about it."

"Got shot up, I'm told. Cilla was the source on that."

"Nicked here and there. Mainly a head wound, thank God. Nothing to harm up there."

MacIntyre nodded. He'd heard that one before.

"Let's get a fresh dram," Godwin said, "and step out on the porch or veranda, whatever the hell they call it." He motioned at the French doors and the stone walk toward the cliffs. "I'd like a word with you about Max. Privately."

The sun was trying hard to pierce the gray low-hanging clouds, and the view was a dim one of gray, brown, and slashes of white where the snow had blown in drifts. The wind whistled out of the trees and up the cliff from the open expanse of the airstrip below. MacIntyre's weathered face seemed impervious to the cold.

"I need to know if Max told you about the mission we went on."

"He said it was risky, whatever it was. I seem to recall he described it as fifty-fifty."

"Ah. They told me it was a piece of cake."

"So much for the concept of trust in time of war."

"Well, they wanted me to go with them and doubtless figured I'd think twice before setting out at fifty-fifty."

"Yes. I suppose everyone had about the same chance of survival."

"Max was wrong by fifty percent." He felt relieved to talk about it. "Everyone was killed. But me, of course."

"It must have been a very bad business." MacIntyre swallowed the scotch after whisking it around his teeth. "Still, Max saved himself a death he wouldn't have liked. He lived out his destiny."

"He wouldn't have much liked growing old and infirm," Godwin agreed. "The long slow decline."

"Oh, he wouldn't have had a long slow decline in any case. That's not what I mean."

"I don't follow you."

"Max Hood was dying and he knew it. He'd been on borrowed time for years. I thought perhaps you knew. I'm quite sure he never told Cilla but I thought in your case . . ." He shrugged.

"I can't imagine what you're talking about. Are you quite sure?"

"That he was dying? Of course. It was a brain tumor. He'd had it for years but it was dormant for quite some time, then it would act up a bit, cause him some trouble. Inoperable. He even had it looked at in the States. I discovered it shortly before his marriage. Later he mentioned he'd had a thorough checkup in Boston and I knew what he meant. For three or four months before he went off on his secret mission all the old symptoms had returned. Headaches, erratic vision, severe depression, references to suicide, lapses of attention, occasional numbness in his limbs."

"When did you say it all began?"

"Just before he married Cilla—that's when he had the first bad attack. First time he told me about it. He may have had some symptoms before then but I didn't know. After that it flared up a few times but then it would pass and he'd feel all right. Once the war began I think he was relieved. He might still manage a hero's death—"

"Well, he did that, I assure you."

"You're very fortunate you didn't share it with him."

"How did it affect his behavior when the attacks hit him?"

"Moody, withdrawn, black humor. . . . He'd try to pick a fight with anyone handy. He told me that he 'behaved badly' to Cilla; he wouldn't elaborate but I gathered he knocked her about a bit. . . . When he was in that condition he'd come up here and hide from the world, you see. Didn't trust himself to be around people."

"Is that what happened to Colin Devitt?"

"He told you about that, did he?"

"I heard about it. One version, anyway."

"Well, you put your finger on it. He was having bad headaches, told me he felt as if his teeth were being yanked out with a red-hot pliers. Cilla was up here, Max heard rumors about young Colin and her, Colin was one to blow his own horn, you know the type—"

"Any truth in the rumors?"

"How would I know? You couldn't believe a damn thing Colin said when it came to women and nobody else was in a position to know."

"Cilla was."

"Well, let's just say I doubt she'd drop her knickers for a boy like young Colin. I've heard stories about Cilla Hood, who hasn't? But I don't put much credit in them. I've always liked the lass. In any case, Max got himself in a bit of a fracas with Colin and some of his mates down at the pub. They were behaving like louts—I was there, you see. A few blows were exchanged. Colin's nose was broken; I patched him up. Then Max shot him."

"Tell me about that. It was an accident, I'm sure."

MacIntyre laughed into the wind. "Are you? Quite sure? Well, you're surer than I am and I was standing next to Max when he pulled the trigger."

"You're telling me it wasn't an accident?"

"I'm just telling you that Max had a brain tumor. That it was giving him a hell of a time. He was severely depressed. He had a tendency toward violence with the pain he was suffering. And a young fool was boasting in pubs about rogering his wife. So what do I think happened at the shooting party that day? I think Max Hood was seeing red, I think Max Hood saw the chance, he had the great sod in his sights, and he blew him to kingdom come. That's what I think."

"What was Cilla's reaction?"

"Why not ask her?"

"I don't want to open an old wound."

"Well, I'll tell you what I think. I think she gave considerably less than two hoots about Colin, dead or alive. She's an actress . . . she may be used to men killing each other over her. Some women are like that. Women who look like Cilla, women who behave like Cilla—she just doesn't give a damn, does she? At least that's this country doctor's opinion."

"And you don't think Max ever told Cilla about his illness?"

"Seems to me he wanted to spare her that. He knew she'd be well taken care of—his money, her career. But it wouldn't hurt if you asked her now, surely."

Homer Teasdale got slightly tipsy and tried to read aloud from one of Godwin's books but Godwin threatened to kill him on the spot if he did so. Roddy Bascomb got a bunch of people to play charades and Lily Fantasia read Tarot cards and that led to Cilla's producing a Ouija board and Monk Vardan told a few ripe Churchill stories and Dr. MacIntyre kissed Homer Teasdale's girlfriend in the billiard room. Vardan claimed to have lost a pound note and then found it in Lieberman's ear. Magic.

They all spoke of the war and drank a bit too much and laughed too loudly and wondered what was going to happen before the war would finally end. They all listened to some new records, Sinatra and Al Bowlly and Hutch, and everyone stayed up late talking and talking and talking.

"Well, Rodger," Homer said, peering through his glasses with his head thrown back and his glasses parked on the end of his nose, "what about your future? Time to think about it. Do you feel well enough to go back to work?"

"I'm all right. But I'm badly out of touch. I'll have a lot of homework to do."

"Do you want to get back on the air?"

"Ease me back into it. I'll stick to the writing for now. Get me on the air once a week. Maybe Sunday night."

Late Saturday night Godwin was climbing the stairs when Monk Vardan stepped out of the shadows and called to him.

"A word, Rodger."

Godwin turned, then went back down the stairs. "I've been avoiding you."

"A fine sensitivity, old man. But perhaps we should clear the air. Partially, at any rate."

"It's up to you, Monk, but make it snappy."

"It's cold here. Come with me and sit by the fire. Let us reason together."

"Bullshit, Monk."

"You are peevish. I understand."

"Peevish doesn't quite cover it."

"Perhaps I can point out a brighter side to things. I think it's quite possible that an accommodation can be reached which will cool your fevered brow. As it happens you've been very lucky, old boy . . . very lucky that so little has surfaced about the mission. Parliament has taken the PM's hints to heart; they have kept their mouths shut. Your humble servant, namely me, has applied more pressure on certain curious members than you can imagine . . . and I have as well lobbied your posish with the PM himself at every opportunity. I am trying to convince him that it's hopeless to try to *do* anything to you, given the fact that you are who you are." He poked at the dying fire. "Now don't get your hopes up but—"

"Oh, for God's sake, Monk!"

"I don't know which way it will go but now that you Yanks are in the war I'd say your future may be a bit rosier. You can be a great deal more useful to the Allies doing what you do—"

"Monk, shove it. Until someone brings me up on charges I'm going to go on doing what I've been doing—"

"But your access can be cut off once you're back at work."

"I'll deal with that then."

"As you wish."

"But I have a question for you, Monk. Can I get a straight answer?"

"We shall see."

"Are you, or the PM, or anybody, going to try to find out what *really* happened to PRAETORIAN? Somebody did betray us. It wasn't me . . . so who was it?"

"Seriously, old boy, I'm not at liberty to say one more word. We haven't had this conversation—my advice to you is to be as inconspicuous as is humanly possible—"

"I want an answer, Monk."

"Stay out of it. Get back to work. I'll try to make it all go away. I'll work on the PM but there are wheels within wheels; there are men who want someone brought to the dock."

"I want to see your master."

"Surely you jest." Monk offered one of his alligator grins.

"I'm going to find out who killed Max Hood . . . who betrayed us."

"I wish you'd stop saying that, Rodger. You're going to do nothing of the kind. You're going to behave yourself and hope for the best."

"Monk, I don't know what's going on. But I owe Max Hood something. I *am* going to find out what happened."

"Rodger, this is from one friend to another—leave it alone."

"I just want you to know my plans. Stay out of my way, Monk."

"That sounds rather like a threat, old chap."

"Only if you're between me and whoever betrayed PRAETORIAN."

Godwin's first broadcast came early in May. It dealt with one of what became famous as the Baedeker Raids, after the series of guidebooks to notable sights. This one was a Luftwaffe attack on the cathedral at Exeter. Many lives were lost, the cathedral sustained considerable damage, and Godwin took a sound man and visited Exeter the next day. He interviewed townspeople, a crusty old fire warden who had a few choice comments about the Heinies, and told the story of the wife and daughter of a doctor serving abroad. Both mother and child were killed. And so it was that the war reclaimed Godwin as if he'd been away for only a moment.

He moved back into his flat in Berkeley Square. He saw Cilla openly, met her at the theater several nights a week and returned with her to the house in Sloane Square for a few hours. Together they went to the occasional party. They were becoming a couple, laying the groundwork for the future together. How often did a woman fall in love with and marry a man who had been a great friend of her late husband's? It seemed a promising storyline.

One night he and Homer Teasdale went to see Bea Lillie's new hit show, *Big Top*, at His Majesty's Theatre. At the interval Godwin was taken by surprise by a familiar voice at his shoulder.

"Rodger, you *are* back in town. I couldn't believe it when I heard it—you hadn't called me." It was Anne Collister, and rather to his surprise the sight of her blond hair and perfect pale face warmed him. He'd been dreading calling her, explaining the situation. But her mocking, reproachful expression, the cool of her eyes, pleased him. He was reminded of how genuinely fond of her he was. "When I visited you in Salisbury you hadn't wakened. Then they told me it would be better to leave it alone."

"I'm just back, getting my feet on the ground. Anne, it's good to see you."

"I've been worried sick. Are you quite all right?"

"Yes, just fine. It's been a slow business . . . I've been out of circulation."

Edward Collister appeared, dragging on a cigarette, hair hanging across his forehead, eyes sunk in purple sockets with dark puffy pouches beneath. He looked rather worse than the last time Godwin had seen him. "Well, Rodger Godwin . . . back from the wars." He spoke wearily. "Subject of rumors, tall tales, campfire songs. Heard you were dead but that must have been some other fella. Anne's missed you like bloody hell, crying herself to sleep—"

"Edward, please! Pay no attention to him, Rodger."

"Well, I've missed you, too, Anne."

"You'll prove it by calling me? Tomorrow?"

"Yes, of course. We'll make a date."

"Sorry to hear about your friend." Edward half smiled.

"My friend?"

"General Sir Max Hood, of course."

"Well, I appreciate that, Edward. It was very bad news."

"That's war, I reckon. Still, every cloud has a silver lining."

"Well, I'm damned if I see one when it comes to Max's death."

Edward Collister nodded. "Perhaps not. I know of a great many chaps who are awfully pleased that Cilla Hood is back on the market. If she was ever really off."

"I wouldn't know about that, I'm afraid," Godwin said.

Godwin did not call Anne Collister, as he'd promised. He didn't want to face the issue she represented and, besides, Cilla was beginning one of her difficult times. She would soon be shooting a film during the day and doing her show at night, a stress that couldn't have come at a worse time. Her behavior was increasingly erratic. She would flail at him in the most painful way and he was helpless to stop her. He could do nothing but withdraw from her life. Neither of them knew how long the spasm within her psyche would last. She knew how badly she was behaving; sadly, she believed it was her true nature, held at bay for a long time, breaking through the fragile membrane of self-control.

He could not risk seeing Anne Collister in the weeks after running into her at the theater. In his despair over Cilla he might do things, promise things he would later have to betray. Anne deserved better than that, better than a man obsessed by a woman he could not trust, a woman he at times actually wanted to kill.

Alone in his flat, composing letters to Cilla he would never send, working on his new book, trying to understand and encompass the war as it lurched and fell and struggled from day to day, he would conclude the work of the day with the constant companionship of Max Hood. Godwin knew he would never be free of Max until, perhaps, he was avenged. He thought of Max knowing he was doomed by the tumor in his head, going off on another mission . . . Max, Max, Max, what was really going on out there that night? Was it really so risky? Had Monk Vardan known of the dangers? Had Churchill? Or was it a piece of cake that had gone bad only because it had been betrayed? Would they have sent Rodger Godwin had they known it was fifty-fifty at best? How could they have failed at least to warn him? What was really going on? No, they couldn't have known. It *was* a piece of cake. Until someone had sold them out. That was a fact and Godwin knew it.

One rainy night he sat alone in a pub in Islington, far from the heartbeat of London and the war. The venue was Alec Rakestraw's idea. "I can't be seen with you these days, Rodger. The word's out. Be reasonable. Wear a false beard and a funny nose and a trilby low over the eyebrows. Vardan has been seen sniffing in corners, talking to everybody you've ever stood pints for. Shall we say leading questions have been asked. So it's the Green Man in the outer precincts of Islington or it's a scratch."

Vardan's inquiries were no surprise to Godwin; he'd heard it from several quarters. And he needed to see Rakestraw, who was a man of some influence and weight at the admiralty. He was sitting in a dim corner, halfway through a pint, ignored by the regulars who listened to war news on the wireless and listlessly pitched darts at a tattered board. There was a sudden blast of wind and rain and there was Rakestraw in the doorway, collar turned up, out of uniform, seeming smaller than usual. He spotted Godwin and scurried over.

"Alec, you're shrinking."

"You're exceedingly fortunate I'm visible at all. Get me my pint and whatever passes for a sausage roll in these parts. I have rather definitive answers to your questions. First, provisions for the hungry sailor. I don't come cheap, as the harlot reminded the bishop."

When Godwin returned to the table and placed the pint and sausage roll before Rakestraw, his guest was carefully smoothing a sheet of notepaper on the table, attempting to avoid the damp puddles of bitter. He took a bit of roll and grimaced, swigged some bitter, ran his finger down the list of names.

"Martin Jellicoe, Cyril Pinkham, Bert Penrose, Brian Qualley, Alf Dexter, Reginald Smythe-Haven, Bill Cox, Lad Holbrook, Anthony Jones, Jim Steele, Boyd Malvern, Oxham Bester . . . that's the list you gave me, Rodger."

"And you checked the service files. So what turned up?"

"It was an extraordinary request. Full of pitfalls."

"Let's say you owed me one."

"Obviously. Otherwise I'd have turned you over and they'd have stood you up against a wall and—"

"Alec, Alec, you *did* owe me. So what did you find out?"

"Nothing. Not a crumb. The cupboard was bare."

"That's hardly possible. They existed. There must be records."

"Oh, I'm sure there *were* records. It's just that there are no records now."

"Lost? Misfiled? What?"

"Gone. How to make you grasp this? These men do not exist in service personnel records. I may not exist simply because I was ill advised enough to ask—"

"I don't believe this. There's a simple explanation."

"Certainly. From somewhere on high the normal files have been snatched away. Not merely stamped secret or eyes only. Not requisitioned by this department or that ministry. They have *gone*. Now let me explain that there are central files where a man's service career is summarized, noted, annotated, and so forth. There are other records where they'd show up in time but that is impossible even to check—it would take months of digging through records scattered across our brave and sceptered isle . . . and I wouldn't recommend that you try to dig any of it out. Unseen and immensely powerful forces are at work here, Rodger . . . dum da-da-*dum* . . . Central Registry's cupboard is clean as a bleached bone and as far as I'm concerned I never asked. It's all forgotten. We never discussed it."

"And the other word I brought up?"

"*Praetorian*, yes. I saved it for last, asked a couple of people I trusted to be discreet. I mean . . . *discreet*."

"And?"

"Nobody's ever heard of it. I can read eyes, too. Nary a flicker. There was no such thing as PRAETORIAN. Take my word for it. Whatever you think you're on to . . . you're not. There never has been anything called PRAETORIAN. Mustard—do you think mustard might improve another sausage roll? Then I really must be off. We'll leave separately, if you don't mind."

Godwin remembered Lad Holbrook: the expert card player who'd wound up with most of the money on the submarine, the man who knifed the German sentry, the man with his arm shot to bits who died a hero's death at Rommel's HQ. Holbrook had told Godwin his father was a clerk in an office somewhere near the docks, that they'd lived way down the King's Road, past World's End.

Godwin found the flat in a brick block, a place of genteel Depression-style poverty inhabited by people who refused to admit their poverty but still only barely managed to live from week to week. The men wore collars and ties, that was what mattered. Antimacassars on the backs of the chairs, weak tea, the smell of boiled vegetables, the electric bar glowing in the tiny parlor, Lad Holbrook's mum and dad finishing up a supper of toast and egg. Their eyes flickered at Godwin's name, though it wouldn't have been proper to admit recognition of a famous man. More tea was brewed. A large-eyed girl with a very up-to-date haircut brought it in on a tray. She poured the tea, the huge eyes catching Godwin's for a moment after the cup was full. Lad's sister, Diana.

"I was a friend of your son's," Godwin said. "I was with him when he died. I can quite honestly tell you that he gave his life heroically and without hesitation." Mrs. Holbrook smiled tightly, a lace handkerchief wound tightly through the fingers of her clenched fist.

"We were given to understand his mission was secret," Oliver Holbrook said quietly. He was a schoolmasterish, lean man who looked as if he'd once been fat. He still wore his suit though evening was upon them and supper was finished. "I'm not at all sure we should be speaking of this now. Not by the book, I'm afraid."

"How did he pass over?" the woman asked. Her mouth melted downward at the corners. There was a small, well-thumbed Bible in leatherette on the table beside her chair.

"Biscuit?" Diana was passing round a plate. No currants, no faces. Not Monk Vardan's favorites.

"He died taking out a bunch of Germans who had a machine gun. He got them all."

"Oh my, oh my. He was always a brave boy."

"Sounds like Laddie," Diana said, crunching a biscuit.

"Here now," Holbrook said. "That's enough. I'm sure you're well intentioned and all, Mr. Godwin, but we've been told that we're not to say a word. This must all remain secret. Quite out of the question to discuss this any further."

"Where did he die?"

"Now, Mother," Holbrook said, fluttering a hand at her. "Enough, I said."

"North Africa," Godwin said. "But your husband is quite right. I wanted to know if you've been told about the mission—now I realize that you haven't. And Lad, I take it, told you nothing."

"Not a word," his mother said. "He was a good soldier."

"Well, I don't believe I've endangered security by telling you what I have, as long as it goes no further."

"I was quite upset that we were told so little." She dabbed at her eyes. "Quite upset."

"Now don't start, Mother. You know what they told us." Her husband turned to Godwin. "No questions, that's what we were told. My good wife wanted to go to our member but they told us, no questions. Very important. Security's security. King and Country, Mr. Godwin. That's our motto."

"I think it's very kind of Mr. Godwin to come here—"

"I liked your son. Hell of a card player. Persian monarchs."

Holbrook gave a muffled laugh. "I taught him that game. He was just a young boy. Holiday at Brighton. You remember, Mother. Persian monarchs and Brighton Rock on a rainy afternoon." He fumbled in his sleeve for his handkerchief. He held it to his eyes. "Happy days, happy days." He stood up, shook Godwin's hand. "Mother's right. It was good of you to come, sir."

Godwin was standing halfway down the block. It would take a long time to walk all the way back to Mayfair. Two hours maybe but, then, he had plenty of thinking to do.

He heard running feet behind him, a voice. "Mr. Godwin, wait a moment." It was Diana.

"What can I do for you?" He smiled at her, liked her immediately.

She was out of breath and her pale cheeks were flushed. "Jolly nice of you to come by that way. I hear you on the radio; you must be terribly busy. Mum and Dad were quite taken by surprise when you sort of materialized, poof, like a genie."

"I wanted to take them by surprise."

"Well, the point is, they didn't tell you everything. And since you are so nice to stop by—I could tell you about the man who came to see us one night. Said he represented King and Country—" She giggled, behind her hand, "sounded like he was representing a pub, you see . . . but you can imagine how that appealed to Dad. King and country. Bells began ringing, he stood at attention."

"Your father is a patriot, Diana."

"No doubt of that. Anyway, this man who came to see us, it was back near Christmas, during the hols. I was reading in the corner and Dad had forgotten I was there. This man told them that Lad's death—they'd already been told he was dead—but they weren't supposed to begin any inquiries. They'd got the wind up because Mum had been to see our MP at his office; she wanted to know what had happened to Lad. Our member, Mr. Spears, told her a few days later that any more information was impossible . . . then this chap showed up at the flat and gave Mum and Dad a packet of money. Not a check, mind you. Money. A big envelope of bills—I couldn't believe it." Her eyes were wide as she walked along looking up at Godwin.

"I don't blame you. It is odd, isn't it? Not the way things are done."

"The man said it was a special payment for their great loss . . . he called it a one-time insurance payment from an appreciative government."

"Anything else?"

"Before he left he told them several times that they mustn't go back to Mr. Spears, they mustn't ask any questions or discuss any of this with anyone. . . . He said it mustn't fall into the wrong ears, something like that." She brushed the hair away from her face and pushed her hands down into the pockets of her peacoat. She was about to become very pretty, as Lad had been handsome. "I saw a movie with George Raft. He gave somebody money to be quiet. They called it 'hush money.' I think what the chap gave Mum and Dad was hush money. A pay-off to keep quiet."

"What did this man look like?"

"Hmmm. He was tall and I think he was quite thin but he wore a sort of cloak. That and the long nose made me think of Sherlock Holmes. He kept calling my father old boy. I doubt if anyone had ever called him old boy before in his life. It was rather funny. What do you think?"

"I think you have the makings of a good reporter."

"No! Do you mean it?"

"You're observant. You've been a great help. I'm not kidding."

"Do you think I might ever become a reporter? Really?"

"Why not?"

He gave her his card and when he looked back she was still there, rooted to the spot, and when she saw him turning to her she waved and cheekily blew him a kiss.

Peter Cobra caught sight of him as soon as he entered the dimness that was Dogsbody's. He shimmered through the crowd. "Rodger, do you realize how beastly hard it is to serve a decent meal at a five-shilling maximum? These new regulations are killing us. We can charge another two-and-bloody-six for cabaret but that means we have to provide this absolutely grisly entertainment! Thus, a gypsy violinist will pass among you. Or his cousin, a Portuguese *fado* singer. Sounds like a cat in the throes of either death or passion. Perhaps a distinction without a difference. What this war has reduced us to! Let's see, your date is back in one of the darker corners." He smiled indulgently, like one who thinks of everything.

Monk Vardan was drinking a martini and looking rather Pre-Raphaelite with his scarf furled about his long throat. He crooked a finger at Godwin and patted the banquette beside him. To Peter Cobra he said: "Keep that violinist away from me or I shan't be responsible for my actions." Cobra shrugged. Vardan said: "So glad you could come, old boy, considering how busy you've been. Now wet your whistle, young Godwin, and prepare yourself, for I would remonstrate with you."

"Just don't talk funny all evening. A martini, Peter, and shake a leg."

Cobra frowned and presently one of his minions appeared with the perfect martini.

"But pleasure before business," Vardan said, dropping the monocle from his eye. "How fares the lovely Cilla? I must say that was a fine weekend up at Stillgraves. Some might have found it a trifle brisk in the wing I inhabited but I call it invigorating. The water in my toilet was frozen. Did I tell you that?"

"You spared me."

"A small thing. So how are you two keeping, then?"

"I haven't seen much of Cilla lately. She's working very hard these days."

"Do I detect a sour note, old chap?"

"She's having one of her difficult times. She'll come out of it."

"She certainly seems to have a tendency toward these periods of—"

"Drop it, Monk. What's on your mind? Why am I here?"

"Because you have been a rather naughty boy. My God, I warned Peter about this gypsy—you there! Skat! Be off! Damn that Peter! I swear he sent him over here on purpose! For God's sake, Rodger, naughty, naughty, naughty. Perverting the course of His Majesty's government. Treason. You really were told to behave yourself and button your lip. We've been frightfully square with you, considering the situation. But you wouldn't listen and you're in the soup again. What are we to do with you? You're dragging other people into your mess. . . . It's not a good plan, old boy. You ought to have known that."

A little shiver scampered along Godwin's spine. "Get to the point."

"Well, there's poor Rakestraw, for one. I mean, he's blotted the old copybook. *Finito*. He'll never go any further and quite frankly it's your fault. Nobody's going to tell him, mind you, but he'll get the idea in the not too distant future. He didn't inform us you'd been onto him, a terrible mistake . . . but some of the people he thought were safe to ask turned out to be people who knew their duty and alerted us to the requests he was making."

"This is very dirty, Monk."

"Wet work, as we say. Well, it's a war, Rodger. Then we come to Oliver Holbrook, an Englishman of the old school. He knew what to do when you called on him. He said you were a fine fellow but he had his duty to do." Vardan lit a cigarette and sucked smoke through the holder. "Now listen to me, Rodger—we can't have you dashing about the landscape planting little seeds which might grow into very large problems. A botched attempt to kill Rommel, everybody dead. . . . We can't have it coming out. Surely you do see that?"

"I'm not planting any seeds, and I'm certainly not going public, though I could by God and nobody would believe your crazy story about my being a traitor . . . I just want to find out how PRAETORIAN was betrayed and who did it. You might as well believe me, Monk."

"To what end? Seriously, old boy, what do you hope to accomplish? This was a highly secret mission; we want its outcome to stay that way. We've asked you to cease and desist—"

"You've accused me, Monk . . ."

"Tell me, Rodger. Have you jumped the track? I'm quite serious. You've had a terrible head injury. Do you think you should be examined? Our doctors are at your disposal—"

"Why do I think if I let you put me in a hospital I wouldn't be coming out again?"

"I don't know what you must be thinking, Rodger. Seems to me it's evidence that you might actually be going off your head. Just a thought."

"If it's made me want to find out the identity of a traitor, then apparently I am mad."

"Well, you worry me," Vardan sighed. "I'm empowered only to tell you—warn you, really, one last time—to lay off. You're interfering in the affairs of state, in the prosecution of the war. That comes to you directly from my boss. If you don't behave yourself, Rodger, the consequence will be your doing, not ours."

"As a friend of mine would say, 'How very dire, dear boy.' "

"The direst, I assure you. Now I have to threaten you again and I really do hate this. However, what one must do, one must do. While you were aboard the good ship *Kismet* headed out of Alexandria for Beda

Littoria, you wrote a letter which was left with the ship's captain, Stanley Wardour. It was *that* sort of letter—chap going off on a dangerous mission, always the chance he might not come back. It was written to Cilla Hood, to be delivered in care of Homer Teasdale. But, as it happened, you didn't die and the letter never reached Teasdale. Nor Mrs. Hood, obviously. With the rest of your effects, it came to me. Being a nosey Parker I read it . . . and a very touching, moving letter it was. A very moving declaration of love for another man's wife . . . and that man leading the mission you were undertaking . . . a rather clear statement of a motive for murder. This letter, Rodger, or a version thereof, might be released mysteriously to some of our less responsible Fleet Street types. You know, it might even be construed as evidence against you and Mrs. Hood, the two of you plotting to kill her husband. Can you imagine what a mess that would be? Oh, it might never come to court, but imagine the damage not only to your career but hers as well—she's just stupid and unstable enough to jump off Westminster Bridge or something equally dramatic. In any case, a particularly nasty scandal would ensue . . . just think about it, will you? Before you decide to play the hero detective again?"

Godwin slid out from behind the table and stood up. "Monk, you amaze me. Does Eton know how you're behaving these days? Another moment in your company and I'm afraid I'd make you eat your martini, glass and all."

"I know," he said looking up at Godwin. "The necessity for my behavior grieves me. It truly does." He shrugged hopelessly. "What a patriot will do for his country."

At the beginning of June 1942 the RAF launched the biggest air raid in history, the thousand-bomber raid over Cologne. Godwin went to one of the aerodromes to interview returning pilots and crewmen for the American audience.

One young Halifax pilot with a sparse, boyish mustache shook his head in wonder at what he'd just been part of. "That many planes fill the sky, as far ahead and as far behind as you can see. We were coming over Cologne at the rate of one bomber every six seconds. Believe me, sir, it was like the traffic at Picadilly Circus, only worse."

Another could hardly believe the devastation. "We were over the coast of Holland on the way home, that's about 140 miles from Cologne and, so help 'em, you could still see the fires behind us. Stands to reason, we toasted the blighters, don't it?"

And a young gunner, white-faced and soft-spoken, half whispered: "You can't help but feel bad for the people down below. I mean, I've got two little sisters, me mum and dad and grandpa, I wouldn't want anything like this to happen to them . . . London at its worst was only a patch on Cologne."

At times Godwin would turn in his Sunday-night broadcasts or in his column to familiar names and places. At times it was hard to comprehend that it was all the same enormous war, from the North Sea run supplying Russia to the opening of the spring offensive in the Crimea to Burma to Malta to the Bay of Bengal to Cologne to those familiar desert names. Out there in the desert a huge tank battle was raging, stretching from Bir Hacheim to El Adem, only twenty miles south of Tobruk. The RAF was playing hell with Nazi tanks but Rommel still aimed at Tobruk. The Brits were holding tight. The official line from Auchinleck's HQ was that "there is no cause for dissatisfaction," an observation Godwin included in his broadcast as an example of British understatement. It became one of his catch phrases. He had a lot of people saying it across America in those days.

The audience was glad to hear his voice and read his columns twice weekly now. He felt pretty good, except for the problems with Cilla which haunted his nights and ate at him twenty-four hours a day. If only he could patch things together with Cilla. He had to believe that it would work out. Somehow.

It was then that somebody tried to kill him.

CHAPTER 24

An American general had given the party at the Dorchester in honor of an American senator known to be well connected to a variety of cleanup hitters in Washington, most particularly to Harry Hopkins, which meant he had an avenue to Franklin Roosevelt's ear. Therefore the crowd was large, military, political, and bureaucratic, with a crucial mix of beautiful women, which accounted for the cluster of admirers around Lily Fantasia.

When Greer and Godwin talked that night, Greer's sense of decorum kept him from mentioning Cilla. Thus Godwin knew that Greer knew about the problems and in that sense he felt almost as if Cilla were hovering just above their heads. Later in the evening, once Godwin had been trotted past the senator who asked for his autograph for his teenage daughter Sue, who thought he was neat, almost like a movie star—after this business was finished, Lily finally pinned him against the wall. She gave his hand a long, hard squeeze, her eyes very sad.

"Oh, come on, Lily . . ." he said.

"Just wait, Rodger, it will all blow over. You knew how it would be, Rodger, you can't claim ignorance . . ."

"What are you talking about? I'm as ignorant as they come and you know it."

"You make jokes, that's Rodger, but your heart is breaking—and she is tearing herself to pieces."

"Well, I can handle it."

"If you need to talk," she said, "I've a friendly ear."

"Thank you, Lily. But I'm made of pretty stern stuff. Quiet sobbing is heard in Mayfair about three o'clock and I'm my usual shiny self come the dawn."

"And of course there is your friend Miss Collister. I was at lunch the other day and someone tried to bet me ten pounds that Anne Collister would be Mrs. Godwin by the end of the year."

"What a peculiar thing to bet on."

"No names. But she claims to be a friend of the Collister family. The family itself seems to be in a state of some indefinite turmoil."

"Lily, I must be going. Did you ever have the feeling that you wanted to go but you wanted to stay? Fits me to a T." Godwin kissed her check. "Besides, I have a case of party head."

She kissed him a second time and he left, trying not to think about the curious look in her eye as she watched him back away. Stefan Lieberman was approaching her and Godwin nodded to him and was gone.

The fog was thick and smelled as if rubber had been burning since the time of Agincourt. It got in your eyes, made your face feel greasy, stuffed your nostrils like a dirty rag. He stood at the corner looking back up Deanery Street angling away from Park Lane and thought better of it. The fog that way looked solid as cement. He struck off down Park Lane and was tempted by Curzon Street. Yes, he knew every inch of Curzon Street; he could do it by touch. Still, there was nothing quite like a London pea-souper and before he knew it he'd somehow meandered off into Shepherd's Market where he stood leaning against a lamppost, trying to get his bearings. The problem was, with the familiar buildings reduced only to vague shapes it was difficult to know which way you were actually heading. He heard footsteps muffled by the fog, they came and went, they stopped, occasionally there was a muttered oath following a misstep, an ankle twisted on a curb that had never been there before, by God!

Godwin was at last quite sure he was correctly aimed at Berkeley Square and set off again, ferrule of his umbrella tapping the paving ahead of him like a blind man's cane. He reached a broad street, more footsteps scuffling along as if afraid to lose touch with the earth. Piccadilly. . . . He had been going in exactly the wrong direction. He stood on the corner of Down Street or Brick Street, whatever the hell they were . . .

Now of course, he did know where he was. He moved cautiously along the edge of the curb, came to what he knew had to be Half Moon Street where Bertram Wooster and the excellent Jeeves had long resided.

"Godwin . . . Godwin? Is that you?"

He heard the voice but it was soft, indistinct, far away, or was it close at hand? "Yes? Who is it?" But there was nothing, no answer. Had it come

from up Half Moon Street? Or from somewhere ahead or behind in Picadilly? He coughed, choking for a moment on the gritty, greasy, oily damp.

He set off up Half Moon Street, familiar territory. No way of losing
his bearings. Right on Curzon Street, then to the left and Berkeley Square.
He was in Anne Collister country, a moment from her place. . . . Now
let's see, surely this was Curzon Street . . .

"Godwin? Are you there? Is that you? I can't see . . . Godwin? Stay
still . . . I'll find you . . ." The voice floated away, came from everywhere.

He stopped, eyes burning. "Who is it? Where are you? Identify yourself. . . . Where the devil are you?" Footsteps faded away on the left, or
was it behind him? Or back along Curzon Street in the direction of Hyde
Park? Then there were other footsteps. Everything bounced off the fog, off
the walls; everything was everywhere at once and he couldn't make sense
of it. The fog tore at his throat like a claw with each breath. Who was
calling to him? Or was it his imagination? Strange things happened in the
fog. You seemed to float this way and that without reference point; it was
like being in one of those plays where everyone was dead but didn't know
it. Maybe he was dead and didn't know it and if he were, who the hell
would care anyway?

He didn't quite know how he got all the way to Berkeley Street on the
far side of the square but he could smell the newly mown grass and knew
he'd made it home. No one was calling to him anymore. He stared into
the fog knowing he was looking across the little park toward his flat. He
had just reached the fence, was feeling it with his fingertips, sliding his
hand along its damp smoothness, when he heard the sudden rush and
clump of footsteps close behind him.

He half turned, his umbrella caught in the fence and was yanked
from his grasp. He was about to say something when he slipped on the wet
curb and felt his ankle twist, felt himself going down, heard cloth rip, his
hands out catching in the man's mackintosh pocket. He thought he'd
ripped the poor bastard's coat, then he hit the street, scraping his knee,
tearing the fabric of his trousers. The other man fell backward, grunted,
and something metal clanged on the pavement, came to rest against Godwin's sleeve where he'd fallen.

He felt it slide or bounce up against him and touched it.

It was a knife, like the hunting knives he'd seen back home when he
was a kid. It was like a commando knife.

Suddenly the figure of the other man lurched like a mountain on
wheels out of the fog, came crashing down on him. For some inexplicable

reason, Godwin felt a terrible blood-red rush of anger, felt something like a kind of superconsciousness, a feeling of pure wrathful imperviousness to danger, and he rolled his own considerable bulk out of the way, swung his foot as hard as he could at the shape as it landed on the wet street, turned to find the knife but couldn't, dropped to one knee hoping to scoop it up, failed, heard and half felt the shape breathing hard and struggling upward but he wasn't quite sure where the shape was and then it was upon him, knocking him backward but Godwin was large and strong and ripped at where he thought the thing's face should have been, found an ear and tore it, felt it pull away from the skull, felt the gush of thick hot blood like a geyser, heard the screaming, felt himself hurled aside as the invisible man was swallowed by the fog . . .

The screaming stopped, the footsteps were gone, Godwin's head swam as he sat down against the fence protecting the park at the center of Berkeley Square. He gagged trying to get his breath. He wasn't thinking quite coherently, wasn't analyzing what had happened to him. Slowly he stood up. His knee was scraped and bloody to the touch. His hand and sleeve reeked of blood from the man's torn ear. There was a gaping tear along the left side of his coat where the knife had slid through coat and lining.

He couldn't find his umbrella. He couldn't see a damned thing. There was nothing to do but follow the railing around to his side of the square. His ankle gave a twinge with each step. His knee felt as if broken glass had been ground into it. His mac was ruined and he had a stitch in his side. He stank of blood. His memory flickered: He smelled like the bloody hallway in Beda Littoria . . .

He was trying to get his key in the lock when he heard the voice behind him in the fog. "Godwin? Is that you? Answer me, man, I'm hopelessly lost . . ."

"Up here. I'm standing at my front door. When you get the smell of blood up your nose just follow it. You can't miss me. Who the hell is it?"

A broad figure loomed out of the fog.

"It's me, Stefan Lieberman. I've been trying to catch up to you. Wanted to talk to you . . . the fog kept getting in the way. Good God, what happened to you? You look like bomb damage—here, let me give you a hand, you're bleeding like a stuck pig!" He came forward, intent on helping out.

"Don't worry. It's not my blood. I just about tore a man's ear off a few minutes ago. I'm surprised he didn't knock you down in the fog—"

"I didn't see anyone."

"He's probably feeling pretty faint about now."

"Why did you do this thing to him?"

"Well, mainly, because he tried to kill me. With a knife. Slipshod workman, fortunately."

"I'd better see you in."

"If you like. I'm quite all right. We'll have a drink."

"But why did this man try to kill you? Was he robbing you? Did he think you were someone else?"

"No, I don't think so."

When Godwin came back into his sitting room, washed up and disinfected and patched and dried off, Lieberman was smoking a cigar roughly the size of a railway tie. He held out a leather case to Godwin. "Have one."

Godwin clipped the end and lit it. He poured some Napoleon brandy older than he was. Lieberman treated it like mouthwash, swallowed, and poured himself some more. "This could be worse," he said, grunted appreciatively. "Nice kick to it. I knew a guy in Los Angeles once who drank a bottle of this stuff a day. Ostentatious kike. Like me. No wonder we were pals." He either growled or laughed. Godwin wasn't entirely sure what he was hearing but it wasn't the Stefan Lieberman he'd known. He seemed to be presenting an entirely new side of himself.

"You? In Los Angeles? This is news—"

"Are you kidding me? Why the hell not Los Angeles? Do you know the kind of money they pay out there? I went three times, wrote some stuff for Louis Mayer, Jack Warner—hell, I even married a Mexican actress Ty Power introduced me to. That lasted two delirious years. She had this habit of pissing at the goddamnedest times. You just never knew when she'd let fly. She was a nut, but she had spirit, she was fun. Every studio liked to have a few European yids hanging around, like tame Jesuits at court. Added some cultcha, as they loved to say, and the guys that ran the studios, they were all Russian-Polish-German yids, made 'em feel important, like they were bringing family to the promised land. But, as you may have noticed, I don't go on about it much here in London, here among the hotsy-totsy Brits. Better to let the other side of Stefan Lieberman show through, the poor fuckin' wandering Jew, the Nazis nipping at his ass—look, it's all true. Both of me, both Stefan Liebermans are real— what London gets is the European refugee/dramatist/screenwriter, not the Hollywood husband of Lupe What's-her-name. It makes sense. You gotta know your audience. Don't let it worry you. What's worrisome is what happened to you tonight. What do you mean, it wasn't a case of mistaken identity? Why would somebody want to kill you?"

Godwin had revised his candid response to Lieberman's initial question in the street. "Well, you must be right, it must have been a robbery or mistaken identity. Foggy night, how could he have known who the hell he was stabbing?"

"Seems a little violent for a robbery. You never know what people will do these days. You'd better report it . . . the man has lost a lot of blood—"

"In the morning," Godwin said. "I'll take care of it in the morning." They spent several more minutes conjecturing about the attack, Godwin stressing the possibility of random violence, being in the wrong place at the wrong time. He listened to Lieberman and marveled at the second personality he was seeing within one man. He much preferred the new one, the ex-Hollywood screenwriter who was playing the Brits for all they were worth. Of course, it was probably true that both personalities were accurate representations, two sides of the same man. But it was the degree of calculation on Lieberman's part which attracted him. You just never knew. You never could tell.

"You said you wanted to talk to me . . ."

"Yes, this goddamned war . . . the world hasn't begun to understand what Hitler is doing." Lieberman rubbed his heavy, overhanging brow, then ran his hand back over the tight curly hair that hugged his skull. His eyes were burning at the center of dark pouches. Up close he looked as strained and tired as Edward Collister. "They've killed over a million Jews so far and they're just getting started. Three quarters of 'em just in Poland . . . I don't think the world outside understands any of it, just what it means to *plan* the extermination of an entire people . . . and to brag about it! So far they're concentrating on the East, but they're well underway in France, Holland, Belgium, and of course Germany. Take Rumania, they murdered 125,000 Jews, and they made the poor bastards sign a paper admitting responsibility for starting the war before they killed them. Czechoslovakia and Hungary . . . if they get to England . . ." He shrugged his massive shoulders. "My family . . . if I think about it I go mad and I think about it all the time. People have got to be made to realize what's going on out there." He waved a long arm, ash dropping from the cigar. "A war is one thing . . . but systematically, carefully murdering a specific group of people—like blue-eyed people, or bald people, or only the people from Iowa, your state—not just the fighting men, but everyone, *everyone*. . . . Imagine it, Godwin, use your insulated, protected American imagination, try to think of the police coming in to Iowa and rounding everybody up, little boys in short pants and sad-eyed three-year-old girls in little pink dresses, holding on to their favorite dolls, loading them all onto railroad cars where they half-suffocate from the smell of their own shit and piss for a few days, and then they unload them and have 'em dig a ditch and jump in and then the Germans machine-gun 'em. . . . Don't think about Warsaw, some ghetto full of Jews you'll never know anyway and wouldn't like if you did . . . think about Iowa, then you begin to get the idea."

It was turning into a very late night. Godwin tipped the bottle again. The mammoth cigars would last another hour.

"Hitler. Everybody's going to have to put up for several generations to come with scholars going on about what a twisted, demented genius he was, evil incarnate." Godwin snorted. "Well, they'll be half-right. He's an evil and demented little shit. But a genius? What a load that is! A jumped up, quarter-educated nut case, a misfit, a disappointed, obsessive creep, who has led a great and frequently noble people into a meat grinder of their own making for the second time in twenty-five years. For some reason, otherwise decent, God-fearing people occasionally respond to the very worst in themselves . . . well, Herr bloody Hitler has brought out the worst in a great people, albeit a people without an overpowering sense of humor—"

Lieberman seemed to be growling softly and may have been doing so for some time by the time Godwin noticed. The brandy snifter dropped from the hairy paw. He wasn't growling. Tears were streaming down his cheeks, from behind his heavy glasses. He swallowed against his sobs, said: "I'm sorry. About the glass. . . . A great and noble people . . . you are not, I hope, referring to the fucking Germans who are stuffing my people into ovens as fast as they get them built, as fast as they can get my relatives jammed into cattlecars and back out of the cattlecars and into the ovens or into the work camps where they work until they fall dead . . . you think of these, these *creatures* as a great and noble people, do you?"

"Bach, Beethoven, Goethe—"

"Hitler, Himmler, Goering—"

"Well, not so noble *lately*. Not *these* Germans. But as recently as the Weimar Republic, they were a model of—"

"Not tonight, my friend, not tonight, my American friend. Don't talk about the good qualities of the Germans to me. Some chap tried to kill you tonight. If you keep telling me what wonderful, noble guys the Krauts are, I'm afraid I'll have to finish the job. What do you think of that?"

"I think I'd better drop the Germans."

Lieberman laughed loudly and banged his hand in a comradely gesture on Godwin's lacerated knee.

. . .

Godwin sat in the darkened room, surrounded by the ominous shapes of unfamiliar furniture, hearing the ticking of a large clock on the mantelpiece, feeling the slight breeze from the open window. It was a warm night and the smells of Victoria Station moved sluggishly, half-heartedly through the flat. Fresh flowers in a vase on the table, painting of a sea battle over a deep chintz-covered sofa, table lamps with fringed shades, a liquor cabinet, books stacked on the floor beside the worn, favorite chair. There was a bedroom beyond, a hallway, the bathroom, a kitchen at the other end of the hall. He heard the trains at Victoria, grinding, clanging. The flat was on the top floor of one of the huge, squat flat-blocks between Victoria and Westminster Cathedral, the great seat of English Catholicism that tourists kept confusing with Westminster Abbey, which was something else altogether.

He'd been sitting there since late afternoon, waiting. He was going to wait for as long as it took. He'd gone to a certain amount of trouble to make sure he was there at all and he wasn't going to leave before he'd had his money's worth.

The fifty pounds had gone to Dickie Flyte, who was the useful sort of guy you ran into if you hung around journalistic sewers and pubs and late-night fish-and-chips joints. He was a fixer. He was also a police informant these days. He picked the lock and supplied the gun.

It was nearly eleven o'clock when Godwin heard the key rattling in the lock. Then the door swung open just out of sight down the hallway and he heard the soft humming of Mendelssohn's violin concerto, heard the umbrella dropped into the boot, heard the beating of his own heart like a triphammer in his chest. The Smith and Wesson .32 felt like a cement block in his lap. He lifted it, held it in his right hand on the overstuffed arm of the chair.

The footsteps came down the hall and the shadowy figure stood still in the archway into the sitting room as if pausing to sniff the air and listen for some familiar, reassuring sound. Then the man came into the room, felt around for the dangling chain of a lamp, the one with the fringed shade. The light snapped on.

"Why, Rodger, what in the world are you sitting here in the dark for? You might have given a man without my nerves of steel quite a fright. You did surprise me, I must say. Did you get yourself a drink? No? Gin and it all right? And what is that great awful thing in your hand? Oh, I say, old boy, you're not going to be a problem, I hope."

"Pull up a chair and sit, Monk. Skip the gin, the tea, the biscuits with the little currant faces, skip all the bullshit. Just apply your ass to that chair. Sit down, goddammit!"

"All right, all right, I'm sitting, though you *are* in my chair. Now, what do you think you're doing?"

"I think I'm going to shoot you if you don't make it all crystal clear to me, Monk."

"It? What is this 'it' to which you make reference."

"Monk, listen to me and listen just as hard as you can. Your life depends on it. You have put me through a wringer. You suckered me into PRAETORIAN in the first place with all that piece-of-cake crap. Max thought it was fifty-fifty at best. Nobody bothered to tell me that Max was dying with a brain tumor—therefore he didn't care maybe quite as much as I did about staying alive. . . . Then everybody got killed and I'm to blame because I wanted to have Max's wife for myself, oh sure, that makes sense, I became a fucking Nazi saboteur so I can make sure that Max gets killed, *everybody* gets killed *but me* for Christ's sake . . . and of course I damn near do get killed but what the hell, a minor flaw in my brilliant plan, but by some cockeyed miracle I pull through . . . at which point you start turning me into a pariah by questioning everybody I've ever known and leaving little hints that I am under suspicion . . . and when I try to find out who actually betrayed PRAETORIAN you wreck the career of my friend Rakestraw . . . but that's not enough—"

"We know who betrayed PRAETORIAN, old boy—"

"—no, that's not enough for you, ruining poor old Rakestraw, then you send some muscle-bound goon to try to knife me in the fog and have you seen him lately? He's half-an-ear short, you can't miss him, and unless you are pretty fucking convincing in the next few minutes you're going to get the scare of your life though you may get lucky like me and pull through—" He stopped for breath. "What did you just say?"

"We know who betrayed PRAETORIAN."

"You're not listening to me, Monk. You've got the wrong guy. You're disappointing me, Monk—"

"No, not you, old boy. Never really thought it was you, of course, but it was important to make you think we did. Do stop pointing that thing at me. . . . Perhaps you're right, perhaps if you point the gun over there at my stuffed woodchuck from childhood, then perhaps I might as well explain."

"Take my advice. This is the time to explain."

"With all due respect, my son, you've been a decoy. A thankless role, but a necessary one. The idea has been to let the word trickle down here and there that you were the one being investigated. We hoped that the real German agent would feel safe enough to continue his activities—how to say this so it doesn't sound like one of Roddy Bascomb's cinema adventures? Where do you think the movies get the plots, old boy? From us, I'm afraid. So, we hint that you were involved with Hood's wife, that you had this personal reason for wanting to scuttle Max, that in fact you may have killed him yourself . . . yes, it's all absolute rot, we know that, but if we could convince you that we were serious and you reacted as you have—" he shrugged, "we may have convinced the real spy. You have done beautifully, by the way. I congratulate you."

"Don't move a muscle while congratulating me." Godwin sighed. "Who is the spy? What was the idea of having your thug trying to kill me?"

"We know the man we're after is called Pangloss."

"Dr. Pangloss? From *Candide*?"

"Alpha-plus. And you an American, too. You surprise me. Unfortunately that's all we know about him—his code name. We can only wait for him to show himself. However, there is something new—according to you he may be half-an-ear short."

The longer he waited to get in touch with Anne Collister the worse he felt and the harder the whole necessary business seemed. It was the sort of thing that happened to other people all the time; still he dreaded it, dreaded the look of pain and self-consciousness and the attempt she'd make to keep the lid on her feelings. She was a good English girl; she knew how to behave. He almost wished she didn't.

They met at the Savoy for lunch on a gray, damp day, the very end of July. It felt like impending rain as he walked along the Strand from the pigeon-infested flurry of Trafalgar Square, imagining what he would say, how he would say it. She was waiting at the far end of the dining room by the window above the deep greenery of the Victoria Embankment Gardens. She smiled brightly and clicked her fingers at him. She was halfway through a glass of very pale wine.

"At long last," she said with a forced gaiety. "I can't tell you how many times I had picked up the phone to call you but my better judgment carried the day. I knew you'd call when you were ready."

"It's been a struggle, a lot of time at the Beeb, getting back into my working habits. The fact is, I had some of the starch taken out of me while I was playing at war . . . I don't have the stamina back yet."

"I'll do my very best not to strain you." Her blue eyes regarded him for an extra second or two. She wore a blue suit, a Paris item from before the war, a sapphire and diamond ring. "But, my sweet, my English reserve and self-control are approaching the breaking point. I *need* you, Rodger. Do you understand what I mean by that? Are you listening to me, sweet?"

"Sure, I understand." He put his hand over hers on the starched white tablecloth. "I'm starved. How about you?"

"Rodger, I am making a very indecent proposal. It's been a long wait. I know you've asked nothing from me, I know that everything I've thought and done is entirely my own doing. But you're back now; it's time we got on with things. Yes, yes, I'll have the sole, some haricots vert—I really don't care what I eat. You order for us, Rodger. Then we'll talk about the war and then you won't be afraid of what I'm saying and then we'll see where we stand—all right?"

Looking at her, he felt as he often did that she deserved so much more than he gave her. As it was, he sought refuge in the war. Everyone was talking about Tobruk.

Tobruk had finally fallen with twenty-five thousand prisoners ending up in Rommel's hands. Ten days later the Allies drew the line for the decisive battle which would inevitably decide the fate of Egypt. They drew the line at a bottleneck sixty miles from Alexandria called El Alamein. The bottleneck was a forty-mile-wide front leading from the escarpment about the Qattara Depression to the water. Here the Eighth Army would make its stand. The soldiers on either side were exhausted from a month of continuous fighting at Tobruk. Either the fury of Rommel's attack would be stalemated by the arrival of Allied reinforcements, or the battle for North Africa would be over. No one seemed to have a very clear fix on how long it was going to take.

"Don't tell me you're going back out there?"

"No, I'm quite sure my days at war are over. I'm a coward, Anne. I don't think I'd go back there at gunpoint."

She smiled slyly: "Are you a broken man, then?"

"Broken enough. I don't want to get broken again."

"Well, I'm glad you're back for good. I'd hate to lose you now. I've come too close already." There was a sudden quaver in her voice. "I thought you were dead. Edward heard things . . . I thought I'd go mad. I felt as if I'd never truly gotten to know you, that you were always holding so much of yourself back. You're hard to get to know—but now we'll have the time to fill in all the blanks. We've all the time in the world, war or no war."

After lunch the rain still hadn't come. Godwin suggested a walk and they went down to the Embankment. The humidity seemed to have smudged the view over the Thames. The Savoy, up behind them, was blurred and glowing. Godwin leaned on the railing over the water and she came to stand beside him. Her voice was less restrained now that they were out of doors. So were her emotions.

"Why haven't you called me, Rodger? Just relying on my good English-girl manners not to make it uncomfortable for you? Just taking for granted my willingness to hang about awaiting word from on high? Can't you at least try to imagine how I feel? People ask me how you are and what am I to say? I don't know how you are, I haven't laid eyes on you. . . . They tell me they've seen you at one party or another and I have to let them see that I know nothing about you or what you've been doing." She was gripping the railing, soiling the white gloves, staring at the water, impenetrable, dirty. "Why are you doing this to me, Rodger? My parents ask me about you; they say I simply must bring you down to the country for a long weekend—what am I to tell them, Rodger? That you act as if you no longer even know me?"

"Anne, there are things I have to tell you. I ought to have told you a long time ago but I didn't know how . . . I didn't know if I should. But now things have changed. Now I've got to level with you. You've been so damned patient with my . . . my—"

"Ambivalence? That's as good a word as any. I knew, of course, that I didn't have your undivided attention." She tried to smile but couldn't. There was a tremor on her lips. "I'm not going to like this, am I, Rodger?" She touched his arm, as if to steady herself.

"No, maybe not, but I've got to—"

"Oh, bloody hell! This isn't a very good time for bad news, I've had rather a lot of bad news lately. No, don't ask, I'm not here to talk about it. And I don't mean to embarrass you . . . I do need to sit down . . ."

She sank onto one of the cast-iron nineteenth-century benches decorated with the famous Egyptian figures, winged and regal. She leaned back, trying to take a deep breath of the thick, stultifying air. "All right, Rodger. You'd better get on with it."

"I'm in love with another woman. I've been in love with her all my life. Now she's free. I simply can't help it. There's no cure. There's no other way to put it."

She was crying quietly, holding a handkerchief to her mouth. Her eyes flickered across his face, then away. "You might as well have driven Cleopatra's ghastly old needle through my heart, Rodger. You must realize that."

"It's not as bad as all that. Try to face this honestly, Anne—we had no agreement, we'd made no commitment, we've been good friends but I never tried to lead you on—"

"Of course, how could I forget the things you didn't do? It's entirely my fault, my imagination. . . . Who is she?"

"Cilla Hood."

"Oh, Rodger, how appalling. You are such a hopeless, utter fool." She had stopped crying, was putting the bit of cambric back in her bag. "She's a well-known whore. She'll make your life a misery. She actually *is* a whore. Everyone knows that. Surely that bothers you . . ."

"Don't demean yourself, Anne. There's nothing you can say."

"I don't think you need worry about *my* demeaning *myself.* You've already taken care of that. I've been demeaned by an expert. It's her mother, you know, she's that mother of hers all over again, you poor simple fool . . . you must stay clear of her for your own sake . . . please, listen to me . . . I heard rumors about you and her, long before her husband was killed—"

"What can you possibly mean?"

"Surely you don't think you can keep something like that entirely secret? Oh, you're such a simpleton . . . but I thought she was an old friend, and Max Hood was an old friend of yours too. I couldn't believe you were blind to what she is, always has been from what I can gather, and I couldn't believe that you of all people, that stalwart Yank Rodger Godwin, would betray his old friend Max Hood, the Hero of the Desert. . . . Tell me, Rodger, did you ever sleep with us the same day? Did you ever dash from her bed to mine? . . . Oh, Rodger, I really did love you. . . . Was I such a clumsy girl, so easy to fool, so easy to use?"

"Anne, it's nothing like that, there's nothing so terrible, it's not that way at all . . . there's nothing so *bad* about it—"

"Oh, but there is. You're going to find out just how bad it is. . . . You've been a swine, haven't you? Well, I'll make sure you realize just how bad it is. I call her a whore but I've been nothing but a whore for you—"

"Anne, for heaven's sake! Don't be silly—we're adults, we've enjoyed each other, what's the point in leaving a bad taste in our mouths?"

"Just go away, Rodger, leave me alone. You've been an utter swine to me and I was in love with you . . . what a fool I've been . . . I thought we could be so happy, Rodger and Anne. . . . Edward warned me, he told me about you, he warned me, he actually warned me about you and Cilla Hood and I laughed at him and said Neddie, don't be silly and melodramatic. . . . Why couldn't I just have believed Ned when he told me but I said oh no, he and Cilla are just old friends, Rodger's known Max

Hood forever . . . and Edward was right about you, right about you all along . . ."

Godwin sat in front of the open window with the warm night breeze rustling the plane trees of Berkeley Square. He was systematically, slowly, calmly drinking a bottle of E'Dradour single malt. He was also systematically charting the peculiar bits and pieces of information which had suddenly begun accumulating. He wondered, as the scotch wafted its happy way into his brain, laying waste to God only knew how many little gray cells—he wondered if he'd forgotten anything important as he'd made his list.

First, the most recent curiosity—Edward Collister, known affectionately as Ned by his sister Anne. How could Edward have warned Anne about him and Cilla? How could he have known? *Nobody* knew. Not even a creature with elaborate antennae, not even Lily Fantasia, who had been urging Rodger to pursue Anne herself just before the mission to Beda Littoria. Nobody had known but Monk. And, apparently, poor, exhausted Edward Collister. How had he found out? Did it matter? Was it something he made up? But why? Why tell Anne? To protect her? That was the problem with questions. Scotch seemed to make them multiply.

Second, someone *had* tried to kill him. Monk hadn't addressed that question at all. But before Godwin had left Monk's *pied-à-terre* that night Monk had sworn that nobody had been sent to kill him. "Really, old chap." He'd laughed. "Perish the thought. If it had been one of Special Executive's lads you'd be dead and we wouldn't be having this charming conversation. You'll just have to believe me, Rodger. I wouldn't lie to you."

"You're the one who told me PRAETORIAN was a piece of cake, Monk. That was a lie."

"That was a mistake. Something else entirely."

If Monk happened to be telling the truth, then who had tried to kill him?

Third, Monk had used him as a decoy. That was the good news. But there was a spy. That was the bad news. But they knew his code name. Pangloss. That was good news. But they didn't know who Pangloss was. That was more bad news. Now, Pangloss . . . If Pangloss thought they believed he, Godwin, were the guilty party, would that make Pangloss relax? Did Pangloss know about Godwin? How could they be sure he did? They didn't know who Pangloss was . . . and they didn't know the answer to the biggest question of all: How did Pangloss know about PRAETORIAN?

He looked at the last item on his list.

Cilla.

Why wouldn't she answer his calls?

The telephone rang.

It was Jack Priestley.

"I've been wanting to talk with you," Godwin said.

"I'm at Brat's. In the smoking room. Come down for a drink. I've picked up an odd bit of information. I'd better pass it on."

When Godwin arrived Priestley was scrunched down in an old, deep club chair. He'd had several drinks and was good-humored volubility itself. He was not alone. "Rodger," Priestley grumbled, "do sit down and stop this constant looming. You know Stefan Lieberman."

"Of course. How are you, Lieberman?"

"Quite foul, now that you ask. And you?"

"Fouler, if possible. I've been drinking."

"So have we," Priestley said, "and I doubt very much if we've finished yet." He motioned to one of the ancient, jacketed retainers who nodded and brought fresh whiskies.

"To ultimate victory," Lieberman said, lifting his glass.

Godwin said: "Victory," and Priestley nodded, grumbling, and drank.

"We've been through the horrors of the damned tonight," Priestley said.

"How's that?"

"Lieberman and I have come from a Ladies' Literary League Meet-the-Authors evening. Imagine, if you will, a red-hot poker slowly inserted in your throat by way of your rectum and I'd say you had the essence of it. By God, we gave as good as we got, I'll say that."

Lieberman chuckled softly, eyes beginning to overflow with laughter.

"We repaired here for a libation." Priestley was sucking a match's flame down into the bowl of his pipe. "And I thought of calling you. . . . Feeling all right, are you, back in the thick of things?"

"Jim-dandy."

"You look half-drunk."

"You smell half-drunk," Lieberman added.

"I am half-drunk," Godwin allowed. "So let's get on with the job, then."

"What's the problem, dammit?" Priestley scowled from beneath his barbed-wire eyebrows. He pursed his lips. He was a notably impatient, irascible man.

"You said you had something to tell *me*."

"Yes, yes, I did tell you that."

"Well, J.B.?"

"Remember that I warned you about Vardan and his crew? I told you they'd turn on you; you're a resource they don't mind wasting. But while they are wasting time with you they're also looking for a Nazi spy . . . well, they've almost got him."

"Really?" Godwin felt as if he were losing feeling in his limbs. It was rather a pleasant feeling. Like floating away.

"Candide," Priestley said, winking. "Code name. Candide."

Lieberman was driving a car he'd borrowed. He made his way unsteadily from the front door of Brat's to the car, flung open a rear door. "Three men in a boat," he said, laughing. "I'll drive you gentlemen home."

"Albany," Priestley muttered. "Not far."

"And Berkeley Square for me."

"Righto!"

But once Lieberman was behind the wheel things began to deteriorate mysteriously. He couldn't seem to navigate properly. Lieberman grew alternately truculent and amused. Priestley was laughing so hard he kept choking. Godwin dozed, smiling. Whenever he woke they seemed to be whirling around the statue of Eros in Piccadilly Circus. Finally Lieberman expelled a howl of frustration.

"Don't worry about Berkeley Square," Godwin said soothingly. "Really. I can walk if you'd just let me out."

"Ten pounds—" Priestley sighed, "says you can't walk across the street without falling down."

In the end Lieberman pulled over in Jermyn Street and stopped the car. "I can go no further. You bastards are on your own. That goddamn Eros thing . . . everywhere I went there was that goddamn Eros thing . . . it was following me, sneaking around after me . . . it's all so bloody English."

Sometime later they sat like the three monkeys at the curbside.

Godwin was staring into space, seeing nothing. Something prodded his brain and he turned to Priestley. "Jack?"

"Hark! Someone calls my name!" The dourest of gazes turned to survey Godwin.

"Not Candide."

"Candide, I say. And they're closing in."

Lieberman said: "No matter where I went, there it was. That awful statue. Let me assure you, I am the soul of sobriety. That statue was moving. Following me."

"Pangloss. That's the code name. Dr. Pangloss. He's *in Candide*—"

"Don't presume to tell me about *Candide*! I know who Pangloss is, you idiot!"

"Where did you hear about Pangloss?"

"Hear about him? I've read the book you fool!"

"No, I mean the spy Pangloss. You heard about him?"

"My God, I *am* J. B. Priestley. I am not in the dark, you know. I hear things. People tell me things."

"Who is Pangloss?"

"You just told me, Godwin—you must be losing your grip! He is Candide's friend, adviser, teacher—"

"No," Godwin said patiently, "who is the spy called Pangloss?"

"How should I know?" Priestley winked broadly. "I've heard it could be you!" Then he very slowly pitched over into the gutter and went to sleep.

CHAPTER 25

He came back to the flat on an August evening and found in his mail a note from Clothilde Devereaux, whose name alone always brought the past flooding back, down the passageways of mind and memory. Sitting at the Parisian cafés on warm summer nights, bringing her bouquets of bright flowers, feeling her body enclosing him and draining him, laughing with her and watching her dance and feeling a pain he couldn't admit when he knew she was with Clyde or with one of her clients. Clothilde Devereaux wanted to give him lunch the next day at her place in Cheyne Walk down by the river. If he could join her he should just show up, and if he couldn't he should call and leave word with her housekeeper. Things were obviously going very well for little Clothilde. Godwin knew she'd come to England, but he'd seen her only in passing—once at a party at Lily's—in several years.

She was in the garden behind the house. The housekeeper led him through the beautifully appointed rooms out into the sunshine. Clothilde was wearing a simple gray dress with no sleeves to show off her lean, slightly tanned arms, a hat with a wide brim, muddy gloves. She turned and dropped the trowel, slid the gloves away, and whisked the hat off. Her hennaed hair was cut short and hung in points across her forehead. Her eyes were large and her teeth prominent when she smiled. It was quite possible that she was prettier now than she'd been as a girl. The lines fanning out from the corners of her eyes and etched into the corners of her mouth seemed to speak of things she'd seen, secrets she'd been told, a life she'd lived and understood with humor. Her lips were soft and warm and she clung to him for a moment as if pinned by memory.

"You're exquisite," he said. "It's been too long—"

"We haven't had a real talk in years," she said. "But now I have you all to myself in my garden. We've grown up, Rodger. We're not children anymore."

"No, but it's still a hot summer day. That's how I always think of us, hot summer days and nights and the flowers in the window box—"

"And I was a poor ballet student. And then I met you—you changed my life, you know."

"Hardly."

"But of course. Think what it meant to me—a nice young American fell in love with me! The great world beckoned. What a summer it was!"

"And now you're not only a famous *chanteuse* but you are obviously rich and live in Cheyne Walk! La-di-da—"

"This from a man who lives in Berkeley Square! Look to yourself, Rodger!" She laughed happily, running her fingers through the cap of reddish hair. She smelled very good. Something French, something pre-war.

"How did you get your hands on this place?" An awning from the back porch caught a momentary breeze off the Thames. Fluffy white clouds dotted the pale sky like barrage balloons. "Bay windows, iron gates, a shiny front door, everything."

"I married it. Lord Bell. I am Lady Bell when I choose to make an issue of it."

"When did all this happen, for God's sake?"

"Back in '40. Isn't it rich, my sweet? The rest of his family is just beginning to speak to us. I might add that my origins and early life are shrouded in mystery and destined to remain that way. It's a perfect match. Percy's my first lord and I'm his first exotic 'bloody Frog,' as his father would have put it before his suicide. No—I wasn't the reason for that, I swear! It's a lovely house, isn't it? Percy bought it for me, a wedding present. It's Georgian, I'm told. Dante Gabriel Rossetti lived right over there and the stories we've been told are so perfectly English. He moved in not long after his beautiful wife, Elizabeth, died of tuberculosis—she'd sat for many of his paintings and he wrote a great many poems about her. She was already half-dead when she married him and when she finally got it done he had some of his poems buried with her. Wrapped in her hair, no less. Such a romantic! Several years later, however, when he realized the poems were worth something, he had her dug up so he could recover the manuscripts . . . not quite so romantic. But, again, so English!"

The housekeeper brought lemonade, then a lunch of cold chicken, salad, wine, all immaculately served on china with her husband's crest at the center of each plate. As you ate, you had the feeling you were slowly revealing the truth.

Clothilde was fascinated by the English. Her store of Rossetti stories was ample. "He kept a couple of kangaroos in a shed. The younger finally killed its mother. And there was a pet raccoon, rumored to have killed the surviving kangaroo later on. However, his favorite pet was the Australian wombat—and, do you know, Rodger, Rossetti was a friend of Dodgson, who was Lewis Carroll, and it is said on good authority that the wombat was the model for the dormouse at the Mad Hatter's tea party!" She paused for breath. "When we have children, I shall tell them that story. He kept armadillos, too. What a peculiar man!"

"And how English," Godwin added for her benefit, leaning back in the chair. "Married. I'd heard something—"

"I tried to get hold of you but," she gave a shrug, "it was impossible. You were elsewhere. I was desolated."

"Where is Lord Bell at the moment? I'd like to meet him."

"He is a sort of scientist. He works with scientists. Something vaguely connected with Cambridge. Or is it Oxford? I can never get them straight —no, it is Cambridge. I'm sure. But my poor Rodger, what is all this I hear about you? Droll stories, amazing adventures, hair-raising escapes. You must tell me everything."

"Well, I don't know what you've heard. Enlighten me."

"Well, I was talking with Clyde the other day and he mentioned having heard you nearly got yourself killed doing something terribly daring . . . he'd heard from Cilla a few weeks ago, you see. Apparently she was going through one of her unhappy periods—you understand? Now this is according to Clyde—for myself, I never found her to be so difficult, well no, that's a lie, I *have* but it doesn't matter, does it? The point is, Cilla spent most of what Clyde described as a very trying day talking mainly about you . . . much crying and tearing of hair . . . Clyde got the impression that you and she are quite an item, by the way. And he came over here to tell me about it and he got terribly depressed thinking about Cilla and then he drank himself into a complete stupor. You know Clyde, always in the grip of the past. He never got over little Priscilla but I expect you know that—"

"Well, we're all in the grip of the past," Godwin said. "Everybody. Or everybody with any brains. It's impossible to escape the past. That's all we are, sweetheart, the sum of our past. It's all we've got."

"Now don't you get morose! I can't stand it. So, did you nearly get killed?"

"More or less. Got shot in the head. But I'm fine."

"It's Max Hood who's dead. I begin putting *deux et deux* together
. . . Are you and Cilla lovers?"

"It comes and goes."

"That must have made things difficult for you and Max. You and he
were quite close, as I recall. Coffee? Lemonade?"

It was hot even in the late afternoon. Godwin drank lemonade. "Max
never knew about me and Cilla."

Clothilde looked up, eyes round, lips pursed between a smile and an
exclamation. "*Mais non!* Rodger, believe me, he *knew!* Oh, yes, he knew.
He knew how you felt about her."

"What do you mean?"

"I knew Max quite well myself." She lowered her eyelashes.

"When?"

"It's rather a complicated story, *cherie.* Can you stay?"

"When do you expect your husband?"

"Not until the weekend and the story isn't *that* complicated. You see,
before I met you back in Paris, I was of some service to Max Hood. You're
blushing, Rodger, just the way you used to . . . well, we must all remember where we began, mustn't we? Max was a client . . . Oh, poor dead
Max, such a life . . ."

"What's that supposed to mean?"

"Max had some problems. We can be frank with one another, no?"

"Of course."

"Max was unable to perform. In bed. After a few visits he stopped
trying. I told him that men go through phases, I tried so hard to convince
him of that. And he was such a gentleman. He still came to see me, he
insisted on paying me for my time, we would talk, he told me about the
time he spent in the desert . . . I think something may have happened
to him in the desert . . . but I don't know, he wouldn't tell me . . . but
when he married Cilla DewBrittain I nearly fainted. I knew how smitten
he was by her when she was a child but I also knew he was impotent." She
said it sadly. "He was mad about Priscilla. And Clyde was completely
besotted by her . . . As soon as they'd been in bed with me, poof, they
fell in love with her! And then—that summer—Max and I were talking, I
think we were waiting for you, having coffee, you were off somewhere with
Swaine, and he said that you were in love with her, with Priscilla, too! I
was crushed!"

"Well, it was nonsense. Max was all wet. I was very fond of her
but—"

"Max said he was sure, he'd been studying your behavior toward her
and there was no question, you were in love with her, too." She held up a

forefinger, stopping his interruption. "But he said you didn't know you were in love with her! Imagine how much effort he put into analyzing the situation—tell me, Rodger, was he right? Were you in love with little Priscilla so long ago?"

"Well, perhaps I was. But he was right, I didn't know it then. It's all quite irrelevant . . . I didn't see her again after Paris until a couple of years ago. I ran into Max in Cairo. He got quite a kick out of surprising me with the identity of his wife . . . It was Cilla, of course. That's how I found out they had married."

"Now, you can be frank with me, Rodger. Remember how close we were, my dear . . . when you saw her again, were you still in love with her? Or did you fall in love with her all over again?"

"Clothilde, what's your game? Where is this going?"

"I told you my relationship with Max was complicated. You see, once I came to England, and Max and Cilla were married, Max found me . . . we became friends again, the way we'd been in Paris—"

"You mean he came to you for sex?"

"Rodger, you're not listening to me. I told you, sex was never an issue between us."

"You're telling me he hadn't gotten through his, ah, phase?"

"I'm telling you Max Hood was impotent. His little soldier would not stand at attention . . . so sad, he *was* such a soldier . . . he was very worried about things with Cilla—he meant sexual things of course. He knew his condition was driving her mad . . . She had a *trés difficile* time with Max, he told me he'd gone into rages, he said he'd struck her—he hated himself for being unable to service her, he hated her for going elsewhere, to other men, to women, he was torn to pieces, Rodger . . . he was never really sure what she was doing but he made logical assumptions—"

"But they have a daughter," Godwin said.

"He said it was possible it could be his. Apparently she was able to . . . arouse him sufficiently a few times, he couldn't bring himself to talk about it . . . but that may have been a lie, maybe he wanted me to believe the daughter *could* be his . . . Could he have impregnated her? Who knows? Certainly not the way he was with me . . . But he told me he'd seen you by chance in Cairo, he was very excited, he said to me, *I love that man*, meaning you, *I helped make a man of him*, he said, *we're brothers, Red*, he called me Red, *we're blood brothers*, and that phrase meant nothing to me, I asked him what it meant, this *blood brothers*, and he said that maybe I had a right to know . . . and he told me . . ."

"What did he tell you?"

"He said it was something that only you two know . . . he told me about the two *flics*."

Godwin stared at her.

"He told me how the two of you killed the two *flics* who had beaten and raped and nearly killed me. He said he'd never told a living soul and he doubted if you had either. He said the two of you had never spoken of it to one another. But he said maybe I should know—he said you would understand."

"Yes, I do."

"Rodger, I feel foolish now . . . I shouldn't have told you . . . but somehow I wanted you to know that I knew about it. Now Max is gone and there are just the two of us left . . . it is a bond between us. I nearly died and you, my sweet defender, my American lover, killed for me . . ." She looked away across the shade-dappled garden where the dog snored peacefully and the bright flowers drooped lazily in their freshly watered beds. She waited, remembering, controlling herself. "Then," she continued, "when Clyde got to talking about you, you'd loved the same woman . . . it made me think of Max talking about the bond the three of *us* shared . . . and I remembered how he'd said that when he saw you in Cairo he realized you still loved Cilla . . ."

"What else did he say about that?"

"Oh, he was very calm, very philosophical, not angry—he said he didn't blame you a damn bit and he laughed very softly. But he was sure about it . . . he was sure you were in love with his wife. He said you would always worship her from afar. He thought it was all rather sad and funny at the same time and then he said, *And now we've got this damn war,* I can hear him now. Rodger, I thought now was a good time to see you, to tell you all this."

"Well, it's even funnier and sadder than Max thought. There's something wrong with Cilla . . . She's gone off the deep end. She suddenly hates me, won't see me, won't return my calls or letters. So," he sighed, "I may love her, I can't help that, but will it ever be right? Will it ever make any sense? I doubt it, Clothilde. There's something wrong with her . . ."

"I have my own theory, of course," she said. "Come walk with me along the river. Danvers needs his exercise. The wind comes up this time of day, cools things off. Come, Danvers, that's a darling boy." The clumber spaniel yawned and got to his feet, picked up the leather leash which lay nearby, and came slowly across the lawn. She leaned down and hooked the lead to the worn leather collar.

Clothilde linked her arm through Godwin's as they walked beside the river. The bright sun shone on the surface, turning it rippling gold.

"Max loved Cilla," she said, "and Clyde loved Cilla, and you love Cilla . . ." She made a wonderfully amusing French face. Bittersweet but amused. "And you all slept with me that summer. I believe Clyde was the only one who was sleeping with both of us at the same time."

"So you know that, too. I'm amazed he told you."

"He didn't. Cilla did, over lunch just after the war broke out. We see each other once or twice a year, we confess things to each other. Strictly woman-talk. She was in a bit of a state, she wore dark glasses all through lunch. She said she had an eye infection . . . later she admitted that Max had struck her. As you can imagine, the whole thing came pouring out. She said she'd had bad luck with men, told me about Clyde and how you had walked in on them one day . . . she told me she fell hard for you back then but you wouldn't pay any attention to her that way. She said Clyde bungled a suicide attempt when she ended things with him. All at fourteen! Even I was shocked. Then Max spent several years refusing to leave her alone, could it have been eight years? She finally married him and he changed. She said he wasn't well. She didn't know what it was but she said he seldom showed any desire for her, wasn't able to complete the sex act . . . and, as we women tend to do, she blamed herself . . . at least most women seem to blame themselves. You see, Rodger, that's the point. She doesn't hate you . . . she hates herself—she blames herself for her problems with men, for her sexual precocity, *for everything* . . . for Max's impotence and now, no doubt, for his death . . . she will never be happy, I'm afraid, and if you love her, poor Rodger, you will never be happy either. Unless you can make her believe in herself—"

"She was so enchanting as a girl," he said.

"She is still enchanting, isn't she?"

"She can be. That's the problem."

"Danvers, we're turning back."

At the house in Cheyne Walk she smiled at him. "Stay with me tonight."

"Old times' sake?"

"Call it what you like."

He stayed. The night was warm. The moonlight shone across the foot of the bed. The window was open.

She woke before dawn and found him staring at her. "What is it?" she asked.

"It's possible to go back in time." He stroked her breast, felt the nipple stiffen. "I never thought it was possible."

"Oh yes, it is possible. But, my dearest Rodger, it is a cheap trick we play on ourselves."

"A trick?"

"An illusion. You can go back, that is true—but only for one night at a time. That is life's little tragedy . . . you can go back but, alas, you cannot stay there. It will crumble before your eyes and when the illusion is gone you're back in the present. It is so sad, isn't it? But there's no changing it. One night at a time only."

It was a hot, still, drowsy day. Heavy clouds had come in and now lay upon the treetops. Godwin went through the war news in the papers, the wire dispatches messengered over from the BBC, wrote his broadcast for the evening.

On the off chance he impulsively grabbed the phone and called Cilla.

She answered, breathless, and sounded all right. All right after a summer of refusing to speak with him.

"Oh, Rodger, I've been meaning to call you. I am conscience stricken—"

"Don't be. A bad conscience is the worst reason for calling." He hated the idea of it. He hated being the awkward burden, the duty: Oh, I must call poor Rodger, I've been ignoring him so . . .

"Well, I have been intending to call, whatever the reason." Listening to her, he flinched: She couldn't say she'd missed him. She hadn't missed him. It didn't matter to her. "I finished the picture, another piece of celluloid for the ages. And I'm rehearsing Stefan's new play, we open in a couple of weeks and there are scenes in act two which are troublesome, I'm afraid, so that's a bit of a worry . . . and Jacob Epstein is doing my bust, well, not my *bust*, but a bust of me in bronze, and I've been sitting for that. Can you believe it, he seems to be immortalizing me? One day, when I'm long dead, people will take a gander at me in some dim museum gallery and they'll think, now who the dickens was this little tart? It's all too ghastly but rather touching in its way, don't you think? We all behave as if we matter so much, and we don't, do we? None of us matters—"

"Don't be silly. It's wonderful. I can see it now. Epstein's bronzes of '42 . . . Churchill, de Gaulle, Ghandi, Cilla Hood—"

She laughed. "You have the proper perspective, as usual. In death we're all equal or words to that effect. Jolly good. Now what have you been doing with yourself? Have you had a nice summer?"

"Carrying on, one way or another. Fella tried to kill me one night—"

"Whatever for?"

"His motivations remain murky. It turns out I haven't really been a suspected spy. All part of Monk's clever plan to throw our enemies into confusion—can such maneuvers possibly work? I suppose they must—"

"Monk! Of course you're not a spy! I never thought of you as a spy, not for a moment! Incredible! What else qualifies as news?"

"I saw Clothilde recently."

"Really?"

"And Lily and Greer and J.B. and I seem to keep running into your Mr. Lieberman. Did you know he's an old Hollywood hand?"

"Isn't it a scream? One never quite knows where one is with Stefan— or exactly which Stefan one is dealing with. I expect that's what makes him such a good writer."

"And Homer," he continued, "and his succession of girls, Rakestraw . . . the same old bunch."

"Aren't you leaving someone out?"

"No, I don't think so."

"You didn't mention Anne Collister."

"Why no, I don't believe I did."

"I'm afraid you were seen."

"At the Savoy? Having lunch?"

"No, but in the vicinity. On the Embankment, by Cleopatra's Needle, and you were making her cry. Shame on you, Rodger."

It was like talking to a friend. Nothing more. He never knew what it meant. Would she see him? Who would she be? Someone he could love or a woman he knew casually?

"I'm afraid I was giving her some bad news."

"I'd like to give her some myself. I *could* give her some myself come to think of it."

"Such as?"

"It was her brother Edward the Fool who's been following me. Remember, I told you about the man I'd seen?"

"Yes, of course."

"Well, I had a private inquiry agent watching me, too. Just like the movies, darling. Well, he found the man who's been lurking and began following him—and it was none other than Edward Collister! Can you believe it?"

"But what was his reason? What did he say?"

"Oh, he denied it, of course, bleated on about things having come to a pretty pass when a Londoner was no longer free to walk the streets. But my man didn't approach him until he'd watched him several nights outside my house. Scared the hell out of him, I must say. So, that mystery is ended. A postadolescent crush on a movie star? Who can say? He hasn't tried it again and that was a month or more ago. Darling, should I come see you? Would you like that? Nanny has taken the children off for the day, some sort of fête, I have a free afternoon. Do say yes, Rodger."

"By all means, come."

"I'll be there in a jiffy." She blew him a kiss.

He was waiting in Berkeley Square when she arrived and she smiled gaily, skipping away from him, too far away to kiss. She wore a cream-and-lavender dress with pleats that swung from her hips like a grass skirt. Her face was almost gaunt, her eyes seeming even larger and more luminescent. The fragility of her face and upper body was more marked, or he noticed it more because he was regarding her so closely, but her legs were strong, she bounced nervously as they walked, she kept turning to face him as they talked, walking backward and counting on him to save her from tripping. He half listened, couldn't take his eyes off her: She might have been fourteen again. Looking at her no one would have believed she was out of her teens. It was as if she knew some secret, as if youth were hers to call upon when she chose. The bending and twisting of time made him nervous, made him feel old. Sometimes he felt as if he might as well be visiting from another planet. Or, perhaps, it was more accurate to say that she was the visitor from some other place.

They crossed Piccadilly and walked in Green Park. It was quiet, Sunday quiet. She had calmed down and fell into step beside him. His heart beat faster simply because he was so near her. He'd have given anything if it hadn't been so, but he would have missed the thrill of it. When he felt the thrill of her being near, he was free of the war, free of the longing for her, free even of Max. She replaced it with herself, her smell, her energy, her laughter, her eyes, the swing of her skirt. How did it work? Why did she erase everything else with a sweep of her hand? Was he mad? Did every man one day find such a woman? Or was it just the saps?

They sat on a bench and watched a couple of boys in short pants try to coax a kite up from the grass. There was no wind and it wasn't going to work. He told her about Monk and the man in the fog and how he'd gone to wait for Monk with the gun.

"Pangloss," she said softly, repeating the name.

"The thing is, how did Pangloss find out about the mission—tell me, think hard, Cilla—did Max ever mention anything about where we were going, what we were going to do? Did he ever mention the code name PRAETORIAN? If he told you, if he let it slip, he might have let it slip somewhere else . . . you might have repeated it, not knowing it was important . . ."

She waited a long time, watching the boys tug the kite along the ground. "No. It was one of his secrets. Not a word. In any case, I'm quite sure I don't know any spies to tell."

"Well, Pangloss is out there somewhere. A real German spy."

"You have only Monk Vardan's word for that. Not much of a guarantee of the truth."

"He had a gun pointed at the top button of his vest. It's the sort of time people tell the truth."

"It's exactly the time I'd lie my head off."

How did she take up so easily where they'd left off? Did time stand still for her? How could she pretend that nothing was wrong? Why did he want to get it out in the open and face it, while she didn't? What made him the one so hungry for an answer?

She told him about posing for Jacob Epstein and about how Lieberman's play was coming, she told him little stories about Chloe and Dilys as if they were his children as well as hers—and that was how he felt, as if they were his. Then the inevitable clouds began darkening and it looked like rain. "Let me walk you home," she said.

She didn't speak as they walked back to Berkeley Square. The bounce had gone out of her step, as if the performance were over.

"Come on up," he said.

"All right. But I can't stay long."

In the flat she leaned back against the closed door, took several deep breaths. "I haven't been here in a long time."

"What's the matter, Cilla?"

"Rodger . . . I'm so sad, so bloody *sad* . . . I don't know what to do about it . . . I was trying so hard and then it just came over me . . . I don't know what's the matter with me . . . sad, I'm just so sad about everything, it all seems such a waste."

She was biting her lower lip. Her eyes darted from his face, picked at the room like blades picking at his life, his things. She was trembling.

He took her by the shoulders, holding on hard as she went rigid. "Cilla, take it easy. Everything's going to be fine. You just get into these pits and there's no one to help you climb out. You think you're all alone, but you're not alone, you and I, we've got each other, you can always depend on me . . . I've always loved you. Remember when we first met in Paris, the day we all went to the tennis . . ." He was just talking, whispering to her, trying to calm her as you tell a restless child a bedtime story. It was dark in the flat. He'd left the radio on. The voice was talking about the war. A million Germans were attacking Stalingrad. B-17s were bombing Rotterdam. The Germans were trying to reach the Mediterranean coastline behind the British Eighth Army. If they did so, several more German divisions were poised to make a run for the Nile. The best news was that Rommel was running short of fuel. The Brits had just sunk a big tanker in Tobruk's harbor. He relaxed his hold on her, kissed her hair, inhaled her. "It's going to be all right." He touched her chin, tilted her face up, her eyes didn't seem to be focusing properly. It was like looking into a mirror laden with dust. The irises of her eyes moved like shadows. His lips touched her face.

She jerked away like someone who'd been jabbed by a live wire. She shot out of his grip, whirled away as if he'd been trying to throttle her, one arm swinging wildly, a milk-glass vase full of flowers smashed against a windowsill.

"Don't touch me," she screamed, flinching at the sound of her own voice, then whispered, "don't dare touch me!" She was crying suddenly, her mouth drawn down, her features were turning scary, a mask he'd never quite seen before. "I don't mean that, Rodger—I should say don't degrade yourself, don't dirty your hands on me. I'm going mad, Rodger . . . I do insane things, pointless, crazy, dangerous things . . . it's worse than it has ever been before . . ."

No matter how she tried, no matter how real all her emotions might be, there was nothing she could do to keep from sounding like one of her movies. Maybe that meant that movies had it right after all. Maybe the movies had learned from life. He watched her, unable to know if she was striking a pose or was swept away by emotion. What would it be like to spend the rest of his life with her, never knowing what was real?

She stared at the pieces of broken vase, knelt slowly and began to gather them together. She was staring at her hands, her voice a monotone that droned on, empty and drained and pitiful.

"I'm quite mad. Maybe it's the war . . . no, of course it's not the war. My mother always says I'm a slut, just like she was, but I believe it's worse than that . . . she was a slut, but I've gone further—she enjoyed it, I'm just—just . . . Can you imagine, Rodger dear, what I did a few weeks ago? There was a man who wanted me, he made it clear that he'd heard stories about me, he was very graphic . . . he said he'd seen some pictures of me, he described them and I knew he was telling the truth . . . so I told him, yes, I'd let him look between my legs while he did it to himself, but before I'd pull my dress up and take off my knickers he had to give me a thousand pounds . . . he was a man from the City, it was enough money to register but not enough to matter to him . . . then he wanted to lick me, put his tongue inside me, and that was another thousand pounds . . . then he wanted me to suck him . . . and then there

were other things he had in mind and I just kept adding on more money
. . . before he finished with me he'd put up seven thousand pounds."
She sniffled, tried to laugh. "I bought some shares. Oh God . . . and
then I refused to see him again. I told him he could never afford it on a
regular basis . . ." She wouldn't look up, kept stacking pieces of sharp-
edged glass in her palm. "You must get rid of me, Rodger, forget Paris,
forget the girl you knew there, just walk away from the mess, you knew
there was something wrong with me even then so just walk away, leave it
for someone else to sweep up, or beat me, beat me until your arms ache
. . . or marry Anne Collister, do anything you can to hurt me. Leave me,
tell people about me . . . oh God, I don't know why I do it . . . I want
to be like my mother, maybe I believe what she has always said about me
. . . I hate her, I hate myself even more, why can't we just die and be
forgotten, we've made no difference . . ."

It was dark in the room. He couldn't see her clearly, kneeling below
the sill, flowers and water on the floor, the sound of the glass against other
bits of glass.

She let out a small cry of pain.

Oh, Cilla, for Christ's sweet sake . . .

He grabbed her, yanked her to her feet. In the light from the window
he saw the sharp edge of glass in one hand, the raw scratches across her
wrist where she'd just been trying to slice her way through to a vein.

He knocked the piece of glass out of her hand.

"Silly bitch!"

"Thatta boy!" She was panting, saliva white on her mouth. "Now
you're getting the idea. Why don't you hit me? Hurt me, Rodger, make
me behave, make me be good."

"My God, you can be a drip," he said. "And you can stop telling me
the boring little horror story of the big bad man from the City—"

"It's true, you bastard!"

"So what? Who cares? You're no mystery to me, not anymore. You're
a drip and you're nuts . . . why am I even bothering to say all this? It's
not going to make any difference to you, it's not going to make any
difference to me. You'll still be a jerk and I'll still be in love with you. I'm
wasting my breath."

"Why don't you kill me? Do me a favor, just kill me."

"I can't."

"Why not?"

"Because you're my destiny. Such as it is."

"And because you're not a killer."

"Oh, I'm a killer, all right."

"Well then?"

"But my destiny is not to kill you. My destiny is to love you." He reached out and she came to him, rested her head on his chest.

"Why? *Why?* Save yourself, Rodger."

"Oh, baby, oh Cilla, I just can't."

"Why not?" One of the cuts on her wrist was bleeding. It was nothing. She flicked her tongue at it. He lifted her wrist and kissed the blood.

"Because it is written."

"Oh, Rodger, that's Max talking. Who says it's written?"

"It doesn't matter. It is written. It's all you need to know."

Godwin was increasingly in the grasp of two obsessions as summer slipped away that year. He had to figure out how to deal with Cilla, a way to keep them both alive, a way to live out his destiny. He'd thrown logic and reason out the window. He had to have her, that was all there was to it. She had been in his heart and mind too long to give her up. He knew perfectly well that his love was now obsessive, even destructive, but there was no point in worrying about it anymore. Wherever it—she—took him, that was where he was going. It was an odd feeling, almost a kind of eerie stillness at his center, as he finally gave himself up to it. Explanations didn't matter now. He thought perhaps it had happened when he saw her kneeling on the floor, tears running down her face, sawing pathetically at her wrists with the piece of broken glass, smears of blood on her pretty dress. In that instant all of his feelings for her crystallized—love, pity, desire, the almost mystical need to protect her from the nightmare she made. He believed, rightly or wrongly, that she would be better off with him than without him. She needed someone to stand between her and the abyss. He didn't realize that he was leaving out any consideration of his own well-being. It didn't matter anymore. And, besides, without her there was nothing, no well-being, an emptiness.

The second obsession which never stopped growing was the need to avenge Max Hood. The more he learned of the complexity of Max Hood's character, the dark, tortured side, the more important it was to find the man who'd arranged his death. He had to give Max some rest, some peace, he'd never had in life. That meant finding Pangloss. But the job seemed next to impossible. Or would have been had it not been for a few odd connections that provided the faintest glimmerings of hope.

First, Vardan had used Godwin to mislead Pangloss. It may or may not have succeeded, but Godwin was part of the equation.

Second, Godwin had been part of PRAETORIAN, once again part of the equation.

Third, Pangloss had found out about PRAETORIAN somehow and told the enemy. Godwin's survival was sheer chance. So, it was personal.

Fourth, someone had tried to kill Godwin in Berkeley Square. Godwin was important, somehow.

Fifth, Godwin's relationship with Cilla Hood had not been quite as secret as he'd thought. There were people who had known. And one of them had threatened to kill him.

So far, Godwin had seen things come to him, bits of this and that. He had no idea who Pangloss was. He couldn't force the issue; he didn't know where to squeeze the tube. All he could do was put himself out there, wait, keep at it. Maybe because he was part of the pattern, the pattern itself might eventually reveal itself.

CHAPTER 26

It was a bright, brisk Friday morning when Monk Vardan called him at home. Godwin was drinking coffee and working on his Sunday-night broadcast and the telephone jarred him out of his thoughts about the American general Dwight Eisenhower newly taking command of a secret operation in London, about the tremendous battle between the marines and the Japanese on Guadalcanal, about the terrible hand-to-hand fighting in the streets of Stalingrad.

"So, have you heard?"

"I don't know what you're talking about."

"Anne Collister. She tried to kill herself last weekend. Are you there, old man? Did you hear me?"

The bottom had fallen out of Godwin's stomach. "Yes, I'm still here." He was suddenly numb, chilled. "I hadn't heard. Knocked the wind out of me. What happened?"

"Despondent, depressed, hiding out at her parents' country home. The usual sleeping pills. Enough to put a battalion under, I gather."

"This is terrible. She's all right?"

"Apparently she'll survive. Hell of a tummyache and quite a head."

"It's hard to believe. She has everything. Family, money, looks—"

"Everything but you. Some women turn to lives of the mind and write sonnets. Others gulp a handful of whatever's handy and wash it down with gin. I don't know which is worse. Still, you must be rather proud. It's not every chap who has lovelorn girls trying to kill themselves over him."

"Monk, you're very lucky you're not within arm's reach right now."

"Well, with your record of poor sportsmanship, I'm always glad of that."

Godwin didn't know what the hell he was talking about and didn't care much. "How did you find out about Anne?"

"Well, it's a very private matter but I happened to run into your friend Eddie Collister over at the Admiralty. He was pretty well out on his feet, hollow-cheeked, an unhealthy shine in his eye. In shock—it seems he was very close to Anne."

"What did he say?"

"He wasn't terribly eloquent. Said she'd been depressed of late, said she'd had some nasty shocks lately, whatever that means. I assumed your departure from her bed was major among them."

"Monk—how do you know a thing like that?"

"My goodness, old boy, your relationship with Cilla is hardly a secret now . . . and I find it hard to believe that a decent upright chap such as yourself would want to juggle women. You are not a deceptive man, Rodger. Your heart is on your sleeve. It's all delightfully American." He sighed.

"Good-bye, Monk."

"Nothing so bad about being used as a decoy. You're being childish."

"I resent your not telling me." Monk was giving him a headache. He squinted out at Berkeley Square. Anne Collister . . . The enormity of it was hitting him slowly. Why had she done it? Could it have anything to do with him? Surely not. It was all too silly and Anne wasn't silly. She'd said that day that she'd had too much bad news lately. But she hadn't said what.

"People act quite differently when they've been told secrets. You're such an open book—you'd never have carried it off. We had to have you actively angry and frustrated and afraid—"

"But did it really make so much difference?" Godwin hated himself for being dragged into the mire again but he couldn't help it. "How would the real Pangloss even know I was under suspicion?"

"You just don't get it, do you, old man—Pangloss is someone who was able to know about PRAETORIAN. *He's close by.* He's drawn from a very small, very select group. Someone we *know* because he knew about PRAETORIAN. I may know him. You may . . . or Max did . . . or Cilla —but then we must assume Max never told her about the mission. Somehow Pangloss found out about a very secure, very secret mission. So, word had to reach him, or he had to observe, your discomfort . . . your falling under suspicion was something he wanted to believe. As far as he knows, you're still the one. The word is still out there. I merely took some degree of pity on you. . . . The idea has been sewn in his mind; now we will wait for him to make a slip. We're watching everyone. Our net is a very fine one. He won't slither through."

The village lay at the bottom of a mile-long road leading down from the main thoroughfare, tight up against the water of ocean and channel. Godwin had arrived, skidding on the slick pavement, in early evening after Saturday's cursory, uneventful sightseeing in Cornwall. He'd climbed puffing like a madman, up and down and hither and yon through the rain-spattered remains of what was said to be King Arthur's castle at Tintagel. It was really a maze of earthworks and what might have once been foundations but which were now overgrown with moss and thick grass. The wind blew like a mad bastard, the rain was cutting, and he didn't draw another deep breath until he was back on the flat and headed for the car. The rag top had developed a new leak and was pulling to the right for some unknown reason. The village looked inviting from the roadway where the wind was blowing the little red car about like a toy. He needed a pint and something to eat. He hadn't looked at his watch all day, and he was deriving a good deal of pleasure from the fact that no one knew where he was, or who he was. Monk and Pangloss and Max and Cilla and all the rest of them had drifted off into the fog for a bit. Welcome relief. He couldn't recall the last time the tension had gone from his shoulders. He was indulging himself in the moment and for that moment there was no war, no Monk, no Cilla, no Pangloss, nobody out there in the fog waiting to kill him, not a damn thing to worry about.

The narrow streets were slick with oily rain and there was no way to escape the booming of the waves against the shore and the huge slabs of rock stretching away at either end of the patch of sand. It was the beach that must have accounted for the existence of the place at all. Otherwise the coastline along this particular spot was pretty foreboding, not much of a place for a holiday or fishing. The rain was blowing off the water, the streets were deserted, the pubs were full as evidenced by the snatches of song and hubbub of chatter when one of the doors swung open.

He settled on the Wheatsheafs and found a place at the bar. Through the window, through the smoke from all the pipes and cigarettes, a lonely, bedraggled palm tree bent in the wind like a lonely sentry, forgotten and left behind by his retreating army. It was that part of England that was always going on about its palm trees, trying to convince the unwary that a warm, southern Paradise lay just at the end of British Rail. Palm trees proved it.

The pub smelled of wet wool and tobacco and beer and the saltwater which, like the constant booming, permeated everything. Out beyond the palm tree lay a wooden dock that pointed in the general direction of the Continent and did so with a dispirited sense of longing, as if it didn't know there was a war on. Godwin sipped his beer and watched the game of darts. He barely sensed the man who took the place next to him at the bar, just another body squeezing in among his fellows needing a pint. He didn't realize for a moment that the man was speaking to him, then he heard his name being repeated. "Rodger . . . Rodger? It's me. What are you doing down in this out-of-the-way place?" Godwin turned and saw that it was Edward Collister. He looked dreary and unkempt. He hadn't shaved and his face looked smudged and empty, his hair was greasy, his eyes bloodshot. His hat was wet and losing its shape and the lighter was trembling in his hand as he strove to connect it with the end of a fag.

"Getting away from it all, Edward. What are you doing here? Quite a coincidence, isn't it?" How was he going to get rid of him? Just the sight of poor Edward was depressing. The good mood—the sense of freedom— was already paling.

"It's not a coincidence, actually, Rodger. I've been following you. I had to talk to you. I've been rehearsing what I planned to say." The cigarette trembled on his lower lip. He was wearing his glasses and they had steamed over so his eyes had disappeared behind enormous filmy cataracts. He slipped them off and rubbed them with the tail end of his scarf.

"Well, Edward, I'm at your service." Someone had won the dart match and there was a loud ruckus as fresh pints were called for. The barmaid, a short stocky redhead, bulled her way through with a tray of heavy knobbed tankards.

"I had to wait to talk to you. I had to make sure I was ready. I had to get my nerves under control."

If he was under control now Godwin wondered what he must have looked like earlier. He drank some beer and dribbled it down his chin. Ash dropped from the cigarette into the beer. Godwin looked away, said: "Well, you know best."

"It's all rather personal. I might tread on some toes."

"Well, you've got me in the dark. Get up your nerve? What could you possibly be talking about?" Godwin smiled, trying to put him at his ease. It was nervous work, like trying to defuse an unexploded bomb. "Look, Edward, is it about Anne? I am terribly sorry—I don't quite know what to say. She's such a positive girl, such a stiff-upper-lipper, isn't she? Monk told me . . ."

"That's a relief. I don't know why I told him, I suppose I was in shock, I'd have told anyone I ran into just then. But we don't want it to become common knowledge."

"You should have told me. I'd have come immediately—or stayed away, or done whatever you thought best. I'm tremendously fond of Anne. You know that. How is she?"

He bit his lip. "She's . . . not so good. I shouldn't bother you with it—"

"But she isn't in any danger, is she?"

Collister frowned. His lip was ragged from chewing. He looked into the beer, saw the ash floating, drank some anyway. "No, she's in no danger this time. But I'm terribly afraid she'll try again. She's horribly depressed. She won't talk about it."

"Look, if I'm responsible in any way, if anything I said or did pushed her over the edge—well, I feel like hell about it. But I tried to be gentle. Maybe I failed. I had no idea she'd take it so—" He couldn't seem to stop apologizing but what the hell had Collister been doing watching Cilla?

"Look, Godwin, don't blame yourself. You didn't hand her the pills, you didn't betray her and make her life a misery—did you?" A crooked grin flickered across Collister's face.

"I swear I didn't. I may have been clumsy, I may have been insensitive. But I never misled her, Edward, I promise you that. I never told her anything and then failed to deliver the goods."

"No, I'm sure you didn't. Not your style at all, is it, Rodger? You're not a duplicitous bloke—I'd never accuse you of that. But it's an old country, we're an old race, and there's duplicity all around you. Count on it." He ground the butt out in a large ashtray, watched the last smoke curl away. There was sweat dimpling his forehead. He finally took off his wet brown hat and laid it on the bar. His hair was plastered to his head. "Anne had a helluva lot on her mind lately . . . she's like you, not duplicitous. Confront her with treachery and her faith in life comes apart."

"Yes, she mentioned something about having had her share of bad news lately."

Collister's eyes flared, burned for a moment. "Did she mention me?"

"You? No, no, not you. Except that she was worried about how hard you were working, how you seemed to be pushing yourself too hard. She was worried about your health—the war was taking such a toll on you—"

Collister laughed harshly, wiped his forehead with his scarf. "That's ripe, really, that's quite good. She was right, God knows. Right to be worried . . . the thing is, you see, Godwin old chum, is that I've gone round the twist—"

Someone had begun singing "The White Cliffs of Dover" and one of the darts players was adding obscene lyrics to much applause. "What are you saying?"

Collister moved closer, nearer Godwin's ear. "I'm saying I think I've gone quite mad. Overwork, looking for answers . . . My morality has been driven through my heart, my brain, like a stake. I'm wriggling." He pointed past the singers. "Let's sit over there. A quiet corner. I can't take this din."

Godwin followed him, wondering if he looked like Dr. Freud. Everybody came to him and told him they were nuts. He was close to having enough of it but there was something about Collister that frightened him. In Cilla's eyes there had been a kind of wild sorrow; in Edward Collister's there was a light of glinting madness. But what the devil had it to do with him? What was this business of following him across the countryside on a preposterous chase?

In the corner behind the fireplace it was dark and quiet. They slid into the nook beneath cobwebs arching overhead against the darkened stones of the chimney. "What do you mean, Edward? You're not making much sense. What about your morality? We're both too tired for riddles. Now, why the hell did you follow me all the way down here?"

"But that's all there is, don't you see it? That's all this war is . . . that's all life is—one bloody goddamn riddle after another and none of them makes any sense. Haven't you noticed all this? Haven't you been paying attention? Nothing is what it is supposed to be—nothing is what it has always been before. I sit there, all through the night, can't sleep anymore, wondering why none of the answers I learned about life—how to live life, how to behave—are right anymore? What's happened? Everything is wrong. Everything is so confused, one doesn't know where one stands anymore . . ." He leaned forward in the exaggerated pose of one confiding the truth of a great conspiracy. "It all began to go wrong—in fact everything began to go jolly crazy—when I learned about Coventry . . . the bombing of Coventry, that's what did it for me . . . It was none of my business, really, there was no way I was supposed to find out. But I did and I've had no peace since—"

"Look, it was a terrible thing, Edward. The bombing of innocents—and this is a war. What do you expect from Hitler? There's no riddle in that. Evil is evil and we're pretty used to it by now, aren't we?"

"No, no, no, I'm not talking about that. Damn, you've got to listen to me!" He wiped his scarf across his forehead again and sipped the beer. He blew out a gust of pent-up frustration. "No, I mean the truth about Coventry. Hasn't a damn thing to do with Hitler. Evil Hitler—that was the old world I understood. Coventry—that was when the unanswerable riddles began. Now *that* was a riddle . . . and young Master Collister came face to face with real Evil . . . and you know what it was, Rodger? It was not knowing what the hell to do!" He shook another cigarette out onto the tabletop, picked it up, tapped the end on the wood. He stared at Godwin. He had a secret.

"You're not making any sense, Edward."

"It eats me, it devours me, Coventry does." He licked his lips, stuck the cigarette on his lower lip. He finally lit it, flicked the burnt match onto the floor. "You see, it's a kind of accident that I know. God wanted me to know or I wouldn't have been put in that position—God, Rodger, remember Him? He put me in the way of the knowledge—that stands to reason, it's obvious. But He didn't tell me what the hell to do about it! I'm not crazy so far, am I?"

"No, not if you accept the existence of God, Edward—"

"But you do, surely?"

"Sure, sure. Why not?"

"Well, He must exist. He has to exist. There is so much evil in the world, there must be a God. A counter-balance to the evil. The existence of evil is proof of God's existence, I'm sure of that. I read that somewhere and it made a great impression on me."

"Calm down, Edward. Just relax. Keep your voice down. You were going to tell me about Coventry."

"Yes, well, normally I'd never have known about it but I got mixed up with these cipher chaps, they put me in charge of these blokes, just filling in, it was just purest chance . . . and that's how I found out about Coventry. All a mistake on the surface, a coincidence, but there's no such thing as coincidence—am I right? I read that somewhere, too. Every coincidence was meant to happen. No, I personally was meant to find out about Coventry . . . but I can't understand *why!* What am I supposed to do? What does God expect of me? Is He offering me some way out of my problems? But how? I'm lost, Rodger—"

"Tell me about Coventry. What did the cipher boys tell you? What's bothering you?"

"The code, of course! They'd broken the German code—they didn't say when, but they'd had it for a while. And having broken the code they knew—you do see that, don't you? They broke the bloody code and they knew about Coventry—"

"Who knew what about Coventry? Edward, calm down—you've got to pull yourself together—"

"We knew, *we* knew, the good guys knew . . . that the Nazis were

going to bomb Coventry, we knew a few days before . . . and we didn't
do anything, we didn't evacuate the city, we didn't warn the people, we
just let them go on with their lives . . . and the bombers came." He
swallowed thickly, rubbed his tired eyes. "So the bloody Germans
wouldn't know we had their codes, we knew what they were doing . . .
those people died but we didn't let the Nazis know we had their codes
. . . Did you know all this, Rodger?"

"No. I didn't know."

"It was a decision made at the highest levels. You understand me?"

"Highest levels."

"The PM. His closest advisers. You know."

"Vardan?"

"Sure. Vardan, God only knows who else. It was decided to let them
go ahead with the bombing." He sighed, staring. "And from that time, my
friend, I began to lose my sense of navigation. Where was I? What was
right and what was wrong? What was good and what was evil? I'd lost my
bearings . . . my sextant had been swept overboard, it was a dark and
starless night and I was lost. And then I began to ask myself the most
horrible question of all. Was anything good? If *they* were evil and *we* were
evil . . . where was good? I lost hope." He lit another cigarette from the
butt of the one that had burned down. "That's when I began to go quite
mad . . . and Anne knew it, of course. There was no hiding it from her,
she knew me too well. She wasn't all that worried about my being over-
worked—that may have been what she told you, but it's a laugh. She was
getting the idea that I was heading for Colney Hatch or Bedlam, double
time. What do you think of that, Godwin? You were sleeping with my
sister and she was in love and she knew I was going nuts . . . Imagine
poor Anne. Very ambivalent position, what?"

"Is this all true, Edward? And what do you mean, you were going
crazy? Fatigued . . . confused . . . exhausted—hell, join the club.
You're not crazy, Edward. You've just grasped the seriousness of the situation. But are you absolutely sure about the Coventry thing?"

"Oh, take it as read, old man. And after that—now this is the part I
want to tell you, just you, you're the only one—after that is when I began
to lose track of things. I'd lose pieces of time. I began to drink and when
morning came I wouldn't remember the night, where I'd been . . . I was
thinking about all of this stuff I couldn't escape, evil and corruption and
the lies, the cesspool we're all swimming in . . . Look, Rodger, you must
listen to me, I'm not just some babbling lunatic." He coughed hard and it
turned into a choking fit. When he'd struggled to get his breath back, he
said: "You don't see it yet, but this is just background . . . you don't

know that it's really all about you and Max and everything. You're going to get very bloody interested before I've done with you, mate, so listen closely."

"I'm listening, Edward. Do go on. I want to know where the story leads."

Collister suddenly stood up, pushing the table away. "I've got to get out of here. Let's go outside. Get some air. The rain's let up. Damn, I do need some fresh air. We're coming to the meat of my story . . . I'm going to tell you just how crazy I am."

"All right, Edward. We'll go for a walk."

The rain hadn't stopped but it felt good after the heat of the pub. The salt air cleared Godwin's head. The boozy singing had been replaced by the echoing boom of the surf against the rocks. The moon ducked in and out from behind the rushing fields of clouds. The rain-blown narrow streets were empty and dark. Walking down along the parade bordering the stony beach, they heard the creaking of the wooden dock like a cry of pain across the hundred yards. With hands plunged deep in the pockets of their macs, the two men strode along the wet paving stones, past the handful of bending palms, lonely figures on a cold wet night.

Edward Collister couldn't stop talking. He was purging himself.

"Morality," he said, "everything I'd grown up with, all of it was out the window. Nothing left. I was starting over with a set of rules I didn't understand. I was terrified. Then there was another blow—another of the things which put the screws to my sister and drove her to . . . what she did last weekend. Money. We'd always believed in our money, the Collister money, a fine old fortune, as bankers are so fond of saying. A fine old family fortune. That's what our parents and their parents always called it. Well, that, too, has been smashed to bits before our eyes—before my eyes first, then I had to tell Anne when it could no longer be avoided. My father was the culprit, poor bastard—I can't even hate him for it. As it turned out he had steadily been losing the fine old fortune, beginning with the crash on Wall Street and continuing on through the Thirties . . . but he never told us, couldn't bear telling us. He kept up appearances by borrowing against our land and losing it a bit at a time. It was like having an arm amputated one year and then an eye plucked out the next and then a foot . . . now there's nothing much left. My father has had a stroke and can't speak, my mother stays in her room and won't come out and talks only to her parents who have both been dead for dog's years. The house is falling to pieces . . . there's nothing, you see, the Collisters have come to nothing and it's late in the day . . ." He stopped, pulled at Godwin's sleeve.

Godwin looked into the pained little eyes, the trembling lips, the mist or tears or both congealing on the pale face with its dark stubble. It was all so pedestrian, so pathetic. The man had money problems. Cut away all the fear and moralizing and shame and it came down to money. But why drag Godwin into it?

They were walking toward the end of the sand, where the beach gave way to the rock formations. There was a narrow pathway ahead, a seam in the rocks.

"You can't understand, can you?" Collister's head was lowered against the wind, one hand holding his hat in place. "You've always earned your way, you have that peculiar ability. I have no idea, no skills, not a clue . . . I'm a mediocre scientist, a passable bureaucrat, these are not ways to hold things together . . . You don't understand a man like me . . ." His voice was hoarse, carrying against the wind. "Did you know I was the one who sent you the letter about your messing about with Max Hood's wife? Did you know that?"

"You said you'd kill me . . ."

"Can you imagine my sending such a letter? How could I have sunk so low? Though, believe me, I was to sink much, much lower later on . . . as you'll see."

"But why, Edward? What was the point? You threatened my life—"

"I should think it's obvious, old man. Why, you're famous. You must make a lot of money . . . a lot of money—"

"Would that it were so," Godwin murmured.

"I wasn't thinking clearly. I thought if I frightened you I could somehow turn it into money . . . I was frantic—it's a joke, really, a bad joke. It's inexplicable except that I was mad, insane. But I began to hate you, I knew you were seeing Anne, I knew she had hopes of you, she was in love for the first time in her life and I didn't trust you . . . so I began spying on you, I watched you, I knew you were seeing Cilla Hood! You swine! I thought I'd put you through the wringer for this . . . I was going to threaten you with going to Max, I'd say that I was going to tell Max everything . . . I was so sure you'd pay me to keep silent! It was then, when I started hatching these insane plots, that I found myself missing whole days, I couldn't remember what I'd done, where I'd been, I was afraid I'd say something about Coventry and they'd have to kill me to shut me up . . . all I could think of was the disintegration of good and evil, the loss of the family fortune, your swinish betrayal of Anne and Max with the slut Cilla—I was being driven madder and madder! Anne was worried about me but she knew nothing of the condition I was really in . . . she thought I might kill myself—God, what a laugh, I'd never do that, but someone else? I might, yes, I think I'm quite capable of killing someone else because now I know there is no right and wrong anymore and besides everyone is dying these days . . . I have nothing to lose anymore. There's no such thing as disgrace anymore, not for my family—I have to have money, you see . . ."

He leaned on the railing, looked at the spray of waves blasting the rocks, catching the moonlight and exploding like a meteor shower overhead. He turned away and trudged on toward the path among the huge stones making up the cliff face. Godwin called his name but he paid no attention and Godwin followed. He had to know the rest of the tale.

"I finally went to see Hood," Collister said, head down against the wind and the spray. "I'd written the note to you but I hadn't delivered it. Before going to you I would go to Hood himself—after all, maybe you were planning on marrying Anne after all, I didn't want you to hate me, I didn't want to throw a spanner into the process—you see?"

"Go on. You went to see Max—"

"Yes, yes, I went to Max, I told him about you and Cilla, I told him I'd followed you, I was sure—"

"Oh, my God . . . when was this?"

"I can't remember. A year ago, last September, that's not the point. I made a bit of a fool of myself, I'm afraid. I told him you were having an affair with his wife, I told him about you and Anne. I pointed out what a scandal it would be if I told people, I told him to think what a fool he would appear, cuckolded by an old friend and a young wife, I painted an ugly picture for him I assure you . . ." They were climbing the path. "You must see this extraordinary view. Moonlit night, ocean rolling in . . ."

"You went to Max, you told him your story . . ."

"I asked him for money, of course. I didn't know if it was to be a thank-you for telling him or to keep me quiet, it made no difference. I told him his secret would be safe with me. He could afford it, his family was enormously rich, you see. You should have seen his face . . . *He laughed at me!* He called me a peculiar little man! Me! He patronized me . . . a Collister! He laughed and said that I apparently wasn't aware that his wife was famous for it, that she was having it off with half the men in London, he said it was in her nature and there wasn't a damn thing to be done about it . . . he said he was rather disappointed in you but, then, you were only human . . . He said he wouldn't pay me a penny, not a farthing. He said none of it made the slightest difference to him, in any case, because very soon he would be dead."

He stopped to catch his breath, leaned against a wet boulder. "Come on, not much farther. I used to play among these rocks as a child, Anne and I did. We owned land near here. No more, of course." He was breathing hard, pushing upward.

Godwin felt the spray cresting the raw teeth of stone. They streamed with water. He was soaked. His mac was leaking. His heart slammed against his ribs like a cannonball.

Collister stopped again just below the summit. He clutched at his side. "My God, I'd forgotten how strenuous . . ." His breath was hoarse, rasping.

Godwin sucked at the wind. "He said he was going to die."

"Yes, he said he had something growing on his brain, inoperable, only a question of time. He said he was damned if he was going to wait it out, he was going to finish it off sooner than that. He was going to pick the time and place, not bloody chance. He said it was written he'd die a warrior—he sounded like a bloody mystic and all I wanted was some money! Put me in your fucking will I said and he found that most amusing, he laughed like hell, and I asked him what he was going to do, how was he going to die a bleeding warrior . . . He told me he was going on a secret mission, a suicide mission, for king and country. We were in a scrofulous pub, somewhere out of the way, over in Elephant and Castle, a dark street . . . he bought me a drink, he said he felt sorry for me . . . Christ, I could have killed the bastard . . . but we kept drinking . . ." The waves boomed.

Godwin strained to hear the voice. The moonlight struck Collister's face. It was decorated with a cunning, demented smile on his thin lips.

"He told me he was going to North Africa, he told me he was going to kill Rommel . . . and he was going to die doing it." Collister smiled at Godwin, his face shining in the moonlight.

Godwin felt as if he were standing off to one side, watching himself and Collister. Saw himself tensing, saw Collister's bitter grin. It was the face of something diseased, a rabid thing. Godwin could scarcely believe it. He was looking at the man who had known what he wasn't supposed to know. And it was Max who had been the leak.

"You knew about PRAETORIAN."

"Yes, that's what he called it. He seemed quite at ease with himself. But he'd had too much to drink. He looked at me and he was awfully sorry, old boy, but he couldn't help me out. But now I knew something of value, surely you see that? I knew a great secret. . . . My money problems were over! I had something I could sell! I was euphoric!"

"You were going to sell what you knew."

"Of course."

"You know you were the one who made it a suicide mission—it needn't have been."

"That's not my concern, is it? So, you see, I found a buyer . . . But the bastards never paid up! Can you imagine that? They bloody well didn't pay me!"

"They left you holding the traitor's purse."

"Traitor? Who the hell are you calling a traitor? What are you talking about? Who can be called a traitor in a world stripped of good and evil? A world of Coventries? Is Churchill a traitor? Don't you see it? Morality is over. It's different now . . . Anyway, Max died right on schedule—and nobody cared about what happened to poor old Edward . . ."

"I care about what happens to you, Edward." Godwin's hands were shaking.

Collister's face brightened. "I knew you would—I knew down deep you were a good bloke. After all, I've taken you into my confidence, I've told you my story . . . I've put myself in your hands. My sister tried to kill herself over you . . . You'll give me some help, you'll help bail old Edward out, won't you?" He was either crying or it was the spray running down his face. "I'm a desperate man, Rodger . . ." He took his fist out of the pocket of his mac. He was holding a gun. He barely seemed to notice it. "I brought this with me. I thought I'd shoot you if you laughed at me, if you told me to bugger off like he did—"

"I'm not laughing at you, Edward."

"My God, he was a swine, Rodger—so superior, so gloriously doomed, and all poor Eddie wanted was a bit of the ready . . ." He gulped a deep breath. The gun was wavering in his small white hand. "So what are you going to do for me? Oh, please, help me out of the mess . . ."

Godwin watched himself standing there, the spray rocketing across them in the moonlight. He watched himself with some interest, as if he were curious as to what he might do for Edward Collister. What was he going to do for the man who killed Max Hood? "Put the gun away, it's an insult to both of us."

"What are you going to do for me?"

"I'm going to put you out of your misery."

He'd thought so often of confronting the man who'd betrayed them and sent them to die. Nothing mattered but that. It had been a suicide mission all right but only in Max Hood's mind. It became one in fact when it was betrayed. He'd thought of what he'd do but it had never occurred to him that it would be so easy, so small a challenge.

Collister nodded. "All right, then. You won't be sorry. I'll be in your debt forever." The hand with the gun was dropping down. Godwin took the gun from the weak fingers. He dropped it, heard it hit the stone and clatter away, fall into the deep darkness between the rocks.

"What the devil—"

Collister was not a large man. The first blow knocked him backward against the glistening rock face. His nose was bleeding.

Godwin smashed his head against the rock, it seemed an effortless thing to do, he felt the bones give way like an eggshell on the rim of a crock.

The body was limp and very light.

Godwin dumped him headfirst into the dark hole where the gun had disappeared.

It was all over.

For better or worse he was square with Max Hood.

PART FIVE

AUTUMN
1942

CHAPTER 27

On the following Thursday Monk Vardan called. He slid away from the pleasantries still sounding utterly casual.

"By the way," he said, "have you seen Eddie Collister this week?"

"No, not in weeks. I'd wanted to tell him how sorry I was about Anne." Godwin wondered if the beating of his heart could be heard by Monk Vardan. His palms were slightly damp and he was exerting considerable will to keep his voice steady.

"I'm rather concerned. He seems to have got himself mislaid since Friday evening. Or misfiled. All rather disconcerting."

"What are you saying? Maybe he's in the country with Anne—"

"Ah, I'm not making myself clear. Let's see. He's gone missing. He did not turn out at reveille. We cannot find the poor old thing."

"I see. He's disappeared—"

"The very nub of the thing, old boy."

"Well, he must be somewhere. Have you looked thoroughly, as my mother used to say?"

"Quite thoroughly, I'm afraid. Now a bit of a manhunt is underway. Haven't found a clue and he was, let's face it, one of the king's men."

"He'll turn up."

"Yes, well, we shall see. He has rather a lot of secrets, bits and pieces, stored in that wee brain. Could be useful to any number of unsavory sorts . . . so do let me know if you run across him—"

"Should I put the word out among my sources?"

"No, don't do that. This is all quite delicate, as I'm sure you will understand. When a man who knows some secrets is suddenly among the missing—well, we can't have it all appearing in the penny press, can we? Just keep an eye out for the silly sod—"

"Look, he's probably just off on a toot, a binge. He'll turn up tomorrow with a head as big as the Ritz."

"I do hope so, Rodger. Well, tinkerty-tonk."

Godwin heard nothing more from Vardan—nor from anyone else, for that matter—regarding Edward Collister during the next several weeks. It was as if he'd been wiped from the face of the earth which, in a manner of speaking, he had been. Godwin felt no guilt whatsoever but rather a sense of relief. Not triumph, however, no, nothing like triumph, primarily because avenging the killing of Max Hood had been very much like stepping on a dung beetle. Edward Collister had gone entirely off the tracks. He had sold out his country, he'd betrayed good men who had died, and to top it off he'd betrayed Godwin to Max Hood. Max, dying, had known the truth. What had Collister said? *Disappointed.* Max had been disappointed in Godwin when Collister had told him. *Disappointed . . .*

Thinking about it would send him into a cold sweat. All the guilt, all the sneaking off with Cilla, all the bloody betrayal—

And Max had known. Dying, he'd known.

For that alone Eddie Collister had deserved to die.

23 October 1942. One of the first great turning points of the war began and Godwin hung around the BBC and the ministries and made calls, buttonholed sources, pieced it all together. And he could smell Egypt, the desert, the camels, the bazaar, the cigarette smoke hanging in the bar at Shepheard's where the boys would be waiting, drinking too much and sweating it out, wondering just what the hell was going on out there. He wished he were there. No. That was a lie. But he imagined what it must be like now.

The second battle of El Alamein was beginning. For twenty minutes, more than a thousand British artillery pieces hammered the Axis lines, a prelude to the ground attack. Montgomery of Alamein—only General Bernard Montgomery as the battle began—was about to be born.

2 November. Operation SUPERCHARGE was begun. A furious attack led by New Zealand's Second Division broke through Rommel's lines at El Alamein, opening the way for the Ninth Armored Brigade. During the next day the Ninth suffered seventy-five percent casualties establishing a bridgehead near the enemy minefields. By 4 November Rommel was in complete retreat.

5 November. Montgomery proclaimed total victory in Egypt. Rommel's second in command, General Ritter von Thoma, was captured along

with ten thousand other Germans and twenty thousand Italians. So, Egypt was saved. On the same day Eisenhower set up his HQ on Gibraltar in preparation for the invasion of North Africa. George S. Patton was studying Rommel's book on tank warfare. A lot of men were going to die in North Africa but so far as the end went, it was written.

8 November. The Allies landed on the Algerian and Moroccan coasts. Germany was denied the west coast of Africa. Most important, a base was established for the eventual, inevitable invasion of southern Europe.

10 November. With the North African invasion accomplished, Churchill spoke. "This is not the end. It is not even the beginning of the end. But it is, perhaps, the end of the beginning."

The war was gathering speed, the power and devastation were growing, steamrollering everything else. When Godwin thought about the things Eddie Collister had told him—the insane Coventry story, for one thing—they all seemed so long ago. He recalled the night he and Anne and Edward had had dinner and it seemed to be fading in the foggy mists of time, one more victim of the rush of events. Like the day he and Cilla had gone down to watch the air war and made love beneath the dogfight in the sky. Like the day he'd driven to Cambridge to meet Monk, the day he'd first heard about PRAETORIAN from Churchill . . . So long ago . . . A year . . . Barely a year . . .

15 November. Half a world away in the South Pacific, the prolonged bloody battle for Guadalcanal was nearly over. The Japanese could no longer resupply their garrison. The Americans had won the big game. The tide was running against the Japanese. Their high-water mark was past, less than a year after they'd bombed Pearl Harbor.

19 November. The Russians began the winter offensive with the relief of the defenders of Stalingrad. The guns roared, the earth trembled, the river Don rolled and bucked from the magnitude of the concussions. The temperature was minus thirty degrees Centigrade. The Germans were a long way from home.

From Norway there was some bad news making the rounds of Whitehall. The Norwegian-British team of saboteurs trying to destroy the Germans' supply of heavy water at the Norsk Hydra plant in Vemork had run into trouble. The word was that nobody got out alive.

22 November. The German Sixth Army, more than a quarter of a million men, was encircled by the Red Army, fifty miles west of Stalingrad.

2 December. In Chicago, beneath the University's abandoned football stadium, Arthur Drompton and Enrico Fermi achieved the first nuclear chain reaction. Technically it was the fission of uranium isotope

U-235. The world at large didn't know what it meant, didn't know that life was never going to be the same again.

In the aftermath of Edward Collister's death, life was getting better for Rodger Godwin. He still thought about Max Hood, still remembered how much he'd loved and respected the man, still regretted betraying him and regretted even more Max Hood's knowledge of that betrayal, but finishing Edward Collister had wiped the slate clean. Life was newly fresh. He was calm. He enjoyed his work. He enjoyed the company of his friends. He was uplifted by the surge of war news.

The avenging of Max Hood's murder set Godwin free, made him more expansive, less worried. He abandoned the policy of hammering himself against the anvil of Cilla's chaotic behavior. He let her be. He took the long view. Time would tell. Meanwhile, he let her be.

Lieberman's new play had opened in September to good notices; better than good for Cilla Hood. She seemed a bit steadier. Lily Fantasia told him that Cilla was "coming round."

A few weeks into the run of the show, after news of Edward Collister's disappearance, Cilla called him and suggested that if he were interested in seeing the play she would arrange it and perhaps they could have supper afterward at the Café Royal. The evening was pleasant if a trifle strained to start. It was quiet. It was devoid of innuendo. It was, as he told Homer Teasdale, "different." Over coffee and Armagnac, Cilla said she was giving up sex for a bit and did he understand? Godwin smiled at that. He told her she should do exactly as she wished. Whatever, it was all right with him. It was her business, after all. His attitude took her by surprise and that pleased him.

Lady Pamela's health worsened during that autumn and it was then that Cilla turned to Godwin. It was her first step toward a reconciliation, her first step—at least in a decisive way—since the Sunday she'd broken like a mirror right in front of him and begun sawing at her wrist with the pieces of glass. She didn't apologize, she didn't explain, she didn't refer to any of the past problems. No one would have known there had ever been anything amiss between them.

She asked Godwin to spend a day with Chloe and Dilys while she went down to see her mother and arrange for more nurses, if that was called for, or transference to a hospital. It was going to be a rather trying day or two and there was no point in subjecting the two little girls to it. Godwin collected the children, told Nanny not to worry, and took them to a church fair in Hampstead. They played several games, visited a frighteningly bewigged fortune teller with a wart on the tip of her nose, and won a cake by guessing the number of marbles in a large cookie jar. The cake was made with real eggs and butter, was of a deliciously lemony flavor, and the thick white frosting was decorated with edible clowns. All in all, the day was a great success, the girls were happily sticky-fingered, lightly bearded with frosting, and sound asleep when they arrived back at the house in Sloane Square. Nanny greeted them as if they were back from the eastern front. The girls were bathed simultaneously, Godwin scrubbing them down with a sponge while they happily floated their rubber ducks and whales to and fro. Godwin couldn't remember when he'd last enjoyed himself quite so much. Maybe he never had. That was a possibility.

He watched Chloe with wonder: She was turning into a replica of her mother. When he looked at Dilys splashing and giggling he saw that she, too, was a copy of the mother he'd seen only as she was dying. His eyes misted over at the thought, at the realization that somehow, in some scheme of things just beyond our understanding, Dilys's mother was alive in her daughter, that something of her endured, that maybe there was life everlasting.

Cilla was responsible for both the little girls, she loved them both fiercely, she'd told Godwin that they were the same, God had given her both of them in His own way. It was the only time he'd ever heard her speak of God and in her voice it was clear that her belief in the means she was given the little girls was not open to question. He'd seen it in her eyes, in the way she dealt evenhandedly with the girls, in her determination that Dilys not be done in by what Cilla called "bloody bad luck." Watching Cilla with the two little girls was embarrassingly emotional for him. They—the three of them—tapped into something within him that was deeply primitive. He watched them and in their sisterhood he saw them as fighters, so determined, pulsing with the life-force. There was nothing so moving as the courage of women—of Cilla battling the demons within her, of Dilys's mother fighting to live long enough to see her daughter into safe hands, of the fragile little girls coming to grips with life and caring for each other and for their mother when they sensed her need. Of the courage of women, the courage of little girls was the greatest, the most irresistible. When he saw Cilla talking with the girls, teasing them or laying down the law or being silly with them, then he knew that he could not love her more, that there was no greater love he could give. He felt as if he had finally recognized the point of his life.

Christmas Eve.

A light snow drifted down on London beginning in the middle of the afternoon. The city was coming to a halt. By the time night fell, London was quiet. An inch of snow had accumulated as Godwin walked through Sloane Square toward the familiar house that was now his haven. In the moonlight the square seemed paved with diamonds. In the street at the corner behind the house the shape of the unexploded bomb that had fallen during the Blitz and been judged safe was growing a halo of snow.

There were no guests for Christmas Eve. Godwin, Cilla, Chloe, Dilys, and Nanny. Family. A fire was burning in the kitchen fireplace. It made the room snug. They'd been saving up rationed staples and there was a good deal of baking going on, and the smell of ginger and cinnamon and apple pie permeated each breath. The girls in their nightgowns and robes were helping to roll out dough and then cut and decorate Christmas cookies in the shapes of camels and trees and Father Christmas himself, of course. A goose and a brace of very large chickens were keeping in the icebox. There was Christmas music on the BBC.

The girls were laughing and yet very serious about their cookie-making duties, blotched with flour, their cheeks rosy, paying close attention to Cilla, who encouraged them, demonstrated several techniques, told them that even the misshapen, strangely decorated runts of the cookie litter were beautiful, maybe the most beautiful of all. Godwin tried to join in and made a mess of things, and the women, all of them, laughed at him and teased him and when he pretended to hurt feelings Chloe and Dilys hugged and kissed him until he solemnly promised that they'd made him feel better.

When the kitchen jobs were done, they all went into the parlor and finished decorating the tree with cookies on strings and Nanny brought in hot chocolate and some more cookies and stayed to talk about the various joys of the season. She, Nanny, told about her childhood Christmases in the West Riding of Yorkshire and how one Christmas she learned to skate on a frozen pond, her father, who was a man in the woolen trade, revealing considerable expertise on the ice much to his daughter's surprise. Cilla asked Godwin to tell them about his Christmases in Iowa as a boy and the girls listened spellbound as he told them of the snow four and five feet deep and the huge roasted turkeys weighing twenty-five pounds and his first two-wheeler bike under the tree with a ribbon tied round the handlebars and tobogganing down Bunker Hill and sneaking down the stairs on Christmas morning when it was cold in the house and the grandfather clock on the landing was ticking loudly, tiptoeing to the tree to see if Santa Claus had put in an appearance. He told them about one Christmas dinner during which his father, after carving the turkey, had been summoned to deliver Mrs. Anderson's twin boys, and when he'd gotten back to the house everyone—twenty people, aunts and uncles and grandparents

—was still at the table, not yet finished. He told them how his mother had warmed up a complete dinner for his father and dinner had just gone on and on until he, Rodger, had been excused to go play with his first type-writer and how he'd written his first story which he'd called "The Doctor's Christmas, 1917." He'd been twelve years old then and for some reason Chloe and Dilys hadn't moved a muscle while he'd told them the story, just sat there listening wide-eyed, their mouths slightly ajar. Finally Chloe announced, "I want a typewriter when I'm twelve. Mummy, do you think Father Christmas might bring me one?" Cilla said she thought there was a very good chance of Father Christmas doing precisely that. After a consid-erable pause, Dilys, who had a natural flair for comedy, heaved a mighty sigh and toppled over, sound asleep, smiling. Cilla, who had a beautiful, low voice, sang "Silent Night" and "Good King Wenceslaus" while they carried the children up and tucked them in their beds. Godwin could almost see the visions of sugar plums and Father Christmas dancing in their sleepy heads.

Downstairs, he was putting on his coat. Cilla was watching him, arms crossed, a faint smile on her jutting lips. Her hair was so thick it looked as if it had been carved and polished.

"Christmas suits you," she said.

"It's good to have a nice Christmas. The kids will remember it."

"I know. Some day, along about 1975, they'll be telling their children about tonight, the Christmas of 1942 during the famous war. They make everything worthwhile, don't they? There's such hope for them. Perhaps they won't muck things up."

"There's always hope, I guess. If there wasn't any hope, I suppose there wouldn't be a war. Nobody would care. But we care about the kids. They're the hope of us all. Sorry, I'm sounding like one of my maudlin holiday broadcasts."

"Rodger . . . I've put you through too much."

He was surprised. He shrugged. He had no idea what to say.

She went on: "It's important that you be aware that I know it."

"Why is that, Cilla?"

"Because I'm afraid I might lose you."

"Ah."

"I love you so much, Rodger, that when I think about it and my guard is down . . . I'm afraid I'll faint. I watched you with Chloe and Dilys . . . I thought my heart would stop."

"I know," he said. "I feel that way when I watch you with them . . ."

"It's all changing," she said. "I'm not sure I understand it. But it's changing."

"I know." The clock in the hallway struck midnight. He kissed her softly, whispered in her ear: "Merry Christmas, Cilla."

She made a small sound, put her hand to her mouth, nodded silently, and wiped tears away.

"See you tomorrow," he said.

Again she nodded.

He walked off into the crisp night, leaving his footprints in the snow. He walked all the way back to Mayfair. It was a wonderful night.

Merry Christmas, Mr. Godwin, and God rest ye, merry gentlemen.

Christmas Day.

Gray, cold, dry snow blowing along the window ledge and across Berkeley Square. In the dark early morning, Godwin stayed in bed drinking coffee and correcting galleys of his new book. Finally he bathed and dressed and drank more coffee and set off for Sloane Square, arriving shortly before noon. The goose and the chickens were in the ovens, Cilla was upstairs getting dressed, and the girls were excitedly shaking the brightly wrapped packages Godwin and Cilla had been sneaking into the house for weeks, urging their mother to hurry up. "He's here, he's here."

Cilla came down wearing a bright red dress, the girls in dark green and white lacey bits. Nanny came in from the kitchen, leaving the dinner to fend for itself for the moment. The children were nearly bursting with the effort to stay calm, opening the gifts, dolls and puzzles and games and books and clothing, each item somehow precisely the one that had been hoped for. Father Christmas was clearly a hero.

Dilys, still so young, had developed a runny nose and Chloe seemed to enjoy taking responsibility for her. Godwin commended her for her attentiveness and Chloe fixed him solemnly with her eyes the color of her mother's, cafe au lait, said: "I am only litt-o, you know." That was how she said it: *litto*. "But Dilys is even litto-er. And sometimes she forgets to use her hankie. She's very good, though, isn't she? Even though she is so litt-o . . ."

Soon the carpet around the tree was obscured by the wrapping paper, and Nanny was burning it among the slabs of coal in the fireplace. While the girls played happily with their dolls and exclaimed over the pictures in the books, Cilla gave Nanny her gifts, a sweater and an exquisite tortoiseshell comb set and a leatherbound scrapbook she'd filled with photographs of Chloe and Dilys. Nanny gave Cilla a set of tea towels and pillow cases she'd painstakingly embroidered. Then, after Cilla hugged her impulsively, as she might have hugged a mother and as she'd never hugged Lady Pamela, Nanny went back to the kitchen which smelled much like heaven ought to smell. Godwin noticed yet again how often his thoughts turned maudlin and weepy these days. Middle-age at hand. And falling in love. Really in love. He sounded like a sophomore to himself but, then, he knew he wasn't a sophomore and hadn't been a sophomore for some time now. Maybe maudlin thoughts, within reason, were good things. Maybe they meant you were having a rite of passage or some damn thing and if so it was about time, goddammit.

Cilla came across the room and knelt beside his chair where the girls were playing, trading dolls, books, clothing, squealing. "I'm such a fool about presents, I didn't know what to get you. So this was what I decided on." She handed him the package.

It was the most beautiful fountain pen he'd ever seen. Worked gold, his initials engraved on the barrel. It glowed warmly in his hand. He'd never seen anything like it. A Montegrappa from before the war.

"Do you like it?"

"Yes. It's quite . . . it's something." He opened the small card where she'd written: *Let's hope it contains all the words in just the right order. C.* She beamed while he read it.

"And this is for you," he said.

It was a baroque pearl ring set in gold. She gasped when she saw it. She slid it onto her finger, held it out, admired it. He stroked her hair.

"What does it mean?" she asked. "A baroque pearl?"

"Oh, it's very special. It has a curious property . . . it means whatever you want it to mean."

"A magic ring." She sighed.

The guests began arriving about three o'clock. The house filled with friends, most of them Godwin's as well as Cilla's, with a sprinkling of movie and theater orphans with no place to go for Christmas Day. Champagne flowed, there was singing and laughter and it was, Godwin thought, more like a scene from a film than something from real life, but it was all right, it was good behavior, it was a shielded moment, away from the war.

Lily and Greer, of course, and Homer and Stefan Lieberman, Robby Bascomb, a swirl of faces and voices and toasts. If it had been a movie it would have been a loving montage, lingering on moments unique to Christmas. Carving the goose, an actor reading from *A Christmas Carol* to people seated quietly around the tree, Godwin finding a moment to stand alone in Max's study thinking of the man he'd avenged and whose place he was taking, Santo Colls and Peter Cobra arriving with fresh magnums of champagne, snow sifting quietly past the window . . .

Clyde Rasmussen arrived late and stayed late, observing that he was feeling very mortal lately and laughing about it, stretching out on a couch with his head in Cilla's lap once the rest of them had finally gone and Christmas was nearly over. "We three," Clyde mused, half-asleep, "we three . . . all these years . . ." His voice trailed off, his eyelids drooping. "Anybody know what it all means? Rodger? You're something of an expert on what things mean . . . No? Cilla? Somebody around here must know. How old are you, Rodger?"

"Closing in on thirty-eight."

"And you, beautiful Cilla?"

"Thirty last October."

"Well, you're both old enough—well, Rodger is, anyway. So why the hell don't you know?"

"I'm just not wise enough," Godwin murmured.

"Well, I know who knows. You know who knows? I'll tell you who knows—you remember Swaine? The editor in Paris?"

"Merle B. Swaine," Godwin said.

"Damn right. Swaine. I'll bet that old bastard knows . . . Christ, I wonder if he's all right? You think he's still in Paris?"

"Who knows . . ."

"Well, I'd like to see him. Ask *him* what it all means. He'd know."

Eventually Clyde roused himself to go. In the doorway, he looked down at Cilla. Then he put his arm around her, leaned down and kissed her on the lips. Godwin's hand was resting on his shoulder. "Lordy, lordy," Clyde said wistfully, "I haven't kissed such a pretty girl since . . . 1927." He was wearing a top hat for some reason, evening clothes, a cape. He went out into the light snow, looked back at them in the doorway. "Cilla, my dear, I tried to kill myself over you."

"You were such a rotten shot."

"Yes, I suppose I was. Only woman I've ever actually tried to kill myself over. I was thinking quite clearly at the time. You're that kind of girl, you know. Yes, you are, but I don't know why. That's the point, isn't it? Why, why, why? It's not your fault but you never let go of a fella. Ain't that right, Rodger?"

"Well, it just happens, Clyde. The girl can't help it."

"You two—what a pair!" Cilla was standing with her hand on one hip, waving their suggestions away. "Go home, Clyde! I'm freezing to death—"

"Well, I love you and it's Christmas and I couldn't leave without telling you. Both of you. You're a good fella, Rodger, even if you did pinch a fella's girlfriend. Water under the bridge, that's what I say. And you're a good fella, too, Cilla. Both of you. Good blokes, I don't care what anybody says. I want it on the record. Merry Christmas, then, wonderful party, and now I must be going . . ."

When the door was closed she led Godwin back into the parlor. They sat before the fire, her head on his shoulder. "Would you stay here tonight, Rodger? It seems silly to be apart . . ."

"Why, that sounds fine. I'll stay."

She nodded against him.

The fire burned down.

She fell asleep like that and he carried her upstairs.

He looked in on Chloe and Dilys. He pulled the blanket up and heard their breathing. They were each surrounded by their favorite presents. He kissed Chloe's forehead. Dilys was on her back, cooing softly. He lifted one tiny fist and held the little fingers to his lips.

For just a moment there he heard Clyde Rasmussen wondering what it all meant, and Godwin thought perhaps he knew the answer.

But in the midst of life we are in death.

Cilla was still emotionally fragile when it came to their relationship, as if during the year just past their roles had been reversed. The year before, Godwin had been brought back to England more dead than alive, hanging in a kind of suspended animation between past and future. He might have gone either way. Now it was Cilla's turn. Grappling with her demons, struggling to rid herself of them, she was fighting a battle Godwin knew he could never affect. He was really no part of it. He waited in the cheap seats, watching, but the show itself was beyond his reach. She never spoke of it. If she lost the struggle, if her darker needs and impulses prevailed, none of it would matter: Then it would be decided and Godwin could choose to stay and endure the torture or go and live with the pain of loss. If she won, if she pulled herself back, then her life—and his—would change in ways unknown to either of them. But for the better, he was sure.

The question he couldn't avoid was unanswerable: Would the battle within her ever be decided?

Whatever the outcome, however, she was delicate now. He believed she was winning, the good side—what else could he call it?—but she needed time and space, whether she knew it or not. So he kept his distance. He lived his life. He was not always available but, then, that was part of her therapy. He wasn't a crutch, he wasn't the faithful hound, he was a man who loved her but had drawn the line, had told her she was frequently impossible and he could do without the histrionics. She would have to grow up, in a phrase of the day, or she would lose him. And he would lose her. It was up to her. Whether intuitively or intellectually he didn't know, but the fact was she was dealing with the issue. Either she was growing up or she wasn't.

She couldn't be protected, no matter how much he wished to shield her, from the harsher realities.

On New Year's Eve Godwin went to a party of BBC types and left at eleven o'clock. Cilla had a performance, had then gone directly home and was waiting for him when he arrived at half-past eleven. Together they toasted the New Year of 1943, just the two of them. Much of what existed between them was unspoken, as if too many words might shatter the peace and calm.

Fifteen minutes after the new year's beginning the telephone rang.

She went into the study to answer it. When she came back he was stoking the fire, sparks rising in the chimney. She picked up her glass of champagne and smiled wanly, took a sip before she spoke. She knelt beside him and held his hand, staring into the fire.

"Lady Pamela is dead, Rodger."

The death of her mother worked a kind of miracle on the daughter. It was at first a tender shoot of a miracle but Godwin watched it take root, saw Cilla's behavior altering. The tension and anxiety seemed to drain off, as if an overload of electrical energy were being shunted away to power some other engine. She grew softer, slower to respond, less jagged at the edges, easier.

The death of her mother freed Cilla Hood from what she'd always believed was her fate. She had lived all her life believing she was another Lady Pamela, trapped forever in the restless, unsatisfied precincts of her soul, certain that she was unworthy of receiving real love. Now her mother was gone and Cilla was, as it turned out, reborn. Rodger Godwin was not a sophisticated man when it came to psychological theory; in his view, her mother died and Cilla was set free. He couldn't make it out any other way.

Cilla knew it was happening, as well. Her view of herself changed. She had lost her mother; Godwin had changed somehow. She was free to win him if she wanted him. In this view she was firmly supported by Lily Fantasia.

She did want him. She was good enough to deserve him. She won him.

It wasn't much more complicated than that.

Monk Vardan wanted to see him urgently. He had that way of making it sound like a command from on high. It was late January, an icy, windy day, hats blowing and grown men falling down on slippery patches. Godwin checked his calendar and told Monk he could make it if it was so important. "But if you spring Churchill and another half-baked secret mission on me, another piece of cake, I can tell you now you're out of luck. I don't care if the fate of the world depends on it."

"Well, don't get shirty with me, old boy. This is your old comrade Vardan speaking. What do you say to Dogsbody's?"

"Who's paying?"

"The King, of course."

"All right."

"Eight o'clock?"

"All right."

"By the way, I'm awfully sorry to hear of Lady Pamela's passing."

"She wasn't in good shape. It was a blessing."

"Ah. Well, a long and active life. Eight o'clock. Toodles."

That night Monk was waiting in the secluded corner when Peter Cobra delivered an uneasy Godwin to the table. "Rodger, old man, a belated Happy Holidays to you. I hope the joys of the season were yours." He waved Peter away. "Strong spirits, the strongest." Cobra bowed imperceptibly. Once Godwin was seated, Vardan fixed him with a twinkling eye slightly magnified by the monocle. "My spies tell me that you and your lady-love are as one. May I say how happy I am to hear it?"

"May I say it's none of your goddamned business?"

"Ah, same old Rodger. But of course you may say anything you like. You harbor a grudge against old Monkton, I see. My advice is, rise above it, old chap. It is unhealthy. It ill becomes you. It wrinkles your boyish countenance."

"Monk, what was so urgent?"

Drinks came, a pâté.

"You recall Brother Collister? He who disappeared, gave us the slip?"

Godwin felt his hair prickling in an attempt to stand up. "Yes, of course, I remember. Don't tell me he's shown up at his desk?" He could barely get the words out, a very bad actor indeed. What if, in fact, Collister hadn't died? Was it possible? Of course it was *possible.* Maybe he'd been revived by the cold water, maybe there had been more space down among the stones than Godwin had thought, maybe he'd somehow righted himself, somehow climbed out with his memory a bit woozie. "Monk, you have that pregnant-with-secrets look. Tell me. He was off on the bender of all benders? Absolutely rat-assed like some of the lads at Dogsbody's?"

"Well, he's turned up. Rather a relief. We were quite worried—"

"He's all right?"

"A bit water-logged, actually."

"Monk, spit it out!"

"Well, he's dead, I'm afraid. Seems he took a bad spill cavorting about on some rocks down south, fell into the channel backwater. Drowned—"

"What a shame!" And he felt it was a shame at just that moment, a shame that the man's life hadn't worked out better.

"He's rather a mess, y'know. Tide's been slamming him back and forth between the rocks, he's been in the water God only knows how long . . . ever since he went missing, for all I know. Badly banged up, bones all smashed to jelly, flesh decomposed. It's a relief. But a sad story."

"Why do you say a relief?"

"We were afraid he might have gone over to the other side. He knew things of a scientific nature, y'know. And the poor devil had the wolf at the door . . . needed money rather badly. He was under observation— oh, nothing constant but we kept the occasional eye on him. I was rather vexed when we lost track of him—in Cambridge, actually. We thought he might take the opportunity away from London to meet his opposite numbers and try on a spot of treason."

"Eddie Collister? I don't believe it."

"Oh, believe it, old boy. We knew he was on the market with some very recent product—you know what that means." He quietly mouthed the word *boom!* and made an exploding, upward gesture with his hands. It was the unspoken subject. The superbomb. "He had contacted some chaps of ours, in the government, tried to sell us some information. It was incredibly ill advised but then Eddie was not top boy in class, was he? No, nothing to do with you-know-what." He made the boom gesture again. "No, he was rather more subtle than that. You won't believe it but he knew all about our little Rommel show. PRAETORIAN. And well you should look as if you'd found a dog turd in the soup—he *knew.* He said he wouldn't let it out to the press, doomed murder mission, all hands lost, on and on, but his silence would be costly. He tried to put some rouge and mascara on it but that was the deal he offered. We told him if he breathed a word of it we'd have his guts for garters and there'd be a treason trial, too. Maybe."

"Monk, you're telling me that Eddie Collister was Pangloss."

"Eddie? Pangloss? Oh, my dear fellow—"

"Well? He knew about PRAETORIAN, he tried to sell it to you and failed—but that doesn't mean he hadn't sold it to the Germans before the fact. He *knew.* Pangloss, by your own definition."

"Oh, no, no, no. Eddie Collister couldn't have found a German agent with a map provided by Hitler himself. No, poor Eddie Collister wasn't Pangloss."

Suddenly Godwin couldn't quite catch his breath. No, Monk had to be mistaken. Monk was fallible. He didn't know every damn thing. He was wrong about Collister. He had to be wrong. He *had* to be wrong. Or Godwin had killed the wrong man. He couldn't speak so it was a bloody good thing Monk was talking.

"Eddie Collister was no Nazi, no Nazi symp, no Nazi dupe. His affections lay entirely elsewhere. Do you know what Eddie Collister was?"

Godwin shook his head. His stomach was lurching, his mouth dry. The words kept rushing past him. What had he done? For the love of God, what had he done?

"He was a Communist." Monk laughed bitterly. "Eddie was a Red. Philosophically, at least. But he wasn't one of the masses. He was the son of a rich family, a Cambridge man. When the money was gone, what did he do? He went running to the Communists . . . to dear old Uncle Joe."

Godwin was thinking slowly. "But why sell PRAETORIAN to the Russians?"

Vardan shook his head. He slipped the monocle from its socket and polished it on the pocket square. Godwin wet his mouth with scotch. "Why, indeed? However, since the Russians have a very difficult time making water come out of a faucet or light come from anything but a candle, since they are trapped more or less in the early nineteenth century, young Collister had something to sell the Ruskies . . . *science*. Secrets of the pencil sharpener, mysteries of the lawn mower, that sort of thing. And our lad knew some other things, as well. He knew what the Americans had accomplished in Chicago in December and he knew how. And he knew how far along we were in the same race. He was putting it up for sale. For all I know, we've got it wrong, but you can be damned certain Ivan in his laboratory, trying to perfect the wheel, wouldn't know it."

"You mean he was a Russian agent?"

"Old boy, you have no grasp of these things. He was a desperate man willing to commit treason for money and his personal inclinations led him toward the Reds. He was a would-be seller. That's why we've had an eye on him. We would have had to do *something*. We were contemplating two courses of action. Some of the more visceral chaps were suggesting what they always suggest—what your Mr. Edward G. Robinson might call cement overshoes in the Thames estuary. I on the other hand, always the spokesman for delicacy, thought a very high-security asylum might remove Brother Collister from the scene . . . while at the same time solving his immediate financial crisis. But Fate intervened, Collister is no more. Presumably no harm done—unless he delivered something to a contact and instead of paying him they killed him. There's no point in worrying about that at the moment, is there? We shall muddle through. Frankly, I rather doubt if Collister's death was simply misadventure—it all seems rather odd, doesn't it? What was he doing down there, I ask you?"

"Where?" Godwin asked.

"Some little dump. Anyway, it's irrelevant." He put his bony forefingers to his chiseled lips. "In any case, Collister's story is over."

"But what about Pangloss?"

"I've told you before . . . forget Pangloss. He's none of your business."

Alone, Godwin knew he'd killed the wrong man. And he played back through that last scene with Eddie Collister, heard him telling the story of Coventry again, how the decision had been made not to warn the inhabitants. And Monk had been involved. Hadn't he said that? Yes, yes, he must have. Godwin wished he could have laid the subject before Monk . . . but he couldn't risk it. Monk would want to know how he'd learned the truth.

He'd killed the wrong man. Collister had been guilty of a great many things, maybe even treason if Monk could be believed, but he had died for something he hadn't done. He hadn't betrayed PRAETORIAN.

Pangloss was still alive.

And Rodger Godwin wasn't done after all.

Rodger Godwin and Cilla Hood were joined together in marriage in June of 1943. Chloe and Dilys were members of the wedding.

Their vows were celebrated after the ceremony at a lavish party given by the Fantasias. Everyone was there. Journalists and politicians and stage and screen performers and old friends and Whitehall ministers and playwrights and novelists and directors and royals and the most famous bandleader in London and, all in all, it was quite a shindig.

The gifts were very creative, as you might expect from such a gathering, but two were particularly striking.

Jacob Epstein presented the bronze of Cilla which pretty much transfixed the guests at the party. The eroticism of her face, her attitude, caught in the curl of her lips, was almost shocking, yet it was a perfectly decorous, accurate representation of the subject.

And Monk Vardan gave them a huge hourglass, three feet high, dating back to the early nineteenth century, nearly one hundred and fifty years before. It was a handsome thing, heavy with age and vast dignity, with a sense of the Vardans, who had commissioned it in the first place and lived with it ever since. Monk had written on his card: A *reminder to enjoy the moment to the fullest because Time is never resting but always running out.*

Charles Hugh Maxwell Godwin was born in London, 16 May 1944.

When Cilla first held her son in her arms and nuzzled his fuzzy head she looked up into her husband's eyes and said: "Oh, Rodger darling, we must do something about Eton. My father was at Eton, you know."

Godwin nodded, kissed her. He'd talk to Monk.

CHAPTER 28

In the early autumn of 1944 Godwin had just about given up hope of ever finding the real Pangloss. Symbolically he'd killed one Pangloss, a traitor, and another man might have called it a day: He had carried out the revenge and how could he know Collister was the wrong man?

It was nearly three years since PRAETORIAN had gone bust and he supposed that another man might have just figured the hell with it and forsaken the search. Max Hood seemed to have died decades before but the fact was, the man who'd killed Max Hood was still alive and well. And that was not acceptable. And it wasn't just that anymore. Godwin had become acutely aware that he had taken Max's place in the scheme of things. He was Cilla's husband, he was Chloe's father now, he was at home in Max's study in the house in Sloane Square. Having betrayed Max and then replaced him, there was a moral necessity—at least as Godwin saw things, since he was an Iowa-born moralist—to avenge him. Having failed once, the imperative to succeed was all the greater.

In his dreams the search for Pangloss had taken on a new form: It had become a cloaked figure, coming out of the fog. It had been a long time since Godwin had given any thought to the mysterious, never-identified man in the fog who had tried to kill him that night in Berkeley Square. But this one night the cloaked figure in his dream metamorphosed into the man in the square and Godwin smelled the fog and the blood and felt the bit of ear he'd stepped on . . .

He woke up, wringing wet, startled, put his hand out and felt Cilla's body sleeping undisturbed beside him. The windows were open and the curtains billowed in the breeze. It was six o'clock in the morning. He threw his legs over the edge of the bed and sat up, still thinking about the man from the fog. Who had he been? *Who?*

Cilla turned toward him, leaned up on her elbows, and yawned. She was having trouble getting her eyes open. "Are you all right? Is that Charlie I hear?"

"I'm fine and it is. I'll go check on the Young Master. You go back to sleep."

She was making a film version of the stage success, *The Widow Weeds*, and this was a rare day off. Smiling, she let herself crash back onto the bed.

Four-month-old Charlie Godwin was raising a hell of a din down the hall and Godwin was still back in Berkeley Square and the man's ear was on the wet pavement. As he went toward his son's room he struggled to banish the man from his mind and then he smelled something Nanny was baking in the kitchen and then he was standing in the doorway, having the first look of the day at the boy.

"Charlie Godwin, what the hell are you up to so early? I ask you. Hungry? My God, man, you're drooling . . . what will they say at the club? And I do believe you've already done your morning business. All right, lad, forget your dignity, let's all pitch in and tidy up your bottom . . ."

Charlie had begun to smile at the sound of his father's voice. Godwin tickled his son's chest and quite soon they were both laughing and for the moment he'd quite forgotten the man in the fog.

By the time young Charlie Godwin had been around for just a month the Allies had invaded Europe, the biggest overseas invasion in man's history, and Hitler had activated his "revenge weapons," as he called them. The English called them V-1s, or buzz bombs or doodlebugs. The pilotless planes were the handiwork of a young scientist called Wernher von Braun and an artillery expert from the Great War, Walter Dornberger. That June of '44 the Nazis fired these primitive missiles—more sophisticated, however, than what anyone else had—from the Strait of Dover in the general direction of London, landing across Kent and Essex and throughout London.

By September the V-1s had given way to the longer-range, more powerful V-2s and the level of terror increased accordingly. The robotic nature of the bombs seemed to make them all the more frightening. It wasn't a skyfull of bombers as it had been during the Blitz. In those days there was at least a rhyme and a reason to the bombing, there were targets on the ground, it all made sense in the context of nations at war and you could predict the nature of the attack. There were young German pilots up there and they were risking their lives. There was a human factor. Not so with the rockets. There was no risk for the Germans once the V-2 was fired. No one knew where it would land. It was random; therefore inexplicably terrible.

Of the thirty main stages in London's theater district only eight remained open. While Cilla was off making a picture, crowds dwindled for *Arsenic and Old Lace* at the Strand, *The Last of Mrs. Cheyney* at the Savoy, and *Blithe Spirit* at the Duchess. More and more children were being evacuated to the countryside for safety's sake. Cilla had sent Nanny to Stillgraves with Chloe and Dilys shortly before the birth of Charlie. Then she and Godwin took their newborn son there for July and August. Leaving the girls behind with Nanny number two, they returned to London in September with Nanny and Charlie for a couple of weeks as Cilla began her film work, but the beginning of the V-2 onslaught unnerved Cilla on behalf of her son, so back Charlie and Nanny went to Stillgraves. It was a hectic period, but somehow they were all so sure they would win through in the end. Cilla and Godwin had found trust and happiness. The children were healthy. The war was being won. They would all make it through.

But still there was no ignoring the constant threat of the V-2s. They might arrive by day or night. But arrive they would, there was no doubt of that. Professionally speaking, the rocket attacks had been good copy for Godwin. Otherwise, they were a constant worry.

Priestley asked Godwin by his Albany flat for a nightcap late one evening in October. He was drinking whisky. His feet were propped on a footstool before the fire. He was grinning like an overage, very cynical cherub, puffing on one of his stubby black pipes. "Pull up a chair, pour a drink. Time for a chinwag."

Along about midnight with chimes booming across the city, Priestley poured himself another drink and handed the bottle to Godwin. "I understand your lady-wife is making a new picture, working with the Lieberman chap again. What do you make of him?"

"What's to make of him? I never know about Europeans. Different points of reference. I never know what they're *thinking*."

"Well, we're talking about an old culture. Persecuted, driven from place to place, needing to depend on themselves to survive. Lieberman, now he's quite a bright chap. Lots of animal energy. Quite a lady's man." Puff, puff. "But then you know that."

Priestley sat on the footstool and poked at the fire. "I ran into another old friend of yours the other day—you remember Anne Collister. She's living in rather reduced circs. Goes about with a youngish barrister, good family. Didn't have much to say—the barrister, that is. I was struck by how much he reminded me of Eddie Collister. Perhaps that's why she's drawn to him. Women are curious creatures. Her mother died about six months ago and her father about a month after that. It seems to me that the mysterious death of young Eddie rather put paid to their lives. One young fella dies and the whole family withers away."

Godwin nodded. "It's a sad story." He was thinking of Anne telling him stories about her father. How the maid or cook or someone in the household had poured the porridge out the window onto a German bomb. Whatever the story, it had amused him at the time. Now they were all gone but Anne.

"Anne asked after you. She'd heard you were a new father. She smiled at that, said she thought you were meant to have a family. She was quite genuinely happy for you, Rodger. I thought you might like to know that."

"I hope the barrister is the right man. God knows, she deserves something nice."

"She said that she missed Edward, said she had come to think of him as one of the war's doomed. Poor girl, she wears her emotions on her sleeve. Very vulnerable. Her brother, mother, and father, bing, bing, bing. Ducks in a row. She must be very close to the edge these days. Still, what else can go wrong for her now?"

"She was right about her brother, in any case. He was one of the doomed. You know, Jack, I . . . do you remember Pangloss? The mysterious Nazi agent who betrayed Max?"

Priestley snorted through a cloud of fragrant smoke. "Of course. I'm not altogether looney, Rodger. It's not a thing one actually forgets."

"Well, you may think I'm looney but I began to learn things about Eddie and pieces began to fall into place and I began thinking he might be Pangloss. When he disappeared, I thought, yes, he knew a great many secrets . . . it's a long tangled story but the details fit—"

Priestley lowered his chin onto his chest, sucked the pipe. "You didn't kill the poor bugger, did you?"

"Jack, for God's sake—"

"Well, you're daft if you think he was Pangloss. He was a bedraggled lightweight, rather pathetic, but hardly a traitor."

"Well, of course, you're right and I was wrong." He wished Priestley hadn't made the remark about killing Eddie. It was the sort of thing that made a guilty man sure that everybody knew the truth.

Priestley stared into the fire, heavy-lidded eyes almost shut, a thin smile curling mischievously. "But how do you know I'm right? How do you know he wasn't Pangloss? Maybe he really was—how can you be sure?"

"I am sure. How would you guess I'd be so sure?"

"Ha! The gray eminence, our friend Vardan! I'm very tempted to put him into a novel or a play. He always reminds me of someone behind the scenes of the French Revolution. He assures you Eddie wasn't Pangloss, does he? Well, well, our Monk is so forthcoming."

"Yes, but I'm left to wonder . . . I thought it was Eddie and it wasn't. So I'm back where I started. I still want to know the truth."

"You don't say—it's all rather a long time ago, isn't it? Why not let it go?"

"It was a long time ago. And it wasn't. He died in my arms, Max did. I saw the flash of the bullet that hit me—"

"What the hell's that supposed to be? Bullets that hit you don't make a flash. They just hit you. The pain, maybe."

"Max died in my arms. I want to know who made it happen. Wouldn't you?"

Priestley shrugged. "But you're such a forgiving, pleasant chap. I'm not, you see."

"I can't forget, I can't forgive. Max and I went back a long way. He made a man of me. It's . . . it's—"

"Personal. Would you say it's personal?"

"I would, Jack."

Priestley sank even deeper into the chair and muttered, almost to himself, tamping the ashes down in his pipe. He was an actor, which was easy to forget. But he'd led the conversation all the way to this point, building a performance, and now he was going to get his money's worth.

"Say again, Jack. What did you say?"

"I said I know who it is. The bloke you're looking for."

"Ah. You'd better explain."

"I know who Pangloss is."

"Jack, it's not a thing to joke about."

"It's no joke. Information has come my way. I've put two and two together. I know who Pangloss really is. A German agent. There's no doubt, really." Priestley smiled slowly, like an arrogant child, his eyes moving slowly toward Godwin. He was a man who loved knowing secrets. He was a man who loved knowing it all. "Would you like to meet him, Rodger?"

. . .

Godwin had been on time in Cable Street and the problem was the fog was so thick Priestley might have been anywhere and still unnoticed. He finally saw the vague outline of a stubby, thick figure in a mac which brushed the pavement and a slouch hat pulled low. The smell of pipe smoke was added to the general fog. It was Priestley.

Together they proceeded to the corner and down the next block to the blurred glow announcing the Lamb and Porter. Priestley muttered with his pipe stem clamped tight. "He comes here to meet his contacts. A pair of Irishmen who are in the pay of the Germans. So far as my friends know, the Irishmen work in and around the docks and pick up whatever bits of information they can. They don't know how Pangloss got in touch with these scoundrels but somehow he did. In any case, he meets them weekly, they talk, they part. I'm convinced he's our man."

Pubs all over London were doing good business during these months of the buzz bombs. Apparently the prospect of dying in the company of your buddies was more palatable than dying in your flat hiding under a table. The Lamb and Porter, though decidedly down at the heel, was full and smokey and hot and might have been any of a hundred other pubs in the East End. The darts were in progress, the beer was flat, the patrons mostly workmen in their stiff, soiled work clothes. There was a greasy map of the invasion of Europe on the wall with men standing around it arguing strategy.

Godwin was anxious and jumpy, in no mood to talk. They sat nursing their beer in the shadows. Priestley, afraid of being recognized, kept his hat pulled low and his head wreathed in smoke. The heat and the warmish beer was giving Godwin a headache to go with his cold. He was wishing he had an aspirin when he felt a nudge. Priestley nodded at two men coming in the door. One large, hatchet-faced, heavy-shouldered, wearing a cloth cap; the other smaller, round-faced with thinning red hair and a squint. They took pints from the bar and sidled into a corner where they could watch the door. They lit fags and sat silently.

"These guys?" Godwin's idea of Nazi spies was taking a beating.

"Take my word for it. Impeccable source."

Twenty minutes later the third man came in, headed for the corner without a glance. He was thick and powerfully built, wore a belted trench coat. He stripped off his gloves and took a seat with the two Irishmen.

Godwin stared at the newcomer, then turned to Priestley. "Are you quite sure?"

"That's Pangloss."

Godwin turned back, watching Stefan Lieberman leaning on the table, accepting a light from the hatchet-faced man.

He mentioned the man casually to Cilla one evening when she'd brought two cups of tea into the study where he was working on a column. She was tired but at ease in a way he'd never seen before their marriage. Now he had grown used to it, the way she seemed to bring a kind of peace whenever she came near him. Still, the usual, momentary question flickered across his mind: Had she once upon a time brought tea to Max Hood, or to unnamed others, in this room, and had she somehow preferred it to this? He didn't suppose such questions would ever disappear: They were reflexive. He would always be jealous of her past and the secrets it held. But it was a benign jealousy: For Cilla more than most, the past was a closed book. So the questions that leapt from the corners of his mind at odd moments truly didn't bother him: They were just there, inevitable, and signified nothing that mattered.

He watched her settle down like a cat at the end of the couch after she'd put his cup and saucer on the desk. She was reading Jane Austen, *Mansfield Park*. She had taken to wearing little tortoiseshell reading glasses at the end of her nose. She was thirty-one now. He was smitten by the idea of spending all the coming years with her.

"Someone was asking me the other day what I thought of Stefan Lieberman. I didn't actually know what to say. Don't know him well enough. Though I feel like he's been around the premises for ages."

"Who in the world was asking about Stefan of all people?"

"Someone at the Beeb. Apparently Lieberman wants to get close to the war now. As a correspondent. The Beeb might send him, I suppose. Maybe they want him to host a program of some sort. Who knows? They work in mysterious ways their wonders to perform. I was thinking, why don't you give me your thoughts about him and I'll pass them on." He sipped the tea, felt the steam clearing his nasal passages. "I mean, you've worked with him as much as anyone. More."

"Well." She put her finger in the book to mark her place. "I've always felt terribly sorry for him. He used to tell the story of his family, those that were left alive, living in fear of the camps. Vienna, wasn't it? Maybe they're dead now. He never mentions them anymore . . . it's so bloody awful, people still dying with the outcome of the war decided now."

"I wonder, has he any way of finding out? He seemed to have some contact over there at one time—"

"I don't know. But he's desperately worried, I know that. I haven't known anyone who's aged so much over the past few years. I expect it's not knowing what's become of them."

"I'll never forget the night he told me about his other life—it's an odd thing, two entirely different lives, almost not touching. It's all so calculated. One life in Europe, then another life in Hollywood, then a third life here during the war. He's quite an actor himself. He'd have to be."

"The American interlude." She made a tolerant, clucking sound. "Yes, he's a bit of a ham, that's true. His whole life is a bit of a performance. I pity his biographer."

"There was something about a Mexican wife, some glamor girl or other—"

"Yes, something rather lurid." She smiled.

"Well, he's said to be quite a devil with the ladies."

"So I've heard. Did your man at the BBC say that?"

"As a matter of fact, yes, he did. Said it as if it were common knowledge. Like Homer Teasdale."

"Well, he is rather attractive, isn't he?"

"Homer?"

"Lieberman, darling. He has a kind of animal magnetism, don't you think? Like the song . . . give me a primitive man."

"What are his politics? You know the Beeb."

"I've never heard him discuss politics. Other than the Nazis, of course."

"How he must hate them," Godwin said softly.

"No doubt. But what comes through more than that is . . . well, I suppose it's fear. He seems to have a very visceral, personal fear of them."

"Maybe it works with the animal magnetism. One never knows about women."

"You probably don't need to tell the BBC man about the animal magnetism." She uncurled herself from the couch and came to stand behind him, her hands on his shoulders. "Drink your tea, my love. It'll be good for your throat." She waited while he drank. "Now come to bed. I have some plans for you . . . we'll sweat your cold out of you . . . if you think you're up to it." She whispered something in his ear, tickling him.

Priestley was on the scent and couldn't leave it alone. He was an adventurer by nature, a man who loved to pretend and felt at home with play-acting. He was so sure about Lieberman he was determined to make Godwin see it. With that in mind he spent some of his immensely valuable time puttering around with a private inquiry agent he'd known for years, trying to turn up any other evidence of Lieberman's perfidy. It took some time but eventually the effort paid off.

Godwin was coming out of Broadcasting House with Portland Place glistening in the rain and the lights of the taxis when Priestley darted out from a doorway and fell into step beside him. "Have you made up your mind yet?"

"Cilla says he's all right. Frankly, Jack, it's hard to see him working for the Nazis."

"I can think of countless reasons. Perhaps he's not the Jew he claims to be. Perhaps he's in it for the money. Or love. Maybe they're blackmailing him. Countless reasons."

Godwin nodded slowly. "Yes, blackmail. There is that."

"Well, I've found his woman. A woman. Not the sort of thing you'd expect of our friend Lieberman. Not a showgirl, not like that at all. But he visits her regularly, once a week at the bare minimum. Small house in Golders Green."

"What's she got to do with anything of interest to us?"

"I don't know, Rodger. But she's tucked away out of sight, he sneaks out there . . . when it's a man you don't trust, then everything he does is interesting. Who is this woman? Why is she a secret? Maybe she's what he's being blackmailed about . . . or maybe she's his spymaster . . . maybe he loves her and they're both Nazis—the point is, let's find out."

"How, Jack?" Godwin wasn't cut out for all of this jiggery-pokery, which is what Priestley called it. Priestley loved it.

"I'm an actor. We'll make a little play of it. There's nothing to worry about."

The house in Golders Green was a detached three-story with a crop of dead flowers gone stalky in front and a creeper winding up the bubbled, blistered stucco past a bedroom window like a broken vein. The windows facing the street were dark but there was a dim glow from the rear of the house. It was cold and wet and no one had been tending the patch of grass or the flaking paintwork.

Priestley leaned on the buzzer, his face losing its animation and settling into set ridges, a grim mask, a grim character in the play. He kept the weight on the buzzer and by the time there was a noise on the other side of the door he had become another man, fully in character. The door opened tentatively and his boot went in and his voice slipped lower and deeper into North Riding dialect. He muttered something about the Metropolitan Police, showed some sort of stage-prop badge or card which was out of Godwin's view, and pushed into the dim hallway. Godwin smelled something like pressed flowers in the cold, inhospitable gloom.

The woman was short and thin and slightly bent, gray hair in a bun, wearing a well-tailored wool dress with a heavy cableknit sweater held across her throat with a chain. Her face was narrow, her head tilted slightly like a flower about to droop on the reedy stem of her neck. She led them down the passage and into a poorly lit dining room, to a table with a yellowing lace cloth but no dishes, no centerpiece. "What have I done?" They were the four most pathetic sounds Godwin had ever heard.

"There are some questions I must ask you, madam. You are acquainted with one Stefan Lieberman, is that right?"

"Acquainted? Of course. Has anything happened? Is he all right?" She had a German accent which was thicker than Lieberman's. She was, Godwin guessed, in her mid-fifties and very frightened. By Priestley posing as a cop? Or by something else, something worse? In any case, she was no show girl, no tootsie Lieberman had stashed away. And she was no Nazi spymaster. She reminded Godwin of someone they might have interviewed when they'd been looking for Nanny number two.

"We are conducting inquiries into the activities of Mr. Lieberman. You may be of assistance. Ah, is that your kettle I hear?"

"For tea—is Stefan all right?"

"A cup of tea, yes, by all means. Take the chill out of the bones. If you please?" She got up, confused, from the table and he stood. "And, yes, Lieberman is perfectly well for the present. Just inquiries, madam. Of a very confidential nature, you understand." He followed her, stood in the kitchen doorway while she took the kettle off the boil. "All you need to do, madam, is be absolutely truthful with us and it will work out for the best for both you and Lieberman."

She busied herself with the tea things, china rattling. "Is Stefan in trouble? You must tell me." Her voice was damp, as if she were on the verge of tears. She might have been back in the Reich. You could hear the fear in her voice, someone who would cower in fear before authority. Somewhere along the line they'd broken her. "I'll do whatever you want of me but, please, don't hurt Stefan, it's not his fault, none of it is his fault . . ."

"Do as I say, we'll do our best by Lieberman. Now let's have a nice cup of tea and get to know one another. Come, come, nothing to be afraid of, we're not the Gestapo you know. Let's sit down and you can tell us all about it. Get it off your chest."

As Priestley suddenly softened his approach, the woman's fear collapsed: She wanted to be friends with her tormentor; it was her only hope.

She hurried with the tea into the dining room and apologized for the cold and poured for each of them, her eyes lingering for one curious moment on Godwin, who smiled reassuringly at her. Godwin saw it all as pure Kafka: He tried to put himself in her place, with no idea as to what was happening, how severe the danger, two strangers taking over her house and requiring tea, it had to be hopeless, she'd been thrust upon the stage without warning, without a clue as to the play at hand, and all she could hope for now was as little pain as possible. Yet Priestley had gone from frightening and official to cozy, just an old dear of a copper slurping his hot tea from the saucer. Was it, Godwin wondered, real? Or was it pure make-believe? Was it just a game for Priestley? Scare hell out of the frightened biddy and get her talking and maybe find out if Lieberman is a Nazi spy? What then for Jack Priestley? Yes, it was a game for Jolly Jack.

Jack wasn't going to have to go out and kill anyone . . .

Godwin's mind had wandered and he came back, startled.

"Describe your relationship with Mr. Lieberman, please."

"Relationship? Well, you obviously know—"

"Pretend we know nothing, that's a girl."

"Well, I'm his sister, of course . . ."

Priestley peered up at Godwin for an instant, then sank back as he jotted notes on a pad. "Of course . . . but are you working with him? Now tell the truth, mind, or it'll go hard with him . . . and, dear lady, hard with you as well, oh yes, we British, we stick at your brother's sort of thing . . ."

She made her last stab at normality, the flutter of wings before the blast from the Purdey.

"My brother writes plays—the British don't like them? It is a crime, writing plays the police don't like?"

Priestley slowly shook his head, lowered his hand onto hers, patted it slowly, like a metronome counting off the final moments of her safety. It was a startlingly ominous gesture and Godwin felt himself shrink away. "No, not writing plays—" He pretended to consult his notes for her first name and she supplied it in the spirit of cooperation: *Renate.* "No, Renate, I can't recall a single playwright we've ever actually hanged . . . and make no doubt about it, Renate Lieberman, unless you help us out, your brother's for the hangman one day very soon. We hang spies in the old country. Once we're through with 'em, of course. Spying . . . it's a jolly dangerous, nasty business. Espionage in time of war, providing the enemy with secrets, the resulting loss of life . . . No, hanging is too good for 'em, I say, but drawing and quartering's a thing of the past, unfortunately—now do what you can to save your brother, Miss Lieberman. Tell us all the naughtiness your brother's been up to . . ."

She tried to fend them off, but the tears came with a rush, a steady, nearly soundless flow down her face. She seemed older, lined, a victim of a nasty prank, thinking a man's life was in Jack Priestley's hands. It was up to her—maybe she could save her brother's life. It was a scene from one of Priestley's plays, like something from *An Inspector Calls*. It was real for her, a game for Priestley.

Poor Jack didn't know. He didn't know a man's life truly was at risk after all.

She began to talk.

An hour later she was cried out, exhausted, and Priestley had kindly patted her shoulder and assured her that she'd saved her brother's life by telling the truth. As long as she said nothing to him the authorities could keep an eye on him and perhaps—just perhaps—his case would never be brought to the Old Bailey. Priestley gave her hope and left the house with his finger to his lips. "Not a word, Miss Lieberman. This little chat never happened. You may never see us again."

They found a pub in a dark, quiet lane off the main road and sat with their pints, exhausted by the performance—Godwin exhausted from watching Priestley's remarkable dismantling of the woman's life and the careful reconstruction.

Priestley's chin had sunk deep into the collar of his mac. He grumbled to himself, under his breath, said: "I'm not proud of that bit of play-acting. It seemed like a good idea at the time but torturing innocents can never be much fun. Damn."

"She's all right. She'd been worried for a long time. Now she thinks she's saved his life. You've made her a heroine."

Priestley grunted without enthusiasm. "Well, at least we know the truth now. He's our man. He's Pangloss. You can't doubt it now."

They went back and forth through the story. It was so simple. The Nazis had his family—Lieberman's wife, his parents, some relatives—and they assured him their lives would be spared. But in return Lieberman must become Pangloss. There was a terrible arrogance to it: all Lieberman had had to go on for years was the word the Nazis gave him. No proof. They might be alive, they might have long ago been gassed in the camps. But if he didn't do their bidding, he could be sure the ovens would be their fate.

"What in the world can they expect him to find out?"

Priestley grumbled some more. "He is a successful writer, he dines out, he hears things, he might hear the useful tidbit on occasion. He knows you. He knows me. He hears things. Beyond that, I haven't the foggiest." He sneezed and rubbed his nose. "He's our man," he repeated. "At least you know who got Max Hood killed."

"But that's just it, Jack," Godwin said. "That's the fly in the ointment."

"Bloody hell, man, what are you talking about?" Priestley sneezed again. His patience was wearing thin.

"He has to be the *right* spy, don't you see? There's just no way I can imagine how he found out about PRAETORIAN."

"Christ, man, you really do want it with ribbons on, don't you?"

"I've got to make sure he's the one, that's all."

Jack Priestley didn't understand.

But that was because he didn't know Godwin had already killed the wrong man once.

CHAPTER 29

One evening in mid-November, just after dinner which Cilla had eaten by herself, one of the damned V-2 rockets landed in the street behind the Sloane Square house and made a hell of a racket. Godwin was at Broadcasting House, talking contracts and pay increases with Homer Teasdale. Both nannies were at Stillgraves with the children. When the V-2 hit, Cilla's hardboiled egg slid off the plate and bounced on the carpet, followed by two triangles of toast. The explosion—a muffled sound fifty yards or so away, maybe more, the sound of distant glass breaking, hardly a *real* sound at all, more of a sound effect—shook some windows in the house and that was apparently that, when suddenly a second explosion, much closer, blew out the back wall of the house, filling the air with mortar and plaster dust and whizzing glass and bits of ceiling. A water main broke and a geyser appeared behind the house and smoke and flame filled the street.

Cilla staggered into the hallway from the library where she'd been nibbling away, went on through the dust and smoke until she saw the flames and spraying water where the wall should have been. The kitchen's rear wall was missing and flames darted at her. She gasped in the dense smoke. People were in the street, calling out, and across the way she saw that a roof was burning. She was confused and stunned, stood quite still for a moment, then grasped the fact that there were no children in the house, no one to worry about, then she threw her sable coat over her shoulders and turned to go back through the foyer when she stopped, listened to a strange, unidentifiable squealing noise overhead. It sounded almost alive. She blinked. The lights were flickering on and off. She felt dizzy, reached out and held on to the bannister for support. The stairway seemed to be moving away from her. She looked up again, the chandelier was twinkling, the crystal bits tinkling merrily, the whole thing swaying and then the lights went out.

In the pitch blackness she turned toward the front entry, took a step, then heard the squealing sound again, realized that the house itself was crying out, heard wood and nails pulling apart, heard a bright cacophony of tinkling glass, and then, in the dark, the chandelier pulled loose from the ceiling fixture and crashed down where she stood. She'd been moving when it fell and the next thing she knew she was flat on the floor, face down, with hundreds of bits of glass exploding all around her. The weight had struck her a glancing blow on the shoulder, knocking her away from the worst of it, but as she shook her head, struggling to stay conscious, she felt the glass cutting her hands, and she was alert enough to pray that it didn't make mince of her famous face. . . .

When Godwin got back to Sloane Square he saw the fire trucks, smelled the burning, the smoke, but the flames were down and for the moment his house seemed intact, undamaged. Crossing the square, past the broken windows of the stationers, he saw a nurse and a doctor kneeling beside someone before his front gate. He began to run, past the gawkers, between the cars. It was Cilla. She was sitting up, talking animatedly when he reached her, while the listeners marveled at their luck, a movie star! V-2s could happen to anybody, you just never knew.

"Rodger! What an extraordinary experience! Our house is rather smashed up. The chandelier fell on me and the back wall isn't there anymore . . . it's going to take a good deal of fixing—"

He kissed her, held her close and then the doctor was shining a light on her face and Godwin saw some shining bits of glass embedded in or clinging to her forehead and cheeks. The doctor was tweezing the more obvious ones, careful of her face. The nurse took Godwin a few feet away. "I don't think there's anything to worry about, Mr. Godwin. I shouldn't think there'd be any significant scarring. She's in a bit of shock at the moment. We'll take her to hospital—you may ride along with her. They'll give her a thorough checking over. But she'll be fine."

He thanked her and saw one of the fire wardens staring at Cilla. Godwin went to stand beside him. He nodded at the house. "My home. Do you know what happened? A V-2?"

"A V-2 down the block took out four houses quick as Bob's your uncle, pieces of bodies everywhere. Down behind your place, guv'nor. It went off and so far as we can tell from talking to your wife here the concussion must have set off an old UXB out back of your kitchen. I'll bet it had been checked and rechecked and declared a dud and forgotten about years ago, during the Blitz." He shrugged, wiped his face with the back of a grimy glove. "Then, *ka-boom* like, you know, guv? Just one of those things. Might as well be philosophical. Your wife there, she's a very lucky lady she wasn't in the kitchen . . . very lucky the gas didn't go, too. It's all capped off now, never fear." He sipped from a mug of coffee someone who lived nearby had brought round to the workers.

Godwin said: "Have you been inside? What shape's it in?"

"Well, you won't be sleeping there tonight. My guess is, you can save it if you get the right builder in double quick. It'll need some bracing, of course. You never know what's happened to the structure itself but those old Victorians knew how to build a house."

Godwin nodded his thanks and went back to Cilla. She had lost a good bit of her vitality. He held her hand while they went to the hospital. She squeezed his fingers every so often and he whispered to her that she was all right, he loved her and she was very lucky and she wasn't to worry.

The doctors were determined to keep Cilla in the hospital for a few days. Observation, they said, concussion, some sprains, scrapes. She could use the rest, they said; she was a bit underweight. Can't be too careful with a national treasure, they said, and Godwin supposed they were right.

Once he knew she was going to be good as new he sank back into his obsession with Stefan Lieberman, trying to leave out the fact that he'd grown fond of the fellow during the past few years. He didn't want to believe that Lieberman was a spy. But he surely was: His sister left no doubt of that, whatever the extenuating circumstances. Godwin wanted to believe that Lieberman was an ineffective spy, a spy in name only. And maybe he was. But Renate Lieberman had said his code name was Pangloss. And Monk Vardan had said Pangloss was the man who betrayed PRAETORIAN. It was all in place and if it hadn't been for what he owed Max Hood, Godwin would simply have gone to Monk Vardan and said that Lieberman was Pangloss, the hunt was over. But he couldn't risk that, he couldn't give Pangloss to Monk Vardan, for then revenge would be lost and what this was all about was revenge. He owed it to Max.

But how could Stefan Lieberman have found out about PRAETORIAN? Who was his guide to the secret back in 1941?

Godwin was at his wits' end when he thought of Lily Fantasia—yes, Lily, of course; she might give him a key to the puzzle of accessibility. She'd made Stefan Lieberman one of her projects, one of Lily's "mascots." She'd spent a lot of time shepherding him through London's wartime social scene. Lily might remember something, might have a clue hidden somewhere in her memory. Dammit, he needed something more, anything to make him feel sure he had the right man . . . a connection . . . then he'd know what he had to do . . .

She was delighted to see him late one afternoon at the Belgravia house. She gave him a hug and brushed his cheek with hers and was pouring sherry at a small table by the window. Dry, brittle snowflakes whipped through the early darkness. There wasn't enough snow to collect on the paving but it was a warning of winter. A fire was going in Lily's personal sitting room and Godwin draped his trench coat over the back of a low couch.

"How is Cilla today? Yesterday when I stopped in with some fresh flowers she had a blazing headache—"

"She's all right. Ribs are painful. Goddamn chandelier. But, look, Lily, I haven't really come about her—"

"Rodger, you look so odd. Not your customary phlegmatic self. Is something wrong? What's troubling you?"

"Well, I've got to ask you to be very, very careful about saying nothing about this visit. Don't ask me any questions and for God's sake don't say anything to anybody else—I just need some answers. Okay? I need your help—"

"Of course, my sweet Rodger. You are upset. Ask me anything you like. You know where I came from. I'm a monument to discretion."

"I need to know about Stefan Lieberman . . . whatever you can tell me, really. For instance, back when you first knew him."

"Oh, Rodger," she sighed, pouting. "Are you quite sure you want to go into this? Why not just forget it." She looked at him almost reproachfully.

But Godwin wasn't really paying attention to her mood. "Back in '41, the autumn of that year. Remember, the screening of Cilla's picture, *Primrose Crescent*, the big party. Tell me about Lieberman then, you said you were making him one of your mascots. Tell me about what he was up to—who was he closest to? What about Monk? Or Max? Or Cilla—"

"But what difference does it make now? Stefan was so glad to be alive, he was flexing his muscles a bit—"

"He got around, right? He knew people, he was round and about—"

"You don't have to dance around the issue like this—did Cilla tell you? Or did she deny it? You've got the wind up and I want to know who did it to you."

"Deny what? No, Cilla didn't deny anything—"

"Well, that just goes to show you. It's not worth denying, it was a long time ago and it's best just to forget about it—"

"Lily, what the hell are you talking about?"

"The person Cilla was seeing a lot of. After all, Rodger, as I recall, you and Anne Collister were quite an item at the time. Cilla was just living her own life—"

"No, no, Lily, that was all over by the autumn of '41. Cilla and I were . . . Lily, what the hell are you talking about?"

"I'm talking about Cilla and Stefan, of course. And I can tell you it was never more than a dalliance—"

"Cilla and Lieberman? You don't mean—"

"Well, of course. Isn't that what we're talking about? You said Cilla didn't deny it—and why should she? It was years and years ago and she was run ragged with work and Max was behaving quite badly which was no surprise but it was still a trial and why shouldn't she have an affair with an interesting man like Stefan Lieberman? Rodger, you do look rather dreadful. But don't be a silly oaf—you and Cilla are the happiest couple I know, I've ever known, and what difference does it make if the path to true love was a bit on the rocky side? Isn't it always? Buck up, don't be silly—"

Godwin swallowed. "You're right, I understand everything you're saying. But I didn't know . . . while Max and I were off trying to be heroes, while Max was getting killed and I was getting shot to pieces, I just didn't know that Cilla was . . . was—"

"Well, put it out of your mind. There's a lot of water over the bridge or the dam or whatever you people say water goes over, there's been a lot of spilt water since then—"

"Milk. Spilt milk. Yes, you're right."

"And our Cilla is an entirely different woman than she was then. Let me give you a word of advice, Rodger. When it comes to matters of the heart, don't hold the past against the one you love. Think of what agonies Greer could go through if he held my past against me. It could ruin his feelings for me—and yet we have been happy and loving and we have a wonderful life and love. None of it would count for a thing if he held my past against me—it would all turn to kindling—"

"Ashes, Lily. It would all turn to ashes—"

"And for no good reason. I am not the same person I was when I was young. I wouldn't do now what I did then. The same is true of your wife. She is your wife, she loves you with every ounce of her energy. She had your child. She is not the troubled, unhappy person she once was—so forget Stefan Lieberman, forget him and cherish your wife. You loved her when she was little more than a child and you love her now as a woman. Let that satisfy you, Rodger. Do you understand?"

"Yes, Lily, I do." He leaned down and kissed her softly on the mouth.

"I understand every word. Nobody has ever given me better advice. I mean that."

"Love her. Nothing is as important as that."

"Lily, my darling girl, you have put my mind at ease."

He walked through Eaton Square, back toward the poor bombed house in Sloane Square, and stopped at one of the locals for a pint. He took out his pipe which Priestley had got him smoking lately, packed it, lit up.

She had put his mind at ease.

With everything she'd said about Cilla.

And because she had tied Stefan Lieberman tightly to the world of Max Hood. Somehow, somewhere, something had slipped. Something had tipped him off. Something Cilla had said. Maybe something he'd seen on Max Hood's study desk. A note, a jotting, a doodle.

For a spy whose family's lives hung in the balance, it wouldn't have taken much.

Now it was time for Rodger Godwin to find his man.

Paris had been liberated in August of 1944 and by mid-October—with the exception of the Nazi's brutal crushing of the Warsaw uprising—the Allies were determinedly rolling eastward, attacking the Siegfried Line, while the Russians were pressing resolutely westward. It wasn't that it was easy: The Germans fought like men possessed in what many realized was a losing cause. It was all so inevitable. Allied bombers kept hammering the Reich. At Dumbarton Oaks in the suburbs of Washington the plans were laid for collective security in the postwar world, to be organized by the United Nations.

14 October. The Desert Fox, Field Marshal Rommel, perhaps Germany's greatest hero of the war, was given the opportunity to commit suicide rather than face a trial and certain execution for his involvement in a plot to kill Hitler. He put himself to death with a poison pellet and the German government announced officially that he had died of combat wounds. Godwin was sorry to hear the news from the Intelligence boys. He remembered the man, the long talks in Paris, the oddball craziness the day Rommel was winning the war on film. He was a good man, though the enemy. Godwin would have enjoyed meeting with him in a world at peace.

20 October. General Douglas MacArthur waded ashore in the Philippines, two and a half years after leaving. In fact, over a period of a few days he waded ashore several times with the cameras rolling just to make sure they got it right. As a result, many people insisted he'd gotten there late,

that they'd seen him arriving several days after his troops. In any case, he was able to make one of his famous, dramatic speeches. *I have returned . . .*

From the twenty-third to the twenty-sixth of October the greatest naval engagement in history was fought in the South Pacific. It was called the Battle for Leyte Gulf. The Imperial Navy of Japan was fatally wounded, losing thirty-five ships, including three great battleships, four aircraft carriers, ten cruisers, thirteen destroyers, and five submarines. The United States Navy lost six ships.

On the last day of October eighteen Allied Mosquitos bombed the Gestapo headquarters in Aarhus, Denmark, destroying it, while sparing a pair of hospitals not a hundred yards distant.

On the seventh of November Franklin Delano Roosevelt was elected to his fourth term as president of the United States.

The Age of the Battleship came to an end on the twelfth of November when thirty-two RAF Lancasters finally sank the mighty *Tirpitz*, scoring direct hits with three six-ton bombs. Henceforth, sea power would stem more from the great carriers rather than the mighty battlewagons.

One after another, the great events tumbled across the fields of history and Godwin caught them on the run, wrote about them, broadcast the stories, tried to keep it all in perspective for his audience. Perspective: that was the part of his job he loved the most, trying as best he could to divine what it all really meant.

Throughout November the Germans fell back across Europe. By the end of the month American B-29s were raining bombs on Tokyo. In Britain the casualties for the month from the rocket attacks were 716 killed and 1,511 wounded, one of whom was Cilla Hood, though her recovery was a speedy one.

No one outside the precincts of the German high command had any inkling that Hitler was already whipping his generals hard, planning to risk all on one final roll of the dice. No one thought the German army and air force had it in them to mount a last great attack. From now on it was going to be a messy mopping up, a grinding offensive that would lead across the blood-soaked fields and towns until at last Berlin fell. No one gave much thought to having once again to go on the defensive.

Stefan Lieberman had pulled strings to get accreditation as a war correspondent. He had departed for Paris to write the story of the end of the war for a very glossy magazine: the story of Paris after the Germans, the first Christmas free of the Nazis in their gray uniforms on the Champs-Elysées, how the French were taking it all, and he would then observe the breaching of the Siegfried Line, the crossing of the Rhine, the final destruction of the Third Reich, and his return to Vienna—to search for the remaining members of his family. He'd said if there wasn't a play in that, then he'd better find another line of work.

Homer Teasdale produced all that information one afternoon when Godwin dropped by the office a block from the Café Royal. "But why do you want to know where Lieberman is?" Homer was pitching cards into a bowler hat, which meant that the week's business was winding down. It was Friday afternoon.

"I'd heard he'd gone over. Lucky bastard. Homer, if he can go over—a playwright for God's sake—then I can go over. You hear me?"

"Let's not go through all this again, Raj. The network boys, the newspaper boys, the Madison Avenue boys—you know what they say? They say they're looking forward to Rodger Godwin coming marching home . . . The conquering hero comes back, radio awaits, television is just around the corner, boom times once this fucking war is over—pardon my French —and you're going to be one of the standard bearers of the new age—"

"So what's this got to do with the price of beans?"

"They think you're accident prone."

"I'm going, Homer. I used to live in Paris. I met Cilla there . . . hell, I met everybody there. I want to go back. I want to see the town again, now the Nazis are gone."

"Look, Raj, nobody can actually stop you. But I personally also think you're accident prone . . . why not wait until the war is over? It won't be long—"

"Homer, anybody can go when the war's over. I *will* go when the war's over. But I'm also going over now. Lieberman's just a playwright . . . now, pretend you're my agent and manager, get started on lining up my credentials, transport, the rest of it."

When he was leaving Teasdale's office Homer said: "Cilla okay?"

"Bit of a headache."

"You're at the Dorchester?"

"Until they put the house back together."

"It's impossible to get into the Dorchester." Teasdale shook his head admiringly. "You and Cilla are so bloody *grand* anymore."

"We owe it to you, Homer."

"Thank you, my liege." He finally got one of the cards into the hat. "This isn't easy to do, you know."

"It's all in the wrist, Homer."

CHAPTER 30

Godwin had never been so cold.

So cold, so tired, so hungry, so scared. Dirty. Exhausted. Scared. The noise, the endless racketing reverberations, the shifting of the earth and the shaking of the walls and the slabs of snow coming off the fir trees like a thousand avalanches, the air always thick with snow and dirt and shrapnel and bits of hurtling debris. He'd lived through the Blitz in London but this was of an entirely different order. And he was sure he'd begun to go deaf. He still felt his stomach growling but he couldn't hear it anymore. He wondered how much time he had left. Was it enough?

He had wandered so long in this blasted, flattened empire of sleet and snow and frozen ruts of mud that had once been roads, stumbled through acres of forests that were now only shredded, broken stumps in a landscape littered with corpses and abandoned trucks and jeeps and tanks —and now he was beginning to lose track of time. Maybe that happened to you before you died. Maybe you no longer cared what day it was when you hadn't slept for a long time and were nourished by fear and rage and had forgotten what it was to not be afraid. The smoke and snow and fog blotted out the sun, night was a different shade of darkness. What difference could it possibly make, which day you finally handed in your lunch pail and called it a lifetime?

He fought the desire to sleep. He straightened his back against the wall and blew on his fingers and thought about making a fire but that might burn the rest of the building down and then where would he be? So he tried to remember what—exactly—was going on. It wasn't easy, getting it all straight . . .

There had been the first night on the road out of Paris in the old low-slung black Citroën, the three of them in search of the rumored German breakthrough in Belgium, trying to catch up with the war, looking through the rain and mud and snow for the front when they hadn't known the front was all around them, constantly shifting as the panzers and the quarter of a million German troops struggled to cross the river Our and break on through to Antwerp, when they didn't know that the whole damn war was collapsing in on them, coming like a steamroller of men and tanks and firepower. The German army was just trying to pull one out, trying to win one in the bottom of the ninth . . .

There had been a night spent in a sawmill after he'd lost track of his companions in some heavy shelling around a place called Manhay, a night in a sawmill breathing in damp wood pulp and the fumes of the Citroën slowly burning in the snow. The sawmill had been operating twenty-four hours a day using timber from the forests near Saint Vith to make lumber to build the winter housing for the Allied troops who would soon be smashing the last bits of the Reich to rubble . . . and at first light every-body was running for their lives as the German panzers came thrashing out of the woods, flattening trees before them, came out of the dense fog and swirling snow, machine guns chattering, hundreds of ghostly troops in white capes coming with the tanks, seeming to float alongside them, the machine guns always snarling as they advanced . . .

There had been nights when he hadn't known where he was, huddled with a few men around a fire in the stark cold drawing room of a once elegant château where American officers had been headquartered a few days before, now empty and smoke-smudged, the walls pockmarked with bullet holes, and a night when he'd stood guard with a lone, frightened GI from Dubuque who'd been given a bazooka and told to hold the cross-roads if Sepp Dietrich's Sixth Panzer Army happened through. It took two men to handle a bazooka, one to aim and fire, the other to load the shells. But the GI's partner had heard hell breaking loose in the trees up around the muddy bend in the fog and had said no thanks, had set off down the road, leaving the fate of democracy and humankind to those better equipped for the job. Godwin had come across the kid with the bazooka just before nightfall. They were both lost and terrified and soaked to the skin, flinching at every sound of battle from the fogbound woods where the snow was knee deep, and together they had guarded the western front that night, and Sepp Dietrich had found some other way . . .

There had been a lot of nights, nights in the fun house, in the house of horrors, and now he was back in Malmédy which had once been a lovely little village and by now had pretty much disappeared from the face of the earth.

The bombing had been going on now for two or three days, what did it matter? For some reason which he no longer understood—if he had indeed ever understood it, in the first place—the Americans were bombing Malmédy. Maybe it was all a dreadful mistake. Or maybe they knew what they were doing and had simply neglected to inform the men of the 291st Engineer Battalion and all the rest of them passing through or dug in in Malmédy. Well, what difference did it make?

As far as he could tell the Americans and the British and the Germans were trying to kill everybody in their way, everybody in Belgium, maybe, and that was what the war had come down to at last, but Godwin wasn't part of the war. Not really. He was on a personal mission. Two weeks before, he'd been in London making his usual broadcast to the United States, writing his newspaper column, contemplating the sixth London Christmas of the war and now, here he was, flat on his ass in a bombed-out building in a village overrun by the German army, a village where he'd watched a bunch of American dogfaces, newly captured, blown away in cold blood by their German captors . . . That was the way the war was going now. Fuck the prisoners, take no prisoners. It was a far cry from the war in the desert but this was what it had all come down to.

He remembered hiding in a basement with a lot of other terrified people in a little place called Trois Ponts, he'd heard the rattle of the machine guns there, too, and felt the house above them shifting on its foundations. An old man had told him that the Huns were using the Big Berthas on them, the biggest cannons ever built, firing from miles away on the other side of the Siegfried Line, fired from special railway flatbeds . . .

And now, for Christ's sake, he was back in little Malmédy, blood and mud and snow and smoke and fog center of the known universe.

He'd had him, then lost him in the madness of the German breakout, but now he'd followed him to Malmédy. Godwin had tracked him to poor godforsaken Malmédy, and now Godwin waited for him to come through the door. Pangloss was going to die.

Godwin wasn't alone in the room. The windows were all blown out, there was snow drifting through the tattered joists and beams of the wrecked roof, and night was falling. Faintly, in the lull of firing, he could hear somebody singing . . .

Godwin lit a candle that flickered in the cold draught, then caught hold and cast its faint light toward the corner where it fell briefly on the other occupant of the room. He was the radio man. He lay on his back, face up, eyes open, three hours dead.

Godwin had thought it was Pangloss, bent over the radio, getting word back to the German HQ on the course of the battle. Godwin had shot him. But it hadn't been Pangloss.

Now Godwin waited, a patient killer surrounded by death. He was holding a German Smeisser machine pistol, waiting for the sound of footsteps in the hallway.

Pangloss must have known about the breakout when they were all back in Paris. That night in Paris a week ago—a week? more? No, a week was about right, yes, tonight was Christmas Eve . . . he remembered and his eyelids grew very heavy as he thought about Merle B. Swaine of all people and Sam Balderston and he tried not to think of the knife edge of cold cutting him off . . .

When he'd arrived in Paris early in December, once again accredited as a war correspondent, the city was damp and cold and gray, pneumonia weather, as unlike the summer he'd spent there seventeen years before as you could imagine. But he visited the old haunts, saw the narrow street where he'd lived with Clothilde, and found the Club Toledo where Clyde had made a name for himself; he stopped at the house where Hugh Dew-Brittain had lived and where Priscilla had reigned so seductively, where she'd changed all their lives. He went to visit the graveyard, where he and Max Hood had killed the two *flics* who had terrorized the *quartier*. Everything had changed except the graveyard, which was just the same. It had been a long time and the world and Paris and Rodger Godwin were all very different now. So far as he could tell things hadn't changed for the better.

After he'd made the rounds of the press offices and begun looking for the man he'd come to kill, after he'd been there several days, he was having a late breakfast at a little sidewalk café across the Seine from Notre Dame. He was the only customer outside, wrapped in his Burberry and with his hat pulled down. The coffee was scalding, the roll was crusty and warm, and before him fog was rising off the river. He'd had no luck finding his prey and he was beginning to doubt if he would. If the man had left Paris he might, in the jumble of the war, be impossible to locate. Pangloss was in Paris as a sort of correspondent himself, an unlikely one, in Godwin's view. If he'd taken off for the front he could be almost anywhere. It was too soon to give up but Godwin was feeling a trifle disconsolate.

Then he heard the voice from the past.

"Either that's Rodger Godwin or I am not Merle B. Swaine!"

The man seemed rather shorter than Godwin remembered and he'd put on weight. His jowls were heavy, dropping over his collar, and his hair had thinned, turned white. His face was red, his plaid tie askew, and his small, shiny eyes were full of glitter and mischief.

"Mr. Swaine! Merle . . . for God's sake, it's you! Come on over here, damn but it's good to see you!"

They talked about the old days, the names from the past, and Godwin told him about how Max Hood had married Cilla and how Max had been killed and how he himself was now married to Cilla. He told Swaine about the birth of Charles Hugh Maxwell Godwin and what little Clothilde was up to and Clyde, as well. And Swaine took it all in and told Godwin how he'd stayed on with the newspaper until the mid-Thirties, then married a French woman, an aristocrat of considerable property and wealth. During the war her brother had been a collaborator and was now on the Resistance wanted list; she had dragged Swaine into the Resistance down near Lyon where her brother had provided her with an excellent cover. She had blown up a bridge and a collaborationist police headquarters. "She's a madwoman, Godwin. Doesn't know the meaning of the word fear. Well, let me tell you, Merle B. Swaine knows the meaning of fear, and I don't have the backbone nor the sense of adventure of a French aristocrat. She damn near got me killed and that's aside from the several near-heart attacks she gave me. But she pulled me through somehow. We're back in Paris now. It was quite a war, wasn't it? As long as it had to happen, I'm glad Merle Swaine didn't miss the damn thing. I'm sixty-four, y'know. Can't believe it! How did it happen? Merle B. Swaine is sixty-four!"

Godwin had dinner at the Swaine home, an elegant house on the Right Bank carefully surrounded by very old money or what was left after the Germans got through. He listened to war stories from Swaine's awesome wife, Marie-Claire, a tall, haughty-looking woman somewhere in her forties. Godwin told them a bit about North Africa and the Blitz about which they knew little. And when the evening was over Swaine walked him—and his own immense poodle, Richelieu—all the way back to the hotel where Godwin had taken up residence, the Ritz. It had been a grand evening.

And for the rest of the night Godwin didn't think of Pangloss. But it was the next day that he found him or, more accurately, it was Pangloss who found Godwin, greeted him with a mixture of surprise and delight in the lobby. "I had no idea you were over here. Staying long?"

Godwin smiled, shook hands, joined Pangloss for lunch and wondered just how and where and when he would kill the son of a bitch.

Then, when he'd been in Paris just two weeks, the balloon went up.

Sam Balderston of *The Times*, who later gained fame on the postwar lecture circuit as Sam "Left-for-Dead-at-the-Remagen-Bridge" Balderston, came in out of the rain and fog while Godwin was sitting in one of the cane chairs at the Deux Magots at three o'clock in the morning of 17 December 1944.

It was a cold wintry night with an icy mist falling and Godwin and Merle B. Swaine were sipping brandies and soda when Balderston came through the doorway and peered owlishly about as the heat steamed up his round spectacles. He wore a ratty old army trench coat that was splotched where the mist had soaked through. For a moment he looked around in some confusion, checking the crowd for the face he wanted. The joint was full. All the joints had been pretty full in the months since the liberation. If the Frenchmen weren't running around killing old collaborators, or endlessly talking about restoring honor and glory, or explaining why the Germans had walked in and crapped on them in the first place, they were hanging out in bars getting stewed by way of proclaiming their independence and freedom. As usual, rumor was going around that Hemingway might be in later. The more things changed, the more they stayed the same.

Balderston polished the lenses on the end of his tie which appeared to be stiff from an encounter with a fairly recent bowl of *boeuf bourguignon*. Spectacles replaced on his round pink face, he came waddling through the crush, dribbling cigar ash down his own burned and stained mac as well as onto everyone in his path.

"Godwin," he shouted, "we go to war again, *mon ami!*"

"How's that, Sam?"

"Hell, man, the bloody balloon's gone up."

Godwin smiled thinly. Swaine was on his right. On his left, the third man at the table, was the man he planned to kill within the hour.

"Calm yourself, my dear fellow, pull up a chair." This was Pangloss. That's how Godwin thought of him now, though he'd known him for years by his real name. Knowing he was going to kill him so soon had made for rather a tense evening.

And now here came Sam Balderston, master of the worst possible timing, unless you were trying to escape from Rommel and had no transport. In those circs, old Sam had been pretty handy. Swaine called for another brandy and soda for the newcomer. Balderston huffed and puffed, wiped his face with a napkin plucked from the collar of a man at the next table, and squeezed himself into the fourth chair, knocking a full ashtray off the table on the other side. He ignored the cry of alarm. Pure Balderston.

"The balloon's gone up," Balderston said again.

"Which balloon would this be, Sam?" Pangloss asked.

Balderston looked from one face to the other. He was out of breath and sweating like a prize sow. His chins obscured the knot in his tie. "The death of the great bloody awful Third Reich which Monty's been dithering on about at such great length lately . . . seems to have been . . . rather exaggerated." He chewed at the wet end of the cigar as if for dramatic effect. "My spies tell me that yesterday—eighteen hours ago, more or less —the Germans unleashed the goddamndest attack of the war in the Ardennes . . . all along the front . . . the Jerries are everywhere, it's snowing, there are Jerries in GI uniforms, it's a nightmare . . . the shit has well and truly hit the fan." He gasped for air. "Fucking Hitler thinks he's going to win the bleedin' war, he does!"

"Belgium."

"I suppose we should have known," Godwin said. "They find something that works and they stick with it. 1870, 1914, 1940, they flooded troops through the Losheim Gap in the Eifel mountains—"

"That's it," Balderston said, slurping brandy and soda, "the Losheim Gap."

"They overran the Netherlands, Holland, Belgium, and France," Godwin said. "They're having another go."

Swaine nodded, ran his hand through the rumpled white hair. "It's a helluva story. All those impossible twisting roads . . . we never believe they'll actually do it, we always think it's a feint, we always think they're trying to trick us, and then they always load up and come hell for leather and lookin' for bear, right through the Losheim Gap. We just never learn."

"Can we quote you on that, Merle?"

"It makes you wonder," Godwin said. "We're like the Bourbon kings. We never learn and we never forget." He looked over at Balderston. "How bad is it?"

"It's bad." Balderston spit bits of wet cigar wrapper. "Americans are being shot to pieces. We're undermanned, the Jerries are coming with these huge tanks. Not just Tigers but Tiger Kings. Sixty tons. Twice as big as our Shermans. *Twice!* And they're using those new planes, those damn jet planes. You can barely see the goddamn things. We're stretched very thin and Jerry is punching lots of holes in the line and it's just beginning. It's Louis and Schmeling again but the Germans are winning. No shit, German soldiers in American uniforms and trained to answer all these typical American questions about your baseball teams and movies and who knows what. A fucking nightmare."

"We have to get up there," Godwin said.

"My thought exactly. Now here's the scoop . . . bunch of boys from the 101st Airborne are here in Paris on leave, I just happen to be their little round limey mascot, they've got a truck and they're heading back to this bloody mess in about an hour. Brigadier General McAuliffe's all of a sudden in charge of the 101st and there's a convoy of four hundred trucks headed for Bastogne . . . these young pals of mine don't want to miss the fun. There's room for us. But it's now or never, lads."

Pangloss looked at Godwin. "I have that great huge Citroën. Wouldn't it be a fine thing to go to war in our own touring car?"

Godwin nodded. "Wherever you go, my friend, I go, too."

"It's decided then. Care to join us, Sam?"

"I'll lay on a supply of cognac."

"And Merle? There's plenty of room, old chap."

"No, thanks. I've had my war. And don't ask my wife because she'd be in the front seat giving directions before you could say Jack Robinson. But include me out."

"Well, we go in style."

Godwin smiled at Pangloss. There was the luckiest man in France. Tonight was not the night he would die.

"Good luck, boy, and remember—Merle B. Swaine will be with you . . . in spirit!"

Laughing, they went off to battle.

And this was where it had brought him. To the cold, dusty, snowy, smoking remainders of a house in Malmédy where he sat with his back against the wall waiting for Pangloss to return.

He checked his watch, shook it to make sure it was still running. Four hours he'd been waiting. The cold had driven the rats in out of the mud and snow and he'd noticed their dainty footprints, like those a bird might leave, in the thick plaster dust. They kept snuffling at the dead body in the corner. Occasionally Godwin would pitch a bit of plaster blown off the wall at them but they were determined. As darkness fell around them he couldn't see them anymore. Unfortunately he could still hear them as they snuffled and chewed at part of the body, doubtless starting on the face, the most exposed flesh. It really didn't bear thinking about. Finally they just ignored the bits and pieces of debris he threw at them and went on with what they were doing.

The bombing had stopped and he began to be able to hear again. The wind blowing, the muttering and stumbling of somebody's soldiers outside in the dark, the occasional moan or curse. He dug in his pocket and came out with a small bit of cheese wrapped in wax paper, a gift from someone in Trois Ponts. He unwrapped the cheese and slowly munched it. It wasn't much.

Somewhere in the night the dogfaces who were dug in had begun singing "O Come, All Ye Faithful." Flames licked up the sides of the buildings, tongues of flame darted across darkened windows, smoke hung in a vast pungent pall over the bombed village, as if it were despair, carried about like baggage. "Silent Night, Holy Night." He found himself singing softly. "O, Holy Night" . . . But were the stars shining brightly? He couldn't see them for all the smoke.

He cut himself off in midphrase, the song forgotten.

He'd heard footfalls on the stair.

The heavy steps of a weary man.

He balanced the Smeisser on his knees. He was shaking with the cold and the realization of what he was about to do.

As the door swung slowly open, creaking on sagging hinges, he thought for just a moment of his wife and his children, his new son, and wished to God he were with them and free of the bloody quest . . .

There in the shadows stood Pangloss, alone at last, ready for killing. Alone. Just the two of them. No one to tell the story.

We three kings of Orient are . . . Outside they were still singing.

"Pangloss!"

"What?"

"This is for Max Hood—"

"What? Who's there? Who is it?"

The gun made a noisy rattle. The kick traveled like electric shocks along his arm, bang, bang, bang, slamming against him.

Lieberman was knocked back into the door frame—if he made a noise it was lost in the afterecho of the gunfire—and pitched over onto the floor where he lay like a bag of wet laundry.

Godwin didn't move for a long time. Then he struggled to his feet and checked the dead man's face with the candle. No last words, no dying questions, just dead.

In the end, there had been nothing to say. No point in talking to the man. No mercy, no apologies. There had been none for Max Hood and his men.

He heard a man's voice.

"Lieberman? Are you up there?" Someone on the stairs. "Did you find Godwin?" He tripped on the stairs in the dark and swore.

Godwin couldn't stop staring at the dead man. It had taken such a long time. Years.

"What the bloody hell's going on here?"

Someone was standing in the doorway. A gust of wind made a swipe at the candle.

The man looked at Godwin, the Smeisser in his grip still, then at the body. "What the bloody hell have you done, man?"

It was Sam Balderston.

Godwin couldn't think of exactly the right thing to say.

There was no great problem with the official explanation of what had happened in that murky, shot-up, and bombed-out building in Malmédy in the middle of the Battle of the Bulge. The surprise wasn't that Stefan Lieberman, poor bugger, got himself killed in the fracas, but rather that Balderston and Godwin got out alive. Everyone agreed on that, and it was also pretty widely believed that they'd been damn stupid to set off from Paris like hare-brained adolescents in the first place. The word going round Fleet Street and Portland Place was that they were damn lucky to get out alive, and more than one glass was lifted to bloody Godwin and his nine lives. Sam Balderston had gone on to write the story of war's end, gone on to keep his appointment with destiny at the Remagen Bridge. Godwin's firsthand story of the fury of the Bulge engulfing him, bumping into the lonely soldier with a bazooka assigned to hold the crossroads against Sepp Dietrich, witnessing what history came to record as one of the Nazis' worst atrocities—the Malmédy Massacre of prisoners—Godwin's eyewitness accounts only increased his stature and guaranteed another raft of awards. But Godwin alone knew that his mission to Europe was accomplished in Malmédy, that there was no need to go on following the carnage to the end.

Lieberman's death made a one-day splash in the London papers and there was a memorial service at a Golders Green synagogue overseen by a gaggle of West End actors. Cilla had read a passage from one of his plays that fit the sad occasion, and Greer Fantasia spoke of the death of a Renaissance man. It all took a little time to pull together since communications from the front were shot to hell there for a while, but by the first week of February all the details had been seen to.

Monk Vardan called Godwin into his cubbyhole of an office in the basement of Number 10 and asked him sternly—rather in the manner of the old days when they'd all been playing at accusing Godwin of being a Nazi agent, a quaint period when glimpsed in retrospect—just what the hell had actually happened over there in Malmédy. He was a trifle put out about the whole thing. He believed he deserved an explanation from Godwin and if he could ever get his hands on that fat scoundrel Balderston

he'd wring the story out of him, too. For that reason—Balderston's eventual stint in the interrogation room—Godwin had to adhere pretty closely
to what he'd told Sam on the spur of the moment when Sam had blun-
dered up the stairs and tripped over Lieberman's corpse. " 'Fess up, young
Godwin, how did our friend Stefan meet his maker?" In the glaring basement light, the monocle looked flat and impenetrable, like an eye patch,
imparting to Monk Vardan a piratical air.

"Well, Monk, you had to be there to get the feel of it—"

"But I shall have to do without that, shan't I? You were there. You are
a writer. Make a word picture for me, tell me the story."

"Well, you see, there was quite a ruckus, Stefan and Sam and I got
split up early on. You can't imagine what it was like—snow, fog, mud, rain,
the shelling, smoke, fire, everybody running around trying to find their
units, those ungodly big German tanks, I saw 'em, Monk, they always
looked like they could see you, like they were coming for you personally—
the trees were getting ripped to pieces by the shelling, bark and limbs and
splinters flying through the air, the snow would come sliding down out of
the trees and it was like a thousand little avalanches, guys looking like
snowmen. I'm telling you, Monk, they just kept coming, like nothing
you've ever—well, anyway, I wandered around and grabbed rides, I was
looking for Stefan and Sam and one time I just stood by the side of the
road when truckloads of German troops passed by and it was like I was
invisible, I was too tired to hide, and I suppose they just saw a confused
civilian standing there like a stump. It seemed like I passed through Malmédy two or three times, maybe more, and then somebody told me Sam
was holed up in this wreck of a building and I figured I'd wait for *him* . . .
a friendly, familiar face, so I went up these stairs to this dark room with
only part of a roof and I could hear soldiers singing Christmas carols . . .
well, I fell asleep or something and suddenly the door slammed open,
somebody was yelling something, sounded loud enough to scare me, and I
woke up all confused and then somebody started shooting . . . Turned
out that there's been another guy in the room, a sleeping soldier, and he
came out of sound sleep and shot the man who was yelling—that turned
out to be Lieberman—and I had picked up this German machine pistol, a
Smeisser, and I grabbed it and started shooting the shooter and then it
was very quiet and I was having a heart attack of some kind and then Sam,
following Lieberman, came up the stairs and discovered us. . . . That
was about it, Monk, a comedy of errors. A tragedy, too, of course."

Vardan sat staring at Godwin for a long time, slowly pursing and
unpursing his lips, as if committing a passage of something not so very
good to memory. The monocle finally fell from his eye and he unfolded

his long, thin body and got it upright. "Certainly a tragedy for our wandering Jew who ought to have gone to ground in Clapham or the Bayswater Road and waited for the war to end."

Godwin said: "He lived in Belgravia actually." Monk said nothing, staring at him. "Well, things happen. It was his unlucky day."

"Things happen," Monk repeated. "Don't they just? Well, that's your story?"

"Yes. And, frankly, I'm sticking to it."

"I'm sure. Well, begone with you."

"Monk, it was an awful mess over there—"

"Yes, yes, I grasp your point."

It was snowing vigorously in the north of England and in Scotland. Train service was suffering occasional disruptions, there were ice sheetings here and there, there were still V-2s raining haphazardly on London and across the southern counties. Repairs to the Sloane Square house were moving sluggishly and life at the Dorchester grew wearisome. The children did their best to cope with the unfamiliar and somewhat cramped accommodations but they were just children, after all. Cilla was physically recovered but winter and the lack of space were closing in on her. There was no play to rehearse, no film on her schedule until later in the spring, and she sensed that something was preying on her husband's mind. He would shake his head and deny it but he couldn't fool her. For Godwin it was a curious time, blending relief with indecision. He was relieved that Max was finally avenged, finished: Now that it was done, he was surprised that relief was his strongest reaction. But it still remained to wipe the slate clean: He would have to tell Cilla the story. The secret was too large, had lasted too long, to live with alone. He needed to know that there was someone on earth with whom he shared it. Cilla, of course, was the one. And he needed some time alone with her to deal with it.

Early in February, shortly after the memorial service for Lieberman, matters resolved themselves. A V-2 landed rather too close for comfort and Cilla and Nanny One decided that the best place for the children was Lady Pamela's place down on the south coast. Used only sporadically for short holidays since Lady Pamela's death, it needed opening up and airing out. Once they'd seen the nannies and the children off with the mountains of luggage, Cilla said she was dreading a couple of parties looming in the days ahead. "Could we get away, too? Off by ourselves—I've been cooped up at the hotel too long . . . Please, Rodger? Let's go to Stillgraves. It'll be cold and snowy and safe and we can go for walks . . . and you can tell me what's on your mind. You know, I think I have an idea what it might be."

"I doubt it," he said.

"You're thinking about the end of the war. It'll be coming soon and everything will have to be reordered, the whole world. And you're thinking about what we'll do then . . . you're wondering what I'll say when you tell me you want to go back to New York." She grinned mischievously.

"That's not it. Not even close."

"Aha! You admit there is something, then."

"Stillgraves sounds perfect. Let's go."

"We'll take the night train. Perhaps we'll be stuck in a snowbank—"

"You think like a movie."

"Thank you, darling."

"The night train. Very romantic."

"It will be wonderful, Rodger. Just the two of us. I'm so glad you're back from the battle again. The war's over for you now, isn't it?"

"I promise."

The Flying Clansman headed out of London in a light snowfall, fully loaded and ready for whatever storms might be waiting for them. After dinner, they retired to their bedroom with a bottle of chilled champagne. The rocking of the train, the old familiar mesmerizing motion, the occasional lights and moaning bells, blurred past outside, the ringing of a bell fading in the night, the beds with the crisp, starched linen turned down . . .

She lay in his arms beneath warm blankets, the lights out, the window frosted with ice. It was time to tell her. It was easier in the darkness where she couldn't see him, couldn't see the expressions crossing his face, where he could let his voice do the work of drawing her into his mind, his life, his code, the need he'd harbored for years to avenge Max Hood.

He began by telling her about the friendship that had grown between him and Max Hood that summer now nearly twenty years before in Paris. He reminded her of what she'd observed herself but he told her more. He told her about the killing of the two *flics*. He explained to her what the two cops had done and why they had had to be killed and he described the bond that had been forged in blood between him and Max. No, she didn't have to understand how such a brotherhood worked: Hell, Godwin himself didn't fully understand how it had happened, or precisely the moment it had become irrevocable, or what it was in his own makeup that had made it so permanent, but the point was the bond was there, it was what it was, it existed, and in the end she had to accept that. "It's like religion," he said. "The Trinity, transubstantiation, fishes and loaves, miracles—it's like believing God is an Englishman. You accept it on faith. There was something between Max and me. Not something we talked about—"

"Like Hemingway," she said softly.

"I knew I had to avenge his death, the betrayal that led to his death . . . it was all the more important because by loving you I had betrayed him as well . . . One man took away his life, I took away what he loved most." He sighed, wishing he knew a way to make it all concrete and sensible and understandable. But sense and reason had nothing to do with it. "My debt to Max Hood was my fate, Cilla. My destiny. I believe in things like that. There are some things that have to be done or we're just wandering around without a hope . . . I couldn't leave the avenging of Max Hood to someone else, to some institution which might, someday, be made to pay attention. I had to play it out or it wasn't going to get done. It was written that I should do this thing. That's all. That's why I finally had to kill Stefan Lieberman."

That took her by surprise, the last thing she'd expected to hear, though if you'd asked her what she did expect she wouldn't have known. It took a minute or two to grasp the essence. She made him repeat it, then lay quietly, then pulled away as if to give herself room to clear her head and sat up, trying to get it straight.

"*You* killed Stefan? *Intentionally?* I don't understand—you said you killed the man who killed Stefan . . . I thought Sam Balderston was there . . ."

He took her through it, moment by moment, describing what had happened that night in Malmédy.

"But why, Rodger? Why kill Stefan?" She shivered at the thought.

He was acutely aware of the rocking of the train, the cold and the darkness and the depth of the night. "Because he was a Nazi agent. He betrayed PRAETORIAN and that's why they were ready for us when we got to Rommel's headquarters. Once I found him, once I knew he'd done it . . . then I had to kill him."

"But . . . oh, no, no, Rodger, that's not right—it can't be right. Not Stefan . . . no, darling, he had a secret, but that wasn't it. He was a *British* agent. I'm sure of that, he *told* me that . . ."

"He *told* you?"

"Yes. That was why he was always going off to see Monk—"

"Monk? Monk hardly knew him."

"That's what I always thought. But he used to say he was going off to play at cloak-and-dagger with Monk and he'd laugh sort of quietly and wink at me . . ."

"What if Monk *believed* Lieberman was a British agent . . ." Godwin felt once again as if he'd stepped unexpectedly into a hall of mirrors. "Cilla . . . you knew Lieberman quite well. Cilla, I know that you were lovers."

She was quiet for a time, then said: "How long have you known?"

"It doesn't matter."

"Yes, we were lovers. I can't explain. Except to say that I was a different person then . . . it was a long time ago. It ended when you came back in a coma and I thought you were going to die. I must trust you to believe me."

"I do believe you. It's the dead past."

"But Rodger . . . you killed him."

"Not because you were lovers. *You* must trust *me*."

"I can't believe you actually killed him. You're not a *killer* . . ."

"A lot of people are killers who never meant to be, never wanted to hurt a soul . . . Stefan Lieberman was a casualty of war. Believe me, he was a German agent and because of him every man on our mission was killed—everyone but me."

Slowly she came back, leaning against him, making him warm, and he told her about finding Lieberman's sister and the story she told about the family held by the Gestapo, about how they'd given Lieberman no choice but to work for them.

Her voice was expressionless when she finally spoke. "The poor bastard. He didn't have a chance."

"Neither did the men who died on the mission."

"What else could he do? Kill his family or kill you and Max and the rest? So you killed him anyway . . . you killed him and all he was trying to do was keep his family alive . . ." She didn't move, didn't pull away, but she was lost in thought.

"Try to understand. I didn't kill him for being a Nazi spy. He didn't have a choice and I'd have done the same thing. But I had to kill him for Max . . . it was for Max. I wouldn't have killed him if it had been the rest of us, I'd have tracked him down, maybe, and turned him in . . . But not when it came to Max. He killed Max and I owed his death to Max." He'd said it so much, so often, it was beginning to sound unnatural. Either she got it or she didn't.

She sighed, said so softly: "I am so sick of Max." It was exhaustion and anger. He heard her. She'd had Max up to here. "Max Hood, the hero of our time. Max Hood, the old soldier. The best friend a man ever had. Max the good, Max the kind, Max the decent. Sir Max. Saint Max. Shakespeare would have written a play about this man. But, Rodger darling, no man is a hero to his wife . . . or is it his tailor? Well, somebody was right, in any case. He helped you commit murder when you were just a boy . . . and now he drives you to murder—yes, yes, it's war, Lieberman was the enemy, have it your way—he has driven you to kill again . . . yet, you revere him."

"My revering him has nothing to do with it. I know he was just a man—"

"I know, I know, he was the man who made you a man, you were blood brothers . . . it's all very manly and wonderful and the result is that Max died a sick and bitter man, you've committed murder, and a decent, frightened man whose life was made a hell by Hitler is dead by your hand. You'll have to pardon my delicate female mind, but is that the legacy of Max Hood?"

"I can't explain it any more than I have."

She breathed softly against the rhythm of the train on the track. "I don't hold it against you, I'm not judging you. You never had a chance either . . . Max made you his. He'd been in the desert with Lawrence—what must all that have sounded like to you at twenty-two? He was an enigma. I don't know . . . maybe it is the perfect legacy for a Max Hood. Spilled blood . . . it's what he was best at." She rested her head on Rodger Godwin's chest. He felt her eyelids fluttering against his flesh. "Try not to be angry with me. I know nothing about your code, what you owed Max or what he made of you . . . I love you, I love your bravery and the way you embrace your fate and I love how you're always trying to do the right thing . . . you're a decent chap, darling, I'm glad, oh so glad, that the children will have you rather than poor old Max . . . I don't mind if you take long walks with young Charlie and tell him about your friend Max Hood and what a grand fella he was . . ." She sniffled against him and he felt her tears wet against him. "That's all right, Rodger, because Max Hood had his moments and he was important to you, far more than he was or could have been to me . . . but for now I just want Max to take a powder. Do you hear me? I want him out of our lives. Let him rest in peace now. Let him die, let him go, let him march off with the bloody immortals, the gods of war . . . just get him out of my life. I had quite enough of Max Hood while he was alive. Now you've carried out your revenge like somebody in *The Duchess of Malfi*. Now we're quits with Max Hood. Now it's just you and me and a new generation. Can you live with that, my darling husband?"

He kissed her hair, her forehead. She was all he'd ever dreamed she might be.

"Just you and me," he said, "and a new generation."

In the darkness he felt her mouth smiling against him.

She relaxed in his arms and went to sleep. He stared out the window into the darkness. At junctions, in swinging lights, he saw the banks of snow, but the Clansman rolled onward through the night.

He couldn't sleep. He still wasn't sure how Lieberman had actually learned of PRAETORIAN. It didn't matter anymore. Cilla was right. It was time for Max to march off with the immortals. He could take PRAE-TORIAN with him.

CHAPTER 31

The day passed in opening the place up, getting fires going and bringing in some wood. Cilla thought it was like playing house, pulling the snow-storm around them like a cloak, making love before the fire in the afternoon, watching through the gathering darkness as the snow kept falling, building up slowly, steadily. The wind was blowing from Hadrian's Wall all the way to the front door of Stillgraves, yowling the whole time. Gusts of snow blew down the chimneys, sparks flying, snow hissing. It was heaven.

Cilla hadn't mentioned the talk they'd had on the train. He knew her well enough, however, to know she was thinking it over, trying to put it all in order. Max, Lieberman, Godwin. She'd work it out. She'd made her peace with it because she loved him and because it was over.

Godwin knew it was over, too. Pangloss was dead and that made it over. He knew he shouldn't be worrying about details. But he couldn't keep himself from wondering about Monk. What was going through Monk's mind now that Pangloss was dead? Godwin had been through it with him, telling the story of Lieberman's death, and Monk had had his chance to raise any questions. And he hadn't. He hadn't mentioned Pangloss. He'd been able to live with Godwin's version of events. How was anyone going to challenge it now? And what if they did? At the worst, he'd killed a German spy in a darkened, bombed-out ruin in the middle of the Battle of the Bulge.

So Monk was doubtless as glad it was over as he was.

But the idea that Monk might have thought Lieberman was a British agent—that off-center possibility wouldn't leave Godwin alone. Did it matter? How *could* it matter? The man was dead. He was Pangloss and he was dead.

He turned it over in his mind, regarded it from every imaginable point of view. It always came out exactly the same way. Max Hood was avenged, a Nazi spy was dead, and Monk Vardan was washing his hands of it and moving on.

Before she fell asleep one night, she said: "You did what you had to do. I want you to know that I understand that much."

In the night he was unable to sleep. He felt overly alert, wound up, as he had at college on the night after the last exam had been taken and the pressure was off and he'd felt as if his life were beginning over again. That was the way it was now: he felt as if his life had been handed back to him to have another go at it. And of course it had. His old life was over. He was invigorated at the thought of the new life awaiting him, more or less stainless and shining and hopeful. The new life would hold so much, more than he'd ever dreamed. And the upshot was, he couldn't sleep. He needed a walkabout. He got out of bed and dressed and went downstairs. It was a little past one o'clock. The embers still glowed.

He was in the kitchen making hot chocolate, trying to get it right, when he thought he heard the sound of an automobile engine snarling and grinding through the wind. He pictured a car stuck and burning rubber trying to get loose . . . but where? He padded into the large sitting room and craned to look back down the private road that connected to the public road which led to the village. The snow was still blowing and the moonlight was spotty at best, coming and going, blue milky shafts here and then gone behind clouds. He could still make out the road leading away from the house, curving, clinging to the hillside, but it was too dark to make out anyone who might be stuck. There was nothing moving out there.

During the daylight he could have seen all of it from the long windows where he stood, but at night it was a mystery solved only by the moon shafts between the clouds. Then it would leap out at him, the clouds scudding, the moon on the snow, the wind blowing a frosting of snow across the crust, and then darkness again.

Then he thought he heard a car door slam. Or a trunk.

No, impossible. Who would be out on such a night? He sipped his hot chocolate, staring into the darkness, the sea of shadows on the strip of road. Poor bastard. Getting a shovel out of the boot to dig himself out . . . somehow off on the wrong road . . . stuck in a storm . . . cold . . .

Godwin found a pair of boots in the box and a sheepskin coat hanging on the peg. He couldn't leave the poor devil out there.

The crunch of snow was loud underfoot. It was bitter cold, the wind stinging, the blowing snow like tiny darts aimed at his face. Once he was on the road he fell down, slipping on the ice beneath the snow cover. Damn, what a fool! He struggled to his feet, slipping and sliding on the ice. He looked up at the ridge of boulders above, barely outlined black against the navy sky and the hurrying clouds. Twenty yards up to the rocks. On the other side another fifty or so down to the flats. He looked up warily once more, hoped to God the damn things didn't come loose.

All the time he kept hearing things but wondered if it was the wind, the cracking of the snow, the creaking of the trees. He couldn't see a damn thing and he wished he'd just minded his own business and stayed inside. And then he saw the car stuck in the snow.

Or was it? It didn't look stuck. It looked as if it had been parked and possibly left. He couldn't see anyone. He approached it, touched the fender, no, it wasn't stuck in a snowbank. Maybe it was out of petrol. It had been sitting there long enough to grow a white moss covering of snow. It was a black Rover. And it was empty. It must have been petrol. He moved carefully around the car, saw tracks leading away from the car. It all made sense. Out of petrol the lone driver had rolled to a stop and then set off on foot toward the house. Godwin followed a few yards in the man's tracks but couldn't see him. He strained to see through the darkness and that did no good. Finally he made a megaphone of his cupped hands and called out, was anybody there? Echoes bounced off the hillside and then silence returned, just the sounds made by wind and snow. He waited and, feeling foolish, called again into the wind and the darkness.

He sensed something fluttering in the snow beside him, like a trick of vision, a feathering of snow. Then the flat crack of a rifle shot. He turned reflexively, slipped and fell, felt and saw another spray of snow beside his hand and heard another crack. It took a second, maybe two, before he got a handle on things. He'd been looking for a stranded motorist and suddenly everything had changed and somebody had taken two shots at him with a rifle. It made no sense, at least not for the moment. All he thought about doing was staying alive. He rolled to the back of the ditch against the overhang of frozen, snow-covered grass. And he thought the nightmare was starting all over again; it hadn't been finished after all.

He lay in the snow, brushing it out of his eyes and feeling it shoved down inside the collar of the coat, and thought that the shots had been fired from well along the road toward the house. That put some space between him and the gunman. He began crawling away in the back edge of the ditch where the damn snow had drifted deepest, pushing himself, trying hard not to panic, wanting only to get away, brain racing, overheating. He burrowed along, drew even with the Rover on his right. He was gasping, soaked through with snow and sweat, without a weapon, nothing to fight with but his wits and the prospect didn't cheer him.

He heard another shot, the bullet skittering through the snow and spraying bits of ice and gravel. Clouds slid across the moon making it as dark as it was going to get. Godwin struggled to a crouching position, wondering how much spring he had in his legs, looking back, trying to get a glimpse of movement or hear even the slightest sound, but he saw nothing and was breathing too hard to hear anything else. Then he got to his feet and began running out onto the road, heading in a zigzag fashion away from his attacker, trying to keep the shape of the Rover between him and the other man. The pounding of his heart and the rushing of breath blotted out everything else. The wind was icy and froze the sweat on his face and he was aware of the peculiar coldness of the plate in his head . . .

He heard the *thunk* of a slug hitting the car, then a whining ricochet of another glancing off. He grinned as he ran. The darkness was his ally and he felt the fear draining away. He wasn't going to die tonight.

As his confidence increased so did his anger. Who was this faceless, anonymous bastard? Was it the man in the fog who'd attacked him once before? Was it some friend of Lieberman's? Was the sister part of the Nazi cell? Had she recognized him and set the dogs loose? Another crack and he veered sharply to the left, adrenaline pushing him hard, and hurdled the drifted ditch, grabbed a clump of scrub and pulled himself up the incline, used a small tree as a brace for one foot, pushed off reaching for another bit of root, kept pulling and pushing himself up the hill until he was sheltered behind one of the boulders edging the spine. He smeared snow across his sweating face, sucked some into his mouth, waited, barely peering around the side of the rock.

The moon slowly unveiled by the passing clouds turned the snowy road below him a dowager blue. The man with the rifle came along past the car, staring into the depression of the ditch, looking for tracks, looking for his quarry. The man's eyes raked the road and then he stopped beside the Rover. He stood looking over the roof at the expanse of shadowed hillside. He knew Godwin was unarmed by now but as he stood, staring at the hill, he seemed to be weighing his options. He didn't know the terrain and Godwin did. Venturing into the shadowy hillside, facing a man fighting for his life . . . A killer doesn't like those odds. He'd lost the chance to take him by surprise, to kill him in his bed. And now he knew that Godwin was watching him. Calmly, with a kind of massive arrogance, he laid his rifle on top of the car, took out a cigarette, cupped his hands around a flaring match, took a deep drag. Godwin watched the wind catch a cloud of smoke and blow it to tatters.

Suddenly, like nausea, a wave of revulsion and rage swept across Godwin. He was shaking, not with fear or cold. He was furious, a dry-throat hair-trigger kind of fury, aching to strike back. . . . Who the hell was this arrogant assassin? Who would dare try to take his life away from him just as he reclaimed it for himself? Who would dare take him away from Cilla and the children?

Finally the man flicked the butt away with a gesture of disgust and dismissal and climbed back into the Rover, flinging the rifle into the back. He didn't turn the lights on but drove slowly toward the house for maybe a hundred yards. The snow held him back, forced the slow pace. He was approaching the widened place in the road, the turnaround, where he stopped and began the painstaking process of backing and edging forward that would finally turn the car around. It was all done so casually, taunting the helpless intended victim watching in the snow.

Godwin leaned on the big rock, four feet high and as many wide. It had to weigh hundreds of pounds, maybe a ton. He leaned on it, braced his foot against a trunk behind him, tried rocking it, felt it move, felt it rock back and forth in its shallow resting place. There were several small, frozen shrubs and clumps of grass on the hillside between Godwin and the narrow road and he had not the slightest idea if any of them would stop or impede the boulder once he'd got it rolling. It was a long shot in any case. Chances were he'd miss the car in front or behind and the boulder would carry over the road and gather destructive speed all the way down to the hangar on the flats and the son of a bitch would be off on his merry way, safe to give it a try later on. But there was always the odd chance that it would hit the car. He didn't worry about what would happen then.

Anger had taken over. He wasn't thinking: He was calculating. The car had turned and was backing into position to make its getaway. The tires were spinning, spraying snow and ice, and then they caught on gravel and Godwin heard the grinding of gears. He'd satisfied himself he could dislodge the boulder. Now it was all in the timing. He faced the fact that he had no idea how to judge the speeds of the car and the rock. The hell with it. He'd depend on the power of ill will.

He watched the Rover gathering speed in the snow and he gave a mighty heave and saw the damn thing on its way, grinding and smashing through the gorse and knocking a tree or two sideways, Jesus Christ, it was off on a tear, it was going too fast, damn, too fast, and then it bounced over the ditch and onto the road.

And stopped with a crunch of snow and ice, a great thumping sound that carried all the way up the hillside, stopped dead like a perfect nine-iron pin high and Godwin stood there riveted to the spot. The Rover was only ten yards away and it was dark and when the driver saw this huge thing dropping out of the sky like the thumb of God he reflexively hit the brake and sent the car into a severe sideways skid. The Rover broadsided the boulder at maybe thirty miles an hour and Godwin heard glass breaking and metal screaming against stone and the car shot forward at right angles to the road and went over the edge of the road and plummeted in a great swirling plume of snow down the steep rock face toward where the hangar slumbered, a rectangular shadow on the snow. He waited, watching the snow rise like a foaming wave on a shore, heard the muffled thudding of the bouncing car. Finally, there was only the whistling of the wind and the Big Ben booming of his heart.

Far below nothing moved. He could barely see the car, nose down, like a hearse sinking in the snow. Slowly, trying not to fall, he went down the hillside, grabbing at scrub and bits of rock to keep from falling, across the road where he inspected the boulder for a moment, then on down the steep slope, scrambling and sliding on the seat of his pants. The car sat desolate in the moonlight, the radiator broken and steam half-heartedly spouting. It looked like a lawn sculpture or a fountain, as if it had always been there surrounded by the apron of snow.

Godwin approached carefully, snow well up his boots and frozen hard on top, crunching. Flurries skittered, eddied up against the Rover. He peered in through the side window. The driver lay still, tilted over onto the passenger seat, his face obscured by shadow. It was incredibly still. The wind had died, the steam dissipated itself. The windshield was broken. Blood was smeared across the glass where his head had cracked it. Godwin wanted to check something and he wanted the gun.

He pulled the door open, yanking it against the snow, stood back. Nothing. The guy had to be dead. No moaning, no wheezing, nothing but silence. Godwin reached into the backseat and finally got hold of the rifle, slid it out, stood it against the rear fender.

Then, grinding his teeth with distaste, he leaned back into the driver's compartment, pulled the body toward him, holding the front of the man's leather jacket, jerking at him frustratedly until he was in a seated position behind the wheel. The head lolled to one side. He turned the head, pulled the head into a shaft of ice blue moonlight, turned it to see the earlobe. It was intact. No one had ripped it off.

He was backing out of the compartment, shrinking back from the lifeless body, when suddenly, with an unearthly, wet growl, the dead man came to life, his fingers grasping at Godwin's face, sliding away, digging at his lip, finally catching in the collar of the sheepskin coat, pulling him back into the car, the awful wet growl and blood spraying from his mouth, hands pulling, tugging Godwin toward the bloody face and he felt the blood sticking to his face, heard himself screaming in sudden terror, unholy mind-bending terror, the cold fingers tugging, raking his throat, and Godwin struck back blindly at the face, pulling away, pulling the man's fingers out of the car, partly through the open door, pulling the head with the staring, bloody eyes toward him, and with his free hand he found the handle on the open door and with a violence born of naked horror he slammed the door and caught the man below the jaw, across the throat, his face outside of the car and the rest of him inside but for the hands, and he was free, he saw the tongue protruding from the black mouth, the teeth sawing at the tongue in a paroxysm of strangulation, saw the hands also protruding at the wrists, and he threw his body again and again against the door until a river of blood ran from the dead mouth and the tongue was left hanging by a raw white thread clamped between clenched teeth and finally he let the door bounce back, watching as the body slowly toppled out onto the bloodstained snow. Godwin was gagging, gasping for breath, standing leaning forward with his hands on his knees, trying vainly not to vomit, then waited until his gut had emptied everything into the snow and when he'd stopped trembling he picked up the rifle and set off slowly, slogging through the snow, across the flats toward the steps leading up the cliff face to the house.

As he went he began thinking about what had just happened. He thought about it all the way up to the house. He didn't like any of it but something had clicked in his mind, he'd begun to theorize, and he'd begun to figure out what might be going on.

But that didn't stop it from being more of a nightmare than ever because he'd killed Pangloss in Germany and still it wouldn't end and he was just beginning to see it whole, the way the odd little pieces just conceivably might fit together.

He wondered if he was on to something. Or maybe he was just losing his mind.

The house was dark and still. It seemed impossible, given what he'd just been through, but it was lucky. Cilla was still asleep. He was alone. He

heated another cup of hot chocolate and built a fresh fire on top of the
embers in the library and sat down, staring out the long French windows
to the terrace. It was three o'clock. He sat still, occasionally sipping chocolate. What to do, what to do . . .

An hour passed and then he picked up the telephone. The lines were
still up, another stroke of luck. The connection wasn't much but he succeeded in getting Monk at home in London. Monk sounded tired and
strained but he said he hadn't slept a wink all night. Waiting for a report
to come in. "What's the matter? What's going on? What's going on up
there?"

"Monk . . . everything's going crazy, a man just tried to kill me, he
was out on the road leading in here, in the snow—he was shooting at me.
Monk? Can you hear me?"

"I hear you, old boy. Go on."

"Monk, it's crazy . . . I wound up killing him!"

"How in the world did you manage that?"

"It doesn't matter. The question is, Why was he after me? Look,
Monk, I've got to tell you something, there's quite literally no one else I
can tell. I killed Pangloss."

"You're raving, old boy—"

"No, listen to me—I killed Pangloss in Germany. I found out who he
was . . . it was Stefan Lieberman. Did you have that figured out, Monk?
Did you know?"

"You killed Pangloss. Lieberman. This is all going a bit fast for me."

"You see, I had every reason to think it was over. Pangloss was dead. It
was over. Max was avenged . . . But someone is still out there trying to
kill me—Monk, this guy tonight was going to come into the house and kill
me and Cilla, too. I just got lucky—what's happening, Monk? You're the
only one I know on the inside. You're going to have to lend a hand."

"Well, I'm not sure—"

"Was Lieberman Pangloss, Monk?"

"Really, I can't—"

"Play it straight, Monk. Just this once."

"All right. Straight. Yes, he was Pangloss."

"Then why is somebody still trying to kill me? I don't get it. I wanted
to kill the Nazi who betrayed Max Hood and PRAETORIAN and Lieberman was the man . . . but Cilla says you knew Lieberman, she says he
told her he was a *British* agent. I don't much like what I'm seeing . . .
But I just want a free pass out of the maze. Monk, I'm in way over my
head. I've killed two men and—"

"Two?"

"Yes, two."

"You're admitting you killed Collister? Well, confession is good for the soul. But we knew that, we knew all about you and poor Collister. Two people in the pub identified your picture, told us you were deep in conversation with him. But that's neither here nor there. Water under the bridge, what? And now you've killed Stefan Lieberman. You're a bit of a public menace, old boy."

"No, *now* I've killed some madman with a rifle intent on killing me. Don't bullshit me, Monk. Was Lieberman your agent? Or was he a Nazi? Do you even know? Is that it? Doesn't anybody know what the hell is going on? Monk, I'm right at the edge up here—I can't go on with people with guns trying to kill me . . . Monk, I don't blame you—"

"Very generous of you, old man."

"And if you can't help me out I'm prepared to pull some strings. I can go directly to Churchill. Is that what I should do? He'd understand, wouldn't he? He was right there, he's the one who briefed me for PRAE-TORIAN and that's when everything began to go wrong. Would that make it easier on you? If I just went right to the top? But I can't wait. Today's the day I finish this."

"Rodger, listen carefully. It's the middle of the night and yours was not the call I was expecting. I've got to get the old noggin on straight—now what shall we do? Well, in the first place, we can't have bogies out there trying to kill you, can we? So old Monk is laying on a plane first thing and I'll bring an armed detachment to back us up. How does that sound?"

"It sounds fine, pal, that's how."

"Forget Churchill. He won't have the foggiest idea what you've been through and what's going on now. I'll get there as soon as I can. I'll be able to fill in some blanks for you. And don't worry about having killed Collister and Lieberman and this latest chap." He laughed. "There's a war on and I hear it's hell. But, on the other hand, try very hard not to kill anyone else? All right? It's not a good habit to get into. Still, I have to hand it to you."

"What are you talking about?"

"Well, you're a dangerous man. A killer. Good God, I've never killed anyone." He paused. "Will you just sit tight? We'll get to the bottom of this."

"I want it over, Monk. All the way over. It's gone on way too long. A joke's a joke, Monk, but this one is old. Very old."

"I'll get started as soon as I get off the phone. And, Rodger, don't worry. I promise you, it's all over. I can feel it in my bones."

Godwin went to the cupboard in the tack room and took the old Webley from the back of the shelf. It had been Max Hood's. Godwin had found it by accident one day while recovering after his stay in the hospital. He'd oiled it up and done some target shooting down on the flat. It was a gun and a half. A hell of a kick and it didn't leave much of a tin can. Now he wanted it near him. He wanted to be ready. It was a gun for killing. Nothing else.

When he finished his hot chocolate he went out onto the terrace and watched the horizon begin to lighten a bit. Far to the left, at the back of the cliff, he saw the black shape of the Rover and his tracks leading back toward the house like an umbilical cord. He didn't think about the frozen body.

He was thinking about the endgame and just how to play it.

It was just past noon, the sky was the color of a silver dollar, and beneath it the wind came and went in an angry mood but the snow had stopped for the moment. Godwin was standing at the long windows looking out across the terrace with its pots rounded with snow down to the flat expanses of the airstrip where Monk would be landing. Cilla had come pattering down the stairs and spoke from the doorway behind him.

"I feel like a delinquent. I've slept the whole morning away." She grinned sleepily, yawned and stretched. "I suppose you've been up for ages."

"Ages," he said. "You're incredibly beautiful."

"Oh, please. Don't look." She was wearing a plaid wool robe with stags, arms folded across her waist, hugging herself.

"You want hot chocolate? Coffee?"

She came and stood beside him, linked her arm through his. "I'll take some coffee back upstairs. I'm going to have a long, very hot soak." She shivered at the sight of the gray-and-white world.

"Light the fire in the bathroom."

"I shall, you may be sure. Is everything all right?"

"Monk's on his way."

"Monk Vardan? Whatever for? You invited him?"

"He has something he wants to talk to me about."

"Tonight?"

"He's flying in, actually. He'll be here anytime."

"It must be terribly important. It's nothing awful, is it, Rodger? It's not something bad?"

"No, no, just some housekeeping. You know Monk. Irons in every fire."

"Must be more than housekeeping if he's flying. Rotten flying weather, isn't it?" Her face brightened. "Maybe he'll crash and we won't have to put up with him."

"Well, the snow has stopped."

"Are you sure you're all right?"

"Yes, of course. Don't worry."

In the stillness, they heard a waspish, high-pitched droning noise which grew into the whine of an airplane engine. Godwin looked at his watch. "It's Monk, right on time."

The plane appeared at last on the gray horizon, above the treetops, coming out of the clouds and haze.

"Well, I cannot possibly put up with Monk at the moment. I'm off for my soak. Maybe he'll be gone by the time I reappear. If not, I'll do my very best at behaving. But do try to send him on his way, darling. Please?"

"I'll do what I can," Godwin said.

He pulled the sheepskin coat on over the turtleneck sweater, turned up the collar, and was standing on the terrace when the small aircraft touched down, bounced on the frozen snow, and settled back on all three wheels. Plumes of snow kicked up as it taxied in the direction of the hangar. Godwin was down the long flight of stairs cut in the cliff face and striding toward the plane as the pilot throttled back and cut the engine. He could see the pilot in his leather helmet and goggles in the cockpit. Monk was sitting behind him.

When the canopy came back Monk was first out, as if his long spidery figure had been spring-loaded. He was wearing a navy blue duffel coat, the hood blowing back off his head. The wind whipped at his trouser legs as he felt for a foothold on the wing, then jumped clumsily down to the snow.

"Cheers, Rodger," he said with a mock salute. "I'm the last man to complain, mind you, but I simply need a larger plane. Or a larger cockpit. Or something. I feel as if gangrene is devouring my lower extremities. Ah," he pointed with his long outflung arm, "is that the Rover from last night? Yes, I thought so. I told Airman Davidson to drive this flying torture chamber on down past the hangar, take care of his tinkering and fondling and have a look at the night's debris."

"Who is Davidson? Not just an ordinary airman—"

"One of the PM's personal flyboys, or so I'm given to understand. Apparently entrusted with the most sensitive undertakings of which this would appear to be one." He looked Godwin up and down, as if inspecting for cracks and bits of breakage. "You're hale and hearty, I take it?"

"I'd like to stay that way, Monk. I've been in the dark about all this for way too long. I'm turning on the lights, coming inside. I'm tired of this game . . . all the games that have been played all around me."

"I understand. Of course you're a bit fed up. But, to be fair, you must admit you've been playing the game with considerable verve yourself. And you will remember, too, I hope, that it was your humble servant, M. Vardan, who repeatedly asked—nay, begged—you to leave it all alone." The engine was feathering and starting to whine, the plane rolling slowly on down the strip. It drowned out some of what Monk was saying and Godwin leaned forward. This was all very important. Missing a word could be dangerous. "I say you've been continuously impetuous and irresponsible. Not a good soldier, old boy."

"I didn't volunteer for any of it," Godwin said. "You sucked me into it, you and Churchill—"

"There's no point in quibbling, is there? Mistakes were made. But the fact of the matter is, you could have declined the invitation. Once you accepted you became a part of the military, subject to orders." He shook his head. His lean face and long bony nose were pink in the wind. Godwin had never seen him look so healthy. "Yet you have steadfastly refused to follow orders . . . I'm only pointing this out because you seem to feel put upon, endangered, and generally angry at what has befallen you. I merely point out that you are as much to blame as anyone . . . and no one, certainly not we in the government, asked you to go about murdering people . . . though," he hurried on, forestalling argument, "the men you murdered were rascals and no one is contemplating pursuing the matter— still, it was very naughty and we have the option of—"

"That would be very unwise, I promise you. I have access to quite a few soapboxes to tell my story . . . the story of what happened at Coventry . . . the story of PRAETORIAN—"

"Come, come, old boy. What story of PRAETORIAN?"

"The betrayal. The fact that it was a suicide mission—"

"All the tales Eddie Collister told you—the old hobbyhorse he rode all the way to his death. I'm not sure it's a story anyone wants to hear anymore. The war is going to be ending. PRAETORIAN is very old news. If it's news at all—more likely the whole period of Rommel has faded from people's minds. Time marches on, old boy. Sad but true. The public is a fickle lot. You'd be wise to accept that notion. And the old war stories told by a murderer—well, be serious, old boy. Why are we threatening each other?" He was clapping his gloved hands together against the cold. "Come on, let's walk. We'll talk this out. We aim to please at Vardan and Company." From the corner of his eye Godwin saw Airman Davidson heading toward the upended wreckage of the Rover.

"You're just beating your gums, Monk. You see your pilot over there? Presently he's going to be looking into the face of a frozen corpse . . . the corpse of a man who tried to kill me last night. This is what my life has come to, killing. How many more killings are there? Who else is looking for me? And why? What the hell is going on? Who was this guy and who sent him? Who was Lieberman? Ours or theirs? I can't think of anyone else to turn to, Monk, but you. You always seem to know what's going on. You and Churchill—you got me into it, you and Churchill, and then you say Churchill decided I was a traitor, an agent of the Nazis or a man who wanted to kill his lover's husband. Monk, I want to talk to Churchill about all this. He owes me an explanation—"

"But that's just not practical, is it? As I told you, he wouldn't know what you're talking about. Actually, I doubt if he'd even remember his briefing you at Cambridge that night. It was a long time ago, Rodger, and he's a very busy man."

"Well then, Monk, you're going to have to tell me the story, aren't you? By the time you're ready to leave Stillgraves, I'm going to know what's been going on. Start wherever you like. But start, Monk. Tell me the whole story. Think of it as a matter of life and death. You're the spymaster—isn't that the truth? Only a spymaster knows all the things you know. So tell me about the spies."

Monk looked away from the sight of Davidson pulling the car door open and looking inside. "You're giving me orders? Rather cheeky, old boy."

"You grasp the essence. I'm all cheek along about now. Tell me everything I've missed."

"Ah, where to start? You really do put me into a most delicate position—"

"Look at it this way. I've grown rather used to killing people. I'm a very dangerous man. Who knows what I might do next? So talk to me. Why not start with PRAETORIAN and where it all went wrong."

"Mine was a rhetorical question, old man. I suppose the matter of Pangloss is the best starting point. Let's see . . . yes, he was Lieberman. One and the same. Yes, he was a German agent at the start, though what they thought he'd deliver for them I'm sure I don't know. Must have been very low level—supposed to pick up the gossip of the Rialto, what any of his fancy celebrity friends might let drop from the conversational banquet table. Very small potatoes, really. They were holding his family hostage, all that's quite true, and we learned it once we interviewed him. Poor Lieberman wasn't much of a spy, hadn't the natural inclination for it, had he? We tumbled to him very early on and we turned him around—do you understand? It's not hard to do, give a chap the choice of working for you or facing a firing squad early some dark, cold dawn. So, he became our man while the Germans believed he was still theirs. But even then he didn't amount to much. He was destined to have a very quiet, uneventful war unless the perfect opportunity arose. It's odd the way it worked out; we really only used him this one time . . ."

Godwin heard the slam of a car door. Airman Davidson had closed the corpse away and was inspecting the car, the surrounding snow. A thorough man. Monk watched while taking a gold cigarette case from the pocket of his duffel coat. He fumbled with his gloves, extracted a fancy smoke he always had made up in Jermyn Street, and lit it. The wind whipped the lighter's flame. A slanting shaft of sunshine hurried furtively between the clouds and glared on the snow. Godwin shielded his eyes, then they walked on, heading toward the line of trees at the far end of the runway. As if by mutual consent no mention had been made of taking this particular conversation indoors. For a moment Godwin thought of Cilla, soaking in the steaming tub, and he hoped that somehow this was all going to turn out all right.

Godwin said: "But it's true that he was also working for his German masters. He found out about PRAETORIAN somehow and the son of a bitch told them."

"Oh yes, he told them, that he most certainly did." Monk's smoke mixed with the clouds of their breath in the cold air.

"I don't understand, Monk. You once told me you didn't know who Pangloss was . . . you told me he was the man you were looking for, the man who'd betrayed us—"

"A disclosure I will deeply regret for the rest of my life. It's the sort of terrible mistake one occasionally makes without realizing it. I needn't have told you at all—it would have saved everyone a great deal of trouble—"

"—but of course you did know his identity."

"Yes, that's it."

"What I don't understand is this: If you knew who he was, and you knew he betrayed PRAETORIAN, why didn't you bring him in? What was the point in leaving him alone?"

"Ah . . . now you've reached the nub of things."

"Tell me, Monk. I'm serious. Remember . . . it's life and death—"

"You must understand, we were—we still are—at war. Everything must be seen against the background of war. *That* was life and death—"

"Believe me, so is this."

"You may remember the plan for the great counteroffensive against Rommel back in November of '41. Churchill was quite excited about it.

We—well, Auchinleck that is—were going to biff the bastard—actually CRUSADER was the key to North Africa as we saw it at the time. A bloody nose for Rommel—"

"You're forgetting our little operation, Monk. We were supposed to kill Rommel on the eve of CRUSADER, throw them into panic and confusion as CRUSADER broke across them."

"Yes . . . well, this is the sticky bit, isn't it? That's what you were intended to believe. You were going in to kill Rommel, yes, that was the story."

Godwin stopped and turned to stare at Vardan, who was squinting into the sun. "You'd better explain this part pretty carefully, Monk."

"Look, this is the part where you have to . . . look beyond yourself, you have to see the big picture, the grand scheme—you have to *understand*. I'm not saying it'll be easy—it was the PM's idea and there was no talking him out of it. CRUSADER was so important . . . that's the key to everything." The cigarette had stuck to his lip and was trembling. He pulled it loose, peeled the paper away. "He said why not give the Germans PRAETORIAN. Have Lieberman—Pangloss—tell them all about it . . . so they'd believe him when he told them that a big push, CRUSADER, was coming *later on*, *after* the first of the year. Well, you must stand back, Rodger—you must see the appeal of this plan." He waited, staring off at the tree line, the tufts of snow blowing off the branches. "Say something, for God's sake. This isn't easy for me . . . I have no business telling you this but you've got to put it all to bed. I've got to be able to tell the PM you're getting out now . . . he's got to know you're safe—"

"Safe? That's all I want to be—safe!"

"No, not the same kind of safe. He wants to know that *we're* safe *from you* because you finally know the truth and understand why it had to be—"

"So," Godwin swallowed in a dry throat, "so you are responsible for betraying PRAETORIAN. You had Lieberman pass them the word." He waited to catch his breath. "It's hard to believe, Monk. That Britain would betray its sons that way. Brave men."

"It wasn't me." Monk's voice cracked momentarily. "You must believe me."

"You're lying, Monk. Not that it matters."

"I wouldn't be telling you if it had been my idea . . . would I? I'm telling you, there's no reasoning with the PM. Once he had the idea . . ." He shrugged.

"I want to hear it from his own lips."

"You'd be dead long before then . . ." He nodded back toward the

Rover in the snow. Davidson was nowhere in sight. "Who do you think sent the man last night? It wasn't the Germans, dear boy. And who do you think sent the man in the fog so long ago? And who do you think picked Airman Davidson? No, no, I suggest you leave the PM all the way out of this one."

"You . . . the PM . . . it doesn't really matter."

"Why would I lie? I'm revealing a terrible secret. I'm committing treason just telling you—"

"You could be blaming it all on the PM to save your life, Monk."

Vardan laughed spontaneously, harshly. "Come on, old boy. You wouldn't kill old Monk—"

"When was the decision made to betray PRAETORIAN?"

"I couldn't give you the exact date."

Godwin reached out, brought his large hand down on Vardan's shoulder and spun him around. "Before or after I was brought into it?"

A look of confusion crossed Vardan's hawklike features. He was trying to come up with the safe answer but didn't know what it was. What did Godwin want to hear?

"You're lying. I hear the lie. You're in a helluva lot of trouble, my friend."

"Rodger, for God's sake! What are you doing?" He looked down at Godwin's hand which was filled by the old Webley. "You mustn't keep on killing people. It's a disgraceful habit, old boy."

"You could have stopped it, Monk, you could have told me at the very least . . . You could have saved all those lives. And you chose not to."

"The Coventry option, don't you see? All for the greater good . . . believe me, I was in an agony over it."

"Pity. It must have been terrible for you—"

"It was. You know it was, I didn't *like* doing it, dammit—"

"It must have been an awful moment when you discovered I'd survived. What an inconvenient survivor."

"You're taking a very unpleasant stand on this, I must say. People die. Missions *are* sacrificed. You've said it yourself—war is hell."

"You sent Max Hood to his death. And all the others. There's blood on your hands, Monk. I don't feel too damn good about it . . . I've killed the wrong people. And now here you are, finally, the guilty party." He tried to read Vardan's face. Was the familiar masque beginning to crack? He looked back the way they'd come, across the snow. The field was empty and dark, solid clouds blocked the sun. "Monk, what am I to do with you?"

"I told you. It was not my doing . . . Do you think I wanted it this way?"

"No. You wanted me dead at Beda Littoria."

"My God, it's all such a ghastly joke . . . the joke's on you and me, it's on all of us. It's the one essential war story. It sums up all of war and treachery and betrayal and it's all a joke. Everything you've done is a joke . . ." Monk had begun to laugh, softly now, shaking his head. His eyes were watering. "And the biggest joke of all . . . you want to kill me because of this idiotic quest of yours! It's so bloody noble and pathetic and silly . . ."

Godwin nodded and motioned Vardan to walk back toward the hangar, far away. He wasn't sure what he would do with Monk. How much of his story was true? What game was he playing at now? Was Churchill actually behind it? Or . . . or . . . but who else could have dared to send PRAETORIAN to its death? Had the PM authorized the killer last night? Or had the PM's authority been usurped by Monk Vardan? Were there any rules at all to the life-and-death game?

Their feet crunching in the snow, the wind picking up, whistling in his ears. Vardan glanced anxiously at Godwin. "Be reasonable, old boy . . . you wouldn't actually shoot me, surely?"

"I might. I'm trying to decide. I owe something to Max . . . I can't get it out of my mind. I betrayed him with Cilla. You threw his life away. How can I betray him again?"

"It's all in your mind, you know. You're quite mad."

"The thing is, he'd have done this for me . . . he taught me, there were times when a man had to do the right thing, whatever it was. He taught me that . . . Otherwise, there was no point in being alive—"

"My God, you're such a bloody fool!"

"Really? Well, at least I'm the one with the gun."

"Oh, how deliciously American! You have the gun! Really, old boy."

"Maybe I'm a fool for believing in something—"

"Exactly! Of all the things you could believe in, what do you choose? Max-bloody-Hood! It's a laugh, mate, that's what it is . . . You've spent years trying to avenge Max Hood and what has it gotten you? You're positively barking mad and it's all been a great fool's errand . . . and now you think you're going to kill me! You are, you're absolutely barking!" He was choking on the absurdity of it. There was a wild look in his eye. "Shoot me, and Davidson puts a bullet in your heart before I hit the ground . . . I happen to know our man Davidson. He's Churchill's assassin, yes, for a fact!—and then we'll all be dead because of your noble quest. The madness of it and you, you great innocent buffoon, you still haven't a clue to the truth . . . You know what was really happening? You know who wanted—no, *insisted*—you go on the mission? The suicide mission?" He wiped the saliva foam from his mouth. "You won't like this, old boy. Better shoot me now, and spare yourself the pratfall . . ." He was watching the gun in Godwin's hand.

"Go on, Monk. I can shoot you later."

"You go on about betrayal, you're obsessed with betrayal, but you don't know the one betrayal that matters . . . all your killing and hunting and stalking . . . and you don't know who was making a joke out of your life . . . It was Max Hood, you hopeless fool! *Max Hood!*"

"What do you mean? Quick, Monk. You're almost out of time."

"Max knew he was dying. He knew you were in love with his wife—or sleeping with her at any rate. He was willing to lead something he knew was a virtual suicide mission—no, no, he didn't *know* about Pangloss, he didn't *know* PRAETORIAN was being sacrificed, but it didn't matter to him anyway—better to die in action . . . You've heard him talk about setting an example, becoming one of the soldier stories men tell later on . . . Well, at the end, not even that mattered, nothing mattered but one thing . . . my God, I'm bloody cold, old man—"

"Go on. What did Max Hood care about?"

"*Killing you!* That was his only stipulation . . . you had to be part of PRAETORIAN. Or he wouldn't go! He had to get you out there in the war with him . . . out where he could kill you."

"That's absurd. Don't try it on with me, you're wasting your breath. He knew how I felt about him—"

"You see? You're obsessed—we're not talking about how *you felt*. We're talking about how *he* felt—two different things. You may have felt you owed him something. *But he didn't owe you a goddamn thing!* He never owed you a thing. You confused your feelings with his. Don't you see it? He knew you were betraying him with his wife. You weren't playing the game, old boy. You weren't following the code."

"I don't believe any of this. You can't talk about Max Hood this way—"

"What you believe doesn't matter. We have proof. We *know* . . ."

"What are you saying?"

"For one thing, you told me yourself. You told me the last bit about what happened at Beda Littoria. You and Max were running away and the Germans had you in the spotlights and Max got hit. You said you could see the bullets hitting him, tearing at his clothes . . . You told me how he reached out to you right at the end and then you saw a blinding flash, the snipers hit you in the head—"

"Stop! No more, shut up, Monk!"

"It always amazes me how otherwise rational men will deny reason, will lie to themselves—a German soldier some distance away shoots at you, you don't see a flash! Max Hood shoots you point-blank, you see one hell of a flash!"

"Stop it! I'm warning you, Monk." The gun was wavering, he felt almost faint. He didn't want to go back to that moment.

"All he wanted was to put that last bullet in your face. But he'd waited too long, he was dying, his strength was ebbing away . . . Your pal, your hero, personally wanted to put you down . . ."

"Monk!" The wind whistled in his ears, he felt far away.

"When they picked you up the report showed you'd been shot at close range, your face was burned by the blast, it was obvious for God's sake! And you've been avenging his death ever since! He betrayed you with the last breath of his life. All this isn't about betrayal . . . you poor bastard, here you stand in the middle of nowhere with a gun pointed at your friend . . . it's about *irony* . . ." He put his hand out toward the gun in Godwin's hand. Slowly it was coming up. "No, no, this isn't the point—you're mad, you've lost your mind, it's me, it's Monk—"

Godwin was holding the pistol at arm's length. Monk was shrinking back, the color gone from his face, his head shaking no, no.

"*Rodger!*"

Godwin tore his eyes from Monk Vardan's face.

Cilla was standing at the top of the stairway leading to the terrace. Her voice carried on the wind, clear and desperate.

"*Rodger! Don't . . . don't!*"

Monk was watching her, too, then looking back at Godwin.

Godwin stared into Monk's face past the end of the barrel.

Slowly he felt the gun begin to slide away, like a massive weight. He took a deep breath, closed his eyes. It was all so sad. He was so tired.

When he opened his eyes he was looking into a pistol Monk Vardan had taken from the pocket of his duffel coat.

"I'm sorry, old boy. You really are the worst kind of risk. I'm authorized to do this . . . you're a danger, you've lost your reason . . . you've threatened to use your position to commit treason . . . you've held me at gunpoint—"

Godwin laughed. It was utterly insane. Most of what seemed to happen in a war was insane. More or less. Godwin watched Monk's finger on the trigger.

"It's up to you, Monk. I'm just too worn out to make a fuss about any of it . . . not anymore . . ."

He turned his back on the gun, saw Cilla on the stairs. She was coming down. He wondered if he would live long enough to touch her.

He heard the flat crack of a gunshot.

Cilla had reached the bottom of the stone steps. She was running toward him across the snow.

She was in his arms, alive and warm and holding on as tight as she could.

He turned, smelling her hair, feeling the cold clean wind on his face. Alive.

Monk Vardan lay on his back in the snow.

Godwin ran back to him and knelt beside him.

Vardan looked up into his eyes. There was a ragged hole in the front of the duffel coat. The life was leaving him. "What a balls up this is," he sighed. "I thought young Davidson was here to kill *you* . . . if you wouldn't cooperate . . . life is full of lessons learned too late . . . surprises . . ."

"War is hell, Monk." Godwin looked up. Davidson was walking slowly toward them. He carried a rifle. Behind him the airplane stood silent, snow eddying around the wheels. He was pulling his leather flying helmet off with his other hand.

Monk was talking, breathing hard. "Listen . . . I never should have let Max talk me into including you . . . he'd have led the mission anyway . . . but I caved in . . . he said he had to be sure you'd die, too . . . then I got the idea to give PRAETORIAN to Pangloss . . . to save CRUSADER . . . it was me . . . the PM never knew . . ."

"None of it makes any difference, Monk. I'd have done it all the same way. Even if I'd known. You don't understand, Monk. I owed it to Max from a long time ago . . ."

"All damn silliness . . . you Yanks . . . code of the West . . ." He coughed. His eyes flickered upward, past Godwin's shoulder. "Cilla . . . sorry you had to see this . . . such a mess . . . I'm bloody well out of it . . . last words . . . All is vanity, old boy, every bit of it . . ." His voice was very weak. His lips moved but Godwin couldn't hear. He lowered his head to Monk's. "One last thing . . . tell Cilla . . ."

She was kneeling beside him. "I'm here, Monk."

But he couldn't see her. His eyes were closed. "Tell Cilla . . . I spoke to the Eton chaps . . . about young Charlie . . . it's all booked, don't worry . . . all booked . . . you'll love him in his topper . . ." He turned his head slightly, as if he were seeing something across the field, something they couldn't see. "I say you chaps . . . wait for old Monk . . ." He was smiling faintly.

Cilla took his ice-cold hand.

He squeezed it and then he was gone.

Airman Davidson stood looking down at the three of them. Godwin took Cilla's hand from Monk's and they stood up.

"Awfully sorry about this, sir." Airman Davidson's voice was very high. He was very young without his helmet and goggles on.

Godwin was staring at him. As he turned to Cilla, something caught his eye. It was beginning to snow and the daylight was going.

"I had my orders to make sure nothing happened to you, sir. He was threatening you, sir. He would have shot you. I was under orders. He was to speak with you, that was all. My masters were very precise, sir. They seemed to think something untoward might happen. The PM wants me to bring you back, sir. At once. He wants to talk to you."

"Ah." Godwin looked at Cilla. "There'll be two of us."

"We can manage that, sir. But . . . as soon as is convenient, sir. All right?"

The snow was falling across Monk's breast like bits of time. He was already in the past, moving away. The snow was turning red and all around them night was closing in.

"Yes, sure, all right. Let us get some things."

"Of course, sir. I'll just tidy up here."

Climbing the stairs to the house, Cilla leaned against Godwin. "It really is over now, isn't it, Rodger?"

"Yes. Monk tried to convince me that it was all the PM's doing. But it wasn't."

"Oh, Rodger, none of it makes sense to me—"

"Then he tried to lay it all on Max, he said Max wanted to make sure I died, he wanted to kill me. He said Max was the one who shot me."

"Is that true?"

"I don't know. It doesn't matter. What I owed Max had nothing to do with anything Monk could understand. It was all about 1927. Back when it all began."

"Are you quits with Max at last?"

"Yes. PRAETORIAN, it was all a fool's errand . . . and it was all Monk's idea. He thought it was a masterstroke. War was all about betrayal and irony . . . life was betrayal and irony . . . and what Monk did was for the greater good. I think it made him feel he was part of the bloody war at last." He held her to him, swore to himself he'd earned her now, by God, and would never let her go. "It was a fool's errand, my love. And it has nearly consumed me, consumed my life."

"Not quite, darling."

"No, not quite."

"It was all written," she said. "Destiny."

"Max would have understood that."

"Yes, darling, I'm sure he would have."

When they came back down the stairs, leaving Stillgraves behind, walking across the snow toward the plane, past the place where Monk had died, Cilla spoke.

"Was Monk a terrible swine?" She was holding on to his arm.

"I don't know. I suppose." Then: "No, he wasn't a swine. Not at all. He believed he was doing what had to be done. Now he's just another fallen Englishman. God, it's been a long war."

"Still, it was awfully nice, what he did."

He looked down at his wife.

"About Charlie," she said. "About our son and Eton."

"Well, Eton meant a lot to Monk."

"Don't worry, darling. Don't be too sad. It's the war. Everything goes to hell during a war and then the war is over . . ."

"And then you have to put it all back together."

"That's it, my darling."

The moonlight was shining on Davidson's solemn, pink-cheeked face, so like a choirboy's, Godwin thought. It was a flawless English face. Except for the left ear. Someone seemed to have ripped the lobe off. Davidson was holding out his hand to help them aboard.

He saw Godwin's glance stop, stick at the ear. He began to blush, then smiled self-consciously. "That night in the fog, sir—" He looked so very young.

"Yes?"

"I'm very sorry, sir. It was all a terrible mistake."

"I'm sorry about the ear, son."

"My fault entirely, sir. I shouldn't have been there. And you were more than I could handle."

"I understand. No hard feelings. War is hell, son."

"Thank you, sir," Davidson said. "Mrs. Godwin," he said, seeing Cilla safely into the plane.

Cilla smiled back at her husband.

"Mr. Godwin," she said softly.

ABOUT THE AUTHOR

Thomas Gifford is the author of *The Assassini, The Wind Chill Factor, The Man from Lisbon,* and other novels. He lives in New York.